NOCTURNAL

NOCTURNAL

A NOVEL

SCOTT SIGLER

BROADWAY PAPERBACKS
NEW YORK

BROADWAY

Copyright © 2012 by Scott Sigler

All rights reserved.
Published in the United States by Broadway Paperbacks, an imprint of the Crown Publishing Group, a division of Random House, Inc., New York.
www.crownpublishing.com

BROADWAY PAPERBACKS and its logo, a letter B bisected on the diagonal, are trademarks of Random House, Inc.

Originally published in hardcover in the United States by Crown Publishers, an imprint of the Crown Publishing Group, a division of Random House, Inc., New York, in 2012.

Library of Congress Cataloging-in-Publication Data
Sigler, Scott.
Nocturnal / Scott Sigler. — 1st ed.
1. Detectives — California — San Francisco — Fiction. 2. Homicide investigation — Fiction. I. Title.
PS3619.I4725N63 2012
813'.6 — dc23   2011040389

ISBN 978-0-307-95275-2
eISBN 978-0-307-95276-9

Printed in the United States of America

Book design by Lauren Dong
Cover design by Jarrod Taylor
Cover photograph: © Andres Rodriguez/Alamy
Author illustration based on photograph by: © Amy Davis-Roth, surlynamics.com

10 9 8 7 6 5 4 3 2 1

First Paperback Edition

For Byrd Leavell, who makes things happen.

*For Julian Pavia and the amazing job he did helping me
make this novel what it is.*

And for A. Kovacs, who keeps me sane.

BOOK I

PEOPLE

Penance

Y ou're not welcome here, Paul."

Most places in the world, a statement like that sounded normal. Unfriendly, perhaps, but still common, still acceptable.

Most places, but not at a Catholic church.

"But someone's following me," Paul said. "And it's cold out." Paul's eyes flicked left, flicked right, too fast to take anything in. He looked haunted.

That wasn't Father Esteban Rodriguez's problem. This man, if he could be called that, would never again be allowed in the Cathedral of St. Mary of the Assumption. Never again.

"You've been told," Esteban said. "You're not part of this church anymore."

Paul's eyes narrowed, cleared. For a moment, Esteban saw a glimmer of the wit that had made Paul so popular, so engaging.

"What about forgiveness?" Paul said. "That's what we're all about, forgiveness of our sins. Or are you better than Our Savior?"

Esteban felt rage — a rare emotion — and quickly fought to bring it under control. "I am only a man," he said. "Perhaps a weak one at that. Maybe the Lord can forgive you your sins, but I can't. You may not seek shelter here."

Paul looked down. He shivered. Esteban shivered, too. San Francisco's evening chill — a wet, clinging thing — rolled through the church door that Esteban blocked with his body.

Paul wore a sagging blue coat that had once probably been puffy and shiny. Maybe it had looked nice on the original owner, whomever that might be, however many years ago that was. Paul's pants were dirty — not caked with filth, but spotted here and there with finger streaks of food, grease, other things. Years ago, this man had helped care for the homeless; now he looked like one of them.

"I have nowhere to go," Paul said to the ground.

"That is not the church's problem. That is not *my* problem."

"I'm a human being, Father."

Esteban shook his head. This disgusting, demonic creature before him thought himself *human*? "You don't belong here. You're not wanted here. This is a sanctuary — one doesn't let wolves in among the sheep. Why don't you go somewhere you *do* belong? If you don't leave, I'll call the police."

Paul looked away, down the street. He seemed to be searching for something, something . . . specific. Something that wasn't there.

"I told the police," Paul said. "Told them someone was following me."

"What did they say?"

Paul looked Esteban in the eyes.

"Pretty much the same thing you did, Father."

"Whatever a man sows, this he will also reap," Esteban said. "Hell has a special place for people like you. Leave, *now*."

Sadness filled Paul's eyes. Desperation, despair — perhaps the final understanding that this part of his life was *over*. Paul looked beyond Esteban, through the door to the church interior. The look of sadness changed to one of longing. Paul had spent many years in this very building.

Those days were gone forever.

Paul turned and walked down the church's wide steps. Esteban watched him reach the sidewalk of Gough Street, then cross and continue down O'Farrell.

Esteban shut the door.

•••

Paul Maloney hunched his shoulders high, tried to burrow his ears into his coat. He needed a hat. So cold out at night. Wind drove the fog, a fog thick enough that you could see wisps of it at eye level. He walked down O'Farrell Street, home to strip clubs, drug dealers and whores, an asphalt swath of sin and degradation. Part of him knew he belonged here. Another part, an *older* part, wanted to scream and yell, tell all these sinners where they would go unless they took Jesus Christ as their Lord and Savior.

The gall of Father Esteban. *Hell has a special place?* Maybe for Esteban, maybe for men like him who purported to preach the Word when they didn't even understand it. God loved Paul Maloney. God loved everyone. Someday, Paul would stand by his side — it would be Esteban who would feel the fires.

Esteban, and the others who had kicked Paul out of the only life he'd ever known.

Paul turned left on Jones Street. Where would he go? He had a constant, churning *need* for human contact that continued to surprise him. Not the type of contact that had changed his life, just the normal act of a kind word, a conversation. A *connection*. He'd spent so many years in the church, so many years in front of a steady stream of people. Even during the long periods of study, of contemplation, his isolation was self-imposed;

people were always a few rooms away. There was always someone out there to talk to if he so chose.

But for the past couple of years, no one had wanted to talk to Paul Maloney. He had to be careful everywhere he went — some of the sinners around here would pass judgment with their fists and feet.

Two in the morning. People were still on the street, especially in this part of town, but not many. No kids out at this hour. A shame.

Behind him, a noise, the sound of metal scraping lightly against brick. Paul whirled. No one there.

His heart hammered. He'd turned thinking he would see the man with the shaggy black beard and the green John Deere ball cap. How many times had Paul seen that man in the past week? Four? Maybe five?

Please, Heavenly Father, please don't let that man be a parent.

The sound came again.

Paul turned so fast he stumbled. What had made that scraping noise? A pipe? Maybe some bag lady pushing a cart with a broken wheel? He looked for the bearded man, but the bearded man wasn't there.

Paul put his cold hands on his face. He rubbed hard, trying to shake away the fear. How had it come to this? He hadn't done anything wrong, not really. He just *loved* so much, and now this was his life: one foot in front of the other, walking through loneliness, until he died.

"I must be strong," he said. "I will fear no evil, because you are with me, thy—"

A whisper of air behind him, the sound of something heavy falling, the slap of shoe soles against damp concrete.

Paul started to turn, but before he could see what it was, strong hands locked onto his shoulders.

Good Morning, Sunshine

As the sun rose, the shadows crawled along the streets of San Francisco, shrinking away into the buildings that spawned them.

Bryan sat on the ledge of his apartment building's roof, watching the dawn. Bathrobe, boxers, a cup of coffee, feet dangling six stories above the sidewalk below — a little slice of the good life. He loved his daily rooftop ritual, but normally his work *ended* with the rising sun.

At dawn, Bryan Clauser usually went to sleep.

He rarely had to work the day shift, a perk of both his seniority and the fact that few other people wanted to pursue murder investigations from eight at night until four in the morning. His beloved night shift would have to wait, however — the Ablamowicz case had stagnated, and Chief Amy Zou had to show some kind of movement or the press would eat her alive.

When a local, loaded businessman is found floating in three separate barrels in the San Francisco Bay, the media wants answers. Zou would masterfully ration pieces of information, steadily feeding the media hounds what they wanted to hear until those hounds gradually lost interest and moved on to the next story.

Zou had a press-conference playbook so predictable that the cops she commanded had labeled the steps — *Step I: Gather Information but Don't Make Assumptions,* then *Step II: Put Our Senior People on the Case.* She had already moved past *Step III: Creation of a Multidisciplinary Task Force* and sailed headlong into the media-pleasing *Step IV: Assign Additional Resources.* In this instance, *additional resources* meant pulling in the night-shift guys. Zou gave orders to Jesse Sharrow, the Homicide department captain, and Sharrow gave orders to Bryan.

So, day shift it was.

Bryan scratched at his short, dark-red beard and his hands came away wet; sometimes he forgot to dry that off. It was getting a little long — not too bad yet, but he'd have to trim it in a day or two or his look would slide from *casually cool* to *newly homeless.*

He pulled his black terrycloth robe a little tighter. Chilly up here. He sipped his coffee and looked north to his "view" of San Francisco Bay. Not much of a view, really: a postage-stamp-size space at the far end of Laguna that showed a strip of blue water, then the dark mass of Angel Island, and beyond that the faraway, starry-light-twinkling of sleepy Tiburon. He couldn't even see the iconic Golden Gate Bridge from here — too many taller buildings in the way. Views were for the rich.

Cops don't get rich. Not the clean ones, anyway.

People called his job "homicide inspector," but that wasn't how it felt to Bryan. He didn't *inspect,* he *hunted.* He hunted murderers. It was his life, his reason for being. Whatever might be missing from his world, those things faded away when the hunt began. As corny as it sounded, this city was his home and he was one of its protectors.

He'd been born here, but his dad had moved around during Bryan's childhood and teenage years. Indianapolis for grade school, Atlanta in junior high, Detroit for his freshman and sophomore years. Bryan had never really felt at home anywhere, not until they moved back to the city for his junior year in high school. George Washington High. Good times.

From his robe pocket, his cell phone sounded the tone of an incoming two-way message. He didn't have to check who it was, because only his partner used that feature. Bryan raised the phone to his ear and thumbed the two-way button, the *bee-boop* sound chiming when he called out, the opposite *boo-beep* sound signaling Pookie calling in.

"I'm ready," Bryan said.

"No, you're not," Pookie said. "You're probably up on your roof drinking coffee."

"No, I'm not," Bryan said, then took a sip.

"You probably aren't even dressed."

"Yes, I am," Bryan said.

"You're an L-L-W-T-L."

Pookie and his made-up acronyms. *Bee-boop:* "What the hell is an *L-L-W-T-L?*"

Boo-beep: "A lying liar who tells lies. It puts on the clothes, or it gets the horn again."

Bryan drained the coffee mug and set it on the ledge to his left. Three other mugs were already sitting there. He made a mental note to grab them the following night. He usually didn't bother with the orphaned mugs until there were five or six sitting there like a little ceramic calendar marking the last time he'd bothered to clean up after himself.

He hurried to the fire escape and started down to his apartment. If he wasn't down on the street by the time Pookie's Buick rolled up, the man would lean on the horn until Bryan came out. Bryan's neighbors just loved Pookie Chang.

The damp metal steps felt cold on Bryan's bare feet. Two flights down he reached the narrow landing just outside his kitchen window and climbed inside.

His kitchen was so small you couldn't fit two people in there and open the fridge at the same time. Not that he ever had two people in the kitchen. Six months he'd lived in the one-bedroom, and he still hadn't unpacked most of his boxes.

Bryan dressed quickly. Black socks, black pants and a black T-shirt. His black Bianchi Tuxedo shoulder holster came next, followed by a nylon forearm knife sheath. He scooped up his weapons from his coffee table. Tomahawk tactical fighting knife for the forearm sheath. SOG Twitch XL folding knife, clipped inside the pants to the left of the crotch, hidden from sight but within easy reach. Sig Sauer P226 in the holster. The SFPD issued the .40-caliber version to the entire force. It wouldn't have been his first choice for a main weapon, but that's what they gave you and that's what you carried. The shoulder holster was equipped with two additional magazine pouches and a small handcuff holster. Bryan dutifully filled these as well.

Where a lot of cops carried a backup piece in an ankle holster, Bryan wanted the full effect of an *onion field gun* — a gun that might be missed by perps should he be taken hostage. His was a tiny Seecamp LWS32, a .32-caliber pistol so small it fit in an imitation wallet and slid into his back left pants pocket. He'd actually *been* a hostage once, been at the mercy of a perp who'd missed several days of meds. Bryan never wanted to experience anything like that ever again.

He shrugged on a black hoodie and zipped it up, hiding his holster from sight. As he slid past still-packed moving boxes and out his apartment door, he heard the faint, steady sound of a car horn.

What an asshole.

Bryan skipped every other stair as he shot down four flights to the old-school lobby, sneakers slapping against chipped marble floors. Right out front was Pookie's shit-brown Buick — double-parked, completely blocking a lane.

Passing cars honked, but if Pookie could hear them over his own car's horn he didn't pay any attention. After six years together as partners, Bryan knew Pookie's attitude all too well. Pookie was a cop; what was someone going to do, give him a ticket?

Bryan shot out the door, onto the sidewalk and around the Buick. As usual, a stack of beat-up manila folders filled the passenger seat.

Pookie Chang did not believe in technology.

Bryan scooped up the teetering mass, held it in his lap as he sat and shut the door.

"Hey, Pooks." Bryan reached across and patted Pookie's belly. "Did the Buddha like his donuts this morning?"

"We can't all have the metabolism of a hummingbird," Pookie said as he pulled into traffic on Vallejo Street. "The choo-choo don't run without some coal in the engine. And *Buddha*? I could have Internal Affairs bring you up on racial intimidation charges for that. How would you like it if I called you a potato-eating Mick bastard?"

"Clauser is a German name, genius."

Pookie laughed. "Yeah, all those members of the Master Race have red hair and green eyes just like you."

Bryan shrugged. "Dark-red. Irish have bright-red. I'm German through and through, going back three generations. Besides, oh sensitive one, I was talking about your big Buddha belly, not your slanty eyes."

"*Slanty eyes*? Oh, yeah, that's so much more politically correct. And I'm not fat. I'm big-boned."

"I remember when you bought that coat," Bryan said. "Four years ago. You could button it then — can you button it now?"

Pookie turned south on Van Ness, then cut across two lanes of traffic for no apparent reason. Bryan automatically pressed his feet to the floor and grabbed the door handle. He heard honks and a few screeches as drivers quickly hit their brakes.

"We Chicagoans like to eat," Pookie said. "You have your tofu and bean sprouts, Cali boy, I'll keep my brats and bear claws. Besides, the ladies love my belly. That's why in our cop show, you're the brooding, mis-understood, tough-guy rebel. I'm the pretty one that gets the babes. In the grander hot-or-not scale? I'm ranked like nine hundred levels above you."

"That's a lot of levels."

Pookie nodded. "Most assuredly."

"How's the script coming?"

Pookie's latest hobby was writing something called a *series bible* for a police show. He had never acted a day in his life, never been involved in show business, but that didn't slow him down in the least. He attacked everything in life the same way he attacked a buffet.

Pookie shrugged. "So-so. I thought a cop drama would write itself. Turns out not so much. But don't worry, I'll lick it like I licked your mom."

"Name the show yet?"

"Yeah, listen to this. *Midnight Shield.* How's that sit in your mouth?"

"Like bad sushi," Bryan said. "*Midnight Shield*? Really?"

"Yeah, 'cause the characters are cops like us, and they work the overnight shift, and—"

"I got the wordplay, Pooks. It's not that I don't understand it, it just sucks."

"The fuck you know about entertainment?"

Pookie swerved sharply to cut off a Prius. He probably did that on purpose — he wasn't a fan of green energy, green technology, or anything else green that didn't come complete with the face of a dead president.

"Pooks, anyone ever tell you that you drive like shit?"

"I may have heard that once or twice, Bri-Bri. Although I stand by my theory that feces can neither apply for, nor pass, a driver's license exam." He accelerated through a yellow-turning-red. "Don't worry, God loves me."

"Your imaginary Sky Daddy is going to keep you safe?"

"Of course," Pookie said. "I'm one of the chosen ones. If we get into an accident, though, I can't say what he'll do for you. You atheists are a bit lower on the miracle depth-chart."

Pookie unexpectedly slowed and got into the left-turn lane at O'Farrell. They were supposed to start the day at 850 Bryant, police headquarters. For that, they'd stay on Van Ness for another four blocks.

"Where we going?"

"Someone found a body this morning," Pookie said. "Five thirty-seven Jones Street. Kind of a big deal. Remember the name Paul Maloney?"

"Uh . . . it rings a bell, but I can't place it."

"How about *Father* Paul Maloney?"

"No shit. The child molester?"

Pookie nodded. "Child molester is too nice a word for the guy. *Was* too nice a word, I mean. He was murdered last night. Call him what he was — a rapist."

San Francisco hadn't escaped the wave of accusations that had crashed into the Catholic Church. Maloney first came to attention because he helped cover up early accusations against other priests who were clearly guilty. As more and more adults came forward about what had happened to them as children, the reasons for Maloney's efforts became clear; he wasn't just protecting pedophiles, he was one himself. Investigations ensued, producing enough clear-cut evidence that Maloney was finally defrocked.

It didn't surprise Bryan that someone had killed the man. That didn't make it right, not by any stretch, but it wasn't exactly a shocker.

"Wait a minute," Bryan said. "Time of death?"

"Word is about three or four A.M."

"So why didn't we get called in?"

"That's what I'd like to know," Pookie said. "We're temporarily assigned to days and all, but the Maloney murder is just as high-profile as Ablamowicz. The press is going to circle-jerk all over this one."

"*Circle-jerk* might not be the best metaphor, considering."

"Sorry, Mister Sensitive," Pookie said. "I'll refrain from sexual innuendo."

"So who got the case?"

"Verde."

Bryan nodded. No wonder Pookie wanted to get to the scene. "Polyester Rich, nice. Your favorite guy."

"I love him so."

"So we're driving to the crime scene, to which we're *not* assigned, to be a pain in Verde's ass."

"You're very deductive," Pookie said. "They should make you a cop or something."

A murder scene, in daylight. That might bring about an uncomfortable situation Bryan desperately wanted to avoid. "Any word on who the ME is for this?"

"Don't know," Pookie said. "But you can't avoid the girl forever, Bryan. She's a medical examiner, you're a homicide cop. Those things go together like chocolate and peanut butter. It's just been dumb luck she hasn't been at one of our scenes in the past six months. Maybe we'll luck out and Robin-Robin Bo-Bobbin's pretty little face will be perched over the dead body."

Bryan shook his head before he realized he was doing it. "I wouldn't call that *lucky*."

"You should really give her a call."

"And you should really mind your own business." He didn't want to think about Robin Hudson. Time to change the subject. "Verde still working with Bobby Pigeon?"

"Verde and the Birdman. Sadly, that *would* be a pretty kick-ass name for a cop show. But Verde is just plain ugly, and they don't make primetime dramas about stoner cops."

Pookie turned left on Jones. This part of the city was a mix of buildings, two stories up to five or six, most built in the 1930s or 1940s and with the city's trademark angled bay windows. Just half a block away, three black-and-whites blocked the area. Pookie reached his hand out the window to place the portable bubble-light on top of the Buick, then pulled a little closer and double-parked.

"This case should be ours," he said as he got out. "Especially if this is some vigilante bullshit."

"I know, I know," Bryan said. "Rule of law and all that."

Five thirty-seven Jones Street was a two-story building sandwiched between a parking garage and a five-story apartment complex. Half of 537 was a locksmith, the other half a mail services building.

Bryan saw little movement inside the buildings. Up above, however, he saw bits of motion.

Pookie pointed up. "The goddamn *roof*?"

Bryan nodded. "Curiouser and curiouser."

A whiff of something strange tickled Bryan's nose. There, then gone.

They ducked under police tape. The uniforms smiled at Pookie, nodded at Bryan. Pookie waved to each, calling them by name. Bryan knew their faces, but most times names were beyond him.

They entered the building, found the stairs and headed up. Pookie and Bryan stepped onto a flat roof painted in many gloopy layers of light gray. A morning breeze hit them from behind, snapping their clothes just a little. Rich Verde and Bobby "Birdman" Pigeon stood near the body.

Fortunately, the ME was not a hot little Asian woman with her long black hair done up in a tight bun. It was a silver-haired man who moved with the stiff slowness of age. He was squatting on his heels, examining some detail of the deceased.

Light-colored roofs aren't a good complement to splattered blood. Long brown lines and streaks marked the rough gray paint, creating a Jackson Pollock canvas of death and dirt.

The body lay twisted in a rather unnatural position. The deceased's legs looked broken — both forelegs and femurs.

"Wow," Bryan said. "Someone had it in for that guy."

Pookie put on his aviator sunglasses, then feathered back his heavy black hair. He'd started doing that since he began the series bible — Hollywood wasn't calling yet, but Pookie Chang would be ready when it did.

"Had it in for a child rapist? Gee, Bri-Bri, I can't imagine a connection like that. What's under the tarp, I wonder?" Pookie pointed to the right of the body. A blue, police-issue tarp flapped in the light morning breeze, its corners held down by duct tape. The tarp lay flat against the roof, no room for body-sized lumps — or even severed-limb-sized lumps — beneath it.

Some of the streaks of dried brown blood led under the blue material. The wind caught an edge of the tarp, just a little, lifting it. Like the flash of a fan dancer, Bryan saw a here-then-gone glimpse of what was underneath. Was that a drawing of some kind?

"Hey," Pookie said, "the ME . . . is that Old Man Metz?"

Bryan nodded as soon as Pookie said the name. "Yeah, that's the Silver Eagle all right. I haven't seen him outside of the ME's office in . . . like five years or so."

"That pisses me off," Pookie said. "I mean, even more than before. Did you know Metz was a consultant on that *Dirty Harry* reboot? Metz knows Hollywood types. And Verde gets to work with him? Verde is a pig-fucker."

Metz wore a blue uniform jacket — gold braid around the cuffs, two rows of polished brass buttons down the chest. Most of the people from the medical examiner's office wore windbreaker jackets for pickups, but not Metz. He still sported the same formal attire that had been de rigueur for his department back in the day.

Metz had been the main guy in the ME's office for thirty years. He was a law enforcement legend. When he walked into a courtroom, lawyers from both sides trembled. Under examination, he often made lawyers look like idiots. He'd written textbooks. He'd been consulted by some of the world's top crime writers. What Metz *didn't* do anymore, though, was go out into the field. The guy was pushing seventy. Even the great ones have limits.

"I'm *pissed*," Pookie said. "You ever see Metz in a courtroom? He's so effing cool. And he's the only one with a better nickname than you."

Some people in the department called Bryan the *Terminator*. "I'm half of Schwarzenegger's size and I don't look anything like him."

"It's not about looks, dummy, it's because you kill people," Pookie said. "That, and you have all the emotional response of a used Duracell. Don't be so sensitive. People only say it because they respect you."

Pookie would think that. He saw the world through rose-colored glasses. Pookie didn't seem to hear the condescending tone with which people used the nickname. Some guys in the department thought Bryan was trigger-happy, a cop who used the gun as a default action instead of as a last resort.

"I'd rather you didn't use that name, okay?"

Pookie shrugged. "Well, work as long as Metz and get that fabuloso gray do, and maybe they'll call you the *Silver Eagle* instead of him. I mean, look at that hair. Home-slice looks like a walking shampoo commercial."

Metz looked up from the body. He stared at Bryan and Pookie for a second, gave a single nod — chin down, pause, chin up — then went back to work.

"He's so cool," Pookie said. "I'd like to be as cool as that when I'm his age, but I think I'll be busy filling my pants and drooling on myself."

"Everyone has to have goals, Pooks."

"True. Oh, that reminds me. Later I'll tell you about my stock tip. *Depends adult undergarments.* An aging boomer population makes that stock gold. Brown gold, Bryan."

"Not now," Bryan said. "What the hell is that under the tarp?"

Rich Verde looked up from the body and locked eyes with Bryan and Pookie. He shook his head. It didn't take advanced skills to read his lips: *these fucking guys.*

Pookie waved, high and happy. "Morning, Rich! Helluva day, ain't it?"

Rich walked over. Birdman followed, already shaking his head slowly and rolling his eyes.

An odder couple you could not find. Rich Verde was pushing sixty. He'd been busting ass back when Bryan and Pookie were in diapers. Verde still dressed in the cheap polyester suits that had been in style when he'd made his bones thirty years earlier. His pencil mustache just screamed *douchebag.* Birdman had been promoted from Vice just a few weeks earlier. With his scraggly brown beard, brown knit hat, jeans and tan Carhartt jacket, he looked more like someone who would be the arrest-*ee* than the arrest-*or.*

Verde walked right up to Pookie until they almost touched noses.

"Chang," Verde said. "What the *fuck* are you two cocksuckers doing here?"

Pookie smiled, reached into his pocket, pulled out a small plastic case and gave it an audible rattle. "Tic Tac?"

Verde's eyes narrowed.

Pookie leaned to the left, gave an upward nod to Bobby. "Hey there, Birdman."

"'Sup," Birdman said. He smiled. The morning sun glinted off his gold front-left incisor.

"Bobby, don't talk to this asshole," Verde said. "Clauser, Chang, get your asses the fuck outta here."

Pookie laughed. "You kiss your mother with that mouth?"

"No, but I kissed yours," Verde said. "With tongue. Far as you know, I'm your daddy."

"If so, I thank God that chronic halitosis isn't congenital." Pookie leaned to the right, looked over Verde's right shoulder. "I see the Silver Eagle came out for this one. That's good, Rich — that means everything will be shipshape when Bryan and I take over."

Verde pointed to the roof door. "Get lost."

The wind reversed direction, bringing with it that smell — urine.

Urine . . . and something else . . .

"Jeez," Pookie said. "Speaking of Depends, did someone forget theirs today?"

Birdman nodded. "The perp *pissed* on him, man. Pretty messed up, huh?"

Verde turned. "Shut the fuck up, Bobby."

Bobby held up his hands, palms out. He walked back to Metz and Paul Maloney's body.

"Hey," Bryan said. "You guys smell that? Not the piss . . . that other smell?"

Pookie and Verde both sniffed, thought about it, then shook their heads.

How could they not smell that?

Pookie offered Verde the Tic Tacs again. Verde just glared.

Pookie shrugged and put them away. "Look, Polyester, do me a favor and be thorough with your report, okay? Once the chief sees the vic's name, you know she's going to give the case to us. We'd hate to have to call you to fill in the blanks."

Verde smiled, shook his head. "Not this time, Chang. Zou put us on this case herself. I wouldn't rock the boat on this one if I was you."

Pookie's ever-present, condescending grin faded a bit. He was eyeing Verde up, seeing if the man was telling the truth.

The roof suddenly shifted; Bryan stumbled left, trying to keep his balance. Pookie caught him, steadied him.

"Bri-Bri, you okay?"

Bryan blinked, rubbed his eyes. "Yeah, just got dizzy for a second."

Verde sneered. "Take some advice, Terminator — save the bottle for off-duty time."

Verde turned and walked back to the body.

Bryan stared after the man. "I hate that name."

"It's only funny when I use it," Pookie said. "Bri-Bri, I want to go on record that I am officially unhappy with this staffing decision."

"Zou's call," Bryan said. "You know that means we have to accept it." Pookie, of course, knew no such thing — he'd be angling for the case nonstop, no matter how exhausting that became to Bryan.

"Come on," Bryan said. "We have to get to the Hall."

Pookie adjusted his sunglasses and re-feathered his hair. "Fine by me, Bri-Bri. Can't really tell which one of them stinks like piss, anyway."

Bryan went down the steps first, that smell still tickling his nose. He was careful to keep a hand on the rail.

The Morning News

The buzz of an alarm clock brought Rex Deprovdechuk awake. He'd been dreaming a great dream that made him feel wonderful inside; he tried to capture it, to lock in the memory, but it slipped away. The nice feeling faded, replaced by the aches of his body and that pain in his chest.

Rex felt so sick. He just wanted to sleep. Wanting to sleep during the day was nothing new — he routinely dozed off during second-hour trig class — but this was different. He'd been hurting for days. His mother wouldn't let him stay home. He dragged himself out of bed. He blew his nose on some crusty Kleenex he'd used the night before, then shuffled out of his tiny bedroom into the hall.

The hallway ran the length of the floor, a blank wall on the left, five doors on the right. The wall held old framed pictures from a time Rex barely remembered — pictures of his dad, of Rex when he'd been really little, even pictures of his mom, smiling. He was glad for those pictures, because he had never seen her smile in person.

Rex walked into the toilet room. The room was barely wider than the toilet tank itself. Wasn't really a *bath*room, because it just had the toilet and a sink. The next room down had the bath — and no toilet — so Rex called that the shower room.

He took care of his morning business and was headed back to his bedroom when he heard it.

From down the hall, a voice on the TV made him stop. Not the voice itself, but the name the voice had spoken — a name both from Rex's unremembered dream and from his unforgettable past. He wiped his hand across his runny nose. He turned around and walked down the hall, past the shower room to the living room, which was just inside the front door.

He entered quietly. His mother, Roberta, was sitting in her chair that faced the television. The screen's glow shone through her wiry hair, silhouetting her skull.

Rex stood there, waiting to hear the name again, because he'd just dreamed about that name, dreamed about that man. And he'd drawn a picture of that man just last night, before he went to bed — he had to have heard it wrong.

But he hadn't.

". . . Maloney was a longtime priest at the Cathedral of St. Mary of the Assumption in San Francisco, until he was caught up in a sex-abuse scandal and removed from that post. Maloney served a year in jail and was on probation. San Francisco chief of police Amy Zou said in a press conference this morning that the force is working to gather information on Maloney's murder, but that it's too early to make assumptions about the killer's motives."

"Father Maloney's dead?"

Rex said the words without thinking. Had he thought, he would have quietly walked away.

She turned, leaning over an armrest to look back at him. The television's light played off her pockmarked face. A cigarette dangled from her skinny fingers. "What are you doing in the TV room?"

"Uh, I just . . . I heard Father Maloney's name."

She squinted. She did that when she was thinking. She nodded almost imperceptibly. "I remember the lies you told about him," she said. "Dirty, *filthy* lies."

Rex stood there, motionless, wondering if she'd get the belt.

"Finish getting ready for school," she said. "You hear me talking to you?"

"Yes, Roberta." She didn't like it if he called her *Mom* or *Mother*. When he'd been little he'd called her those names, but sometime after his dad died she told him to stop using them.

Rex quickly walked out of the TV room before she could change her mind. Once out of her sight, he ran down the narrow hall to his bedroom. His room had a bed, a little TV with a video-game console, a dresser and a small desk with a stool — the sum total of his existence. He threw on his clothes and grabbed his backpack, remembering to get his notes for Freshman English off the floor as he did. No time for a shower; he had to get out of the house before Roberta thought of a reason to get mad at him. He hoped he didn't smell like pee — some bum was using the alley outside Rex's window as a bathroom. Not that it really mattered; sometimes Roberta wouldn't let him shower at all.

Before Rex left, he picked up the drawing sitting on his desk, the one he'd made last night. The picture showed a much larger Rex, a Rex with muscle-bound arms and a big chest, using his bare hands to snap Father Paul Maloney's left leg. Now Father Maloney was dead. The drawing made Rex feel funny. Funny, and *wrong.*

Rex put the drawing in the desk's drawer. He closed it, then looked at it to make sure no part of the drawing stuck out.

Time for the long walk to school. Rex prayed he could avoid the BoyCo bullies.

Father Paul Maloney was dead, and that was awesome. Maybe, for once, Rex could make it to school and back without getting his ass kicked, and the day would just keep getting better.

All in the Family

The San Francisco Hall of Justice takes up two full city blocks. The long, featureless, seven-story gray building located at 850 Bryant Street houses most divisions of the San Francisco Police Department — Gang Task Force, Homicide, Narcotic/Vice, Fraud, Operations and, of course, Administration. SWAT and Missing Persons have offices elsewhere in the city, but by and large most cop-related things that don't involve a local precinct happen at the Hall.

Bryan set his weapons and keys on the conveyor belt, then walked through the metal detector. He recognized the old uniform on the other side. Recognized the face, anyway — Bryan was shit with names.

"Clauser," the white-hair said with a nod.

Bryan nodded back, then collected his gear. Pookie came through next.

"Chang," the cop said.

"Lawrence," Pookie said. "How's that artificial hip treating you?"

"They think the screws on the ball part are coming loose," the man said. "Feels like someone is scraping a knife in my hip every time I take a step."

"Terrible," Pookie said, shaking his head in sympathy. "You suing?"

"Naw," Lawrence said. "I just want it fixed."

Pookie gave the man's shoulder a squeeze. "Good man. You change your mind, holla at your boy. I know some great lawyers. Oh, and happy anniversary. Tell Margaret I said congrats on number . . . is it twenty-three?"

Lawrence's hard face split in a smile, which lasted only a few seconds until he turned to glare the next person through.

Bryan and Pookie headed for the elevators.

"We gotta get you on *Jeopardy*," Bryan said. "How the hell do you remember this crap?"

Pookie pushed the *up* button, then shrugged. "Not all of us are as antisocial as you, my black-clad little buddy."

•••

Teddy Ablamowicz had been one of the city's financial golden boys. A heavy contributor to the San Francisco Opera, the ballet, GLBT charities and just about anything involving a park, Ablamowicz had been a well-known philanthropist, a mover and a shaker.

He had also been a money launderer. His murder — and the simultaneous disappearance of his wife — created reverberations throughout the organized crime community.

Bryan and Pookie walked into the conference room for the morning status meeting. Their fellow task-force members were already there. Because money laundering was a financial crime, the task force included Christopher Kearney from the Economic Crimes Unit. Kearney was okay except for that fact that he dressed in sweater vests like some Ivy League grad, and he insisted on being called *Christopher*. So, of course, everyone called him Chris.

A case of this magnitude also necessitated participation from the district attorney's office, hence the presence of Assistant DA Jennifer Wills. No charges had been filed as of yet — the task force didn't even have a suspect — so Wills was just there to keep tabs on the case. She mostly stayed quiet, only piping up if a planned action might get a perp off the hook somewhere down the road.

Since it was a murder investigation, Homicide took lead. Inspectors Stephen Koening and Steve "Ball-Puller" Boyd — also known as *the Brothers Steve* — ran the fieldwork. Koening was as cool as cool got, a stand-up guy by all accounts. Ball-Puller Boyd, on the other hand, seemed to be oblivious to the fact that he was quite repulsive: the sweaty, porn-stached, self-touching man had little concept of personal space.

Assistant Chief Sean Robertson ran the show. He was second in command for the entire SFPD. Bryan liked him. Robertson made people walk a fine line, but he was fair and didn't let the power go to his head. Everyone knew Robertson was being groomed as the future chief. Zou was in her late fifties. Another six years, maybe, and the whole department would probably be Robertson's.

Bryan had seen all these faces before. Today, however, he noted a new one — a guy in a three-piece talking to Robertson. Bryan nudged Pookie.

"Pooks, check out the suit. Fed?"

Pookie looked, nodded. "Yeah, but no way he's a gunslinger. Guy looks like he farts tax code. Excuse me for a moment, Bri-Bri, Daddy has to see about getting himself a date."

Pookie put on his best smile and closed in on Wills, the room's lone female. She was taking advantage of the premeeting lull to go over a legal pad full of notes.

"Jen-Jen," Pookie said. "Stylish, as always. That outfit new?"

She didn't bother looking up. "I'm not your type, Chang. But good eye — it is new."

"Of course it is. I could never forget seeing something that fetching. The shoes really set it off. And what do you mean you're not my type?"

Jennifer looked up, brushed her blond hair out of her face, then held up her left hand and wiggled her fingers. "No ring. Word on the streets is you only like the married ladies."

Pookie leaned back, put a hand on his chest. "Assistant DA Wills, I am hurt and offended by your insinuation that I contribute to infidelity."

She again bent to her legal pad. Pookie walked back to Bryan.

"Smooth," Bryan said.

"Sexual tension," Pookie said. "Vital to any good cop drama." He tapped his forehead. "It all goes in the vault to someday be played out in my brilliant scripts."

Steve Boyd walked up to Bryan and Pookie. He had a cup of coffee in his left hand. His right hand scratched at his balls. Where Polyester Rich's upper-lip scraggle looked like it belonged on the face of a 1950s movie villain, Boyd's walrus mustache was so thick you could barely see his mouth move when he talked.

"Clauser, Chang," Boyd said. The man tilted his head toward the suit. "Word is the nerd brought us a lead on the hitter."

Pookie sighed. "The *hitter*? Ball-Puller, you been watching the AMC gangster movie marathon again?"

"Never miss it," he said. "I hope he's got something. We've been shaking down all of Ablamowicz's clients, haven't come up with jack shit."

Robertson clapped three times to get everyone's attention. "Let's get started," he said. Robertson's thick brown hair had recently started to go gray at the temples, a color that matched his glasses. He always looked half rumpled: neither sloppy nor neat. His blue tie and bluer button-down shirt didn't quite hide a growing gut. That's what a desk job would do to you.

"Let's make it quick and get you back on the streets," he said. "I want to introduce Agent Tony Tryon, FBI."

The three-piece-suit man smiled. "Good morning. I'm here because I've spent the last five years watching Frank Lanza."

Ball-Puller Boyd started laughing. "*Lanza*? As in, the Mafia Lanzas of the Long-Ago Time?"

The FBI agent nodded.

Chris Kearney crossed his arms over his sweater-vest-covered chest and glared at the FBI agent. Bryan wondered if Kearney doubted the man or was just jealous of the tailored suit.

"The mob hasn't been here since Jimmy the Hat died," Kearney said. "The Tongs and the Russians pushed them out."

Jennifer clacked her pen against the table, *tap-tap-tap*. "Wait a minute — did you say *the hat*? His mob nickname was *the hat*? Not exactly frightening, is it?"

Tryon smiled at her. She smiled back. Bryan noticed Pookie scowl at the FBI agent.

"James Lanza frightened people just fine," Tryon said. "He ran the La Cosa Nostra in San Francisco for almost forty years. His dad, Francesco, founded the whole thing back in Prohibition."

Tryon picked up a folder off the table and walked to a corkboard at the end of the room. He pulled out black-and-white photos and started pinning them to the board. Pictures of four men went up in a row, with a single face on top. The face in that photo showed a man in his early forties, short black hair parted on the left side. Even in the still shot, Bryan thought the man looked smug and condescending.

Tryon tapped that top picture. "Francesco Joseph Lanza, known as *Frank*. Son of Jimmy the Hat, grandson of the first Francesco. For years, we've known Frank has been asking for permission to take back San Francisco. Looks like he got it. We think he's been here for six months, maybe more."

"Bullshit," said Ball-Puller Boyd. "We'd have heard he was in town."

Tryon shook his head. "Like his father, Frank doesn't draw attention to himself. He's probably not here for the clam chowder, if you know what I'm saying."

The FBI agent smiled at the other cops, as if waiting for them to laugh at his joke. No one did. His smile faded. He shrugged. "Anyway, Frank Lanza has been here for about six months. He brought a few guys out with him." Tryon tapped the faces below Lanza as he called out the names. "The big fella with the shaved head is Tony 'Four Balls' Gillum, Frank's right-hand man and bodyguard. The guy in the middle with the oft-broken nose is Paulie 'Hatchet' Caprise. This one is Little Tommy Cosimo. Last but not least, and the real reason I'm here" — he tapped the final picture — "is this sleepy-eyed gent, Pete 'the Fucking Jew' Goldblum."

Pookie raised his hand. "This guy's nickname is *the fucking Jew*?"

"At least it's better than *the hat*," Jennifer said.

"Goldblum is bad news," Tryon said. "No convictions, but he's got several hits to his name. If Lanza was behind Ablamowicz's murder, you can bet Goldblum did the deed."

"But why Ablamowicz?" Pookie said. "Taking out an *accountant*? Accountants don't mean shit. No offense, Chris."

"It's Christopher," Kearney said.

Pookie hit his forehead with the heel of his hand. "Aw, damn. Sorry about that."

Kearney looked at Pookie, then used his middle finger to rub his left eye. Pookie laughed.

"This *accountant* controlled cash flow for several organized crime outfits," Kearney said. "Ablamowicz worked for the Odessa Mafia, the Wah Ching Triad and Johnny Yee of the Suey Singsa Tong. More recently, Ablamowicz was moving a lot of cash for Fernando Rodriguez, leader of the Norteños."

All those gangs were serious business, but Bryan's role in Homicide brought him face-to-face with the Norteños more than any other outfit. For decades, the gang had spent most of their energy fighting their main rival, the Sureños. Under Fernando's guidance, however, the Norteños were expanding operations. Fernando was known for his smarts as well as his boldness — he would order a hit on anyone, anywhere, at any time.

"Ablamowicz controlled money," Kearney said. "If you want to mess up cash flow in San Francisco, he was a good a place to start."

Tryon again tapped on the picture of Frank Lanza. "Maybe Lanza offered Ablamowicz a deal. Maybe Ablamowicz didn't take the offer."

Robertson stood and smoothed his tie. "Thank you, Agent Tryon. That gives us more to look at. Tryon has copies of these photos for all of you, and he's been kind enough to share addresses and hangouts for Lanza's people. Brothers Steve, go talk to Paulie Caprise and Little Tommy Cosimo. Clauser and Chang, track down Goldblum and see if he has anything to say."

Everyone started to file out, but Pookie hung back. Bryan waited to see what his partner wanted.

"Hey, Assistant Chief," Pookie said. "Got a minute?"

Robertson nodded, then shook Tryon's hand. Tryon walked out, leaving Robertson with Pookie and Bryan.

"What's up, Pooks? You have some thoughts on Lanza?"

"No," Pookie said. "We've got thoughts on Paul Maloney."

Robertson nodded as he pushed his glasses higher on his nose. "Ah, I should have seen that coming."

Bryan's throat felt scratchy and dry. He needed some water — hopefully Pookie's whining wouldn't take long.

"We want this one," Pookie said. "Come on, man. It went down in the middle of the night. It's *ours*."

Robertson shook his head. "Not going to happen, gents. It's Verde's case."

"Don't get me wrong," Pookie said. "I like Rich Verde. I also like my grampa. My grampa drools a lot and tends to shit himself. Not that I'm making any association with Rich's age, mind you."

Robertson laughed. "The fact that Chief Zou wants you guys on the Ablamowicz case is a compliment to your skills. Be happy with that. Now go talk to Goldblum. Find me something."

Robertson walked out.

Pookie shook his head. "I hate this L-I-T-F-A shit."

"L-I-T-F-A?"

"*Leave it the fuck alone,*" Pookie said. "The guys who *should* be on the case intentionally kept off it? An ME that hasn't left the office in half a decade assigned to work the body? Strange things are afoot at the Circle-K, Bri-Bri."

Pookie had a point, but a couple of *strange things* didn't add up to a conspiracy. Sometimes the brass made decisions that didn't go your way.

"Forget it," Bryan said. "Come on, the sooner we find Goldblum, maybe the sooner we get back on nights."

Robin-Robin Bo-Bobbin

Robin Hudson backed her Honda motorcycle into the thin parking strip on Harriet Street just outside the San Francisco Medical Examiner's Office. Several bikes were already there, some owned by her co-workers. The guys had 1200s; the women mostly had scooters — Robin's ride sat right in the middle at 745ccs.

The morgue van was already backed into the unloading dock. Maybe it had been a busy night. She walked past the AMBULANCES ONLY sign and up the ramp toward the loading dock. She liked to enter work every day the same way her subjects did — through the doors where the bodies were rolled in.

It surprised her to see her boss get out of the van and gingerly step down to the ground.

"Doctor Metz! How are you this morning?"

Metz stopped to look at her. He gave his trademark single slow nod. "Good morning, Robin."

"Did you go out on a pickup?" When she'd started working here seven years ago, Metz had gone out on pickups three or four times a week, whenever there was a really bad killing or something unusual about a body, something interesting. As the years had passed, she'd watched him go out less and less. These days, he rarely left the office at all. He still ran the department, though, expecting his people to display the same dedication and perfection that he had shown for almost four decades.

"I did," he said. "I'll do the x-rays myself, right now, then I'll be in the private exam room for the next few hours. I don't want to be interrupted. Would you mind handling the department?"

"Sure, no problem." Robin tried to keep her voice neutral, but she couldn't help but feel a little excited by the request — yet another sign that he was grooming her to replace him. She had a lot of work ahead of her and a long way to go to qualify in his eyes, but everyone knew the chief medical examiner job was hers to lose. "Happy to do it," she said.

"Thank you. And I will want to use that RapScan machine. You received the training on it, yes?"

She nodded. The rapid DNA tester was a potential sea change in law enforcement. DNA samples were usually taken at the morgue, then shipped off to labs for processing. Depending on the test, it could take weeks to get results — sometimes even as long as two months. The new portable machines, however, could be taken right to the body and provide a reliable DNA fingerprint in a matter of hours. Rapid Analysis, the Rap-Scan 2000's manufacturer, had given San Francisco a model because of Dr. Metz's nationwide reputation in forensics.

Metz had asked Robin to master the device. For all the RapScan 2000 could do, the size still amazed her — it was no bigger than a typical leather briefcase. Labeling and data entry were done on a built-in touch screen. That same screen displayed results. Sample cartridges were the size of a matchbook, and the machine could process up to four samples simultaneously.

"It's easy," she said. "You could have taken it with you into the field, you know. It's small enough to fit right in the back of the van. That's the point of it, Doc — if you'd started the process while you were in the field, it would probably be kicking out the results right now."

He thought about that, then gave his single slow nod. "That would have been helpful. Call the Rapid Analysis company and tell them I want a second test unit. But do that *after* you show me how to operate it."

"Sure thing, Doctor Metz."

Why was he in such a hurry? She peeked past Metz to the body on the cart. The white body bag hid any details of the corpse, although the form inside it did look a little misshapen. She detected a whiff of urine. Not unusual for a body to void itself upon death, but it had to be pretty saturated for her to smell it through the thick material. She tilted her head toward the bagged corpse. "Something interesting in there?"

Metz looked at her for a few moments, as if he was thinking of saying something but then decided against it. He spoke a fraction of a second before the stare would have become uncomfortable.

"Maybe," he said. "We shall see. A case like this . . . it's delicate. Maybe I'll tell you about it. Maybe soon."

"When you do, boss man, I'm all ears."

"Oh, I saw your boyfriend while I was out. How is Bryan these days?"

Robin's smile faded. "Bryan and I broke up."

Metz's eyes saddened. "Recently?"

"About six months ago."

He looked at her, then looked away. This time it *was* uncomfortable. "Yes. You've told me about this before. Now I remember."

Not knowing what else to do, Robin just nodded. Metz rolled the body into the morgue one slow step at a time. Even at his age, he liked to handle everything himself.

It was hard to watch him forget things. Had to be murder for him — a man whose life and identity rested squarely on his intelligence — to see the first signs of his memory slipping away.

Robin walked through the receiving area where bodies were declothed, weighed and photographed. She entered the offices, which consisted of a dozen gray cubicles that made the old yellow carpet look brighter by contrast. Printouts and paper clippings were tacked up to the cubicles' fabric, showing news coverage of various murders or high-profile suicides. Any photo that showed someone from the examiner's office in action immediately went up as a trophy.

She put her helmet and jacket in her cubicle, then retied her long ponytail as she looked at the chalkboard. That was how the San Francisco ME Office tracked incoming bodies and assignments — not on computers, but on a three-foot-wide, six-foot-high green chalkboard. The board was divided into three-by-three sections that slid up or down, one under the other. The top board listed last night's work; ten names scrawled in chalk, all reading the time of arrival, the examiner assigned to the body, and "NC" for *natural causes.*

The board on the bottom was today's work, already four lines deep. Two of those listed *NC,* while the other two listed a question mark — a question mark meant a probable homicide.

She saw the line on the bottom with Metz's name in the "assigned" column. The stiff's name was *Paul Maloney.*

Robin let out a long, slow whistle. Father Paul Maloney. That was high-profile. Was that why Metz had gone on the pickup? That made sense. And yet, she felt like he'd wanted to tell her something else, something he'd ultimately decided she wasn't ready for yet. What that might be, she didn't know.

Whatever it was, it would have to wait, because according to the board *Singleton, John, NC* and *Quarry, Michelle, ?* were waiting for her.

Pookie's Sister

Pookie parked the Buick on Union Street, next to Washington Square Park. As he got out, his hands did their automatic four-pat — a pat on the left pants pocket for his car keys, the right pants pocket for his cell, left breast for his gun, and rear-right pants pocket for his wallet. Everything was in its place.

Bryan was leaning on the Buick's hood, left hand pressed against the chipped brown paint.

"Bri-Bri, you okay?"

Bryan shrugged. "Might be coming down with something."

That would be the day. "Dude, you never get sick."

Bryan looked up. Beneath his shaggy, dark-red hair, his face looked a bit pale. "You don't feel anything, Pooks?"

"Other than guilt at hogging most of the universe's available supply of awesome, no. I'm fine. You think you caught something at the Maloney site?"

"Maybe," Bryan said.

Even if Bryan had caught something, they'd been there only a few hours ago. Flu didn't set in that fast. Maybe Bryan was just tired. Most days, the guy hid in his darkened apartment like some nocturnal creature. Three day shifts in a row had probably played havoc with Bryan's sleep patterns.

They walked down Union toward the corner of Mason Street. There lay the Trattoria Contadina restaurant. According to Tryon's info, one Pete "the Fucking Jew" Goldblum had been seen there several times.

"Bri-Bri, know what's bugging me?"

"That Polyester Rich has our case?"

"You're psychic," Pookie said. "You should be one of those fortune-tellers."

"Just leave it alone."

Like hell Pookie would leave it alone. Why would the chief want her best two inspectors off the Maloney case? It just didn't make any sense. Maybe it had something to do with whatever was under that blue tarp.

Paul Maloney had deserved a lot of bad things, but not murder. His end couldn't be considered *justice*, no matter what crimes he'd committed. Maloney had been tried and convicted by a jury of his peers — the court's punishments had not included the death sentence.

Bryan coughed, then spit a nasty glob of yellow phlegm onto the sidewalk.

"Lovely," Pookie said. "Maybe you *are* sick."

"Maybe," Bryan said. "You should be a detective or something."

They passed San Francisco Evangelical Church. After arriving from Chicago ten years ago, Pookie had given that one a whirl. Not his taste. He'd tried several churches before finding his home at Glide Memorial. Pookie preferred his sermons served up with a side of soul music and a touch of R&B.

He realized he was walking alone. He looked back. Bryan was standing there, his face in his hands, slowly moving his head side to side like he was trying to shake away a thought.

"Bri-Bri, you sure you're okay?"

Bryan looked up, blinked. He cleared his throat, let lose another goober-rocket, then nodded. "Yeah, I'm fine. Let's go."

Trattoria Contadina was only a block away from Washington Square. Concierges knew the restaurant and sent tourists there to dine, but for the most part the place belonged to the locals. Simple white letters on a dingy-green, bird-crap-strewn awning spelled out the corner restaurant's name along both Union and Mason. A bell over the door rang as Bryan and Pookie walked inside.

The smell of meat, sauce and cheese smacked Pookie in the face. He'd forgotten about the place and made a mental note to come back soon for dinner — the eggplant antipasti was so good you'd slap your sister to get some. And Pookie liked his sister.

About half of the linen-covered tables were full, couples and groups talking and laughing to the accompaniment of clinking silverware. Pookie was about to pull out the pictures Tryon had provided when Bryan lightly elbowed him, then nodded toward the back corner. It took Pookie a second to recognize the half-lidded eyes of Pete Goldblum, who was sitting with two other men.

Pookie walked to the table. Bryan followed, just a step behind. That was the way they handled things. Even though Bryan was smaller, he was kind of the "heavy" of the partnership. Pookie did most of the talking until the time for talking had passed, then Bryan took over. The Terminator had a coldness about him that people couldn't ignore.

Pookie stopped at the table. "Peter Goldblum?"

All three men looked up with that stare, the one that said *we know you're a cop and we don't fucking like cops.* They all wore suits. That was unusual; the era of the well-dressed mafioso had largely passed by.

Nowadays, dressing flashy was for gangbangers — most of the really powerful guys dressed as inconspicuously as possible.

Goldblum finished chewing a mouthful of food and swallowed it down. "Who's asking?"

"I'm Inspector Chang." Pookie showed his badge. He tilted his head toward Bryan. "This is Inspector Clauser. We're with Homicide, looking into the murder of Teddy Ablamowicz."

Bryan walked around to the other side of the table. The three men watched him, their attention naturally drawn to the more dangerous-looking of the two cops.

The man sitting opposite Goldblum spoke. "*Clauser?* As in, *Bryan* Clauser?"

Pookie recognized the other two men just as Bryan answered — the arrogant face of Frank Lanza, the broad shoulders and shaved head of Tony Gillum.

Bryan nodded. "That's right, Mister Lanza. I'm surprised you know my name."

Lanza shrugged. "Someone told me about you. From what I hear, you're in the wrong line of work. You should be one of those" — he squinted and looked to the ceiling, pretending to try and remember something — "Tony, what's the name of those guys they have in those silly gangster movies? The guys who kill people?"

"Hit men," Tony said. He spoke with a voice so deep he might very well have the four balls of his nickname. "He should be a hit man, Mister Lanza."

"Right," Lanza said. "A hit man, that's it." He looked at Bryan. "I heard you killed what, four people?"

Bryan nodded. "So far."

The one-liner made the men pause. Damn, Pookie had to write that one down for later — that kind of stuff could make a script sing.

"Mister Goldblum," Pookie said, "we'd like to ask you some questions about Teddy Ablamowicz."

"Never met him," Goldblum said. "He the guy in the paper?"

Lanza laughed. "He's in *three* papers, if you know what I mean. Parts of him, anyway. At least that's what I heard." Lanza picked up a piece of bread and smeared it in the sauce on his plate. He shook his head dismissively, as if Pookie and Bryan were a trivial annoyance that had to be temporarily tolerated.

Were these guys for real? The suits, all of them together, in public like this, and in an Italian restaurant? Maybe they had been quiet for six months, but stealth seemed to be over — they wanted people to see them, to know that the LCN was back in town.

"This isn't Jersey," Pookie said. "I don't know how you run things back east, but maybe you don't understand who Ablamowicz was working for, or what happens now."

Bryan stared at Lanza, then picked up a piece of bread and took a bite. "He means you should lie low, Mister Lanza. Not be out like this, where anyone can roll up on you."

Lanza shrugged. "We're just out for a meal. We didn't do nothing wrong. You think we did something wrong?"

Bryan smiled. The smile was even spookier than his stare. "Doesn't matter what I think," he said. "What matters is what Fernando Rodriguez thinks."

"Who the fuck is Fernando Rodriguez?"

It took Pookie a second to realize that Lanza wasn't making a joke. Maybe God loved Frank Lanza, because it had to be a miracle that an idiot like this had lived so long.

"He's the boss of the Norteños," Pookie said. "Locally, anyway. You should know these things. Fernando is a man who gets things done, Mister Lanza. If he thinks you were involved with the Ablamowicz murder, odds are you guys are going to have visitors. Real soon."

Goldblum picked his napkin out of his lap and dropped it on his half-eaten dinner. "Fuck that," he said quietly. "I'm a taxpaying citizen. Think I'm concerned about some chickenshit wetback outfit?"

Oh, man, these guys hadn't done their homework. Underestimating the Norteños could win you an express ticket to the morgue. Pookie felt compelled to bring Pete in — for his own safety more than for the crime.

"Mister Goldblum," Pookie said, "I think you should come with us."

Goldblum's eyebrows raised, but his eyes stayed half lidded. "You arresting me, gook?"

Pookie shook his head. "I'm from Chicago, not Vietnam. And, no, we're not arresting you, but why make things difficult? You know we're going to have that conversation downtown sooner or later, so let's just play nice and get it over with."

Lanza laughed. "Yeah, right. Like you guys are so different from East Coast cops. You *never* get it over with."

Pookie heard the tingle of the front door's bell. Bryan's eyes snapped up, then narrowed.

Uh-oh.

Pookie turned quickly. Two Latino men, approaching fast. Thick workingman jackets. Knit hats — one red with the white N of the Nebraska Cornhuskers, the other red with the SF logo of the 49ers. Tats peeked out from their T-shirt collars, running right up to their ears.

Each man had a hand in his jacket.

Each man was staring at Frank Lanza.

Jesus H. Christ — a hit? *Here?*

"Pooks," Bryan said quietly, "get back here, *now*."

Pookie stepped around the table before reaching into his jacket for his Sig Sauer, but the men were faster. Their hands came out of their jackets — one raising a semiauto, the other leveling a sawed-off pump shotgun.

Before the men even cleared their weapons, Bryan drew his own Sig with his left hand, reached out and grabbed Lanza with his right. In the same motion, he kicked the table over so the top faced the gunmen, sending plates of food flying. Bryan shoved Lanza down behind the overturned table.

The sawed-off roared, shredding linen and splintering wood.

Bryan's pistol barked twice, *bam-bam*. The shotgun guy twitched, then Bryan fired for the third time in less than a second. The man's head rocked back and he dropped.

Screams filled the air. Pookie found his gun in his shaking hand. The other attacker backpedaled for the front door, firing wildly toward the table. Pookie aimed — *people on the floor, ducking behind tables, too crowded, traffic outside, people on the sidewalk* — but didn't fire.

A gunshot to Pookie's right. Tony Gillum, firing as the perp ran out the restaurant door.

Bryan came at Tony from behind, grabbing Tony's right hand and lifting it, pointing the gun to the ceiling even as Bryan drove his left foot into the back of Tony's right leg. Tony grunted and fell to his knee. Bryan twisted sharply, throwing the bigger man facedown onto the food-strewn linoleum floor.

Bryan remained standing, Tony's gun still in his hand. He ejected the magazine and pulled back the slide, then walked four steps forward and kicked the sawed-off shotgun away from the downed gunman.

"Pooks, cuff Tony and call this in."

The fear finally hit home. It had all gone down in four seconds, five at most. Pookie pointed his weapon just to the left of Tony's back.

"Don't move! Hands behind your head!"

"Relax," Tony said as he obliged. "I got a permit."

Pookie set his knee into the small of Tony's back, making the man carry his weight. "Just stay right there. Bryan, you going after the other gunman?"

"No way," Bryan said. "We wait for backup. First guy to peek his head out that door might get it shot off." He then shouted to the restaurant patrons. "San Francisco Police! Everyone just stay where you are! Is anyone hurt?"

The patrons looked at one another, waited for someone to talk. No one did. A chorus of shaking heads answered Bryan's question.

"Okay," he said. "Nobody move until backup arrives. Stay down, stay calm. *Do not* try to leave the building, the gunman might still be outside."

Ten seconds of panic had rooted the patrons in place. They didn't relax, not even close, but they obediently stayed put.

As Pookie cuffed Tony Gillum, Bryan knelt next to the would-be assassin and opened the man's jacket. Glancing over, Pookie saw two spreading red spots staining the perp's white T-shirt, blood circles merging into a solid figure-8. Blood also oozed from a spot just under the man's left nostril.

Two to the chest, one to the head.

Pookie called for backup. He also requested an ambulance, but unless someone got a splinter from the ruined table the paramedics wouldn't have much to do — Bryan's perp was already dead.

"Holy shit," Lanza said. "Holy shit."

Bryan sighed, closed the gunman's jacket. He looked back at Lanza.

"They were after you, Lanza," Bryan said. "Like I told you, you probably want to lie low, if not just throw in the towel and go back to Jersey."

A wide-eyed Lanza nodded. "Yeah. Lie low."

Bryan walked to Lanza and helped the man to his feet.

"You owe me," Bryan said.

Pookie watched. Bryan had just killed a man, yet he acted like that was about as upsetting as opening the fridge to find someone had drunk the last of the milk. The casual nature and the cold stare seemed to shake Lanza up as much as the shooting itself.

"You owe me," Bryan said again. "You know that, right?"

Lanza rubbed his face, then nodded. "Yeah. I . . . holy shit, man."

"A name," Bryan said. "We want a name for this Ablamowicz thing."

Lanza looked back to the dead gunman lying on the floor at Bryan's feet, then nodded.

Pete Goldblum had hit the deck as soon as the shooting started. He stood and wiped spaghetti sauce off his suit coat. "Mister Lanza, you don't owe this cop shit."

"Shut up, Pete," Lanza said. "I'd be a grease spot right now. You and Four Balls didn't do a god-damned thing."

"Hey," said a facedown Tony Gillum. "I got a round off."

"Sure, Tony," Lanza said. "You're like a regular Green Beret."

Pookie heard his own long release of breath before he knew he was letting it out — the situation was contained. It wasn't the first time he'd seen Bryan Clauser in action like that, but he hoped it would be the last.

Bryan's Lie

The sun had hidden itself somewhere behind the apartment buildings. Bryan was only minutes away from his bed and sleep. Usually he had trouble sleeping at night, but not today — he'd be out like a light.

"Riddle me something, Bri-Bri."

Bryan's forehead rested in his right hand; his elbow rested on the inside handle of Pookie's Buick. Whatever bug he had was rapidly getting worse: fatigue and body aches, the start of sniffles, throat full of razor blades, a first hint at a monster headache.

Bryan leaned back and yawned. Pookie had been talking nonstop since they left the restaurant. That was in a manual somewhere — keep the shooter talking after the incident, don't give him time to get all introspective.

Pookie meant well, for sure, but Bryan just wanted silence. He couldn't tell his friend and partner why. Some things you just couldn't share. They were almost back to Bryan's apartment, then he'd be done with Pookie's constant chatter.

"Bri-Bri? You hearing me?"

"Yeah, sure. What's the question?"

"How does a grown man not have a car?"

Bryan had to clear his throat before he could talk. "Don't need a car. I live right in the city."

"You don't need a car because I schlep you all over the place."

"Also a factor."

Pookie double-parked in front of Bryan's building. Horns behind them started honking instantly.

"Bri-Bri, you going to be okay? I can hang here tonight if you want."

Bryan put on his best fake-solemn expression. "Thanks, but no. This ain't my first rodeo. I just need to be alone and think this through."

Pookie nodded. "All right, playa. But call me if you start wigging out, okay?"

"Thanks, man." Bryan had to coax his exhausted body out of the car. He stumbled into his building. What a day. A shooting, handling the crime scene, giving his statement, the preliminary shooting review — too damn much. There would be more long days to come. With all those witnesses, with a gunman opening fire in a crowded restaurant, Bryan wouldn't catch any shit for this. That didn't mean, however, that he didn't have to go through the motions. A full shooting review board was already scheduled. That was always such a good time.

And at the crime scene itself, before he could even leave, there'd been the mandatory chat with the police shrink. Was Bryan okay? How did the shooting make him feel? Did he think he could be alone that night?

Bryan said what he always said — that killing a man felt awful.

And, as always, that was a lie.

Did he enjoy killing people? No. Did he feel bad about it? Not in the least. He knew that he *should* feel something, but just like the last four times, he did not.

The guy had fired a shotgun. If Bryan hadn't put him down, it could have been Lanza in the body bag. Or Pookie. Or Bryan himself.

Lanza, such an idiot. Maybe on the East Coast people respected the Mafia enough to give them leeway, but not out here. Jimmy the Hat had been a sharp cat. His son? Not so much. Frank and his buddies dressed up like they wanted the golden age of crime to come back overnight. Well, now they knew a different story.

Adrenaline had kept Bryan pumped from the shooting right up through the talk with the shrink. But during that whole time, his body had been sneakily breaking down. Once the buzz of excitement wore off, he'd felt completely wiped out.

Bryan pressed the button to call the rickety old elevator. Instead of a click and the whir of machinery, he heard nothing. Dammit — the elevator was broken again.

He pushed his body up the stairs, each step feeling like he was lifting someone else's much-larger foot. He reached the fourth floor and paused. Muscle pain you could ignore. Most of it, anyway. Aches, throbbing, fever . . . but now he felt a new pain that demanded his attention.

A pain in his chest.

Bryan ground his teeth, then rubbed his hand hard against his sternum. Was he having a heart attack? No . . . it felt like it was a little *above* his heart. But what did he know about heart attacks? Maybe that's where they started.

And then, suddenly, the pain faded away. He took a long, deep breath. Maybe he should call a doctor, but he was so damn tired.

It was probably nothing. Just the flu, messing with his system. Maybe he was more stressed about the shooting than he knew. If his chest felt like that the next day, he'd call a doc for sure.

Bryan walked into his apartment and started stripping off his weapons. He managed to remove most of his clothes before he crashed into his bed and fell asleep on top of his covers.

Fade In, Fade Out

The musty dampness of rotting cloth.

The stench of rancid garbage.

The pulsing heat of the hunt.

Two conflicting emotions fighting for dominance — the overpowering, electric taste of hatred juxtaposed against the pinching, tingling sensation of creeping evil.

Even as he hunted, something hunted him.

Bryan stood motionless, using only his eyes to track the prey.

One womb.

They hurt him. Just like the other one had.

We have waited so long.

Even through the blurry, nonsensical images, he recognized the street: Van Ness. Shifty streaks of people with indiscernible, blurred faces; moving swaths of fuzzy color that were cars; headlights and streetlights that made the fog glow.

Bryan watched his target, a target made up of abstract impressions of hazy crimson and dull gold, of wide shoulders and floppy blond hair, of scowling eyes made of evil.

Not a man . . . a *boy.* Big, but still young. The boy had a certain walk, a certain . . . *scent.*

Bryan wanted this boy dead.

He wanted them *all* dead.

One womb.

Hunting, but also . . . hunt*ed.* Bryan searched the skyline, looking for movement. Even as he did, he felt a deep, cold knowledge that he probably wouldn't see death coming. He needed to make the mark, the mark that kept the monster at bay.

Bryan felt a tap on his shoulder. He sighed in frustration, knowing he could take the prey if only there weren't so many people around. But he had another job to do — this target would have to wait.

Turning now. Moving. Everything a blur. Fade in, fade out. Refocused. Looking down at an alley. Must be high up. Looking down at a beat-up blue dumpster. Something behind the dumpster, mostly hidden from view, but not hidden from *smell.*

Bryan recognized this scent as well. Not as good as the boy, not as healthy. More . . . *worn-out,* but still good enough to make his stomach rumble. Bryan looked closer — a bit of red and yellow behind the dumpster. A blanket. A red blanket. The yellow looked like something familiar . . . a little bird . . .

Fade out, fade in, fade out again. The dream slipped away.

In his bed, Bryan turned once, opened his eyes and wondered where he was. The room's darkness seemed a living thing, ready to sting him with blackened barbs. Sweat dripped from his face, soaked into his sheets.

His sheets. *His* bed. He was in his own apartment.

He'd left the dream, but the fear of the monster that hunted him came along for the ride. His chest hurt, far worse than it had on the stairs. Was that ache from dream-terror, or from the flu that made him burn and sweat?

Bryan reached out and turned on his nightstand lamp. He winced at the sudden light, but not for long.

He had to find some paper, find a pen.

He had to draw.

Rex Wakes Up

Rex Deprovdechuk woke up hot and sweating.

Excited. *Terrified.*

For a brief moment he remained lost in the dream's power, his heart hammering, his breath short and fast. Then the aches faded back in like a vise slowly squeezing every part of his body. The pain, the fever . . . he'd never been this sick before.

His pants felt funny. He reached down and touched, felt something *stiff.* He pulled his hand back — what was that down there? Embarrassment swept over him, making his skin feel even hotter.

He had a *boner.*

He knew what boners were, of course. Kids at school talked about them all the time. People talked about them on TV. He'd even seen them in Internet porn. Seen them, sure, but he'd never *had* one. Watching porn hadn't given him one. Neither had the girls at school. Rex had always known he was *supposed* to have them, yet they had never come. Nothing had ever turned him on before.

But the dream had.

He had been stalking Alex Panos, the biggest of the bullies who made Rex's life hell. Stalking him, like a lion would stalk a zebra. The dream-smells still filled Rex's nose — rotting cloth, garbage — and those conflicting feelings: burning rage against the bully, and mind-numbing fear of the thing lurking in the shadows.

One womb.

What a great dream. He'd almost jumped down from some building to attack that asshole Alex. Wouldn't that have been great?

There had been other people in the dream, people who were hunting side by side with him. Two people . . . two people with strange faces. Dreams were crazy like that.

His dick throbbed so bad it hurt. It was a different kind of hurt than the sickness that overwhelmed his body. *Growing pains,* Roberta had told him. He still didn't know about that. The pains had come out of nowhere just a couple of days ago. But maybe she was right — he'd just had his first boner ever, so maybe he was growing. Maybe he'd grow a *lot* and wouldn't be the smallest freshman in the school anymore.

Maybe . . . maybe he'd get big enough to beat up the bullies.

The boner brought with it a huge wave of relief. In that way, at least, he was like the other boys.

Rex climbed out of bed, careful to move quietly lest the squeaky floorboards wake his mother. If Roberta woke up at this hour, it would be real bad.

He reached up and tenderly touched his nose. Still sore. That wasn't from the body aches, it was from where Alex had punched him in the face yesterday. Just a little punch, and it had put Rex down. If Alex ever hit Rex as hard as he could . . .

Rex didn't want to think about that. He walked to his desk and turned on his lamp. He had to draw a symbol he'd seen in the dream, something that he knew would make the fear fade away. He'd draw the symbol, and then something else — one of those strange faces he'd seen in the dream, a face that should have frightened him but did not.

Finally, Rex would draw Alex. Alex, and all the things Rex wished he could do to him.

The sketch pad waited.

Rex drew.

Aggie James, Duckies and Bunnies

Aggie James pulled the dirty sleeping bag tighter around his body. Even the two cardboard boxes underneath him couldn't keep away the ground's chill. He'd wedged himself behind a dumpster that blocked at least some of the light wind, but San Francisco's night mist permeated his clothes, saturated every breath he drew into his lungs, even soaked into the sleeping bag he'd been so lucky to find. The sleeping bag was red, with duckies and bunnies on it. He'd found it draped over a trashcan not too far from here.

He felt the cold, the dampness, but those were distant, just faint echoes of something that might concern him. Weather didn't matter, because he had scored. Scored *big*. And it was good shit, too — he'd felt the horse kick in before he'd even pulled the syringe out of his arm.

This was his favorite sleeping spot, in the back doorway of some old furniture store on Fern Street, just off Van Ness. They called it a *street*, but it was an *alley*. No one really bothered him here.

A numbing warmth spread all over his body, even down to his toenails, man, even down to his *toenails*. So it was cold out, so what? Aggie was warm in the way he *needed* to be warm.

He heard a light thump, then a heavier rattle, like something had landed on the dumpster.

"Pierre, you retard, try to be quiet."

"You sthut up."

The first voice sounded raspy, like sandpaper on rough wood. The second rang deep. Deep and *slow*. The sounds echoed through Aggie's head. He hoped these guys would just pass on by. Sleep was coming whether he wanted it or not. *Damn*, but this was some good shit.

"This him?" The sandpaper voice.

"Uh-huh," said a third voice. This one sounded high-pitched. "We gotta clean him up, but for sure he's a won't-be."

The sound of someone sniffing, and that sound was close. When Aggie heard it, he felt a cool trickle of air across his cheek. Was someone *smelling* him?

Aggie tried to open his eyes. They cracked, just a little. He saw a blurry image of a kid's head, maybe a teenager?

The teenager smiled.

Aggie's eyes slid shut, returning him to the delicious darkness. Had he dropped a tab? Maybe he had after he shot up, then forgot about it. Had to be something — horse had never made him hallucinate before. Well, maybe a little, but not like *that.* Had to be acid. Only acid could have made him see that teenager with big black eyes, skin as purple as grape juice, and a smiling mouth full of big fucking shark teeth.

Just say no to hallucinations, thank you very much.

"I been watching him," said the high-pitched voice.

"He looks sthick," said the deep voice. Something about that voice, something wet and slurry. It reminded Aggie of Sylvester, the cat from Looney Toons, the way he'd spit and slobber while working out *suffering succotash.* The guy sounded like he had a tongue that just didn't know its place.

"He's not sick," said high-pitch.

"He looks sthick. Thly, you think he's sthick?"

"I dunno," said the sandpaper voice.

High-pitch sounded offended. "He's not sick. He's just stoned. We can clean him up."

"He better not be sick," said sandpaper voice. "The last one you picked must have had the flu. I shit chocolate milk for a week."

"I said I was sorry about that," said high-pitch.

Sandpaper voice sighed. "Whatever. Pierre, pick him up. We need to get back."

Aggie felt strong arms slide under him, lift him effortlessly.

"I'm staying out tonight," said high-pitch. "We have lots of time before dawn. I got to do my thing."

The sandpaper voice again. "Chomper, you need to come back with us."

"No. The visions. I . . . I can *sense* him."

"Yeah, so can we," said sandpaper. "I told you not to talk about it. You want Firstborn to beat you again?"

"No. I don't want that again. But those assholes *hurt* him, I can feel it."

Him. Whoever it was, he sounded important.

"I have someone watching over him," sandpaper said. "You stay away, or you could bring the monster down on him."

A pause. Aggie felt like he weighed all of five pounds. Maybe even five *negative* pounds, because you don't weigh anything if you float.

"I'll stay away," high-pitch said. "But I'm not going home. Not yet."

"Just don't draw attention," said the sandpaper voice. "And *stay away* from the king. Hillary said he's not ready yet. You get us caught, Firstborn will kill us. Pierre, let's go, we're due back."

"Okay, Sthly."

Aggie felt like he was falling, only for a second, then he went *up.* So fast, herky-jerky, *pop . . . pop . . . pop . . .* like someone taking the stairs three at a time, yet the arms holding him felt gentle, like the guy carrying him was being careful — much like you would be careful carrying a dozen eggs you just bought from the store.

Aggie struggled to open his eyes again. He was on a rooftop. He could see Van Ness far below, his attention drawn to a green Starbucks sign. Not that a Starbucks sign was much of a landmark; those things were everywhere.

Then, the world lurched under him. Up, then down, then up, then down.

Despite the motion, the horse — that goddamn *fine* horse — finally caught up with him. Aggie James let himself slide into the warmth and the darkness, into the one place where the memories didn't haunt him.

The Belt

ut I feel sick."

Roberta Deprovdechuk crossed her arms and stared. "Get up, boy. You go to school."

The very word *school* did, in fact, make Rex feel sick. Sick inside, a cold sensation that made him want to crawl into a hole and hide forever.

"Honest, I really don't feel good."

She rolled her eyes. "You think I was born yesterday? You're not sick. Those kids pick on you because you're obnoxious. You leave them alone and they'll leave you alone. Get up and get to school. And no skipping! You skip school like some good-for-nothing burnout, sit here and draw all day. I let you put your stupid pictures up on your walls, don't I? Now *get up.*"

She grabbed the blankets and yanked them off. He had a horrid, frozen moment of exposure, of his boner pushing his underwear out in a little tent. Rex slammed his body into a fetal position, hands over his underwear-clad privates.

"You *filthy* boy! Did you touch it?"

Still curled up, he shook his head.

"Rex, did you *touch yourself*?"

"No!"

He heard the familiar hiss of leather sliding through denim belt loops. He closed his eyes tight in anticipation of the pain to come.

"Roberta, I didn't touch it! Honest, I—"

The *crack* of leather on his back cut his words short.

"You little liar."

A second *crack*, this time on his legs. Despite the stinging pain, he stayed curled up. Rex knew better than to cry out, or to try and get away.

"I told you *never* to be like the other dirty boys, didn't I?"

Crack, his shoulder lit up.

"I'm sorry! I won't do it ever again!"

Crack, on the thin underwear fabric covering his ass. That one made him lurch, twitch, his body screaming at him to *run*, but he fought himself back into a tight ball.

If he ran or resisted, it would only get worse.

"There," Roberta said. "I'm helping you, Rex. You need to learn these things. If you're not ready for school in five minutes, you get more. You hear me talking to you?"

She walked out, slamming the door behind her.

The pain faded a little, but the cold feeling in his chest would not leave. He still had to go to school.

Rex sat up on the bed. His boner had gone away. Roberta had always told him boners were bad, and the lingering stings on his back, his legs, his ass told him she was right.

He'd dreamed again, and this time he'd remembered more. He'd been watching Alex Panos, waiting for a chance to *kill* Alex. And that was what made Rex feel funny. Not girls, not even boys — the *stalking* gave him the boner. Hunting Alex felt exciting, *arousing*, but the dream also carried a dark fear that someone was watching Rex, waiting in the darkness to *hurt* him.

Dream-Rex had turned away from Alex. Instead, Rex and his friends had grabbed some random homeless guy. Grabbed him, *taken* him, but taken him where? Rex couldn't remember.

He stood. That fear, it sat in his stomach like a block of ice. It wouldn't go away. He picked his jeans up off the floor. As he slid them on, he looked over at his desk, at his latest drawing of Alex Panos and the bullies.

The drawing wasn't finished.

Maybe he could finish it in history class. Rex had read the whole textbook the first week of school and got 100 percent on every test — Mr. Garthus didn't care if Rex did any work, as long as he kept quiet. No time to finish the full drawing, but Rex felt an urge to sketch that symbol again. He *had* to sketch it, right now.

When his pencil completed the symbol's final half-circle, the lingering dream-fear finally eased away. Rex's more familiar, ever-present anxiety remained, however. Roberta was wrong; it didn't matter if he minded his own business or not, the bullies would come for him no matter what he did.

Rex shivered. He wanted to skip school, but he didn't dare. Whatever beating the bullies had for him, it couldn't match what Roberta would do if she switched from the belt to the paddle.

Rex rubbed his new welts. He finished dressing. He gathered his books, then slid them, his pencils and his art pad into his bag.

Maybe today would be better.

The Drawing

Bryan opened the Buick's door, moved Pookie's pile of folders, then sat. "Pooks, you ever clean up this crap-ass car?"

Pookie leaned back, affected an expression of hurt. "My goodness, did someone wake up on the wrong side of the bed?"

Bryan shut the door. Pookie pulled into traffic.

"I had some messed-up dreams," Bryan said. "Couldn't sleep for shit."

"That could explain why you look like the wet side of a half-dry dog turd."

"Thanks."

"Don't mention it. But seriously, folks, you do look awful. And trim that beard, man. You're starting to look like a gay hipster. I've no room for such nonsense in my life."

Bryan's chest pain had faded from sharpness to a dull, nagging ache, like a jammed finger, or a knot in his spine that refused to crack. He dug his right fist into his sternum and rubbed it around.

Pookie looked over. "Heartburn?"

"Something like that."

"Not sleeping, pale as a ghost, and chest pains to boot," Pookie said. "If we weren't meeting Chief Zou, I'd drive you back to your apartment and tell you to take a sick day."

Chief Zou would already have the preliminary overview from the shooting review board. A full investigation was under way — standard procedure — but the early overview would determine if Bryan stayed on normal duty or was relegated to a desk until the final report came in.

There was also the option that Zou could just suspend him altogether. For most cops, that wouldn't be a worry. Most cops, however, hadn't just killed their fifth human being.

"I'll be okay," Bryan said, which was a lie. His fever had grown during the night. He felt hot all over. He was still a little dizzy, congested, and on top of that the body aches were even worse. His knees and elbows, his wrists and ankles, all his joints felt like they were filled with gravel. His muscles throbbed with an entirely different feeling, as if someone had spent hours pummeling him with a meat tenderizer.

"Don't breathe on me," Pookie said. "You get me sick, I'm kicking you in the nuts. Tell me about these messed-up dreams. Anything involving either a naughty cheerleader, detention with the MILF-a-licious assistant principal, or a shy-yet-stacked nun questioning her life choices?"

Bryan laughed, a short, choppy thing that drew a raspy cough. "I wish. Weren't those kind of dreams."

"Nightmares?"

Bryan nodded. "Dreamed I was with a couple other guys. I don't know who they were. We were hunting this kid as he walked down Van Ness, and at the same time something was hunting us. Something real bad, but I never saw it. Then we were going to do something to this old bum. I was still scared out of my gourd when I woke up. I had to draw something from the dream."

Bryan pulled the sheet of paper out of his pocket, opened it and passed it to Pookie. Pookie looked at the image: an unfinished triangle with a circle slicing through the lines and under the points, a smaller circle in the center.

"Wow," Pookie said. "Your father and I are so proud, honey, we'll put it right on the fridge next to your report card. What is it?"

"No idea."

"And . . . what happened after you drew it?"

Bryan shrugged. "The fear went away. So did most of the dream. But I think I remember *where* the dream took place."

"You recognized the spot?"

"Uh-huh. Pretty sure it was Van Ness and Fern."

"Crazy. You want to check it out?"

Bryan shook his head. "We have to get to the chief's office."

"We've got fifteen minutes to spare," Pookie said. "Come on, this could be good material for our cop show. I can see the log-line now — *an overstressed rebel cop can't escape nightmares of the hit man that got away.*"

"I didn't dream about a hit man."

"Dramatic license," Pookie said. "Come on, Bri-Bri, this could be like a whole episode for me. Or even a three-episode mini-arc. You in?"

Bryan remembered the crawling sense of creeping death, the fear that had gripped his stomach even as he descended on the bum. But he didn't feel that fear anymore. And besides, it was just a dream.

"Sure," he said. "Let's check it out."

Pookie changed lanes again. He left angry honks in his wake, and — as usual — he really didn't seem to care.

Bryan looked around the alley. So damn familiar. Maybe he'd been here before. *Had* to have been here before. He couldn't know this place from a dream.

Pookie lifted the lid of a beat-up blue dumpster and peeked inside. Seeing nothing of interest, he shut the lid, brushed off his hands and adjusted his sunglasses. He kept looking around the alley. "So you saw a bum. And some kid wearing crimson and gold?"

"Not sure," Bryan said. "The kid could have *been* crimson and gold. It was a dream, Pooks."

"Yeah, but this is cool. Episode is practically writing itself. It's rare for a dreamer to think of a specific spot and not have there be some kind of a connection."

"And you know this because of your doctorate in dream-ology?"

"Discovery Channel, asshole," Pookie said. "There's more to life than reality TV."

Pookie pulled out his cell phone and checked the time. "All right, we better get rolling. Can't be late for your chitchat with Zou. Maybe the Brothers Steve already tracked down Joe-Joe. The Steves find Ablamowicz's killer, and we go back on nights and can grab the Maloney case away from Polyester Rich."

Lanza had made good on Bryan's demand for a name. That name? Joseph "Joe-Joe" Lombardi, another of the guys who had come out from New Jersey. Bryan and Pookie had immediately turned that info over to the Brothers Steve. Was that Ablamowicz's actual killer? Bryan couldn't say, but it was a lot more information than they'd had twenty-four hours ago.

"Let's get out of here," Bryan said. "My stomach is a mess. If I have to smell that dumpster anymore, I'm going to blow chunks."

They walked out of the alley back to the Buick.

"Pooks, you need to get with reality — Zou won't give us the Maloney case."

"The hell she won't."

"Polyester Rich and Zou go way back. I heard they both made inspector about the same time."

Pookie got in and started the car. "Mark my words, young Bryan Clauser. You and I will get this case. And when we do, we *will* nail Paul

Maloney's murderer. I simply won't stand for pee-freak vigilantes in my town."

Bryan slid into the passenger seat. He looked back to the dumpster and saw something he'd missed.

Underneath the dumpster, was that a blanket?

A red blanket.

With pictures of brown bunnies and yellow duckies.

. . . a little bird . . .

As Pookie drove away, the nightmare's cold echo blossomed anew in Bryan's memory. Bryan took a breath, tried to forget about the blanket. He hadn't *really* dreamed about a red blanket with duckies and bunnies, he was just reverse-imprinting or something. For now, he had more important things to worry about — things like Chief Zou's take on the shooting review board.

But maybe, when that was done, Bryan could find a quiet place to draw that weird picture again and make the cold feeling go away.

Rex ran.

They were faster than him, but he ran anyway, hoping against hope that he could find a way out or a place to hide.

Sometimes they got him, sometimes they didn't. Every now and then he got lucky, made it to a street with lots of pedestrian traffic, saw a cop car or something else that would make his constant pursuers break off and wait for another chance.

Today was not a lucky day.

They'd been waiting for him after school. They knew which path he took to walk home. Sometimes he'd go fifteen or twenty blocks out of his way, taking different, random streets, but this time he just wanted to get back to his room.

That fat, ugly meth-head April Sanchez had seen his drawing. April bought her drugs from Alex. She was rich. Rex hated her. She'd recognized the people in the drawing and said she was going to tell Alex. Rex had known, instantly, that he was in major trouble. April wanted to be Alex's girlfriend. Something like the drawing was a chance to get Alex's attention.

Rex had spent the last hour of school terrified, waiting for the bell to ring so he could get home fast. He should have gone *away* from his house, to one of his many hiding places, even to his favorite park, but in his fear he'd taken the direct route home.

Big mistake.

He'd made it two blocks when he saw them, all four of them, on the corner of Francisco and Van Ness. Their crimson, gold and white clothing stood out bright and clean in the afternoon sun. Rex instantly turned and ran back down Van Ness, past the football field, toward Aquatic Park. He should have run somewhere with more people, but he'd just run *away*.

They chased him. They laughed.

The four boys. Always the same four.

Jay Parlar . . . Issac Moses . . . Oscar Woody.

And the worst of them all, Alex Panos.

They caught him just past the parking lot that funneled the two divided three-car lanes of Van Ness Avenue into a normal two-lane road. An arm wrapped hard around his shoulders, a hand clamped over his mouth. The boys packed in close around him, carrying him.

Rex tried to yell for help, but the hand was too tight. The bay was off to his right, the greenery sloping up to Fort Mason on his left — and no one was around. They carried him to the left, into a shady spot, and threw him down on a dirt patch.

Rex tried to scramble up, but they surrounded him. Someone kicked him in the side and he fell. They dragged him behind a utility van parked beneath an overhanging tree, out of sight from the mostly unused street. He wound up on his back. Someone hit him in the face, once, twice, three times. His nose buzzed with a numb, confusing pain. Tears filled his eyes, making everything look shimmery and fluid. He was dumb enough to call out for help, then something hit him in the stomach and all wind left his body.

Someone sat on his chest, pinning him to the ground.

"I heard you were drawing fag pictures of me, you fucking faggot."

Rex didn't need to see; he knew that voice. Alex Panos. A deep voice, far deeper than it should be for a sophomore in high school, but still it cracked on the first syllable of *drawing*.

Rex tried to talk, to apologize, but he couldn't pull in enough air to speak.

"Hey, here's the drawing!" Jay Parlar's voice. "Lookit, Alex. Hey, *ha ha*, I'm in it, watching you get your ass kicked. Wow, I look totally scared."

"Gimme," Alex said.

Rex blinked away tears. He could see again. Oscar Woody was the one on his chest. Oscar's curly-poofy black hair stuck out from beneath a white baseball cap with a gold-lined, crimson *BC* on the front. Above Oscar, standing there looking down — Alex Panos.

Alex, with his movie-star blond hair and his big strong body, a body that Rex would *never* have. Alex held an unfolded page from a sketch pad. He looked up. His eyes narrowed. He turned the drawing around, so Rex could see it.

Rex's drawings were getting pretty good — no mistaking that Alex was the boy in the drawing, the boy getting his arm cut off with a chain saw held by a muscled version of Rex Deprovdechuk.

Alex smiled. "So you think you can kill me, faggot?"

Rex shook his head, the back of his head grinding against dirt, twigs and dried leaves.

Jay peeked over Alex's shoulder. Sixteen years old and Jay already had a goatee, although it was as thin and red as the hair on his head. "Seriously, Alex, that's a good drawing! Looks just like you!"

"Jay," Alex said, "shut the fuck up."

Jay's shoulders drooped. He seemed to suddenly shrink from a five-foot-ten stud to a five-foot-six weakling. "Sorry, Alex. I didn't mean nothing."

Alex's eyes never left Rex. Alex crumpled the paper, then tossed it aside.

"Boys," he said, "hold his arm."

Rex tried to scramble up, but Oscar was too heavy.

"Stay still, pussy," Oscar said.

Someone grabbed Rex's right wrist and yanked it hard, painfully stretching his arm. Rex looked at this attacker — blue-eyed Issac Moses, his strong hands locked on Rex's little forearm.

"Jay," Alex said, "go grab those two chunks of wood, I want to try something."

Rex finally managed a few words. "I . . . won't draw . . . anymore."

"It's too late for that," Alex said. He looked to his right. "Yeah, those are the ones. Put a chunk under his elbow, and the other one under his wrist."

Rex felt something hard shoved under his elbow, raising it a few inches off the leaf-scattered dirt. He watched Jay slide a piece of wood under his wrist, then looked up at the surprised face of Issac Moses, who had yet to release his hold on Rex's arm. Issac's mouth was always turned down, and his nose seemed too small for his face.

"Oh man, don't do this," Issac said. "That's going to hurt him bad."

Alex's smile faded. He looked hard at Issac.

"Shut up and keep holding him," Alex said. "If you don't, you're next."

Issac's mouth opened, perhaps to say something, then he closed it and looked down.

Alex took a step forward. His feet straddled Rex's elevated arm. Alex looked like a towering god, blond hair hanging down, a few locks gleaming from the beams of late-afternoon sun filtering through the tree's shade.

"I have to teach you a lesson, Rex. I have to teach you about pain."

The tears flowed. Rex couldn't help it. "You guys hurt me all the time!"

Alex's smile widened. "Oh, them was just love taps, faggot. You probably even liked it. Now? Now you get to learn about *real* pain."

Alex weighed over two hundred pounds. He was bigger than most of the teachers. He raised his leg knee-high, letting his military boot hover above the center of Rex's forearm. Alex smiled, then stamped down hard. Rex heard a muffled *crunch* sound, then had the odd sensation of feeling his forearm grind into the dirt while his wrist and elbow were still elevated a good two inches off the ground.

Then came the pain.

He looked before he cried out. His arm made a shallow V, an extra joint between his wrist and elbow. Oscar got off of Rex's chest. He stood there, black curls puffed out from under his hat. Oscar was part of the circle that surrounded Rex, the circle that blocked out what little sun filtered through the overhanging tree, the circle that cast the wounded boy in complete shadow.

Tears streamed down Rex's cheeks, down his chin, washing through the blood that smeared his face. It *hurt* so bad. His arm . . . it *bent* where it wasn't supposed to bend.

Alex put his foot on Rex's stomach.

"Tell anyone about this and you're dead," Alex said. "I know a hundred places to hide a body in this city. You got me, you little faggot?"

Overwhelmed with pain, humiliation and helplessness, Rex just cried. No one was coming to help him. No one ever would.

He wanted to hurt them.

He wanted to *kill* them.

A size fourteen boot kicked him hard in the ribs.

"I said, do you get me, Rex?"

Thoughts of hatred and revenge vanished, replaced by the more-powerful and ever-present fear.

"Yeah!" Rex screamed, a mist of blood and tears flying off his lips. "Yeah, I hear you!"

Alex lifted his big boot. Rex had time to close his eyes before the heel hit him in the face.

Chief Zou's Office

When Bryan and Pookie entered the chief's office, four people were already there. Chief Zou sat behind her desk, her blue uniform free of the slightest hint of a wrinkle. Assistant Chief Sean Robertson stood a little behind her and a little to her left. To the right of the desk, in chairs against the wall, sat Jesse Sharrow, the Homicide division captain, and Assistant DA Jennifer Wills. Sharrow's perfectly pressed blues were a dark contrast to his bushy white eyebrows and slicked-back white hair. Wills had her legs crossed, making her skirt look even shorter than it was. A black pump dangled provocatively from an extended toe.

Zou wasn't much for decoration. A big, dark-wood desk dominated the room. Commendations hung on the walls, as did several framed pictures of Chief Zou shaking hands with various police officers and elected officials. Two of those pictures showed her with governors of California, both the current and the former. The room's largest photo showed Zou shaking hands with a smiling Jason Collins, San Francisco's heartthrob of a mayor. Behind Zou's chair, on angled wooden poles, hung the U.S. flag and the dark-blue Governor's Flag of California.

Her desktop looked larger than it was because there was almost nothing on it other than a three-panel picture frame — a panel for each of her twin daughters and one for her husband — and a closed manila folder.

It wasn't the first time Bryan had been in here, staring at a folder just like that one. Zou's office felt more ominous than he remembered, the air thick with an oppressive potential of career destruction. Maybe he was justified in the shooting of Carlos Smith — now they knew the would-be shotgun assassin's name — but justified or not, fourteen years as a cop hung in the balance.

Chief Zou gestured to two chairs in front of her desk.

"Inspector Clauser, Inspector Chang, have a seat, please."

Bryan walked to the chair on the right, his eyes never straying from the manila folder. Its edges perfectly paralleled the edges of the desk. It couldn't have been more dead-center if Zou had used a tape measure.

Bryan sat. So did Pookie.

Waves of nausea bubbled in Bryan's stomach. He would have to stay focused. His whole body throbbed, but he could deal with that — what he couldn't deal with was losing his breakfast in the office of the chief of police.

Robertson nodded at Pookie, then gave Bryan a small smile. Was that a good thing?

Amy Zou had held the chief position for twelve years, an infinite tenure by San Francisco standards. While many, *many* in-house seminars had taught Bryan the evils of reacting to a woman's looks, he couldn't deny that Zou was quite attractive. By the numbers, anyway — despite being in her late fifties, Pookie said that Zou would have been officially "MILF-a-licious" if she ever learned how to smile.

She picked up the folder, opened it for a second, then put it down again and straightened it, making sure it was perfectly centered. She already knew the results, obviously; checking them again seemed more of a nervous tic than anything else.

She stared at Bryan. He tried to sit still.

Chief Zou left the folder on her desk as she opened it again. This time she leaned forward and read aloud from it.

"Regarding the incident of January first," she said, "the use of lethal force against Carlos Smith, a resident of South San Francisco. Preliminary findings indicate that Inspector Bryan Clauser acted in a manner appropriate with the situation. Inspector Clauser's actions saved lives."

She closed the folder, straightened it, then stared at him. "We still have to go through the formal review board, but I can't imagine there will be an issue. Based on the eyewitness accounts I read, I will communicate to the review board my opinion on the situation."

The breath slid out of Bryan's lungs. He was off the hook. "That's great, Chief."

Robertson came around the desk, clapped Bryan on the back. "Come on, Clauser," he said. "You knew this was a righteous shoot."

Bryan shrugged, tried to play the part. "I keep winding up in the wrong place at the wrong time."

Robertson shook his head. "You did what had to be done, and this isn't the first time. You saved lives. You had no choice."

Zou turned to Jennifer. "Miss Wills? Any further comments from the DA's office?"

"No, Chief Zou," Jennifer said. "Considering Smith's record of violence, even the usual San Francisco protester crowd will probably ignore this one. We'll be ready for the inevitable lawsuit from Smith's family, but between the witnesses and the security camera footage, we're in the clear."

Zou nodded, then turned back to Bryan. "I have some more good news. Steve Boyd investigated the apartment of Joseph Lombardi, also known as Joe-Joe Lombardi. Boyd found evidence to make Lombardi our lead suspect in the Ablamowicz case. We have that name because of you and Pookie."

Bryan nodded. Lanza had given up Joe-Joe, true, but it remained to be seen if anyone would ever see Lombardi alive again. Lanza needed someone to go down for the crime, to show the Norteños that blood had been settled with blood. Odds were that Lombardi would turn up dead.

The white-haired Sharrow stood. "Chief Zou, does Clauser need to be on desk duty while this case is with the shooting review board?"

"No," Zou said. "This was a clean shoot. Inspector Clauser, you and Inspector Chang will continue to work on the Ablamowicz task force. We need you guys too much right now to put you behind a desk. That's it, people. Get back to it."

He felt so relieved it almost made him forget about his sour, churning stomach. Bryan didn't care about Carlos Smith, but he did care about his job. Anything could happen in a shooting review. Ignoring his body's numerous complaints, Bryan stood, thanked everyone for their support, then walked out of Chief Zou's office, happy to still be a cop.

The White Room

arm.

Toasty warm. Blankets. Soft blankets, *dry* blankets. Clean clothes that slid against his skin, skin that was scrubbed free of dirt and grime and sweat for the first time in months.

Aggie rolled over . . . and heard a metallic rattle.

He blinked a few times as he woke. Was he wearing . . . *pajamas*? He flashed back to his childhood bed in Detroit, to his mother gently waking him with loving words and hugs, the smell of pancakes filling the small house. But this place didn't smell like pancakes.

It smelled like paint. It smelled like bleach.

He was on his side, the blankets bunched up around him, lying on a mattress so thin he could feel the hard floor beneath. The world seemed to move, to *wave*, but he knew from long experience that was just the horse talking. He opened his eyes and blinked — yeah, he was still more than a little high.

Was this really happening?

Just inches from his face was a wall made of broken bricks and rounded stones, all coated with a glaze of bright white enamel so thick the surface must have been painted over and over and over again.

Something heavy hung around his neck.

Aggie's hands shot up to find a flat, metal collar. There was barely enough room to slide a finger between the collar and his neck, but inside he felt a soft leather strip to cushion the metal against his skin.

More metallic rattling.

His hands reached behind the collar, found a chain.

He sat up, hands pulling the chain around where he could see it — stainless steel, its chromelike sheen reflecting fluorescent lights from above, each quarter-inch-thick link showing a tiny, curved reflection of his black skin and shocked face. He looked down the chain's path. It led into a stainless-steel ring mounted flat into the white wall.

Oh, shit. Please, let this just be a bad trip.

"Ayúdenos," a man said.

Aggie turned away from the white wall, toward the voice, and saw a family: small boy clinging to his mother, mother clinging to him, father with arms protectively wrapped around them both.

The woman and the boy looked terrified, while the man stared with eyes that promised death to anyone that came near. Black hair, tan skin — they looked like Mexicans.

All three of them wore pajamas: pale blue cotton for the man, fuchsia silk for the woman, pink flannel with blue cartoon puppies for the boy. The clothes looked clean but well used, the same way clothes looked in the Salvation Army store on Sutter Street.

Like Aggie, they all wore stainless-steel metal collars with chains leading into holes in the wall. Aggie stood and started walking around slowly, his chain rattling across the stones beneath and behind him.

"Por favor, ayúdenos," the man said. "Ayude a mi familia."

"I don't speak beaner," Aggie said. "You speak English?"

The man shook his head. "No speak."

Figured. Fucking people coming to this country without speaking the language.

"What is this place?" Aggie said. "What the hell are we doing here?"

The man shook his head. "No entiendo, señor."

Aggie looked around the room. The walls shimmered, shifted — the smack made it hard to focus. He wasn't sure if he was seeing reality or not, but the circular room looked like it had a curved ceiling, sort of like a dome, about thirty feet across with a high point maybe fifteen feet off the floor. The floor looked the same as the walls: rocks and bricks laid down in a rough, flat pattern, repeatedly slathered with enamel paint. Aggie felt like he was inside a big stone igloo.

On the far side of the room stood a door of bright white bars: a prison door.

Ten mattresses lay on the floor, one for each of the circular rings Aggie counted in the walls. Chains led out of four of the rings, connecting to Aggie and the three other people. Several loose blankets lay on each mattress. The blankets, like the clothes, had that secondhand look. But everything — from the clothes to the blankets to the mattresses to the walls — looked *clean.*

A one-foot, circular, stainless-steel flange marked the center of the room's floor. Aggie saw three rolls of toilet paper sitting on the flange. Was that where he was supposed to shit?

Something really fucked-up was going on here, and Aggie wanted out. He might be a bum, might have phoned in all pretense of a real life many years ago, but the significance of being a black man in a collar and chains was not lost on him.

The woman started to cry. The little boy looked at her, then started to do the same and again buried his head in her bosom.

The man kept staring at Aggie.

"I got no idea what's goin' on," Aggie said. "If you want help, ask someone else."

A metallic noise rang from the walls and echoed through the small room. Three heads looked around: Aggie, the man and the woman, eyes searching for the source of the sound. The little boy didn't look up. Another clang — Aggie realized it came from the holes in the wall.

Then the sound of chains rattling: Aggie's collar yanked him backward. He stumbled and fell, banging his elbow, then choked as the chain dragged him across the hard, bumpy ground. He reached out, hands grabbing for anything, but his fingers found only blankets that offered no resistance.

The woman slid across the floor, her hands clutching her child tight to her chest. "Jesús nos ayuda!"

The man tried to fight, but the chain dragged him along as easily as it did the woman.

The little boy just screamed. The chains pulled him away from his mother. Their arms grabbed at each other, but they were powerless against the steady, mechanical force.

Aggie felt his back hit the wall, then felt himself pulled *up* the wall, the collar's edge digging into his lower jaw, pressing against his throat and cutting off his air. He managed to get his feet under him just as the chain pulled the collar against the wall-ring, where it *clanged* home with a metal-on-metal authority. The yanking stopped. Aggie sucked in a deep, panicked breath. He grabbed the collar and tried to lean forward, but the chain wouldn't budge.

All four prisoners were in the same predicament: collars pulled tight against stainless-steel rings. Hands grabbed at necks, feet pushed against white walls, but none of them could move away.

They all stood there, waiting.

"Mama!" the boy screeched, finally finding his voice. "Qué está pasando?"

"No sé," she said. "Sea valiente. Lo protegeré!"

For some reason, Aggie recognized that last bit of Mexican. *Be brave. I will protect you.*

But the mother couldn't do anything. She was as powerless as the boy was.

The sound of a big key ratcheting open a metal lock silenced them all. The white prison gate swung out.

Was this really happening? Everything seemed to blur; the walls blazed with a white that couldn't possibly exist in the real world. *A bad trip, a bad trip, that's all this is, I'm tripping.*

When he saw what walked through the cell door, Aggie's instincts took over. It didn't matter if he was high, dreaming or stone-cold sober — he pulled harder than he'd ever thought possible, pulled so hard he almost choked himself out . . . but still the collar refused to budge.

Men in hooded white robes with rope belts tied around their waists. Only they weren't *men* — they had the faces of monsters. A pig, a wolf, a tiger, a bear, a goblin. Twisted, evil smiles, beady eyes blinking away. Something primitive and raw inside of Aggie screamed for deliverance. Pig-Face carried a wooden pole, perhaps just over ten feet in length. The pole ended in a stainless-steel hook.

The five robe-covered monsters moved slowly toward the boy.

The boy, their child, like my daughter was my child, with her skin as smooth as melted chocolate. My daughter, please don't kill my daughter . . .

The Mexican man screamed with rage. Aggie blinked, shaking away the memories that he'd worked so hard to leave behind.

The woman screamed, too, hers one of heart-wrenching fear. Her son mimicked the sound, his all the more hurtful for its high-pitched terror.

The boy saw the monsters coming for him. He thrashed like an epileptic, spit and blood dribbling from his mouth, his eyes so wide that even from fifteen feet away Aggie saw the boy's full brown irises. The boy clawed at his collar, his fingernails cutting into his own soft skin.

The man continued to shout threats that Aggie didn't understand, protective rage roaring out and echoing off the white walls.

The white-robed men ignored him.

They stopped a few feet from the boy. One of them produced some kind of remote control and hit a button. The boy's chain loosened. He shot forward, but only made it four feet before the chain yanked taut again and his feet flew out from under him. The boy fell hard on his back. He rolled to his hands and knees, screaming, crying, bleeding, trying to get up, but the five were on him. Black-gloved hands reached out from white sleeves and held him tight. Pig-Face reached down with the pole and slid the steel hook through the back of the boy's collar.

The one with the remote control hit another button. The boy's chain went completely slack and slid free from the hole in the wall. It hit the floor with a cascading rattle, one end still connected to the collar, the other end connected to nothing.

Pig-Face gripped the pole and walked to the door, dragging the boy along behind him. The loose chain trailed along like a dead snake, links ringing against the stone-and-brick floor.

Aggie wanted to wake the fuck up, and wake the fuck up *right now.*

The mother begged.

The father roared.

The boy's clutching fingers left thin red smears against the white floor. Pig-Face walked out the door. He turned right and vanished behind a corner. The boy slid out behind him, dragged by the pole. The last sight of him was his chain, pulled out of the room with a final, thin ring when it clanged against the open, white jail-cell door.

The other monsters walked out. One by one, they turned the corner and were gone. Goblin-Face was the last to leave. He turned and pushed the cell door shut behind him. It clanged home, the metallic sound echoing and fading as the mother's screams went on and on.

Rex Gets in Trouble

Rex sat in the waiting room of St. Francis Hospital, a new cast on his broken right arm. The cast ran from above his elbow down to his hand, wrapping across his palm, leaving his thumb peeking out of a white hole. Stupid thing would be on for at least four weeks.

A feeling of pure dread hung in his chest and head, dragging his chin down almost to his sternum. The arm had been bad, real bad, but now Roberta was coming.

Alex Panos had nothing on Rex's mother.

He sniffled back tears. They didn't have money for this. They didn't have insurance. But Alex had *broken his arm . . .* what was Rex supposed to do?

She came through the doors, saw him immediately and made a beeline right for him. Roberta: too skinny, nasty wiry hair that smelled like cigarettes, and that disgusting skin.

She stood in front of him. His chin tried to dig itself even deeper into his chest. She stared. He wanted to just die.

"So you were fighting again?"

Rex shook his head no, but even as he did it, he knew better.

"Don't lie to me, boy. Look at your goddamn nose. You were fighting again."

He felt the tears coming. He hated himself for crying. He hated her for making him cry. He hated Alex for all of it.

He hated his life.

"But they attacked me, Mom, and—"

"*Don't you call me that!*" Roberta's voice carried through the waiting room of St. Francis, drawing stares from the walking wounded awaiting treatment. She saw the glances, lowered her voice to a nasty hiss. "You just stop it right now, *Rex*. Do you have any idea what this is going to cost me?"

Rex shook his head again. The tears streamed down his face.

Roberta huffed and strode over to the billing desk. Rex tried to slink even deeper, but there was nowhere left to go. Roberta and the woman behind the counter exchanged words, then the woman handed Roberta a bill.

Roberta read it.

Then she turned to look at him, and the world grew colder.

Rex hid his face in his uncasted hand, tears wetting his palms. He rocked back and forth. He didn't want to go with her, but he had no place else to go.

He had no one.

Sharrow Sends Bryan Home

Clauser."

Someone shook his shoulder. Bryan tried to say something to the effect of *leave me alone or I'll kill you*, but all that came out was a three-syllable mumble.

Another shake.

"Clauser!"

Captain Sharrow's voice. Bryan blinked awake.

"Clauser, this isn't the place for a nap."

Damn . . . he had fallen asleep at his desk.

"Sorry, Captain."

Jesse Sharrow glared down. His white hair and bushy white eyebrows framed his weathered scowl. Bryan started to stand up; his butt cleared only one inch of airspace before aching muscles and bones froze him in place, then promptly dropped him back down on the chair.

"Good God, man," Sharrow said. "Wipe that drool off your chin, will you?"

Bryan touched his cheek: cold and slimy. Well, that was certainly a way to score points with your boss. He wiped away the spit.

Sharrow pointed to the stack of paper on Bryan's desk. "Reprint that."

Spots of drool had soaked into Bryan's report.

"Sorry," Bryan said.

"Go home, Clauser. You're a dumb-ass coming in here like this, bringing your germs in with you. You want to put the whole department down?"

"I wasn't planning on making out with anyone, Captain. Except for you, of course."

"Blow it out your ass," Sharrow said. "You're so ugly you make my wife look hot. And that's saying something."

"It sure is."

Sharrow snarled and pointed a finger a Bryan's face. "Watch it, Clauser. Don't talk bad about my wife."

"Yes, Captain."

"Seriously, go home."

"But, Cap, I still have paperwork for the shooting review board to—"

"Shut your piehole. Get out of here. In fact, don't bother reprinting that report, just email it to me — I don't want to touch anything that's come anywhere near you. Be out of here in the next ten minutes."

Sharrow turned and stormed off.

Bryan hadn't taken a sick day in four years. But falling asleep at his desk, drooling on paperwork . . . maybe it was for the best if he cleared out. With both hands flat on the desk, he pushed himself to a standing position, every muscle screaming the biological equivalent of horrid obscenities.

A crumpled-up twenty-dollar bill landed on his desk.

Bryan looked up. Pookie had thrown it.

"Take a cab," Pookie said. "I'm not driving you."

"Don't want a sick guy in your car?"

Pookie let out a *pfft* noise of disgust. "You've already been in my car. I'm not driving you because you said you'd make out with Sharrow and not me. I have feelings, you know."

"Sorry about that."

Pookie shook his head. "Men. You're all pigs. Do I need to call you an ambulance instead of a cab?"

"No, I'm good."

Bryan shuffled out of the office and headed for the elevator. The sooner he got to sleep — in an actual bed — the better.

Robin Gets the Call

A rare, quiet moment at home.

Robin was taking advantage of the time to sit on her couch and do nothing. Nothing but scratch the ear of her dog, Emma. Emma's head rested on Robin's lap.

Emma wasn't supposed to be on the couch. She knew that, Robin knew that, yet neither of them was motivated enough to do anything about it. Robin was home so little these days she didn't have it in her heart to scold the sixty-five-pound German shorthair pointer for wanting to be closer. Robin slowly swirled the dog's floppy black ear. Emma moaned in happiness with a doggie equivalent of a cat's purr.

As Robin's responsibilities grew, so did her time at the morgue. Thankfully, her next-door-neighbor, Max Blankenship, could almost always swing over to take care of Emma if Robin worked late. Max would take Emma to his place to play with Billy, Max's gigantic pit bull. Max was sweet, kind, clever, handsome, sexy as hell and had a key to her apartment — the perfect man, if not for the small fact that "Big Max" was as gay as gay gets.

Robin's cell phone rang. She looked at it, but didn't recognize the incoming number. She thought of ignoring it, but it might be work related so she answered.

"Hello?"

"Doctor Robin Hudson?" asked a woman's voice.

"This is she. Who is calling, please?"

"Mayor Jason Collins's office. The mayor would like to speak with you. Can you hold for a moment?"

"Uh, sure."

The phone switched to elevator music. The mayor's office? It was ten o'clock at night. And more than that, *the mayor's office*? Why would the mayor be calling her?

Because it was the mayor who appointed the chief medical examiner.

Oh, no . . . had something happened to Dr. Metz?

The on-hold music clicked off. "Doctor Hudson?"

She'd heard his voice dozens of times on newscasts. This wasn't a prank. Holy shit.

"Yes, this is Robin Hudson."

"This is Mayor Collins. Sorry to bother you so late at night, Doctor Hudson. Do you prefer to be called *doctor* or can I just call you Robin?"

"Robin is fine. Is Doctor Metz okay?"

"Sadly no," the mayor said. "Doctor Metz suffered a heart attack earlier this evening. He's at San Francisco General."

"My God." Her heart suddenly pounded at the thought of never seeing her friend again, of death taking him away forever. "Is he going to make it?"

"They think so," the mayor said. "He's in stable condition, but he's not out of the woods yet. I'll have my office put you on the notification list. The hospital calls me with any information, I'll be sure to relay that same information right out to you."

"Thank you, Mister Mayor."

"I assume you understand why I'm calling?"

Robin nodded to herself, scratched Emma's ear. "Someone needs to run the Medical Examiner's Office."

"That's right. I'm hoping our famous Silver Eagle will make a full recovery. If he is unable to return to work, we'll launch a nationwide search for a new chief medical examiner. Until we know if he'll be okay, however, can I count on you to run the ship?"

Was she ready for this? Could she run the department and not screw it up? There wasn't any time to doubt herself — Metz would expect her to handle things in his absence.

"Of course," Robin said. "I'll keep everything running smoothly, just the way Doctor Metz likes it."

"Excellent. Now I know this is upsetting news and a lot of information to process, so I'll let you go. I will say that I'm pleased a representative of our active Asian American community is there to take care of things in the interim."

Were she not so shocked and saddened by the news of her mentor's heart attack, Robin might have laughed — Mayor Collins would find a way to spin this into votes. Asians made up a third of San Francisco's voters. He probably didn't know she'd grown up in Canada, the daughter of an immigrant Englishman. Still, she'd inherited her mother's looks, and that meant she'd make a good potential photo op for the mayor. Not that she'd mind taking a picture with a hunk like Collins; with his tailored suits, expensive haircuts and big-jawed smile, the handsome mayor had topped *most eligible bachelor* lists for years.

"Something else to think on," he said. "While we will, if necessary, do a search for a new chief ME, you're in charge right now. If you want that job long-term someday, this gives you a hell of a leg up."

She was already being considered for the top spot? "Of course, Mister Mayor."

"Just one more thing, Robin. The Paul Maloney case is sensitive. Delicate. I know Doctor Metz finished the examination, so I'm having Maloney's body removed from the morgue."

"And you're taking it . . . where?"

"Somewhere safe," he said. "I'm too worried that, with Maloney's past, victims or relatives of victims might want to desecrate the body."

Someone would try to break into the San Francisco morgue?

"Mister Mayor, I don't think you need to worry about that."

"I *am* worried about it," he said. "I know the morgue is at the Hall of Justice, but remember that cops are parents, too. With Doctor Metz out of commission for the first time in recent memory, someone might get ideas. I want to remove the temptation. Maloney's body will be gone when you arrive tomorrow morning. Understand?"

She didn't understand. At all. The processing of the deceased was done under a strict protocol. But maybe this was how politics worked. At any rate, Jason Collins was the boss, and she wasn't going to rock the boat so soon, not when her future career might be on the line.

"Yes, Mister Mayor," she said. "I understand."

"Great. Robin, I'm thrilled you're on this. We'll let you know when Doctor Metz can have visitors. Good night."

"Good night," she said. She hung up and stared at the phone. She stared at it so long that Emma wondered what was going on, thought the phone might be a treat, so she stared at it as well.

Robin put the phone down, then scooched both of Emma's ears. The dog's eyes narrowed sleepily and she growl-moaned with pure love.

"Hear that, baby girl?" Robin said. "I'm sorry, but it looks like you might be seeing more of your uncle Max. A lot more."

Hunter's Blind

Like any good hunter, Bryan waited. He didn't know how he'd come to be here, but he recognized the place. He was on Post Street, his back to an abandoned, boarded-up laundromat at the corner of a little alley called Meacham Place. A gate of square, ten-foot-high black bars blocked the entrance to the alley. Beyond those bars, he would take his prey.

Covered by a damp, smelly blanket, he lay perfectly still. Streetlights lit up most of the concrete sidewalk, but couldn't chase away all of the darkness. Shadows flexed and moved in time with the passing of late-night cars and taxis.

The blanket covered every inch of his body, everything except for a narrow slit through which he could watch. People ignored his presence, and why not? Just one more nasty-ass bum sleeping on the streets, an everyday sight in San Francisco. People walked past, only a few feet away, oblivious to the concept that death hid beneath tattered, filthy, third-hand fabric. Many times on nights just like these, he had grabbed such people and dragged them into the darkness.

He waited for the boy with the curly black hair.

Hail to the king.

First had come the visions. Visions of hateful faces, tastes of fear and the flush of humiliation, of helplessness. Waking dreams made Bryan feel what it was like to be bullied by a pack of boys, to be beaten by a woman who should have protected, to be violated by a man who promised love.

All of those people had wronged the king. All of those people had to be punished. How dare they hurt him, how *dare* they. Bryan and the others searched, they watched, they hunted, until the faces of dreams matched faces of flesh and blood.

The priest had been first. He could only die once, so they had made it last.

Now the bullies would pay the same price.

Bryan wanted the blond boy, the leader, but he was hard to find. He was difficult game. The curly-haired boy, though — he was predictable. He often came this way.

It would not be enough to just take the curly-haired boy away, to make him disappear. There was too much rage for that, too much anguish: like with the priest, the world had to know.

Hail to the king.

The curly-haired boy turned the corner. Bryan stayed calm, stayed motionless inside his hunting blind, moving nothing except his eyes. Bryan wasn't the smartest, he knew that, but he could hunt like no one else. As big as he was, the prey never saw him coming.

The boy walked down the sidewalk like he owned the whole street. His turf, his neighborhood, his territory. Big enough that most would avoid him. Young enough to think he controlled his life, to think that no one wanted to mess with him.

One womb.

The heat of the hunt boiled inside Bryan's skin, a feeling so primitive it bordered on lust. Bryan wanted to kill, *needed* to kill.

The black, curly hair stuck out beneath the boy's white baseball hat. He wore a dark-crimson jacket with the big, angled letters *BC* on the left chest. An eagle — forever paused with wings back and talons outstretched — sat in the middle of those letters.

The boy drew closer. Bryan breathed slowly. The boy glanced at Bryan's blind, then wrinkled his nose and looked away. The boy drew even with Bryan, took two steps past, then came the voice.

"Help . . . me . . ."

That voice came from behind the black gate. The boy stopped, looked through the gate's bars into Meacham Place's still shadows. Bryan knew what the boy would see. On the right, scraggly, ten-foot-tall trees growing up out of the narrow sidewalk, trunks only a foot from a brick wall, their leaves casting down lightless pools of deep black. On the left, the laundromat's crumbling masonry, broken windows and layers of grafitti. And in the middle, lying on the cracked pavement, a bearded man in a white tank top.

Bryan waited. There were enough cars passing by that if the boy ran, Bryan would have to let him go. If the boy went into the alley, Bryan and the others would move.

Take the bait.

The boy looked down and to his left, again examining Bryan's blind, again deciding the unmoving, blanket-covered homeless person wasn't worth worrying about.

The man in the alley called out a second time, so softly that no one but the boy would hear. "Help me . . . please. I'm hurt."

Take the bait . . .

The boy gripped the gate's black bars. He quietly climbed over, careful to avoid the pointy spear-tops, and dropped down on the other side.

Bryan moved without a sound, turning his head slightly to look down Post Street — empty enough to act. He quietly stood, but remained hunched over. Bryan was careful to keep the big blanket looped around his face, like a hood, so that no one could see what was underneath. The rancid fabric cut off his peripheral vision, but that didn't matter: it was almost over.

A crawl of fear washed over him. The monster was always out there, somewhere. Bryan looked up, scanned the buildings above, looking for movement, for an outline.

Nothing.

He had to draw the symbol, and soon, or the monster would come for him.

"Mister," he heard the boy say. "You okay?"

Was the boy going to try and help? Or was he just looking for an easy victim?

It didn't matter.

Bryan bent slightly, then jumped. He sailed over the gate and came down silently on the other side.

One womb. One family.

The man in the white tank top lay on the ground, his beer-gut spilling out from under the shirt and over his dirty jeans. He wore a green John Deere ball cap. He reached up a chubby hand toward the boy who stood a few feet away.

"Help . . . me. *Please.*" Marco was a good actor. Really good.

The boy moved closer. "You got any money, asshole?"

The heat of the hunt bubbled Bryan's soul. He took a step toward the prey. When he did, his foot ground a small rock against the asphalt, making a slight *skritt* sound that caused the curly-haired boy to turn.

Bryan smelled fear. The boy realized he'd made a mistake — he was cut off, trapped between two men. His hands clenched into fists, his eyes narrowed and his head dipped down a little, as if he might lash out at any second. Like most trapped animals, the boy growled a warning.

"Fuck off," he said to Bryan. "Don't fuck with me, you piece-of-shit bum."

Behind the boy, Marco silently rose to his feet.

Bryan finally stood tall and let the filthy blankets drop to the ground.

The boy's face changed. The haughty look slowly slipped away, his angry, icy stare melting into puzzlement.

He took a step back, right into Marco's belly.

The boy turned, found himself face-to-face with Marco. It was hard to see anything under that beard, but Bryan knew Marco was smiling.

Marco reached behind his back. When his hand came out again, it held a rust-spotted hatchet. The alley's feeble light flickered off the sharpened edge.

"Don't," the boy said. He didn't sound that tough anymore.

Bryan heard the flap of fabric, of things falling from above. The others landed on either side of the boy. One remained tucked under a dark blanket, his face hidden save for the glint of a yellow eye.

The other let the blanket slide free.

Bryan saw a nightmare. A man with purple skin, with big black eyes. It stared at the boy for a moment, then smiled wide a mouth full of big, white, triangular teeth.

The one still hidden inside a blanket spoke. "Pierre," he said in a voice that sounded like sandpaper on rough wood. "This one is yours. Take him."

Sly had kept his promise.

Hail to the king, motherfucker.

Bryan rushed in. He took the bully from behind, teeth sinking into the prey's shoulder. Bryan's mouth filled with the vibrations of crunching bone, the nylon taste of the crimson jacket and the sweet heat of squirting blood.

•••

Bryan opened his eyes. His heart mule-kicked in his chest.

Adrenaline pumped cactus-prickle through his veins and muscles and skin. His pulse blasted away, undeniable in one place more than any other. He sat on the edge of the bed, staring off into the dark room, his rock-hard erection pitching a tent in his underwear.

The dream had gone farther than the last. Bryan hadn't just stalked, he'd *attacked*. He had tasted blood. He could *still* taste it. So why was he vibrating with excitement when he should be vomiting in disgust? Why did he have a boner so hard a cat couldn't scratch it?

And why did he feel like *he* was being watched by someone who wanted to kill him?

"What the fuck is wrong with me?"

No one answered, because there was no one else in the room. There was never anyone else. He was alone in his silent apartment, as he had been every day since he'd moved out of Robin's place.

He reached over to his nightstand to grab the pen and the notebook he'd left there. He drew. A few scraggly lines. He didn't even know what it was, only that it wasn't quite right. Still, that feeling, that *being watched* feeling, it faded away.

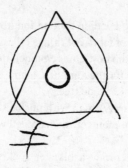

Bryan let out a long, deep breath, then set the pad and pen back on the nightstand.

He stared at it for a moment, then picked it up again and wrote down two words.

Meacham Place.

He set the pad down a second time, then snuck a peek in his underwear — boner diffused. He felt better, but there was no point in trying to go back to sleep: he could still taste that kid's hot blood in his mouth.

And it tasted good.

He pulled the bed's comforter tight around his shoulders and stumbled to the living room, feeling a sudden urge to watch Creature Features on cable.

Pleasant Dreams

ex woke suddenly, sat straight up in bed. His chest heaved, his face dripped with sweat that cooled in the night air.

In the dream, Rex hadn't feared Oscar.

Oscar had feared *Rex.*

Then the grabbing, the biting, and that taste . . .

The taste of blood.

Rex pushed back the damp covers. The air cooled his sweaty skin. It also cooled a spot *down there.*

He looked to his bedroom door. It was closed. He looked at the clock — 3:14 A.M. Roberta would be asleep.

He pushed the covers down past his legs. In the alarm clock's faint red light, he saw a darker spot on his underwear.

Rex reached down and touched.

Wet.

He looked at the door again. In his sleep, he had done the bad thing, the *naughty* thing. Would she find out? If she did, she would beat him.

Rex started to shake. He slid the underwear off, then stuffed them in the bottom of his book bag. He grabbed three sheets of Kleenex and cleaned himself up. Eyes constantly flicking to the door, he put on a fresh pair of underwear.

So weird that he'd dreamed about Oscar.

Rex quietly walked to his desk. A streetlight outside his window cast a dim glow on his most recent drawing — a pencil sketch of Rex using a sledgehammer to crush the skull of Oscar Woody.

How he wished *that* was reality, that he could strike back at them, make them pay. But drawings and dreams weren't real life. Rex felt tears welling up in his eyes. He grabbed the paper, crumpled it into a ball and threw it in the trash.

He then crawled back into bed, his sheets still wet with his own sweat.

Rex threw his head down on the pillow and pulled the covers up tight. His eyes squeezed shut. Shaking and alone, he cried.

Bryan Clauser: Morning Person

The brown Buick cut across three lanes of traffic. Bryan covered his face, trying to ignore the chorus of horns sounding in the car's wake.

"Jesus, Pooks. Try not to kill me before we go back on nights, will ya?"

"Pussy," Pookie said. "Hey, I have some more ideas on our series bible."

"It's *your* TV show, Pooks, not *ours*. I'm not writing anything."

"You're an executive producer," Pookie said. "No one knows what the hell executive producers do, anyway. Here's my idea — we make the chief's wife this smoking-hot MILF. She's ignored by her work-obsessed husband, so to fulfill her need to feel sexy and wanted she uses her feminine wiles to tease the Young Rebel Detectives. But it backfires on her when the good-looking detective — based on me, of course — finally beds her with the Chang Bang."

Bryan couldn't help but laugh. The *Chang Bang* was from Pookie's previous pet project, a coffee-table book called *69 Sex Positions the Kama-Sutra Forgot*.

"Is the Chang Bang the one with the trapeze?"

"No, the trapeze is only used in *Granger's Golden Snitch*. The Chang Bang is the one with the hula hoop and the semi-inverted angle on the bar stool."

Bryan sighed and looked out the window. "The hula hoop. How could I forget?"

"Anyway, we check-mark-yes for hot sex scene, but we also get ongoing dramatic tension as our one-night fling turns into a torrent love affair."

"Torrid."

"What?"

"Torr-*id*, not torr-*ent*."

"That too," Pookie said. "The Staff Sergeant with the Heart of Gold finds out and tries to give wisdom to the Young Rebel Detective. And it makes things dicey between Young Rebel Detective and his nemesis, the Crotchety Old-Guard Chief of Police."

"Your show seems to be more about sex than police work," Bryan said. "You getting laid these days?"

Pookie shook his head. "Nope. I put Junior and the Twins into a hiatus while I work on the series bible."

"Well, then maybe you should lay off the *torrid* scenes for a while, or you're going to wind up with blue balls."

Pookie's head snapped to the right. He stared at Bryan. The car swerved into the left lane.

Bryan pointed at an oncoming truck. "Dude!"

Pookie saw the truck, slammed the Buick back into the proper lane as the truck shot by, horn blaring.

"Pooks, what the fuck?"

"Sorry," he said. "But that's it. You did it."

"I did what?"

"Came up with the name."

"Of?"

"Of the TV show," Pookie said. "You know, the thing we've been talking about for the past fifteen minutes?"

"And that name is?"

"Blue Balls."

It would have been a good joke, but the man looked serious. "Pooks, you're going to name your TV show *Blue Balls*?"

Pookie nodded.

"You can't name a show *Blue Balls*."

"Like hell I can't," he said. "Half cop drama, half soft-core porn. Just think of all the classic TV shows that have lasted more than three seasons — which puts them into syndication, where the big bucks are, by the way — that have the word *blue* in the title. *Hill Street Blues. NYPD Blue. Blue Bloods. Rookie Blue.*"

"Those are cop terms," Bryan said. "Blue balls has, like, a *totally* different meaning."

"Right, it's *sexier.* That means HBO might pick it up, then we can show titties. Holy shit, Bri-Bri, this is the ticket. I got to email that to myself."

Pookie drove with one hand, thumbed his cell-phone keys with the other.

Bryan's gaze nervously flicked between the road ahead and Pookie's phone. "Is there any point in me reminding you texting and driving is illegal?"

"No," Pookie said. He hit the last button and put the phone back in his pocket. "Speaking of plot lines, Bri-Bri, any more of those dreams last night?"

Bryan paused, then shook his head.

"L-L-W-T-L," Pookie said. "Let me hear it. Similar to the first one?"

Bryan closed his eyes. The tangy taste of blood echoed on his tongue. "No. Worse."

"Talk to a brotha. What happened?"

"Not really sure," Bryan said. Then, in barely a breath: "I think I tore his arm off."

He couldn't bring himself to say what he really remembered: *I BIT his arm off, and it tasted better than anything I've ever known.*

"You tore his arm off," Pookie said, nodding as if that was the most normal thing in the world. "Nice. And what did you do with said arm?"

Bryan closed his eyes, trying to crystallize his fuzzy dream-memories. "I don't know. I woke up after that part. It was weird in another way, too."

"How so?"

"I woke up sporting wood."

Pookie let out his *pfft* sound. "That's new? I wake up with wood every day. Can't even pee in the toilet. It won't point down. Gotta whiz in the shower or it's golden rainbows for all."

"Thanks for sharing."

"So you woke up with a rager, so what?"

Bryan chewed on his bottom lip. "Because I'm pretty sure I was turned on by the killing."

Had the first dream also aroused him? No, not that he could remember. But murdering the kid, all that hate mixed up with lust, lust for pain, lust for *fear* . . . Bryan tried to push the thoughts away.

"Was it in the same place?" Pookie said. "The dream, did you recognize the location?"

Bryan started to talk, then paused, remembering the red blanket at Fern Street — he'd seen it in his dream, and then, impossibly, found it in real life. What if there was something from last night's dream waiting for him, something far worse than an abandoned red blanket with yellow duckies and brown bunnies?

All it would take was one quick trip to set his mind at ease.

"Post and Meacham Place," Bryan said.

"Roger, Adam-12," Pookie said. "See the man, see the man at Post and Meacham."

Pookie suddenly changed lanes for no reason, cutting off a Volkswagen as he headed for Post Street.

Bryan's Dose of Reality

Pookie eased the Buick to a stop. Meacham Place looked quiet, empty. Beyond the black gate, the alley seemed undisturbed. Bits of trash dotted the cracked pavement. On the alley's right side, four narrow trees stretched up, waiting for the brief window of time when the sun would be overhead and send light down between the two buildings.

Bryan stared at the abandoned, one-story building on the alley's left. Paint- and graffiti-covered boards covered the old laundromat's three arched windows. Across the alley from the urban ruin was a three-story, narrow brick building — well-kept, neat as you please. Decay on one side of the street, finery on the other: plenty of that to go around in San Francisco.

At the bottom corner of the abandoned building, where the sidewalk turned under the black gate and into the alley, Bryan saw the place where he had hidden under

       [a hunter's blind]

              a blanket watching for

                    [the prey]

                         the boy to walk past.

Bryan rolled down his window . . . and *smelled* it.

A scent, thick and rich, billowing out of the alley, carried by a breeze that slid into his nose. It was the same odor that had made him dizzy up on the roof with Paul Maloney and Polyester Rich.

The same, but also unique.

"Pooks, you smell that?"

He heard Pookie sniff. "Maybe. Smells like piss?"

Piss. Yes. Piss, but also something else.

Bryan looked to the four scraggly trees growing out of the narrow sidewalk. At the base of the farthest tree, wedged between the trunk and the building . . .

A blanket, dark and rumpled.

"Bri-Bri?"

A blanket, covering something about the size of a man.

A man . . . or a big teenage boy.

No. It was a dream. Just a dream.

His tongue tasted the memory of hot blood. His mouth salivated.

"Hey, seriously," Pookie said. "Are you okay?"

Bryan didn't answer. He got out of the car and walked to the black gate. He held the square bars the way a prisoner holds his jail-cell door. The pointed tops of the bars were a good three feet above his head. In his dream, an effortless, standing jump had carried him over this gate, but in the waking world he saw that would be impossible.

The dark blanket looked . . . wet. Wetness on the sidewalk. Streaks of it. Wetness on the brick wall, in lines and patterns, in symbols and words. He vaguely recognized these things, but only saw bits of them out of the corner of his eye — he could not look away from the blanket.

The gate rattled as Bryan climbed it.

The sound of a car door shutting.

"Bryan, answer me, man."

Bryan dropped down on the other side. He walked toward the blanket.

Behind him, the gate rattled again, followed by sound of big dress shoes hitting the pavement.

"Bryan, this is *blood*. It's everywhere."

Bryan didn't answer. That scent, so overpowering.

"It's on the walls," Pookie said. "Jesus, I think they painted a picture in blood, right on the fucking walls."

Bryan reached for the blanket. His fingers clenched on fabric, *wet* fabric.

He yanked the blanket away.

A ravaged corpse. Its right arm had been ripped off. A piece of collarbone jutted out from near the neck. The stomach had been cut to pieces, intestines dragged out then shoved back in like dirt stuffed back into a hole. *So much blood.*

And that *face*. Puffy and swollen. Missing eye. Shattered jaw. The boy's own mother wouldn't recognize him.

But the hair . . . Bryan recognized the hair.

Black, curly, wiry.

To the left of the body, a white baseball hat streaked with blood spatter.

"Bryan."

Pookie's voice again. Something in his tone forced Bryan to turn. Pookie was staring at the mutilated body. He looked up at Bryan, his expression one of disbelief, perhaps even shock.

"Bryan, how did you know about this?"

Bryan didn't have an answer. The smell of piss was so strong, it made his head spin.

Pookie's right hand moved a touch closer to the left flap of his sport coat. "Bryan, did you do this?"

Bryan shook his head. "No. No way, man. You know I couldn't do something like this."

Pookie's eyes looked so cold. Was this the face perps saw when he took them down? A happy-go-lucky man, unless you were in his sights, then Pookie Chang became serious business.

"Step out of the alley," Pookie said. "Slowly. And keep your hands away from your gun."

"Pooks, I'm telling you that I didn't—"

"You *knew*. How could you know?"

That was the million-dollar question. If there was an answer, did Bryan really want to know it?

"I told you," Bryan said. "I had a dream."

Pookie took a breath, then nodded. "Right. A dream. If you had *knowingly* done this, for whatever reason, you wouldn't have told me about it, and you sure as hell wouldn't have brought me right to the body. But it doesn't change the fact that you *knew*."

"Pooks, I—"

"*Shut the fuck up,* Bryan. Here's what's going to happen. I'm going to believe my instincts and not my eyes. You're going to step out of this alley and stay out until I tell you to move. I'm going to call this in. We're going to gather evidence and see if anything points to you. Meantime, you don't say *a word* to anyone about your dreams or anything else. I'm going to wait and pray that my best friend, my partner, is not a fucking murderer."

Pookie suspected him? But Pookie knew Bryan, knew him better than anyone.

"I'm not," Bryan said. "I'm not a murderer."

Pookie raised his eyebrows. "Yeah? Are you *sure* about that?"

Bryan opened his mouth to answer, but nothing came out.

Because when it came down to it, he wasn't sure at all.

Pookie and His Partner

ookie Chang had seen a lot of nasty things in his day. He was no stranger to dead bodies. Back in Chicago, his second homicide case involved a man who had killed his mother, then tried to dispose of the body by chopping it into chunks small enough to fit into the kicthen sink's garbage disposal. You're never the same after you see something like that — it changes you. He'd handled cases that showed just how evil people could be, cases that made him doubt his faith. After all, how could a loving God allow things like this to happen? Yes, he had doubted God, doubted his own ability to do the job, and on more than one occasion he'd doubted the justice system itself — but in their six years of partnership, he had *never* doubted Bryan Clauser.

Not until now.

Cops on the scene had cordoned off Meacham Place and just one of Post Street's three lanes, allowing the one-way morning traffic to continue along. Two SFPD cruisers were parked at the curb. Two more were parked on the sidewalk, one on either side of the alley. A half-dozen uniforms milled about, keeping people away, calmly instructing pedestrians to use the other side of the street. Bubble-lights flashed blue and red. The morgue van sat silently, like a scavenger, waiting for the CSI personnel to finish their work before it could claim the corpse as its own.

Pookie stood on the sidewalk outside the now-open black gate. He stayed close to Bryan. Badges hung from both of their necks. Pookie stared into the alley, watching crime-scene investigators Sammy Berzon and Jimmy Hung do their thing. They wore dark-blue windbreaker jackets with SFPD in white across the back. What they found might nail Pookie's best friend to the wall.

But the truth had to come out.

Bryan looked horrible, his green eyes and pale white skin a harsh contrast to his dark-red beard. The guy seemed to be in shock, but this could not wait, could not be put off until he felt better.

"Tell me again," Pookie said. He spoke quietly, loud enough only for Bryan to hear. "Where were you last night?"

Bryan tilted his head closer, responded in kind. "My apartment. I went straight there after Sharrow sent me home."

Pookie remembered Bryan falling asleep on his desk — Bryan, who'd never missed a day of work or even exhibited the slightest sniffle.

"You were sick yesterday," Pookie said. "Feel the same today?"

"Worse. Whole body hurts. I think I have a fever or something."

Pookie nodded. Could the fever be so bad that Bryan somehow went out last night, during the dark hours the guy loved so much, and butchered this kid? And on top of that, didn't even remember doing it?

"So you went home," Pookie said. "What happened then?"

"I went right to bed. I slept pretty hard, I guess. The nightmare woke me up about two-thirty, maybe three A.M. I woke up, drew some pictures, went back to sleep."

"And no one to verify that? No girls, neighbors, landlords, nothing?"

Bryan chewed on his lower lip, shook his head. Of course the guy didn't have an alibi. He lived alone. He hadn't even been on a date since he'd moved out of Robin's place.

Bryan had led them right to this corpse, even *described* the state of the body. For him to have that kind of detailed knowledge, he had to have spoken with someone who saw this go down, someone who actually did it, or . . .

. . . or the obvious answer: Bryan had done it himself.

Impossible.

But was it impossible? People called Bryan *the Terminator* for a reason. He was cold, detached, and — most important — deadly. Had the Lanza scene pushed him over the edge?

Pookie couldn't believe that. If it weren't for Bryan Clauser, Pookie wouldn't even be alive. Maybe Bryan was a bit robotic, sure, but he was also everything a cop should be — brave, dedicated and self-sacrificing. He wasn't a murderer.

Not a murderer, maybe, but he sure is a killer, isn't he?

Pookie couldn't think of anything else to say, to ask. He looked back into the alley. The boy's body still lay under the tree's shade, lit up every few seconds by the flash of Jimmy Hung's camera. The severed arm was nowhere to be found. In its absence was a ragged, gaping, negative-space wound that ran from the neck down to just under where the armpit would have been had the arm still been attached. Part of the collarbone jutted out, red-streaked white gleaming bright every time Jimmy snapped another picture.

On the brick wall, between the thin trees, two-foot-high reddish-brown letters spelled out a message in graffiti, graffiti made with the victim's now-dry blood:

Pookie gently nudged Bryan, pointed to the letters.

"And that? Ring any bells?"

Bryan looked, and when he did, Pookie saw the telltale signs of recognition. The words had meaning to Bryan. Would he talk about it, or would he lie?

"Something like that in my dream," Bryan said. "Can't remember, exactly, but there were some words . . . or thoughts, maybe . . . they were banging through my head like someone was sending a message."

"A message like a phone call?"

Bryan shook his head. "No, not like a phone. Like . . . *inside* my head. Crazy, right?"

Yeah, *crazy.* That was the word Pookie kept trying to avoid. It was more palatable than *psychotic,* but still not a term one wanted attributed to one's best friend.

Pookie nodded toward the boy's body. "Maybe before we found him, it would sound crazy. But right now I'm ready to consider anything. Tell me more."

Bryan licked his lips. Pookie waited.

"Something about a king," Bryan said finally. "No, not *a* king, with *the* king."

"You sure? Was that what you heard in your dream?"

Bryan Clauser turned away from the gory scene. He stared at Pookie. Bryan didn't look all blank and emotionless anymore — the guy was scared.

"Pooks, you're talking to me like I'm a suspect."

There was no sugar-coating this. It was all Pookie could do to not call for the other cops on the scene, have them help slap cuffs on Bryan and take him in for questioning.

"You *are* a suspect, and you know it," Pookie said quietly. "You led us right to the body. You even told me what we'd find."

Bryan shook his head. "Just a dream. Just a fucking *dream*, man. Shit like this doesn't happen, it *can't* happen."

Pookie glanced around at the uniforms, seeing if any of them were trying to listen in. They weren't. "Just keep it together, Bryan. Don't say another word about it. We'll figure this out."

Pookie started to walk away, but a strong hand grabbed his upper arm and pulled him back. Pookie turned to face Bryan, to see the look of anguish in his partner's eyes.

"Do you really think I could do something like this?"

The logical part of Pookie's brain said *yes*, but that, too, was crazy. Why the hell would Bryan have killed this kid? Where was the motive?

"If I didn't consider you a suspect, I wouldn't be worth a squirt as a cop and you know it," Pookie said. "You shouldn't even be standing here, and you know that, too. You should be in an interrogation room. But you're my friend and I've been doing this job for a long time. We'll figure this out, but for now just shut up and *don't touch anything.*"

Pookie looked back into the alley and watched the CSI team. Sammy walked slowly, with very small steps. He had his head down, a camera around his neck and in his hands. When he reached the far side, he would turn ninety degrees to the right, still looking down, take one step, turn another ninety degrees, then start slowly recrossing the alley. Every three or four steps he would stop, point his camera down and take a picture, then bend to pick something up with tweezers. He'd drop the object into a brown paper envelope, seal it up and label it. Finally, he'd write on a small folded piece of white cardboard and put that in the object's place.

Jimmy hovered around the body, shooting the grizzly corpse from multiple angles: far back, tight shot, practically sticking the camera *into* the missing shoulder, on and on. The blue windbreaker was too big for Jimmy's tiny frame, making him look even smaller than he was.

Sammy stopped walking. He straightened. Still looking down, Sammy used the back of his gloved hand to wipe a few strands of blond hair out of his eyes. Moving only his head, he looked left and right, taking in a wider area. He looked up at Pookie and Bryan, then carefully walked out of the alley.

"Sammy," Pookie said. "How's Roger?"

Pookie didn't feel like making small talk, but it was an automatic impulse. Sammy's brother had been in a car accident a few days ago. Pookie didn't remember where he'd heard that. He had no idea why such information always stuck in his head.

"He's all good," Sammy said. "Out of the hospital tomorrow, I'm told. As for your one-armed bandit back there, I got an ID for you."

Sammy reached into a pocket and pulled out a plastic bag with an open wallet inside. A driver's license showed a kid with thick, curly-black hair. It seemed impossible that this young, healthy face had once belonged to the one-eyed, mutilated corpse in the alley.

"Oscar Woody," Sammy said. "Pretty sure that's him, based on the stats. We'll get confirmation as soon as we can. He's had that license all of two weeks. Happy sixteenth, eh?"

Pookie watched as Sammy turned the wallet for Bryan to see. Bryan's eyes widened, just a little. Had he recognized the picture?

Sammy put the wallet back in his pocket. "That body is a real piece of work, eh?"

Pookie nodded. "You can say that again. What do you think ripped that kid's arm off?"

"In the absence of any industrial machinery, I'd say a big animal. We found some brown hairs, about an inch long. Looks like dog fur to me."

Pookie looked to the body. The kid had to be five-ten, maybe one hundred seventy-five pounds. "That's not a toddler, Sammy. Tearing an arm off ain't no easy thing. How big would a dog have to be to do that?"

Sammy shrugged. "Pit bull, maybe? Probably more like a rottweiler. Get a rottie that weighs one-thirty or so, could happen. Mastiffs can top two hundred pounds. Tear that arm off easy."

Possible, but still . . . the patrol officers had already canvassed the area looking for witnesses and come up empty. Hard to imagine no one hearing a scream if a two-hundred-pound dog had bitten the kid's arm off.

"I'm guessing the dog had help, though," Sammy said. "There's a security camera mounted up the building. The nice building, not the old laundromat. It was pointed into the alley, but it's broke to shit. Looks like it was recently smashed. If the camera had been working, it would have caught everything that went down in the alley."

Maybe the camera had been broken just before the murder. Maybe this wasn't some random act of passion — maybe the killing had been planned. Pookie would track down whatever footage it had recorded, of course, but he already knew he'd probably find nothing of use. "Was Woody alive when the arm came off?"

"Oh, for sure," Sammy said. "Blood splashed around like a fuckin' fire hose, man. That's what I want to show you. Come here and take a look."

Pookie started following Sammy, then stopped when he realized Bryan had remained on the sidewalk. Bryan seemed to be waiting for permission. Pookie tilted his head sharply toward the alley: *get over here, now.*

Pookie Chang had seen many things that can and did change a person, but so had Bryan Clauser. Maybe Bryan had seen one thing too many.

Bryan walked into the alley. Pookie let him pass, then followed — he wanted to keep Bryan in sight at all times.

Nothing to See Here . . .

Bryan followed Sammy Berzon into the alley. He felt like he was returning to the scene of a crime — a crime he'd committed.

But he hadn't done this. *Couldn't* have.

Sammy held up a hand showing Bryan and Pookie where to stop. Then he pointed down. Not with a single finger, but with a palm-up, sweeping gesture that said *take a look at all this.*

"I can see how you guys missed this one," Sammy said. "I mean, any bigger and it wouldn't fit into the friggin' alley, eh?"

On the pavement were two drawings, done in tacky dry blood clotted with dirt, pebbles, bits of flesh, pieces of trash and even a used condom. Each drawing was about fifteen feet wide, as wide as the alley, large enough that Bryan had mistaken the bigger picture for random, individual streaks of blood. Two big circles, both with lines through them, and was that . . . a triangle? . . . lines also running through that, maybe . . .

The image clicked home. Clicked *hard.*

Bryan knew one of the images all too well, because he'd made it himself.

And there was a second drawing, one he didn't recognize.

"Interesting," Pookie said. "Isn't that triangle drawing interesting, Bryan? It looks familiar to me, but I couldn't say why."

Bryan said nothing. He had to force himself to take a breath. He'd sketched that same thing, and here it was, done in the blood of a murder victim. His body hurt. His face felt hot. He just didn't want to think about any of this for one minute longer.

"You two are *great* observers," Sammy said. "I mean, these drawings are only fifteen fucking feet across, eh?"

"Piss off, Sammy," Pookie said. "Not a good time for sarcasm."

Bryan stared at the two symbols. They were different, but both had that curve with the two slashes. What did it mean? What did *any* of it mean?

"And there's *two* drawings," Sammy said. "But anyone could have missed them, right? I mean you two geniuses could—"

Pookie turned fast, grabbed the shoulder of Sammy's coat and shook, jostling the smaller man. "I said, *shut up*, Sammy. You got it?"

A shocked Sammy nodded. Pookie let him go.

Bryan looked around. All cop conversation had stopped. Everyone was staring at Pookie. Pookie, who never lost his cool. Pookie, who never said an angry word.

Pookie saw the other cops looking. He turned, glared at Bryan, then walked off to talk to the uniforms.

Bryan walked back out the black gate, careful not to tread on the blood drawings. He stood on the sidewalk, alone, wondering if Pookie was already regretting the decision to believe in his partner.

If so, Bryan couldn't blame the man.

He felt a breeze on his face. He wiped the back of his hand across his forehead — he was sweating. Finding the body had brought on a big blast of adrenaline. Now that the surge was fading, his nausea, aches and chest pain once again fought for attention. He felt ten times worse than he had that morning.

Pookie returned. He was smiling, but Bryan could see it was fake — Pookie was putting on a show of normalcy. As far as the other cops would see, it was just good-ol' Bryan and Pooks, working the case and doing their thing. *Nothing to see here, please move along . . .*

"The driver's license picture," Pookie said in a whisper. "You recognized that kid, didn't you. You knew that face."

Bryan thought of lying, but nodded. "Yeah."

"From?"

Bryan shrugged. "From my dream, man. I don't know what else to say."

Pookie pursed his lips and nodded, an expression of anger, of frustration. "Go home," he said. "Just for a couple of hours, okay?"

"But I have to help you with this, I have—"

"I'll finish working the scene," Pookie said. "We'll have to talk to friends and family, so I'll come grab you before it's time to bang on doors. We're not that far from your place, so just walk. I think it's best if you're not here right now."

Pookie's stare was hard and unforgiving. This wasn't open to debate.

There had to be an explanation for this, but neither of them had any clue what that might be.

Bryan turned and started walking.

Robin and Spoiled Milk

obin Hudson finished tucking her hair into a hairnet as she stood in the prep area, watching the van back into the loading bay. The back of the van opened. Robin was surprised to see Sammy Berzon and Jimmy Hung get out. They removed a cart loaded with a white body bag.

As crime-scene investigators, Sammy and Jimmy usually didn't help bring a body back to the morgue — that was normally done by Robin's co-workers in the ME's office.

Robin smoothed out her disposable gown and hung a digital camera around her neck. She slid her face-shield rig onto her head, but left the clear plastic flipped up.

The men rolled the cart into the prep area.

"Fancy meeting you two here," Robin said.

"Hello, pretty lady," Sammy said. "Do you mind if we help with this one? We got a hundo riding on what did the killing. I say rottweiler or big dog, Jimmy is betting a more exotic animal."

"Tiger," Jimmy said. "Definitely a tiger."

Robin nodded. "Sure, you can assist. Whatever floats your boat."

"Awesome," Sammy said. "I'll load the crime-scene photos into the system as soon as we help prep the body." He held up a clear plastic bag containing a blanket. "This was covering the vic." He set the bag on the end of the cart.

Robin leaned down to look. Inside the bag, she saw that the blanket was covered with short, brownish hairs. No wonder Jimmy thought it was a rottweiler.

She picked up the bag. "I'm pretty good at identifying dog breeds from fur. I'll take a closer look after we finish with the subject. You guys get ready while I handle the x-rays."

•••

Robin shot x-rays while the corpse was still in the body bag. The digitized images immediately showed major damage: missing arm, jaw dislocated and fractured in at least two places, missing teeth, shattered right orbit. Bright white bits glowed from within the soft, multihued gray representation of his lungs — the boy had aspirated some of the teeth.

She finished the x-rays and rolled the cart into the prep area. Sammy and Jimmy were waiting. They had donned their own protective personal equipment: gowns, face shields and fresh gloves.

"You boys bring me the nicest presents," she said. "Just what I needed to pep up my afternoon."

Sammy smiled. "That's what we do. Great case for your first day as the boss-lady, huh?"

"I'm not the *boss-lady*, guys. It's only temporary."

Jimmy shrugged his little shoulders. "We'll see. I love Metz, but a heart attack at his age? Hard to come back from."

"He'll be back," Robin said. She wanted the top job, absolutely, but she knew she wasn't ready for it yet. Just another year or two with Metz, maybe, then she would be.

"Okay," she said, "let's get this party started."

They unzipped the body bag. Instantly, she smelled urine. Strong, and somehow unique — *the same smell as when Metz brought in Maloney.*

"He's a ripe one," she said. "Must have had a full bladder when he died."

Sammy shook his head. "Guess again. The perps pissed on him. Or the rottweiler did."

"Tiger," Jimmy said.

When a body died, the muscles in the bowel and bladder relaxed, often resulting in a corpse releasing feces and urine. That was why she hadn't thought twice about Maloney's body smelling as it had when Metz brought it in. But this scent was so unique — aside from this corpse and Maloney, she'd never smelled anything quite like it. Was it possible Maloney's killer had urinated on him as well?

"This could help us," she said. "If it was the animal's handler that urinated on him, we might be able to get something out of that."

Sammy reached into the body bag and pulled out a bloody, dead hand. They ran fingerprints, then weighed and measured the corpse.

"We have a preliminary ID from a driver's license," Sammy said. "Oscar Woody, age sixteen. We'll get confirmation quick, he's got a record and his prints are in the system."

"Already?" She found it endlessly sad that kids went bad so early in their lives. Had it always been that way? Probably. It just seemed more drastic now — as she got older, teenagers seemed progressively younger and younger.

Jimmy cut away the victim's clothes and started placing them in bags.

"We got what we think are saliva samples," he said. "All over the shoulder area. Probably from the tiger."

"Rottweiler," Sammy said. "Robin, thanks for letting us help. If you want to prep your table, we'll bring him in to you."

Robin nodded. "I'll go do that."

She walked out of the prep area and into the long, rectangular, wood-paneled autopsy room. Five white porcelain exam tables lined the room's length, the tables' long sides paralleling the room's short sides. At the moment, the tables sat empty. Robin had seen many days when all five tables were in simultaneous operation, with even more bodies backed up in the big walk-in refrigerated transit locker.

Most morgues used stainless-steel tables. The Hall of Justice, to which the morgue was attached, had been built in 1958. This examination room — original white porcelain autopsy tables and all — hadn't changed much in the last fifty-odd years. Metz often told her that other than the ashtrays being removed from the walls, it basically looked the same as it had on his first day of work four decades earlier.

Sammy and Jimmy rolled the metal cart into the room. They slid the body onto the first porcelain table. As seasoned as she was, Robin couldn't help but wince at the carnage.

When the arm came off, the outer third of his clavicle had been sheared away. The stumpy bone stuck out of the ravaged pectoral. Blood on the clavicle's jagged end was already a dry brown. She saw scrapes on the broken bone; gouges from teeth, probably. No teeth marks on the face, though — that damage had been done by blunt-force trauma: fists, elbows, feet and knees, most likely.

Severe lacerations covered his abdomen. Severed pieces of intestine dangled out like bloody gray-brown sausages speckled with yellow globs of fat. She realized that the intestines had been pulled out, torn up, then crammed back in. That was the work of a person — animals didn't stuff your guts back in for you.

"Any evidence that could lead to the perps?"

"Tons," Jimmy said. "Sick bastards used the vic's blood to write *long live the king* on a brick wall, and make some weird occult drawings. It's all in the photos for you."

"Good," Robin said. "So, where's the arm?"

Sammy shrugged. "We couldn't find it."

Jimmy checked his watch. "Well, that does it for me today. I'm heading home. Robin, if you have any questions, call me, but I'm sure Bryan and Pookie can answer anything."

The sound of his name stopped her cold. "This is Bryan's case?"

"He and Pookie were first on the scene," Jimmy said. "I'm out. Later."

Robin threw the departing Jimmy a half-wave. She pushed away any thoughts of Bryan Clauser and focused on her job. She did a slow walk around the white table. Oscar had been a big kid. Five-ten, would have been about a hundred and eighty pounds if the arm had been attached. Hopefully the arm was discarded somewhere and would soon turn up. If the perp still had it, that probably meant he was keeping it as a trophy. A trophy-taker could mean a serial killer. Or, perhaps even more messed up, the arm had been an *atta-boy* treat for the attacking animal.

"Soft-tissue damage looks like it extends to the back," Robin said. "Let me look at the scapula. Sammy, can you flip him over?"

He did. The scapula remained intact, scraps of tacky human meat still plastered to the bone. She saw two long, parallel gouges about three inches apart — matching lines that curved and zigzagged. She lifted her camera, leaned in and snapped a picture. Sammy would have a complete set of shots for this and everything else, but Robin liked to record key areas with her own eye and angles.

She let the camera drop to her chest, then reached out and gently probed the torn shoulder.

"You guys are probably right about an animal," she said. "These parallel gouges would be consistent with marks made by canines, like something bit him and shook him."

Sammy smiled at her. "Like I said, rottie, eh?"

She gave a noncommittal shrug. "Maybe." She looked at the wide space between the parallel teeth gouges, tried to imagine the size of a dog that owned those teeth. "Jimmy might win the bet after all. I won't rule out a big cat, as weird as that would be in the middle of San Francisco."

"Fascinating," Sammy said. "You know, this sounds like great conversation material. Why don't we talk about it over dinner. Say, tomorrow night? I'll pick you up at eight."

Robin looked up from the body and smiled. "Sammy Berzon, did you guys *really* have a bet on what kind of animal killed this boy, or did you connive your way in here to ask me out on a date?"

He smiled and held up his right hand. "Guilty as charged. I know this café on Fillmore with outside seating, so we can take your dog."

She laughed, felt her eyebrows rise in surprise admiration. "Wow, you're *good*. Invite the dog, too?"

He gave a half-bow. "You have to know the battlefield, my dear, but you make it pretty easy. Your desk is covered with pictures of the pup. He's cute as hell."

"*She.*"

"Sorry, *she.* So, how about dinner?"

Sammy was a handsome man. He had rugged features, although maybe he spent a little too much time on his blond locks. Robin's mother had always said *don't ever date a man who spends more time on his hair than you do.* As a criminalist, Sammy knew the horrors she dealt with on a daily basis. They had that in common. And he'd catered to her near-obsessive love of Emma. Obviously, he was a perceptive guy. She looked back down to the corpse. Sammy would undoubtedly be a great date, but she just wasn't up for it.

"Thanks, but . . . uh . . . I don't think I'm good dating company."

"Come on. You and Bryan split up six months ago. Live a little, eh?"

She felt her anger rising, but fought it down — he *was* asking her out, after all. "You know how long it's been since we broke up?"

Sammy smiled. "Of course. Six-month rule. I couldn't ask you out for six months out of respect for the Terminator."

Her smiled faded. "Don't call him that."

His smile faded as well. He knew he'd made a mistake. "Sorry," he said. "I mean, it's not really an insult, you know?"

She nodded. She hated the nickname. It insinuated that Bryan was cold-blooded, a machine that could just kill without remorse. She knew that wasn't true. Still, in the bizarre world of male logic, the nickname was a compliment and Sammy hadn't meant anything by it.

She tried to change the subject.

"And what do you mean by *the six-month rule*?"

"You can't ask a brotha's girl out for six months," Sammy said. "It's man law. The six-month rule is kind of like an expiration date in reverse."

Men. Impossible to understand. "So . . . I *was* sour milk, and now I'm fit to serve?"

"You got it. How about instead of telling me *no,* you just take a rain check on dinner?"

"Fine. I'll take a rain check."

Sammy's wide smile returned. "Works for me. Later, gator."

He walked out of the morgue.

Robin wondered how many people knew Bryan had moved out six months earlier. Everybody in the medical examiner's department, probably, and obviously even more than that. Big city, big police force, but still a relatively small group of people that dealt with the steady influx of dead bodies.

She turned her attention back to the one-armed boy. The shoulder wounds were definitely from a big animal, but she'd test the collected saliva just to confirm it.

She'd start with a short tandem repeat analysis test. The STR would come back within hours and provide a genetic fingerprint of the victim and the attacker or attackers — if those attackers were human, that was. That test would find thirteen key loci in human DNA that she could run against CODIS, the FBI's genetic database of known criminals. Sometimes it was just that easy — process the evidence, isolate the DNA, submit it to CODIS and get a hit.

Robin hoped they'd get lucky and identify the killer right away. Such savagery was beyond even the normal gunshot, knife and blunt-force trauma deaths she dealt with all the time.

This was part of the reason she'd chosen an ME career instead of continuing on in medicine. In a world heading down the drain, she was part of the solution. Her job was intel, really. Intel in the war against crime. She provided the data that helped the guys on the front line — guys like Bryan and Pookie.

Bryan. Not the time to think of him. He'd moved out, and she'd moved on.

Robin closed her eyes, cleared her thoughts. She had a job to do. And if someone actually *had* taken the arm as a trophy, a very important job.

Rex Gets Good News

School had started an hour ago, but Rex wasn't there for it. No way he was going there. *No way.*

The cast on his arm was a badge of shame, a brand of weakness. Some would snicker; others would outright laugh at him. Everyone in school would know who broke his arm. That didn't matter to Roberta — all she cared about was getting him out of the house. He'd pleaded with her to let him stay home, even cried a little, and all he got for his trouble was a slap in the face and a brief-but-intense lecture about being a crybaby.

He hated the BoyCo bullies. *Hated* them.

Roberta didn't know about his secret places, his hidey spots. He walked toward his favorite — Sydney Walton Square, down by the Embarcadero. There he could sit with his back against his favorite oak tree. His backpack held his sketchbook, pencils, and his tattered copy of *Game of Thrones* by George R. R. Martin.

Maybe he could read a little later, read about empires and knights and kings and queens, but first he had to draw. Draw more of what he'd seen in last night's dream. Draw more of what had made his pants wet. It was wrong to want more of that, very wrong, but he *had* to draw it.

If only that dream had been real.

If only he was big enough, *strong* enough, to get an ax or a knife or whatever, use it on that stupid asshole, cut into his belly and drag out all his guts, *hurt* him, break his jaw so he couldn't scream, couldn't cry for help, could only whimper and make quiet begging noises. If only he were man enough to kill Oscar Woody.

Whatever Rex had been in that dream, it most certainly was not a man. He didn't care. It had been the best dream ever. *Ever.* Oscar going over that black gate. Oscar turning . . . oh, the look on his face! And something with Oscar's arm . . . Rex couldn't quite remember. Had he broken Oscar's arm?

It had seemed so real. But it wasn't. He'd never be free of those bullies.

Rex wasn't strong. He was weak. A wimp. *Pathetic.*

And that's all he'd ever be.

The sun peeked out behind the tapering point of the Transamerica Building as Rex walked east on Washington Street. He looked up just enough to see where he was going. The rest of the time he kept his gaze firmly affixed on his shoes and the two or three yards in front of them.

It wasn't until he reached Kearney Street that he looked around, and when he did, he saw a *San Francisco Chronicle* headline screaming at him from inside a beat-up newspaper rack.

Rex stopped cold.

GALILEO STUDENT BRUTALLY MURDERED
16-Year-Old's Arm Torn Off, Still Missing

Those words called to Rex, but not as much as the picture that accompanied them. A small school photo of a smiling Oscar Woody.

Oscar Woody was *dead*? His arm . . . *torn off*?

An older couple walked by. Rex ignored them. Dream-recollections flooded his thoughts, crystallizing the visions of smashing Oscar's face, throwing him to the ground, stepping on his chest, grabbing his arm and *yanking* until there was a muffled cracking sound and the arm gave way.

Rex felt his dick stiffen a little in his pants.

My dream . . . I did this. I MADE *him die.*

Rex's pulse hammered through his body. His face felt hot. He grabbed the newspaper rack and pulled. The locked door just rattled. He dug in his pockets, but he had no change. He had no money at all. He turned in a near panic, eyes scanning for the ever-present bums. He didn't have to look far. An old man with a dirty beard and even dirtier clothes sat on his knees in front of the concrete steps that led into Portsmouth Square park. Head down low, hands cupped together and held at chest level, the kneeling bum waited for suckers to walk by.

Rex sprinted to the man.

"Give me your change," Rex said. "Give it to me now."

The bum ignored him.

"I said give me your change!" Rex reached back his right foot and kicked. His sneaker landed in the bum's ribs. The old man cried out. What a baby — Rex hadn't kicked him that hard.

The bum fell to his side, his face screwed tight in pain. "Ohmygod ohmygod . . . you broke my ribs."

Rex leaned in until his face was only inches from the bum's, so close Rex could smell breath that combined fruity alcohol and decay.

"Give it to me *now*, you motherfucker, or I will *cut you*!"

The bum shrank back, tried to bring his hands up in a defensive posture, but his face scrunched tight again and his hands shot to his side, where Rex had kicked him.

"*Please*, boss, don't hurt me!"

Rex felt electric — this man, this *grown man*, was *terrified*. Rex's dick stiffened, throbbed.

"Hey!"

The voice came from down the street. Rex looked up. A half-block away on Washington stood a big man with a beer gut straining a white wife-beater shirt. He had a thick black beard that hung down to his chest. He wore a green John Deere baseball hat, and he was looking at Rex.

Looking so strangely.

"Hey," the man said again. "You can't do that when people are looking."

Rex stared. More images, flickers of his dream phasing together in ghostly echoes. He'd seen this man before.

He'd seen this man in the dream.

Rex's rage vanished. What the hell was going on? How could he see a man who had been in his dreams?

Then, a strange feeling blossomed in his chest. A *warmth*, a *buzzing*. It felt so good. The guy looked like a pedophile from a TV show, but the sensation in Rex's chest made it feel like he could trust this stranger.

The man held out his hand. "I'll help you. Come with me."

Rex stared, then shook his head. The man was coming from where Rex had been walking . . . had the man been *following* him?

Rex turned to run, stopping only long enough to wind up with his right foot and kick the bum again, this time right in the face. The bum's head snapped back, shaking hands reaching up to cover a mouth that already gushed blood.

Blood. I made him BLEED *. . .*

Rex sprinted down Washington, thumbs hooked under his backpack straps. He saw a Chinese restaurant and ran inside, pushing past anyone who got in his way. He slid past the tables, saw a door in the back and ran through it into the kitchen. People were yelling at him in Chinese or whatever, more in surprise than anger. Moments later, he found a door that led to a back alley.

He sprinted away from the restaurant, away from the bum, away from the bearded man. The emotions that pounded through his body, his brain, were exquisite in intensity and texture.

He had *hit* someone.

For the first time in his entire life, Rex had *fought back*.

Black Mr. Burns

John Smith focused on his computer screen, using a stylus to hand-trace the lines of a photo from new graffiti found in the Western Addition neighborhood. He didn't recognize the artist's work by sight — perhaps a new tagger from an existing gang, or, more likely, the markings of a brand-new outfit. John was so intent on mapping the image that he didn't hear the office door open, didn't even realize someone was there until that person spoke.

"Black Mister Burns," said Pookie Chang. "How's life sniffing the silicon ass of the digital dog?"

John turned and smiled at his former partner. "Computer work is just fine, thanks."

John reached out to shake Pookie's hand. Pookie had to juggle his ever-present overflowing manila folders to answer the shake. Some things never changed.

Years earlier, Pookie had used the unusual nickname to try and get a rise out of John. To most people, being compared to a character on *The Simpsons* would be less than flattering. Most people, sure, but not to a man who had the most common name in America, *and* in England.

John loved his moms, but when other black mothers were naming their children sweet names like *Marquis, Jermaine, Andre, Deshon,* or even something crazy like *X-Ray,* his mom settled on the rather unoriginal *John.*

When Pookie started calling John *Black Mister Burns,* it didn't bother John at all. Then the rest of the cops picked up on it, laughing at how John's overbite, long nose and his mottled bald head did, indeed, make him look like a black Mr. Burns.

John had loved it.

It was something people could remember — a name that wasn't shared by over half a million American men. And for that, seeing Pookie always put a smile on John's face.

"Burns, you look good," Pookie said. "Only *mildly* anorexic this time. How's that bike restoration coming? Eighty-eight softail, right?"

John's smile faded, then he forced it back into place. "Finished it two years ago."

Pookie winced. "Damn, I knew that. Sorry."

Pookie Chang remembered the most obscure facts in the world. That he'd forgotten about John's project showed how far apart the two men had grown in the six years since they'd last worked together.

"We got something for you," Pookie said. "Could use your help on this."

"Cool," John said. "Where's the Terminator?"

John was still a bit jealous that Pookie's career had not only continued, but had skyrocketed with another partner. John couldn't bring himself to be mad at Bryan Clauser, however — the Terminator had saved his life.

"Bryan's at his apartment," Pookie said. "He isn't feeling so hot."

"Sick? *Bryan?*"

Pookie shrugged. "Yeah, I guess there's a first time for everything."

"Well, then stay away from me," John said. "I know you guys were probably in the back of that Buick swapping spit and rubbing tummies."

"Kissing dudes is my business and business is good. Now if you're done fencing with your rapier wit, I need your help with this."

"Is it from that body on Meacham this morning?"

Pookie nodded, looked for a place to set down his stack of folders. John cleared out a space. Pookie set them down, opened the top folder and handed John several printed crime-scene photos.

John took them, made a show of waving them so the paper made noise. "Pooks, you know you can email this shit, right?"

"Electrons are the work of the devil," Pookie said. "We found that graffiti at the murder scene."

"What makes you think it's related to the murder?"

"It was drawn in the vic's blood. So was this."

Pookie handed over another photo showing the words *long live the king* scrawled in dripping letters on a brick wall.

John's eyebrows rose. "Yeah, that'll do it."

"You recognize that symbol?"

John stared at it, waiting for a flicker of recognition. A round eye inside a triangle, which itself was inside a circle. Didn't ring any bells.

John's main role with the Gang Task Force was to track gang memberships and relationships. That meant database work, analyzing online activity such as email and social media interactions, and that staple of gang communication — graffiti. Graffiti painted a picture of which gangs controlled various parts of the city. What looked like random vandalism was often a complex code of who ran the streets, who was marked for death and who would do the killing.

Computer work was about all John was good for, these days. Six years ago, he'd caught a bullet in his belly, then lay there, bleeding out, while the sniper — a dirty cop named Blake Johansson — kept him pinned down and stopped anyone from reaching him. The incident had left John with a blinding fear that made even the daily drive to work a challenge. Going out and being an actual cop? Forget it.

But if sitting behind a computer was the only way he could contribute, he would do it better than anyone else. Everyone in the department played a role. John knew his and accepted it.

When you're a coward, you do what you can.

John shook his head. "I've never seen this symbol before. You got pictures of the victim?"

Pookie pulled out more printouts and handed them over. John had seen a lot of damage in his career, but this was among the worst. Such *savagery*. The colors of the victim's jacket clicked home.

"He was in Boys Company," John said.

"That a gang?"

John nodded. "Small potatoes. Just kids. Runs mostly out of Galileo High in the Marina."

"They at war with anyone?"

"Not that I know of. Like I said, they're small potatoes. A little B and E, some fighting, maybe a little dealing in the school. More like a club than a gang. If BoyCo went up against a serious outfit like MS13, they'd get slaughtered."

Pookie pointed to the picture. "That sort of fits my definition of *slaughter*."

"Good point. I'll start digging, but I'm sure no one is at war with BoyCo."

"How do you know he's from BoyCo?"

"The jacket," John said. "Boston College. Initials are *B* and *C*, same as Boys Company. That's how they show their colors."

"So why not the Boston Celtics? That's *BC*."

"Green and black are the colors of the Latin Cobras," John said. "Anyone wearing Celtics gear is going to get fucked up by the Cobras, or any of the gangs that are fighting with the Cobras. Pretty much every gang has some sports team affiliation, either with colors or initials."

"Go team," Pookie said. "Dare I ask what happens if I wear the colors of my beloved Chicago Bears?"

"You get beat up by Raiders fans. That's the worst of it, though. I don't think any gangs use the Bears. Kids got to be real careful of what color clothes they wear to school these days — the wrong colors in the wrong spot can get you killed."

Pookie nodded absently as he thought. "If it's not another gang, what about someone just fighting back? Maybe BoyCo roughed up the wrong kid?"

"Possible, but not likely," John said. "These lower-tier gangs are usually smart enough to only pick on the weak. They target kids who aren't in a gang or related to gang members, who aren't on the wrestling team or football team, anything like that."

"And *long live the king*? Could that be some gangsta's street name?"

John shrugged. "Maybe, but that doesn't ring any bells, either. We could have a new player in the mix. Let's take a look at the BoyCo file."

John sat at his computer and called up his database. The file had hundreds of tabs, one for each of the gangs that ran through the Bay Area. Some, like MS13 or the Norteños, were seriously bad news, connected on a national and even international basis. Other outfits were local but just as dangerous, like Westmob and Big Block in Hunters Point; 14K Triad and Wah Ching in Chinatown; Jackson Street Boys all over the city; or Knock Out Posse and Eddy Rock in the Western Addition.

John clicked on the tab for BoyCo. A file appeared with four photos.

Pookie looked over his shoulder. "Just four kids?"

"That we know of. Oscar Woody, Jay Parlar, Issac Moses and the leader, Alex Panos."

"Four kids is a gang?"

John shrugged. "Like I said, more of a club of bullies, really. Barely even on our radar."

Pookie pulled out another photo. A particularly gruesome shot, it showed Oscar Woody's full body: arm ripped off, stomach torn open, face beaten so badly it barely looked human.

"This isn't just some mugging," Pookie said. "The mutilation, the writing on the wall — someone is sending a message. Sure it couldn't be MS13? Don't they cut off limbs?"

"And hands and heads," John said. "But MS13 uses machetes. Look at that kid's body, Pooks. He wasn't *cut* apart, he was *torn* apart."

"Could it be a new gang? What about that blood-graffiti symbol?"

"That's where we'll start. Let's get this scanned in and see what the computer says."

John scanned in both the photos, then opened them up in his computer and accessed the Regional Information Sharing System. RISS coordinated nationwide gang data, including suspects, organizations and weapons as well as visual imagery of gang members, gang symbols and gang graffiti.

"Huh," Pookie said. "And I thought the Internet was for porn."

"Oh no," John said. "We don't look at porn down here, Pooks. There are filters and then if you're caught—"

"Kidding," Pookie said. "Jesus, man, you haven't changed a bit."

John sighed. Even when they'd been partners, he only caught about half of Pookie's humor. "Anyway, the RISS software identifies key points much like a fingerprint, marking the degree of curves, the thickness and relative length of lines. It breaks down individual segments of the symbols into a hundred minisymbols. Then I feed it into the database and it searches for matches, partial or full."

"Does this crap really work?"

John nodded. "Oh, hell yeah. It's amazing. It can even build a graphic profile on individual artists so accurate we can tell the genuine artist from an imitator."

The computer beeped.

John opened a window to read the results. "Huh. Nothing in San Francisco."

"Anywhere else?"

John scanned the results. "Looks like one hit in New York City a couple of decades ago. A serial killer. Looks like he murdered four women, then killed himself. That's all it says. I'm sure there's more info, but we'd have to reach out to the NYPD to get it."

As John read the lines of information, he saw something strange. "This is weird."

"What is?"

"Well, I see incoming links on these symbols from that old case in New York, but what those links connect to was deleted from our system. Oh, look at this! Here's a local request. It's old, must have been the early days of the SFPD's efforts to computerize. Let's see . . . twenty-nine years ago. But there's no images associated with it, so we can't know if the request was answered."

Pookie absently scratched at his jaw. "Why would someone delete info on this symbol?"

"Probably a mistake," John said. "You have thousands of people accessing this stuff. Systems and software conflict, databases purge, things can get accidentally erased."

"That local request," Pookie said, "Can you tell me who made it?"

John looked. He followed database links to a dead end. "No, those fields aren't there. The information is too old. Probably migrated from sytem to sytem to system as the department continued to modernize. I can keep looking, though. Give me a couple of days, I'll see what I can find."

Pookie sighed. He gathered his papers and pictures, stuffing them once again into the abused manila folder. "While you're at it, can you get the details on the New York City case?"

"Sure thing."

"One more favor," Pookie said. "Keep all your searching on the down-low. Polyester Rich has what might be a similar case, and I want them both. Don't need him hearing about you looking into it."

Pookie's rivalry with Rich Verde was still alive and well, it seemed. "Not a problem, Pooks."

Pookie opened the door to leave, then turned, a grin on his face.

"Come on," he said. "Do it for me just once."

John laughed, then affected an evil smile. He held his hands in front of him like claws, touching the tips of his left fingers to the tips of his right.

"Excellent, Smithers," John said. *"Exxxxcellent."*

Pookie nodded sagely, as if John had just said the most wise words in all the world. "Mister Burns should have been black."

"He *is*. The networks just decolorize him because America fears a rich black man."

Pookie nodded, then walked out the door, leaving John to look at the symbols scanned into his computer.

Pookie's Flashback

It had been almost two decades since Pookie Chang's high school graduation, and yet a principal's office still gave him the creeps.

Pookie had given Bryan a few hours to himself. That hadn't seemed to help much — when Pookie picked Bryan up, the man still looked scattered, a little freaked out and sick as a dog. At least Bryan hadn't fled. Maybe it would have been easier if he had. That would have forced Pookie's hand, saved him from deciding if he should either trust Bryan or arrest him.

You just couldn't *dream* crime-scene details like that. Could someone be setting Bryan up? Maybe, but how would that work? Was someone hypnotizing him? Maybe drugging him, then sneaking into his apartment and whispering sweet nothings in his ear? Could this be some massively convoluted revenge plot from someone Bryan had put away?

Maybe, sure, or maybe Pookie could pull his head out of his ass and accept the obvious answer — that Bryan Clauser had gone out last night and butchered Oscar Woody.

No way. I've known that man for six years. NO WAY.

That thought echoed constantly through Pookie's head, fighting for space against *but he's already killed FIVE people*. The bottom line, however, was that Pookie owed Bryan Clauser his life. So did Black Mr. Burns. Therefore, Bryan got the benefit of the doubt. However unlikely, there could still be a valid reason why Bryan knew those crime-scene details. To find that answer, Pookie had to do his job — beginning with Kyle Souller, principal of Galileo High.

"Principal Souller, we need to know who Oscar Woody may have had a beef with."

Souller had the tired look of a man who knew his entire career involved fighting a losing battle. His suit seemed to hang on him like a convict's stripes.

Souller threaded his fingers together, rested the clasped hands on his desktop. "You think a student did this?" He didn't say that with shock or disbelief, just a sense of resignation. "We have violence here, like any school, but this is on a different level."

"Could be a student," Pookie said. "A stronger possibility is a student hired someone to do it. We understand Oscar had incidents here?"

Souller let out a single, sad laugh. "Yeah, you could say that. We don't have much of a gang problem at Galileo. That lets a pissant operation like BoyCo kind of rule the roost. They pick on a lot of kids."

"Which kids?" Bryan said. "We need names."

Souller sat back in his chair. "Inspector, I can't just give you names of everyone BoyCo has crossed. I'm not going to subject those kids to police questioning when they've done nothing wrong."

Bryan started to talk, but he winced before any words came out. He cleared his throat — painfully, judging by the expression on his face — then tried again. "Don't give me that civil rights bullshit," he said. "We need leads. We . . ."

His voice trailed off. He closed his eyes and leaned back. He rubbed his temples.

Pookie reached out and supportively squeezed Bryan's shoulder. "You okay, man?"

Bryan slowly shook his head. "Yeah, I . . . got a headache. Is it hot in here?"

Souller pointed to his office door. "There's a water fountain in the hall. Quite cold."

Bryan nodded. "Yeah, that'll help. Pooks, you mind?"

"I got this," Pookie said.

Bryan stood and walked to the door. He moved slowly, swaying just a little bit. Maybe he had a split personality taking over. Maybe he was going out to tear off someone's arm, poke out their eye, rip out their guts and then stuff them—

Pookie shook his head once, quickly, as if to chase away the thoughts.

Bryan shut the door behind him.

Pookie turned back to Principal Souller, who looked less than pleased.

"*Civil rights bullshit?*" Souller said. "You guys are subtle."

Pookie shrugged. "Cut him some slack, man. Oscar's body really shook him up."

Souller sighed and nodded. "Yeah, I guess that would shake up anyone. But I can't just give you a list of names."

"Principal Souller, we have concerns that the other BoyCo members could be in trouble. Alex Panos, Issac Moses and Jay Parlar deserve our protection."

Souller's eyebrows rose. "You already know their names? Nice. Are you telling me that you really care about a bunch of bullies?"

"It's my job," Pookie said. He looked around the room. "And let's just say I spent a significant amount of my high school years in an office that looked a lot like this."

"As victim, or victimizer?"

"The latter," Pookie said. "I know these kids are bad news, but they're still *kids*. They can straighten out. I did. Oscar Woody will never have that chance. You know the students and the staff here better than we do. Anything you can do to save us time could matter."

Souller nodded. "Okay. I'll go through the records, see if anything comes up. I'll talk to the teachers individually."

Pookie stood and handed over his card. "Please call me if you find anything at all."

They shook hands. Pookie walked out to find Bryan bent over the drinking fountain, water splashing against his face.

"Bri-Bri, you okay?"

Bryan stood, wiped the water from his face. "Yeah, that did the trick. I feel better. Ready to go talk to Oscar Woody's parents?"

You've killed five human beings was what flashed through Pookie's head.

"Sure thing" was what came out of his mouth.

Hair of the Dog

obin lifted her head from the microscope.

That *couldn't* be right. She must have mistakenly used a human hair.

She reached for the tray that contained the inch-long brown hairs she'd collected from the body and the blanket. With a tweezers, she carefully selected one that had been embedded in Oscar's wound. She picked it up, held it close — yes, that was one of the animal hairs.

But it looked the same as her current sample.

She held them side by side: *exactly* the same.

She put the new one under the microscope. Just as she had done with the first sample, she started at low magnification to see the entire shape. The hair had a tapered end, as would be expected from animal fur. Ends of human hair were almost always *cut*, something that could easily be seen under a microscope, while most animal fur *tapered* to a point because the strands of fur wore down on their own.

At higher magnification, things got weird.

Hair or fur has three parts: the *cortex*, the *cuticle* and the *medulla*. Comparing it to a pencil, the cortex is the wood, the medulla is the lead and the thin coat of yellow paint is the cuticle.

The cuticle is a layer of cells that covers the shaft, like scales on a snake. The pattern of scales differs from species to species. Crownlike scales, called *coronal*, are common among rodents. Triangular *spinous* scales indicate cat hairs.

The sample Robin examined had *imbricate*, or *flattened*, scales.

Dog fur had imbricate scales, but those scales were thick sheets that wrapped all the way around. The scales on the sample from the blanket, however, were thinner, finer and tighter than would be found in dog fur.

This type of imbricate scales were found on *human* hair.

She checked a third strand, a fourth, then a fifth. All had fine scales, all had tapered ends.

Maybe the attacker had hair that grew very slowly. Maybe he rarely, if ever, had to get it cut. Maybe the strands were from a man with a receding hairline, his follicular growth slowed to a near standstill. Guys who were balding didn't like trimming what little hair they had left.

Possible, but then there were the bite marks, the parallel gouges on Oscar Woody's bones. Those *had* to be from an animal. A *big* animal. Sure, a handler and a big animal working together could account for the damage, and the handler's hair could have been in the wound, but with that level of contact so would some fur from the animal.

The STR results from the saliva would soon be finished. If that came back as human, it would correlate with what she saw in these hairs. She could *confirm* the hair as human, however, by finding samples that still had follicles attached to the root end, then running the tests on those follicular cells.

Human or animal, soon she would know for certain.

Pookie's Pimpin' Gear

W e need your help, Alex," Pookie said. "Can you think of anyone who would want to get back at you for anything?"

Pookie waited for an answer. He and Bryan sat in chairs, while Alex Panos and his mother, Susan, sat on the couch across from them. A coffee table with a vase of fresh flowers separated the pairs. A pack of cigarettes and a box of Kleenex lay on the table in front of Susan, but she had yet to light up and seemed to favor the already well-used wad of tissue clutched in her hand.

Alex wore jeans, black combat boots and a brand-new crimson-and-gold Boston College Eagles jacket. He glared at the cops in his living room, his lip all but curled into a snarl. Susan Panos watched her son, her hands nervously working the wad of tissue now so ravaged and wet with tears that little shreds of it broke off to drift down lightly to the brown carpet below.

"Alex, honey," she said, "can you answer the man?"

Alex looked at his mother with the same expression of bored disdain he'd affixed on the cops.

She dabbed her eyes. "Please?"

Alex leaned back into the couch, his mouth making a little *psh* sound. He crossed his arms over his chest.

The kid was a real prize, the kind that Pookie wished he could just *shake* some sense into. Alex was big enough that most people stayed out of his way, giving him an overly inflated sense of badassery. He was also young enough to think he was bulletproof.

They sat in Susan's two-bedroom apartment on Union Street, just east of Hyde. It was a nice, sixth-floor place in a somewhat upscale ten-story building. Susan either had one very good job or two decent ones. Mr. Panos, if there had ever been one, wasn't around. He'd probably been a big guy — Susan was a skinny five-four, while sixteen-year-old Alex was just under six feet and thickly muscled. He was bigger than Bryan. Give the kid another three or four months and he'd be bigger than Pookie.

Pookie and Bryan had first gone to Jay Parlar's place. Jay wasn't there. His father didn't know where he was. His father didn't want to talk to the cops. Quite the wonderful family scene, really. Issac Moses was next on the list, but for now, Pookie and Bryan had to deal with an uncooperative, arrogant Alex Panos. Alex didn't seem all that put out by his gang-mate's death.

"Try to understand," Pookie said. "This was a particularly brutal murder. You don't usually see this kind of thing unless there's motivation. *Personal* motivation. Have you guys had run-ins with other gangs? Latin Cobras? Anyone like that?"

"I got nothin' to say," Alex said. "I'm a minor and I haven't done anything, so I can tell you both to go and fuck yourselves. What do you think of that?"

Bryan leaned forward. "What do I think? I think your buddy is dead."

Alex shrugged, looked away. "So Oscar wasn't tough enough. Not my problem."

Pookie saw anger in the boy's eyes. Oscar's death clearly *was* Alex's problem. Alex probably thought he was going to find the killers himself.

"You don't get it," Bryan said. "Oscar's arm was ripped off his body. They cut his belly open, pulled out his intestines."

Susan covered her mouth with the tissue. "Oh my God."

"Then they stuffed his guts back in," Bryan said. "They broke his jaw, knocked out his teeth. They tore out his right eye."

Susan cried into her disintegrating Kleenex and started rocking back and forth. Alex tried — and failed — to look indifferent.

"There's more," Bryan said.

Pookie cleared his throat. "Uh, Bryan, maybe we should—"

"They *pissed* on him," Bryan said. "You hear me, Alex? They pissed all over your supposed friend. This wasn't a random act. Someone hated him. Tell us who hated him, maybe we can find his killer."

Alex stood, stared down with angry eyes. "Are you guys arresting me?"

Pookie shook his head.

"Well, if you're not arresting me, I'm leaving."

"You should stay here," Pookie said. "Whoever killed Oscar could be after all of you. You could be in danger."

Alex let out that *psh* sound again. "I can take care of myself."

Susan reached over and pulled lightly on the crimson sleeve of Alex's jacket. "Honey, maybe you should listen to—"

"Fuck *off*, Mom." Alex snapped his arm away. "You like these pigs so much? Why don't you just blow 'em already? I'm gone."

Alex walked to the door and slammed it shut behind him.

Susan kept crying, kept rocking. Her shaking hand reached for the pack of cigarettes on the coffee table.

Pookie automatically found the lighter in his pocket, pulled it out and offered her the flame. He didn't smoke, but he'd made a lighter part of his standard pimpin' gear long ago — dress nice, talk nice, buy drinks and the ladies loved you. Amazing how a little act of kindness like lighting a cigarette could break the ice, show a woman that you were interested. If you didn't mind kissing an ashtray, lighters got you laid.

She took a drag, then set the tissue on the table. Pookie and Bryan waited, quietly. Susan composed herself quickly; quickly enough that Pookie could tell crying over Alex was a regular occurrence.

"I'm sorry about him," she said. "He's . . . hard to control."

"Yes, ma'am," Pookie said. "Teenage boys can be difficult. I know I was."

She sniffed, smiled, ran her fingers through her hair. Pookie knew that gesture as well, and it saddened him — her son was in serious trouble, his friend had been murdered and Susan Panos was still concerned about her looks. Were this some random night, were Pookie out for a beer instead of investigating a murder, he would have instantly put his chances of taking Susan Panos home at about 75 percent.

"I knew Oscar," she said. "He's been Alex's friend since they were in grade school. He was a good kid, until . . ."

Her words trailed off. It had to be hard to know that a nice kid had traveled down the wrong path because he hung out with the wrong people, and that *your son* was among the wrong people in question.

"Missus Panos," Pookie said, "we know Alex is in a gang. A small one, but still a gang. Do you know anyone who would want to hurt your son and his friends?"

She sniffed, shook her head.

Bryan coughed, a wet, rattling thing. He grabbed two tissues from the table and wiped his mouth.

"How about *payback*?" he said. "How about any of the kids that BoyCo victimized?" Bryan's words and tone were harsh and unforgiving. He clearly blamed Susan for letting Alex grow up to be such a flaming prick. Bryan *would* feel like that: he grew up with a perfect family. Bryan had lost his mom as a kid, but until she died she'd loved him. His father still worshipped the ground he walked on. People from perfect families have a hard time understanding the concept that sometimes, no matter what parents do, some kids just go bad.

Back in the day, Pookie had been heading down the same road as Alex. Pookie's parents were great — loving, attentive, supportive — but Pookie just grew too big too fast. He'd been a bully. He'd enjoyed the power, enjoyed making other kids afraid of him, right up until he screwed with the wrong guy and got his ass kicked. *Shamus Jones.* Who the hell names their kid *Shamus?* Apparently it was akin to naming your boy *Sue,* because once Pookie started in with Shamus it turned out Shamus not only knew how to fight, he knew how to fight dirty. It was the first time Pookie had been beaten with a lead pipe. It also turned out to be the last — broken ribs, a concussion and a night in the hospital proved to be fantastic learning aids.

"Anyone?" Bryan said. "Any of those kids your son beat up, any of them stand out?"

Susan took a drag on her cigarette, blew it out of the corner of her mouth away from Pookie and Bryan — that strange "courtesy" smokers seem to think helps. She picked up the wad of Kleenex. She shrugged. "Alex is just a boy. Boys get into fights."

Pookie pulled two fresh tissues out of the box on the table and offered them to Susan. She seemed to see the disintegrating wad in her hand for the first time. She put that in her pocket, then smiled as she took the fresh tissues.

"Missus Panos," Pookie said, "any information you can give us could help. Nothing is too trivial."

"It's *Susie,* not *Missus Panos.* I haven't seen Alex's father in five years. Look, this isn't the first time cops have talked to me about my son, okay? He's a wild kid. Uncontrollable. Sometimes he's gone for days."

Pookie nodded. "And when he is, where does he go?"

"I don't know."

"Bullshit," Bryan said. "How can you not know?"

"Bryan" — Pookie held up a hand to cut him off — "not now." He turned back to Susie. "Ma'am, where does your son go?"

"I told you, I don't know. He's got girlfriends. I've never met them, but I know he stays at their places. And no, I don't even know their names. I can't control that boy. He's too big, too . . . *mean.* Sometimes he comes home when he needs money or food or clothes. The rest of the time . . . look, I have to work two jobs, okay? Sometimes I pick up extra shifts. I'm gone twenty hours at a time. I gotta do it, we need the money. If Alex doesn't want to come home, I can't make him."

The hurt in her eyes told the story. *If he doesn't want to come home* really meant *if he doesn't love me.*

Bryan stood. "Fuck this. I'll wait outside." He left the apartment, slamming the door almost as loudly as Alex had.

Susie stared at the door. "Your partner is an asshole," she said.

"Sometimes, yeah." Pookie reached into his sport-coat pocket, pulled out his card and offered it to her. "Your son could be in real danger. If you see anything, hear anything, anything at all, let me know."

She stared at him, her eyes a window to the soul of a heartbroken single mother. She took the card. "Yeah. Okay. I can text you at this number?"

Pookie pulled out his cell phone and held it up. "All calls and texts go right here. I never leave home without it."

She sniffed, nodded, then put the card in her pocket. "Thank you, Inspector Chang."

"Yes, ma'am."

Pookie left the apartment.

Bryan was already downstairs, waiting in the Buick. "We have to get to Eight Fifty," he said as Pookie slid in. "Captain Sharrow called."

"Right now? We still have to talk to Issac Moses's parents."

"Yeah, right now," Bryan said. "Chief Zou wants to see us."

The Babushka Lady

Aggie James sat on his thin mattress, pajama-clad arms around his pajama-clad knees. He was rocking back and forth a little bit, which he knew had to make him look nuts, but he didn't care because he couldn't help it.

He wasn't high anymore. He still didn't know if what he'd seen had been real. He figured he'd been down here for a day, maybe two, but it was hard to tell — in the white room, the lights always stayed on and time had already lost meaning.

The place still smelled of bleach. The chains had again drawn Aggie and the others back, then a hooded, white-robed monster with a dark-green demon face had rolled in a beat-up metal mop bucket. The thing had mopped up the long, bloody streaks left by the Mexican boy's clutching hands. The demon hadn't said a word, had ignored the Mexican parents' endless pleas. Once the mopping and bleaching were done, the white-robed demon left.

There had been no visitors since.

The collar was driving Aggie crazy. His skin chafed beneath it, the muscles and flesh sore from being dragged across the floor by his neck. The bottom edges of his jaw, both left and right, felt swollen and bruised to the bone.

He needed a hit. That would make him feel better, so much better. Itchy tingling crawled up his arms and legs. His stomach felt pinched and nauseated — he'd have to shit real soon. Maybe whoever had taken him would let him get back on the streets and find what he needed.

All he had for company was the Mexican couple. The woman barely talked. Sometimes she would cry. Most of the time she just sat against the wall, staring out into space. The husband tried to encourage her, his tone ringing with *don't lose hope, our son is still alive*, but she either didn't hear him or just didn't care to respond.

Sometimes, though, the woman would turn to the man, say something so quiet Aggie couldn't hear. Whenever she did, he would slowly walk as far from her as his chain and collar would permit. Then he would stand in that spot, still as a stone, just staring at the floor.

For now, they said nothing. The man sat on his ass. His wife was asleep, her head in his lap. He slowly stroked her hair.

Aggie's stomach suddenly flip-flopped, a sour, acidic feeling that was like an internal alarm bell. He lurched off his mattress and crawled to the metal flange set in the white floor's center. His neck chain trailed behind him, the tinny sound bouncing off the stone walls.

He pulled down his pajama bottoms as he turned and squatted over the hole. Cold shivers rolled over his skin. His body let go a blast of diarrhea. The wet, slapping sound echoed through the room. Cramps clutched his stomach. Sweat broke out on his forehead, bringing a wave of chills. He had to put one hand on the ground to steady himself, a three-point stance/squat, his naked ass hovering over the hole. A second ripper tore out of him, smaller than the first. The cramps eased off, just a bit.

"Usted es repugnante," the Mexican man said.

Was that Mexican for *repugnant*? The beaner's son had been taken by monster-men, and he was worried about poop?

"Go fuck yourself," Aggie said. "If I didn't have these chains on, I'd beat your ass."

Which was a total lie. The man looked like a construction worker — thin, but with wiry muscles. And all them beaners knew how to box. Hard to box when you're chained up like an animal, though.

Maybe the guy had to say something to someone — he'd lost his boy.
You know that feeling, so cut him some slack.

A metallic noise echoed from within the walls. Were the monster-men coming back? Aggie grabbed a wad of toilet paper and quickly wiped himself, then pulled up his pajama pants and sprinted for the hole where his chain led into the wall. Another cramp hit hard like a fist in the gut. He turned and pressed his back to the white stone — when the chain yanked his collar tight, it only jerked him a little.

The man and woman had been pulled back as well, dragged to their spots along the wall. Rage twisted the man's face. The woman's expression combined terror with sleepy confusion.

The ringing of the chain retractors stopped.

The white cage door opened.

Aggie held his breath, expecting to see the white-robed demons come through, but instead it was an old lady pushing a slightly rusted Safeway shopping cart. She rolled the cart into the white room, one wheel squeaking out a slow, high-pitched rhythm.

She was chubby and a bit hunched over. She shuffled along with short steps. A plain gray skirt covered her wide ass and hung down to her calves. She also wore a brown knit sweater, simple black shoes and loose gray socks. A scarf — dirty yellow, printed with pink flowers — covered her head, leaving just her wrinkled face and a little of her gray hair exposed.

She wore it like a babushka, tied under her chin so the two ends hung down past her breasts.

She looked perfectly normal, like some old lady he might see waiting at a bus stop. She smelled of candles and old lotion.

She stopped her squeaking Safeway cart a few feet away from him. Inside the cart, he saw Tupperware containers and sandwiches wrapped in clear plastic. She set a red-lidded container and one of the sandwiches on his mattress. She reached into the cart again — a juice box joined his lunch.

She looked at him. Something about her deeply wrinkled face, her deep-set, staring brown eyes, made Aggie want to run, *fast,* to go anywhere his feet would carry him.

She shuffled closer.

"Lemme go," he said. "Lady, just lemme go, I won't tell no one."

The old lady leaned forward and *sniffed him.* Her nose wrinkled, her eyes narrowed. She seemed to hold the sniff for a moment, think about it, then she blew out a breath. She turned, waving a hand dismissively at him as if to say *you are not worth my time.*

She pushed the cart to the Mexicans. She left a container, a sandwich and a juice box on each of their mattresses. She walked to the man, but stayed an inch or two out of kicking distance. She sniffed deeply, then shook her head. She turned toward the woman.

The babushka lady sniffed again. She held it in.

Then she smiled, showing a mouthful of yellow, mostly missing teeth. She nodded.

She turned and pushed her squeaky cart out of the cell. She slammed the white-painted door shut behind her.

The chains relaxed. Withdrawal made Aggie feel like shit, but he grabbed the sandwich and tore off the wrapper. He wasn't worried about poison — if they were going to kill him, they would have done it already. He bit off a big chunk. The welcome tastes of ham, cheese and mayo danced across his tongue. He opened the Tupperware container — hot, steaming brown chili that smelled beefy and delicious.

His stomach pinched hard, and he set the food down.

He already had to shit again.

Golden Shower

Pookie Chang sat in a chair in front of Chief Amy Zou's desk, patiently counting the minutes until he could text Polyester Rich Verde a detailed variation on YOU ARE MY BITCH. That would be a brief moment of joy in an otherwise messed-up situation.

Bryan sat on Pookie's right, slumped in his chair, a withdrawn ghost of himself. They'd been in this same spot just over twenty-four hours ago. One day later and their world had changed.

Once again, Chief Zou sat behind her immaculate desk. And once again, in the center of that blank desk, sat a manila folder. Nothing else except for the three-panel picture frame showing her family.

Assistant Chief Sean Robertson stood on the chief's immediate left, almost like he was waiting for her to get up and go to the bathroom so he could sit down and take over. He also held a manila folder.

To the right of Zou's desk, Captain Jesse Sharrow sat in a chair against the wall. He, too, had a matching folder in his lap. Whatever the hell was going on, it was clear that Zou, Robertson and Sharrow were all using the same playbook. Sharrow sat ramrod straight. He definitely had something on his mind, something that didn't make him happy. Even his usually immaculate blues looked a tad rumpled.

Chief Zou opened her folder. Pookie saw what was inside — his case report on the Oscar Woody killing from that morning. She flipped through it.

She looked up at Pookie. "It says here you two were just driving by?"

Pookie nodded. "Yes, Chief. We were just driving by. Bryan . . . ah . . . saw the blanket, so we stopped."

She stared at him. Stared long enough for it to become uncomfortable.

"So you just *stopped*," she said. "For what looked like a homeless man in an alley? I didn't know you were such a humanitarian, Chang."

"I smelled it," Bryan said quietly.

Goddamit, Bryan, shut the fuck up.

Zou turned her stare on Bryan. "You smelled *what*, Clauser?"

Bryan rubbed his eyes. "I . . . I smelled something, something that—"

"Urine, Chief," Pookie said. He flashed Byran a glance. Bryan blinked, then leaned back in his chair — he got the message: *let Pookie do the talking.* Pookie didn't want Bryan to say another word. If the guy slipped up and mentioned his dreams, he'd be screwed.

"We were at the Paul Maloney scene," Pookie said. "We smelled urine there. When Bryan smelled urine at Meacham Place, and we saw what looked like a prone guy under a blanket, we just stopped. Call it cop instincts."

Zou again looked at the case report.

She probably just wanted to get everyone on the same page. Oscar was a kid, his murder particularly brutal, and that meant the media was all over it. The *Chronicle* had already done a special edition — Oscar's high-school photo stared out from newspaper racks all over the city. Oscar's body had been pissed on, as had Maloney's. If word of that connection ever got out, the case would turn into a media circus.

Of course, Pookie was banking on that connection. He and Bryan had been first on the scene for Oscar. Zou would connect the two cases and give them both to her best team — which meant Polyester Rich could go fuck himself with a cactus.

Chief Zou kept reading. She seemed to be staring at the crime-scene photos for far too long.

Pookie glanced at Robertson. Robertson had the report open to the same page. He was staring intently at it, his gray glasses halfway down his nose.

And Sharrow as well, the report open on his lap, his bushy-white-eyebrowed eyes focused on the blood symbol.

The way they all stared, so intently . . . it was spooky.

Chief Zou looked up. "Who have you talked to so far?"

"We canvassed the area," Pookie said. "We couldn't find anyone who saw or heard anything that night. We talked to Kyle Souller, principal at Galileo High, where Oscar attended. We tried to speak with Oscar's parents, but they're too upset to talk about it yet."

Zou's eyes flicked to the framed picture of her twin girls. "I can only imagine how they must feel right now."

Pookie nodded. "They were pretty shook up. We also talked to Alex Panos, who runs BoyCo, the gang Oscar was in, and to Alex's mother, Susan. We still need to talk to Issac Moses and Jay Parlar, the other gang members."

Zou pulled three photos from the folder and set them side by side in a neat row above the report. Pookie had included the photos from Black Mr. Burns's gang database. Once again he looked at the details, memorizing the faces: Jay Parlar with his scraggly red goatee; Issac Moses with his crooked nose and blue eyes; the blond hair and arrogant sneer of Alex Panos.

Zou nodded, looked at the report. "And these symbols, Inspector Chang? What have you found about those?"

Sharrow and Robertson both looked up from their reports. They stared at him. Pookie felt like a lab rat with three scientists waiting to see how he would react to new stimuli.

"Uh, we searched the RISS database," he said. "It came up with nothing."

"Nothing?" Zou said. "Nothing at all?"

"Nothing local, I mean."

She nodded. Three heads again bent to look at the report, at the symbols.

He'd been joking about *cop instincts* earlier, but they were real; they suddenly lit up like his own version of Spidey-Sense. There had been information about those symbols in the system, but that information had been deleted — Zou, Robertson and Sharrow probably had the access privileges to do just that.

At this point, it was best not to let on that Black Mr. Burns was still digging deeper. But John's name was already in the report — if Pookie didn't at least mention John's work, Zou might call him to the office next.

"There was one hit," Pookie said. "A serial killer from New York, but that case has been closed for twenty years. We showed the symbol around the neighborhood where Oscar was killed — no one has seen it before. John Smith in the Gang Task Force said it wasn't associated with any local gangs. In short, we couldn't find shit."

Zou leaned back, ever so slightly. Had that information made her relax? Just a little?

"You didn't find anything else?"

Pookie shook his head.

Zou looked at Bryan. "How about you, Clauser? Anything to add?"

Bryan also shook his head. She stared at him until the air again became uncomfortable, but Bryan didn't look away. Finally, Zou looked back down to the report.

Pookie waited. Zou was meticulous, sure, but she had a flair for quiet drama.

Assistant Chief Robertson also waited, his folder open in his hands, his eyes fixed on Zou.

Pookie glanced at Sharrow. The white-haired captain had closed his folder. He held it in both hands. The folder trembled slightly. He still sat ramrod straight, but his eyes were closed.

What the hell was going on?

Zou looked up. "The urine," she said. "Similar m.o. to Paul Maloney — murder, mutilated body, the perps urinated on the corpse. Inspector Chang, do you think the two are connected?"

Pookie nodded. "I'd bet my balls on it, Chief. It can't be a copycat because the news didn't report that someone gave Father Paul a golden shower."

Her eyebrows rose.

"Sorry," Pookie said. "I mean, *urinated on the deceased*, of course."

She shut the folder and looked up.

"I agree," she said. "The two cases are related. Give all your information and contacts to Rich Verde and Bobby Pigeon."

No, he had *not* just heard that correctly. "Chief," Pookie said, "shouldn't they be giving their info on Maloney to us?"

"Did I stutter? You guys are off the case."

"But, Chief, we were the first on the scene!"

Robertson closed his folder with an audible *snap*. "Just give Verde your information, Pookie."

Not only were they not getting the Maloney gig, but now Verde would have a case that Bryan was somehow connected to? Verde was an asshole, sure, but he was good at the job. He would dig and dig hard. If he found info that could tie Bryan to this . . . Pookie *could not* let the man get this case.

"Chief," Pookie said. "Oscar Woody is *ours*. We found him, we were first on the scene. Birdman just came over from Vice. He's seen, what, *four* murder cases?"

Captain Sharrow stood. He held his folder at his side. His hands had stopped shaking. "Knock it off, Chang," he said. "Pigeon is good. And Verde was busting murderers when you were still in diapers."

"But, Cap, we *want* this case!"

Chief Zou straightened the report, making sure it paralleled the desk's edges. "Inspector Chang, that's enough."

"But, Chief, you—"

"Done," she said, slicing her hand sideways like a knife through air. "Chang, this time you are going to *listen* and *obey*. This isn't going to be another Blake Johansson situation."

She was bringing that up? "And by *Blake Johansson situation*, you mean the dirty cop that I uncovered, right?"

"You were told to leave that case alone," Zou said. "You were told that Internal Affairs would handle it, but you wouldn't listen. John Smith almost died as a result and his career has never been the same." She glanced at Bryan. "Blake Johansson *did* die."

Pookie ground his teeth, trying to keep quiet. Internal Affairs had seemed to be part of Johansson's payoff chain — they ignored Johansson just as Johansson ignored the gangs who paid him off. Pookie had gone for the bust — it wasn't his fault that Johansson decided to shoot it out instead of going quietly.

At least that's what Pookie told himself every time he saw Black Mr. Burns stuck behind a desk instead of out chasing perps.

"Inspector Chang, this time, you *will* listen," Zou said. "My orders are not open to debate. Go see Verde and Pigeon, give them everything you have. If that principal you talked to finds anything, he is to call *them*, not you."

She turned her stare on Bryan. "And you, Clauser, let me hear it — let me hear you understand that you guys are *off this case*."

Bryan stared back at her. Other than the fact that he looked like he might vomit at any moment, his eyes showed nothing.

"We're off the case," he said. "Our ears work just fine."

Zou nodded once. "Good day, gentlemen."

Bryan walked out of the office. Pookie stood to follow him. This didn't make sense. Even if Verde and the Birdman ran both cases, Pookie and Bryan should have been assigned to support them, not booted to the curb altogether. Did Zou know something Pookie did not? Maybe something about Bryan's dreams?

The thought made him stop and turn. He looked back, but Captain Sharrow, Chief Zou and Assistant Chief Sean Robertson didn't notice him doing it. They had their folders open again. All three of them were staring at the symbols.

Robin Runs the Show

Three more bodies had come in that afternoon. Two looked like natural causes, while the other one was clearly from a gunshot wound to the temple. The morgue seemed busier than ever. Even with Metz gone, his policies and training were still in place and things ran fairly smooth.

Robin finished up one of the natural causes cases, freeing her up to finally check the STR results from Oscar Woody's killer. She walked from the autopsy room to her desk in the admin area. She sighed and looked over at her pictures of Emma. It was almost seven o'clock. Robin wanted to get out of there, get back to her apartment, crawl into bed and have Emma curl up beside her. Sure, the dog would shed all over the bedspread and probably fart something horrible, but when it came to nap time, Emma was Little Miss Lights-Out. Emma couldn't sleep on the empty side, of course, she had to lie *right on top* of Robin. But that was the point, really. Robin didn't have a man in her bed anymore — Emma's weight, her breathing (hell, even the farts in a weird way), they were comforting beyond anything Robin knew.

She turned to her computer and called up the STR results. Yes, confirmed — the saliva sample found on Oscar Woody came from a human, as did the material taken from the hair follicles. Due to the signs of mauling there *had* to be a large animal involved, but there was no longer any question that a human killer had left DNA on Oscar's body.

The computer system had automatically submitted the STR test results to the CODIS system. That check didn't produce a match; whoever the killer was, his DNA had never been entered into the FBI's database.

But there was something strange about the sample. In addition to a genetic fingerprint, the test also indicated a person's sex by detecting a gene known as AMEL. AMEL is on the male and female sex chromosomes, but it isn't quite the same on both. Men have two sex chromosomes — X and Y — while women have two Xs. The STR test didn't show the actual chromosome, only another test known as a *karyotype* could do that, but it did show spikes indicating the presence and relative number of AMEL genes on each sex chromosome. If the test only showed a spike for AMEL-X, the subject was female. If it showed two equal spikes, one for AMEL-X and one for AMEL-Y, that meant the subject was male.

This sample, however, showed AMEL-X and AMEL-Y spikes that were *not* equal. The X spike was twice as high as the Y spike. That suggested the presence of a second X, which would mean the killer could have *three* sex chromosomes.

It wasn't a contaminated sample — she had run enough parallel tests to know, for certain, that the material came from just one killer. Robin felt a rush of excitement: either the killer was XXY, or he had an even more rare condition she had yet to identify.

She heard people approaching. She looked up to see Rich Verde and Bobby Pigeon walking toward her desk. Bobby smiled at her. Rich just scowled. Good God, but Rich was a horrible dresser.

"Hudson," Verde said. "I'm here to talk to you about the Oscar Woody case."

She felt a deep twinge of disappointment. "I thought this case belonged to Bryan Clauser and Pookie Chang."

Verde shook his head. "Case is mine. Covered in piss, right?"

There was a question you didn't hear every day. She nodded.

"Mine," Verde said. "Normally Metz would handle a case like this."

"Well, I assure you I'm perfectly qualified to—"

"Whatever," Rich said. "This case will run a little different than maybe you're used to. Special deal. Call the chief right now. She's expecting to hear from you."

Robin's eyebrows rose. "Call Chief Zou?"

"That's right," Verde said. "And make it snappy, I got shit to do."

Metz frequently talked to Chief Zou. Robin was the temporary head of the department, so it made sense she'd be the one to answer any questions Zou might have. Robin picked up her phone, then started scanning a list tacked to her cubicle wall to find the chief's extension.

Verde reached across her and dialed the phone for her.

"There you go," he said.

She glared at him as she waited for someone to answer. Like he couldn't have just told her the extension number?

"Chief Zou's office."

"This is Robin Hudson from the ME department. I was told—"

"One moment, Doctor Hudson, the chief is expecting your call."

Chief Zou came on the line, her words as terse and clipped on the phone as they were in person. "Doctor Hudson?"

"Yes."

"Rich Verde is in charge of the Oscar Woody case," Zou said. "This case is of particular interest to me. I don't want anything getting out to the media, understand?"

The Medical Examiner's Office and the police department worked closely together, but Zou was not Robin's boss. Robin tried to think of how Metz would handle the same situation. The Silver Eagle would be polite, but firm. "Chief Zou, you know we don't release anything to the media."

"And yet the media somehow gets information from many places," Zou said. "Doctor Hudson, I'm not insinuating anything, I'm asking. Please limit any access to information on Oscar Woody. Move his body to the private examination room, the one Doctor Metz uses. Access to any electronic records are for Inspector Verde's eyes only. The mayor said you can call his office if you have any questions."

Call the mayor? Well, that was a hint and a half. *If you want the top spot, play ball.* But was Chief Zou really asking for anything unusual? Maybe there was a good reason for her secrecy. *Covered in piss,* Verde had said. Robin again thought of Paul Maloney. Maybe her initial hunch was right and the two cases were related — a potential serial killer could be out there. Any leaked information might compromise finding that killer.

"Yes, Chief," Robin said. "I'll use the private room and keep things quiet."

"Thank you for your time, Doctor."

Chief Zou hung up. A strange call. It nagged at Robin, the way Zou seemed to be dangling the potential chief medical examiner position as a reward for playing along. Or . . . was it more of a threat of punishment, that *not* playing along would cost Robin the job?

Robin turned to Verde. A *told you so* sneer twisted his mouth to the left.

"You know, Rich, she's not asking for anything crazy, so you don't have to be such a sanctimonious dick about this."

"When I want your opinion, I'll ask for it," Verde said. "Just do your job, file the report, and don't go blabbing about this case with your girl-friends at the watercooler. Come on, Bobby, let's go."

Verde turned to walk away. Bobby looked at him with confusion, the same confusion, probably, that Robin felt.

"Wait a minute," she said. "I found some really interesting things that will help in the investigation. Don't you want to know what they are?"

"It was an animal attack," Verde said. "I'll read your report."

"It wasn't just an animal attack."

He sighed. "Okay, fine, there were people involved who used the ani-mal to kill the kid. Whatever. The death was due to mauling, and that's that. Sammy Berzon's preliminary crime-scene report said there was dog fur all over the body."

"It wasn't dog fur." Robin said. "The hair samples were human."

Verde's eyes narrowed. He seemed almost ... *bothered* by the information.

"It's some kind of animal," he said. "Your results are wrong."

What a pompous ass. "And you know this because you got your medical degree where, exactly? You don't get to dismiss my results because you don't like what they say, Rich."

Verde threw up his hands in annoyance. "The boy was attacked by a guy, a couple of guys, whatever. They beat him and sicced a fucking animal on him. The animal tore off the kid's arm, the kid died, done deal. If it looks like a duck, walks like a duck, and—"

"It doesn't *quack*," she said. "And it doesn't *bark* either. All the DNA I recovered was definitely human."

Robin had given case results to Rich many times before. He was always a bit of an asshole, but normally he seemed interested in every detail. Why didn't he care about the details now?

"I only have evidence for *one* assailant," Robin said. "I have saliva and hair from a *person*, Rich — can your little mind process that?"

Bobby was smiling, and not the way men did when they thought she was pretty. He seemed to be enjoying the fact that she pushed back. The veins in the sides of Rich's thinning temples throbbed and pulsed — they looked like they might pop at any moment.

She'd lost her temper a little, but now she seemed to have Rich's full attention. He looked angry. Calm, but angry.

"So," he said, "you're telling me this *can't* be an animal attack?"

Robin paused. She had genetic evidence of a human killer, but the tooth marks were definitely from some kind of animal. There had to be some element of the animal on Oscar's body, she just hadn't found it yet.

"I'm sure an animal was involved, but what I'm telling you is I have specific evidence that can help you find the guy responsible for Oscar's death," she said. "I found indicators of *three* chromosomes, two Xs and a single Y."

"Three?" Bobby said. He seemed to perk up at the first mention of genetics. "You said it was one killer. Guys are XY. Wouldn't three chromosomes indicate a second killer?"

Verde glared at Bobby.

Bobby shrugged at him. "Rich-o, seems like we'd need to know this stuff, don't you think?"

Verde's jaw muscles twitched. He turned back to stare at Robin. "Go ahead, busy bee — tell me what you found."

He'd looked angry before. Now he looked downright furious.

"If there was a second male assailant, I'd have found evidence of another Y chromosome," she said. "Even if a second assailant was female, I'd have at least found evidence of a third X chromosome. That leads me to believe Oscar's killer is *trisomal,* which means he has three sex chromosomes instead of the normal two. If the assailant is XXY, he probably has a condition called Klinefelter's syndrome."

Bobby nodded. He had the same look in his eye she'd often seen in Bryan — to guys like them, clues were crack cocaine that got their pulses racing. "I've heard of Klinefelter's," he said. "But that's not the only possibility, right? I mean, couldn't two people have identical chromosomes? Like twins? Not the identical kind, but fraternal twins?"

Robin smiled in surprise. For a layman, that was a brilliant question.

"It's possible the killers could have been male and female twins," she said. "And technically, normal brothers with the same father have the same Y chromosome. However, I'm almost positive the samples show we're dealing with a single killer. I'll run a different kind of test to be sure."

Verde's eyes narrowed. "And what kind of test would this be?"

"It's called a karyotype," Robin said. "We need living cells for that, but the saliva on the body was only a few hours old, so we have plenty. A karyotype shows the total number of chromosomes in an organism. You, me, Bobby, pretty much every person you know has forty-six chromosomes — that's normal. If the test shows the perp has forty-six, that means my extra X is from a second killer. But if the test shows an individual with forty-*seven* chromosomes, it means we have just one killer with a unique genetic disposition that will help you track him down."

Bobby smiled. "Sweet," he said. His gold tooth made him look like a pimp.

"Metz didn't run tests like that," Rich said. "You shouldn't, either. And we don't need that test — we've got some leads we can't talk about."

She noticed Bobby suddenly look at Rich in surprise. If there were such leads, it was news to the younger of the two partners.

Robin crossed her arms over her chest. "Are you telling me you don't want *more* leads? If our guy has Klinefelter's, he could be confused about his gender or possibly express sexual deviation that's been recorded. You could look for mixed-gender support groups, or—"

"Do *your* job," Verde said. "You get paid to look at stiffs. You *don't* get paid to solve cases. Leave the detective work to the detectives. Just do the basics. Bobby, let's go."

Verde stormed off. Bobby rolled his eyes and smiled apologetically before following Verde out.

Robin spun slightly in her chair, watching them go. So strange — why wouldn't Rich want to exhaust every angle to solve a horrific murder? Maybe that was a question she didn't need to ask. Verde had the authority of Chief Amy Zou behind him, and he was right about one thing — solving crimes wasn't her job. So maybe Rich had her there, but on the other hand, he wasn't her boss. Neither was Chief Zou. They could make suggestions, but they couldn't tell her what tests *not* to run.

Robin could use the new RapScan machine to run the karyotype. All she had to do was load DNA samples into the machine's cartridges, which took about fifteen minutes. From there, the whole process was automated — it only took a few hours to complete. She'd start the test now, then pack up the work she could finish at home and get out of there.

When she came back in the morning, the karyotype results would be waiting for her.

The Artist and His Subject

Rex drew. He was a good drawer, he knew that. Mrs. Evans, his art teacher at Galileo, she said he had *potential*. No one ever said that to him, about anything. Not since his dad had died, anyway.

Mrs. Evans was okay, but he had to hide his best drawings from her. The ones with the guns, the knives, the chain saws, the ropes — things like that. She'd seen some of those drawings and pretty much flipped out, so Rex just kept them to himself.

He also now knew he couldn't let other kids see his pictures. Not *ever*, or BoyCo might hurt him even worse than before.

But if they did come after him again, Oscar Woody wouldn't be with them.

Because Oscar Woody was dead.

Rex had made so many drawings. He'd even drawn one of the strange faces he saw in his dreams. That one had gone up on the walls with all the others, labeled with a name that he heard most often during those visions: *Sly.*

Rex drew. His pencil outlined the oval of a head, then the shapes of eyes, the contours of a nose. Quietly, he worked away, adding lines and shading. Gradually, the face became recognizable.

The sound of pencil on paper picked up speed. A body took form. So did a chain saw. So did splashes of blood.

Rex felt warm. His chest tingled inside.

Erase that part of the nose, redraw . . . adjust the corners of the mouth, coax the lines and shapes and shades into expressions of agony, of terror.

He felt his own heartbeat pulsing in his neck, bouncing through his eyes and forehead.

Erase the bicep, darken that line . . . the chain saw had just passed through the arm, severing it in a splatter of blood.

Rex felt himself stiffen in his pants.

He moaned a little as he erased the eyes. They weren't quite right. *Make them wider. Make them full of fear.*

Fear of Rex.

He had drawn Oscar Woody, concentrated on Oscar Woody, and now Oscar Woody was dead.

Maybe it hadn't been coincidence.

And, maybe, Rex could make it happen again.

The new face?

Jay Parlar, the boy who had put the pieces of wood under Rex's wrist and elbow.

Rex drew.

Big Max

Home at last. Robin juggled a stack of mail and a bag of last-minute groceries — dog treats, dog food, milk, a bottle of Malbec and some Twinkies — as she struggled to find her apartment key on an overfull key chain. Quite honestly, she didn't know what half the keys were for. They probably opened old mailboxes, storage lockers, gym padlocks, etc. She could never bring herself to throw any of them out because she knew as soon as she tossed one, she'd wind up needing it the next day and would be summarily screwed.

A door opened just down the hall. A gigantic man stepped out and stood still while sixty-five pounds of whining white-and-black whirlwind shot past him into the hallway, ears flapping and claws digging into carpet.

Emma jumped up, almost knocking Robin over. Groceries spilled on the floor. Robin grabbed for the milk, but the plastic quart container bounced on the carpet without breaking and rolled to a stop.

Robin cupped her hands around Emma's floppy ears and dug her fingers in just enough to shake the dog's head. Wild-eyed, Emma's tongue lolled — her body seemed to want to go in five directions at once.

"Baby girl! I missed you," Robin said. She pushed the dog away, then knelt to pick up the groceries — a strategic mistake. Emma jumped again to kiss Robin's face. The dog's paws hit Robin's shoulders, knocking the kneeling woman on her behind. Emma's feet pranced as she launched rapid-fire kisses on Robin's face.

"Easy, girl," Robin said, laughing at the dog's desperate intensity.

Suddenly Emma's weight was gone. Robin looked up to see Big Max holding the sixty-five-pound dog in his left arm, big hand scooped under Emma's butt, her head at his shoulder. Emma's tail thumped against Max's leg.

"Goodness gracious, girl," Max said. "That dog just kicked your ass."

Robin nodded. She put the groceries back in the bag and gathered up the scattered mail.

"Thanks, Max. Thanks for everything."

"Don't worry about it, honey. I'll watch this little thing any old day."

Emma just sat there, totally comfortable and relaxed cradled in Max's huge arm. *Huge* wasn't really the word for his arms — *gigantic* might be more appropriate. Max looked like an effeminate version of a roided-out professional wrestler. Big arms, thick legs, huge barrel chest (which was waxed, of course). The head on top of his beer keg of a neck sported deep laugh lines. A blond goatee formed a dainty point, and the same-color hair sat on his forehead in a moussed swirl.

One glance told you Max was gay, and that was always somewhat of a bitter feeling — the man was a Grade-A hunk. He made for a very interesting neighbor: dog lover, well versed on local politics, worked nights as a bouncer and was trying to break into erotic films. Not a run-of-the-mill guy by any stretch of the imagination.

That was Robin's best friend: a gorgeous, badass, gay pornstar-to-be.

"Hey," Robin said. "How did your audition go at Kink-dot-com?"

Max smiled. "Pretty good," he said. "Were you asking because you're a polite sweetheart, or do you want to know the gory details of my shoot?"

Robin laughed and blushed. "The former. Not sure I could handle the details."

"Ah, you modest Canadian girls."

A second dog came out of Max's apartment. This one made Emma look tiny — ninety pounds of pit bull with gray fur, white feet, and the sweetest face you could ever see.

Without missing a beat, Max reached down with his right arm and scooped up the pit bull. He cradled one hundred fifty-five pounds of dog like a couple of feather pillows.

"Hello there, Billy," Robin said. She gave the pit bull a kiss on the nose. Billy's thick tail swirled in an uncoordinated circle.

Max leaned toward her, breaking the three-foot cushion. His eyes narrowed as he stared at a spot just below Robin's eyes.

"Honey, look at those circles. That job is going to be the death of you."

Robin put the mail in the grocery bag (why she hadn't done that to start with, she had no idea) and finally found her apartment key. She opened the door and walked into her entryway. Max followed her in, still carrying the dogs.

"Tell me about it," she said. "You should have seen the poor kid they brought in today."

"Bad?"

"Beyond bad." Robin set the bag down on her dining room table. "His arm was . . . wait, are *you* asking because you're a polite sweetheart, or because *you* want the gory details? Because these details are actually gory."

Max set both dogs down, then waved his hands palms-out. "Oh, I'm just being polite. I like to watch *CSI* because it's fake, but your stories make my balls head for high water. Is the case important?"

"It is to me."

Max smiled, a left-corner-of-the-mouth-curling-up thing that Robin could only hope they put on the covers of his posters, or web pages, or whatever they used to advertise porn.

"I see," he said. "And would Mister I Dress All in Black be involved?"

Robin felt her face flush. "I didn't say that."

"You didn't have to. I can see it in your eyes. Maybe you should invite him over to discuss the case. You haven't been laid since he moved out."

"Max! That's none of your business. And how do you know I haven't been laid? Maybe I'm a regular trollop."

Max reached up a big fist, rapped his knuckles against the wall that separated their two apartments. "These things are pretty thin. I'd know if you were knocking boots. I certainly knew every time that you and Bryan were . . . shall we say . . . *discussing a case.*"

A swirl of thoughts stopped Robin cold: embarrassment at Max having heard her with Bryan; memories of Bryan making love to her; echoes of the happiness they shared in this very apartment; still-fresh memories of the arguments, of her yelling at Bryan while he just stared back, infuriatingly calm and maddeningly distant. The yelling . . . Max had to have heard as well.

"The Man in Black and I are finished," Robin said. "And I'm too busy to worry about sex right now."

The big man shrugged. "My mom told me there's two things you should never be too busy to do."

"Pay taxes and vacuum the carpet?"

"No," Max said. "You're never too busy to pet a puppy, and never to busy to make love."

"Your *mom* told you that?"

He nodded. "Sure. Before I came out, I mean. Now she focuses mostly on the puppy part. Look, there's nothing wrong with getting a booty call from an ex. You should have Bryan go old-school fifties-movies on you. You know, shake you around a bit, maybe a little slap or two, then the ravaging."

Robin rolled her eyes. "He's not like that, Max. He's a softie."

Max laughed and shook his head. "Honey, Bryan may be a *gentleman,* but he's no *softie.* He has a mean streak in him a mile wide."

Bryan was standoffish, sure, but *mean?* Nobody besides her — and maybe Pookie — seemed to know the real man. Or maybe everyone *did* know him, and it was Robin who was clueless. "You've only met Bryan a couple of times," she said. "How can you tell that about him?"

"It's my *job* to tell. I'm a bouncer, remember? Your little Johnny Cash is not someone I'd want to meet in a back alley."

"You outweigh him by at least fifty pounds, Max."

"Size isn't everything. Outside of porn, I mean. I like my teeth right where they are, so I've learned to watch out for guys like Bryan."

What a ridiculous concept. Max was so . . . well, *big.* Bryan was lean and strong, sure, but was he mean enough to take on a bruiser like Max? It didn't matter. She didn't want to think about Bryan Clauser anymore.

"Thanks for watching Emma, Maxie. I owe you dinner."

"Seven," he said.

"Seven what?"

"Seven dinners. That's only for the past three months."

"Seven? *Really*?"

Max nodded. "I don't mean to tell you how to run your life, honey, but Emma is starting to like me more than she likes you."

"Oh no she is not!"

Max smiled, then walked toward the door. Emma trotted along after him.

"Emma! Where are you going?"

Emma stopped and looked at Robin, then looked back at Max.

Max shrugged at Emma. "Don't worry, boo-boo, I'm sure I'll be seeing you soon."

He shut the door behind him. Emma stared at the door, then let out a little whine.

Robin clapped her hands once to get the dog's attention. "Emma baby, do you want treats?" The dog came running.

Maybe Bryan Clauser didn't love Robin, but Emma sure did — and if Robin had to buy that love with dog treats, that was just fine. A treat, maybe two (or three, or four), and then it was time for bed.

Pookie Phones a Friend

Sweat started to pool in Pookie's armpits. Carrying a grown man up four flights of stairs was a surprising and unwelcome workout. His stupid partner needed to find an apartment with an elevator that worked.

"Bri-Bri, if you puke on me, I'm going to punch you in the taint."

Bryan mumbled something unintelligible. He didn't weigh all that much, maybe one-seventy, but the guy could barely walk. Bryan was sweating, too, but from a fever as opposed to exhaustion.

Pookie was making bad choices and he knew it. Helping Bryan up to his apartment? This guy could be a killer. Not a *sniper from fifty yards* kind of killer, but rather the type that tears a kid's arm off and paints pretty pictures with it.

They reached the fourth floor. Legs exhausted, undershirt sticking to his sweaty skin, Pookie half helped, half dragged Bryan to the door.

"Come on, Bryan, try to walk."

"Sorry," Bryan said. "Man, I hurt all over."

"You sure you don't want me to call an ambulance?"

Bryan shook his head. "Just sick is all." He dug into his pocket for his keys, tried to unlock the door with a shaking hand. Pookie had to take the keys and do it for him.

"Just sick," Bryan repeated as they stepped inside. "Feel like the inside of a donkey's butthole."

"Live donkey or dead donkey?"

"Dead."

"Ah yes," Pookie said. "I hate that feeling."

"Tell me about it. Lemme go. Going to bed."

Pookie slowly released his hold on Bryan. Bryan made it three steps before he stumbled over one of the dozens of unpacked boxes cluttering the small hallway. Pookie stepped in quick and slid under Bryan's shoulder, stabilizing him.

"Wow, Bryan, unpack much?"

"I'm getting to it."

Pookie helped Bryan around the boxes and into the small bedroom. It had to be a little bit of a shock to move from Robin's spacious two-bedroom apartment to this tiny one-bedroom affair, but six months on and he still hadn't fully settled in? Bryan had set up the TV and the couch, hung up his all-black wardrobe, and that was apparently all the guy needed.

Pookie gently hip-tossed Bryan into the bed.

Bryan opened one puffy, bloodshot eye. "You gonna undress me, Daddy?"

"Don't think so, fag."

"Homophobe."

"And proud of it," Pookie said. "Bible's pretty clear on that one, big guy. I'm whipped, brother, so either you get nekkid on your own or you sleep in your clothes."

Bryan didn't answer. Just like that, he'd already fallen asleep.

Pookie felt sweat cooling on his forehead. He wiped the sweat away with his hand, then wiped his hand on Bryan's pant leg. Whatever bug Bryan had, Pookie now surely had it as well.

Pookie stared down at his partner. He wasn't going to leave Bryan alone tonight, that was for sure. Besides, if someone was — somehow — putting thoughts into Bryan's head, they sure weren't beaming them in with a magic wand. Had to be something in the apartment. While Bryan slept, Pookie would tear the place apart.

Bryan's Sig Sauer was still in its shoulder holster. Pookie gently pulled the firearm free. Then, he took the Seecamp wallet from Bryan's back pocket. Best not to leave him with knives, either — Pookie pulled the combat knife from the forearm sheath, and finally, gently removed the Twitch knife from Bryan's belt. Who wore a knife right next to their Jimmy Beans?

Psycho killers, that's who.

Pookie looked at the pile of weapons in his hands and couldn't help wondering if one of those knives might have cut open Oscar Woody's belly.

Two things sat on the nightstand next to Bryan's bed — a small, framed picture showing Bryan, Robin and her dog, Emma, and a cheap, spiral-bound notebook. The notebook was open to a drawing.

A drawing of a triangle and a circle, with a smaller circle in the middle, a slashed curve beneath.

Pookie walked into the kitchenette and set the arsenal on the small table.

Bryan just couldn't have done that horrible thing.

Couldn't have.

Pookie was playing games with people's lives. Bryan Clauser was a goddamn *suspect*, yet Pookie was acting like his nursemaid. If only he could look deeper into Bryan's soul.

Maybe there was one person who could do just that.

Bryan's fridge held some leftover pizza, some leftover Chinese, half a leftover burrito and one Sapporo. Pookie opened the beer, then leaned against the kitchen counter. He pulled out his phone and dialed.

A sleepy voice answered.

"Hello?"

"Robin-Robin Bo-Bobbin. How're they hanging?"

A sigh, the rustle of covers, the soft clink of a metal tag on a dog's collar.

"Pookie, they don't *hang*. In fact, I don't even have *they*. It's late, and I'm exhausted. Are you okay?"

"Right as rain," he said. "I hear you're running the show at the ME office while Metz is out. Congrats, girl."

"Doesn't mean anything yet," she said. "Just more work. But thanks. In the past forty-eight hours, I've talked to the mayor and Chief Zou. She called to tell me Verde had the Oscar Woody case."

"He does," Pookie said. "Bless Verde's black, black heart."

A pause. "Why does he get it and not you guys?"

Pookie took a sip of beer. "To be honest, Bo-Bobbin, I'm not really sure. It's kind of . . . well, it's kind of weird."

"Yeah," she said. "Kind of weird on my end, too."

"How so?"

"It's Verde. I've worked with him before. He's usually okay."

"He's an ass-hat."

"Yes, but as far as ass-hats go, he's an okay ass-hat. You know what I mean. Anyway, he's not my favorite guy or anything, but he's fine to work with. Except for this case. He seems super . . . *intense*. And it feels like he's rushing things."

Rushing things. Pookie hadn't realized it until now, but that's exactly how he felt about Chief Zou's actions. She was trying to hurry the case along as fast as possible.

"Bo-Bobbin, truth be told I wasn't calling about Oscar Woody."

"Then get to the point so I can get some sleep."

Pookie hesitated. If Bryan found out about this call, he'd feel betrayed. *Bros before hoes*, even though Robin Hudson was about as far from a *ho* as one could get.

"Robin, do you think Bryan could ever hurt someone? Like, *really* bad, and not just in self-defense or doing his job?"

Now she paused. "He never laid a hand on me."

"Of course not," Pookie said quickly, apologetically. "That's not what

I mean. I'll just say that he's going through a tough time, and I really need the take of someone who's close to him."

"*Was* close."

Pookie used a quick sip to hold back his laugh.

"That's a good one," he said. "If I say I believe that, will you also try to sell me a bridge? Come on, you guys are kidding yourselves."

"Pookie, I don't need a lecture on—"

"Sorry," he said. "Not trying to play matchmaker. Just please, for me, answer the question. Do you think Bryan is capable of a revenge attack? Or maybe even something unprovoked?"

He waited. The beer didn't taste like anything.

"Yeah," she said in a whisper. "Yeah, I do."

He'd known what her answer would be, because he'd already come to the same conclusion. But believing Bryan was *capable* of it didn't mean that Bryan had *done* it.

Pookie would not turn his back on his friend.

"Thanks, Bo-Bobbin."

"You're welcome. Take care of him, Pookie."

"I'm trying, darlin', I'm trying. Night."

He hung up.

Please, God, don't let me be wrong about him.

Mr. Sandman . . .

This boy wasn't as stupid as the other one. This boy kept looking around, kept to the shadows, tried to stay out of sight.

One womb.

Bryan looked down at the boy. He looked so tiny, like a little mouse. From this high above, everyone seems small. The boy had a thin, red goatee. He wore a crimson jacket with gold trim. A white sweatshirt hood was up over a crimson ball cap sporting the gold initials *BC.*

The colors marked him, marked him as a tormentor, as a torturer.

The colors marked him for death.

Bryan felt that heat, that flush of stronger-than-life passion for the hunt. This boy was already on the run. He knew someone was out to get him. That would make him more dangerous prey.

The boy looked up, but not *at* Bryan. The boy turned his head this way and that, looking at every window, every doorway, even up to every rooftop, his head moving steady and smooth and nonstop. This boy knew his surroundings, he knew his turf.

The whole CITY is our turf, asshole.

Bryan stayed very still. He let the prey waste its energy. Bryan's soul tingled; his mind swam with the knowledge that this was the way life was meant to be lived.

He'd been born for this.

The boy walked west on Geary. He crossed Hyde, heading toward Larkin. Bryan moved back, like a shadow, out of sight from anyone on the street. Clutching his blanket tight around his body, he jumped, a silent wind, moving from the roof of a parking garage to the tarred, flat top of the Ha-Ra bar. There, Bryan paused, freezing in place. He scanned the rooftop, the other buildings, looking for any sign of movement, any sign of the monster.

He saw none, and that made him happy.

With the barest of movements, Bryan leaned out over the brickwork to look down to the street twenty feet below.

Prey spotted.

One womb, you motherfucking bully.

There were very few people on the streets, but still enough to make it difficult. The boy wasn't far from Van Ness. Even in the predawn hours, that road had enough traffic that you couldn't just grab prey and drag it into the shadows or pull it up onto the roofs. If the boy reached Van Ness, they'd have no choice but to wait and watch.

"He's a smart one," said the sandpapery voice to Bryan's right.

"You got that right, Sthly," Bryan said.

Bryan turned — and saw a nightmare. A thick man with a heavy, dark blanket draped over his head and shoulders. The blanket covered him, but not *all* of him; a green face with a pointy snout caught the dim light, yellow eyes narrow with anticipation. The thick man smiled, revealing razor-sharp, neon-white teeth.

The nightmare spoke.

"This one is going to taste sweet."

• • •

Bryan woke up screaming.

He was going to kill that boy.

No-no, not *him* . . . that *monster.*

Blood pounding. Adrenaline surging. His cock as hard as a railroad spike. Every ounce of him ached. Invisible jackhammers, pounding away at his flesh. Even his *bones* hurt.

His bedroom door flew open. Pookie slid in, gun in hand, eyes darting first to Bryan then around the room. Pookie knelt to look under the bed.

Bryan shook his head. "No one here. A dream."

Pookie stood. He looked scared. Scared of Bryan. Maybe he should be.

"A dream," Pookie said. "Like the last one?"

Bryan coughed, nodded. So hot. He'd never felt this sick, felt like something was attacking every ounce of his body. "Yeah. Like the last one. I think it's happening again."

Pookie stared, blinked. "You're telling me that someone's being murdered right now? That you *dreamed* it?"

Bryan pushed his body out of bed. Heavy feet — still in his shoes — landed on the floor with a thump.

"Not yet," he said. "Stalking him."

"*Who* is stalking him?"

"I am. I mean . . . someone is, and I think I was in that someone's head . . . something like that, anyway."

Pookie's face showed he was having a hard time believing this. "You're telling me someone is stalking this kid, right this second?"

Bryan rubbed his eyes, tried to breathe through aching lungs, tried to think. "They're going to take him down. He's at Geary and Hyde. We gotta go."

"I'll call it in," Pookie said. "You're not going anywhere."

Bryan's hands drifted to his shoulder holster . . . empty. "I need my weapon."

"I'd rather you went without."

Pookie didn't trust Bryan with a gun? Considering what Bryan had put him through that was probably smart, but Bryan didn't have time to argue.

"Bryan, forget it. You're in no shape to—"

"No time," Bryan said as he brushed past Pookie and stepped into the hall. He found his weapons piled up on the kitchen table, put them where they belonged. He turned back toward the front door, to leave the apartment — and found Pookie blocking his way.

Pookie's gun was in his right hand, the barrel pointed at the ground.

"Bryan, I can't let you go."

Bryan paused. His own partner had drawn on him. He didn't feel offended or insulted. Instead, he actually felt instant sympathy for Pookie's difficult position — but there just wasn't time for this.

"Pooks, I *will not* let that boy die. Call for backup, come with me or stay here, but whatever you do, get the fuck out of my way."

Pookie's hand flexed on his Sig Sauer. Was he going to point it at Bryan? Had it come to that?

Bryan turned and ran into his tiny kitchen. A second later, he heard footsteps behind him as Pookie reacted.

The narrow kitchen window was hinged on the left side. It swung open like a door that led to the fire escape. Bryan stepped out the window to the metal-grate platform outside, the night welcoming him back to its dark embrace. It had rained while he slept — the metal rails felt icy-cold on his hands. Before Pookie had even reached the kitchen, Bryan had slid down to the third floor and was already descending to the second. By the time Pookie crawled out of the kitchen window, Bryan's feet hit the first-floor landing . . .

. . . and slipped.

His feet shot out from under him. The fire escape's wet, rusty metal smashed into his forehead. That pain added to his aches and fever, but he didn't let it stop him. He got back to his feet. Instead of lowering the collapsible ladder to the sidewalk, he just hopped over the rail.

"Bryan! Stay there!"

Bryan's feet hit concrete. He ignored his partner. The kid from his dream was going to wind up just like Oscar Woody. Bryan had to stop that from happening.

He felt blood sheeting down his face. His Nikes slapped lightly against wet sidewalk as he sprinted toward Van Ness Avenue.

•••

Bryan ran south on Van Ness, the six lanes of sporadic 3:00 A.M. traffic moving along on his right. What few pedestrians there were got the hell out of his way — a black-clad, sprinting man with a Sig Sauer in his hand and blood streaming from his forehead didn't exactly court conversation.

Despite his pain, his legs worked just fine. Long, loping steps threw him along. Everything whipped by so fast. As soon as this was over, he'd puke his guts out, he promised himself, but for now he had to ignore everything and get to that kid.

Bryan planted at Geary and turned left, momentum actually curving him off the sidewalk and into the road before he corrected. He heard sirens approaching — probably patrol cars already responding to Pookie's call. The sound echoed through the nighttime city-canyons.

Bryan didn't know where to go, so he kept running. He crossed Polk Street, dodging a car as he moved from sidewalk to blacktop then sidewalk again. Building walls shot by on his left, parked cars on his right.

Movement from above . . .

A burning body sailing off a rooftop four stories above. It blazed orange against the black night sky, a flailing comet trailing a tongue of fire that smashed into a white van, deeply denting the roof. Another flash of motion from up there, but whatever it was

    [snake-man]

                  slipped out of sight behind the roof's edge.

Bryan ran to the van and jumped. He found himself on top of the deeply dented, smashed-in roof — the man was facedown, small flames licking at his blackened clothes. Bryan whipped off his jacket and covered him, patting him down, snuffing out the flames. The man moaned.

"Hold on, buddy. I got ya."

The sirens grew louder.

Bryan realized the man's jacket — where it wasn't blackened and melted — was crimson and gold.

BoyCo gear.

It wasn't a man, it was a boy . . . the boy from his dream. Hurt, but not dead.

Bryan pulled out his cell and hit the two-way button.

Bee-boop: "Pookie, you there?"

Boo-beep: "I'm here." He sounded out of breath. "I'm a block and a half away, I see you."

Bryan looked down Geary. He saw Pookie running toward him.

Bee-boop: "Get an ambulance."

Bryan slid the phone back in his pocket. Streetlights reflected off of the blood slowly pooling around the wounded kid, wet-red smearing the van's white paint.

"Just take it easy," Bryan said. "I'm a cop. Help is on the way." He didn't want to move the boy, but broken bones or an injured spinal column didn't matter if Bryan couldn't find the wound and stop the bleeding. "I'm going to roll you over. I'll do it slow, but it'll hurt. Did someone throw you off the roof?"

"Jumped," the boy said, his words muffled because his face rested against the van roof. "Had to . . . get away."

"Get away from who?"

"Devil," the boy said. "Dragon."

Bryan rolled the boy over. Wide, frightened eyes stared out from a face covered with third-degree burns. Swollen blisters — some shiny-white, some raw-red — clustered on his cheeks, his nose, his mouth, his forehead, on almost every bit of exposed skin. His eyebrows and eyelids were gone, as was most of the hair at his temples and on top of his head. Blackened clothes — the jacket and what looked like a football jersey — had melted onto him. A small but steady pulsing of blood bubbled up from the boy's abdomen.

Bryan moved to apply pressure, but something on the boy's face froze him in place. A bit of red hair on the boy's lip, a bit more on his chin . . . the remnants of a scraggly goatee. Most of it had burned away, but enough remained for Bryan to see the blistered face anew. A small part of him knew this was Jay Parlar. A bigger part of him, the part that took over, it recognized something else entirely.

That part recognized the prey from his dream.

One womb, motherfucker.

A wave of hatred instantly bubbled up and boiled over into blinding, murderous rage. Bryan stood and straddled the kid, his feet balancing on the dented, blood-streaked white metal.

He reached to his shoulder holster, pulled his pistol, then pointed the barrel right between the boy's eyes.

A charred hand rose up, palm out, as if flesh and bone would stop a bullet.

"You're a bully," Bryan said. "I'm going to kill you."

The boy's oozing lips struggled to form words. "Please, *no*." He didn't even have the energy to fight for his life.

Bryan thumbed back the P226's hammer until it clicked. "Long live the king, asshole."

The boy's eyes widened. "That's what the devil said."

Bryan leaned in. He rested the muzzle against the boy's forehead. The boy squeezed his eyes tight.

"Bryan! Put it down, *now*!"

Pookie's voice. Pookie's *screaming* voice. Bryan blinked, looked down to the sidewalk. Pookie . . . his chest, heaving . . . his gun, drawn . . . his feet, spread in a shooter's stance.

Why the hell is my partner aiming at ME?

"*Drop it*, Bryan! Drop it *right fucking now* or I will put you down!"

Bryan's rage evaporated into the cool night air. There was something in his hands. He looked. He was holding his gun, pressing the barrel against the forehead of a badly wounded sixteen-year-old boy.

Bryan decocked the Sig Sauer, then slowly slid the weapon into his shoulder holster. The gun's muzzle left an indented ring on the scorched, blistered forehead. The last of the boy's energy seemed to fade away like a long, final breath — he closed his eyes.

He didn't move.

Pookie scrambled onto the van's hood, then up onto the now-crowded roof. The boy's abdomen no longer pulsed blood.

Pookie grabbed the boy's wrist, feeling for a pulse. "Nothing, *shit*." He looked up at Bryan. "What the fuck were you *doing*, man?"

Bryan didn't answer.

Pookie turned back to the boy. Left palm on the back of his right hand, Pookie started chest compressions. Bryan's gaze drifted toward the buildings on the other side of Geary Street, at heads and bodies silhouetted in lit-up apartment windows. People were watching.

As Pookie pumped, he again looked at Bryan. "Were you going to kill this kid?"

Bryan blinked a few times, trying to collect his thoughts, then the impact of Pookie's words hit home.

"No," Bryan said. "He fell, he was on fire . . . I put out the flames. I didn't touch him!"

Pookie's hands kept pumping. "Didn't touch him except for putting your fucking *gun* against his forehead, *right*? And I saw you. I saw you jump up on this van. Eight feet up and you landed standing? How the hell did you do that?"

What the fuck was Pookie talking about? Bryan couldn't do that. No one could.

The fever swept over him again, hotter than before, as if it was furious at being ignored and wanted payback. The aches pinched his joints, his muscles. His face felt wet and sticky. He touched his fingertips to his forehead — they came back covered in blood.

Pookie kept pumping, his arms straight, his hands on the boy's sternum. He stopped to press his fingers against the boy's neck.

Bryan waited, hoping Pookie would feel something there, but Pookie's shaking head told him otherwise.

"Still no pulse." Pookie returned to chest compressions.

The oncoming sirens screamed louder. Couldn't be long now. Bryan watched Pookie try to save the boy. Maybe this was still the dream. Maybe if Bryan had given first aid right away instead of putting a gun in the boy's face, the boy would still be alive.

"Bryan, get off the van," Pookie said.

Red and blue lights cut the night as patrol cars turned onto Geary. Bryan looked down at the boy again — horribly burned, young body smashed from a four-story fall. If Bryan hadn't dreamed about the kid, would this have happened? All that rage, all that *hate* . . . how could he feel that for someone he'd never even met?

"Bryan!"

Pookie's yell yanked Bryan back into the moment.

"Get *down*," his partner said. "Let me handle this. You keep your mouth shut, let me do the talking, got it?"

Bryan nodded. He slid off the van. Next thing he knew, he was sitting with his ass on the concrete sidewalk, his back against the building from which a flaming Jay Parlar had fallen to his death.

Up on the van roof, Pookie kept pumping away on the boy's chest. Pulse or no pulse, he would continue to do that until the paramedics arrived.

Bryan closed his eyes.

This was what it felt like to go insane.

Alex Panos Gets Gone

A half-block east of the ruined van, two teenage boys stood at the corner of Geary and Larkin, their heads peeking around just enough to watch the scene — four police cars, an ambulance and cops all over the place. One of the boys was much bigger than the other. The smaller one wore a black sweatshirt, hood pulled up over his head. His name was Issac Moses.

The other boy wore a crimson jacket with gold sleeves and a gold *BC* on the chest. His name was Alex Panos, and he wanted to know just what the hell was going on.

"Holy shit," Issac said. "Alex, that cop, I thought he was gonna shoot Jay."

Alex nodded. "I recognize those pigs. The one in black is Bryan Clauser. The fat one is Pookie something or other. They were at my house."

"At your *house*? Holy shit, man, holy *shit*. What are we gonna do?"

Alex didn't know. He glanced at his friend's plain black sweatshirt. Issac thought someone wanted to kill anyone wearing BoyCo colors, so he didn't wear them. Alex had called Issac a pussy for that, but after seeing what happened to Jay, maybe it was a good idea to lose the Boston College gear after all.

"Alex, man, I'm scared," Issac said. "Maybe we should go to the cops."

"Dumb shit, those *are* cops."

"Yeah, but you said they were in your house, and they didn't try anything, right? And that cop in black, he didn't actually shoot Jay. Besides, both cops were on the ground — they didn't set Jay on fire and throw him off the fucking roof of his own building, right?"

Alex looked back down the street. One of the cops that had visited his apartment, the one that dressed all in black, was in the back of the ambulance. A paramedic was working on his face. The other one, the fat chink, he was also around somewhere but Alex didn't see him.

Jay was still on the van roof. It didn't look like he was moving. A second paramedic was up there with him, but he didn't seem to be in much of a hurry.

"I think Jay's dead," Alex said.

Issac's face wrinkled, his blue eyes narrowed and started to tear up. "Dead? *Jay*? Holy *shit*, man!"

"Be quiet," Alex said. "I gotta think."

Issac was right about one thing: the cop hadn't actually shot Jay. But maybe that was only because Jay was already dying from the fall. If Alex and Issac had been just a couple of minutes earlier, would they be dead as well? What really mattered was that those two cops had come to Jay's place at three in the morning, and now Jay was dead.

Issac tugged at Alex's sleeve.

"Alex, come *on*," Issac said. "Let's go to the cops. Other cops, I mean. We're in a lot of fucking trouble."

Alex shook his head. "No way. Whatever cop we talk with, those two are going to know, and then they'll come for us. Cops stick with cops — they don't give a shit about the law or justice or whatever. We have to find a place to hide for a while. That, and we have to find guns."

Alex ducked back behind the building, out of sight of the cops swarming around Geary Street. He started walking north on Larkin, then stopped, reached back, grabbed Issac and dragged him away from the corner.

Another Day, Another Body

Pookie went through the motions. Part of his brain paid close attention to details. Another part directed the other cops, sending uniforms where they needed to go to collect information. And yet another part was lost in the bizarreness of his partner, of what this all meant.

Pookie was overweight, out of shape and slow, but he wasn't *that* slow. He'd been maybe two blocks behind Bryan. Pookie had turned the corner just in time to see Jay Parlar's flaming body sail into the night air. Bryan was down on the sidewalk when the kid's body smashed into the van. No way Bryan could have thrown the kid off that roof.

Pookie had closed in, his chest burning, his stomach heaving — he really had to do something about getting back into shape — and then, Bryan's crazy leap. To leap that high, maybe Bryan had jumped up, then pushed off the side of the van or the van's door handle, like those parkour guys who could run up the side of a building. Bryan had been far away, it had been dark save for the streetlights, the boy had been on fire . . . plenty of variables to play tricks with what Pookie had seen.

Because a man couldn't jump *eight feet* straight up.

Bryan's feet had cleared the van roof. He had dropped down lightly, one black Nike on either side of the facedown, burning kid. Bryan had whipped off his jacket and used it to smother the flames. He'd been *helping* the boy.

But when Bryan had rolled the kid over, everything changed. Pookie knew — he *knew* — that if he hadn't gotten there when he had, Bryan would have put a bullet through Jay Parlar's brain.

The crime-scene investigations team was already finished with their work. According to them, Jay would have died even if he hadn't been set on fire and tossed off a four-story building. The boy had been stabbed while still up on the roof, severing an artery — he never had a chance.

When the morgue van took the body away, Pookie had gone up to the roof to see things for himself. There, he'd found symbols written in Jay Parlar's blood.

The same symbols they'd found written in Oscar Woody's blood.

Back down on the street, Pookie found Bryan sitting in the back of an ambulance, a paramedic examining his head. He looked dazed. No one gave that a second thought, though — the other cops automatically wrote it off as a natural reaction to seeing a burning kid thrown off a building.

Pookie scratched the stubble on his cheek as he stared at his partner. He'd tried hard to rationalize all of this crap, tried to come up with a normal explanation, but it was time to accept what he'd witnessed with his own eyes.

The dreams were for real.

It was no trick, no gimmick. Was Bryan psychic? Pookie wasn't ready to believe that just yet, but after tonight he couldn't rule it out. He'd been in Bryan's apartment when Bryan dreamed about Jay Parlar. No evildoer had slipped in and whispered in Bryan's ear. There were no microphones in the wall, no electrodes in the pillow. Bryan had dreamed a kid was in danger. Then, he'd shot out of the apartment, tried to save that kid just as any cop would do. An abnormal method of discovery, but a normal reaction.

As fucked up as it was, Pookie felt infinitely better. Bryan had not killed Jay Parlar — if he hadn't killed Jay, then he probably hadn't killed Oscar Woody. *Probably.* Bryan had no alibi for Oscar. He could have killed Oscar and someone else could have killed Jay.

Which would mean, what? That Bryan had accomplices? That maybe he was working with other killers? Even if that was true, *why* would he murder those kids? Pookie spent at least fifty hours a week with Bryan. Before last night, Bryan clearly hadn't know a thing about Oscar Woody or Jay Parlar or BoyCo. There was no motive.

Fuck. None of this made any sense.

Patrol officers were already in buildings on both sides of the street, knocking on apartment doors, looking for witnesses. Pookie didn't have any hope of finding someone who had been up at three A.M. and had seen the deal go down.

There were no witnesses.

Wait . . . that wasn't right — there was one person who had seen Jay Parlar up on that roof.

Bryan had. In his dreams.

Pookie walked to the ambulance. The paramedic was just finishing up, wiping down the cut on Bryan's forehead. Bryan's black clothes helped hide the fact that he'd bled like a stuck pig, even left a trail of droplets all the way from his apartment to here.

Pookie leaned in and looked at the sutured wound. "Hey, is that just *three* stitches?"

The paramedic nodded. "Yeah. Not too bad."

"Three stitches for all that blood? Bryan, what are you, a hemophiliac?"

Bryan shrugged.

"I asked him the same thing," the paramedic said. "Seemed like a lot of blood, but it appears to be clotting normally. No problems. Maybe it was from his sprinting here, I'm not sure. Scalp wounds always bleed like hell, though. He's fine."

"Thanks," Pookie said. "Can you give us a minute?"

The paramedic nodded and walked off.

Pookie sat next to his partner in the back of the ambulance.

"Bri-Bri, you good?"

Bryan shook his head. "Far from it. Panos and Moses are next if they're not dead already. You put out a call to have them picked up?"

Pookie nodded. "Ball-Puller Boyd already tried the Panos place, but Alex wasn't home. Susie doesn't know where he is."

"Shocker," Bryan said.

"I know, right? A patrol car is at Issac Moses's place, but he's also nowhere to be seen. I called a BOLO for both of them."

Bryan nodded and seemed to relax. The call to *Be On the Look-Out* went out not only department-wide, but across the Bay Area. Someone would find those kids and bring them in.

Pookie took in a slow breath. He had to ask the hard question. Asking it somehow made all of this real, and he wished to God it *wasn't* real, but he couldn't beat around the bush any longer.

"Okay, Bryan, spill it — tell me what you saw."

Bryan pointed out the ambulance's open back doors toward the ruined white van. "I turned the corner, started running down Geary, and—"

"No, not *that* what you saw. In the dream. Tell me what you saw in the dream."

Bryan looked down — not at Pookie, not at the floor, just *down*. When he spoke, it was in little more than a whisper. "I saw Parlar. He was walking. It was like I was looking down from above. Like I was tracking him . . . *stalking* him."

"From above," Pookie said. "Maybe, four stories above?"

Bryan looked at Pookie, then up to the apartment building's roof. He nodded, understanding. "Yeah. Maybe four stories above. Only, it wasn't me that saw him. It was and it wasn't. I was on the roof, with this . . . other guy."

"What did the other guy look like?"

Bryan paused. "I don't remember."

"Bri-Bri, you lie about as well as I do when I tell a woman I'll call her in the morning. Start talking."

Bryan reached up, his fingertips lightly touching the three tiny black stitches. "You'll think I'm crazy."

"Dude, I'm already *positive* you're crazy. So tell me what the guy looked like."

Bryan looked down again. "He had a blanket over his shoulders, his head. From what I could make out, he . . . he looked like a snake."

"What, you mean shifty? Like those fucking Italians?"

He shook his head. "No, I mean *like a snake*. Green skin and a pointy nose."

Pookie stared at Bryan. Bryan continued to stare at the ground.

"Green skin," Pookie said. "Pointy nose."

Bryan nodded.

Pookie didn't want to laugh, but he couldn't stop a small one from slipping out. "Man, I'd love to see the lineup if we catch this guy. Will number three step forward? No, not the werewolf, the snake-man."

"It was just a dream, okay? It's not like I saw a snake-man in real life."

"Okay, okay," Pookie said. Bryan was taking this hard. Who wouldn't? But Pookie still had to treat him like any other witness — walk him through the situation, rephrase questions and ask again, and so on. "So what do *you* think is going on, Terminator? Did you know these boys?"

"No."

"Before we found Oscar Woody, had you ever heard of the Boys Company?"

"No."

"Then how did you know someone was trying to kill Jay Parlar?"

Bryan sighed. He probably wanted to believe all of this even less than Pookie did. "I already told you, Pooks. In my dream I was stalking him. I wanted to kill him, just like I wanted to kill Oscar in that first dream, although I didn't know who Oscar Woody was at the time."

Pookie closed his eyes and rubbed his face. He had to start making the smart decisions. Bryan hadn't killed Jay Parlar, fine, but there was no longer any question that — somehow — he was involved in these murders. Partner or no partner, he *belonged* in interrogation, getting grilled like any other suspect in a murder case. But Pookie just couldn't do that to his friend. There had to be another angle here.

"Bri-Bri, you said there were others with you in the Jay Parlar dream. You said the same thing about the Oscar Woody dream, right?"

Bryan nodded.

"So do you think you could describe them to a sketch artist?"

Bryan thought for a second, then shook his head. "No, I don't think so. I can't really visualize them, you know? It was just a hodgepodge of messed-up features."

A young uniformed officer approached. Pookie slid out of the ambulance to meet him. "Officer Stuart Hood, good to see you. Your mom win that cook-off last month?"

"Took second," Hood said. "I'll tell her you asked."

"Aw, she got robbed. You tell Rebecca she should have won the blue ribbon. And tell her to make me some more of those hazelnut cookies you brought in. Like little slices of heaven, those things."

Hood smiled. "I'll tell her. Turns out we have a woman who saw something suspicious, Inspector. Tiffany Hine, sixty-seven years old."

"A witness at three A.M. in this part of town? Nice work, Officer Hood. I'm surprised you didn't find a ring-tailed lemur first."

Hood smiled, laughed a little. "I wouldn't get too excited, Inspector."

"Oh, you think this is a funny situation?" Pookie said. "This is high comedy to you?"

"If I'm sad and melancholy, is he going to suddenly spring back to life?"

"*Melancholy?* That's a big word for you, isn't it? Just tell me what Hine said."

Hood bit his lip, trying to hide a smile. "She said she saw a werewolf take the boy."

The last thing Pookie needed right now was a standup comic moonlighting as a cop. "Officer Hood, I'm really not in the mood for jokes, you get me?"

Hood shrugged. "I'm not joking. That's what she said."

"She said, *a werewolf*?"

"Well, she said the guy had a dog-face, anyway. That sounds like a werewolf to me. But Wolfie wasn't alone, he had . . . a partner." Hood's chest jiggled from a suppressed laugh. "She said . . . she said it was a guy with . . . with . . . a *snake-face*."

Pookie looked at Bryan, then back to Hood. "A snake-face? You're sure?"

Hood nodded. He coughed, still trying to cover up his laughter. "Uh, Inspector Verde is en route. He said the case is his because of the symbols on the roof. He's coming to take over the scene. Should I give him this crazy . . . excuse me, I mean this *valuable* witness?"

Polyester Rich. As soon as he arrived, Pookie and Bryan would be locked out of the case. If Pookie wanted answers, he had to get them now. "What's Verde's ETA?"

"He said fifteen minutes."

"We'll take the witness," Pookie said. "Where is she?"

Hood pointed to the green apartment building across the street from the white van where Jay had died. "Apartment 215," he said, then walked away.

Bryan stepped out of the ambulance. "We have a witness that saw a snake-face?"

Pookie nodded. "So it seems."

That old excitement flashed in Bryan's eyes, but only for a second. He looked down again. "Look, man, I don't know what's going on, but I'm putting you in a really shitty spot. So here's your out — if you say the word, I'll go downtown and turn myself in. I'll tell the chief all about my dreams and let her figure out what to do next. You want me to do that?"

It shocked Pookie how badly he wanted to say *yes.* Shocked him, and filled him with guilt. Bryan Clauser had saved his life. They were partners. They were *friends.* And, God help him, Pookie just flat-out believed that Bryan Clauser was innocent.

He looked to the green building across the street. Could the witness in there somehow validate what Bryan had seen in his dreams?

"Come on," Pookie said. "I have to talk to this woman. You're my partner, so you get to tag along."

Bryan looked up, looked Pookie in the eyes. He nodded. They both knew that Pookie was putting his career on the line.

"Thanks," Bryan said. "I mean it. Thanks."

"Don't thank me yet, Terminator. Maybe you and this Tiffany Hine both wind up in a straitjacket before sunrise. Polyester Rich will be here soon, so let's make this quick. Who knows? You might actually get your monstery lineup after all."

The Only Thing We Have to Fear Is . . .

He had a flashlight pinned under his right armpit, its oblong of illumination dancing madly off a drawing of Jay Parlar taking a fire ax to the stomach. The beam danced because of what Rex was doing with his left hand. It was *bad*, it was *unclean*, but he couldn't stop. His cast-clad right hand rested on the edge of his desk, the only thing stopping him from falling down.

Rex's left hand did the nasty thing. Even though he'd never done it before, he knew it felt wrong.

He was right-handed.

Come on, come on . . .

He'd woken up all wet, his blankets soaked with sweat, his breath ragged and his heart beating so loud he heard it. *The dream.* It had been so real.

He'd watched Jay Parlar die.

And that had made his dick hard, so *painfully* hard.

Naughty, awful, *bad*. Dreaming it was shameful, but now he was making it worse *just stop it Rex just stop it* but he could not.

The fingers of his right hand curled tight against the cast across his palm. He couldn't think. *Come on come on* couldn't think *come on come on come on . . .*

The flashlight dropped to the floor. He grabbed at his right hand, pulled, tore, smashed his right arm into his desk making a big *bang*, then pulling and tearing again, and then *it feels so good come on come on come on.*

The flashlight no longer lit up the desk, but that didn't matter; he saw his drawing in his mind — a pencil sketch of Jay Parlar, eyes wide and wet, snot hanging from his nose, mouth open and pleading for his life.

Die you bully I will kill you I will come on come oncomeoncomeon . . .

"Hate . . . you . . ." Rex said, then his breath locked up in his throat and his thoughts faded away. All sensations vanished, all but the sound of Jay Parlar's final scream.

Rex's knees buckled. He caught the edge of the desk to stop from falling. Sweat dripped down his forehead.

He picked up the flashlight and pointed the beam at his drawing. Oh, no . . . he'd jizzed right on the picture of Jay Parlar's pleading, terrified face. What did that mean? Rex felt tears well up — what was wrong with him? Why did he have to do the thing that Roberta told him was bad, that she said was *sinful* and *dirty*?

His right arm tingled with cool dampness.

Rex held his right hand in front of the flashlight beam.

The cast was gone.

The skin on his arm goosebumped, still tacky with sweat that had built up inside the plaster. He pointed the flashlight at the floor. The cracked, floppy ruin of his cast lay on the carpet.

He looked at his right arm again. He made a slow fist. The spot where Alex had stomped . . . it looked fine. It didn't feel broken anymore. The doctor had said he'd be in the cast for weeks.

The doctor had said that the day before yesterday.

Rex suddenly realized that the aches he'd suffered for days, his pains, his fever . . . all of it was gone.

Gone.

But that didn't matter right now. He had to clean up before Roberta saw what he'd done. Just leaving his bed unmade got three hits with the belt — how bad would she beat him if she saw he'd been jacking off? He'd get the paddle for sure. He was in trouble, *so much trouble.* The pieces of his cast went into the trash. He could dump that tomorrow while Roberta watched the morning news. He grabbed tissues from a box of Kleenex and wiped at the picture. Some of the pencil lines blurred, smudged. Would Roberta know? Probably not, she never looked at his pictures anyway.

And that cast had been *expensive.* Roberta would freak out that he'd ruined it. Rex looked around his room. Nothing really seemed out of place. Sometimes she went days without coming in here at all. Sometimes he slept in the park and didn't even come home. Once he'd been gone for two nights in a row and she hadn't even noticed.

Maybe he could do that again, go hide in the park or something. Maybe in a few days he could tell her the cast just fell off.

Rex wiped snot away from his nose. He crawled into bed and pulled the blankets tight around him. He shouldn't have done that nasty thing, but now he felt better. He'd gotten it out of his system. Imagining Oscar's murder, jizzing to it, that was a onetime thing. It was bad, but he would never do it again.

Never.

But still, what if Roberta *found out*?

Rex's breath suddenly stopped. He stared at the ceiling without really seeing it. A thought, so new, so shocking, so . . . *revolutionary* . . . had flashed through his head, grabbed him and wouldn't let go.

What if Roberta found out? No. *So what* if Roberta found out. *So what?*

Father Paul Maloney.

Oscar Woody.

Both of them had hurt Rex. Rex had drawn them, and now they were dead. Roberta hurt Rex all the time . . . he could draw her, too.

Maybe Rex didn't need to be afraid anymore.

And tonight, he'd drawn Jay Parlar. Would Jay still be alive tomorrow?

Rex closed his eyes, a smile on his lips as he fell asleep.

Bryan Lets Pookie Do the Talking

Sixty-seven-year-old Tiffany Hine didn't look a day over sixty-six and a half. Bryan thought her apartment smelled exactly the way you'd think an old lady's apartment smelled — stale violets, baby powder and medicine. She had a high, soft voice and frizzy silver hair long past a glorious prime. She wore a yellow flowered robe and worn pink slippers. Her eyes looked clear and focused, the kind of eyes that could see right through the bullshit of any child (or grandchild, for that matter). Those eyes sported deep laugh lines. At the moment, the lines on her face showed real fear.

She was old, but she looked sharp. She looked *sane*, and that was what Bryan desperately needed to believe.

Pookie and Tiffany sat next to each other on a plastic-covered couch. Bryan stood by, looking out the living room window to Geary Street below — and across the street, to the van where Jay Parlar had died. Bryan's sour stomach threatened to twist him in knots. His head swam so bad he had to keep a hand on the wall to stop from swaying. It was usually best to let Pookie do the talking; now, it was a necessity.

"Just take it from the beginning, ma'am," Pookie said.

"I already told the other man, the one with the uniform," Tiffany said. "You don't have a uniform. And I might add it's time for you to get a new jacket, young man. The one you're wearing probably stopped fitting you twenty pounds ago."

Pookie smiled. "I'm a homicide inspector, ma'am. We don't wear uniforms. But I still eat lots of donuts, as you can tell."

She smiled. It was a genuine smile, although halfhearted and a bit empty. What she had seen affected her to the core. "Fine, I'll tell you. But this is the last time."

Pookie nodded.

"As you can see, my window looks out on Geary. I look out on the street a lot. I like to watch people go by and imagine what their stories are."

Outside the window, morning sunlight was just beginning to hit the blacktop. This woman had really been staring out the window at such a convenient time? Bryan wanted Pookie to get to the point, get to the part with the *snake-face*, but Pookie had his own way of doing things and Bryan had to be patient.

"At three in the morning?" Pookie said. "Kind of late for people watching, isn't it?"

"I don't sleep well," Tiffany said. "Thoughts of mortality, you see. Of how everything is just going to . . . *end*. Don't worry, young man, if you aren't thinking about it already, you will soon enough."

Pookie nodded. "Thoughts of mortality come with my job. Please continue."

Tiffany did. "So I'm looking out the window, and I see this young man across the street, wearing a crimson jacket. I've seen him before. He and three other boys wander the streets at all hours. I recognize them because they all wear the same colors — crimson, white and gold. But tonight, it was just the one boy."

Pookie made a few notes on his pad.

"The boy was walking fast," Tiffany said. "That's what caught my attention. He kept looking behind him, like he thought someone was following him, perhaps. Then the bums dropped down."

Bryan turned away from the window. *Dropped down?*

"Dropped down," Pookie said, echoing Bryan's thoughts. "You said bums *dropped down*? Dropped down from where?"

Tiffany shrugged. "From the roof of that apartment building across the street, I imagine. It was like they . . . like they fell, from windowsill to windowsill. But not an accident. On purpose."

"I see," Pookie said. "And you got a good look at them?"

She shrugged again. "As good as I could, considering the light and how fast they moved. They dropped down, grabbed him, then went up again."

Pookie scribbled. "And how did they go up? Fire escape?"

She shook her head and stared off to some spot in the room. "They went up the same way they came down. Window to window. I've never seen people jump that high. It wasn't as if they stuck to the walls like Spider-Man, mind you — it was more like watching a squirrel scramble up an oak tree. They went up four stories so fast I couldn't believe it."

Bryan looked to the building across the street and tried to visualize what she had seen. Even if someone could climb from windowsill to windowsill, some acrobat or whatever, no one could climb those four stories with any kind of speed.

Pookie nodded and wrote, as if hearing about someone scrambling up the side of a building were an everyday occurrence. "That's fine," he said. "And could you describe the men, please?"

Tiffany cleared her throat again. "They were big, maybe a foot taller than the boy. Maybe even more. They both had these dirty blankets draped over their shoulders."

"You called them bums?" Pookie said.

"That was my first reaction," Tiffany said. "I mean, if I saw those men on the street, all bundled up like that, I probably wouldn't even notice them. You see people like that all the time, the poor souls. But these men . . . well, the blankets seemed to . . . to loosen up, maybe. The blankets slid away from their faces a little." She stared off to a corner of the room. She continued in a barely audible whisper. "That's when I saw the one with green skin and a pointy face. Like a snake. The other one" — Tiffany mimed pulling at her nose, pulling it out a foot from her face — "had a long snoot, and it looked like he had brown hair all over it. I also saw he had brown legs, covered in hair, the same as his face."

Bryan breathed slowly. Dirty blankets, just like in his dream. And brown hair. Like the brown hair Sammy Berzon had found on the blanket covering Oscar Woody's corpse. If she had actually seen this, then maybe he wasn't crazy after all.

"Oh," she said. "There was one more thing. The one with the brown legs was wearing Bermuda shorts."

"Bermuda shorts," Pookie said, writing it down in his notebook. "The one that looked like a werewolf was wearing Bermuda shorts?"

Tiffany tilted her head and narrowed her eyes. "I never said *werewolf*. I only got a glimpse when he grabbed the boy, when the blanket loosened up a little. The big snoot . . . it was like a dog's, but the jaws didn't line up right. He had a long tongue that hung off one side. People . . ." she stopped, looked down to her carpet, the fear now totally in control of her face and voice ". . . people don't look like that."

"Then what happened?"

She licked her lips. Her hands were shaking. "Then I didn't see anything for a bit. Then there was this fireball from up on the roof. I saw the boy engulfed in it."

"Did you see what caused the fireball?"

She shook her head. "No, it was too bright. I only saw the boy because he was silhouetted. Then he was burning. There were others on the roof, in the blankets. The boy . . . he was still on fire and he . . . he *jumped*. Whatever was up there with him, he chose to kill himself rather than face it."

Pookie lowered the notepad. "Ma'am, this has been very helpful. Would you mind if a sketch artist came over?"

She shook her head violently, instantly. "As soon as you boys leave, I'm not talking about this again. Ever."

"But this could be helpful to our—"

"Leave," she said. "I did my part."

The front door opened, and they all turned to look. No knock, no buzzer, just Rich Verde storming in, resplendent in a dark-purple suit. Where the *hell* did that guy shop? Behind Verde walked Bobby Pigeon, and behind Bobby came Officer Stuart Hood. Hood had a look on his face like he'd just been reamed out good and proper.

"*Chang*," Verde said. "What are you doing here?"

Pookie smiled wide. Despite the horrible circumstances, Bryan knew Pookie wouldn't pass up a chance to get under Verde's skin.

"Just interviewing the witness," Pookie said. "On account of how we were here first because you were probably getting your sleepy time."

Rich glared at him, then walked up to Tiffany. He flashed a smile as fake as the fabric of his clothes.

"Ma'am, I'm Inspector Richard Verde. I'd like to ask you a few questions about what you saw tonight."

Tiffany sighed and shook her head. "Please leave my home."

"But, ma'am," Polyester Rich said, "we need to—"

"I've told my story," Tiffany said. She pointed to Hood. "I told him" — she pointed at Pookie — "and I told him. Hopefully, Mister Verde, your co-workers take good notes because I'm never speaking of this again."

Tiffany's voice carried the authority of a disciplinarian mother. She didn't take shit from anyone.

Rich started to protest. Bryan saw Pookie tilting his head toward the door. Time to get out while the getting was good. Excellent idea.

Bryan quickly walked to the door, followed Pookie out, and the two all but ran down the stairs.

"Fuck Verde," Pookie said. "He'll get my notes, but when I'm damn good and ready to give them up."

"Doesn't work that way, Pooks. He's the lead. Give him your info."

"Yeah-yeah-yeah," Pookie said. "He'll get Hood's notes, for starters. Of course I'll give him mine, but I'll make him say *please* first. That will drive him crazy."

They reached the ground floor and stopped in the building's entryway.

Pookie looked at his notepad, read something, then looked at Bryan. "You know that old biddy's story is nuckingfuts," he said. "She took the express train to Looney Land."

Bryan nodded. "Totally crazy."

Pookie rubbed his chin. Bryan could barely breathe.

Pookie slapped the notepad against his open palm. "I mean, guys scaling down the wall, and back up again? I'm supposed to assume it was . . . I don't know . . . stuntmen in Halloween costumes snatching a kid?"

Pookie stared at the notepad again. Bryan waited, letting his partner work through this. Tiffany's testimony was close to Bryan's dreams, too close for coincidence. After her description, if Pookie *still* didn't believe, he probably never would.

"Pooks, she used the words *snake-face*. I didn't prompt her — you know that, right?"

Pookie nodded, slowly. "Yeah. Kind of specific. Not the same thing as saying *it was a black guy*."

Bryan needed Pookie to believe him, believe *in* him. If Pookie did not, Bryan would truly be in this all alone.

Pookie sighed, smiled, looked to the ceiling. "I've got the testimony of a senile old woman who was probably tripping on acid, who saw something for three seconds, and I've got your dreams. I'd have to be an idiot to believe you."

"She's not senile," Bryan said. "And I didn't see any Deadhead stickers in there."

Pookie took a deep breath and let it out in a cheek-puffing huff. "Yeah," he said, nodding. "Maybe I need to take the short bus to work, but I believe you. This doesn't mean it's a guy with an actual face of a snake, Bri-Bri. These are dudes in costumes. I can't explain your dreams, but the scaling the building thing? It was late at night, Tiffany could have missed cables, ropes, your general circus paraphernalia."

Bryan nodded, but he knew there hadn't been ropes. And he knew there hadn't been costumes. That didn't matter — what mattered was that Pookie believed he wasn't crazy. For now, that was enough.

Pookie's cell phone buzzed. He checked the caller ID, then answered.

"Black Mister Burns," he said. "Why are you calling me at five-thirty in the morning?"

Bryan waited as Pookie listened.

"Yeah, almost done here," Pookie said. "No, just tell me. For real? Sure, no problem. Know where Pinecrest Diner is? No, genius, the diner is closed and I want to hang out by its front door like a skater kid. Of course they're open. Fine. I'll be there in thirty minutes."

He hung up.

"What's happening?" Bryan asked. "He figure something out with those symbols?"

Pookie held up a *just wait a second* finger as he dialed another number with his thumb. He smiled as he waited for the other end to pick up.

"Hi, it's Pookie," he said, then paused to listen. "Oh please, you were probably about to get up anyway. Listen, Bryan wanted me to call. He's on his way over for breakfast."

"Hey," Bryan said. "Don't promise someone that—"

"Twenty minutes? Great. He's looking forward to it. Bye-bye."

Pookie folded the phone and slid it back into his pocket. "Black Mister Burns has something he wants to share. He doesn't feel good broadcasting it over the police radio."

"Cool, let's go."

Pookie shook his head. "Nope, just me. You need to chill out for a bit and get a bite to eat."

"Pooks, I'm not in the mood for breakfast. I still feel like I got hit by a steamroller, and you think I can *chill* after all this?"

Pookie shrugged. "Whether you can or you can't doesn't matter. Mike Clauser sounded excited. He's probably already cooking the kielbasa."

Bryan's teeth clenched tight. Sometimes Pookie thought he knew better than anyone else. "You told my dad I was coming over for fucking breakfast?"

Pookie shrugged. "You need a break, man. I know you didn't do these things, okay? I know it. You need to *stop thinking* about all this for a couple of hours. You need to unplug for a bit. Go or stay, but you know how fired up Mike gets."

Bryan's father would already be excited to have his son drop by for a visit. If Bryan didn't go, Mike Clauser would be crushed.

"Hey, Pooks," Bryan said. "You suck cock."

Pookie smiled. "All I can get."

They heard three sets of heavy footsteps on the stairs a few flights up.

"Polyester returns," Pookie said. "Seriously, man, just go hang with your pops for a bit. I'm off. Catch a cab."

Pookie walked quickly out of the building and headed for his car.

Bryan thought about chasing him, trying to go with him, but Pookie was right — Mike Clauser would already be cooking the only dish he knew how to make.

"Asshole," Bryan said once more, then walked out of the building.

A Visit from Chinatown

The sound of rattling machinery and chains dragging across stone brought Aggie out of a cold sleep. He had to *move* — he fought nausea and disorientation as he crawled toward the white wall. He didn't make it in time before the chain drew tight, yanking on his neck and dragging him across the floor. He got his feet under him just in time to stand and turn his back to the flange.

The collar clanged home.

The white door opened, and this time it wasn't the little old babushka lady.

Five white-hooded, white-robed monster-men came through. The last two carried a long pole, from which hung an unconscious man tied to it by his wrists and ankles. He looked like one of those old guys from Chinatown — sun-wrinkled face, black hair flecked with strands of gray, red flannel shirt over a faded Super Bowl XXI shirt, blue jeans and well-worn brown work boots.

Like Aggie and the Mexicans, the man had a metal collar around his neck.

Aggie stared at the monster-men. He squeezed his eyes shut, then opened them again. He'd been high as fuck last time. He wasn't high now.

Those weren't monster faces . . . they were rubber Halloween masks. A pig and a wolf, like before, but now he saw the goblin was one of those green-faced things that guarded Jabba the Hut in *Return of the Jedi*. There was also a Hellboy with the red skin and stubby horns, and a white-faced, black-whiskered Hello Kitty.

The robed men wasted no time. Hellboy had that remote-control thing and used it to get some slack from a chain to Aggie's right. Pig-Face and Hello Kitty untied the man's wrists, hooked the chain to the man's collar, then left him lying on the floor.

He lay there, unmoving.

The masked men turned and walked toward the Mexican couple, who had been pulled to their respective places along the wall.

"Devuélvame a mi hijo," said the Mexican man, his tone a plea thick with despair. "A Dios le pido!"

The robed men said nothing. Their monster masks showed no emotion. They ignored the Mexican man.

Instead, they closed in on his wife.

Five sets of black-gloved hands reached for her, grabbing at arms and feet. She screamed.

"*No!*" the man shouted. "*Déjenla en paz!*"

She tried to fight, but she had no chance.

. . . His wife . . . Aggie remembered his own wife . . . remembered the gunshot . . . the blood . . .

The Mexican man's voice betrayed shredding vocal cords. "Chinga a tu madre!" Spit flew from his mouth. His eyes blazed wide with murderous insanity. "Le mataré! *Le mataré!*"

Hellboy hit a button on the remote control. The woman's chain went slack, just as it had with her son. The masked men dragged her to the ground, her body half hidden by their white robes.

Aggie stood there, helpless. He couldn't help her. All he could do was draw attention to himself, and if he did they might take him instead. He stood as still as he could.

The Mexican man's fingers clawed at his collar. He pulled, tried to slide his fingers inside the metal and leather. He lurched forward, choking himself. His eyes bulged from rage, from a lack of oxygen.

The woman's bloodied hand shot up through the pile of white robes, clawing at air, reaching for her man.

"*Hector!*"

The Mexican man — *Hector* — could not help her.

Hellboy pocketed the remote control. He picked up the wooden pole, then stuck the end of it into the pile of wiggling bodies and hooked the woman's collar. Like a trained work crew, the masked men quickly grabbed the pole and dragged her across the floor.

Hector shouted a stuttering something that wasn't a word in any language. He lurched again and again, trying to pull at a collar that would not give. Threads of blood flew from his screaming mouth. Every vein on his face stood out in bas-relief. His wet lips pulled back in a sneer of helpless anguish.

The white-robed men walked out of the jail-cell door, dragging the woman out of sight.

The cage door shut. The chains went slack.

Chest heaving, a nonsensical roar rolling from his mouth, Hector ran forward at full speed. He made it ten steps, just past the shit hole, before the chain snapped taut with an accompanying ring of metal. His feet shot out from under him and he landed hard on his left side.

Hector didn't try to get up. He started to cry.

The woman's screams echoed, steadily growing fainter, fainter, until they faded away for good.

Aggie slowly shook his head from side to side. This couldn't be happening. *Couldn't be.* But it was, and he was stone-cold sober.

This was real.

He was fucked. Totally fucked.

Coal for the Engine

Pookie and Bryan usually worked the wee hours of the morning, when most restaurants had closed for the night. Pinecrest Diner was open twenty-four hours a day. The place had become their go-to spot when they needed to sit and talk through a case. Pinecrest was a little touristy during the day, but at two or three in the morning you could avoid the dozen people wearing I ♥ SAN FRANCISCO or ALCATRAZ PSYCHO WARD OUTPATIENT shirts.

Pookie hoped Black Mr. Burns had good info. They needed a break in this case something awful. Ball-Puller Boyd hadn't been able to track down Alex Panos or Issac Moses — both were still missing. Those boys were either already dead, their bodies waiting to be found, or they were in hiding. Pookie guessed the latter.

And Bryan . . . a couple of hours of downtime with his old man would do wonders. Mike Clauser had a way of making you forget about everything but Mike Clauser. Bottom line: Bryan hadn't killed those boys. Now that Pookie believed in his partner's innocence, he needed Bryan to stop moping and get back on his A-game.

Pookie walked into the diner and saw Black Mr. Burns sitting at a booth, a tablet computer in front of him. John's shoulders were up, his head was down — even coming to a public place like this was hard for him. Once upon a time John Smith had been a standout cop. Now he was afraid of his own shadow, and that was a genuine tragedy. The man had unwittingly provided his own comic relief, though: he wore a dark-purple motorcycle jacket.

A few other patrons were in the place. Three working-class guys sat in a booth, getting a carb-loaded head start on the day. A trio of hipsters sat on the diner's round stools, leaning on the black stone counter. The latest trendy after-hours spot — that you probably haven't heard about, because it's so obscure — must have finally shut down, and these fellas wanted to finish off the night with a stack of pancakes.

Pookie slid into the seat across from his old partner. "What's up, Purple Rain?"

"Huh?"

"The jacket," Pookie said. "You rode your hog here and you're wearing purple? Hello?"

John sighed. "So a black man in a purple jacket *has* to look like Prince?"

Pookie nodded. "Exactly. How's Apollonia and those crazy kids in the New Power Generation?"

"Your minority-on-minority hate is a sad thing," John said. "You're letting the white man pull your strings. Listen, I have some serious business to talk about. I found some odd stuff."

"Odd *stuff*? You know, you can swear around me. I'm not going to tell the teacher."

"I'm family friendly."

"Some things never change. So what couldn't you tell me over the phone? I have to admit, in fifteen years of police work, this is the first time someone has called me for a sneaky-spy meeting. Except for your mom, of course."

"Yeah, she told me about that," John said. "She said you had a small penis."

Pookie shook his head. John tried to partake in witty repartee, but the guy was just such a flaming nerd. "Try it with a little more slang next time, BMB. You can't put humor on a spreadsheet."

John shrugged. "Yeah, well, whatever. I got the info on that New York City case. Not much there. The killer targeted women in their twenties. He got four that they know of. Maybe more, because he targeted working girls, usually ones that operated solo. That triangle-circle symbol was at each crime scene. Seems he liked to eat their fingers."

"Delightful," Pookie said. "What was his name?"

"They never found out who he was," John said. "Media called him the Ladyfinger Killer."

"Cute."

"Very. Anyway, when they found the fourth body, they also found the killer. He was just as dead as his victim."

"How did he die?"

"Asphyxiated. *His* fingers had been cut off, and he choked on them."

Poetic justice. "So we have the symbols clearly associated with a serial killer in New York. Anywhere else?"

"That's it," John said. "No other cases before or since. Now, here's the sneaky-spy part." He leaned closer. "Remember how I told you it looked like the files that included those symbols had been accidentally erased from the SFPD system?"

Pookie nodded.

"They weren't. Accidentally, I mean."

"Someone deleted info on purpose? You're sure?"

"Yeah. It was really methodical."

That was a game-changer. The symbols had been *intentionally* removed from the system. It seemed Bryan's strange dreams were a part of something much bigger.

"Impressive, BMB," Pookie said. "But I'm guessing you don't know who did the deleting, or you would have told me already."

John nodded. "Unfortunately, you're right. I can't tell who did it. What little info I have came from old indexes, and those didn't log user names."

"What's an index?"

"It's like a computer map that points to different locations on storage drives. Sometimes if you delete the files, the *pointers* to those files remain, and those pointers have certain information."

"Okay, so why didn't they also delete the pointers?"

John smiled and raised his eyebrows. "Because they didn't know the pointers were there. Whoever deleted the files has high-level access, but they don't know shit about computers. The fact that the index files remain means they didn't even talk to the IT guys about it, and they sure as hell didn't hire some hacker. A hacker would have wiped out everything."

"So it's not a programmer," Pookie said. "A cop did this?"

"At least someone working in the department, yeah."

Pookie thought back to the meeting in Zou's office, to the way Zou, Robertson and Sharrow had stared at the symbol pictures.

"You mentioned high-level access," Pookie said. "How many people in the department have that kind of access?"

John thought about that for a second. "I'm not sure. I know a lot about the system, but I'm just a mid-level user. People like me wouldn't have the access privileges. We can count out the IT guys, they would have done it right. So between administrators, their support staff . . . I'd guess thirty or forty."

A waitress brought menus. Pookie ordered coffee. John just asked for water.

The waitress walked away. Pookie grabbed a handful of sugar packets from a little bin at the back of the table and started stacking them into little piles. He couldn't exactly investigate thirty or forty cops. John's work gave him some great info, but nothing he could act on.

"What about the Oscar Woody crime-scene photos?" Pookie said. "Sammy Berzon took about a hundred shots of those symbols. Those are still in the system, right?"

John shook his head. "Not anymore. They were deleted shortly after they were entered. I saw links to them in the index files, but the actual images are gone."

Pookie flashed back to that blue tarp at the Father Paul Maloney scene, to Verde being in such a hurry to get Pookie and Bryan off that roof. Had that tarp been covering another blood symbol? Baldwin Metz had been there, the first time anyone had seen him outside of the morgue in going on five years. Then Metz had a heart attack. He wasn't available when Oscar died. Maybe that was the connection — Metz hadn't been there to run things, to stop Sammy and Jimmy from processing the Oscar Woody scene. Sammy and Jimmy had followed protocol and entered the photos of the symbols into the system. Then someone found out about the photos and deleted them.

But Zou had seen those photos. So had Sean Robertson and Captain Sharrow. Zou would have also seen the photos from the Maloney murder. If there *had* been a blood symbol under that tarp, than Zou *knew* the two cases were related.

She'd have known there was a possible serial killer out there. Known, and taken her two best guys off the case. She should have already *formed a task force* and moved on to *assigning more resources.* Instead, she'd given it all to Rich Verde.

"Don't look so glum, chum," John said. "I also brought you some good news."

"You can make my penis grow two inches in a week or less?"

John laughed, a soundless thing that made his bony shoulders bob up and down. "Stop believing your spam emails. Remember that local request for information on the symbols, the one that was twenty-nine years old? In the archives I found these old database printouts. They were all in binders, the kind of thing that's been sitting around forgotten long enough that no one knows if they should throw them out or not, you know? I spent about twelve hours in a truly Herculean effort of page-by-page data hunting, and I found the name and address of the guy who made that request. He's still alive, working out of the same place he was then. He's a fortune-teller in North Beach."

A name and an address. Goddamn. An actual lead.

"John, that's amazing," Pookie said. "You still got it, brother."

John's smile faded. He looked out the window onto Mason Street. "Still got it? I can barely leave my apartment, Pooks. I almost had a panic attack coming here to see you. I mean . . . it's still *dark* out, you know?"

Pookie didn't know. He could only imagine what it felt like to go from being a cop on the streets to — for lack of a better word — to *cowering* behind a desk and not being able to do anything to change it.

"You do what you can," Pookie said. He instantly felt like a dick for trying to put any kind of positive spin on it.

John kept staring out the window. No amount of words was going to help.

"Let's eat," Pookie said. "Had the chocolate-chip pancakes here? I swear they are made of crack dipped in gold."

"Aren't you and the Terminator going to go talk to the fortune-teller?"

"Priorities," Pookie said. "Without coal, the choo-choo train just sits on the tracks. And I doubt a fortune-teller is up at six A.M. What's this guy's name, anyway?"

"The name on the FOI was Thomas Reed, but he goes by a different name for his fortune-telling crap."

"Which is?"

"Mister Biz-Nass."

"Interesting," Pookie said. "Come on, order something. Hey, is it racist if I suggest you get the fried chicken and waffles?"

"Incredibly racist," John said. "And it sounds delicious. I'll get that."

They ordered. Pookie tore open one of his sugar-packet piles and dumped the contents into his coffee.

"One more thing, Mister Burns. Considering the deleted files, I think it goes without saying, but—"

"Keep this to myself?"

Pookie nodded. "I think things could get dangerous."

John shrank in on himself a little, his head again lowering as his shoulders again rose up. "I'm not stupid. We're digging up what someone wants to keep buried. If they find out, they might try to bury us, too. I know the risks. I might not be your partner anymore, but I still have your back."

Pookie wished he could go back in time, to six years ago, to that night in the Tenderloin when he'd had the drop on Blake Johansson. Pookie could have taken Johansson out, but he'd hesitated. Because of that hesitation, John Smith wound up with a bullet in his belly, a bullet that took a great cop off the streets.

"Order up, BMB," Pookie said. "Breakfast is on me."

Like Father, Like Son

Bryan sliced into the second kielbasa link. A little jet of fat shot out and landed on the back of his thumb. It was hot, but not enough to burn. He grabbed a slice of rye bread, dabbed up the fat with it and shoved it into his mouth.

"Glad to see your manners haven't changed much, Son."

Bryan smiled despite a mouth full of food. Considering his dad had a bottle of Bud Light in one hand, a Marlboro in the other, and was sitting at the table in a threadbare T-shirt, white boxers and black socks, he wasn't exactly the poster boy for social protocol.

Bryan didn't care that his throbbing body and sour stomach told him this meal was coming up later. The food tasted amazing. It tasted like *home*. He scooped up a forkful of sauerkraut. "Dad, when you write your book on etiquette? I'll be first in line to buy it."

His dad laughed. *That* was what Bryan needed, some normalcy — Mike Clauser in a T-shirt and boxers, drinking beer and feeding Bryan kielbasa and sauerkraut at 7:00 A.M. because that was the only thing Mike knew how to cook. When Bryan had been a little kid, he'd sat with his father at this same chipped Formica table. Breakfast with his dad was a giant step away from the insanity of psycho dreams, burning kids and dealing with butchered bodies.

"So, my boy, want to tell me what's going on? You're wound up pretty tight. I know the job is hard and all, but . . . well . . . you kind of look like shit. You feeling okay?"

"Been a little sick," Bryan said. He couldn't tell his father any of it. Mike wasn't a cop and he just wouldn't understand. "And some stuff at work is getting to me, stuff I don't really want to talk about."

Another kielbasa quarter went under the knife and into his mouth.

"Work," Mike said. "Sure it's not girl troubles?"

Oh, man, were they going to go over this for the umpteenth time? "Leave it alone, Dad."

"When are you bringing Robin over for dinner again? I'll order Chinese."

"You know damn well I moved out of her place."

Mike Clauser waved the Marlboro-holding hand in front of him as if his son had just cut a nasty fart. "Son, I love you to death, but no way you can do better than that girl."

"Gee, thanks for the compliment."

"You're welcome."

"What am I supposed to do? She told me to move out."

"Why? Did you cheat on her?"

Bryan tossed his fork and knife onto the plate. He wasn't going to talk about this, either. Why had she told him to move out? Because she'd wanted to hear the words *I love you, Robin,* and Bryan hadn't been able to say them.

"Son, I grew up with your mother. I asked her out in grade school and she said no. I asked her out in junior high and she said no. I asked her out in high school and she said no. That's when I started calling her Stubborn Starla Hutchon." Mike jabbed out his cigarette in an overfull ashtray, then slid his hand under his shirt to scratch his hairy belly. "I bet she turned me down ten times, at least, but I didn't care. I asked her to our senior prom, and she said yes. The rest is history."

Bryan nodded at his father's gut. "How could she possibly resist the physical specimen I see before me?"

Mike laughed. "Exactly!" he said, then lit another smoke. "Just remember, Son, women are basically retarded. It's not their fault. It's genetic. They have no idea what they want when Madison Avenue spins their little heads around."

"A more rousing endorsement of women's rights I've never heard."

"What can I say? You can listen to Doctor Phil or those stupid broads that tell women to *be strong* and *be independent* and all that crap, or you can listen to a man who's been happily married for forty years."

"*Thirty,* Dad. Mom's been gone ten years now."

Mike waved away another imaginary fart, then pointed to his chest. "I'm still married right here. She loved me like nobody's business. I know you're a skeptic, or whatever you Godless heathens call yourselves these days, but when I kick off and leave this splendor behind, I know I'll be with her. Someday you will, too — she loved you so much."

When Mike talked about his wife, that ever-present light in his eyes faded, dulled. It was hard to see him so sad. Her death had left a deep hole in the man.

"I miss her too, Dad."

Mike stared off for a few moments, then the shit-eating grin returned. "Robin reminds me of your mother. She's got that spark, one of those broads that laughs before she stops to think about if she *should* laugh or not, you know?"

Troubles with his love life weren't high on Bryan's current list of priorities. The more he avoided Robin, the better. He felt like he was already dooming Pookie, somehow — he didn't need to spread his poison to her.

"I know, Dad, Robin is great. But let it go. It's over."

"So what now? You going to go find someone else?"

Bryan sagged back in his chair. He wasn't going to find someone else, because he didn't *want* to find someone else. If it couldn't work with Robin, it wasn't going to work with anyone.

Mike leaned across the table. For just a second, Bryan had a flashback to the look his dad gave him back in the day, when Bryan came home from yet another fistfight.

"You're not *hearing* me, Son. So she booted your ass to the curb. Get over it. Forget your pride. You only have so many days to spend with a woman like your Robin or my Starla, and no matter how many days you get, they aren't enough. So you're going to promise me, right now, that you'll start up with Robin again."

"Dad, I'm a grown—"

Mike slapped the table, making Bryan jump.

"Don't *Dad* me, boy. You're too focused on your work, and what horrible work it is. You need something else in your life before this crap eats you alive. You promise me, *now.*"

The look on his father's face made it clear they'd talk about this, and nothing else, until Bryan conceded.

Bryan was dealing with a probable serial killer, psychic dreams of murder that made his dick hard, strange symbols drawn in human blood, and it was all he could do to coax his agony-filled body through the day — yet despite these things, he still had room to feel *guilty* because his dad was mad at him?

Maybe thirty-five years old wasn't really all that far from thirteen.

"Okay, Dad. I'll talk to her."

Mike's face relaxed. He nodded. "Fine. Now that I've won that battle, you want to tell me what's going on at work? No offense, Son, but I know twenty-four-hour hookers that look like they get more beauty rest than you."

Bryan picked up his fork. He stabbed a piece of kielbasa, then absently moved it around the plate in a slow circle.

"Bryan, I know I'm not a cop, but I can still listen."

His father had always been able to read his mind a little bit. It was spooky.

"The stuff I'm seeing now, it's . . ." Bryan's voice trailed off. Maybe he couldn't tell his dad everything, at least not yet, but it would feel good to share some of this burden. "It's pretty bad. I kind of have some . . . thoughts."

"What kind of thoughts?"

Bryan stopped his kielbasa circle, then reversed it the other way. "Like that there are certain people who deserve to die."

"There are," Mike said. "Fuckin-A right there are. This about that gangbanger you killed in the restaurant? Pookie called me about that, you know."

"You don't say."

"Don't go busting his chops about it," Mike said. "If your partner didn't call me once a week, I wouldn't have any idea what was going on in your life. It's not like it would hurt you to pick up the phone once in a while."

"Who is this little Jewish grandmother before me and where did she hide my manly-man father?"

"Fuck you," Mike said. "Know how your mother is gone forever? I'm not that far behind her. You don't stop by enough."

There was no smart-ass answer for that. Bryan was lucky enough to have his father in the same city, yet he stopped by Mike's place maybe twice a month at most.

"Sorry," Bryan said. "I'll do better at that. But it's not about that gangster in the restaurant. This is something . . . something else."

"Son, just remember that you're a Clauser. I can't pretend I know what it's like to do what you do for a living. But at the end of the day, you're a good man. You walk a line so that fat slobs like me can live in all this splendor. You have to weigh these bad thoughts against all the good that you do. Understand?"

His father had no idea what he was talking about. And yet, in a misguided way, the words made sense.

"Yeah, Dad. I understand. Look, I don't want to talk about it anymore. Do you mind if we just talk about the 'Niners?"

Mike Clauser leaned back in his chair, tilted his head back and wrinkled his face like someone had not only farted this time but also crammed a turd nugget up his left nostril.

"The 'Niners? Good God, Son, don't get me started!"

The next thirty minutes rolled by without one thought of bodies, dreams, symbols or death as Mike Clauser effortlessly solved all of the

San Francisco 49ers' problems and guided them to Super Bowl glory the following season.

Goddamn Pookie. He'd known just what Bryan needed. Most of the time it sucked having a partner who thought he knew everything. But sometimes? Sometimes, it was fantastic.

obin Hudson had awoken that morning after a whopping three hours of sleep, walked Emma next door for a play-day with Big Max and his pit bull, Billy, grabbed a large coffee from Royal Ground (no sugar, a single girl has to watch her waist), pounded it like a sorority girl in a drinking contest, then rode her motorcycle into work.

When she arrived, work was waiting for her in the form of a list of five names up on the green chalkboard. Four *NC*s, and one question mark for *Parlar, J.*

She walked to the body locker, opened the door and pulled out the sliding tray that held Parlar's body. A question mark didn't seem necessary — not much of a chance this was due to natural causes: broken bones and contusions; multiple lacerations on his abdomen; and about 20 percent of the body had been burned, from the abdomen up to the chest and face.

The worst of the burns were on his face and hands, where there had been no clothes to protect him from the heat. Blisters covered his palms and the underside of his fingers — he'd had his hands up in a defensive position when the flames hit. An explosion or fireball of some sort, obviously. His hair was more burned off on the left side of his head than the right — he'd instinctively turned away when it happened.

Robin read the crime-scene investigator's preliminary report. Bryan and Pookie had been first on the scene again? They'd found a murdered teenage boy for the second morning in a row. Weird. The report said that *Parlar, J.*, had not only been stabbed three times and badly burned, he'd also suffered a four-story fall onto a van.

"Sorry, Jay," she said to the corpse. "Rough way to go."

Robin thought back to Pookie's call last night, asking if Bryan was capable of real violence.

She looked at the body.

What, exactly, was Pookie asking? If Bryan could do something like this?

No. That was impossible. Clearly, Pookie was talking about something else altogether.

Robin pushed the tray back in, shut the door, then walked to her computer. The karyotype results from Oscar Woody's killer were waiting for her.

The spectral karyotype showed four rows of fuzzy, paired lines, each set a different neon color. The image represented the twenty-three paired chromosomes of the human genome. The last pair, the one that determined sex, was usually an XX for female or an XY for male.

Oscar Woody's killer had an X, all right, but its partner chromosome didn't look like an X *or* a Y.

"What the hell?"

She had never seen anything like it. It didn't make any sense. Was it a bad test? No, the rest of the karyotype looked perfectly normal.

It wasn't Klinefelter's syndrome; this was something else altogether.

The information would help Rich Verde and Bobby Pigeon's investigation. But Verde had basically told her *not* to run the test, and Chief Zou also didn't seem that interested in getting to the truth.

Maybe Rich wasn't interested, but she knew someone who would be.

Robin pulled out her cell phone and dialed.

Too Cool for School

Rex Deprovdechuk walked down the hallways of Galileo High. Not along the sides, not slinking around the edges the way he'd used to with his head hung low, hoping no one would see, wishing he were invisible.

No, not anymore.

Rex walked down the *middle* of the hall.

He'd heard it on the news that morning. Jay Parlar was dead. Alex Panos and Issac weren't in school. Maybe they knew what Rex could do. Maybe they would just stay away.

Or, maybe Rex would *find* them.

He walked with his head high, staring at everyone who looked his way, *daring* them to make eye contact. These people had all stared at him, talked about him in whispers as he walked by, thought they were so much better than him. They despised him. They treated him like garbage.

But now Rex had friends.

He didn't know who they were, not yet, but they did what he wanted them to do. They made his pictures come true. They killed his enemies. They gave Rex Deprovdechuk control over life and death.

They gave Rex the power of a god.

So he walked down the *middle* of the hall. People didn't exactly get out of his way, but they weren't knocking him around, either. Did all the other kids know? Did they know that Rex Deprovdechuk — Little Rex, *Stinky Rex* — could wish them dead? Did they know that if he drew their picture, they were doomed?

He didn't belong here anymore. He had *never* belonged here. Fuck school.

Rex headed for the front doors. He'd been here for two hours already, and that was plenty.

Tonight, maybe he'd draw some more people.

Maybe he'd draw Roberta.

Rex was done being a victim. Those days were over. No one was going to hurt him, not ever again.

The Rulebook

Robin Hudson checked her appearance in the body refrigerator's steel door, behind which lay the corpse of Oscar Woody.

The reflection wasn't flattering.

Big Max was right — she did have circles under her eyes. She wasn't in her twenties anymore; age and the job's long hours were catching up with her.

She ran a hand through her black hair, untangled it as best she could manage. She hadn't talked to Bryan in six months, and this was how he'd see her?

But why should she care how she looked for him? He'd moved out and hadn't even called her once since. Two years they had shared her apartment. They'd dated six months before that. Two and a half *years* together. She hadn't nagged him about getting married, even though she would have accepted his proposal without thinking twice. All she'd wanted was to hear the words *I love you.*

But he hadn't said it. In all that time together, he'd never said it once.

The two-year anniversary of his moving in with her triggered some kind of realization that she needed to hear him say it. She couldn't think about anything else. He loved her, she knew it, he just needed a little *push* was all, something to make him look deep inside and realize what they had together. She'd made it simple for him — if he couldn't *say* he loved her, then he wasn't *in* love with her, and he had to go.

But even with that ultimatum, he still hadn't said the words. Only at the end did she realize she'd projected her desires onto him. She wished she could forget that final fight. How she had screamed, the things she had said, and he just stood there, calm, quiet, barely saying a word as she raged at him. Cold-eyed Bryan. *The Terminator.* He hadn't loved her. Hell, maybe he wasn't capable of love.

She'd told him to leave and he had. Unlike in the movies, he hadn't come back.

He was probably out fucking anything that moved. She should be doing the same, but she just didn't want to. Six months later, she still wanted only him. The way he could make her feel — no one else had ever been able to do that to her. She was afraid that no one else ever could.

The morgue door opened. Bryan Clauser and Pookie Chang came through.

"Hey, Robin," Pookie said. "Damn, girl, you look *sexy*."

"Right. I've had about four hours of sleep, but flattery will get you everywhere."

Pookie grinned. "Come on, if I really wanted to get in your pants, I'd do something like pick you up those oatmeal biscuits from Bow Wow Meow that Emma likes so much."

"Yeah, that would probably work."

Pookie reached into his pocket and pulled out a zippered baggie filled with thick biscuits. "*Cha-ka-pow!* There you go, toots, now lose the bra."

She laughed and took the bag. "What, you carry around my dog's favorite treat?"

He shrugged. "Knew I'd see you sooner or later. They were in the car."

"Pookie, how the hell do you remember this stuff?"

He pointed to his head. "There's a lot of useless information floating around in here."

"Well, I thank you, and so does Emma." She put the bag in her pocket.

Robin turned to look at her former lover. "Bryan."

He nodded once. "Robin."

That was it. No *God it's good to see you*, or *I hope you've been well*, just a simple *Robin*. Something on his forehead caught her eye.

"Stitches? What happened?"

"I fell in the shower," Bryan said.

He needed to trim that beard of his, and he looked so tired. Not so much the bags under his eyes as a pallor to his skin, an expression that seemed . . . lost. What was he going through?

There was something about Bryan she'd never been able to define, never been able to ignore, and despite his sickly appearance, that something still burned hot. Her attraction to him hadn't dulled in the least.

She stared at him. He stared right back with those beautiful, distant green eyes.

"Guys," Pookie said, "I know y'all have a bit of backstory to work out, but can we lay off the wistful gazing? This ain't a Joan Wilder novel, if you dig what I'm saying."

Robin looked away from Bryan and back to Pookie. Pookie smiled apologetically, but he was right — this wasn't the time to play *who hurts more* with her ex.

"Okay," she said. "So I know I have to give all this info to Rich and Bobby, but it's weird . . . it seems like Rich isn't really that interested in the case. Bobby is, I think, but Rich calls the shots. What I discovered is kind of a big deal. Since you guys found both bodies, I figured you might have a vested interest. But can you keep this quiet? Chief Zou asked me not to talk about the case, to anyone — if she finds out I did, it could jeopardize my candidacy for the chief ME position."

Both men nodded. Pookie mimed turning a lock in his lips and throwing the key behind him. Maybe Bryan wasn't the best boyfriend in the world, but he never went back on his word and neither did the incorrigible Mr. Chang.

Robin led them to her desk and called up the karyotype test results on her computer.

"We isolated samples from Oscar Woody's body," she said. "I'm ninety-nine percent confident that all of the samples come from a single person, meaning Oscar had just one killer. That killer's DNA exhibited evidence of an extra X chromosome. Because of that, I ran another test assuming I would see XXY. Instead I found this."

She pointed to the bottom of the karyotype.

Bryan leaned in to look, so close that his chest touched her right shoulder. He felt warm.

Pookie leaned in over her left shoulder. "I recognize that Y-thingee from my science classes, but what is that next to it?"

Robin shrugged. "I'm calling it a *Zed chromosome*."

"What the hell is a *Zed*?"

"It's like a Z," Bryan said. "Only with higher taxes and with universal health care."

"Ah," Pookie said. "Canadian-speak."

They all stared at the strange result; a Y and something else, something significantly larger. An X chromosome did, indeed, look like an "X" — two lines crossed up high, pinched together like a twisted balloon animal. Naming the male sex chromosome "Y" was a bit of a stretch, as far as name-equals-appearance went: two short, fat chunks came together, with a tiny ball of material where they joined.

The new chromosome looked like a chain of three sausage links. Sharp bends at the two joints made it *sort of* look like a Zed — or maybe that was just the first thing that popped into Robin's mind after years of looking at Xs and Ys.

"This is totally unheard of," she said. "There's a Z chromosome in birds and some insects, but in those animals the chromosome is a little blob — it doesn't actually *look* like the letter Z. So I'm calling this *Zed* to differentiate. This is the genetic code of Oscar Woody's killer. It isn't a fluke — this is a legitimate chromosomal aberration."

Pookie stood straight and raised his hand. "Teacher, which weighs more, a *fluke* or an *aberration*? Or in other words, *what*?"

"I mean this isn't random genetic damage," Robin said. "It's in *every* cell. The killer was born this way."

Pookie crossed his arms. "Are you trying to tell us we're dealing with some kind of fleshy-headed mutant from Planet Six or something?"

"Maybe not that, but something strange," Robin said. "Come on, I've got something else to show you."

She led them back to the body refrigerator. She opened a door and rolled out the tray holding Oscar Woody. Robin gloved up, then pointed to the parallel grooves on Oscar's ravaged scapula. "This scoring appears to be from incisors spaced three-point-five inches apart. Average spacing for an adult man is one to just *two* inches, tops."

Pookie looked up. "But those marks aren't from a man. Jimmy and Sammy said a dog did it. There was dog fur all over the place."

And here it was, the moment where she actually had to say it. She wondered if it would sound as crazy out loud as it did in her head. "That fur wasn't *fur* — it was human hair. I've seen enough evidence that I'm convinced that there was no animal at all."

Pookie stared at her, then looked back to the body. "A dude did this?"

Robin breathed deep, then let it out in a puff. "Yeah, that's what I'm saying."

"It would have to be a seriously big dude, then," Pookie said. "Or a perp with a really wide mouth."

"Or both," Bryan said.

Pookie nodded. "Or both. Awesome. Not to insult your magnificent intellect, Bo-Bobbin, but I'm not buying this. You're saying the killer is big, with wide teeth, strong enough to tear off a guy's arm with his mouth, *and* that he's fucking furry?"

"Imagine that," Bryan said. "I mean, someone might describe that as werewolf-like, right?"

Pookie looked annoyed. "Big dudes can wear costumes, too, Bri-Bri."

Bryan shivered, then coughed hard. He sounded like hell. He cleared his throat, then hovered his hand above Oscar's scapula, using his thumb and forefinger to show the spacing of the parallel grooves. Bryan brought his hand up and held it in front of his own face — the space between the tip of his thumb and forefingers was as wide as his cheekbones.

"A costume that comes complete with big, killing teeth? Come on, Pooks."

Was Bryan arguing that a *werewolf* did this? Just how bad was his fever?

Pookie turned to Robin. "Are you *sure* those marks are caused by teeth? Could it have been some other kind of weapon?"

She nodded. "I suppose, but it would be a weapon designed to act just like a pair of jaws."

"There's a name for a weapon like that," Pookie said. "It's called *fake teeth*. Something that might come complete with a Hollywood-grade monster costume."

Bryan rolled his eyes and laughed. "You're really reaching, Pooks. And you can't put a costume on a chromosome. You made a joke that this was a fleshy-headed mutant, but based on what we've seen, maybe that's not a joke at all."

She knew both men well — Bryan prided himself on being rational. He didn't believe in monsters or the supernatural. The fact that they were arguing about this seemed completely out of character for him.

"Talk to me," Robin said. "What did you guys see?"

"Nothing," they said simultaneously.

So, they weren't going to confide in her? Just like Rich Verde, maybe they thought her job was to examine bodies, not solve crimes. She wondered if this secret information had anything to do with Bryan's wretched appearance.

Robin slid Oscar back into the rack and closed the door. She walked back to her desk. Bryan and Pookie walked with her.

"Technically, Pookie is right," she said. "By definition, we're looking at a mutation. The perp could have other physical deformities as well. There's no way of knowing."

She slid into her chair. They stood at her sides, again looking at the strange image of a new chromosome.

"Hey, Robin," Bryan said. "Why does the Zed chromosome have two hubcap doohickeys, while the Y and X chromosomes only have one?"

He put a finger on one of the Zed's two joints.

"Hubcap doohickey?" she said. "Oh, that's a centromere. But a chromosome can't have two cent—"

She suddenly saw what Bryan had seen.

"Jesus," she said. "How did I miss that?" Bryan had no scientific training, but he was an excellent observer. Far better than she was, apparently.

"Miss what?" Pookie said. "Let's say the only reason I got an A in biology was because I banged the teacher. Fill me in, Bo-Bobbin."

"Chromosomes are made up of two paired columns of densely coiled

DNA," she said. "Each column is called a *chromatid* and represents the copy of the chromosome from one parent. The *centromere* is where the two lines meet, where they fuse together."

Pookie touched the screen, his fingertip on center of the Y chromsome.

"So this spot," he said. "Or the crossing point of the X. That's a centromere?"

She nodded. "It is. Unless a cell is dividing, and the ones I tested were not, it has just *one* centromere. The Zed has *two*. I've never seen anything like this. Neither has anyone else. Ever."

They fell quiet. Together, they stared at the screen.

"Dibs," Pookie said finally. "If it's a new species, I get to name it."

Robin laughed. "Doesn't work that way, Pooks."

"Too late," he said. "I already named it *fuckifino whathehellthatis*."

Bryan nodded. "That's a good name."

Pookie's cell phone buzzed. He pulled it out and checked the caller ID. "It's Chief Zou," he said. "Be right back." He answered his phone as he walked out of the building, leaving Robin alone with Bryan.

Without Pookie in the room, things felt suddenly awkward. She'd hated Bryan for months, but now that he was here, that hate was nowhere to be found.

"So," she said. "How you been?"

"Busy. The Ablamowicz case and all. And then those guys tried to kill Frank Lanza."

Yes, the shooting. Bryan had taken yet another life. She could have been there for him, helped him deal with it. But, apparently, he didn't need her help. More accurately, he just didn't need *her*.

"Yeah, Ablamowicz," she said. "That case has been going on for, what, two weeks? How have you been for the past six *months*, Bryan?"

He shrugged and looked away. "You know. Lots of corpses. Never a dull moment in Homicide."

He was going to play it like that? Well, she wasn't going to let him off that easy. "Bryan, why haven't you called?"

He stared at her again. She wanted to see some emotion in those eyes — pain, want, need, shame — but he looked as blank as ever.

"You told me to move out," he said. "You told me not to call you. You were very specific."

"Okay, but six months? You could have at least called to see how I was doing."

"And your phone is broken? I'm not sure where in the rulebook it says that phones only work when men use them."

She bit the inside of her lip — she would not cry. She *would not.* "You're right. I did tell you not to call."

Bryan shrugged. "It is what it is. Believe it or not, I'm happy to see you again." He looked down, then spoke quietly: "I missed you."

It hurt to hear that. He could have called her a stupid bitch and it would have hurt less. How could he miss someone he didn't love? His words were meant to be nice, but they landed like a boot in the stomach — a boot she couldn't get enough of.

"Tell me again," she said.

He looked up and forced a smile. "Look, I'm happy to see you, but I'm . . . I'm going through a lot of heavy shit right now. Can we just keep things professional?"

His face remained an expressionless shell. Bryan was right — it was what it was. Sometimes things just weren't meant to be, no matter how bad you wanted them.

She nodded. "Sure, professional. Can I at least ask how your dad is?"

"He's fine," Bryan said. "Saw him this morning. Oddly enough, he made me promise to start up with you again."

"And do you always keep your promises?"

"Professional, Robin."

"Right, sorry," she said. She bit the inside of her lip again. "If I come up with anything else, should I call Pookie . . . or you?"

His eyes narrowed, just for a second. The way his skin crinkled when he did that, so goddamn sexy. Was that a look of annoyance, or one of . . . *hurt?* Well-well-well, maybe there *was* some emotion in that cyborg body after all.

"You can call me," he said.

Pookie came back in, wide-eyed and looking upset.

"You okay?" Bryan asked.

"I'm going to expand my investment with the makers of Depends," Pookie said. "I hope they have adult undergarments for people with more than one sphincter, because Zou just ripped me a new asshole. Bri-Bri, we got to get out of here, fast. Verde told Zou we interviewed Tiffany Hine. Zou feels like we ignored her order to stay out of the case."

"But we found a body," Bryan said. "What are we supposed to do, step over it on the way to getting donuts and coffee?"

Pookie nodded. "I guess. She knows we were told Verde was on the way, but we kept at it anyway and that pisses her off. If she finds out we're here to look at Oscar, she'll bronze our balls and put them on her desk next to the picture of her family."

Robin didn't know much about internal police politics, but there had to be much more to the story. Would Zou really be *that* opposed to Bryan and Pookie being involved in this case?

Bryan ground his teeth. Frustration was an emotion he didn't bother to hide. "So what now?" he said. "Do we turn the fortune-teller lead over to Verde?"

"*Hell* no," Pookie said. "In fact, I just called Mister Biz-Nass and he's expecting us in twenty minutes. Listen, Robin, we gots to go. Mum's the word on this visit, right?"

"Of course," Robin said. "Like I said earlier, I shouldn't have told you anything."

Pookie walked out. Bryan looked at Robin for a long moment, then followed his partner. Robin stared after him, already trying to read meaning into his words, and already hating herself for doing it.

Mr. Biz-Nass

North Beach, San Francisco's "Little Italy," sits right next to China-town. As a little boy, Bryan had often walked through both neighbor-hoods with his father. The change from one to the next is so abrupt, so distinct, Bryan thought that gates manned by international border guards wouldn't have seemed the least out of place. One minute you're walking through dense throngs of Chinese people picking through the fruit- and vegetable-packed crates outside tiny grocery stores, all signs and conver-sation in Asian languages, the next minute you're looking at calm side-walks with café tables full of people drinking espresso, old dudes letting out snippets of conversation in Italian and every lamppost ringed with stripes of green, white and red.

North Beach primarily supports two types of street-level businesses: an endless supply of food represented by restaurants, bakeries, butchers and candy shops, and then the kitsch, represented by stores full of souve-nir crap, overpriced clothing and even more overpriced art. Above those numerous food and kitsch shops sits the second layer of North Beach, represented by faded signs in the windows that advertise importers, ex-porters, olive oil merchants, tailors and more.

Mr. Biz-Nass had one of those second-story stores, just a flight up from Stella Pastry & Café. His sign wasn't faded — a blue neon eye set in a red neon hand with the white neon words *FORTUNE TELLER* curving beneath.

"Convenient," Pookie said. "Once we're done talking to this guy, we come downstairs for some Sacripantina cake."

"The choo-choo needs gas?"

"The metaphor is *coal*, actually," Pookie said. He adjusted the four overstuffed manila folders under his arm just before their contents spilled onto the sidewalk. "Brains require chemicals, like potassium and sodium. Sugar is also a chemical, Bryan, ergo, my brain needs sugar. It's what they call *science*."

"The guy who believes in the Invisible Sky Daddy is quoting science?"

"Yep," Pookie said. "And he's about to have a nice chitchat with a black-magic pagan. Confession will be a bitch this week. By the way, I didn't tell Mister Biz-Nass we were cops."

Bryan nodded. "Always good to surprise 'em a little."

"Far as I'm concerned, this guy is a suspect," Pookie said. "But I don't want to move too fast. He's the only person of interest we have."

Bryan wasn't going to get excited about this, not yet. The fortune-telling Thomas Reed, a.k.a. *Mr. Biz-Nass*, had only been looking for info on the symbols. That meant he might have some connection to the case, or, more likely, he'd just seen the symbols somewhere and wanted to know more. Still, people didn't make requests to the SFPD and to the city out of pure curiosity.

"Pooks, what kind of a name is Biz-Nass, anyway?"

"Maybe he's like Elvis," Pookie said. "As in, *taking care of business.* Ready to get some answers?"

Bryan was. He'd take just about *any* answer at this point. He had a small headache, and that was the least of his pains. His rebellious body tried to drag him down, but he refused to give in. At least for now, he could muscle through and ignore the fact that it hurt to move, even hurt to *breathe.*

They entered the ground-floor door, then climbed the stairs. The smell of incense from above mixed with the smell of pastries from below. No question which upstairs door belonged to Mr. Biz-Nass — it was bright red, with a blue eye icon painted on it. They walked in.

Inside was a man dressed in red robes with blue trim, and a blue turban decorated with glass rubies. He had to be sixty; if his face was any benchmark, every one of those sixty years was hard. He sat in a red, thronelike chair. In front of his chair, a blue crystal ball rested on a table draped with a red velvet cloth. Two cheap, blue plastic chairs sat on the other side of the table.

His outfit was something one might find on a 1960s Hollywood prince of India, but his face looked anything but royal: thrice-broken nose, pallid, wrinkled skin and a left eyelid half hanging over his iris in a perpetual stop-action wink.

The man waved them in. In his left fist he held a small, cylindrical object. He pressed the object to his throat.

WELCOME, he said in a mechanical voice. PLEASE COME IN.

Bryan and Pookie stopped, stared.

DON'T MIND MY HANDICAPS. I AM VOCALLY ASSISTED.

"A voice box," Pookie said. "A fortune-teller with a voice box."

"Handicaps?" Bryan said. "Plural?"

I ALSO HAVE A MILD CASE OF COPROLALIA.

Bryan and Pookie exchanged a look.

TOURETTE'S SYNDROME.

"Of course," Pookie said. "A fortune-teller with a voice box and Tourette's."

IT'S ON MY FACEBOOK PAGE. DO SOME RESEARCH NEXT TIME *SHITTY-BALLS! FUCKLESNIFF!* DON'T MIND MY CURSING, IT IS JUST MY HANDICAP. COME AND SIT.

Bryan and Pookie sat on the blue plastic chairs.

WHICH ONE OF YOU IS POOKIE?

Pookie raised his hand. "That's me."

Mr. Biz-Nass leaned forward and circled his right hand over the blue glass ball. He stared into it, scowling like he saw the fires of hell inside. If Bryan hadn't already been so taken aback by the guy's handicaps, he would have laughed at the overly dramatic act.

TELL ME WHAT YOU WANT TO KNOW. I AM IN COMMUNICATION WITH THE *PRICKERDICKER* SPIRITS.

"We're cops," Pookie said. "We need to ask you some questions about a case."

Bryan held out his badge. Pookie did the same.

The hand stopped in midwave. Mr. Biz-Nass looked up without moving his head, eyes peeking out from beneath gray-speckled brows. The scowl vanished, replaced by a wide-eyed *oh shit* expression.

COPS?

"Take it easy," Pookie said. "We just want to ask you some questions."

Biz-Nass looked at them both, eyes flicking back and forth. He seemed to be waiting for something. When whatever that was didn't come, he spoke again.

HHMMMMM QUESTIONS ABOUT WHAT?

"Twenty-nine years ago, you submitted a request to the SFPD about information on some symbols."

The man's eyes widened in fear.

MMMMM I DON'T WANT ANY TROUBLE. DON'T ROUGH ME UP.

Bryan wondered why the guy was so nervous. What kind of an operation was he running up here? Besides the obvious scam of pretending to know the future in order to bilk the gullible out of their money, of course.

"It's no big deal," Pookie said. "We're working on a case. We need some help, we're not here to hassle you."

The eyes flicked back and forth again. YOU JUST WANT TO KNOW WHY I MADE THE REQUEST? THAT'S IT?

Pookie nodded. Biz-Nass seemed to relax, just a little. His expression grew hopeful.

I WAS WORKING ON A BOOK.

"Nice," Pookie said. "An author. A fortune-telling author with Tourette's and a voice box. What's the name of your book?"

I DIDN'T FINISH IT. WHAT DO YOU WANT?

Pookie opened one of his manila folders. He took out the photos of the bloody symbols and gently slid them across the table.

Mr. Biz-Nass looked at them. His eyes grew wide. The guy recognized those symbols, and they scared the hell out of him.

COCKITYTWAT COCKITYTWAT COCKITYTWAT.

"Take a breath, Biz," Pookie said. "Easy, man, just take a breath."

Mr. Biz-Nass dropped his voice box. It rolled across the red velvet surface. He put both hands palms down on the table, then took three long, slow, deep breaths. That seemed to calm him. His face relaxed. He looked at Pookie, then at Bryan, like he was waiting for them to do something.

When they did nothing, Biz-Nass eased back in his throne. He reached out a shaking hand, picked up the voice box off the table and held it to his throat.

NEVER SEEN THOSE BEFORE.

Bryan laughed. "Of course not. That's why you almost shit yourself. Or is incontinence another one of your handicaps? A little late to pretend you don't know what those are."

Mr. Biz-Nass glared at him.

Was the man scared of the symbols, or scared that cops knew about the symbols and had come a-calling? Biz-Nass was a fortune-teller, a psychic . . . could he have projected the dreams into Bryan's head?

Bryan instantly wanted to punch himself for thinking such ridiculous thoughts. Fortune-tellers were scam artists, nothing more. Still, Mr. Biz-Nass knew something about the symbols. He had to have some answers.

Bryan leaned forward and rested his elbows on the table. "Come on, where have you seen these symbols?"

Biz-Nass looked back and forth between the two cops, seemed to size them up.

I DON'T KNOW *DICKER PRICKER* NOTHING.

Pookie reached into a folder and pulled out a picture of Oscar Woody's mutilated corpse. He slid the picture across the table.

Biz-Nass shook his head like he didn't want to believe the picture was real.

"People are dying," Pookie said. "We need to know what you know. If you don't want to talk here, we can take you downtown."

That concept seemed to scare Biz-Nass even worse than the pictures. He started to breathe rapidly, bordering on hyperventilating.

"Take it easy," Pookie said. "All you have to do is talk to us, and this stays right here."

The man gently rubbed his crooked nose. He looked up, that doubtful expression back in his eyes. DID YOU TELL YOUR PIG BOSSES YOU WERE COMING? DOES ANYONE KNOW YOU'RE HERE?

Bryan sat very still, as if the tiniest motion might spook the guy. Pookie seemed to be playing it perfectly.

"One other guy knows," Pookie said. "But that's it. He's not our boss, just a guy who looked up the symbols in our computer system. No report has been filed or anything like that. I take it you want this conversation to stay between us?"

NO ONE KNOWS MY NAME. *SHITTYBALLS! FUCKLESNIFF!*

Pookie crossed himself. "We promise."

The fortune-teller reached out his left fist. WORD IS BOND?

Pookie reached out, bumped fists. "Word is bond."

Mr. Biz-Nass nodded. Finally, he looked down at the photos.

TELL ME WHERE YOU FOUND THESE.

"Murder scenes," Pookie said. "Two teenage boys. Both in a gang called Boys Company. One died two nights ago, one before dawn this morning. Aside from your information request, we couldn't find these symbols anywhere in police records. Tell us what they are."

Biz-Nass looked up, shook his head.

Bryan felt his patience slipping away. He stood up. "Listen, asshole. You're about ten seconds from going from *person of interest* to my number-one suspect."

PRICKER DICKER FUCKER SUCKER.

"What did you say to me?"

"Bryan, relax," Pookie said. "It's a condition."

YES IT IS A CONDITION. I AM SORRY *DICKER PRICKER LICKER.*

"Bullshit," Bryan said. "This guy doesn't have a condition."

I'M DISABLED.

A hand on Bryan's arm. "Chill," Pookie said. "Let the man talk, okay?"

Bryan sat back down and crossed his arms over his chest.

THESE SYMBOLS ARE FOR MARIE'S CHILDREN. IT IS A CULT. *MMMM* YOU ARE COPS; YOU HAVE HEARD OF THEM.

Pookie shook his head. "I've been with the SFPD for ten years. I've never heard of Marie's Children."

Bryan hadn't heard of them, either. He remained quiet — Pookie was making progress.

Biz-Nass stared, as if he was waiting to be the butt of a punchline. He waited for a few seconds, then shrugged.

A WITCH NAMED MARIE AND HER SON, CALLED FIRSTBORN, ARRIVED IN SAN FRANCISCO DURING THE GOLD RUSH. THEY AND THEIR FOLLOWERS WERE SUPPOSEDLY RESPONSIBLE FOR MULTIPLE MURDERS IN THE CITY. SOME ACCOUNTS CLAIM THEY WERE CANNIBALS. *SHITTYBALLS! FUCKLE-SNIFF!* A GROUP CALLED THE SAVIORS ROUNDED UP DOZENS OF MARIE'S CHILDREN, *MMMMM* BURNED THEM AT THE STAKE IN 1873.

Bryan's bullshit detector went off big-time. "*Dozens* of people? Burned at the stake? Even that long ago, no way that happened and we've never heard about it."

PEOPLE DON'T WANT TO KNOW ABOUT THE BAD PARTS OF HISTORY. NOT SOMETHING YOU PUT ON THE TOURIST PAMPHLET, BUT COPS SHOULD KNOW.

"Why?" Pookie said. "Why should the cops know?"

BECAUSE MARIE'S CHILDREN HAVE BEEN KILLING EVER SINCE. QUIETLY FOR THE MOST PART, BUT THERE HAVE BEEN SOME HIGH-PROFILE SERIAL MURDERS. AND SOME *SHITTYBALLS!* RUMORS THEY DID ASSASSINATIONS FOR THE MOB.

Bryan closed his eyes and rubbed his temples. The minor headache had blossomed into something that threatened to put him down.

"I'm not buying it," he said. "How high-profile could they be if I've never heard of them?"

Biz-Nass stared at Bryan. YOU'VE HEARD OF THE GOLDEN GATE SLASHER?

Bryan and Pookie exchanged a glance. The Slasher was the city's biggest serial killer, a monster that had slaughtered children. He'd murdered more victims than better-known psychopaths like the Zodiac Killer, David Carpenter and Luis Aguilar.

Biz-Nass tapped the photos. THESE SYMBOLS WERE FOUND WHEN THEY CAUGHT THE GOLDEN GATE SLASHER.

"No way," Bryan said. "There's no way that's true and we never heard about it."

Biz-Nass stood and walked to his overflowing bookshelves. He pulled out a photo album, flipped through it, then put it back. He did the same twice more, then on the fourth volume he found what he was looking for. He walked back to the table and handed the open album to Bryan.

DICKER PRICKER FUCKER SUCKER READ THIS.

It was a newspaper clipping. The dateline was from thirty years ago. Even protected in the binder, the paper looked yellow, faded and old. To the right of the columns of text, a black-and-white photo showed a symbol drawn in the dirt. It was the circle and triangle symbol from Bryan's dreams, the same symbol they'd found at the scenes of two savage murders.

GOLDEN GATE SLASHER KILLED BY POLICE

A horrible mystery drew to a close early this morning when a man police identified as the Golden Gate Park Slasher was slain in the very park he terrorized for 10 months.

Police have not identified the man. Sources inside the force speculate that the killer's identity may never be known.

Inspector Francis Parkmeyer of the San Francisco police said that fingerprint checks had already placed the John Doe at the scene of all eight Golden Gate Park child murders that took place from Feb. 18 to the last victim on Nov. 27.

John Doe was found near a Bowie knife, a weapon police had long ago claimed was the instrument of death in all the murders. Preliminary reports indicate that distinguishing marks on the blade matched marks found on the victims' remains.

"I have no doubt that we've found the Golden Gate Slasher," Parkmeyer said. "The prints match, and so does the weapon."

The body was found at 5:15 a.m. this morning by a park maintenance crew. Ramon Johnson, a crew member, initially claimed that the presumed killer was stumbling through a grove of trees with an arrow sticking out of his back. After talking with police, Johnson said he had mistaken a stick for an arrow shaft.

Parkmeyer denied the presence of an arrow.

"It was before dawn and the witness's eyes played tricks on him," Parkmeyer said. "The John Doe committed suicide. This nightmare is over. We have our city back."

Pookie looked up from the article. "I don't get it. This is a multiple homicide, one of the biggest ever, and that symbol isn't common knowledge in the department? *Why?*"

Bryan looked to the corner of the clipping. The *San Francisco Chronicle*'s logo seemed darker than the other letters on the page, as if the paper's name itself was more resilient to the ravages of time.

He pointed to it. "Maybe the *Chronicle*'s archives will have more information."

Mr. Biz-Nass smiled. THAT'S A GOOD IDEA. LOOK IN THE ARCHIVES.

Bryan stared at the faded newsprint-photo of the symbol. There it was in black and white. It had been in a major metro newspaper, for one of the biggest cases ever, and yet that wasn't recorded in the SFPD system?

Black Mr. Burns had discovered deleted information, but this . . . this was another level entirely. Was someone protecting a serial killer? Protecting this Marie's Children cult? Or even both at the same time?

PARKMEYER LIED ABOUT THE ARROW. I TALKED TO RAMON JOHNSON. HE'S DEAD NOW *DICKER PRICKER* OF NATURAL CAUSES, BUT I TRACKED HIM DOWN AND INTERVIEWED HIM BEFORE HE DIED. HE SAID HE SAW AN ARROW IN THE KILLER'S BACK. HE SAID THE KILLER DREW THE SYMBOL IN THE DIRT EVEN AS HE WAS DYING.

Biz-Nass took the scrapbook and flipped to another page. He handed it over.

Bryan noticed the dateline — May 5, 1969. The headline read, WAH CHING MASSACRE. Below the headline, a faded, yellowed, black-and-white photo showed three dead men covered in black-spotted white sheets.

The black was blood, and there was a lot of it.

On a wall behind the bodies, slightly out of focus, Bryan again saw it — the circle and triangle symbol from the Oscar Woody murder, the symbol from the Jay Parlar murder, the symbol from his dreams.

What the hell was he supposed to make of this?

Biz-Nass took the scrapbook, closed it and put it back on the shelf. He walked back to his throne and sat. I'VE GIVEN YOU INFORMATION. I'M DONE.

"We need more," Bryan said. "We need *more*."

Biz-Nass shook his head. I CAN'T. I GAVE YOU MORE *SHITTYBALLS!* THAN YOU *FUCKLESNIFF!* HAD BEFORE.

The man had given great info, but now the fear was back in his eyes. What was he afraid of? Bryan looked to Pookie.

"Biz, baby, this is great," Pookie said. "You gave us a lot, and we thank you."

Biz-Nass nodded.

"Give us one more thing," Pookie said. "This thing I ask for, it's like nothing. You researched this, so I'm betting you know what these symbols mean."

Biz-Nass thought for a moment, then leaned forward and looked closely at the photos on his table. He used his right index finger to trace parts of the symbol as he talked.

He started with the slashed curve that was part of both drawings.

MMMM THIS IS A SYMBOL FOR THE SAN FRANCISCO BAY. THE TWO LINES REPRESENT THE ENTRANCE TO THE OCEAN BETWEEN THE TWO PENINSULAS.

He pointed to the symbol that showed a lightning bolt going through a circle, with the two half-circles on either side.

THE CENTER CIRCLE REPRESENTS THE EGG FROM WHICH THE WITCHES WERE SPAWNED—

[*one womb*] flashed through Bryan's mind

—THE HALF-CIRCLES USED TO BE ARMS REACHING OUT TO PROTECT THE EGG. SOMEWHERE ALONG THE LINE THEY WERE SIMPLIFIED. THE JAGGED LINE REPRESENTS HUMAN BLOOD. THIS IS THE SYMBOL OF MARIE'S CHILDREN.

Bryan leaned in. "So, the symbol at the site of the murders means Marie's Children killed the boys?"

THAT'S EXACTLY WHAT IT MEANS.

"I don't get it," Pookie said. "The boys were in a minor gang. Why would Marie's Children go after them?"

Mr. Biz-Nass shrugged.

"We think the killers might be wearing masks," Pookie said. "Costumes and the like. That ring any bells?"

STORY GOES THAT MARIE'S CHILDREN DRESSED UP TO LOOK LIKE MONSTERS, TO TERRIFY VICTIMS BEFORE KILLING THEM.

"I knew it," Pookie said. "Hear that, Bryan?"

Bryan said nothing. Costumes could explain what he'd seen in his dream, what Tiffany Hine had seen, but could it explain what Robin had found?

Pookie picked up the photo of the lightning-bolt symbol. "Biz, you *sure* this is the work of Marie's Children? Could someone be faking it?"

MOST CERTAINLY. OR MAYBE SOMEONE THINKS *SHITTYBALLS!* THEY ARE MARIE'S CHILDREN.

Bryan touched the picture of the triangle symbol, the one that scared him so bad it was like touching a blow-up photo of a spider that might come alive and bite you. He pushed it toward Biz-Nass. "And what about this one?"

MMM FIRST RECORDED INSTANCE IN 1892. CIRCLE REPRESENTS AN EGG, BUT ALSO REPRESENTS THE EYE OF A HUNTER. THE UNFINISHED TRIANGLE IS A SYMBOL OF PROTECTION AGAINST THE DEMONS THAT HUNT MARIE'S CHILDREN.

"Demons?" Pookie said.

THE SAVIORS. IT IS A SYMBOL OF PROTECTION AGAINST THE SAVIORS.

Bryan remembered the fear from his dreams, could feel it even at that moment, a cold fist below his heart. "How about that. The killers have a boogeyman all their own."

I HELPED YOU. NOW LEAVE.

Bryan started to ask for more, but before he could Pookie shook hands with the fortune-teller.

"Biz-baby, you're a good man," Pookie said. "If we have more questions later?"

Biz hesitated, then reached into his jacket and handed Pookie a business card. There was nothing on the card but a number.

THAT IS A PREPAID PHONE. NOT TRACEABLE TO ME.

"A prepaid phone?" Bryan said. "What are you, a drug dealer?"

IT'S MY BOOTY-CALL PHONE. A LOT OF LONELY HOUSEWIVES COME TO GET THEIR FORTUNES READ, IF YOU *YOU'RE A PRICKER-DICKER-FUCKER-SUCKER* KNOW WHAT I MEAN.

Pookie nodded respectfully. "A playa's gotta play, Biz, a playa's gotta play. Thanks again. We'll be in touch. Bryan, let's go."

Pookie quickly walked to the door and held it open. Bryan hesitated, staring at this charlatan who had surprised him with real information. He knew that Biz had more to share, but maybe Pookie was right — maybe this was all they could get for now.

Bryan walked out the door and headed down the stairs to Columbus Avenue.

•••

Bryan watched Pookie slide a fork into his second piece of yellow Sacripantina cake. He put the fork in his mouth, then hummed as he chewed.

"This is so good," he said. "It's like a Twinkie on steroids. Sure you don't want a piece?"

Bryan still regretted the kielbasa that sat like a sour brick in his stomach. He could smell the sugar, the flour, even the lemon flavoring in

Pookie's cake. One bite of that and his swirling stomach would rebel. He shook his head. "I'm tripping, Pooks. Our best lead, and what do we have to work with? I mean, a witches' coven? Mob hit men? A hundred-year cover-up of some kind? Come on."

"Why not? There's a reason Oscar and Jay were killed. Some kind of occult connection is as good a lead as anything else. I'll start digging into the Golden Gate Slasher case. And by *I'll start digging,* I mean I'll get Black Mister Burns to do it for me."

"Do you ever do your own detective work?"

"Yes," Pookie said. "I can detect cock-knockers. Wait . . . I detect one sitting across the table from me now. Sure you don't want some cake?"

"No," Bryan said. "I don't want cake. I want to find out what's going on."

Pookie nodded slowly. "We'll get this figured out, Bryan. The dream thing doesn't make any sense, and I know that's messing with you, but I need you to try and relax so your brain works right."

"I don't want to relax."

"Come on, trust Doctor Chang. Did you feel better after seeing your dad?"

Yeah, I actually felt sane again.

"No," Bryan said. "I didn't."

"L-L-W-T-L. Look, man, if there's a cover-up, and the chief of frickin' police is involved, then you *know* we need to move carefully. Patience, Daniel-san."

Patience? Easy for Pookie to say. And yet patience was exactly what they needed — Bryan was a hunter. If he lost his shit now, he might spook the prey.

Someone was responsible for all of this.

Bryan wouldn't rest until he found out who that was.

Hector's Revenge

Aggie James picked up the Tupperware container that had been tossed his way. It hurt to do even that. His body ached. He needed a hit. Something. Anything. Drying out sucked.

He opened the container and smelled it. His trembling stomach rejoiced at the scent of the brown stew filled with carrots, potatoes and thick chunks of some stringy meat.

The old lady had come with her cart again. They hadn't drawn his chain all the way back this time. He could move enough to reach the food. That made him potentially dangerous, he supposed, but the old lady didn't seem to worry about him. She came close, leaned in, then sniffed.

This time her scarf was pink with big red spots. She wore a brown skirt instead of gray, but the sweater and shoes were the same.

"This stew looks good," Aggie said. "What's in it?"

She stopped sniffing him long enough to look him in the eye. "Is good for you. Eat."

She had spoken to him. It was the first English he'd heard in days. "Lady, what's your name?"

"Hillary."

She reached into her cart and threw a sandwich to the Chinaman wearing the Super Bowl XXI shirt. He caught it and ripped open the brown paper. He said something that sounded like *shay-shay*, then shoved a big bite into his mouth as he crawled forward on his knees until his chain pulled taut.

"Please," he said to Hillary as he chewed. "I no talk. I leave. Please. *Please.*"

His sandwich looked like egg salad. The man was terrified. He had tears in his eyes, yet he still crammed the food into his mouth, chewed and swallowed as fast as he could. Aggie recognized that behavior all too well — if you didn't know when or where your next meal might come from, or if someone was going to kick your ass and take your food away, you ate as much as you could as fast as you could.

"Please," the Chinaman said.

Hillary just stared at him.

What a group they were: Aggie the bum, Hector the Mexican and the hungry Chinaman. Hector had two sandwiches lying in front of him. He hadn't touched them. Hillary had come twice since the masked men had taken his wife. Hector didn't move a lot anymore, just lay there in a fetal ball. Aggie couldn't blame the guy — wife and kid, gone.

And you know exactly what that feels like.

"Please-please," the Chinaman said to Hillary. He shoved the last of the sandwich into his mouth, then pushed his fingers and palms together, like he was praying. "I no talk. *Please!*"

Hillary rattled off a sharp, short phrase of what sounded like that chinky-chong talk, and the Chinaman shrank away. He fell to his ass, then back-crawled until he hit the white wall.

"Damn, Hillary," Aggie said. "What did you say to him?"

"I told him I'll bring egg rolls next time," Hillary said without looking away from the man.

"You've got egg rolls?"

She looked at Aggie again. "You don't seem as scared as he does. Why?"

Aggie shrugged. "Doesn't look like I'm going anywhere unless you let me go. Besides, I got nothing to live for. I'm pretty scared, I guess. If I'm gonna die, I'm gonna die."

And maybe you've been trying to kill yourself for years, but you don't have the balls to do it right.

"There are different ways of dying," she said. "Some worse than others. You don't know what's going to happen to you."

Aggie shrugged again. "What's gonna happen is what's gonna happen. Maybe I'm a little" — he paused as a shiver ripped him from toes to nose — "a little preoccupied right now."

"You're already feeling better, I can . . ."

Her voice trailed off, but somehow Aggie knew that she'd been about to say: *you're feeling better, I can smell it.* Had the Mexican woman smelled better, too?

Aggie decided to stop thinking about that. He didn't want to know if he was right.

"I'd be better still if I could get my medicine," he said. "How about it, lady? Can I get my medicine I had on me when I came in?"

"No."

"But I need my medicine. I'm sick."

Hillary shook her head. "You don't need it, or you won't soon. We've had many like you here before. You'll be fine in another day or two."

Aggie had dried out before. Sure, the shakes would be gone, as would the shits and the pukes, but he'd be far from *fine.* Losing the shakes didn't help you *forget* — the smack did.

"I need it," Aggie said.

Hillary smiled. "Perhaps in a few days, this *need* will be the least of your problems."

The white jail-cell door swung open with its grinding, metallic squeak. Six white-robed men came in, hoods pulled up over monster masks — Wolf-Face, Pig-Face, Hello Kitty, a bug and a demon-face. The last one through wore the black-skinned, red-lined face of Darth Maul.

Wolf-Face carried the pole with the hook. Demon-Face held the remote control.

The Chinaman stared and muttered rapid-fire words that Aggie didn't understand. The guy had been unconscious when they brought him in — this was his first time seeing the freak show.

The white-robed men closed in on Hector.

Hector didn't move. He remained in a fetal position.

Demon-Face pressed a button on the remote. The chains started to clank. Aggie hustled back to the wall, scooping up his chain as he went. He rested his neck against the hole, letting the chain play through his fingers so it wouldn't loop his foot or anything like that.

The Chinaman was freaked, but not so freaked he didn't mimic Aggie's actions.

Hector's chain pulled tight, started dragging him, and still he didn't react. The monster-faced men closed in. Even as he slid, four sets of hands grabbed at his arms and legs. The wooden pole descended, its metal hook reaching for his collar.

Then Hector's chain rang with a strange new *clank*.

It stopped retracting.

Aggie looked to the hole that led into the wall. There, his chain was balled into some kind of a knot large enough that it wouldn't fit through the stainless-steel flange.

The monster-faced men looked too, their black-gloved hands stopping in midmotion around the Mexican's hands and feet. In the brief, still silence that filled the white room, Hector spoke.

"Ahora es su turno cabrones."

His hand shot out under a white robe, grabbed a foot and yanked. Pig-Face went down hard, feet pulled out from under him like some cartoon character walking into one of those rope traps, his head *thonking* audibly off the floor's white stones.

He tricked 'em. He was just playin' possum.

Hector moved like a pissed-off street cat fighting a pack of small, slow dogs. He shook off their grip and with the same motion was on his feet.

He kicked out, planting his foot hard into the stomach of Bug-Face. Bug-Face let out a grunt, then dropped.

Two men down in less than a second.

"Hit 'em!" Aggie screamed. "Hit 'em!"

Hello Kitty grabbed Hector's left arm as Darth Maul pulled a lead pipe out of his sleeve and swung it in a low, horizontal arc, aiming for Hector's knee. The Mexican twisted at the last second, like those guys in that Ultimate Fighting stuff, bending his knee away from the pipe and taking the hit in the crook of his leg. His face wrinkled up — that hit hurt, but not as bad as if it had taken him in the kneecap.

God*damn* but that beaner was fast.

Hector reached out with his free right hand and ripped the wood pole out of Wolf-Face's hands. Darth Maul brought the pipe back for another knee shot, but the Mexican jabbed the stick's butt into Maul's latex mask. Darth Maul let out a scream the likes of which Aggie had never heard — high-pitched and clicky. Black-gloved hands shot inside the hood as Maul fell to the ground, little feet kicking.

The Mexican put the end of the stick on the white floor, then drove his foot through the shaft, snapping it in half and leaving him holding a long, jagged shard of white wood.

Hector snarled. He jammed that shard right under the Hello Kitty mask.

Blood sprayed.

From the floor, Pig-Face grabbed Hector's feet. Wolf-Face dove in and wrapped his white-robed arms around Hector's chest. Demon-Face snagged the lead pipe off the floor — it went up fast, then came down faster in a vicious arc ending on the Mexican's head.

Hector sagged. He disappeared beneath a flurry of white robes, punching black fists, kicking feet and a swinging pipe that did not stop.

Aggie couldn't look away, couldn't stop seeing, couldn't stop *hearing*. Over and over again, the repeated *whiff-gong-crack* of the pipe coming down on the Hector's shins, his knees, his feet, his hands. Each time the metal met flesh and bone, it was answered with a cry of agony.

Hector stopped moving, but the beating continued.

Infinite moments later, Wolf-Face and Pig-Face grabbed the Mexican's shattered hands and dragged him out of the room. Blood-soaked pajamas left long red smears against the white floor.

Two more white-robed men appeared: the Joker and Jason Voorhees. They helped Pig-Face and Bug-Face drag away the still-twitching Hello Kitty and the unmoving Darth Maul.

Hello Kitty's blood ran a zigzag curving path between the cobble-stones' low points until it drained into the same hole Aggie and the others used to shit and piss.

Hillary calmly rolled her Safeway shopping cart out the door. The wheels still squeaked, but only a little. She stopped and looked back at Aggie. "An *ouvrier* will come mop this up soon," she said.

She shut the cage door behind her. Silence filled the bright room, broken only by the soft whimpers of the Chinaman.

Hector had fought like a motherfucker with nothing to lose. Aggie James also had nothing to lose, but he couldn't fight for shit.

When the masked men came for him, he knew he wouldn't be able to stop them.

Blue Balls

People were going to start talking.

For the second night in a row, Pookie had to help Bryan to his apartment. The guy was beyond sick. How he'd managed to put on a good soldier face during the meetings with Biz-Nass and Zou was beyond Pookie's ability to relate.

Three days of this sickness, yet Pookie still felt fine. Those flu shots came in handy.

"I feel like crap," Bryan said. "I don't want to go to sleep. I don't want to dream anymore."

Dreaming might be a necessary evil, because sleep was exactly what Bryan needed. The guy couldn't keep going without rest. That kind of thing wore a body down.

So does jumping eight feet into the air, huh, Pooks?

No, Pookie wasn't going to rehash that crap again. What he'd thought he saw couldn't be, and that was that — just heat-of-the-moment memories playing tricks on him.

Pookie leaned Bryan against the hallway wall while he opened Bryan's door. "Clauser, you're a real rocket scientist, you know that?"

"Why?"

Pookie helped him inside. "Because you've got a fat Chinese dude with a Chicago accent taking care of you, when you could have a hot little brunette medical examiner giving you a sponge bath instead."

"Really, Pooks? You want to ride my ass about Robin *now*?"

"You and Robin are made for each other," Pookie said. "It's like math."

"You hate math."

"My hate doesn't make it any less accurate. And remember my grandfather's advice: you can fuck your math teacher, but you can't fuck math."

Bryan fell onto his bed, lay there for a second, then started sitting up. "I don't think your grampa said that."

"Well, someone did. Maybe it was me."

"I'm so surprised."

Bryan slid off the bed. His knees wobbled and he almost fell.

"Bryan, go to sleep."

He shook his head. "I told you, I'm not sleeping. I can't, Pooks."

If Bryan didn't get some serious rest, the dreams and Marie's Children and the murders wouldn't really matter to him anymore — he'd die from exhaustion. Pookie had to talk him down.

"Tell you what," Pookie said. "Your bad dreams usually come in the wee hours of the morning. I'll wake you up at midnight."

Bryan stared out from sunken, bloodshot eyes. His dark-red beard had been borderline unkempt three days ago. Now he was starting to look like Charlie Manson; not a good image, considering.

"Midnight? You promise?"

"Yeah," Pookie said. "And I'm staying right here. Just don't walk in your sleep and try to get some, because we both know you've been after me for years."

Pookie eased Bryan back onto the bed. A sweaty head hit a cool pillow. Pookie had cast his lot with his partner. He would ride this out to the end.

"I got your back, brother," Pookie said. "I won't fail you."

Bryan didn't answer.

"Bryan?"

A snore. He was already asleep.

Pookie turned off the light, stepped into the box-strewn hall and closed the bedroom door. Another night on his friend's couch. Pookie hadn't slept on couches this much since he'd been married.

He turned on Bryan's TV and watched a little local news. Jay Parlar's death led. The anchor looked so upset. And the street reporter outside of Jay's place, yeah, she looked real somber as well. Reporters were fucking vampires that lived off the blood of others.

Pookie turned off the TV. He took off his jacket. Might as well get comfortable. He pulled his notepad from his jacket pocket.

Things were crazy, his partner was a total mess and there might very well be a murderous conspiracy afoot in the San Francisco Police Department, but that didn't mean Pookie could just ignore his other vital duties.

"Blue Balls, Blue Balls, take me away. In Hollywood, everything works out just fine for the cops."

He started scribbling notes for his series bible, hoping the work would let him tune everything out, at least for a little while.

Roberta

Rex drew.

Alex Panos this time. No axes, no chain saws, and no monsters. Just Alex.

Alex, and Rex.

It felt good to draw it. Rex felt his dick stiffen as he sketched a look of pain in Alex's eyes.

The pencil flew, a *skritch-scratching* sound so fast it was a constant hiss. Shapes formed — circles, ovals and cylinders that became faces, chests, arms and legs.

Curves became blood.

Yeah, yeah it was good it was *good.*

Rex's breaths came faster, shallower. His face felt hot. His heartbeat hammered inside his head. Maybe he wasn't supposed to get turned on by this, but he didn't care anymore. The blood and pain and death spun him up and now he knew why the boys at school talked about porn all the time.

More lines. Rex grabbed a colored pencil. Alex's severed hand took shape, flash-frozen in a spray of red. Rex drew with his right hand. His left hand reached down, unzipped his pants and slid inside.

This would be his best drawing yet. His best drawing *ever.*

Moments went by and time vanished. Rex saw only lines to be drawn and shapes to be made.

His bedroom door opened, breaking the trance.

Rex's head snapped up.

There stood Roberta. She was already holding the belt. Her gaze slid down, her forehead furrowed. Rex looked down as well — his little, hard dick was in his hand.

Oh no.

"The school called me," Roberta said. She stepped into his room, slammed the door shut behind her.

Rex was trapped.

"They said you skipped school, *again.* So I came to teach you better, and what do I find? I find you being a *nasty* boy. Dirty, *nasty,* touching yourself."

"But Mom, I—"

"*Don't* you call me *mom*! You're no son of mine, you nasty, *nasty* thing!"

Rex looked down and started to zip up when he heard a *crack* sound and felt the sting across his left cheek. He sucked in a half-breath of surprise. His hand touched his face. The skin hurt.

"That's right," Roberta said, the belt dangling from her right hand. "I'll teach you to be a dirty, sinning boy in my house."

The belt snapped out again. Rex ducked away but tripped on his desk stool. He and the stool fell — the back of his head *thonked* against the floor.

"Don't you duck, you *sinner*! You take what's coming to you!"

He tried to get up. His arms and legs seemed to move in slow motion.

Crack across his forehead, then on his nose; he brought his arms up in front of his face.

"Dirty!"

Crack on his shoulder, a deep stinging.

"Nasty!"

Rex grabbed the overturned stool, tried to use it to help him scramble to his feet.

Crack across his back, the flash of pain so bad he cried out.

"I'll teach you, you worthless little—"

Rex stood and swung, did both things so fast he didn't even know what he was doing. There was a sound like a bat hitting a softball, then he heard something crash on the floor.

Rex blinked away tears. He opened his eyes.

He was holding his stool by the base of one leg. The edge of the rounded seat . . . it had blood on it.

And on the floor, Roberta. Moving slow, like she was drunk. Bleeding bad from her right cheek, her eyes glazed and unfocused.

The belt was still in her hand.

"Nas . . . tee," she said. "Getting my . . . paddle . . ."

This pathetic *thing* was the woman who had beaten him so many times? Why had he let her do that? For the same reason he had allowed BoyCo to ruin his life — because he'd been a coward, because he'd been *afraid*.

But Rex wasn't weak anymore.

"You're a bully," he said quietly. "I *hate* you."

She puckered her lips and then puffed out, like someone trying to blow away a long strand of stray hair. Flecks of blood sprayed from her lips. She tried to sit up.

She didn't get far before Rex put a foot on her chest and pushed her to her back. He reached down and tore the belt from her hands.

Roberta blinked; the glazed look vanished. She looked up at him with enraged eyes, grabbed his leg and tried to push it away.

His leg didn't move. How had he once thought of her as strong? Her hands and arms, so *weak*, they couldn't even budge him.

"Let me go!" She dug her fingernails into his calf.

This time, Rex saw the pain coming. He let it happen and found it wasn't that bad. He pressed his foot down harder.

Her eyes widened. She dug deeper with her nails, so he pressed harder still. Now her eyes scrunched tight, her mouth opened in an airless scream. Her hands slapped at his foot and leg.

Rex smiled. How *exciting*. All the things he'd felt when he made the drawings, they were nothing compared to the thunderstorm in his chest, the hurricane in his head.

He dangled the belt so that the end slid across her face.

"You like this belt, *Roberta*? You like it so much? Let's see how much you *really* like it."

He took his foot off her chest, then swung the belt as hard as he could. The leather *cracked* across her face, leaving an instant red mark.

Roberta screamed. She flipped onto her belly and scrambled for the door, crawling even as she started to rise.

She's running!

His excitement spiked up to an impossible level. Rex ran after her. She stumbled into the hall and almost reached the front door before he kicked her feet out from under her. She fell hard, her face hitting the hardwood. He moved in front of her and blocked the door.

"Where are you going, *Roberta*? Aren't you going to teach me a lesson?"

She lurched to her right, crawled into the TV room.

He followed her. He caught her next to her TV chair. She started to beg, but only got out a few words before Rex wrapped the belt around her neck. Her eyes bulged, her hands shot to the cracked black leather.

Yeah, yeah that's it, come on, comeoncomeoncomeon . . .

Rex pulled the belt tighter.

The Golden Gate Slasher

The department's electronic records of the Golden Gate Slasher case had been spotty, at best. That didn't surprise John Smith. The case was old enough that all initial reports had been done on typewriters or word processors, before the SFPD implemented a database.

Reports that old had to be scanned or hand-coded into the system. With hundreds of thousands of pre-database cases, even high-profile records didn't always get transferred. Vast amounts of the SFPD's records still existed only on paper: slowly fading, degenerating, slipping away into the untouchable realms of lost history.

The Internet didn't give up much, either. The Golden Gate Slasher wasn't even on Wikipedia. In a culture fascinated by murderers, a culture that celebrated crime, this serial killer had gone surprisingly unheralded.

So John had come down to the archives to see the real McCoy. A white cardboard box in a climate-controlled room was all that remained of one of San Francisco's ugliest summers. Crime-scene reports, medical examiner notes, evidence tags . . . a ton of information, although it seemed very scattered and disorganized.

Maybe John was too damn scared of his own shadow to provide any real help, but he could make himself useful digging through these files.

He hated who he had become. Once upon a time in fairy-tale land, he'd been a real cop. He'd been a *man*. Now he was a glorified secretary. Every night he woke up in a cold sweat. Not with nightmares, exactly, but rather with playback memories so real they made that moment come to life all over again.

Pookie had been obsessed with exposing a dirty cop named Blake Johansson, who was taking payoffs from gangs to ignore certain cases. Chief Zou had told them to leave Johansson alone, but Pookie wouldn't let up. He kept digging for dirt, kept banging away for that bit of evidence that would put the guy away. John had also wanted to let it go, let Internal Affairs handle it, but Pookie refused to stop — and like a good partner, John had been there every step of the way.

A tip led them to the Tenderloin, where they hit gold — Johansson taking a payoff from Johnny Yee, boss of the Suey Singsa Tong. Pookie had rushed things. Instead of calling for backup, he went in. There had been a moment when Pookie had Johansson dead to rights, but that moment passed. Johansson drew. Pookie should have put him down, but he didn't. John would never understand why Pookie hadn't pulled the trigger at that moment. If he had, things would have turned out different.

It got crazy from there. Johannson fired, Pookie fired, John fired, then Johansson ran out the back door. When John followed, he took a bullet in the belly. He never saw the shooter, didn't know where the shooter was, didn't even know if it was Johansson.

John crawled fifteen feet to a big plastic garbage can for cover. During the crawl, he took a second round, this time in the left calf. Pookie called out — he'd been hit in the thigh. He was pinned down, unable to come to John's aid.

For fifteen minutes John Smith cowered behind that garbage can, shoving his fist into the agonizing wound in his belly to try and stop the bleeding. That whole time, bullets kept on coming. John tried to find the shooter, looked at the buildings surrounding him, at the windows, at corners, at trees, but couldn't see anything. He learned that plastic isn't exactly the best bullet-stopping material in the world.

Bryan Clauser had been the first to respond to *shots fired* and *officer down*. Bryan, somehow, found the shooter and found him fast — that exchange lasted all of a few seconds and ended with three new holes in Blake Johansson: two to the chest, one to the forehead.

Since that night John's life had never been the same. He couldn't go outside without staring at every window, every door, without thinking that every stranger had a gun and was watching him, waiting for him to look away.

The shrinks couldn't do shit. John *knew* he was being crazy, but knowing it and fixing it are two different things. The constant, numbing fear made it impossible to be a cop.

Months later, Chief Zou had reassigned him to the Gang Task Force as a graffiti expert. Same pay, same rank, but now his days were filled with computers and spent safely behind the walls of the Hall of Justice. Chief Zou had taken care of John when many people would have cut him loose.

He sorted through the box containing case files for the Golden Gate Slasher. What he saw briefly made him glad he didn't have to visit crime scenes anymore. Eight children, ages six to nine, murdered over a ten-month period, yet the case hadn't drawn the same kind of attention as other high-profile serial killers. In fact, it had received almost no national attention.

John didn't want to think of the probable reasons for the lack of media coverage, but it was obvious — all the murdered children had been minorities. Six black kids, an Asian and a Latino. Back then, the media didn't really give a shit about niggers and spicks and slants.

Not that things had changed all that much in the last thirty years. He could turn on cable news any day of the week and see the bias in full effect. A missing pretty white girl? National news for months on end, driven by angry women wearing too much makeup who screamed about it on cable. A missing black girl? Local paper, page five, running under an ad for Doritos, if she was mentioned at all.

John flipped through a forensics summary report.

"Holy shit," he said quietly. "How can people be like this?"

The report showed a detail that the cops had managed to successfully keep out of the papers — the children's bodies had been half eaten.

He thought of the Ladyfinger Killer. Both the Slasher and Ladyfinger were dead, cases separated by a decade and two thousand miles, yet both had that symbol, and both involved cannibalism.

Forensic reports of the Slasher case also showed fork-and-knife marks on the children's little bones. Some bones even showed *gnaw* marks. All eight children had been missing their livers. Most had limbs cut off . . . some limbs appeared to be *chewed* off.

It was the chew marks that gave a positive ID. SFPD had matched the Slasher's right upper molars to grooves in the bones of four victims. That reminded John of what Pookie had told him about Oscar Woody's body, about marks made by too-wide incisors. John dug through the box until he found the perp's dental charts — he didn't know much about dentistry, but the charts seemed to show a perfectly normal set of teeth.

John started putting the box's contents into neat piles on a table: one pile for each child and a final pile for the killer. The crime-scene report for the Slasher's death was missing. John found the autopsy report's summary page. That report — signed by a much younger Dr. Baldwin Metz — said that the perp had committed suicide with a self-inflicted knife wound to the heart. John looked through the box again — yes, just the summary page . . . where was the rest of the autopsy report?

He quickly flipped back through the files for each victim. Each case had missing information, particularly the initial scene descriptions where inspectors would have recorded strange drawings or symbols. Any paper file would be missing *some* information, sure, but this?

This was systematic.

John went back to the perp's death report, or what little of it there was. Maybe he could find the name of the investigating officers. If they were alive, Pookie could track them down and get more details.

He found what he was looking for — the Slasher task force's lead inspector had been Francis Parkmeyer. John had checked that name right after Pookie called with an update about the fortune-teller meeting; Parkmeyer had passed away five years ago. No lead there.

John read through the other names on the task force. Most had to be long since retired, if not dead.

Then he saw the last two names.

He read those names a second time. Then a third.

"Ho-lee shit," he said.

John started putting the files back together. He still had to get over to the *San Francisco Chronicle* offices. Considering the sorry state of the police records, the newspaper archive was the only place left that would have the information Bryan and Pookie needed.

A Picture Is Worth a Thousand Words

Rex Deprovdechuk sat in his living room. The TV played an infomercial. Something about speed-reading.

Roberta wasn't moving. She was never going to move again.

Rex didn't have to worry about her anymore.

Or Oscar Woody.

Or Jay Parlar.

Rex drew. He drew Alex Panos. He drew Issac Moses.

Rex didn't know how it worked, but he didn't have to. Oscar and Jay were dead. Issac and Alex would be next.

He'd skipped school again. He wasn't ever going back.

Rex drew.

An Offer Aggie Can't Refuse

Hands shook Aggie James awake.

He was old, recovering from addiction, hadn't slept worth a crap in days, but there was no grogginess, no confusion.

He knew exactly where he was.

He knew what the hands meant.

The masked men had come for him.

Aggie jerked upright, his threadbare blanket flying away, his hands waving about in total panic without direction or purpose. He started to scream, but only managed to take in a big breath before a hand smacked him in the face, smacked him *hard*, snapping his head back as he fell to his ass. The room spun. His face stung like someone had pressed a hot iron against it. He blinked a few times, feet automatically pushing him away, sliding his butt across the floor until his back hit the white wall.

A flash of pink fabric with white spots, a hand clamping on the back of his head, another across his mouth. He smelled household cleaners and faded smoke. In an instant, he registered her raw power — her hands were steel skeletons covered with warm flesh, hands that could snap his neck with no effort at all.

Aggie stopped struggling. He stared at the old woman who held his head tight.

"You be quiet," Hillary whispered. A pink scarf with the white polka dots covered her thin gray hair. The scarf's tied ends dangled below her chin. So many wrinkles on that face. Aggie thought about striking out, but she held him so hard he couldn't move his head, couldn't even open his mouth.

"You be quiet. I can kill you, easy-peasy, you understand?"

"Mm-mm," Aggie said.

"Good," she said. "Tomorrow night, we come for the Chinaman."

She turned his head so he could see the Chinaman, who was sound asleep.

"I let you go now," she said. "You make any trouble for me, they will take *you* instead. Understand?"

"Mm-mmm," Aggie said.

She let go of his head, but her face stayed close to his. "After the *ouvriers* come for the Chinaman, I will come for you. I will show you what happens if you do not do what I ask."

Aggie shivered, both in fear and in hope. "You mean . . . you mean maybe I don't die?"

Hillary nodded. "Maybe. If you do what I say."

Aggie nodded violently. "Anything," he whispered. "Anything you want. What do I gotta do?"

She stood and stared down at him. "You help save the life of a king," she said. "You do this, *maybe* you live."

She walked away. Aggie couldn't stop shivering. He'd resigned himself to a brutal end where those freakish masked men dragged him out of the cell. But now, her words allowed a sliver of hope to pierce his soul. He gently fingered his jaw. It was already swelling.

Maybe he could get out of this insane dungeon.

Maybe . . . maybe he could *live*.

All he had to do was help save a king.

BMB, B & P Trade Notes

Pookie watched Bryan shovel a forkful of chocolate-chip pancakes into his mouth. Before even chewing, syrup still dripping from his beard, Bryan also crammed in two full strips of bacon.

"Yeah, Bryan," Pookie said. "Now I see why a hot piece of ass like Robin Hudson can't stay away from you. It's the charm."

"Fa you," Bryan said, chewing with his mouth open.

"And dirty talk, too? You're the total package, Clauser."

Bryan grabbed a piece of toast with his right hand, smashed it into a ball and shoved the whole thing into his mouth.

"So sexy," Pookie said. "Are you still sick?"

Bryan nodded, then shook his head. He took a big sip of coffee to wash down the obscenely huge mouthful of food. "I still hurt all over, but not as bad," he said after a big swallow. "I'm not feverish anymore. I think I'm over it, whatever it is. Man, I'm so *hungry*."

"Eat all you want, little fella, as long as you don't hurl on me."

Bryan answered by shoveling in more pancakes, more bacon, and another balled-up piece of toast.

Pookie felt a sense of relief. Bryan was clearly feeling better. He still looked tired and pale, but the spark had returned to his eyes. He really had to trim that beard, though. Despite the improvement, Bryan still wasn't back to normal. Pookie wondered if *normal* was something Bryan could ever be again. Hell, had he *ever* been normal? Still, an alert Bryan was the Bryan that Pookie needed. The case wasn't going to solve itself.

Pookie heard the roar of a motorcycle engine approaching. The sound lowered to a gurgle as a purple Harley pulled up outside. The driver backed it into a parking space, then took off a dark-purple helmet to reveal the bony face and mottled, bald head of one Black Mr. Burns.

"That bike looks awesome," Bryan said. "He did that work himself?"

"I think so, yeah," Pookie said. "The guy is great with mechanical stuff."

"At least he's awesome with something."

"What's that supposed to mean?"

Bryan slathered red jelly on a piece of toast and shrugged. "You and he went through the same shit. I don't see you driving a desk."

The comment pissed Pookie off and also stirred up his guilty feelings.

Bryan was being dismissive of a friend and former partner. That made Bryan a dick. Pookie was probably an even bigger dick, because as much as he hated to admit it, sometimes he felt the same way about John.

"The guy got shot," Pookie said.

"So did you," Bryan said. "You're out there every day, walking the line."

Pookie didn't really have an answer for that. "What the fuck do you want the man to do, Bryan? If he could be out there, he'd be out there."

Bryan shrugged again, ate half the toast. "He's drawing the same salary as you," he said as he chewed. "Same salary as me."

"Yeah, because he *earned* it," Pookie said. "Here he comes, so shut up about this, you got it?"

Bryan crammed the rest of the toast in his mouth and nodded.

John's dark purple motorcycle jacket matched his helmet. Both items looked fresh off the rack, but Pookie knew John had bought them about four years ago.

John started to slide into the booth next to Bryan, but Pookie stopped him.

"Hold on there, BMB. I think you should sit on this side, with me. Bryan is getting his grub on."

John looked at the three empty plates of food, as well as the crumbs dangling from Bryan's fuzzy beard. "I guess so."

Pookie slid over as his former partner slid in. John's gaze flicked to all corners of the diner, lingered on every patron in the place. Even here, even with two other cops, the guy couldn't relax.

"And keep your hands off the table," Pookie said. "I can't hold Bryan responsible if he eats them."

"Fa you," said a chewing Bryan.

John took a deep breath and calmed himself. He closed his eyes for a moment. When he opened them, he ignored the restaurant and focused only on Bryan and Pookie.

"I got something," he said. "I looked at the Golden Gate Slasher file in the department's archives, but tons of information was missing."

"It's an ancient case," Pookie said. "That's not surprising."

"But *what* is missing *is* surprising," John said. "Pictures of the perp? Nope. Pictures of the crime scenes, where we might see those symbols? Nope. Descriptions, anything with detail that could tie those murders to what's going on now? All of it, gone."

Pookie felt simultaneously disappointed and excited. Disappointed because he needed that information. Excited because — just like the missing symbols in the database — this was more evidence of a strategic cover-up.

Bryan started to talk, but the words caught in his throat along with his last piece of toast. He gulped coffee, then continued. "Why just take parts? Why not just chuck the whole case file and be done with it?"

John's eyes narrowed. And a smile tilted up the left corner of his mouth. For a moment, Pookie saw a flash of the whip-smart inspector that Black Mr. Burns used to be.

"Because if the whole file was gone, someone might notice," John said. "Remove the entire file for one of the biggest cases ever? Once someone realizes it's gone, questions get asked."

Pookie reached over to the sugar bin. He started piling packets, balancing the little rectangles of stuffed white paper. "What about cause of death? That article Mister Biz-Nass showed us said witnesses saw the Slasher was killed with an arrow. But in the same article, Francis Parkmeyer claimed it was suicide."

John nodded. "The autopsy report also said suicide. Signed by the Silver Eagle himself, although I'm guessing he wasn't *silver* thirty years ago."

Pookie thought back to Baldwin Metz making a rare appearance in the field to process the body of Father Paul Maloney.

"It gets better," John said. "Guess who else was on the Slasher task force with Parkmeyer? Polyester Rich Verde and Amy Zou."

Pookie looked at Bryan, who nodded knowingly. Connections were coming together: Zou, Verde, Metz, all connected to a case involving the symbols some thirty years ago.

"Zou and Verde," Pookie said. "Were they inspectors at the time?"

"Both were just newbies," John said. "From what I could gather, Zou was basically a glorified gopher on the case. But get a load of this — six months after they find the Slasher's body, she gets promoted to inspector. She was the youngest person *ever* to be promoted to that rank, a record that she still holds."

Bryan shook his head. "Wait a minute. You're saying you think she did something during the Slasher case that got her the promotion?"

"Maybe," John said. "Hard to tell with all the information that's missing, but the timing fits. Now, here's the really messed-up part. You also asked me to look into the *Chronicle*'s archives on the case. I did, and I didn't find anything."

"Wow," Bryan said. "You really knocked that one out of the park, John."

Pookie glared at Bryan, but John didn't seem to catch the sarcasm.

"It's not that I didn't find anything, there was nothing to find," John said. "There should have been all kinds of stuff. All the back issues that covered the Slasher turning up dead, they're gone. Hard copy, microfiche, scans, electronic copies of the stories — anything to do with that case is nowhere to be found. And before you ask if the *Chron* archive is missing a lot from that time period, it isn't. Just like with the Slasher case files, the removal is targeted and specific. I also checked the library's archive and found exactly the same thing. On top of that, I tried to find info on that gangster killing the fortune-teller showed you — that's missing as well, from both places."

Pookie leaned back. The SFPD files, the *Chron* archives, the library . . . this wasn't just keeping something quiet, it was an effort to wipe history clean of anything involving the symbols.

"Doesn't make sense," he said. "The Slasher was a serial killer. Mister Biz-Nass says the symbol was found with the Slasher. Now it looks like we have a new serial killer that's also using the symbol. Why would anyone cover up clues that could help stop a goddamn serial killer?"

No one answered. Bryan looked at Pookie's plate, then at Pookie, then raised his eyebrows.

Pookie slid the half-eaten plate of scrambled eggs across the table. "Go crazy, Mister Pigerson."

Pookie's cell phone rang. He answered.

"This is Inspector Chang."

"Inspector Chang, Kyle Souller."

"Well hello, Principal Souller," Pookie said.

Bryan stopped chewing. He waved his hand inward: *let me hear.*

Pookie thumbed up the volume and held out the phone. Bryan and Black Mr. Burns leaned in.

"Mister Souller," Pookie said, "hopefully you're not calling to give me detention. Unless, of course, I'm detained in a room with a naughty schoolgirl."

"Inspector, that might not be the best joke to use on a man who's responsible for the safety of *actual* schoolgirls."

"Good point," Pookie said. "The jury is instructed to disregard that remark. How can I help you, sir?"

"I asked around as you requested," Souller said. "I got something from Cheryl Evans, our art teacher."

"Do tell."

"She said she's seen drawings by a student named Rex Deprovdechuk. The drawings showed Rex chopping up Alex Panos."

Son of a bitch. A new lead. "The same Alex Panos that is in BoyCo with the former Oscar Woody and the former Jay Parlar?"

"That's the one."

"This Rex, Deprov . . . what was that last name again?"

"Dee-*prov*-deh-chuk."

"Right. He a big kid?"

"Hell no," Souller said. "Tiny. Couldn't weigh more than eighty pounds, tops."

"Is he rich?" Maybe Rex had hired someone to take out Oscar.

"Strike two," Souller said. "Single mom, I don't know if she works. His teachers said Rex wears secondhand clothes, sometimes has body odor the other kids complain about. I doubt he has two nickels to rub together. I've had him in the office a few times. I know he's had run-ins with BoyCo, but he refused to name them."

Pookie started to ask for Rex's address, but stopped himself. "Mister Souller, I told you I'm no longer on the case. Have you contacted Inspector Verde, by chance?"

"I did," Souller said.

Pookie gave the table a little bang with his fist. If Verde knew about Rex, Pookie and Bryan didn't dare talk to the kid.

"I called you anyway," Souller said. "In the education business, we have a technical term for people like Verde."

"Which is?"

"*Fucking douchebag,*" Souller said. "I was hoping you were still on the case along with him. He rubbed me the wrong way."

Pookie laughed. Polyester Rich couldn't rub the right way if there was a neon arrow flashing the proper direction. "Inspector Verde might be a little brash, but he's very good at his job. Thank you for letting me know, though."

"You're welcome," Souller said. "I can tell that you actually care, Inspector Chang. I think that's pretty uncommon. I hope you get put back on this case."

"Thanks for calling," Pookie said, then hung up.

Bryan's eyes narrowed in annoyance. "Pooks, you didn't get the kid's address."

"Because Verde already has it, and he already tattled on us once to Zou, remember? And you heard Souller — Rex is small and poor. He couldn't have done the killings and couldn't have hired someone to do them. Is he a valid lead? Yeah, but Verde already knows about him. It's Verde's case, Bri-Bri, there's only so much we can do."

Bryan leaned back and glared. He wasn't happy. Pookie couldn't blame him for that.

"How about this," Pookie said. "We give Verde a day or two to talk to Rex, then after Verde moves on, you and I find a way to accidentally run into the kid."

Bryan looked out the window. "I'd rather get on it now."

"And I'd rather collect a paycheck," Pookie said. "The *chief . . . of . . . poh . . . leece* told us to steer clear, Terminator. Unless you want to end up out of a job, we need to play the hand we've been dealt."

Bryan paused, then nodded. Pookie tried to relax. The better Bryan felt, the more stubborn he would become. Pretty soon, Pookie wouldn't be able to talk him out of following his instincts.

Terminator wasn't the only one feeling frustrated. The cover-up involved murderers. At least two kids were already dead. If Zou hadn't been playing these games, would those kids be alive? And whatever was going on, Verde was neck-deep in it — Verde, who knew about the case's only remaining lead.

Pookie started making a new stack of sugar packets. All he could do now was wait. Wait, and hope that Rich Verde wasn't covering up for a psycho.

Verde & the Birdman

Rich Verde got out of the car, then brushed some lint off the sleeve of his blue suit. He shut the door and waited for Birdman to get out.

He was always waiting for Birdman. The kid moved in slow motion. This was what the force was coming to? Kid had hair like a dirty mop. He wore sloppy clothes. He had a goddamned gold tooth, for the love of Christ. Bobby Pigeon looked like a pimp on a four-day bender.

"Birdman, come on. Move it."

Bobby nodded. Even his nod was slow. "I'm comin', boss."

They started up Pacific toward the Deprovdechuks' house. Verde had parked a block away, at the corner of Wayne Place. Sometimes walking up to a perp's place gave you more options, was less conspicuous. Subtlety, calmness, keeping things as quiet as possible — that was how the job got done.

Souller's call had come out of the blue. Pookie had developed that source. Rich would have done the same thing, of course, but it still chapped his ass that Pookie's work had produced a lead. Not that the lead mattered. This was nothing more than a coincidence. The BoyCo kids were assholes, beating up on anyone they could. Rex Deprovdechuk got his ass kicked a few times, so what?

Nowadays everyone wanted to raise kids in a goddamn airlock, protected from anything and everything. Everyone gets a goddamn trophy. When Rich had been a kid, you either learned to fight back or you ate the shit sandwich you were served. So the kid had drawn mean pictures about BoyCo members? So what. It had nothing to do with the killings. He knew it, Zou knew it, but Zou still wanted to dot the *i*'s and cross the *t*'s.

Whatever Amy Zou wanted, if it was in Rich's power to give, Amy Zou got.

"Rich-O," Birdman said. "Riddle me something, brother. Seems to me we're kind of half-assing this case. Why'd we get it, anyway? Terminator and Pookzilla are Grade-A prime, man."

"We're not?"

Birdman shrugged. "I'm game, dog, don't get me wrong, but this is some high-profile shiz. I'm kind of new for that, you know?"

"You're fine. I'll carry you. Just watch and learn, son."

"You didn't answer the question," Birdman said. "Why us? And I know I'm just tagging along, so more accurately, why *you*?"

Rich wasn't going to share that answer. Zou could when the time was right. Verde hoped Birdman would work out, because they needed some new blood. That was why Zou had partnered them up — Bobby was a good cop, but he clearly didn't believe in strict interpretations of the letter of the law. When it came to Marie's Children, to the symbols, what mattered was how a cop would interpret the gray areas. Clauser and Chang were too goddamn goody-goody to play ball, but hopefully Bobby could be more realistic about how the world truly worked.

Rich focused on the task at hand. It was the little things that got a cop killed, like routine traffic stops or just talking to the wrong person at the wrong time. In this line of work, survival meant assuming that everyone who saw you wanted you dead.

He approached the Deprovdechuk place. A few people — mostly Chinese, mostly old — moved along the sidewalks. Verde angled around an old lady that had to be ninety. Her steps were so tiny she looked like a bobble-headed stop-action character.

This was the Chinatown for the locals, not the Chinatown for the tourists. Many windows were open, filled with shirts and pants drying on hangers or dangling from improvised clotheslines. Some store signs were mostly in Mandarin with a little bit of English beneath, while others had no English at all. Massage parlors, beauty shops, art galleries that never seemed to be open, all in storefronts squashed down by the three- and four-story apartment buildings above them. He'd made calls to some of those apartments. The Chinese could pack ten, eleven, even fifteen people into a standard one-bedroom.

Rich stopped when he saw 929 Pacific. "This is it," he said.

"Huh," Birdman said. "I bet they're the only round-eyes in this building, if not the whole neighborhood."

The Deprovdechuks lived in a tenancy-in-common, or "T.I.C." The three-story house had two parallel columns of typical bay windows. Automobile soot smeared and darkened once-white walls. Seven concrete steps led to three side-by-side wooden doors. One door would lead up to the third floor, one to the second, and the last entered into the Deprovdechuks' ground-floor flat.

"Let me do the talking," Rich said as he pressed the door buzzer.

"Don't I always?"

Verde heard footsteps coming from inside the house. Little footsteps.

The door opened a couple of inches before a snapping chain-lock stopped it. Halfway down, a tiny face looked out.

Verde's nose caught a faint, ripe smell, just a trace of it. He knew that smell . . .

The boy's face wrinkled with distrust. "Who are you?"

"Inspector Verde, San Francisco Police," Rich said. "Are you Rex?"

The boy's jaw dropped, his eyes widened. He slammed the door shut so hard the wood rattled and the glass cracked. The slam made the air swirl, and another whiff of that odor tickled Rich's nose.

He recognized it: unforgettable, unmistakable.

The smell of a corpse.

Rich drew his Sig Sauer. Before he could say anything, Bobby drew his own. At least the kid was fast when it mattered.

Rich slid to the right side of the door, shoulder on the frame, gun in both hands and pointed up. "Do it!"

Bobby lifted a big Doc Marten and push-kicked. The door slammed open, ripping the metal chain free and sending it spinning down the hallway's hardwood floor. Bobby went in first. Rich followed, saw Rex sprinting down the long hall. The boy ran through the last door on the left and slammed it shut behind him. Bobby ran after him. Just inside the front door, Rich glanced into the living room on his left — a woman's body, faceup on the floor, a belt wrapped around her neck. Eyes open and staring. Splotchy facial bruising. Purple discoloration around the skin just above and below the belt. A gray pallor covered the corpse's other exposed areas.

Rich saw all this in a half-second glance. He looked back down the hall, saw Birdman kick through the bedroom door and point his gun inside.

"Lie down on the floor!" Bobby screamed into the room.

That's when Rich felt the footsteps behind him.

He turned, but too late. Something smashed into his back, driving his head into the unforgiving wall. As he fell, he had a glimpse of a man racing past — long black beard, white wife-beater, green baseball cap.

The man carried a hatchet.

By the time Rich hit the floor, the bearded man had closed in on Bobby. Bobby saw the man coming and turned to fire. The hatchet slid through the air.

Two shots, so close together they sounded like one.

The hatchet hit Bobby on the right side of his neck and drove down into his sternum. Rich would never forget that sound, that *whiff-crunch* sound of the blade digging home.

Rich scrambled to his knees. He raised his gun and fired, *pop-pop*, but watery eyes and wobbly hands threw off his aim. The bearded man gripped Bobby's shoulders and turned *fast*, putting Bobby's back toward Rich.

The tip of the hatchet stuck out between his partner's shoulder blades.

That cut his heart in half.

The man yanked the hatchet free and stepped backward into the room, grabbing Bobby's gun as he did.

Rich couldn't move. He couldn't breathe.

Bobby's right arm hung down low, swinging sickly from the gaping wound as if it had no bones at all. He took a single, short, staggering step, then his legs gave out. He fell face-first. Rich saw blood pour out of him, spreading across the wood floor.

That cut Bobby's heart in half. You can't help him. Get out. Get out. Get back up.

Rich found his feet under him, found himself backpedaling, right hand pointing his gun, left hand grabbing his radio.

"Eleven ninety-nine! Eleven ninety-nine! Officer down! Officer down at nine-twenty-nine Pacific, get me some fucking help, *now!*"

He backed out of the door and into the evening air.

Marco

Rex's heart beat so fast.

He looked at the bloody man standing in his bedroom. The man held a gun in one hand, a blood-dripping hatchet in the other. Two red spots dotted the chest of his white tank top, at least where Rex could see it beneath the tangled beard that hung down to the man's belly. The man's green baseball hat said JOHN DEERE in yellow letters.

Rex recognized him — the man from the street, the man who had tried to stop Rex from getting the bum's change.

The bloody man should have seemed like a walking nightmare. He'd just killed a cop in Rex's hallway. He had weapons. Rex had nowhere to run. But instead of feeling afraid, Rex felt a warmth blossom inside his chest, a vibration that went *ba-da-bum-bummmm.*

The vibration told Rex that everything would be okay. He just knew it.

"Hello," the man said.

"Hi," Rex said.

The man stared down. He looked nervous. "My name is Marco."

"I'm Rex."

The bearded man quick-peeked back into the hall. He nodded, as if satisfied with what he saw or didn't see out there. He faced out the door, his hands in front of him. Was he . . .

Was he undoing his pants?

He was. Rex heard a quick trickle of pee hitting the body in the hall, then the man zipped up and turned back into the room.

"You *peed* on him?"

The bearded man nodded. "Yeah. Had to mark it, you know? Uh . . . I think you should maybe come with me."

"Why?" And why wasn't Rex afraid?

"Sly told me to watch over you," Marco said. "I saved you from those cops. But cops are like bugs, there's always more on the way."

Sly. Rex knew that name. He had sketched it on one of his drawings.

"You're very important," the man said. "Please, come with me. I'll take you home, to your family."

Rex stared at the stranger. Family? That was crazy. His dad had died when Rex was little. Roberta was also dead — Rex had seen to that. That was his "family" . . . so why did Rex *know* this bearded stranger was telling the truth?

The man quick-peeked again. Seeing nothing in the hall, he continued. "We've waited a long time for you. A real long time. We can protect you." The man pointed to Rex's desk, to the drawing of Alex and Issac lying there. "We can protect you from them."

Rex looked at his own drawing. He felt raw fury blossom up again, push out the good thoughts, the nice feelings.

"I hate them," he said. "I want . . ."

"You want to what, my king?"

King?

Long live the king.

Rex stared at the stranger, looked into his eyes. In there, Rex saw love, acceptance and devotion.

"I want to kill them," Rex said. "I want to see Alex and Issac die."

The man smiled. "Then come with me."

Rex felt a new sensation, one he knew from his dreams.

He felt the thrill of the hunt.

Rex made his decision. "Okay, let's go. The backyard opens up into—"

"I know," Marco said. "I've been watching."

Marco's hands moved faster than Rex could see, lifted him, tucked him under one blood-splattered arm like a running back tucking a football.

Rex's old world rushed by in a blur.

He couldn't wait to see his new one.

• • •

They moved through another alley, into yet another building's dark basement. The fourth building so far, and Rex hadn't seen a person in any of them. Marco moved like he knew the places, like he'd been through these paths a hundred times before.

They came out the other side of the basement into a strange space: long, narrow, filled with brown plastic trash cans and bits of garbage. Rex could see the sky through metal grates about ten feet above his head. Was he under a sidewalk or something? He didn't have time to look because Marco moved fast. Rex followed, his shoes grinding damp dirt against the uneven concrete.

Two steps down on the right led to a dented metal door set in an old stone archway. On the door, Rex saw a shiny, new Master Lock. Had they hit a dead end?

Marco reached. Not for the door's locked handle, but for the outside edges of the door's frame. He slid his fingers between that frame and the stone arch surrounding it, then grunted as he swung the whole thing open. That was so smart — everyone would try the handle and find it locked; they wouldn't think to move the whole door, frame and all. Even if someone did figure that out, they probably couldn't budge it — it looked *really* heavy.

Marco stepped aside, holding the thing open for Rex.

"Through here, my king."

Rex stepped through. Marco slid in after him, then pulled the door back into place, shutting off all light.

"It's dark in here, but I know the way," Marco said. "Hold my hand."

Rex reached out. His tiny hand vanished inside of Marco's. The man's skin felt warm. His hand was rough and calloused. Marco gently pulled Rex along the dark, cramped tunnel.

Minutes later, Rex heard the grinding sound of an ill-fitted metal door opening against concrete. Marco pulled Rex inside and let go of his hand. The grinding sound again, then the sound of Marco's steps.

A light came to life.

Another basement. This one seemed completely unused. Rex looked around the place. It was a real crap-hole. There wasn't even furniture, just a back corner strewn with blankets and a beat-up wicker chair. A single naked bulb hung from the ceiling, held up only by its long, black electrical cord. A pile of clothes sat in one corner.

This place was scary. This was the kind of place you'd think child rapists took children. But Rex knew Marco wasn't a rapist. Rex also knew you didn't need a grungy basement to rape a kid.

Father Maloney hadn't needed one.

Since fleeing the house, Rex had been running behind Marco. Now that they were face-to-face, Rex saw that the bloodstains on Marco's white wife-beater had spread, making the man's shirt pinkish-red although he didn't appear to be bleeding anymore. Marco didn't seem concerned about what looked like a serious wound.

"Place is a mess," Rex said. He didn't know what else to say.

Marco froze. His eyes grew wide. "I'm sorry. You want me to clean?"

"Uh, no. It's fine."

Marco let out a huge sigh of relief. How funny — this man had killed a cop with a hatchet, but he was afraid of what Rex thought? It didn't make sense, but then again, nothing did. So much happening, all of it so overwhelming — Roberta, that cop, Oscar, Jay, the dreams, the drawings, this man, the gun . . . now this man's dirty place in the basement of some building Rex didn't know.

This strange man, who seemed to . . . to *worship* Rex.

Marco stripped off his ruined shirt. He tossed it to the floor and walked to the pile of clothes. He dug around for a second, then found another wife beater and put it on. It wasn't "clean" by any stretch of the imagination, but at least it wasn't bloody.

"Marco, how long are we staying here?"

"Until dark," he said. "Best to move at three or four in the morning. I shouldn't have killed that cop, my king. Cops will be missed. But I didn't know what else to do. He was pointing a gun at you."

Rex remembered the shaggy-haired, gold-toothed cop kicking in the bedroom door, aiming that gun at his face, telling him to lie down on the floor. That cop had wanted to hurt Rex. *Everyone* wanted to hurt Rex.

Everyone except Marco.

"You saved me," Rex said. "Thank you."

Marco looked down and away. "Anything for you, my king."

"Why do you keep calling me that?"

"Because it's what you are." Marco breathed deeply through his nose. "I can smell it. We'll stay here. Then Sly and Pierre and others will come."

Those names again, the names from his dreams. "Are they the ones that killed Oscar and Jay?"

Marco nodded. "I helped. We want to hurt the people that hurt you, my king."

My king. This wasn't a trick. This wasn't a game. These strangers had killed for him. Killed the people who had made his life hell.

"How did you know about Oscar and Jay?"

"We felt your hate," Marco said. "It started a few days ago. Maybe a week — I'm not so good with time. We saw images of the people who hurt you. Only those of us who walk on the streets, though. The others, they ain't felt nothing. I've never felt anything like it, my king. Sly thinks we were seeing parts of your dreams."

A week ago. That was about the time Rex got sick. He'd started dreaming a few days after that.

"We felt your hate for the preacher," Marco said. "And for those other boys. We searched every night. We found them all. At first, Sly told us to wait, because Firstborn wouldn't want us to act."

Firstborn . . . had Rex heard that name in his dreams? "Who is Firstborn?"

"He runs things," Marco said. "He'll be so mad when he finds out, but . . . well, people *hurt* you. We had to kill your enemies."

Marco said that last sentence like it was the most obvious thing in the world, something as natural and inevitable as drawing a breath.

Father Maloney. Oscar and Jay. Rex wished he could have seen them die.

"The people who hurt me," Rex said. "There are more of them, the ones in the drawing in my room. Alex and Issac. Do you know where they are?"

Marco looked down again. He said nothing.

"Marco, are they still alive? Do you know where they are?"

Marco nodded. "Yeah, we know where they are. Sucka is following them."

Rex didn't know that name, but if Alex and Issac were being followed, maybe Rex could watch them die. They'd beat him. They'd tortured him. And why? He'd never done anything to them. People like that *deserved* death. Rex thought of the strength he'd felt when he wrapped that belt around his mother's neck.

He wasn't the same helpless kid who couldn't stop Alex Panos from breaking his arm. That kid was gone forever.

"Take me to them," Rex said.

Marco shook his head so hard his long beard flopped from side to side. "No, my king! Sly would want me to keep you safe. I need to call him when he comes out again, so we can take you home."

Rex wasn't going home, not ever again. Then he realized that Marco wasn't talking about Roberta's house.

"Home? Where is that?"

Marco looked down again. "It's where we live."

Maybe Rex would live there, too. It was probably a lot different from the only *home* he'd known for thirteen years.

"Marco, how did you know where I lived?"

"Sly told me."

"How did Sly know?"

Marco shrugged. "Sly says that's not important. But I think maybe Hillary told him where to go."

Hillary? Another name that didn't ring any bells. Who *were* these people? And why did they think Rex was their king?

Maybe . . . maybe because Rex really *was* a king. Maybe he'd *always* been a king, and just hadn't realized it.

But right now, none of that mattered. What mattered was the hate burning in his chest. Hate for Issac, hate for Alex. He couldn't stop thinking about revenge. Rex had power now, and those two would pay for what they had done.

He wouldn't accept anything less.

"I want to know where Issac and Alex are," Rex said. "I want to watch them die."

Marco shook his head. "No, no, Sly would kick my ass!"

"Marco, am I your king?"

Marco stared, then nodded slowly.

Rex felt so confident, so *strong*.

"If I'm you're king, then you have to do what I say. Tonight, we're going to get Alex Panos."

Aftermath

A news helicopter hovered overhead. A uniformed cop waved Pookie's shit-brown Buick between two black-and-whites that blocked off Pacific Street. Outside this improvised perimeter, a mostly Chinese crowd gathered, staying as far away as they could from the scowling cops while still being able to see the action in front of the house.

Inside the perimeter, more police cars — marked and unmarked — were already parked, their lights flashing.

An ambulance sat silently. Its lights were off. The paramedics just stood there.

Cops were everywhere, and they all knew they were too late.

Bryan sensed the tone: angry, somber, vengeful. Bobby Pigeon was dead. Every cop here, Bryan included, wanted to find the bastard responsible and make him pay.

Pookie parked. Bryan got out. He and Pookie ducked under yellow police tape and approached the house.

Only minutes earlier, most likely, the area had been a flurry of activity bordering on chaos. When the call for *officer down* had gone out, every cop within twenty blocks had stormed in. Stephen Koening and Ball-Puller Boyd had been the first homicide cops to arrive. They were running the scene.

Bryan and Pookie started up the seven concrete steps. Atop the steps, there were three doors side by side; the one on the left hung open. Ball-Puller Boyd was standing in the doorway, phone pressed to ear. He saw them coming, then quickly finished his call and put the phone in his pocket.

"Clauser, Chang," he said. "Koening and I got this one. He's inside with the CSI guys. What's your role here?"

"We had the Oscar Woody case," Pookie said. "I'm guessing Sharrow will put us back on it again, considering. Verde was here because the Deprovdechuk kid might be involved. We'll stay out of your way while you look for Birdman's killer, and we'll feed you whatever we find."

Boyd nodded. "Works for me until we hear different from Sharrow. The kid's room is the last one on the left. Okay, here's what we've got so far. Birdman's sidearm is unaccounted for. Verde said Birdman got off two rounds, and we found two forty-caliber shell casings. We found one bullet in the wall. It went through the perp and into a picture frame. No trace of the other bullet — I hope it's still in the fucker."

Bryan hoped so, too. It would be fitting if Bobby managed to kill his own killer.

"How about a description?" Bryan said. "Verde get a good look?"

Ball-Puller stroked his walrus mustache. "Yeah. Six feet plus, long black beard, big gut, white wife-beater, jeans, boots. Might be carrying a hatchet, and/or Birdman's Sig Sauer. We've got a BOLO out on that description, plus one for the Deprovdechuk kid. Looks like the kid strangled his mother with a belt sometime yesterday. His picture is already all over the news. We'll get him."

Pookie nodded. "How's Verde?"

"Alive and uninjured," Boyd said. "Other than that, not good."

Rich Verde had failed to protect his partner. Right now, he'd be feeling guilty and worthless, like any cop would feel in the same situation.

Boyd reached into his pocket for his phone. "If you guys want to take a look, make it fast. Robertson is on the way, I don't want the house full of feet and fingers when he gets here."

He stepped aside and started dialing. Bryan and Pookie walked in.

Bryan smelled death. Faint and growing, but he knew it was a human corpse.

Far down the hallway, just past an open door, Bobby "Birdman" Pigeon lay facedown in a wall-to-wall puddle of his own blood. Even from fifteen feet away, Bryan could see the bloody wound that split his body from the right side of his neck down just past his sternum.

If Zou hadn't taken him and Pookie off the case, would Birdman still be alive? Or might that have been Pookie lying there instead?

Bryan looked left, into the living room. There, Jimmy Hung and Stephen Koening were looking over a woman who'd been dead at least twenty-four hours. She was the source of the corpse smell.

"Rex did that," Pookie said. "I guess I was wrong when I thought he wasn't a threat."

Bryan nodded. "I guess so."

He sniffed again. That smell of death, sure, but there was something else in this house . . .

"Come on," Pookie said, "let's check out Rex's room."

They walked down the hall, being careful about where they stepped. This many people in the house was a problem. Feet and hands threatened to destroy evidence, to accidentally trample on some key bit of information that could lead to the perp. But at the same time, everyone knew the hard facts — murders are usually solved with speed and logic, not with weeks of evidence analysis. If a killer isn't caught in the first forty-eight hours, odds are he won't be caught at all. They needed as much information as they could get as fast as they could get it.

Bryan saw blood on the hallway wall, spattering the white paint and some of the picture frames. The picture frame with the most blood had cracks radiating away from a hole just left of center.

That new smell grew stronger.

To get to Rex's room, he had to step over Birdman's body. Bryan reached out with a big step to avoid walking in the puddle of blood. Once on the other side, he started to turn into the open bedroom but stopped in the doorway. The door — handle ripped off, wood white and splintered where the latch used to be — had a drawing thumbtacked to it.

The blue-lined notebook paper had been torn out of a spiral binder. A line of frayed holes ran down the left-hand side. On that paper, a symbol:

I dream of a better day.

It was the same drawing Bryan had sketched after waking up from his hunting dreams. The same drawing found painted in the blood of Oscar Woody, and of Jay Parlar.

Scrawled beneath the drawing were the words *I dream of a better day.*

"Pooks," he said, his voice barely a whisper.

Pookie was at his side, talking quietly. "I see it. Keep cool, man. Look at the rest of the room."

Rumpled red blankets lay twirled up on a twin mattress. A small, beat-up wooden desk sat next to the bed. Sammy Berzon was under the desk, using a pen to poke through a small garbage can. A little TV sat in the far corner, a video-game console on the floor in front of it along with one controller. The room's lone window looked out on a narrow alley filled with square plastic garbage cans. A dirty brick wall on the alley's far side was barely more than an arm's reach away. A three-drawer vertical dresser and a tiny closet were the room's only other features. Bryan saw two books on the dresser, the tell-tale strip of white on the bottom of the spine showing they came from a library: *On a Pale Horse* and *The Book of Three.*

And then, Bryan noticed the walls.

Walls *covered* with drawings.

Drawings of guns, of people shooting each other, stabbing each other. Drawings of chain saws, axes, knives and medieval weapons, of torture devices and burning bodies. Most drawings showed a teenage boy with big brown eyes and kinky, dry brown hair. Every drawing showed this boy with rippling muscles and confident movements, using every weapon imaginable to kill Alex Panos, Jay Parlar, Oscar Woody or Issac Moses. Bryan saw Pookie staring at a drawing of an older man, his legs being broken by the snarling teenage boy.

"Holy shit," Pookie said. "That's a dead-ringer for Father Paul Maloney."

Bryan took them all in, the drawings of pain, the drawings of death.

His eyes fell on one, and he could not look away. It was a man with a snake-face, the same thing Bryan had seen in his dreams. The drawing stared back at him from the wall, as if it wanted to come alive and talk. Narrow yellow eyes seemed to laugh at him.

Beneath the face was one word, written in a superhero-style typeface: *Sly.*

"Bryan, you okay?"

Pookie's voice sounded distant. Bryan's breath finally slid out in a long huff. He breathed in through his nose — that new scent flooded him. So much stronger in here, in the room where Rex had slept and played and drawn. The smell made Bryan relaxed and excited all at the same time; it made him want to do something, but he didn't know what that something was.

A hand patting his back. "Bri-Bri, you okay?" Pookie leaned in and whispered: "Is it the drawings?"

Bryan nodded toward the snake-face. "You asked if a sketch artist could draw what I saw in my dream? Well, there you go."

Pookie looked at the drawing of Sly.

"That's messed up," Pookie said. "There's a lot of messed up going on around here today."

Sammy Berzon finally stood up. He dropped a crumbled piece of tissue into a clear evidence bag. "You guys see Birdman's wound?"

Bryan and Pookie nodded.

"It's terrible," Sammy said. "Poor Bobbie, eh? You know how strong a guy would have to be to put a hatchet through the clavicle and three ribs?"

"Damn strong," Pookie said. "Probably as strong as you'd have to be to rip someone's arm off."

Sammy thought, then nodded. "You guys thinking this is the same perp who took out Oscar Woody? He'd have to be like a pro football player or a bodybuilder or something."

Pookie pointed to the many drawings of the brown-haired muscle boy. "That kid looks like a bodybuilder."

"*That* kid, sure" — Sammy picked up a framed photo off the dresser and handed it over — "but not *this* kid."

Bryan looked at the photo. It was clearly the muscle-boy sketched in the drawings, only much skinnier, much smaller, and much dorkier. Something about that face . . . familiar? Bryan hadn't dreamed of this kid. Or had he? He found himself waiting for some kind of reaction to the photo, but the image did nothing.

The picture doesn't affect you, but what if he was here and you SMELLED *him?*

"We have to find this kid," Bryan said. "He's our man."

Pookie took the picture and studied it. "Our *boy*, anyway. Sammy, the gunshot blood in the hall might tell us if Oscar's killer was the one who got shot, right?"

Sammy nodded.

"Cool," Pookie said. "We also need some DNA from this Rex kid. He had run-ins with Woody and the BoyCo gang."

"Kid lived here, DNA is all over the house," Sammy said. He held up the bag. "But I got you covered with this."

Pookie leaned in, squinted. "What's that? Snot rag?"

"Better," Sammy said. "Jizz. Still wet, even."

Pookie leaned back. "That's nasty, Sammy. Nasty."

Sammy shrugged. "If it's from Rex, it's what you wanted, eh? Listen, I'll get it to Robin, but how about you guys clear out? I've got work to do."

Bryan and Pookie walked out into the hall and carefully stepped over the body once again. Seconds later they were out of the house, heading for Pookie's car.

Bryan couldn't quit thinking about that smell. At a level he didn't understand, he now knew his dream-hate, his lust for hunting those boys, it all came from Rex Deprovdechuk — a boy that Bryan had never met, never even known existed until just a few hours ago. What had the scrawny thirteen-year-old done to bring about the deaths of Oscar Woody and Jay Parlar? Was he sending out thoughts or something? Was he telepathic? That was completely impossible, and yet there was no question that Bryan Clauser was somehow bonded to this boy.

They got into the Buick. Pookie had just started the car when a man leaned into the open driver's-side window.

"Shut it off," said Sean Robertson.

Pookie turned off the engine, then sat back so Robertson could see both him and Bryan. Robertson pushed his glasses higher up his nose. "What the fuck are you guys doing here?"

"Our jobs," Pookie said. "Officer down, we responded."

"It's Verde's case," Robertson said. "You were told to stay out of it."

Bryan suddenly wanted to smack those glasses right off his face. A cop had been hacked to death, yet Robertson was going to keep playing this game?

"Birdman is dead," Bryan said. "Verde's a mess. You gotta put us back on it."

"I *gotta*? No, Clauser, what I *gotta* do is kick your asses out of here."

This was madness. What the hell was wrong with Robertson and Zou?

"Assistant Chief, listen to us," Pookie said. "Rex Deprovdechuck had the same symbol in his room that was found at the Woody and Parlar murders. This is all connected. You can't just ignore this."

Robertson nodded slowly. He seemed like he was trying to balance understanding against authority. "We're not ignoring anything. There's a BOLO out for Rex. The entire force is looking for him. We'll get him."

Bryan leaned over in his seat to get closer to Robertson. "There's a BOLO out on Alex Panos and Issac Moses. Has the *entire force* tracked down those kids yet?"

Robertson's lips pressed into a thin line. "Not yet, but that's not your concern. You're both fresh out of warnings. I see you anywhere near this case — and that includes anything involving symbols, Oscar Woody, Jay Parlar, Bobby Pigeon, Rich Verde, Rex Deprovdechuk or this house — and I'll suspend you on the spot. Now get lost."

Robertson stood and walked toward the house.

Bryan tried to control his anger. Robertson was part of it — whatever *it* was. And this bizarre cover-up seemed to extend to protecting cop killers.

"Pooks, get us out of here."

"Where to?"

Bryan shrugged.

"I could go for a beer," Pookie said. "The Bigfoot?"

Leave it to Pookie to find just the thing. They'd been shut out of every angle involving this case — a beer sounded good.

"The Bigfoot," Bryan said.

Pookie started the Buick and drove away from the scene.

The Long Night

The cold rain poured down, soaking sweatshirts, jeans, shoes and even socks — it made Alex Panos miserable.

Alex and Issac walked north on Hyde Street, their sweatshirt hoods up and their heads down. They were careful not to bump into anyone. The Federal Building rose up on their right, part of a world Alex didn't understand and didn't care about.

What he did care about was staying alive. To do that, he had to start taking some chances.

"Alex," Issac said, "I don't wanna do this."

Alex's lip curled up. "You should shut up now, Issac."

Of all the people to be stuck with, he had that whiney bitch Issac. Issac should have been the one to fall to his death, not Jay.

"This rain *sucks*," Issac said. "It's been days, man. I'm cold and I'm hungry. Maybe we should just go to the cops."

Cops like Bryan Clauser? No way Alex would go to the police. No way.

Without the Boston College gear, Alex and Issac were just two more teenagers walking the streets. They'd found places to sleep, but they had been careful not to break in anywhere or to do anything that would attract attention.

Because someone wanted them dead.

"Come *on*," Issac whined. "If you're going to your mom's, let me go see my parents. I got to at least let them know I'm okay."

Alex stopped and turned. Issac stopped, too, wide-eyed with the instant knowledge he'd pushed it too far.

"You're not going home," Alex said. Issac was a big kid, but Alex had a good three inches and at least twenty pounds on him. They'd scrapped once. After the beating Alex had dished out, Issac wasn't going to try it again.

"We stay together," Alex said. "We're going to my mom's because we need the money."

"You spent like five hundred bucks on that gun," Issac said. "That was all we had. And I don't even get to carry it."

Alex nodded. No, Issac didn't get to carry it. That was the breaks. Alex reached behind his back, patted the gun under his sweatshirt where he'd tucked it into his belt. He was checking it every five minutes, it seemed, just to make sure it didn't fall out.

He'd always wanted a Glock but had been afraid to get one. Being busted as a minor in possession of narcotics was one thing — being in possession of a gun was another. But now someone was trying to kill him, someone connected with the cops. Alex wasn't going out like Oscar, and he sure as hell wasn't going out like Jay.

Issac looked like he was about to cry. "I know we need money," he said, "but can you really rob your *mom?*"

"I'm not going to put the gun to her head, stupid," Alex said. "She probably won't even be there. I know where she keeps the money. I'm done with your whining, man. If you're going to act like a bitch, I'm going to treat you like a bitch. You got it?"

Alex stared, waiting for an answer. He couldn't let Issac go to his parents. That would bring the cops. Alex would do whatever he had to to stay safe, stay hidden. If Issac had to be shut up for good, well, that's the way it was.

Issac nodded. "Okay, man. I'm down for the ride."

"I know this sucks," Alex said. "We don't have a choice. Do this with me, then I think we can sleep in a house tonight. April's parents are gone for a couple of days."

Issac smiled. "*Shrek?* Dude, no way."

Alex laughed and punched Issac in the shoulder — playful, but Alex wanted it to hurt a little, just a reminder of who was in charge. Issac winced, then forced a laugh of his own.

"She's putting us up," Alex said. "So you call her *April,* not *Shrek.* We'll get Mom's cash, then we'll go to April's place."

"What then? What do we do when April's parents come back?"

Alex wished he knew. Maybe it was time to get out of San Francisco. They had a gun now. They could rob places, get money, just keep moving until he figured out what to do.

"I'll tell you later," Alex said. "All I know is that tonight, when you're all warm and dry, you'll feel like a douchebag for making fun of me about April a few weeks ago, huh?"

"I guess," Issac said. "I mean, she does kind of look like an ogre."

"Yeah, and I'll be the one getting my dick sucked tonight. You won't be getting shit. She'll do whatever I tell her. I might even tell her you get to watch."

Issac's blue eyes widened. "Oh, wow, man."

Alex couldn't tell if that was an *oh wow* of excitement or fear. Didn't matter. Doing stuff in front of Issac would embarrass the hell out of April. Some girls liked humiliation.

They passed a boarded-up doorway. A homeless guy completely

covered in a soaking wet blanket lay there, trying to avoid the worst of the rain. Alex didn't know who had it worse, him or the bum. Unlike the bum, Alex was young, strong, and would find a way to stay alive — but at least the bum didn't have someone trying to kill him.

The rain kept pouring down. Alex and Issac kept walking north.

•••

Pookie walked back to the table with a second round of beers — an Elizabeth Street Brewery IPA for him, a Bud Light for Bryan. Bryan had no taste in beer.

Bryan sat on the bar stool, his elbows on the small, round table, his head in his hands. The table was right next to the bar's namesake — a twelve-foot-tall wooden statue of Bigfoot himself. The statue made Pookie think of drawings of snake-men, and of an old lady talking about building-climbing werewolves.

Pookie set the beers on the table.

"Buck up, little Terminator," he said. "Turn that frown upside down. Also, just insert your favorite peppy euphemism here."

Bryan lifted his head. "A do-it-yourself pep talk?"

"Absolutely," Pookie said. "The night is darkest before the dawn. Pull yourself up by your own bootstraps. If you don't drink, I'll keep talking."

Bryan picked up his bottle and drank.

Pookie's partner was angry and confused, and rightfully so. Bryan wanted to *fight,* he wanted to lash out at something. He was damn close to going off like a bull in a china shop. But it was Chief Zou's china shop, and that would not end well.

"Bri-Bri, we'll get this figured out."

"You keep saying that. It just gets worse. A cop is dead because of this shit, Pooks. And Robertson gives us the boot?"

"We'll find the guy who did this," Pookie said. "We'll find out what's up with your dreams, Rex's drawings, the symbols, all of it."

Bryan moved his bottle in slow circles on the table. "I think I made those drawings because of Rex, because I saw the same stuff he saw."

Pookie couldn't see how such a thing was possible, but he wasn't about to rule it out. At some point, you have to believe what your eyes are telling you. Seeing the snake-face drawing in Rex's room proved that there was some kind of connection.

"Astral projection, Bri-Bri? Telepathy? Mind-controlling little green men?"

Bryan shook his head. "I got no idea, man. All I know is Rex hates BoyCo. Hates them with everything he's got."

"Hate is a valid motive to kill Oscar and Jay," Pookie said. "But did he have the means?"

"You saw Bobby's body. Someone in Rex's house did that, and it wasn't his dead mom."

Pookie shook his head. "Sure, but it wasn't Rex. Kid is a buck-ten after two trips to the pasta buffet. He's working with adults, and big ones at that. Let's not count your dreams for now. Based on what Tiffany Hine saw, and based on what Mister Biz-Nass told us about Marie's Children wearing costumes, we have to assume that Rex is mixed up in that cult."

Bryan made more beer-bottle circles. "He's thirteen. He's an outcast. Maybe he gets recruited by Marie's Children. Maybe he makes some kind of deal with them to kill his enemies. That's plausible, but it doesn't explain my dreams. More important, it doesn't explain why anyone would cover this up. The body count is up to three."

"Four," Pookie said. "Oscar Woody, Jay Parlar, Birdman and don't forget Rex's mom."

"Right, four," Bryan said. "Why would Zou and Robertson let this happen? If Marie's Children are behind the killings ... maybe Zou is part of the cult?"

That same thought had been rattling around the back of Pookie's mind. It seemed that Zou *had* to be involved, somehow, but to think that the city's top cop was part of some wacko witches' coven? The idea shook Pookie's beliefs to the core.

"She's been a cop for thirty years, Bryan. How would she have got hooked up with them?"

"Maybe on the Golden Gate Slasher case, she found something. Or maybe something found her. Look at her career. She started out on patrol, she works a case with the symbols, winds up as an inspector" — Bryan snapped his fingers — "just like that."

Pookie nodded, trying to work through the possibilities. "Yeah, okay, so maybe she's a shit-kicking rookie who gets a break on the Golden Gate Slasher case. That case brings her into contact with the occult freaks behind the killings, assuming that the John Doe didn't act alone. Marie's Children recruit her, or indoctrinate her, or make her wear a fez hat like those Shriners, whatever, and *bam* — they have someone on the inside of the SFPD."

Bryan slow-motion-slid his bottle from his left hand to his right, then back again. "Doesn't get more inside than the chief of police. Someone with a lot of power gets control of Zou, then moves her up the ranks until she controls what cops get assigned to murder cases."

"Maybe," Pookie said. "But it still doesn't add up. We think Verde is in on this with her. Birdman was Verde's partner, so wouldn't that mean Birdman was in on it as well? Why send Verde and the Birdman somewhere they could get killed? And the BOLO out on Rex is no joke — every cop in the city is looking for that kid. If he's in Marie's Children, and Zou is in Marie's Children, why wouldn't she pull the BOLO?"

The connections just weren't there. On top of that, it didn't jibe with Pookie's instincts.

"Chief Zou has been a superstar cop for thirty frickin' years, Bri-Bri. She's done every job, from patrol to inspector to administration. She's been shot twice in the line of duty. She's won every award the department has to offer. And we're thinking she'd take money to cover up for serial killers? I can't buy it."

"Might not be money," Bryan said. "Blackmail, maybe."

Pookie's cell phone buzzed: a text. He pulled out the phone and read it. It was from Susie Panos.

SUSIE PANOS: ALEX IS HOME. HURRY!

He showed the text to Bryan.

Both men slid off their stools and ran for the door, leaving their beer and the giant statue of Bigfoot behind.

•••

Night had fallen. Under a small tree just inside Sharp Place at the corner of Union Street, Rex and Marco waited. Waited and watched. They each had a blanket. Not the warm kind, either — Rex's blanket was already soaked. It stank. Marco said that was important, the stinky part. It made sure people kept on walking.

The blankets were more complicated than Rex had thought. They were heavy because they were actually four blankets sewn together at one edge. Like the pages of a book, you could flip them so that a different color faced out: dark gray, brick-red, black and dark green. All the colors had lots of stains. The blankets also had hidden pockets. Marco kept his hatchet in one, safely out of sight.

On the way to this spot, Marco had stopped to show Rex how the blankets worked. When Marco picked the right color and slid into a shadowy area, then sat perfectly still, he all but disappeared.

Marco had also shown Rex how to wrap the blanket around his head, almost like a hood. Rex could see out, but for someone to see in they'd have to get real close.

Rex was cold, wet, shivering, and he'd never felt this amazing. The cold, the wet, those things didn't matter — he was waiting, he was watching.

He was *hunting*.

"Do I get to meet Sly tonight?"

"Probably," Marco said. "He'll call when he comes out. He'll be very happy to know I have you."

"Why don't you just call him?"

"No cell-phone reception at home," Marco said. "Just wait, my king — Sly will call."

Rex kept looking up at the window across the street.

"Sixth floor, you said?"

Marco nodded. "I followed Alex here myself a few days ago. He likes to hang out on the fire escape, so I know which apartment is his."

The fire escape ran up the face of the ten-story building. A row of bay windows rose up on either side, close enough to the fire escape that someone could step out of them right onto the small, metal landings.

Alex could be in that building. Rex was so *close*.

"What is Sucka going to do?"

"Kill him," Marco said. "Sucka has been waiting for his chance. Pierre got to kill the first one. I helped, but Pierre got him. Chomper and Dragonbreath got the second."

Chomper? Dragonbreath? Such cool names. *Sucka* was also a cool name, but Rex didn't want him to kill Alex unless Rex could see it happen. He wanted to watch Alex suffer. He needed to hear Alex *beg*.

"Marco, tell Sucka to bring Alex out here."

The bearded man's eyes widened. "My king, we can't bring him out here! It's too early, people are around, we'd be spotted!"

"Then take me inside. I need to see that bully die."

Marco shook his head. He looked pained, like he might cry at any moment. "You're my king and I'm supposed to obey, but I gotta keep you safe! We can't go in. Please just stay here and let Sucka do it for you."

If Rex was the *king*, then people had to do what he said. He'd spent his whole life being told what to do — now he would do the telling.

"I said *I want to see it.* Tell Sucka not to kill Alex until I get there."

Marco just stared. He didn't seem to know what to do. After a few seconds, his blanket slid aside a little. His hand came up with a cell phone.

"We get these at CVS," Marco said. "Or Walgreens. Just buy them and turn them on. It was Sly's idea, 'cause they can't trace them back to us or nothing."

He started to dial, then stopped. "My king, what about other people in the apartment? What if the boy's mother is home?"

Rex thought about that. He closed his eyes and remembered the leather belt tightening around Roberta's neck, how she had struggled and scratched.

His dick started to stiffen.

"He can kill the mother," Rex said. "And he can kill Issac if he has to, I guess, but you tell Sucka not to kill Alex until we come up there. I . . . uh . . . I *command* that, or whatever."

Marco dialed.

Rex tried to sit still. He waited.

●●●

"No fucking way, Mom," Alex said. "Issac and me ain't going to the cops!"

She was crying. The bitch was *always* crying.

Alex packed clean clothes into a duffel bag. Issac looked through Alex's dresser, searching for dry clothes that wouldn't look all baggy on his smaller frame.

His mom was doing that thing with the tissue paper again, wadding it up and pulling little bits out of the ball.

"Alex, honey, the police say your life is in danger. Just stay here with me. We'll call them together."

He walked closer to her. He towered over his mother.

"I'm not going to the cops, and you better not call them. You got that, Mom? Just give me some money, we have to get out of here."

"Alex, baby, *please.*"

"Mom, we saw Jay die. We were on our way to get him. Remember that cop in black that came here? He was pointing his gun in Jay's face. The cops are the ones that want to kill us."

His mother's upper lip quivered. Snot dripped out of her left nostril. So goddamn pathetic.

"But, Alex, baby, that doesn't make any *sense.* Why would the cops want you dead? What have you done?"

He still didn't have an answer to that. He and the boys had done some bad shit, for sure, but definitely nothing worth killing Oscar and Jay over.

"It's raining, baby," his mother said. "It's cold and wet out. Can't you just stay here till it stops?"

Issac nodded with way too much enthusiasm. "That's a good idea. Just till the rain stops. Don't you think that's a good idea, Alex?"

Alex stared at Issac until the smaller boy looked away. Then he stared at his mom. She was hiding something. He looked down — she had her phone in her hand.

He grabbed her wrist, lifted it up hard.

"Ouch! Alex, stop it!"

He ripped the phone out of her hand. She grabbed for it, but he pushed her. She fell back hard against his bedroom door.

He called up her texts. The most recent one read:

ALEX IS HOME. HURRY!

She'd sent it right after he and Issac had slipped in the building's back door and come up to the apartment. Sent to *Pookie Chang, SFPD*. Alex's stomach felt tight — those cops were coming. How could his own mother have sold him out like that?

He knelt and shoved the phone into her face. "This guy you just texted? He was there when Jay died! He's *partners* with the one that shoved a gun in Jay's face, you stupid whore!"

"Alex! *Please!*"

He wanted to punch her in the mouth, but he couldn't — she was still his mother. He ran to the living room, grabbed her purse and brought it back. Inside he found fifty bucks and a small bag of weed. He threw the purse at her; it hit her in the face. She covered her mouth, and then — of course — started crying again.

"Backstabbing bitch," Alex said. "Issac, get up. We've got to—"

The sound of splitting wood: someone had just smashed through the apartment's front door.

•••

Rain poured down even harder, but that became a background thing as Rex saw the sixth-floor window open. He saw a big body climb out onto the fire escape, black sweatshirt and jeans making him blend into the night. As soon as that person climbed out, another followed.

"Marco," Rex said. "That looks like Alex and Issac."

Marco worriedly pulled at his ear. "Uh-oh. Where's Sucka?"

"I don't even know who Sucka is, so you tell me."

Marco looked at his phone, as if by doing so he could make it ring and tell him what was happening. Raindrops splashed off the illuminated screen. He looked back up at the boys on the fire escape. "I'm not sure what's happening."

Rex felt confused — Marco had acted so quickly back at Rex's house, but now the man seemed lost, unsure. Maybe he needed specific orders or something?

Alex and Issac climbed down the fire escape's steep switchback stairs, moving from the sixth floor down to the fifth. If they got away, would anyone be able to find them? They would escape and that wouldn't be fair, not when they were *right there*.

"Marco," Rex said. "Get them."

Marco looked at Rex, then at the phone again, then to Alex and Issac. "It's not even midnight yet," he said. "This is too public. There are rules."

Alex reached the fourth-floor landing. He was going to get away.

Rex reached out and grabbed Marco's wet beard, pulled the man's face close. "I don't care about your stupid rules. *Get Alex!* And don't you *dare* kill him, you hear me talking to you?"

Marco's eyes narrowed — not with anger, but with purpose. He put the phone away and stood. Blanket still over his shoulders, he reached into the hidden pocket and pulled out his hatchet.

Timing the traffic, Marco tucked the blanket tight around him, stepped out into the rain and started crossing the street.

•••

Bryan held on tight. Pookie turned the Buick in a squealing right off Larkin onto Union. Wheels slid across wet pavement as windshield wipers tried to clear away the heavy rain. A block ahead, Susie's building rose up into the night air. At ten stories high, it dominated the surrounding four- and five-story buildings.

The car's tires slid, then caught. The Buick leveled out, rocking Bryan back to the right. They'd left the siren off — they didn't want to warn the kid they were on the way.

Up the street, through the dark drizzle and fuzzy streetlight glow, Bryan saw movement on the front of the building; two figures descending the fire escape.

"That's them," Bryan said, pointing. "They're already running."

The boys stopped. Bryan saw one continue down, while the other reversed direction and started climbing up.

"They made us," Bryan said. "You take the one on the fire escape, I'll take the one about to hit the ground."

Pookie swerved into the wrong lane to pass a truck, then cut in front of it just in time to miss a head-on with a black Acura. He ran a red light at Hyde, but the lights turned red as far as they could see and traffic slowed to a stop. Pookie locked up the brakes to keep from slamming into the cars ahead.

Bryan held the dashboard as the Buick's momentum pulled him forward. As soon as the car rocked back, he was out the door.

The late hour and the rain combined to leave little foot traffic on the sidewalks. Just one person, in fact, moved across the water-sheened blacktop, crossing from one side of the street to the other.

A big mound of a person — a person *covered with a blanket.*

That person was crossing the street and heading for the bottom of the fire escape.

Holy shit this is really happening I'm not dreaming this time.

As Bryan ran, he looked to the fire escape. Even in the dim light and heavy rain, he recognized the thick build of Alex Panos standing on the bottom landing. Alex hit a lever; a ladder rattled down to the concrete.

Alex descended.

Bryan was twenty feet away from the blanket-covered man, who was still thirty feet from the fire escape. Alex reached the sidewalk and took off.

The shambling mound of a person moved faster. The blanket flapped away for a moment, and in that moment Bryan saw a glint of metal.

He drew his gun and sprinted faster.

•••

Pookie scrambled up the cold, wet metal as fast as he dared. He looked up, blinking against the rain hitting his face, and was surprised to see a figure crawl out of a sixth-floor window and jump onto the fire escape. The person was little more than a shapeless shadow thanks to the heavy blanket that covered him. High above, at the eighth floor, Pookie saw a smaller figure — Issac.

Pookie's feet hit hard on the fire escape steps. He had to get to Issac before that blanketed man did.

•••

Bryan saw Alex running as fast as he could, big body lumbering, big arms swinging. The man chasing him moved much faster; he closed in on Alex, the gray blanket trailing behind like a heavy cape.

Goddamn he's fast!

Still sprinting hard, Bryan raised his gun.

"Police! Get down!"

The man either ignored him or couldn't hear over the rain.

Bryan thought of stopping, chancing a shot, but if he missed, he might hit Alex.

•••

Pookie had made it to the seventh-story landing when the man chasing Issac vanished from sight onto the roof. The nearly vertical climb already had Pookie's legs and lungs burning in complaint.

From up on the roof, he heard gunshots.

His foot slipped on a step and his knee banged hard into metal. He climbed on despite the pain.

Cold wind blowing, jacket and hair already soaked with driving rain, Pookie reached the ninth-floor landing — just one more short flight to reach the roof. He drew his Sig Sauer and started to climb.

•••

Marco heard a man yelling somewhere behind him. Police. *Again.* Sly was going to be so pissed, and if Firstborn found out, Marco would get such a beating. There were no tunnels around here. The nearest hidey-hole was the old Russian Hill reservoir, but that was five blocks away. Besides, Marco couldn't just run — the king had given an order.

Marco knew that if he could grab the boy, he could then scramble up a wall to the roof and the cop wouldn't be able to follow. The king had commanded the boy not be killed, but that didn't mean Marco couldn't wound him.

Still running, Marco raised his weapon.

•••

Bryan saw streetlights reflect off the wet blade.

A hatchet.

Bobby Pigeon's killer.

Bryan stopped running, aimed, then fired twice. The man stumbled forward and landed on Alex, sending both of them face-first into the sidewalk.

•••

Pookie heard two noises — a double tap from back down on the street, and a deep, bass *thong* from up on the roof. He swung his pistol over the roof's brick retaining wall, letting the gunsight lead his vision through the pouring rain. The bottom of his forearms rested on the narrow wall's flat top, leaving only his hands and head exposed to danger.

What the fuck?

A snap-sequence of visuals — a man wearing a mask with a long, curved beak, an arrow sticking out of his shoulder, rolling weakly in a puddle on the black-tar rooftop. And a second body, this one wearing a black sweatshirt, lying facedown and motionless: Issac Moses. Past them both, barely visible on the dark roof, a man standing, holding a bow, wearing some kind of . . . hooded cloak?

The standing man turned toward Pookie. The deep hood hid his face in shadow. He let go of the bow and reached into his dark green cloak, reached in *so fast.*

The bow hadn't even hit the roof before the man drew two pistols and fired. Pookie pulled his trigger twice even as he dropped behind the wall, bits of masonry spinning all around him.

•••

Bryan sprinted in, gun raised before him. The blanketed man rolled off Alex. Bryan saw blood staining the back of the man's white tank top — he had taken at least one round.

Bryan rushed in to see if he could stop the bleeding. As Bryan reached for him, he felt a strange warmth in his chest.

What the hell . . .

He didn't see the big boot kicking out until it was too late. The sole drove into his stomach and sent him flying backward. *So strong!* Bryan knew he'd lost his wind before he even landed. The Sig Sauer was still in his hand. His ass hit hard on the concrete. He let the momentum carry him in a backward roll. At the apex, Bryan pushed hard with his head and shoulders, bouncing himself into the air and letting him land on his feet.

He brought up the gun.

The bearded, bleeding man reached for the wet hatchet lying on the sidewalk.

"Don't do it, asshole! Don't even move!"

The man stopped and looked up at Bryan. Then his eyes widened and his mouth opened in an expression of pure shock.

•••

Pookie's heart kicked inside his chest. He'd been *shot at.* He couldn't just sit here, he had to move, he had to *act* and do it *now.* He licked the rain off his lips, sucked in a fast breath, then stood just enough to swing his gun over the wall.

The cloaked man was only a few feet away, rushing forward, bow in his hand. Pookie again ducked behind the wall as the cloaked man sailed overhead, out into the night.

Pookie clung to the fire escape as he turned to watch the man plummet to his death, but the man *didn't* plummet — cloak flapping behind him, the man sailed through the air, legs and arms kicking and pumping like an Olympic long jumper. It was like watching a special effect, a high-wire movie of someone arcing down through the rainy night.

The man soared clear across the street. He hit the flat, black roof of a four-story building and rolled once, twice, three times. Pookie watched in disbelief as the man stood and walked back to the building's edge.

Fifty feet away and six stories down, the bowman was little more than a mound of dark green fabric that blended into the black roof. And yet, Pookie could see the man was staring at the street. Pookie snapped a glance in that direction; on the sidewalk ten stories below, Bryan Clauser had his gun pointed at a man lying on the ground.

Then, Bryan slowly lowered his gun.

Pookie looked back to the man on the roof — he felt a dagger of horror when he saw the man holding the bow, drawstring pulled all the way back to his now-exposed cheek. Before Pookie could say a word, the man released.

The arrow ripped through the air.

•••

Bryan and the blanketed man stared at each other. What the hell was this?

That blossoming warmth in his chest, so *peaceful.* It beat a rhythm, *ba-da-bum-bummmm,* the sensation overwhelming in its intensity.

A staccato hiss, a half-second whisper of something passing scant inches from his ear, then an even shorter crunching noise.

Both men looked down.

An arrow shaft stuck out of the bearded man's chest.

Bryan instantly turned, his brain following the arrow shaft's angle, his gun whipping around to point up and across the street. There, a shape that might be a man

[*savior! monster!*]

and an outline that might be a bow.

His finger flicked the trigger

[*kill it now kill it NOW*]

five times before his training kicked in, before he realized he was shooting at a building that had people in it.

The muzzle flashes screwed with his vision for just a second. By the time he could focus on the roof again, the outline that might have been a man was gone.

The rain poured down.

Bryan turned back to look at the bearded man, at the arrow sticking out of his chest. Only then did he think to look for Alex Panos.

But Alex was nowhere to be seen.

• • •

The arrow had missed Bryan. *Thank God.* Pookie looked back to the archer's position, but now the roof was empty — the cloaked man had vanished into the shadows.

Had he just seen what he'd thought he'd seen? No. *No way.* Shit like that couldn't happen. Maybe someone had slipped some acid into his coffee. Maybe he was tripping balls right this very second.

Bryan Clauser was still standing. With no archer/sniper in sight, Pookie had to deal with the situation at hand. He climbed over the wall and onto the roof.

Issac Moses was still there, but the wounded man wearing the mask was gone.

Pookie's gun snapped up to eye level. He quickly walked toward the center of the roof, to the small hut there that probably led to the building's internal stairs. Pookie circled the hut, letting his barrel lead his vision. Nothing. He tried the handle: locked.

There was nowhere else on the roof a person could hide. The roof door was locked. Pookie had come up on the fire escape, the only other way down.

So where was the masked man with the arrow in his shoulder?

The rain kept pouring. Pookie moved back to Issac.

Oh, God . . .

The kid's chest and stomach were flat on the roof, but his head had been turned 180 degrees — Issac's dead eyes stared up into the night sky.

Susie Panos

ookie stood inside the apartment, looking down on Susie's body. She was on her back, eyes wide open, an expression of shock etched onto her still face. Something had punched a half-inch circle through her chest and into her heart. Her pajama top had been driven into the hole as well; the blood-soaked fabric lined the newly exposed flesh and bone.

Outside, patrol cars blocked the street. An ambulance had already arrived, but the paramedics had made quick work of declaring all three bodies dead on the scene, and all three as homicides. Crime-scene investigators were on the way, as was someone from the ME's office.

Such insanity. The things Pookie had seen — the jumper, the guy with the mask, Issac's head turned the wrong way — hard to process it all. Alex Panos was poison. Whoever wanted that kid had followed him here, and now his mother was dead because of it.

Pookie looked up as Bryan walked through the apartment's shattered front door. Bryan paused to look at the exposed white wood where the hinges had once connected, then down at the cracked door lying on the living room carpet. He seemed to mentally catalog these things, then walked over to join Pookie at Susie's body.

"I called in a BOLO on the perp," Bryan said.

"Really," Pookie said. "And how did you describe it?"

"A guy in a green cloak, maybe six feet tall. Carrying a bow. That about right?"

Pookie nodded. He kept staring at Susie's corpse. Maybe she wasn't the best mother, but she'd tried. She didn't deserve this.

"Sammy and Jimmy are here," Bryan said. "Jimmy is down with the bearded guy. Sammy's on his way up here."

Bryan knelt next to the body.

"She looks really pale," he said. "Maybe like she's lost a ton of blood."

Bryan was right. Pookie had seen the corpses of people who had bled to death. They looked a lot like Susie.

Bryan pointed to the hole in her chest. "Who did that to her?"

"A guy wearing a blanket and a mask came out the window and chased Issac up the fire escape. Maybe the guy had just finished doing this to Susie."

Bryan nodded. "This the same guy that twisted Issac's head the wrong way?"

"Could be," Pookie said. "Either him or the bowman."

"You'd have to be strong to break someone's neck like that. This guy with a mask . . . you sure it was a mask?"

"Not now, Bryan," Pookie said. "I can only handle so much of this shit at one time, you know?"

Bryan held up his hands palms-out. "Easy, Pooks, easy. Just tell me what the mask looked like."

It looked so disturbing my balls hid inside my chest was what Pookie wanted to say, but he didn't. "Ever see the pictures of those plague masks doctors wore in the Dark Ages?"

"I think so," Bryan said. "Long, pointy nose that points down? Kind of like a beak?"

"Yeah," Pookie said. "Kind of like a beak."

Bryan pointed to the hole in Susan's chest. "Something stabbed her there. You think this *mask* could have been strong enough to do that?"

Pookie knew what Bryan was getting at — how likely was it that a hooked-beak mask could punch through a chest? About as likely that the fake teeth of a werewolf mask were strong enough to rip off an arm.

"Pooks," Bryan said, "I know I'm the last person in the world who should ask a question like this, but are you *sure* you saw that bowman jump across the street? The world-record long jump is something like thirty feet — the space between the two buildings is at least *twice* that."

"I know what I saw," Pookie said. "Believe me, I wish I hadn't seen it at all. I don't know a damn thing about archery, but that guy hit the perp from across the street, ten stories up, in a rainstorm, at night, and he put that shot right over your shoulder."

Bryan nodded. "Unless he was aiming at me, and missed."

Pookie thought back to his brief shootout on the rooftop, to the cloaked man pulling two guns and blazing away. He'd had Pookie dead to rights — how could someone be that good with a bow and that bad with a gun from point-blank range? The answer was: *he couldn't be.* He hadn't killed Pookie because he hadn't *wanted* to kill Pookie.

"The archer wasn't aiming for you, Bri-Bri. He was aiming for Bobby Pigeon's killer."

Bryan's eyes narrowed. "Are you saying that since the guy is Bobby's alleged killer, it's okay to put an arrow in his heart?"

"Did I *say* it was okay?"

Bryan stared, then shook his head.

"The archer is just another murderer," Pookie said. "Far as we know, he killed Issac, too. It gives us one more person to look for — Rex, Alex and the archer. We have to focus and get what info we can, because Robertson could show up at any minute and kick us out of here."

Sammy Berzon walked into the room, a metal case in each hand.

"Fellas," he said. "Never a dull moment with you two around, eh? Jimmy is heading up to the roof. I got seniority, so his bitch-ass gets the rain. *Boom.* We're done with the stiff down on the sidewalk. Shot through the heart, and who's to blame, right?" Sammy's head rocked back in a silent laugh. "We found a cell phone on him, but it's a pre-paid. I'll have the boys start running the call history, but don't get your hopes up."

Pookie knew that Sammy was right; the phone would probably reveal nothing. Perps were smart enough to buy pre-paids with cash, meaning there was no personal information associated with them. A pre-paid phone calling only other pre-paid phones left almost no trail. The only thing they were likely to get were GPS locations of calls made and received. That might reveal a pattern, or possibly produce a specific place to investigate.

"Get us call locations as soon as you can," Pookie said. "What else you get off him?"

"Nothing yet," Sammy said. "We're done with him. Hudson the Hotness has him now."

Bryan's head snapped up. "Robin's down there?"

Sammy nodded. "That's the fact, Jack."

Bryan started walking out. Pookie followed him.

"By the way," Sammy said just before they exited the broken door. "Whichever of you two comedians called in a BOLO on a guy in a fucking *cloak* should watch out. Robertson just canceled it. He said someone was in deep shit for playing games at a murder scene. FYI, eh?"

Bryan snarled, then turned and walked out.

The assistant chief of police had just canceled a BOLO on a murderer. Pookie wanted to be shocked and outraged, but he wasn't that surprised; he was just too damn tired to get fired up about it.

Pookie took one last look at Susie Panos. She'd tried to save her son, and in doing so proved an old adage — no good deed goes unpunished.

Post-killing Scene

obin Hudson knelt next to the body. To her right, streetlights danced off rainwater that flowed fast down the gutter. The water spilled into a thick iron grate half clogged with leaves and bits of trash. Bubble-lights flashed from stationary cop cars, casting red and blue glows against the buildings and the wet black pavement. Sammy and Jimmy had set up portable lights to illuminate the body. They had put up a little tent over it as well — just four poles with no sides and a peaked roof, the kind of thing you might see at a street fair. A light breeze snapped at the tent top.

The rain had soaked the victim long before they'd put up the tent. Beads of water stood out on his thick beard. His blue jeans looked nearly black from the wetness. An arrow shaft stuck up out of his sternum. Water had diluted the red stain surrounding the shaft, turning the blood-soaked white fabric a diluted pink.

Robin was about to start her examination when she saw Bryan and Pookie approaching. The pair had been first on the scene — again. It was getting to be more than coincidence. She needed to find out exactly what was going on.

"Robin," Pookie said. "Don't you look official."

She started to ask him what he meant, then she remembered what she was wearing. "Oh, the uniform?"

Pookie nodded. "No sloppy windbreaker for you, I see. Just like the Silver Eagle."

She smiled and looked back to the body. Yes, she wore the formal ME's jacket, even though the windbreaker was an acceptable option. If Metz felt the uniform was an important part of the job, then so did she. And besides, she liked brass buttons and the gold braid around the cuffs.

Bryan knelt down next to the body. Robin couldn't help but look at him, at his green eyes, at the dark-red hair that looked rumbled and ratty, the way it had when he'd spent the day in bed with her. Then she remembered that there was a corpse on the ground between them. How blasé had she become? This wasn't the time for a love connection.

Pookie leaned in. "Long beard, wife-beater, hatchet — he fits Verde's description perfectly."

Robin pulled out a collapsible probe. "Verde's report said Bobby shot his killer at least once. That was a few hours ago." She slid the probe under the tank top's left strap and lifted. "Take a look, fellas — aside from the arrow, there's no bullet holes in the chest. I don't think this is the guy."

Bryan stared at the body. He seemed so distant, even more so than normal. Whatever ordeal he was going through, it had gotten worse. "Maybe Bobby hit him somewhere else," he said.

"Maybe," Robin said. "I'll be able to tell when I get him on the autopsy table."

Bryan reached out and gently took the probe. He dragged the tip lightly across the arrow's feathers. As soon as he did that, Robin saw what had caught his attention.

"Real feathers," she said. "Aren't they usually plastic?"

He nodded. "I think so." He looked up at Pookie, who leaned over both of them. "Don't most arrows have plastic feathers?"

Pookie made his *pfft* noise. "Why are you asking me? Do I look like a fletcher?"

Bryan's eyes wrinkled in annoyance. "A what?"

"A fletcher," Pookie said. "A dude that makes arrows for a living."

Bryan shrugged. "Maybe all fletchers are pudgy Chinese dudes, for all I know."

Pookie rubbed at the belly that stretched out his white button-down shirt. "Naw, there's only so much of that sexy to go around. Bo-Bobbin, I'll be shocked if this isn't Bobby's killer. What's the status on the blood samples taken from Rex Deprovdechuk's house?"

"Already running," Robin said. "They came into the morgue with Bobby's body. I also started running Rex's sperm sample, so we'll know if the blood is his."

"It's not," Pookie said. He nodded toward the bearded corpse. "It will match this guy. And I bet it will also match the samples you took off of Oscar Woody."

"You think this man killed Oscar?"

"Probably," Pookie said. "He tried to kill Alex Panos, so odds are he whacked Oscar and Jay Parlar as well."

It seemed obvious when Pookie laid it out. "I'll start this guy's tests right now with a machine we have in the van. You should have all three results in about an hour."

Bryan nodded, then slid the probe up the feathers again.

Pookie took the probe and did the same thing, as if he just wanted to see for himself.

"Maybe this arrow is custom-built," he said. "The way that guy shot, I'm guessing he doesn't buy his archery supplies from a discount bin at

Dick's Sporting Goods. If we find out who made this, maybe we can find out who bought it. Robin, how soon can you get it out of his chest?"

She leaned in, turning her head this way and that to examine the wound. She lightly touched the notch just above the feathers, then gave it an experimental push. The shaft itself flexed a little, but the arrowhead didn't move a bit.

"It's in there good," she said. "I'm going to need a bone saw to get it out."

"Shit," Bryan said. "How fast can you make that happen?"

First Zou had rushed things, then Verde, now Bryan and Pookie? It was their investigation, but it was her job to do things correctly, methodically.

"Guys, Sammy said there's another body upstairs and a third on the roof. We have to get all three in the van and take them back, so I'm going to be here awhile."

Pookie knelt. Now all three of them were low around the body, as if the corpse were a small campfire on a freezing night.

Pookie looked around quickly to make sure no one was near, then spoke quietly. "Robs, you're in charge of the department, right?"

She nodded.

"We need help," he said. "Can you get wife-beater here to the morgue right away, then have another ME come and handle the other bodies?"

"But keep it quiet," Bryan said. "Don't tell anyone you're taking this guy back, just load him up and go. Can you do that for us?"

She looked at the two men. That kind of action wasn't illegal per se, but it wasn't protocol. If people started questioning her decisions, and those questions got back to the mayor's office, it would damage her shot at permanently taking over Metz's job. But at the same time, Pookie and Bryan had never asked her for anything like that before. They seemed desperate.

"That's not how we do things," she said. "I could make it happen, but before I go off the reservation, you have to tell me what's going on."

"We can't," Bryan said. "Just do this for us. It's important."

It's important, and so is your health, Bryan — so is your sanity.

"You guys want something from me, I want something from you. I need to know more."

Bryan's eyes hardened. "It's best you don't. Just trust me."

She shook her head. "You guys are asking me to do something that could jeopardize my career. So cut the *let's protect the delicate flower* bullshit. Convince me."

Bryan stared at her, then looked over at Pookie. Pookie shrugged.

Bryan turned back to Robin, looked at her over the body on the ground between them. "We think Chief Zou and Rich Verde could be part of a cover-up," he said. "She's protecting someone involved with the murders of Oscar Woody, Jay Parlar and maybe even Bobby Pigeon. She could also be involved in a cover-up of those old Golden Gate Slasher murders."

Bryan and Pookie both looked intense, focused — they weren't kidding. But the chief of police? Covering up murders? "Why would Zou do something like that?"

"We don't know," Pookie said. "We only have theories, and don't have time to go into them now. If Zou or Sean Robertson or Rich Verde shows up here, we'll lose the chance to learn more before they shut us out. We *need* a good look at this arrow. Please, get this guy back to the morgue and start the autopsy immediately."

Autopsies weren't usually done at night. Bodies collected in the evening went into the storage area for the MEs to work on the following morning. Another deviation from the norm, another potential question about her reliability as the next chief medical examiner.

Not so long ago, she had trusted Bryan Clauser more than she'd trusted anyone in her entire life. Maybe he wasn't the most emotional creature in the world, but he was a world-class cop — he wouldn't ask for this if he didn't believe it was absolutely necessary.

She nodded. "All right. I'll take the body back, then send someone else to pick up the other two. Meet me at the morgue in an hour."

Bryan smiled at her. It was forced, but it was still a smile. He and Pookie walked off, giving Robin room to do her job.

The Hunt

Rex stopped walking. He knelt to the sidewalk and leaned against a building wall. He sat very still.

Rex waited.

A block ahead, a boy in a dark sweatshirt stopped and looked back. His head moved, his eyes searched, but after a few seconds, the boy turned away and kept moving down Laguna Street.

Rex waited a few seconds, then he followed.

Even in the rain and the wind, Rex smelled something that made his brain buzz, made his chest all vibratey.

He smelled blood.

Alex's blood.

Marco was probably dead. Rex felt sad about that. Marco had been a nice guy. He had *obeyed*. Rex had watched the brief fight between Marco and the man in black, then that arrow hit Marco in the chest. And just after that, Rex saw Alex running away.

Maybe Rex could have helped Marco, but he could not, *would not* let Alex Panos escape.

Rex had followed Alex, using the night, the rain, the wind and the blankets to stay as hidden as possible. He couldn't believe how well the blankets worked — when he did pass people on the sidewalk, they steered clear. No one wanted to talk to a stinky bum. Rex was a shadow, like those black panthers in the jungle that moved so quiet no one saw them.

He had nowhere to go. The cops would know he'd killed Roberta, so he couldn't go home. He couldn't go back to Marco's basement — what if Marco had ID on him with that address? The cops would look there, too. Rex didn't even have a place to sleep.

And he didn't care, because sleep didn't matter.

What mattered was the *hunt*.

Rex felt *alive*, Rex felt *strong*, Rex felt like he could walk all night and into the next day. Sooner or later, Alex Panos would stop.

And then, Rex would make him pay.

The Arrowhead

Robin prepped for autopsy.

She'd had the overnight ME staff help her shoot the x-rays, then brought the body into Dr. Metz's private autopsy room. Once the body was prepared, she sent the overnight staff out to pick up the bodies of Susan Panos and Issac Moses, leaving her alone in the morgue.

The RapScan machine was almost finished with the tests on Rex Deprovdechuk's sperm and the blood from Bobby's assailant. She carried the machine into the private autopsy room so she'd get the results as soon as they came up.

The private room was just a smaller version of the larger main room. It even had the same old-school wood paneling. There was enough space for a single autopsy table, an area to walk around it, and counters and cabinets along the walls.

Robin was already regretting her decision to do what Bryan and Pookie had asked. Rushing a murder scene, *leaving* the scene — that was not the behavior of a senior medical examiner. And only now did she realize they hadn't given a shred of proof to back up their claims.

Had she really been foolish enough to think she didn't love Bryan anymore? She would do anything for him; it had always been that way, probably always would. He didn't return that love, and that hurt, but it didn't change the fact that she would never be able to let him go.

In the parlance of Pookie Chang, unrequited love sucked donkey balls.

Time to get down to business.

Despite Rich Verde's dead-on description, she knew this wasn't Bobby Pigeon's killer. The body on the table was that of an out-of-shape slob, beer gut and all. There was no way he had the sheer strength needed to drive a hatchet through Bobby's clavicle, part of his scapula, three of his ribs and an inch into his sternum. She also doubted the bearded man would have had the upper-body strength needed to tear off Oscar Woody's arm. And, most of all, his teeth were perfectly normal — he didn't have the wide incisors necessary to make those parallel grooves on Oscar's bones.

So this man hadn't killed Bobby *or* Oscar.

Robin flipped down her face shield. She stepped on a button that started her audio recorder, then picked up a scalpel from the tray next to the table.

"Beginning autopsy on John Doe. Caucasian male, approximately thirty years old. One hundred eighty-six centimeters tall, one hundred four kilograms. Subject appears to have been killed by an arrow that penetrated the heart."

She saw two small, pink, puckerish scars on his chest. Her gloved hands traced them. She hadn't noticed those in the dark and the rain. Could they . . . no, they were almost healed, they couldn't be wounds from Bobby Pigeon's final two bullets.

"Subject appears to have two small puncture wounds on his left pectoral, incurred possibly a week ago. The first is at two o'clock and ten centimeters from the left nipple, the second is seven o'clock and seven centimeters from the right nipple."

She looked at her notes, checking positions of the two bullet wounds on the man's back from where Bryan had shot him. Other than those wounds and the two marks on his chest, the man didn't have a scar or a scratch on him.

But those healed marks on the corpse's chest . . . had she seen something on the x-rays?

She reached over to the portable computer stand next to the porcelain table and called up the x-ray images. A bright white spot glowed directly under the healed wound near his right nipple. Could that be a bullet?

Bobby's bullet?

She shook her head. Bryan had shot this man twice in the back; one of those bullets had probably bounced off a rib and come to rest here.

She looked at the x-rays again. That was strange . . . there were *three* white spots.

But Bryan had only shot him twice.

Something else on the black, white and gray image caught her attention.

"Subject's ribs appear to be thicker than expected. In fact, *all* bones appear to be abnormally thick. Possible high bone density due to a mutation in LDL-receptor-related protein five. Will examine more closely after initial autopsy is complete."

None of this mattered if she didn't get that arrow out of there in time for Pookie and Bryan to use it. That urgency now felt silly. What was going to happen? Would Chief Zou kick in the door to the private autopsy room and chase Robin out?

She picked up a scalpel with her right hand, a small hose with her left. She sliced from the right shoulder to the sternum, spraying the wound with water as she went. Diluted blood ran down the body to the white porcelain surface, then flowed into the grooves that carried it to the foot of the table, where it finally passed through a hole and into a drainage sink. She made an identical incision on the left side, creating a V anchored by the arrow shaft sticking straight out of the man's chest. From the bottom of that V, she sliced down to the pubic bone.

Robin then peeled and cut, peeled and cut, her scalpel scraping against the sternum, the ribs and the clavicle, separating skin, muscle and soft tissue from the bones. As she grabbed, pulled and tugged, she realized the corpse's flesh felt different than she was used to . . . it felt strangely heavy.

"Subject's muscle mass feels denser than normal. Subject may have LRP5 mutation. Again, will examine in detail after initial examination is completed."

That mutation wasn't uncommon; she'd read about it in several journals. Denser muscle could mean more cells per square inch, and more muscle cells meant more strength. Maybe she'd been wrong — could this guy have had the power necessary to inflict those horrible wounds on Bobby Pigeon and Oscar Woody? If he *was* Oscar's killer, could the Zed chromosome be responsible for these mutations? And possibly for other mutations she hadn't seen yet?

Hell, if she didn't get the CME position, she could probably make a living on the Zed chromosome alone. Nobel Prize winner Dr. Robin Hudson? That had a nice ring to it.

She lifted the V-flap up over the perp's face, exposing the neck muscles, then spread the side flaps open to expose the rib cage.

Time for the bone saw.

She lifted the solid, metal power tool. Its high-pitched buzz filled the air as she cut through the ribs where they curved down to the man's sides. Blade on bone produced the smell of burning hair. After so many years at this job, that odor didn't really bother her anymore.

After she finished with the saw, she set it aside and rinsed the body down. She sliced through the diaphragm, then lifted the now-severed, arrow-pierced rib cage away from the body.

The rib cage felt far heavier than she would have expected. Did the thicker, denser bone exist to withstand the stresses generated by stronger muscles?

Holding the pierced rib cage in her hands, she examined the embedded arrowhead.

"Arrowhead is a three-bladed broadhead configuration, approximately seven centimeters from tip to attachment point. Each blade's cutting edge is approximately seven-point-eight centimeters. The blades are serrated. The bottom corner of each blade has a small hook, curving up toward the point."

Such a horrible weapon. The point had penetrated John Doe's sternum, driving right into the heart. The arrowhead probably would have punched clean through were it not for those little hooks. That seemed counterintuitive, as it would do more damage the farther in it went. The way this was made, the way it embedded in the rib cage . . . it looked like the designer wanted it to *stick*.

She set the rib cage aside.

Robin reached for the heart — then stopped.

The broadhead had sliced into the right ventricle, nearly severing the pulmonary artery. A kill shot, no question. But it wasn't the heart that stopped her cold.

"What the *hell* is that?"

The private room's door opened. Bryan and Pookie walked in.

"Robin-Robin, Bo-Bah . . ." Pookie's voice trailed off when he saw the corpse on the table. "Ew. That's nasty."

She lifted her visor and waved them over. "Guys, look at this!"

Bryan looked her up and down. "Don't we need to suit up or something?"

"Screw OSHA," Robin said. "Come here."

The small room fit three comfortably. The boys walked up to the body. She pointed to the bloody, open chest, to a glossy, purple shape just above the heart. "What the hell is *that*?"

Bryan and Pookie looked at it, then at each other, then at her. She saw Bryan's right hand move to his chest, his palm lightly resting against his sternum, making a slow-motion circle there. He again looked at the purple shape, then leaned back a little as if the sight horrified him.

Pookie didn't look horrified; he looked excited. He leaned in close. "That's his heart, right? Do I get a prize?"

"No, you idiot," Robin said. She pointed to the maroon-red heart. "*That* is his heart, and it looks normal." She again pointed to the purple shape. "I'm talking about this thing. I've never seen it before."

She slid her left hand into the body and cupped her fingers under the strange bit of flesh — if felt firm, yet giving. Her right hand reached in with the scalpel. She carefully cut the purple thing free.

"Blargh," Pookie said.

Robin lifted it out of the body. It was a shallow disc about the size of her palm, purple and slimed with tacky blood. She held it for Bryan to see.

He wrinkled his nose in disgust. "Is it a tumor or something?"

"I don't think so," Robin said. "If it is, it's not like any cancer or tumor I've ever seen, or even heard described. It could be an ectopic dysplasic organ — that's a malformed organ that winds up in a different spot in the body than is typical. Sometimes, dysplasic organs are even functional, but . . . there isn't any known organ that looks like this."

Pookie tried to lean in and look but he clearly didn't want to come close enough to touch it. "What does it do?"

Robin shrugged. "I have no idea."

She walked a few feet to the scale. She had to weigh all the organs, might as well start with this curiosity.

"Hey," Pookie said. He pointed to the man's crotch. "This guy has no balls."

Bryan let out a dismissive huff of a laugh. "Figures you'd look there first."

"I'm serious," Pookie said. "Look at Mister No-Nuts."

Robin did. She'd been in such a hurry to get the body in here and re-move the arrowhead that she hadn't paid much attention to the subject's genitalia.

"You're right, Pooks," she said. "I see no testicles."

"Ball-less," Pookie said. "And he's not going to get any dates based on the rest of what he's got, if you know what I'm saying."

The subject's penis was barely larger than that of a small boy. Robin lifted it and felt underneath.

"No scrotum," she said. "And there doesn't appear to be any scar tis-sue, so he was probably born that way."

Pookie shook his head. "The poor, poor bastard."

"He has multiple mutations," Robin said. "Thick, oversized bones, ab-normally dense muscle and an *unknown* organ. You guys, this is a really big deal."

Bryan looked up to a clock on the wall. "It sounds important, but we need to hurry. Can we get the arrow?"

"Sure, sorry." Robin left the organ in the hanging scale's tray.

She picked up the bone saw and made a few more cuts to the severed rib cage, freeing the arrow. She held it point-up so they could all look at it. The room's powerful lights cast glaring reflections off the bloody arrow-head's bright metal. Robin noticed lines in the flats of the blades — blood had coagulated in them, showing an engraved symbol. It looked like a cross with little *V*s at the end of each point.

Bryan took out his cell phone and snapped a picture.

Pookie poked the blade with a pen. "Bri-Bri, you seen this cross symbol before?"

Bryan shook his head. "I'm . . . I'm not sure. I've never drawn it."

Drawn it? Robin had lived with Bryan for two years. She had never seen him draw so much as a doodle. She'd also never seen him *afraid* in that time, of anything, yet each new discovery from this John Doe's body seemed to affect him even more.

Pookie pointed his pen at the arrowhead's base, where it connected to the wooden shaft. Robin saw another symbol there, a different one: it looked like a knife or a sword, pointing down, the blade partly hidden behind a big circle with a smaller circle in the middle.

"Looks like a dagger," Pookie said. "And the circle . . . that look familiar, Bri-Bri?"

Bryan nodded. "It's an eye."

It was a circle in a circle. In context with the dagger, Robin thought the circle might represent a shield, but Bryan seemed very sure. "How do you know it's an eye?"

"We've seen other symbols like it," he said. "Stuff that's directly related to the case. We'll tell you about it later, I promise." He pointed to the hooks at the base of the arrowhead. "This why it stuck in Blackbeard's chest?"

Blackbeard. She liked that. Much better than *John Doe*.

"I think so," she said. "I can do some math on it later — mass of the arrow and arrowhead, distance traveled — try to come up with some force calculations, but I'm sure this arrowhead is *designed* to partially penetrate, then stop. Stop and *stick*."

"That's weird," Pookie said. "Wouldn't it do more fucking-shit-up if those big-honkin' blades just went all the way through?"

Robin nodded. "If the arrow hadn't lodged in Blackbeard's sternum, it would have sliced his heart in half."

Something caught her eye. She reached out with her scalpel and scraped the flat of one of the broadhead blades. The gooey blood moved, of course, but the scalpel tip also made a tiny trough — not in the metal itself, but in a gray smear on top of the metal.

"There's some kind of paste on here."

Bryan leaned in. "Poison?"

"I don't know," she said. "We'll have to analyze it."

"Sure," Pookie said. "Of course. Why not? If the giant-ass broadhead won't kill a brotha, you better poison him too, right?" He pulled out his cell phone and snapped several close-up photos. "I'm going to call Black Mister Burns and have him run these new symbols."

Pookie walked to the door, opened it, then turned and smiled. "I'll just go call him right now. Don't you kids do anything I wouldn't do while I'm gone. See what I did there? 'Cause I would do all kinds of stuff. It's clever in that I'm saying you can fuck if you wanna."

Robin couldn't help but laugh.

Pookie closed the door behind him.

"Amazing," Bryan said. "There's a cracked-open body on the table, and he thinks we're going to play spin the bottle?"

She was alone with him again. She didn't know if she'd get another chance to help him open up, to find out what was happening to him. It wasn't the time to be selfish and focus on her own needs, her own feelings — Bryan needed someone. Even if it hurt her to the core, she would be there for him.

"There's more to this than a cover-up," she said. "I know you, Bryan Clauser. I know who you are and how you think, or at least I did until all this started happening."

"What does that mean?"

"It means I know you're scared."

He turned away, not looking at anything in particular, just looking away from her.

"Bryan, whatever this is, you can tell me. We broke up, sure, I get that, but I will *always* love you."

He turned to face her. She expected to see his usual blank stare, but instead there was pain in those eyes, pain and frustration.

"Robin, I . . ."

Come on, let me in. Let me help you.

She waited.

He closed his eyes, rubbed at them slowly with his left hand. He dropped his hand and blinked a few times, seeming to gather himself.

"Okay," he said. "Man, where do I even start? This seems impossible, but—"

In the corner of the room, the RapScan machine beeped. Robin looked at the briefcase-sized machine; the karyotype tests had finished.

She turned back to Bryan. "Go ahead, you were saying?"

He tilted his head toward the machine. "That's the results from Bird-man's killer?"

Robin sighed. The moment had passed. No way he'd talk now, not with those results waiting. Well, she'd tried. She wished he would confide in her, but that wasn't what he wanted. It *hurt*, and it was out of her control to do anything about it.

She stripped off her gloves and stepped to the machine. Bryan followed.

The top of the monitor showed a notification icon:

BOBBY PIGEON ASSAILANT SAMPLE COMPLETE.

"This sample is from the blood spatter in Rex's apartment," she said. "The other two samples will finish any second now. Let's see what we have with this one."

She hit a key to bring up the karyotype results. The colorful horizontal lines played across the flat-panel screen. Bryan pointed to the last box, the one that displayed the sex chromosomes. "A Zed," he said. "So Bobby's killer is also Oscar Woody's killer?"

When she looked at the markers, she felt a rush of excitement, of pure discovery. She pointed to the second sex chromosome. "This is an X. Bobby Pigeon's killer is Zed-X. Oscar's killer was Zed-Y. Bryan, this means we have *two* people with the Zed chromosome!"

"So . . . they're related?"

Related? One case, two killers, both with the never-before-seen Zed chromosome — what were the odds they *weren't* related?

"Hold on." She worked the touch-screen to enter new commands. "I'm telling the machine do a high-level scan for common sequences."

"What will that do?"

"It will tell us if their Zed chromosomes are identical. If they are, they're brothers."

"Brothers?"

Robin hit *enter.* The machine returned a result almost instantly — the Zed chromosomes were identical.

"Brothers," she said. "At least half-brothers. They either have the same mother or the same father."

The machine beeped again. At the top of the screen she saw a notification icon:

R. DEPROVDECHUK SAMPLE COMPLETE.

She pressed the icon. The screen blanked out, then displayed the new karyotype.

Robin just stared.

"Uh, Robin? What the hell is that?"

She didn't know. She really didn't have a goddamn clue. Rex wasn't XY, as a normal boy would be. He wasn't XZ, and he wasn't even YZ, for that matter.

Rex Deprovdechuk's sex genes? XYZ.

"He's trisomal," she said. "I mean, that can happen — at first I thought Oscar's killer was XXY, but this . . . I don't know what to make of it."

"What about his Zed? Is it the same as the other two?"

Robin tapped the screen again. The machine responded even faster this time.

"It's the same," she said. "Rex is the brother of both Blackbeard here and Oscar Woody's killer."

Bryan chewed at his lower lip. He stared at the RapScan's screen. "This seems pretty convenient. You tell me no one has ever seen the Zed before this case, yet now they come up everywhere we look? Could the machine be on the fritz?"

"I doubt it. I ran the results on Oscar Woody's killer three times and ran control groups of normal male and female samples as well. The control groups came up just as they should, while the results of Oscar Woody's killer replicated the same each time. What that means is, just trust me — the machine works fine."

Bryan turned to her. "What now?"

What now? She had no idea. Where to even begin? She wasn't even finished with the autopsy of the bearded man on the table. Her brain felt stuck in neutral. She couldn't be seeing what she saw, yet it was all there in living color.

The machine beeped a third time.

> ARCHERY VICTIM SAMPLE COMPLETE.
> ALERT! MATCH FOUND.
> GENETIC MATCH WITH: BOBBY PIGEON ASSAILANT SAMPLE.
> MATCH PROBABILITY: 99.9%.

They both turned to look at the body on the table.

"That's impossible," she said. "The first sample came from a bullet that Bobby shot *through* the chest of his attacker, but the guy on the table . . . he didn't have bullet wounds on his chest."

The door to the small room opened. Pookie walked in, eyebrows raised in apologetic alarm. Walking in right behind him: Chief Amy Zou.

Robin's heart sank. *Oh, shit. There goes my chance at chief medical examiner.*

"Inspector Clauser," Chief Zou said. "Fancy meeting you here. Step out of the room, please. I'd like a word. You, too, Doctor Hudson."

They were *so* busted. Robin followed Bryan and Pookie out of the room and into the long, main autopsy area. There she saw more people — Rich Verde, Mayor Jason Collins, Sean Robertson . . . and Baldwin Metz.

Robin ran to him, her hunger for the department's top position forgotten at the sight of her friend and mentor. "Doctor Metz! Oh my God, it's good to see you!"

She reached to hug him, but Robertson gently held up a warning hand. She stopped, then realized that Metz was leaning on Robertson's other arm. Dr. Metz looked like he could barely stand at all. His normally perfect silver hair looked a bit mussed, a bit frazzled. His skin had a sickly pallor. Sunken eyes stared at her with both anger and exhaustion.

"Doc," Robin said, "what are you doing here? You belong in a hospital bed."

He forced a smile. "Duty calls, my dear." He looked at Zou with an expression that seemed to say *it's your show.*

Zou nodded. She turned to Rich Verde. "Can you step into the private room and tell me if that is Bobby Pigeon's killer?"

Verde glared at Pookie and Bryan. The man's pencil-mustached lip curled into a half-sneer. His expression combined utter rage and deep sadness — maybe Verde had yelled at his partner in public, but Birdman's loss weighed on the man's soul.

He walked into the private room. After only a few seconds, he stepped back out.

"That's him," he said. "No question."

Mayor Collins cleared his throat. His tailored suit and perfect hair seemed out of place here, a place where people rolled up their sleeves and did the city's dirty work. He walked over and put a hand on Verde's shoulder. Verde's head snapped around, but his angry expression faded when he saw the look of concern on the mayor's face.

"A tragedy, my friend," Collins said. "I'll make sure the city pays proper respect to Inspector Pigeon."

Verde looked to the ground. "Aw, fuck this," he said, then strode out of the morgue.

Chief Zou walked to the door of the private room. She held it open, then looked at Bryan and Pookie. "Both of you, wait for me in here."

Bryan and Pookie looked at each other, then to Robin. They didn't know what to do. Neither did she.

"Now," Zou said.

Pookie and Bryan did as they were told. Chief Zou shut the door, closing them in. She turned and looked at Collins.

Mayor Collins nodded, then he looked at Robin. "Doctor Hudson, Doctor Metz will take over from here. I'm disappointed in your performance tonight. I thought we could trust you. Apparently, I was wrong."

Metz waved a hand in annoyance. "Oh, shove it, Jason. Now is not the time for that. We're going to need her anyway."

Need her? Need her for what? What the hell was going on?

The mayor looked back at the ill Metz, then nodded. "Sure, we'll talk about that, but not right now. Take care of this, please."

Metz let out a tired sigh. "Robin, go home. I'll finish the autopsy."

She shook her head. "No way, Doc. I don't know what's going on, but you need to be back in bed. You're in no shape to—"

"*Enough*," Mayor Collins said. "Doctor Hudson, your boss just asked you to leave. If you want *any* kind of job in this department, do what he says. *Now.*"

Was he threatening to *fire* her? She looked at Dr. Metz. He smiled apologetically, then gave her a single, long nod. *Just go, I'll explain later,* the gesture said.

This whole thing was insane. Metz could barely stand — he was in no condition to finish the autopsy. But if that was the way he wanted it, then she had to respect that.

She walked out of the main autopsy room and to her desk in the administration area. She took her motorcycle jacket from a peg on the cubicle wall and shrugged it on. She removed her helmet from under the desk and started to leave . . . but her gaze lingered on her computer. All the genetic information she'd just run in the RapScan, that would be in the department database. She could just grab an external drive, copy that over, and—

"Doctor Hudson?"

Robin turned quickly. Chief Amy Zou was standing right there, a cold, blank expression on her face. "Did you need anything else, Doctor?"

Robin's heart kicked in her chest. The woman had been right behind her.

"Uh, no," Robin said. She held up her helmet. "Just needed my gear."

"And you've got it," Zou said. "So drive safe. It's late."

Robin nodded and quickly walked out of the Medical Examiner's Office.

Pay the Piper

Bryan stood in the corner of the private autopsy room, as far away from the open body as he could get — which wasn't far. What crap was Zou going to pull now?

Pookie stood next to the table, looking down at the bearded man with the missing chest. "Did Robin say this hunka burnin' love was Birdman's killer?"

"Yeah. Her tests confirmed this is the guy Bobby shot. But he's *not* Oscar Woody's killer, so that guy is still out there. If Zou is protecting Marie's Children, or whoever the killer is, then—"

"She's not," Pookie said. "I mean, yeah, she's protecting a *killer*, but not some cult. She caught me out in the main autopsy room. She was on me like a bum on a baloney sandwich. I'm looking at her, and for once I'm not thinking about how she'd be in bed, and then some pieces clicked. Remember how I told you that the bowman drew down on me, but missed on purpose?"

"Yeah. How does that connect with Zou?"

"Think about it — first time the arrow thing comes up is thirty years ago, when the Golden Gate Slasher turns up dead. Cops bury the case, they remove any and all mentions of an arrow. We now know Blackbeard is a murderer, and he was killed by an arrow. These archers think they're vigilantes — *that's* who Zou is protecting, not serial killers."

"That doesn't add up. Zou took us off the case to keep us from catching Oscar and Jay's murderer."

"Close, but no cee-gar," Pookie said. "She got us out of the way so *someone else* could find the murderer." He held a palm-up hand toward the body on the white porcelain table. "Someone who would do this, unburdened by laws, rights and procedures. Metz is in on it. He fudges the autopsy reports to eliminate any presence of the archer, just like he did for the Golden Gate Slasher case."

Bryan looked at the body, thought of Pookie's angle. If Zou wanted to protect a vigilante, that would explain the missing parts of the Slasher case files. Verde could pay lip service to finding the killers. Once a killer was taken out, Metz could handle the rest. If that was what was going on, Robertson was also in on it . . . but was the mayor?

"What about Collins? If you're right, why would he be involved?"

"Maybe this is *really* big," Pookie said. "Maybe the mayor, or someone else way up, makes sure the right people run the police department, so that no one goes after the vigilantes. Remember that a bunch of Marie's Children were burned at the stake over a hundred years ago? What if that was the same vigilante organization we're dealing with now? What if we're talking about a group dedicated to taking out Marie's Children whenever they show their little masked heads?"

Bryan remembered how Sharrow and Robertson had stared at the blood symbols from Oscar Woody's murder scene, how they'd played right along when Zou took Bryan and Pookie off the case. There had been symbol-killer cases before: the Golden Gate Slasher, that mob hit from the sixties, that serial killer in New York City. Maybe there were even more cases that Zou and company had made disappear. Father Paul Maloney? Verde had been on the scene, Metz at his side. Maybe if it wasn't for Bryan's dreams leading him to the murder site, no one would have ever known about Zou's game.

The door opened. Chief Zou came in, as did Baldwin Metz helped by Sean Robertson. Zou closed the door. She, Metz and Robertson stood on the side of the room near the RapScan computer. Bryan and Pookie were on the other side. The hacked-up body separated them.

Zou looked at the body for a few moments, then she looked up and spoke. "Congratulations, Clauser. You brought down the BoyCo killer, the man that also killed Inspector Pigeon."

Here we go, she isn't wasting any time. Well, fuck that . . .

"I didn't kill this guy." Bryan pointed to the arrow resting on the body. "Someone put that through his heart."

Chief Zou looked over at Metz. "Doctor?"

He reached out a trembling hand, picked up the arrow, then set it on a counter behind him. "That's not the instrument of death," he said. He pointed to the portable computer rack. "Assistant Chief, would you mind?"

Robertson reached out and rolled the rig closer so Metz could get at it. The old man tapped some keys. An x-ray appeared on the screen. He stared at it, then pointed to a bright white dot below the right nipple.

"Bullet," he said. "I'm sure it's forty-caliber and will match the ballistics of Inspector Pigeon's weapon." He examined the picture again, then pointed to two slightly fainter white spots. "And in my expert opinion, these will be forty-caliber bullets from Officer Clauser's weapon."

Robertson reached across the body, held his hand palm up. "Clauser, your weapon, please."

Bryan looked at Zou. "Am I suspended?"

She shook her head.

"But you want my gun," Bryan said. "What am I supposed to use on the street, harsh language?"

"Pick up another tomorrow," Zou said. "Give the assistant chief your firearm so we can run ballistics."

"Ballistics are on record," Bryan said. "They are for every police-issued weapon."

Zou smiled. "We just want to be thorough. You know how the media can be."

She and Metz would cook the evidence. Bryan's gun would be confirmed as the weapon that killed the bearded man on the table. He looked to Pookie, who shook his head slightly: *don't fight now, we can't win.*

Bryan drew his Sig Sauer, ejected the magazine, then pulled the slide back and checked the chamber. He handed the weapon and the mag to Robertson.

"Your lies won't hold up," Bryan said to Zou. "Too many loopholes."

She pursed her lips. "Really? Rex Deprovdechuk was being bullied by BoyCo. Roberta Deprovdechuk hired an aspiring hit man to kill the bullies. That hit man is lying on the table before us. Forensic evidence will confirm that this man killed Oscar Woody and Jay Parlar. It seems that Roberta refused to pay for services rendered, so the hit man killed her as well. The hit man didn't know what to do about Rex, so he waited at the Deprovdechuk home and kept Rex hostage. Inspector Verde and Inspector Pigeon were investigating the murders of Woody and Parlar. They tracked a lead to Roberta and found the hit man at her house. Gunfire was exchanged. Inspector Pigeon died in the line of duty. The hit man was wounded, but he escaped. Rex fled the scene and has been missing ever since. The hit man decided he needed to protect his newfound reputation by completing his original contract, so he went after Alex Panos and Issac Moses. The hit man killed Issac. Alex's mother got caught in the crossfire. Alex got away, but I'm sure we'll find him. We'll find Rex as well."

She was so smooth, so quick. Her story wasn't just plausible, it connected all the dots in a seamless, streamlined fashion. The doctored "evidence" would make it real.

"There's witnesses," Pookie said. "A lot of people saw that arrow sticking out of the body. Paramedics, Doctor Hudson, bystanders, other cops . . . how you going to explain that?"

Zou smiled. "I don't think the paramedics want to contradict me. As for Robin Hudson, she has a pretty impressive promotion coming up and I'm betting she wouldn't want to risk that. I'll also talk to every cop on the scene, personally, to make sure they remember things correctly. This man on the table killed Bobby Pigeon — do you think your fellow officers will care about the *details* of how a cop killer died?"

She was right about that, too. Even if word got out about the archer, most cops would want to give him a medal, not try and throw him in prison.

But Bryan wasn't *most cops*.

"I care," he said. "A vigilante is killing people, and we're going to get him."

Metz started tapping keys on the RapScan touch screen. Bryan saw the karyotypes come up on the screen, then vanish, one by one — he was deleting the information.

Zou rested the knuckles of her fists on the edge of the porcelain table. "Bryan, this is the *sixth* person you've killed while on duty. And, I might add, the second in the last week."

He stared at her, not knowing what to say. Where was she going with that? "But I didn't kill this guy."

"You did," Metz said. "I hope you get a commendation for it."

Zou smiled and nodded. "He will. So will Inspector Chang. Clauser, the department needs you. You're too good to lose. You'll have to go through the usual review board, as well as some counseling. Considering the brutality of these attacks on the BoyCo members and the death of a cop, however, I'm thinking that I can make the review board perfunctory." Her smile faded. "Or I can suspend you pending a full review, a review that I assure you won't go well. Considering you've killed six people, I imagine the recommendation will call for you to be dismissed and barred from ever again serving in law enforcement."

She would have him banned from being a cop? She had to be bluffing. "Chief, this vigilante is a *murderer*. He's got to pay. You have to see that!"

Pookie crossed his arms and shook his head. "You know that Oscar Woody's *real* killer is still out there. So is the killer of Jay Parlar and Susan Panos. You *can't* tell us you're just going to wrap this up."

Zou leaned closer. Her eyes seemed to soften a little. "Men, I'm asking you to let this go. I can't tell you why, but this is the best thing for the city. Trust me."

Bryan threw up his hands. "*Trust* you?" Trust you to handle a case with those symbols like the way you handled the Golden Gate Slasher?"

He regretted the words as soon as he said them. He'd played a card they needed to keep close to the vest.

The softness slowly faded from her eyes, replaced by her normal, stone-cold expression. "The board might dig into your older incidents," she said. "What if there was a mistake in the review of one of your prior shootings, and they uncover some new evidence? Why, you could wind up in prison."

Prison? He looked at her, waiting for her to flinch, to fold — but her expression didn't change. Zou meant every word she said.

All this time, Bryan and Pookie had been playing checkers while Zou had been playing chess. Metz's flawless reputation would let him create any evidence Zou needed. In trial, any district attorney would paint Bryan as a power-mad cop, killing at will. Even if that wasn't enough for a jury to convict, Bryan's career would be over.

A hot, sudden rage swept over him, the likes of which he'd never felt anywhere outside of his fucked-up dreams. He'd hurt people before, sure, but he'd never *wanted* to hurt them. Now, however, he felt the urge to smash her face in, knew how good it would feel to grab her throat, to *squeeze*, to—

Pookie's strong hand gripped the back of his right arm, fingers and thumb digging into his biceps. The urge faded away. Bryan blinked in shock — had he really been thinking such horrible thoughts?

"We understand," Pookie said. "Chief, you've made your position clear. And our positions, apparently. If there won't be anything else?"

Zou flicked her hand toward the door. "Go."

Bryan stumbled when Pookie yanked him around the table and through the door. The larger autopsy room was empty save for the five white tables. Pookie kept squeezing, kept pulling, dragging Bryan into the administration area and toward the main door.

"Pooks, you want to ease up on—"

Pookie suddenly stopped and turned. His nose was only an inch from Bryan's. His eyes went wide with anger and frustration.

"Bryan, not another word until we get where we're going, you got it?"

His partner was furious, maybe even madder than Bryan was if such a thing was possible. He'd never seen Pookie like this.

"Sure," Bryan said. "Where are we going?"

"We're making a social call. Time to gather the troops."

Robin Has House Guests

Emma ran to the apartment door, skidding across the hardwood floor as she slid to a stop. She jammed her nose at the base of the door, her tail moving faster than her butt could manage. Usually, the dog barked like mad when someone knocked — but not when that someone was Bryan.

Robin opened her apartment door to a bleary-eyed Pookie and an intensely focused Bryan. She'd seen Bryan like that before, usually on a big case, usually when he felt he was tightening the noose on a suspect. Emma barked once at Pookie, then alternately turned in circles and threw herself against Bryan's legs.

Bryan reached down and picked the dog up, holding her under the front arms. Her rear legs dangled, unmoving. The position looked uncomfortable, but he'd always held Emma that way and she didn't seem to mind. Her tail moved a mile a minute and her tongue flicked at Bryan's face.

"Oh, knock it off, Emma-Boo," Bryan said, turning his face away. "I missed you, too."

Pookie stepped in and gave Robin a hug. "Robin Bo-Bobbin, how are ya?"

"I have no idea how I am," she said. "And I still don't know what happened in the morgue." She leaned in and spoke quietly: "John's already here. He's pretty upset."

Pookie sighed. "Yeah, I'm sure he is. I didn't give him much of a choice, you know? I bet he hasn't been out at night in six years."

Bryan let out a huff of disgust, set Emma down and walked into the dining room.

Was he really that insensitive to John's phobia? "Pooks, what's Bryan's problem?"

"Mister Fearless doesn't have much tolerance for us mere mortals."

Robin crossed her arms. She didn't like the thought of Bryan being that callous. "Well, *Mister Fearless* seems to have developed some fears of his own."

Pookie nodded. "That he has, my dear. You tell John about the Zed chromosome like I asked?"

"I did. I'm not sure if he believes me. I think he's waiting for a punch line or something."

"Yeah, it's a regular laugh-riot," Pookie said. "I think we should get this party started." He held out a hand, gesturing *ladies first.*

Robin walked into the dining room. Bryan was already seated at the table, as was John Smith. Emma's front paws were on Bryan's thigh, and she kept pointing her nose up to kiss his face. Bryan basically ignored it, letting the dog do her worst. John still hadn't taken off his dark-purple motorcycle jacket. His chin hung down to his chest, and his helmet was right next to his chair as if he wanted to keep it close in case he needed a quick getaway.

Pookie sat, as did Robin. She suddenly realized how messy the apartment looked — dishes in the sink, dog hair on the carpet. She knew she had more important things to worry about at the moment, but still . . . Bryan's first visit here in six months, and she hadn't had time to pick up for him. He was so focused, however, she probably could have painted the place pink for all he'd notice.

"Robin," Pookie said. "You got any beer?"

"It's three in the morning."

He smiled. "It's happy hour somewhere."

Bryan stood and walked into the open kitchen. He grabbed a bottle opener out of a kitchen drawer, then reached into the fridge and came out with four Stellas. He opened the beers, passed them around before he sat down again. He did all this with automatic ease, like he'd never moved out at all.

"Zou's crooked," he said. "We know it for sure."

John lifted his head and crossed his arms, making his leather sleeves creak. "What, *exactly*, do we know?"

Bryan looked at Pookie.

Pookie shrugged. "Tell 'em. They might as well know what we're asking of them."

Robin listened as Bryan talked about what had gone down in the private autopsy room. The more he said, the angrier she became. When he finished, Robin had an urge to find Chief Zou and punch her right in the nose.

"So she used the word *prison*?" Robin said. "That was her actual word?"

Bryan nodded. "Not a lot of gray area."

Robin believed Bryan and Pookie, and yet . . . the concept of Chief Zou threatening her own people seemed beyond the realm of plausibility. "Can she do that? Could she cook the books and get you accused of something?"

Pookie laughed and shook his head. "Hey, Robin, you like that guy Metz?"

She nodded.

"So do DAs, judges and juries," he said. "What do you think will happen if the Silver Eagle delivers evidence that implicates Bryan?"

Robin said nothing. She wanted to say *Metz would never do something like that*, but after what she'd seen in the morgue a few hours earlier, she wasn't sure.

John nodded. "Pookie's right about that. Heck, Metz could get Jesus thrown in jail. All right, Terminator, looks like you're screwed if you don't back off. So back off."

Bryan shook his head. "Vigilantes don't get to decide who lives and who dies. I don't care if it sounds corny — I took an oath to uphold the law, and that's exactly what I'm going to do."

She knew that was no idle promise. The look in his eyes . . . he was going after the chief of police, the mayor of San Francisco, the chief medical examiner and anyone else who had helped them. He wanted it so bad she could almost see it burning off of him like a corona. What was it about this case that made it so deeply personal to him?

Hadn't she put her career in jeopardy enough for one night? She could just ask them to leave. Robin had worked her ass off for years; if that effort wasn't already lost, it surely would be if she helped Bryan and Pookie go after Zou. Not just Zou . . . they would be going after Metz as well. Metz, her mentor, her friend. But if Zou and Metz *were* crooked, if they were covering up murders, how could Robin ignore that?

"Hypothetically, let's say John and I help you," she said. "What would you need from us?"

Bryan again looked to Pookie. Pookie leaned forward, spoke directly to John.

"Mister Burns, we need your help, but it doesn't look like Zou knows you're involved yet. You back out now, you're probably fine. But if you keep poking your long, hooked nose into things, Zou will be on you like ugly on a baboon's ass."

John stared back, thinking. "What happens if she finds out I'm helping you guys?"

"I think you lose your privileged position in the Gang Task Force," Pookie said. "She might make you walk a beat in the 'Loin."

Robin hissed in a breath. The Tenderloin was where John had been shot.

John looked down to the table. "I have trouble even leaving my apartment," he said. "Took everything I had just to drive here. If it wasn't for Zou, I wouldn't even be a cop anymore."

Robin's heart broke for the man. Pookie and Bryan were asking him to put everything on the line against a woman who had backed him in his time of need.

John sighed and nodded. "I owe her, but I won't stand behind her if she's breaking the law. I'll help."

Bryan smiled as if he were pleasantly surprised. He tipped the neck of his beer bottle toward John. John raised his own bottle and they clinked — the equivalent of a blood contract in man speak, apparently.

Robin felt a bit of shame. She was a doctor; she could get a job anywhere. If this went wrong, John's career would be over, and yet he was willing to do the right thing. She had to step up.

"I'm in," she said.

Bryan leaned back. "Robin, we just need to bounce ideas off you. It's okay. You don't need to get involved."

Her feelings of shame shifted to anger — she'd forgotten about Bryan's misplaced sense of chivalry. John got a beer clink, but Robin wasn't valued enough to help with something this important?

"Getting involved is *my* decision, not yours," she said. "If Zou is playing judge, jury and executioner, then . . . well then fuck her right in her fucking fucker."

Bryan glared at her, but John started giggling, a soundless thing that only moved his hunched shoulders.

Pookie raised his eyebrows. "Hey there, sailor, you just arrive on shore leave or something?"

Robin felt her face flush red — they were *laughing* at her? "You guys swear all the time."

Pookie nodded. "Yes, but we're trained professionals. Dropping three f-bombs in one sentence is punching above your weight class."

Bryan wasn't laughing. He shook his head. "Robin, Zou is done with warnings. Things might get physical from here on out, and I can't let you be part of this."

"You *can't let me*? Oh, I'm sorry, should I be wearing my burqua and averting my gaze from you brave men? Or maybe can I run to my bedroom, toss on a nice gingham dress and bake all you brave warriors some cookies? Because that's where women belong, right? In the kitchen?"

The room suddenly felt uncomfortable. Bryan just wanted to protect her, sure, but he didn't *own* her. Robin was the only one who understood the depth and breadth of the Zed discovery, and how that information might help catch the other killers.

"Well then," she said, "since you three wild stallions are going to play lone wolf, I guess you don't need to know what I've figured out in my pretty little head."

"Hold on there," Pookie said. "First, that's two animal metaphors in one sentence. I think that's against union regulations. Second, I am also not wearing a burqua, so Bryan doesn't speak for me. I'd find your help to be most excellent."

Bryan turned on him. "Do you mind, Pooks? This shit is going to get bad. You want Robin getting hurt?"

Pookie shrugged. "Of course I don't want her hurt, but she's a big girl. She's smart enough to understand the risks."

Robin gave Pookie a single nod. "Thank you, oh elevated one."

Pookie winked. "Plus, you got a hot ass. What cop team is complete without a hot ass?"

Bryan stared at her. He chewed on his lower lip for a moment, then nodded to Robin's right. "That purse on your chair, you take that to work today?"

She looked down at it, then understood what he was saying. "Yes, dear, that is my purse and yes, *dear,* I am packing heat."

"Show me."

God, this man could be infuriating. She unhooked her purse, reached in and pulled out her Kel-Tec P-3AT handgun. Bryan had given it to her on their third date. Nothing spells love like a subcompact .380. The gun weighed only half a pound and was just over five inches long. She could even get decked out for an evening on the town and put the weapon in a clutch, the perfect accessory for the nightclubbing girl on the go.

She ejected the magazine, then pulled back the slide to pop out the round. She held the weapon butt-first and offered it to Bryan. "Happy?"

He looked at the weapon, but didn't take it. "Happy that you're armed, yes. I'm not happy that this could put you in harm's way. But I guess you're going to do what you're going to do, so can we at least *try* to keep you off Zou's radar?"

Robin remembered how Zou had been standing right behind her, and how that had scared her silly. Staying off of Zou's radar sounded like an excellent idea.

"Yes, Daddy, I promise to be a good girl."

"Nice," Pookie said. "Now that we're done with invitations, Robin, do you think you could say *daddy* again? I think I jizzed in my pants a little."

"Me too," John said. "More than a little, actually."

Robin sighed. Responsibility and immaturity were not mutually exclusive traits, it seemed. She slid the magazine home, racked the slide to chamber a round, then put the P-3 back in her purse.

"There will be no repeat of the daddy incident," she said. "I've got some mind-blowing stuff to show you, and it might impact what you decide to do next. Mind if I go first?"

All three men nodded. Robin walked to a cabinet drawer and grabbed a pad of paper and a black pen. She sat back down at the table.

"I've been trying to process all the weird genetic info we've found so far," she said. "First off, the guy we had in the morgue today, that was Bobby Pigeon's killer. So where were the wounds from Bobby's gun? They were there, two small scars on his chest — I think the bullet wounds healed."

"Hold on," John said. "Maybe I'm late to the party, but you can't heal a bullet wound in a few hours. Trust me, I know."

"We're dealing with something new," Robin said. "Blackbeard had the Zed chromosome. We have no idea what that chromosome is or what it codes for. We already know we're dealing with people who are strong, have abnormal muscles, abnormal bones, may have abnormal mouths, *and* have an internal organ no one has seen before. Based on the observed data, I have to make the hypothesis that the Zed chromosome also allows people to heal very fast."

Bryan's fingers drifted to his forehead, fingertips tracing the line of three black stitches.

"There's more," Pookie said. "Tonight I saw a guy jump from a ten-story building to a four-story roof, and that jump was across a street. Two lanes, plus parking, plus sidewalks. Sixty feet at least. I saw him land, roll, and he was fine. Oh, and he carried a bow and was wearing a cloak like Robin Hood or something."

That was impossible, yet Pookie clearly believed what he was saying. Bryan believed it as well.

John looked at Pookie, then at Bryan, then at Robin. "If the three of you are messing with my head, just tell me now. You win, I lose. A new chromosome? A guy who can jump across a street?"

"In a cloak," Bryan said.

"Like Robin Hood," Pookie said.

John rubbed his face. "Yeah, sure. In a cloak. Like Robin Hood." He tapped the table twice with his finger. "From this moment on out, if you say *ha-ha, we punked you,* I will probably shoot someone in the face." He turned to Bryan. "And yes, *Daddy,* I'm definitely packing."

Bryan leaned back and laughed. "Shit, Black Mister Burns, maybe you're not so bad after all."

"It happened," Pookie said. "John, you and I go way back. You'd know if I was bullshitting. Am I bullshitting?"

John stared at Pookie. Robin waited and watched. She couldn't believe the story, but why would they lie? Pookie must have misinterpreted what he'd seen.

John sighed and sagged. "You're not BS-ing, Pooks," he said. "At least that much is true." John turned to Robin. "Well, keep going. Might as well let me hear all of it."

She could try to explain physics to Pookie later. For now, she had real information to share.

"I've got a theory," she said. "The fact that Blackbeard had no testicles got me thinking."

She drew a box on the pad, then a vertical and horizontal line through it, making four smaller squares. Across the top, she put an X above one column, a Y above the other.

"A Punnett square?" John said.

Robin nodded. "You use this to predict the outcome of a breeding experiment. Men and women have two sex chromosomes. A sperm or egg cell, known as a *gamete,* gets just one of those chromosomes. Bryan, know what this XY represents?"

"A man," Bryan said. "He can give an X, or a Y."

"That's right." She drew an X on the outside of each of the two left-hand boxes. "Pooks? Know what the XX represents?"

"A woman," he said. "With gigantic hooters and questionable moral judgment. Oh yeah, I took Biology 101, girlie."

Robin laughed and shook her head. "Sure, Pooks, sure. It's a female, so her gamete can only carry an X."

She put the letter from each column header into the boxes below it, then added the letter from each row header, "So we wind up with two possible combinations of XY, two of XX. On average, half the kids will be male, half will be female. Got me so far?"

All three men nodded.

"Now we saw that the Blackbeard was just that, a *guy.* His sex chromosomes were Zed-X. Normally, the Y chromosome codes for male, but testicles or no testicles Blackbeard had a beard and a penis, so he's a guy.

That means the Zed chromosome has to have some elements of the Y chromosome."

She drew a new four-squared box. She drew XZ across the top, then on the left she drew two Xs. She filled in the squares, resulting in two with XX and two with XZ. "So, if Blackbeard had functional sperm — which he could *not* have had without testicles — he would produce these possible offspring. You guys see the problem with this?"

Bryan pulled the pad in front of him. "There's no YZ," he said. "Oscar Woody's killer was YZ."

"Bingo," she said. He'd always been so good at putting pieces together. "To get a Y-Zed, we *have* to have a female who can provide a Zed chromosome."

Pookie reached out and tapped the pad. "Couldn't the YZ — Oscar's killer — couldn't that be a female?"

Robin shook her head. "In primates, *every instance* of a Y chromosome means *male*. This includes XXY, which is Klinefelter's and for the sake of argument is always male, and XYY syndrome, which also results in a male. We have to assume that Oscar's killer is male, *not* female."

Robin drew a third Punnett square, this time with three columns and two rows to make a total of six squares instead of four. "That brings us to Rex, who is X-Y-Zed. Every one of his sperm cells had what is called *nondisjunction*, which means they had *two* sex chromosomes. Primate sperm cells are supposed to have just *one*."

Above the columns, she wrote XY, XZ and YZ. On the left side, she drew Xs next to the rows. She turned it so the boys could see.

Bryan leaned in for a closer look. "If someone like Rex had a child, the child gets . . . what . . . one chromosome from the mother, two from the father? The mother would always provide an X, and all his children would have three sex chromosomes instead of two, right?"

Robin nodded. "That's right. Three sex chromosomes is called *trisomy*."

Bryan again pulled the pad in front of him. "Well, since the only other two Zed examples we have are *not* trisomal, that means someone like Rex couldn't be their father."

"You got it," she said. "So, if Rex mates with a woman . . ." She pulled the pad back in front of her and she filled in the six boxes: two XXYs, two XXZs, two XYZs. "The XXY is Klinefelter's. I have no idea what an X-X-Zed would be, but maybe it's a female version of Rex. We know Rex was an X-Y-Zed, so at least in Rex's case, X-Y-Zeds appear to be normal people."

Bryan stood and walked to the kitchen. "So Rex could make more Rexes," he said as he pulled four fresh beers from the fridge. "But someone like Rex *can't* make an XZ or a YZ." He opened all four bottles and passed them out before he sat. "So what makes those combinations?"

"Now for the really crazy part," Robin said. She'd walked them through the other Punnett squares to introduce the basic concepts. Now they were ready for the bomb to be dropped.

She turned to a fresh piece of paper and drew a box with two columns and three rows. She put an X and a Y above the columns. To the left of the three rows, she drew an X, a Z and then a second Z.

Pookie rolled his eyes. "Sorry to be a downer, Robin, but this is kind of boring. Can you get to the point?"

"I'm almost there," she said. "Just bear with me. Say the father is a normal male" — she circled the XY — "and the mother is X-Zed-Zed" — she circled the XZZ. "Let's say that — unlike Rex — this X-Zed-Zed mother can give only a *single* chromosome to her gamete" — Robin filled in the squares as she talked — "*then* you can get the X-Zed combination of the Blackbeard *and* the Y-Zed combination that killed Oscar Woody."

"Ewww, that's *nasty*," Pookie said. "You're saying the two killers we know about, they have a mutant-Zed-chromosome mommy who is getting it on with regular dudes?"

Robin nodded as she finished the Punnett Square: two XZs, two YZs, an XX and an XY. "You could even wind up with normal boys and girls. But what you *couldn't* get is another X-Zed-Zed. There's only one way to get that. Now, at the Oscar Woody killing, someone painted *Long Live the King* on the walls, right?"

Bryan nodded. "Yeah, and I think Rex is the king in question."

She looked at John. "You were waiting for a punch line? Here it is, but I don't think it's all that funny — if you have a *king*, maybe you also have a *queen*."

Robin flipped to a new page and drew — three columns and three rows for nine squares total. "So, you take a king" — she marked the columns XY, XZ and YZ — "and a queen" — on the left side, she marked the first row X, the second and third each with a Z — "and something interesting comes up." She filled in the boxes, making an alphabet soup of combinations: two XZZs, two YZZs, three XYZs, an XXZ and an XXY.

She circled the two XZZs.

Bryan looked up, the expression on his face one of shocked realization. "If the XZZ is a *queen,* then the only way to make a new queen is for her to mate with a king."

"Ex*actly,*" Robin said. "If this is the way it works, then you have a eusocial structure with a breeding pair."

John shook his head in annoyed denial. "Wait a minute. Kings? *Queens?* Not like English royalty kings and queens but like . . . *termites?* Eusocial means one breeding pair producing all the offspring for an entire colony, like ants and bees, right?"

Robin nodded.

"Rex and the others are *people,* which means they're mammals," John said. "Eusocial creatures are insects."

"There's at least two species of eusocial mammals," Robin said. "The naked mole rat and the desert rat. They have a single queen, breeding males, and the rest of the colony are sterile workers."

Pookie pulled the pad in front of him. "I could live with fleshy-headed mutants, I really could, but come on . . . a king? A *queen?* Besides, ant colonies have more than just kings or queens, they have workers and drones, right?"

"Right," Robin said. "Those are called *castes.* There's one more caste you didn't mention. Blackbeard had no testicles. He was *sterile,* couldn't have passed on his genes to a new generation. But he was strong, he was dangerous, and he could heal fast, which would let him recover from damage. Guess which caste is most likely to get damaged?"

Bryan stared at her. His eyes widened. He leaned back. "Holy shit."

Pookie looked back and forth from Robin to Bryan. "What? Come on, tell me."

Bryan sagged in his chair. "She's saying Blackbeard is like a soldier ant," he said. "Soldier ants *can't* breed — they just live to protect the colony."

They all sat in silence. Robin felt better for having shared the strange hypothesis. It was the only thing she could find to explain the limited data they had.

Pookie took a long drink of beer, then let out a belch. "Attack of the ant-people," he said. "Awesome. Just *awesome.* But then what's with the costumes?"

Robin picked up the pen, started making a random, back-and-forth doodle on the pad. "The costumes *might* be there to hide physical deformities. We really have no idea what we're dealing with. The thing is, I think those teeth marks on Oscar Woody were exactly that — *teeth marks.* Not some tool designed to look like teeth. If that's true, we'd be talking about someone with a wide mouth and two big incisors, so big you'd see it instantly. Maybe the masks and blankets hide more physical abnormalities?"

Bryan shook his head, so slightly Robin wasn't even sure if he knew he was doing it.

John drained his beer in a long pull, then set the bottle on the table. "This new chromosome means we're talking about a specific *people,* a genetic and possibly ethnic minority. As far as we know, someone is wiping out that minority — *genocide* — and Amy Zou is complicit in that act. Maybe there's a damn good reason these ant-people have stayed hidden."

John brought up a good point. Technically, the Zeds weren't a separate species, not as long as a queen could breed with normal men, or a king could breed with normal women. They were human . . . sort of. But what if they were *all* killers?

"We don't know enough," she said. "We need to find that vigilante. Zou won't give us information, maybe he will."

Bryan pulled out his phone, tapped it a few times, then held it out so everyone could see — it was a picture of the bloody arrowhead. "I watched Metz clear out the computer system. All of that data is gone. I'm betting they won't let any of us anywhere near the bodies of Blackbeard, Oscar Woody or Jay Parlar. We won't be able to search Rex's house. That means this arrow is our only lead. Pooks, I think we have to go back and talk to the guy who literally wrote the book on the subject."

Pookie nodded. He reached into his wallet and pulled out a white business card. There was nothing on it but a phone number. He called, then waited for someone to answer.

"Biz, this is Pookie. Sorry to clog your booty-call phone with a non-booty-call message, but we need to see you. Call me back ASAP."

Pookie put the phone away.

"Who was that?" Robin asked.

"Mister Biz-Nass," Pookie said. "Your friendly neighborhood Tourette-syndrome-afflicted, throat-cancer-surving fortune-teller who speaks with a voice box."

Maybe he wasn't making up the thing about the guy jumping across the street, but she knew damn well *that* one was bullshit.

Pookie turned to Bryan. "Bri-Bri, it's three-thirty in the morning. I suggest we don't sit here and wait for Biz-Nass to call us back. Everyone is cashed out. I need some sleep, Bro. Let's all go home and hit it in the morning."

Bryan's jaw muscles twitched. Robin knew he didn't want to wait for even a second, but he trusted Pookie.

"All right," he said. "Tomorrow."

Robin saw the three men out.

The Monster

So much *pain*.

The dream's blurry swirl engulfed him, lulled him, but the pain in his belly, the *fire* in there — that felt more real than anything Bryan had ever known. How could anything hurt so much? Being dragged, being kicked . . . what would happen to him now?

He shouldn't have gone out alone, and now it was too late.

Savior had him.

What would death be like? Would he go to the Hunting Ground like the old people said, or would he just *end*? The religion, it was all a lie, he knew, because he'd drawn the ward to chase the monster away and yet the monster still got him.

Bryan's hands and feet pulled against the restraints, but he was already too weak. The thing in his mouth muffled his cries for help.

Sliding on the ground now, across grass, his stomach screaming with agony. Where was the monster taking him?

Bryan looked ahead. He saw a cellar door, the angled kind that led down into a basement.

The monster released him. The monster in his cloak, a faceless man-shaped thing of dark green, it opened the cellar door. Inside, shadows.

The monster turned, grabbed Bryan by the neck and dragged him to the door. Bryan slid off the grass and onto concrete steps. The monster pulled him down, *thump-thump-thump* along the steps, rough edges digging into Bryan's shoulder and hip as he slid. The shadows grew, engulfed him, swallowed him up until there was nothing but blackness.

•••

Bryan woke to someone pounding on his apartment door.

He opened his eyes, blinked — was he still dreaming? If so, he was dreaming about his messy apartment and the cardboard boxes he had yet to unpack.

He sat up on his couch.

The door pounded again. From outside, a yell: "Bri-Bri, rise and shine!"

He stood, shuffled to the door and opened it. Pookie walked in, two cups of steaming coffee in hand.

"Pooks, what are you doing here?"

"We have to go see Mister Biz-Nass. We left him a message last night, remember?"

Pookie stepped inside. Bryan shut the door. He was still groggy, but now he recalled Pookie calling Biz-Nass the night before. "Yeah, I remember. Sorry, I'll get ready."

"Answer your phone much?" Pookie said. "I was getting worried that I'd find you in the center of one of those bloody symbols."

Did that mean Pookie worried Bryan would be a victim, or the perp? Maybe that was a question best left unasked.

"I guess I fell asleep on the couch," Bryan said. "I was watching TV."

The exhaustion, the stress, the uncertainty — those things had been weighing on him, combining with the last remnants of the physical aches, joints that felt like they were stuffed with broken marbles and the lingering

> *[it's not cancer it's an organ]*

chest pain.

But he didn't feel those things anymore. In fact, he felt no pain at all.

"Bri-Bri, you get any sleep?"

Bryan shrugged. "Four hours, maybe?"

"Well, you look better," Pookie said. "Way better, in fact." He handed Bryan the coffee. "Here's your milkshake. Four sugars, three creams, just the way you like it."

"Thanks."

Pookie walked to the coffee table in front of the couch. On it was Bryan's pad, a pencil, and a scattering of hastily scrawled protection symbols. "Bryan, did you have another nightmare?"

Bryan started to say no, but stopped. He had vague wisps of something grabbing him, beating him, maybe even stabbing him. He couldn't lock it down.

"I did," he said. "Worse than the others."

"*Worse?* Ummm, do we need to drive somewhere, then? See if there's a body?"

Bryan shook his head. "Not unless the body is mine. I didn't stalk anyone. This time I think something got me."

"Got you? Like, *killed* you?"

Bryan tried to remember. A few more fuzzy images filtered to the surface of his thoughts. "Yeah. I dreamed about the guy in the cloak, Pooks. The archer. In the dream his name was Savior."

"Savior? Wasn't the *Saviors* the group that Biz-Nass said burned Marie's Children at the stake?"

Bryan nodded. "Yeah, you're right. This guy in the cloak, he messed me up pretty bad. He dragged me down some steps. I'm not sure what came next. All I know is that I don't think I've ever felt so afraid in my life. He was going to do something to me."

Pookie nodded. He looked worried, like he was waiting for the other shoe to drop. "What happened then?"

Bryan shrugged. "Don't know. I woke up, drew some symbols, felt better, then went right back to sleep. I didn't go out and put a gun in a kid's face, if that's what you're asking."

Pookie forced a smile. "Of course not. Drink your coffee and shower up. Biz said he was making an exception to see us this early, so let's move it."

Mr. Biz-Nass and the Arrow

HELLO AGAIN OFFICER POOKIE . . . HELLO OFFICER *FUCKER FUCKER DICKER PRICKER*.

Pookie smiled wide. Biz-Nass was actually happy to see them. "Biz-*Nass*, old boy, how they hanging?"

LONG AND RED AND READY FOR BED . . . COME IN COME IN.

Pookie and Bryan sat in the blue plastic chairs. Pookie was keeping a close eye on his partner. The night before in the private autopsy room, Pookie had thought Bryan was about to snap. The man's pain seemed to be gone, but he hadn't gone back to the reserved, emotionless guy that Pookie knew and loved. Now Bryan's eyes showed a steady state of simmering anger, and he had an aura of impending violence that seemed a tiny spark away from erupting.

THIS BETTER BE IMPORTANT. IT'S TEN IN THE MORNING AND I DON'T EVEN KICK MY BITCHES OUT OF BED UNTIL WELL PAST NOON.

"We found something else," Pookie said. "Maybe you can tell us what it means. Bryan, show him."

Bryan thumbed his phone, calling up a picture of the bloody arrowhead. He set it faceup on the table's red velvet, then slid it forward. Biz-Nass didn't move — he just stared down at the screen. He finally looked up, first at Pookie, then at Bryan.

Biz-Nass started to pant. He tried talking without putting the voice box to his throat. Pookie couldn't make out the hissing whisper, but he was pretty sure there was a *fucker* and *pricker* in there somewhere.

Bryan pointed to Biz's throat. "Your hardware, man. Don't forget your hardware."

Biz-Nass stared at Bryan with real fear, then remembered his voice box. He lifted the device to his throat.

SORRY I *FUCK-FUCK* . . . I MEAN I *FUCK-FUCK* . . . I FORGOT MYSELF.

"You've seen this before," Pookie said. "Why does it scare you so bad?"

I'M NOT SCARED . . . I DON'T KNOW WHAT IT IS.

"Biz," Pookie said in a calm voice, "that article you have on the Golden Gate Slasher, it's been wiped out of existence everywhere else. You know about the symbols. You know about Marie's Children. You were writing a fucking *book* on the subject, Bro — there's no way you didn't research the arrow that killed the Slasher."

Mr. Biz-Nass looked at each of the cops, then spoke in a tone so pleading even the mechanical effect couldn't hide it. I HAVEN'T TALKED. I SWEAR. MMMMM PLEASE DON'T HIT ME.

Maybe Biz faked his Tourette's, maybe he didn't, but Pookie knew he wasn't faking this. Wide eyes, fast breaths, open mouth, hands clutching — Biz thought he was about to get his ass kicked.

"We are *not* going to hit you," Pookie said. "People are dying. We need to know how to stop it."

Biz-Nass just shook his head.

The first time Pookie and Bryan had visited, Biz-Nass had thought they'd come to rough him up. He'd thought that when they mentioned the symbols. Biz had formally requested info on the symbols twenty-nine years ago — requested that info from the SFPD.

Pookie suddenly thought of Chief Zou, leaning forward, her knuckles on the autopsy table, threatening Bryan Clauser with career destruction if not jail.

"Amy Zou," Pookie said. "You ever have a run-in with her, Biz? Or how about Rich Verde?"

Mr. Biz-Nass set the voice box down and put his hands flat on his velvet table. He took a deep breath, tried to collect himself. His left hand put the voice box back to his throat, while his right hand pointed to his thrice-broken, crooked nose.

MMMMM WHO DO YOU THINK DID THIS TO ME?

Bryan leaned forward. "Zou and Verde did that to you? Why?"

SHE TOLD ME TO STOP WORKING ON THE BOOK. MMMMMM SHE *BITCHY-BITCHY-BITCHY-CUNTY-CUNTY* TOLD ME IF I DIDN'T LEAVE IT ALONE, SHE'D KILL ME.

Amy Zou, beating the hell out of a civilian. A week ago, Pookie wouldn't have believed it for a second. Now? It sounded par for the course.

"Biz," Bryan said, "we're going after Zou. She's protecting a vigilante killer. You help us find him, you help us bring her down."

Biz-Nass stared, his eyes narrowing in disbelief. He looked at Pookie.

MMMMM IS THIS TRUE?

Pookie put his right hand on his heart. "Scout's honor."

Biz licked his lips, then nodded. He reached out a trembling hand, picked up Bryan's cell phone and stared at the picture.

WHAT KIND OF BODY DID YOU FIND THIS IN?

"Caucasian male," Pookie said. "A cop killer. Six-foot-one, two hundred and thirty pounds. Full beard."

WAS HE WEARING A COSTUME?

"No," Pookie said. He looked at Bryan. "But we think others who might have been working with him were."

Biz-Nass nodded, as if that was what he expected to hear.

THIS V-CROSS IS THE SYMBOL OF THE SAVIORS. THERE SHOULD BE ANOTHER SYMBOL ON THE SHAFT . . . AN EYE WITH A DAGGER THROUGH IT.

Bryan took the phone, flicked to the next photo — the arrow shaft — and set it on the table in front of Biz-Nass.

The fortune-teller stared, then nodded.

SAVIORS KILL MARIE'S CHILDREN. YOUR COP KILLER WAS IN THE CULT. THESE SYMBOLS ARE ON ALL OF THE ARROWHEADS. HE HAND CARVES THEM.

"*He?*" Pookie said. "You know who makes these?"

Biz-Nass nodded. IF I TELL YOU, PROMISE YOU WON'T COME BACK IN A FEW MONTHS AND BEAT ME SILLY?

"Why would we do that?"

The fortune-teller shrugged. THAT'S WHAT AMY ZOU DID. I TOLD YOU SHE ROUGHED ME UP. SHE CAME TO ME JUST LIKE *DICKER PRICKER* YOU GUYS ARE NOW. SHE WANTED INFO ON THE ARROWS, WANTED TO KNOW WHO MADE THEM. I TOLD HER. TWO YEARS LATER, SHE AND VERDE BEAT ME UP, TOLD ME IF I DIDN'T *SHITTYBALLS!* STOP WORKING ON THE *FUCKLESNIFF!* BOOK THEY WOULD KILL ME.

Amy Zou had been tracking down an arrowhead. Had she been tracking the person who killed the Golden Gate Slasher? If so, why had she then come back and forced Biz-Nass into silence?

"You have our word," Pookie said. "We're not going to lay a finger on you."

Biz-Nass held out a fist to Pookie. WORD IS BOND?

Pookie bumped fists and nodded. "Word is bond."

The fortune-teller then held a fist out to Bryan. WORD IS BOND?

Bryan rolled his eyes. "What are you, sixteen years old? I'm not bumping fists, for fuck's sake."

Biz-Nass didn't move his hand. Bryan looked to Pookie.

"Just do it," Pookie said.

Bryan sighed, then bumped fists. "Word is bond."

Biz-Nass nodded and smiled. THE GUY'S NAME IS ALDER JESSUP.

Pookie's skin tingled. Now they really had something. "Biz, if Alder Jessup *makes* the arrows, who *shoots* them?"

I NEVER FOUND OUT THAT PART, I SWEAR.

Bryan reached out and gently took his phone. "That's okay. Know where this Alder Jessup lives?"

Biz leaned forward, waved his right hand over the blue crystal ball. I SEE SOMETHING IN YOUR FUTURE, OFFICER *DICKER PRICKER FUCKER SUCKER.* SOMETHING WE MYSTICS CALL A GOOGLE SEARCH.

He looked up. THAT'S ALL I KNOW. GOOD LUCK.

Bryan offered his hand. "Thank you." Biz-Nass shook it, then raised his palm and extended it toward Pookie.

UP HIGH, MY NIZZLE.

Pookie gave Biz-Nass a high five, then followed Bryan out of the office.

Pookie already had his cell phone in hand. "No coal for the choo-choo today, Bri-Bri. I'm calling Black Mister Burns and telling him to get anything he can on this Alder Jessup."

Bryan nodded. He seemed to be focusing on staying calm — as if he *had* to focus or he'd wind up kicking the holy hell out of the first person to cross his path.

Alder Jessup

For the first time in his career, Bryan hoped things would go bad. He hoped this Alder Jessup would start some shit, or maybe just turn tail and run. That would give Bryan an excuse to take him down. Someone had to pay, and if Jessup wanted to find out how bad Bryan could hurt someone, well, Bryan would be happy to oblige.

He and Pookie sat in the parked Buick, looking out at Alder Jessup's residence — 1969 California Street. The place stood out like a road whore at a convent. The wall-to-wall line of houses on that street all wore colorful paint — white, yellows, pastels and terra-cotta brick. Nineteen sixty-nine, on the other hand, was gray — completely devoid of color. It looked like a haunted English mansion taken from some soggy countryside estate and jammed into the neighborhood like a fat man dropping his big ass onto an already packed bus bench.

Half of an English mansion, that was. Just the left half. The right side of the house rose to a peak that just *stopped*. Below that peak was a half-arch that once might have been intended as an entryway for servants or horses. Where the mirror half of the gray mansion should have been sat a modern three-story brick apartment building trimmed in white.

"Peppy," Pookie said. "Martha Stewart doesn't use dungeon-gray enough for my taste."

"Looks expensive," Bryan said. "What do you think it's worth, two million?"

Pookie laughed. "You don't get out much, buddy. This thing is fifteen mil if it's a penny. And it's not a penny, in case you suck at the multiple choice. Black Mister Burns said Alder Jessup has lived here for at least sixty years. That's all we have for now."

Sixty years? Well, maybe Bryan would have to cool his jets. No matter how churned-up he felt inside, it wouldn't be cool to beat the shit out of a senior citizen.

"It's enough to get started," he said. "Ready?"

Pookie scooped up his stack of manila folders. "Yep, let's go."

They slid out of the Buick and crossed the five lanes of California Street. Four concrete steps led to an archway door that looked like it belonged in a church. An intentionally rusted gate made of crossed diagonal half-inch iron bars blocked the archway. Behind the gate, more stairs, at the top of which sat a fancier door into the house proper.

The gate looked like a high-security rig, although you could reach right through the diagonal spaces between the rusted bars. In the middle of the gate was a small, cast-iron image of Sagittarius — the half-horse, half-man archer.

Pookie gripped the iron bars and gave the gate a shake. "It would take a tank to get through this."

There was a buzzer to the right of the door. Bryan pressed it.

Moments later, the interior door at the top of the internal stairs opened. The man that descended was not what Bryan expected to see greeting them at a multimillion-dollar Pacific Heights mansion. The man stopped behind the gate. He looked at Pookie, he looked at Bryan, then he sneered.

"Who the fuck are you two ass-clowns?"

He was in his early twenties, five-eight, about a buck-fifty. He wore a black KILLSWITCH ENGAGE concert T-shirt. A black belt with a silver skull buckle held up heavy black jeans. Black combat boots completed the ensemble. His short sleeves showed off intricate tattoos running up both arms. Silver bracelets decorated both wrists: some thin loops, some thick bands with detailed engravings. A dozen small, silver earrings pierced each ear. He also had a silver loop in each eyebrow, one through his lower lip, and a thick one dangling from his septum. His pitch-black, sculpted hair hung down over his left eye.

"San Francisco Police," Pookie said. "I'm Inspector Chang. This is Inspector Clauser. We'd like to talk to Alder Jessup."

"About what?"

"About a murder."

The tattooed man sneered. "Got a warrant, bitch?"

Bryan instantly disliked this kind of person, the type that hated cops for the intolerable sin of enforcing the law. Best to let Pookie handle this, or Bryan knew he'd want to rub the guy's face against the concrete sidewalk.

"We don't have a warrant," Pookie said. "But if we have to go get one, someone is going in the back of a marked car, in cuffs, in front of the whole neighborhood."

"You think I care if any of the zombies around here see me in a cop car?"

"Are you Alder Jessup?"

"No," the tattooed man said. "I'm his grandson, Adam."

Pookie rolled his neck, like he was trying to loosen a deep kink. "Adam, no offense, but you look like the kind of guy who's familiar with the back of a squad car. Am I right?"

Adam nodded.

"I'm guessing Grandpa Alder isn't. Am I right about that one, too?"

Adam stared hatefully, then nodded again.

"Fine," Pookie said. "Now, unless you want me to come back here and haul Grampy Alder off in cuffs, stop busting our balls and let us come in."

Adam thought it over for a second, then he opened the metal gate. He led Pookie and Bryan up the steps, through an ornate oak door and into a foyer.

"Wait right here," Adam said. "I'll go get Grampa."

Bryan watched Adam bound up a beautiful staircase, the railing of which was so lacquered and polished it could pass for wood-toned glass. The man's piercings clinked as he ran.

The foyer's furniture, paintings and sculptures looked expensive. Bryan felt like he was standing in a museum wing. Everything, from the art to the marble floor to even the intricate wood trim on a velvet couch, exhibited some kind of archery theme: bows, arrows, arrowheads, archers.

Moments later, Adam Jessup helped his grandfather down the stairs. Alder wore an immaculate brown three-piece suit. He walked with a long wooden cane topped by a silver wolf's head. Most of his hair was long gone, leaving a mottled scalp and a ring of fine white around his temples.

"Inspectors," Alder said in a light, airy voice. "You need to speak with me?"

Pookie introduced himself and Bryan again, then got to it. "We're looking for information on an arrowhead that you may have made."

Bryan watched the Jessups carefully. Alder showed no reaction, but Adam's eyes dilated a little — he was nervous.

Pookie opened a manila folder and handed over a printout showing Bryan's cell-phone picture of the arrowhead. Alder took the printout. Adam's eyes went wide.

The old man squinted, then reached into his breast pocket and pulled out silver-rimmed glasses. He put them on gently and looked again. "No, I'm afraid I don't recognize this."

Alder was a cool customer. Bryan knew his kind well, the kind that could lie with confidence and ease. His grandson, however, didn't have that skill.

"But you do make arrows," Bryan said. "And bows, and all kinds of custom archery stuff."

Alder smiled. "You've been looking into us. How flattering. We do make custom weaponry. Or rather, Adam here does." Alder looked at his grandson and beamed with pride. "My hands and eyes aren't what they used to be. Adam has the talent, though. His father, alas, does not. My son can barely do the dishes without chipping the china . . . bad hands, you see. Twitchy. Certain skills can skip a generation."

"I know what you mean," Pookie said. "My father is a whiz at Mad Libs, but my vocabulary is a bit thin to say the least. A tragedy for me, but perhaps my future children will have the gift."

Alder sighed. "One can only hope, Inspector Chang."

Bryan, impatient, pointed to the printout. "You're *sure* you guys didn't make this?"

"I would certainly know if we did," Alder said.

Pookie's cell phone buzzed. He pulled it out, looked at a text. Bryan peeked at the screen — the text came from Black Mr. Burns.

Bryan couldn't wait for Pookie's slow-play anymore. He wanted to shake these guys up. "Mister Jessup, is that the same story you told Amy Zou twenty-nine years ago? And what do you know about Marie's Children?"

Pookie looked up from his phone with an expression on his face that said *what the hell are you doing?*

Alder took two cane-supported steps forward to stand face-to-face with Bryan.

"Young man," Alder said quietly, "whatever you think you know about Marie's Children, you don't want to know more. Just leave it alone."

Everything about the old man screamed *wisdom* and *patience*. He was the kind of person you listened to, even if you'd just met him. Too bad Bryan didn't give a rat's ass about listening to anyone.

"I won't leave it alone," Bryan said. "And if you're tied up in it, you're going to find that out the hard way."

Alder seemed to sag, just a bit. He leaned heavily on his cane. Adam caught the old man, stopped him from falling.

"Leave," Adam said. "Don't come back without a warrant."

Bryan wanted to punch them both. "The *old guy gets tired* bit? Give me a break."

"Bryan," Pookie said, "we should go."

"But he—"

"We've overstayed our welcome, Bryan," Pookie said. "Let's *go.*"

Bryan ground his teeth. He took one more look at the Jessups, then turned and walked out the door.

•••

He needed to hit someone, and his partner was about one snide comment away from the nomination. Bryan slid into the Buick and slammed the door.

"Hey," Pookie said as he got in. "Easy on the merchandise."

"Nice fucking job having my back in there. You know those guys made that arrowhead, right?"

Pookie started the car. "Yeah, I know. But there's more to detective work than yelling at an old man."

"Yeah? Like what?"

"Like that house," Pookie said. "Black Mister Burns ran the property records. The Jessups don't own it."

"Who does?"

"An esteemed gentleman by the name of Jebediah Erickson. In fact, that house has been in the Erickson family for a hundred and fifty years. So has one other house in town, a house very close to here."

Why was Pookie chasing property records when the Jessups clearly had answers? "So someone else owns the house . . . why would that make you want to leave when they were about to give up the goods?"

"Because Mister Burns found something else about Jebediah Erickson," Pookie said. "Thirty-six years ago, Jeb won a gold medal at the Pan Am Games. Take a guess in what sport?"

Bryan's anger started to fade. "Archery?"

Pookie smiled and nodded.

"Wait a minute," Bryan said. "Thirty-six years ago? So even if the guy was in his mid-twenties when he won, he's at least sixty. Probably not a guy who can do the things you saw."

"Probably not. But we have a gold-medal archer who owns the house of a man who makes custom arrowheads. Think that merits a visit?"

It sure as hell did. "Where is Erickson's place again?"

"Five blocks away," Pookie said. "Let's go see if he's home."

Jebediah Erickson's House

There was something familiar about Erickson's house, but Bryan couldn't place it. He must have seen it before. It was on Franklin Street, a three-lane one-way that pumped traffic from downtown up to the Marina neighborhood. If you went north, you took Franklin. So sure, he'd probably seen the house in passing hundreds of times.

Like the Jessups' place, this house was fairly colorless — gray trim against slate-blue walls. The house faced east, toward Franklin. A small yard sat south of the house, with a driveway at the lot's southernmost end.

Where the Jessups' place looked like an old English manor, this house was all San Francisco Victorian. A round, four-story, window-covered turret rose up from the house's front-right corner, peaked cone-roof soaring high into the air. The entryway was a good fifteen feet above the sidewalk level, at the back of a ten-by-ten porch that itself was covered by a steeply peaked roof supported by ornate, gray-painted wood columns. The stairs started about ten feet to the left of the porch; seven weathered marble steps perpendicular to the street led to a small, square landing, then ten more steps running parallel with the front of the house.

They walked up the steps. Bryan took in the intricate, waist-high railing that lined the porch. At the back of that porch sat beautiful double doors made of thickly lacquered oak.

There was something familiar about the place all right, and more familiarity than he could know from just passing by. The place carried an aura, a disturbing feeling Bryan couldn't nail down.

The answers to everything were inside that house. He *knew* it, deep in his gut.

"Look at this place," Pookie said. "What an awesome set for an episode of *Blue Balls*."

"Not in the mood to talk cop shows, Pooks."

To the left of the double doors, Bryan saw an ornate brass doorbell fixture with a scratched black button in the center. He pressed it. The disturbed feeling grew stronger.

As they waited, Pookie rocked back and forth on his toes and heels. "You weren't a Negative Nancy about the show name this time. That mean you're down with *Blue Balls*?"

"No," Bryan said. "It means I don't want to talk about cop shows."

"If you don't like my name, why don't you propose one?"

Bryan sighed, cleared his throat. Pookie was trying to be helpful, trying to lighten the mood.

"Fine," Bryan said. "How about *Bryan and Pookie*?"

Pookie shook his head. "That sounds like a pedophiliac puppet show."

Bryan pressed the door buzzer again.

They waited. Still no answer.

"Come on," Pookie said. "Give me another one, Mister I Know Show-Business."

"Fine. How about last names? *Clauser and Chang*? You know, with that curly ampersand thing?"

Pookie shook his head. "No, won't work. First of all, I'll be the one nailing all the lonely wives of the murdering big-business guys. That means my name has to come first."

"Chang and Clauser?"

Pookie shook his head again. "That *could* be a police drama, if the show was about two gay cops that moonlighted as interior decorators."

"I'd watch that," Bryan said, forgoing the doorbell to pound four times on the oak door. "It would be like my favorite show of all time."

They stared at the door, but nothing happened.

They turned and walked back down the steps. Bryan felt a sense of loss as he walked away, as if the mystery might vanish without him ever knowing the truth. "Pooks, I *have* to get in there. This house, Erickson, this is the key to everything."

"How do you know?"

Bryan shrugged. "I just know."

"That's not much to go on," Pookie said.

"Yeah, neither was a dream about some kid being killed at Meacham Place."

Pookie nodded. "Good point. It's risky to press our luck, though. Zou will be informed of any warrant we try to get."

"Fuck warrants," Bryan said as he opened the Buick's door. "If she won't play by the rules, neither will we. We have to do this. I mean, unless you still think I'm crazy?"

Pookie slid into the driver's seat. "Well, I wouldn't exactly let you babysit my kids, if I had any. Listen, Bri-Bri, I haven't forgot what I saw on the roof of Susan Panos's building. I couldn't forget that if I drank a gallon of Jack three times a day for a week straight. I don't know biology, but I've bought into Robin's social networking species thing."

*"Eu*social."

"Whatever. The point is, I'm with you on this. I'm down for the gunfight. We'll figure this out, but you are going to *promise* me that you will not roid-rage your way into that house. We have to think about our next step."

"Pooks, you don't understand—"

Pookie slapped the dashboard. "Shut *up*, Bryan."

Pookie wasn't smiling now. Bryan closed his mouth. His friend wanted to be heard.

"I've stood by you," Pookie said. "You owe me. You're not going in there without a plan, even if I have to knock you out myself."

"You can't knock me out."

Pookie waved his hands dismissively. "That's irrelevant. We're going to get the vigilante, we're going to expose Zou, we're going to find the Zed-Y killer that's still out there and anyone else who helped him. We'll get to the bottom of this Marie's Children bullshit, but I've known you for a long time and you're way over the edge. Right now you'll make bad decisions. I won't. So we do this *my* way, agreed?"

Bryan felt an urge to get out of the Buick, run back up those steps, kick in the door and let the chips fall where they may. He took a breath and fought that urge down. Pookie had backed him through all this crazy shit. That couldn't be ignored. Pookie was right — Bryan owed him.

"All right," Bryan said. "What's the next step?"

"Let me think for a minute."

They drove in silence. Pookie didn't cut anyone off. He turned at random, obeying all the signals. Finally, the Buick turned down California Street, heading toward the Financial District. The setting sun cast an orange-juice glow on the horizon, a glow that back-lit the enlongated pyramid that was the Transamerica Building.

"We need more info on Erickson," Pookie said. "Black Mister Burns is digging as we speak. I'll also have Robin test the waters at the Medical Examiner's Office, see if she can find anything."

"Okay," Bryan said. "What about me?"

Pookie smiled, nodded. "You, my little Terminator? I'm not going to ask you to stay away from Erickson's house, because I saw how you were looking at the place. I don't really want to hear you lie to me and tell me that you'll steer clear. So, you do a stakeout, but you just *watch*, you *do not* approach. Give me your word you won't move without backup."

It was one thing for Pookie to believe Bryan wasn't a murderer, but another for him to go all-in like this. If the man had his head on straight, he should have cut ties long ago and moved on. Pookie showed loyalty, true friendship — you back your boy no matter what. And for that level of dedication, was Pookie really asking for that much in return? No matter how bad Bryan wanted to go in that house and find answers, he'd do what Pookie asked.

"I just watch," Bryan said. "I promise."

Pookie reached out his right fist. "Word is bond."

Bryan laughed, and the sound surprised him. "Dicker pricker fucker sucker," he said, and bumped fists.

Bryan felt better. And, he had to admit, Pookie's way was just flat-out smarter — the archer had survived a six-story drop, then promptly killed a man with a freakin' arrow. If that didn't fit the description of *bad motherfucker*, nothing would. He was too dangerous to take one-on-one.

Bryan settled back and looked out the Buick's window. He watched the setting sun sink behind the Transamerica Building, counting the minutes until he could get out and *hunt.*

Amy Zou's Tea Time

Chief Amy Zou took a sip of tea. The tiny porcelain Miss Piggy cup held only imaginary tea, of course, but nothing could taste sweeter.

"Hmmm," she said. "This is *very* good. Which one of you made this?"

Her twin girls giggled.

"We *both* made it, Mom," they said in unison. It spooked the hell out of Amy when they did that.

She sat in a little pink chair at a little pink table. Her daughter Mur sat on her left, her daughter Tabz on her right, and her husband, Jack, in front of her. He also sipped at a tiny teacup, his pinkie properly extended, a pink flower hat pinned to his thinning blond hair. The girls wanted him to wear it, so wear it he did.

"Mmmmm," Jack said. "I do believe this is possum guts tea? Tastes delightfully rotted and smells divinely stinky."

The girls giggled. They looked adorable in their little party dresses.

Amy felt at peace. *Almost* at peace; she didn't get many moments like this, and even when she did an internal voice taunted her, said *these days are almost gone and you've pissed most of them away.* With her job, she could never fully relax. And that job was never far away — her cell phone sat on the tabletop, looking horribly out of place so close to teacups and the Kermit the Frog tea pot.

Tabitha reached for an imaginary piece of cake. Mur didn't like the imaginary cake; she had said as much after the first imaginary bite. Tabitha preferred to be called *Tabz* because, as she put it, it was *funner.* Mary demanded to be addressed only as *Mur* for reasons Amy and Jack had never been able to pry out of the girl.

Jack looked at the girls with a narrow-eyed glare of suspicion. "Wait just a cotton-picking minute. Did you two spike this tea with runny elephant poop?"

The girls squealed with laughter, throwing their heads back and rocking in their chairs.

"No, *Daddy,*" Tabz said. "It's not elephant poop, it's *monkey* poop."

Jack set his cup down with comedic rage, then crossed his arms and sat back, shaking his head hard enough to make the pink flower hat wiggle. God, but the girls loved that man.

Amy realized with a start that Tabz was wearing her heavy, silky black hair in long pigtails. She had never worn her hair like that before. She'd always worn it down, like Mur's was now. They had inherited Amy's hair, not a trace of her husband's thin blond locks.

"Tabitha, honey, your hair looks nice."

"Thank you," she said, and took a sip.

"Did you try that hairstyle out today just for the tea party?"

Mur laughed and pointed at Tabz. "*Ha-ha-ha*, you've been wearing those stupid things for *three* days!"

Tabz sank into her chair, little chin tight to her chest. She looked crestfallen.

"Mur," Jack said, "that's not nice."

Mur didn't catch the hint. "Mommy didn't even *notice*," she said to Tabz. "I *told* you it was stupid to try and be different."

Amy slapped the table, rattling the cups in their saucers. "Mur! You stop that!"

Mur's eyes widened. She shrank into her chair.

Amy's tone echoed in her own ears. She'd talked to Mur not like a mother to a daughter, but like the chief of police to a subordinate. Amy hated herself at that moment — couldn't she put the cop away and just be a mom, even for a few minutes?

Tabz stood suddenly and threw her teacup across the room. It landed noiselessly on her bed. "You didn't *notice*, Mom, because you're *never home*!"

Tabz ran from the room, her little dress swishing with each little step. Jack stood. He took off his flower hat and tossed it on the table as he followed Tabz out. Jack would talk to the girl, leaving Amy to deal with Mur.

"Mary, honey, I shouldn't have yelled like that."

The little girl's eyes narrowed hatefully, as only a little girl's can do. "Don't call me that. I like *Mur*. And why did she have to go and ruin the party? We *never* get to see you."

"Honey, I know, but you have to understand that Mommy's job is—"

Amy's phone let out a tone. A special tone, three dots, three dashes, three dots. S.O.S. That tone represented only one person.

She picked up the phone. He had texted her a picture. High angle, looking down onto a marble porch she recognized on sight and would never forget. The picture showed two men waiting in front of a closed door.

Pookie Chang and Bryan Clauser.

The text beneath the picture read:

THEY ALSO STOPPED BY ALDER'S PLACE. TAKE CARE OF THIS.

Amy felt her temper rising. She had *told* them to keep away. She had given them a chance.

Even before the BoyCo murders, Robertson had wanted to bring Bryan and Pookie into the loop, wanted to tell them everything. Amy had said no, trusting her instincts that the men weren't the kind of people who could properly manage the gray areas. The picture Erickson had texted showed — quite clearly — that her instincts had been dead-on. Bryan and Pookie were by far the best inspectors on the force, but they just wouldn't listen.

Just like another cop almost thirty years ago, right, Amy? Remember how you wouldn't listen when Parkmeyer told you to back off? Remember what happened because you didn't?

She became aware she was alone in the room. Mur had left. Amy looked at the tea set, at the empty chairs. She was missing her daughters' childhoods. They had been born only yesterday, it seemed. When had they grown so big?

She wanted to be with them, but she had a job more important than anyone could ever know. Not even Jack knew all of it. Amy stood, gave the table one last, longing look, then headed downstairs.

Time to put an end to this.

Closing In

Rex sat in a plastic garbage can. Rex waited. Rex watched.

Where had this sensation been all his life? How many hours had he wasted drawing pictures, when the real thing made him feel alive, made him feel complete?

His tummy tingled inside.

His boner had been hard for hours.

The garbage can was across the street from April Sanchez's house. It was one of those big brown kind, wedged into a space between two houses along with the blue recyling kind and the green one people were supposed to use for compost. The garbage can smelled, but Rex didn't care. There had only been one bag inside, which he'd moved to another can. Squatting inside, he could peek out just under the lid and watch for April.

April the meth-head. April the *slut*.

She had rich parents. They didn't own *part* of a house, not just a single floor — they owned the whole thing, all three stories *and* a garage.

The kids in school talked about April behind her back, talked about how ugly she was. They called her *Shrek*. She wasn't fat like Shrek, most druggie girls weren't, but her face bore a passing resemblance. April had been the one who told Alex about Rex's drawing. It was *her* fault Alex broke his arm.

The cops had to be looking for Alex, and here he was with a perfect place to hide. Last night, Rex had followed Alex here. Since then he hadn't seen anyone but April enter or leave. She fetched pizza, bags of groceries, probably whatever Alex wanted.

Darkness was falling, but even then Rex would wait. Marco had said not to move before midnight. Rex hadn't listened to Marco, and now Marco was dead because of it. Rex had learned a valuable lesson from that — some things needed to be done in the dark.

Marco had also told Rex that there was a real family out there some-where, a real home. But without Marco, how was Rex going to find it?

He didn't want to be alone.

His dreams had reached out and connected with people, made them do the things he wanted done. Rex wondered — could he do the same thing when he was awake? It was worth a try. And anyway, it was a long time until midnight and he had nothing else to do.

How could this work? Did he . . . what . . . *throw* his thoughts? Maybe if he just focused, really concentrated on his *need* to find these people.

Rex closed his eyes.

He took a long, deep breath.

Find me, he thought. *Find me.*

The Stakeout

Bryan walked around the block for the sixth time. West on Jackson, south on Gough, east on Washington, north on Franklin. Then reverse, go back the other way. A slow walk, looking all around at everything, looking for places to hide.

There were eight- and ten-story apartment buildings on the other side of Franklin Street. He could go up on those roofs and watch the front of Erickson's house. But big apartment buildings meant a lot of windows, and that meant any number of people could be looking out those windows at any hour of the night. If the archer wanted to enter or exit the big gray Victorian, he wouldn't go out the front where so many people could potentially see. He'd have an exit behind the house, or maybe out on the roof and down the side . . . something *hidden*.

Bryan used his phone to call up a satellite map of the house and the block. The top-down view might give him ideas. Erickson's house had a backyard, a pretty big one by San Francisco standards. Tall buildings surrounded that backyard, hiding it from view. Could he get up on one of those buildings? He flicked his fingers on the screen, zooming in on the map. There, on Jackson Street, a tree that looked taller than the building it was next to. He traced the route with his fingertip — if he could scale that tree, he'd be on the roof of a building that abutted Erickson's backyard. Bryan would be four stories up, giving him a perfect view of the rear of Erickson's mansion.

He nodded. Yes, that was the spot.

He couldn't shake a persistent adrenaline buzz. This guy, this *Savior,* he was a real challenge.

Big game. He's big game because he's a killer — that flips all your switches and turns all your dials to eleven.

Bryan walked to Jackson Street to check his target. He slowly walked past his tree, following the trunk up with his eyes, seeing how he'd climb it to reach that roof. It wasn't dark enough yet, but soon he'd circle back, climb to the roof, and set up his hunting blind.

Then the fun would begin.

Tard

High up on an apartment building across the street from the mansion, a very still, very *quiet* person watched the man in black circle the block again. The man was checking out the monster's house, Tard just knew it.

How exciting!

Tard watched the monster's house every night. Aside from regular bursts of sheer terror when the monster left, or sadness when the monster came back with one of Tard's badly wounded brothers or sisters, nothing interesting ever happened.

But *this* was interesting.

Who was this person?

What did he want with the monster's house?

Tard watched the man in black turn left on Jackson and vanish from sight. Would he be back again?

Tard hoped so.

The Delivery Boy

Pookie showered, hoping the hot water and rough scrubbing might somehow take the edge off his lack of sleep. A nice, thirty-minute shower, the perfect way to finally get a little alone time. Delivery kung pao shrimp was on the way. Some food, a twenty-minute power nap, and he'd be right as rain.

Sure, as if he could ever be *right* again.

Mutants, vigilantes and murderers. *Oh my.* Add in Bryan playing fast and loose with sanity, and Pookie considered his dance card quite full, thank you very much. Bryan did seem better, though — following the clues from Biz-Nass to the Jessups to Erickson's house had given the guy direction and purpose.

No longer were they just reacting to a batch of random dreams; now they had a target. Even though this wasn't an official investigation, they would still use the process and tactics they'd use in any other case. What would they do when they found evidence they could actually use? Were judges in on this? Was the DA?

Maybe, but maybe the *assistant* DA wasn't in on the loop, just like Robin hadn't been in on it. Pookie would have no choice but to arrange a meeting to make sure of that.

Well-well-well, Miss Jennifer Wills from the Land of Sexy Shoes and Short Skirts, maybe you and I will be spending some time together after all. With our clothes on, sadly, but the journey of a thousand Chang Bangs begins with a single coffee . . .

Pookie stepped out of the shower and toweled off. He would make some calls and put Robin and Mr. Burns to work, mow down on the kung pao, then promptly take a nap. Nap, shower and food: the magical trifecta that could right all wrongs.

He tucked the towel around his waist, then found his cell phone and dialed Robin.

She answered immediately. "Pooks, you guys okay?"

"We're fine," he said. "You know, just doin' that poh-lice work thing. How about you?"

"Good news and bad," she said. "The good news is I went to work this morning like normal, and no one said a peep. Metz wasn't there. I got an email from the mayor saying I was expected to carry on as before."

At least Robin wasn't fired. That was something. "That's great. So were you able to get any more info from the bodies?"

"That's the bad news," she said. "Seems there was a little *clerical error* at the morgue. The bodies of Blackbeard, Oscar Woody and Jay Parlar were cremated this afternoon. All their personal effects are gone as well, including Blackbeard's phone."

Pookie's heart sank. Metz had deleted the computer records, and now all physical evidence was also gone for good.

"Two positives, though," Robin said. "Metz apparently didn't call the RapScan people to tell them I'm persona non grata. I snuck one of the portable DNA analyzers out of the morgue. If you find any other likely candidates, we can use the machine to test for the Zed chromosome."

Ah, that Robin — such a clever girl.

"How long will we have that gadget?"

"Don't know," she said. "Metz and I were the only ones to use them so far. When he returns, I'll have to sneak it back in. We probably have it for as long as he's out."

Pookie's phone chirped with the theme music from *The Simpsons* — Black Mr. Burns calling.

"Robin, I gotta go. Great job, but there's nothing else you can do right now. Lie low and don't make waves."

"Got it," she said. "Take care of Bryan for me."

"Will do."

He switched to the other line. "Black Mister Burns, tell me you have more info on Erickson."

"Do I ever," John said. "Jebediah Erickson has a criminal record that you're just going to love. And in case you couldn't tell by his real estate holdings, he's loaded. Old Jeb is actually Jeb *Junior*. Between cash, holdings, the Jessups' place and the house on Franklin, Jeb Senior left his boy around twenty million bucks."

"Rich kid with a criminal record? What did he do, steal monogrammed towels from the country club?"

"Slightly better," John said. "Fourteen allegations of assault and three of resisting arrest. But here's our trump card — he was charged and acquitted of one murder, *convicted* of another. Take a wild guess what the murder weapon was."

Pookie tried to calm the surge of excitement — a gold medal for archery was one thing, a murder conviction was another. "I'll take *what is an arrow* for two hundred, Alex."

"Nicely done," John said. "And now for our bonus round, where the stakes really add up. The arrow thing wasn't in Erickson's SFPD records, no surprise there. Maybe Zou has the City by the Bay on lockdown, but her power *doesn't* appear to extend to certain correctional facilities. I found Erickson's case files at the California Medical Facility in Vacaville."

Pookie leaned back, shocked. "The CMF? The same place they kept Charlie Manson and Juan Vallejo Corona?"

"Yeah, as well as Ed *the Co-Ed Butcher* Kemper and Kees *the Deadly Dutch* Marjis. Jeb Junior was declared unfit to stand trial, so they incarcerated him in the last stop for serial killers. They put him away twenty-eight years ago. After eighteen months of incarceration, a certain Baldwin Metz uncovered new forensic evidence that wound up overturning the murder charge. Erickson walked out a free man."

That would have put him back on the street just over twenty-six years ago . . . right about the time Amy Zou and Rich Verde put a whoopin' on Mr. Biz-Nass.

A knock on his door.

"Burns, my kung pao is here. Daddy needs coal for the choo-choo. Anything else?"

"That's all I've got," he said. "I'll keep looking, though."

"Pookie, *out.*" He folded the phone, grabbed his wallet and opened the door.

Standing there was a uniformed Amy Zou.

Oh, shit.

"Chief," Pookie said, "I know budgets are tight, but moonlighting as a delivery boy?"

"Inspector Chang," she said, then walked inside. "Shut the door. We need to talk."

She looked as neat and pressed as she did in her office at the Hall. Pookie looked at the clock on his wall — 9:07 P.M. Did this woman ever put on a friggin' pair of jeans?

He shut the door. He suddenly thought of Mr. Biz-Nass's thrice-broken nose. His eyes flicked to the polished gun holster hanging from Zou's polished belt.

His gun was in the bedroom. And he was wearing nothing but a towel. Awesome.

Zou brushed off Pookie's couch, then sat.

Her eyes bore into him. "I told you to leave it alone."

Pookie thought of lying, but why bother? She wasn't here for a slap and tickle.

"Chief, we know about Marie's Children. We know you deleted the symbols out of the database. We know you ripped up case files, we know you took all the Golden Gate Slasher info out of the newspaper morgue."

She crossed her legs. "The law doesn't care about *knowledge*, Chang. It cares about *proof*. You have none."

She was right, and it pissed him off to no end. How could she be so callous about it, so *casual*?

"We know about the Zed chromosome."

She smiled. "Do you even know what that means?"

"Not really."

"Neither do I," she said. "But it doesn't matter, because that information went the way of the computer records and the newspaper articles."

Pookie shook his head. This woman disgusted him. "How do you justify letting a vigilante run free, above the law, *murdering* whoever he thinks did something wrong? How can you look your daughters in the eye when you kiss them good night?"

The mention of her daughters hit a chord. Her eyes narrowed in anger. She stood.

"How can I justify it? *Because I saw the bodies!*" Her hands balled up into fists. A lifetime's worth of repressed rage seemed to explode. "Have you ever seen a half-*eaten* six-year-old? No? Well, I have, Chang. *Dozens* of them. Have you ever seen an entire *family* of five *gutted*, their intestines used to make *art*? Have you ever seen a row of severed heads in different stages of decomposition, the fucking *trophies* of a psycho killer the cops couldn't find?"

The outburst left him speechless. So much for the stone-eyed Chief Zou — she vibrated with anger.

"Well, Chang? *Have you?*"

He shook his head.

"Until you have, don't judge me, you got that? And I don't have to *justify* anything to you. I am the goddamn San Francisco *chief of the goddamn police*! I'm sworn to protect this city and that's exactly what I do! This *saves lives*, and you are trying your best to fuck that up!"

She stopped suddenly, her lips curled back, her chest heaving.

Pookie had never heard her raise her voice, let alone blow up like this. She made Bryan look positively sane by comparison.

Zou opened her hands, let them fall to her sides. The cold expression returned. "Sometimes, Chang, the right thing isn't written in the law books."

"We don't get to make that decision," he said. "Cops *enforce* the laws, we don't pick and choose which ones count."

She shook her head and laughed. "Jesus, you sound just like I did." Her hands smoothed her coat at her stomach, a motion to help her regain control rather than to adjust her uniform. "I'll give you one thing," she said. "I'll give you this one thing, then you never speak of it again. You know about Erickson, don't you."

Pookie nodded. "Yeah. He was committed for murder."

Zou paused, seemed to think her words through. "Then look something up for me. Oh, pardon me, have John Smith look it up for you. Tell him to analyze San Francisco's murder rate when Erickson was in the asylum. And by the way, you're fired."

"*What?*"

She held out her hand. "Gun and badge."

"Fuck you."

"I warned you. You're done. So is Clauser. Now, give me your *gun*, and your *badge*."

Pookie remembered the look of rage on Bryan's face when Zou had confronted them over Blackbeard's body. Remembered it, because Pookie knew he now probably wore that very same expression.

He walked to a tray he kept next to his TV. He picked up his badge in its leather bifold and tossed it to her. She caught it, put it in her pocket.

"And the gun," she said. "No, actually, just tell me where the gun is."

"Nightstand next to my bed."

She walked into the bedroom. He'd imagined getting the chief into his bedroom more times than he could count, but not this way. *Fired?* Bryan was going to shit an egg roll.

Zou walked back into the living room, then stopped and stared at him. "Step away from the door, Chang."

He realized he was blocking her path. He stepped aside, giving her plenty of room.

She opened the door, made it halfway out before she turned. "You and Clauser are finished in San Francisco. Bay Area as well. Let's just go ahead and say all of Northern California. But with one phone call, I can get you both homicide jobs in any city in the country. Think about where you'd like to go. That's what you get from me if you stop all this bullshit and stay away from Erickson."

"And if we don't?"

"Then maybe you should look into employment as a prison guard," she said. "Because that's the only way you're going to see Bryan Clauser again."

She stepped out, then shut the door quietly behind her.

Well, this had turned into one gigantic Mongolian cluster-fuck. *Fired.* What was next, a bullet in the back of his head? He didn't have a shred of proof to go against her. No matter what he and Bryan said, it was their word against hers. Who would she have on her side? Only a chief medical examiner who the world thought walked on water, the assistant chief of police, and the goddamn *mayor.* What could Pookie counter with? An overly lethal homicide inspector, a medical examiner who would be portrayed as coveting the CME's job and willing to discredit him to get it, and a computer nerd who was afraid of his own shadow and should have left the force years ago.

Zou held all the cards. She also held his gun.

Pookie reached behind the TV, felt for his backup and found it. He pulled the Glock 22 holster off its Velcro strips. At least he was armed again.

It was over. Amy Zou had won. She had gotten away with it and would continue to do so. Pookie had to break the news to Bryan and hope Bryan didn't go ape-shit crazy in the process. Maybe some extra info could take the edge off, something to put a positive spin on this turd-in-a-punchbowl of a situation. What had Zou told him to look up? Oh, right: the murder rate when Erickson was in the loony bin. Whatever that was, maybe it could help make things more palatable.

Pookie dialed Black Mr. Burns.

And where the *fuck* was that kung pao shrimp?

Come and Play

Bryan waited.

Bryan watched.

He sat on an old five-gallon paint bucket he'd found on the roof, his head just high enough to see over the roof's low wall. He'd positioned himself so a smokestack rose behind him — no silhouette, no outline. Six stories above Erickson's backyard, just past midnight with a starless sky, and Bryan Clauser was all but invisible.

He watched the back of the old Victorian, at least what he could see through the darkness and the trees. The small green space looked almost like a terrarium: trees reaching up high but hemmed in on all sides by concrete, glass and painted wood far taller than the trees themselves. The surrounding buildings left the backyard in shadow most of the day — at night, the area under the trees was as black as the overcast sky itself.

He could see something through the trees, something soaked in deep shadow at the base of the house, something . . . *slanted.* The leaves and branches obscured the shape, but that shape bothered him. It was important; he didn't know why.

At the back of the yard, opposite the Victorian, a narrow space slid between the building Bryan was on and one across from him, a thin alley of grass and trees that led into other backyards. He'd checked the satellite map and knew that one could come out the back of the Victorian, go through the backyard, walk between the buildings and — coated in shadow the entire time — reach Gough Street to the west. A perfect setup. The archer could use that path to come and go unseen.

To go out and hunt.

He's just like me. He hunts killers, the deadliest game there is.

Movement at the base of the house drew Bryan's attention.

Through the obscuring tree, he saw a change in the shape that disturbed him so. The shape . . . it was *opening.* He sucked in a breath and held it, eyes wide with the fresh fear of last night's terrifying dream.

The shape was a cellar door.

A cellar door that led *down.*

Drenched in thick shadow, he saw something come out of that door. The door shut, then that something moved. Smooth movement. *Effortless* movement.

In his pants pocket, Bryan's cell phone let out a *boo-beep.* He twitched a little, suddenly afraid the something would hear, would come for him, but he was six stories up and the phone's sound was little more than a whisper.

The moving shadow crossed the yard, then stopped, vanishing beneath a tree. Bryan waited. The shadow moved to another tree, where it stopped again.

The shadow was making sure no one was watching.

Another few steps, almost between the buildings now. A thin bit of light fell upon the figure and Bryan saw it—

A dark green cloak.

The cloak hung almost to the ground, big hood pulled up over the wearer's head. Slipping beneath the cover of nighttime trees, the cloak was a silent shape sliding across the grass.

The cell again let out a *boo-beep.* Pookie, trying to reach him. Bryan ignored it.

The shape moved to the base of Bryan's white building. Bryan leaned out, carefully, but couldn't see anything in the shadows down there — the cloak, and whoever was in it, had vanished.

Bryan hadn't seen a bow. Had there been one somewhere under that cloak? He knew better than to give chase; by the time he got down to the street the perp would be blocks away in an unknown direction. Calling in a BOLO would be futile — Zou or Robertson or Sharrow would just cancel it, and know exactly what Bryan was doing.

The cloaked figure was gone, but the *house* wasn't going anywhere. This could be Bryan's chance to find some answers. Maybe the vigilante had information on Marie's Children. At the very least, he might find some custom-made arrowheads that could connect Erickson to Blackbeard's murder. *Something* that would let Bryan and Pookie push back against Zou.

No one is above the law.

The cell phone let out a third *boo-beep.* Bryan looked once more to make sure he'd lost sight of the cloaked figure — he had — then pulled out the phone. He didn't want to mess with the stupid two-way button, so he just dialed instead.

"Bryan!" Pookie answerd. "You okay?"

"Pooks, I saw him, he's moving."

"I'm already on my way," Pookie said. "I'm in the car now. Don't do anything."

Bryan forced himself to whisper, as it was the only way he could control his excitement. "I can't believe it, I saw a guy in a big-hooded green cloak. He came right out of these storm-cellar doors in the back of Erickson's house, and the way he *moved*, man, like a . . . wait, you're already on the way?"

"Ten minutes, tops."

Something was wrong. "Why are you on your way before I called you to come get me?"

A pause. A long pause.

"Pooks," Bryan said, "answer my question."

He heard Pookie let out a big breath. This didn't sound good.

"Bryan, it's over. Zou came to my apartment. She's kicking us out of San Francisco. She said if we quit now, she can get us a job anywhere in the country."

No. Not now, not when he was so close. The nightmares, the killings, the connection with Rex, the weird Zed chromosome . . . the answers might be right inside that house.

"Bryan? It's not so bad. I hear Hawaii is great. *Honolulu Homicide* has a real nice ring to it."

Zou had fired them? But the house . . . there *had* to be something in the house.

"Bryan? You there? We're done, did you hear me?"

"I think the house is empty, Pooks."

"Do *not* go in there, man. If you go in there, we're done as cops, *for good*, and trust me, she will send your ass to prison. Just get the fuck out of there."

None of that mattered. Bryan knew he was on the edge of madness. He didn't care about his job. He didn't care about prison.

All he cared about was finding the truth.

"Bryan, dude, I am *begging* you. Wait for me, *please*."

The slate-blue Victorian called to Bryan. *I know what you don't, come and play . . . come and play . . .*

"Bryan! Answer me, man. You *can't* go—"

Bryan hung up. He turned the phone completely off, put it in his pocket, then headed for the tree that led down to the sidewalk.

Tard's Job

Tard tried to put it all together, but it was confusing. His skin itched. This roof always made him itchy. But he dare not scratch, dare not even *move*, because the monster had left the house.

Tard's job in life was to be terrified. Every night. *Every single night* he watched the monster come out of the house and disappear somewhere out on the streets. Tard never knew where he went. The monster could double back somewhere, close in on Tard and then it would be too late — Tard would feel an arrow, or a knife, or a bullet.

The only time Tard could breathe easy was for about five minutes when the monster returned to the house's back door, but then the feeling slipped away — maybe the monster had another door, a *secret* door, maybe it slipped out, circled around the block, scaled a building, and . . .

Tard forced the thoughts away. Focus. This was an important job. Sly had told him so. Important, and tricky, like James Bond. That's what Tard wanted to be, like James Bond, all smooth and stuff.

Tard's hands trembled as he reached down — slowly — to pick up the cell phone. He couldn't have it on his body, not when he was hiding, so he just set it on the ground.

He dialed.

Sly answered on the second ring.

"Chameleon," he said. "How goes your mission?"

Chameleon. That's what Tard wanted to be called, but no one called him that. Not without laughing, anyway. No one except Sly. Sly never laughed.

"Sly, he left the house."

"Good man," Sly said. "Just stay there, call me when he comes back in."

"But can't I join you guys this time?"

"You need to stay," Sly said. "Something glorious is happening, Chameleon. It's happening tonight. We must know when the monster returns. We can't do this without your bravery."

Tard wanted to go with Sly and the others. He was sad he could not. But Sly said this job, the watching, was very important.

"Okay, Sly, I'll stay. I'll be brave. Has Marco come back yet?"

"No," Sly said. "We think the monster got him."

Sadness. Tard wanted to cry. First Chomper, now Marco. The monster murdered people. And Tard was up here all alone.

"Sly, I'm scared."

"Just stay there," Sly said. "If you stay still, the monster won't find you. And if you move around, what happens if Firstborn finds out where you've been all these nights?"

Firstborn. Firstborn could make you go away. Forever. And Firstborn had said no one was to go near the monster's house.

"Do you really think he'll find out?"

"Not if you stay there," Sly said. "When the monster comes back, call me."

Sly hung up.

Tard slowly set the phone back down on the roof. *So* slowly — if you didn't want the monster to take you into his basement, it was best to not move at all.

Fear of the monster. Fear of Firstborn. The *need* to go out, to find a won't-be. Wanting to be brave so Sly would like him, so Tard could make some friends. Too many things to think of.

Sly had said only the bravest of Marie's Children could watch the monster. The monster had killed everyone who went near the house. Many brothers and sisters had tried to kill the monster, sometimes with guns and everything. None of them ever came back. So watching the house, well, even that was just dang dangerous. But if you could do it, if you could watch, Sly said, then everyone would know you were brave and everyone would *like you*.

Except Tard couldn't tell anyone about his job, because Firstborn said no one was ever to go near the monster's house. Sly said it was okay, though, to ignore Firstborn's orders, as long as no one found out.

Movement. Down by the monster's house. By the back door. It was the man dressed in black, the man who had been circling the block earlier. How *exciting*! Tard stayed very still, because he was good at that.

Tard watched.

Cowardice

John Smith checked the caller ID: POOKIE CHANG.

What now? Pookie had just called thirty minutes earlier with that murder-rate research project. John loved Pookie and would always have his back, but truth be told the guy was more than a little too quick to delegate detective work.

John answered. "Pooks, you gotta give a guy a chance. I haven't even started to search the database yet, let alone start tabulating stuff. This isn't—"

"John, I need you, right now."

Pookie never called him *John*. "What's happening?"

"Bryan's having a meltdown. I need you at Erickson's house, ASAP."

John looked to his apartment window even though he knew what he'd see — the blackness of night, lit up only by streetlights and the glowing windows across the road.

"It's dark out," John said.

"I *know* it's dark out, John. Bryan is going in there without a warrant, and if he does, Zou is going to screw him right to the wall. I don't know if I can stop him on my own — I need your help."

John stared at the window. Stared and shook his head. He wanted to help Bryan, he did, but *it was dark outside* and Pookie wanted him to go to the house of a killer?

"Pooks, I . . . I just can't."

"The *fuck* you can't! Your black ass would be *dead* if it wasn't for Bryan. I'm so sorry for what happened to you, I am, but you get your gun, get on that Harley and move."

John nodded. Hard to breathe. Bryan needed him. Erickson's. It wasn't all that far, not at this hour, using the bike to slide between traffic, if there was any traffic . . .

"Yeah, okay, I can be there in fifteen minutes."

"Make it ten," Pookie said. "And don't forget your gun. This isn't about you anymore. Man up, or just stay in your goddamn apartment for the rest of your life."

Pookie hung up. John closed his eyes tight. *Breathe. You have to go, you* HAVE *to.*

He reached into his desk drawer and pulled out his Sig Sauer.

His hand was already trembling.

The Kill

The sound of a shutting door made Rex snap awake.

Had someone found him?

He was still in the brown garbage can. The lid was still closed. What had happened? He had just closed his eyes, tried to think of his people finding him. Had he fallen asleep? It was totally dark out. Was it past midnight? He didn't have a watch, didn't have a phone.

He heard a *click-click-click* sound. He rose slowly, the top of his head lifting the hinged lid so he could peek out under it. There was April, walking away from the house, a big smile on her face. Her high heels *clicked* on the concrete. Maybe she had just fucked Alex. Maybe she had given him a blowjob. She looked dirty. *Unclean.*

There was no one else on the street. There were no cars. She was walking away, fast, like she was *fleeing* him. It spun him up to think that she was trying to escape.

No one else on the street — his attempt to make his so-called family come had failed. Maybe it didn't work that way, he didn't know. What if April didn't return? What if she was going to get help? What if she was going to get her parents? What if Rex wouldn't have another chance?

She would have a key. Alex would be alone in the house.

Rex quietly crawled out of the garbage can. Blanket wrapped around him, he walked after April. Could he get her? He'd killed Roberta . . . Roberta was bigger and stronger than April the meth-head.

His feet carried him after her. He *had* to get her.

Click-click-click.

Rex's feet made no noise. He reached out for her, locked his hands around her neck and *squeezed.* She grabbed at his fingers. She tried to turn, but he wouldn't let her. She made little grunting noises — not enough air for a real scream. Her nails raked the backs of his hands, so he squeezed as hard as he possibly could.

April twitched, she kicked out weakly . . . she stopped moving.

Rex was so turned on, so *damn* turned on. He pulled her into an apartment building entryway and gently set her on the ground. He wouldn't have long. Rex looked in her little purse and found the keys.

He couldn't hide here forever. He had to face Alex, Alex who had stomped on his arm, *broken* it. Alex, who had punched Rex in the face so many times, kicked him in the stomach . . .

Rex shook his head. He wouldn't be afraid anymore, he *wouldn't*. He was the *king*.

He looked around again to see if anyone saw him. The street was silent. There was no movement. Rex walked to the house. He tried to breathe. Alex was inside. Rex's hand caressed the front door's white-painted wood.

He had killed two women — Alex Panos wasn't a woman. Alex was big and strong. Rex couldn't run now, couldn't stop himself from going in. One way or another, Alex's endless torment ended now. Rex's breath came in deep, ragged spurts.

Kill Alex. Kill Alex. Kill Alex.

Rex's hand slid down to the brass doorknob. Cool to the touch. He tried a key: didn't fit. He tried another, staying as quiet as he could. The third one slid in. He turned the key, then turned the handle.

Rex stepped inside. There was a room to the right. Coming from inside that room, the blue/white flashes of a TV playing in the darkness.

From that room, a voice: "Did you get me my Chocodiles? You better have my Chocodiles, girl."

Rex walked into the room. Alex Panos — big, *strong* Alex Panos — sat in a chair facing a huge TV screen.

Alex stood up quickly. He looked across the room, somewhere to Rex's right, then looked back at Rex. Alex's hands curled into fists.

"You little faggot," he said. "What are you doing here?"

The voice froze Rex's feet in place. He couldn't move. He couldn't think of anything but the fists smashing against his nose, the knees breaking his lips, the boot snapping his arm.

The flickering light from the TV played off of Alex's blond hair. "The news said you killed your mom," he said. A statement with an underlying meaning: *you killed your mom, are you here to kill me?*

Yes. That's exactly what Rex was there to do.

His feet came unglued. He took one step forward.

"Don't," Alex said. "Get out of here, or I will fuck you up. Did you tell anyone where I am?"

Rex took another step.

Alex looked to Rex's right again. There was something there Alex wanted, but Rex wouldn't take his eyes off the prey even for a second.

"You better run away, motherfucker," Alex said. "Go now, or I'm going to hurt you real bad this time."

The voice of anger, the voice of *hate*, but there was something new in there: *fear*.

Rex breathed in deep through his nose. He didn't just *hear* Alex's fear, he *smelled* it.

Alex suddenly ran to his left, crossing in front of the TV. Rex shot forward before he even knew what he was doing. He slammed into Alex, driving the bigger boy back into the TV. Plastic cracked, something sparked, and they both hit the ground hard. Alex cried out, a squeal of pain very unlike his manly words of threat.

Rex started to stand, then felt a fist slam into his mouth. *So hard.* He fell back and landed on his ass. A boot crunched into his stomach, crushing the air out of his lungs, making Rex's body curl up into a ball. All the fear came rushing back. The terror of beatings past consumed him, because he knew this one would be worse than all the others — he shouldn't have come here.

A big fist hit him in the back of the head, bouncing his face off the wood floor.

"You ruined April's TV, you asshole!"

A steel-toed boot hammered his ribs. Rex started to scream, to cry out, but he clenched his teeth together — it didn't hurt as bad as he remembered it.

Rex opened his eyes. Right in front of him, a foot, a shin, a knee. He reached out, grabbed Alex's heel and yanked.

Alex went down fast, the back of his head *cracking* off the floor. His eyes scrunched tight and his mouth opened in a silent gasp of confused pain. He rolled to his side, hands holding the back of his head.

Blood dripped from his fingers.

Rex had done that. He had made Alex *bleed*.

Rex stood on shaky legs. He felt blood trickling from his own nose, his own mouth. He stepped forward and raised his foot.

Alex looked up just as Rex's heel smashed down. The bigger boy let out a noise, part fear, part rage, part agony. He rolled away, blood pouring from his now-ruined nose. He looked confused, shocked.

Rex smiled a bloody smile, the smile of a fighter. His hands curled into fists.

"It's your turn, bully," he said. "It's your turn to hurt."

Alex scrambled away on hands and knees. Rex started to follow, but stopped when he heard a loud noise from above. Several noises. Something landing on the roof?

Both boys looked up to the ceiling, eyes searching for the source of the sound as if their eyes could penetrate wood and plaster.

"Shit," Alex said. "The fuck is this?"

Rex's chest started to thrum — *ba-da-bum-bummmm . . . ba-da-bum-bummmm*, the same feeling he'd experienced when he met Marco.

His family had arrived.

How perfect.

Rex looked back at Alex, but Alex had moved. He was standing to the right of the door, next to a small table. He held a gun. Too late Rex realized that's what Alex had been glancing at while they had talked. The gun had been on the table the whole time, just an arm's reach away, but Rex hadn't looked.

No, no fair, I beat him I beat him I had my revenge no fair—

"Fuck you, faggot," Alex said, then pulled the trigger.

Something slammed into Rex's belly. His legs gave out. As he fell, he heard a combination of sounds — splintering wood, another gunshot, and then the screams of Alex Panos.

The Basement

Bryan Clauser stood in the shadows of trees that were themselves drenched in the shadows of tall buildings. He flexed his hands, fists making his leather gloves creak. He stared at the back of the gray house.

He stared at the cellar door.

The basement. Whatever bad thing was happening, it was in the basement. He had to know.

The cellar door waited for him, a demon mouth ready to open and bite, to chew and shred and tear and crunch. Dream-memories blurred his reality, merged and shifted with what he saw until he wasn't sure what was actually there.

Come closer, the house seemed to say. *Come, little fool, save me the trouble of reaching out to pull you in . . .*

His Nikes slid across the grass, carrying him to the door. He bent, reached out a hand, touched. It wasn't wood. Heavy-gauge metal, painted to look like the same wood as the rest of the house. In the door's upper left corner, a key-pad lock. The thing was bomb-shelter solid — he couldn't open it.

Was he dreaming? Was this really happening?

Did you think it would be easy? the house said. *You'll have to work harder to find your death . . .*

Bryan closed his eyes and rubbed them hard with the heels of his hands. He wasn't crazy. He *wasn't*. He had to get in there.

You think a house is talking to you. Sounds crazy to me . . .

"I'll burn you to the ground," Bryan said. "Burn you and piss on the coals."

Then you'll never know what's inside . . . neverknow . . . neverknow . . .

Bryan bit hard into the heel of his left hand. The pain rose up, clearing his thoughts. That helped. He wasn't crazy. He wasn't.

He walked to a window and peeked in. Beyond the glass, the dull gleam of metal revealed some kind of inside shutter. It looked just as tough as the cellar entrance.

He'd have to try the front door.

Bryan drew his Sig Sauer and walked down the side of the house, his left shoulder almost touching the slate-blue wood, shadows curling around him in a lover's embrace.

•••

Pookie turned onto Franklin Street, then floored it. The Buick's engine roared. He kept to the middle lane as much as he could, swerving left or right when he needed to, running red lights with little care for what might happen.

He'd dressed for the occasion. No ill-fitting suit jacket this time. Black jeans, black shoes, a black sweater stretched over his gut, and the black Glock 22 in the black holster attached to his black belt. It was a fashion statement that would win the Bryan Clauser seal of approval. Pookie didn't use the bubble-light or the siren. Couldn't draw attention. If any other cops showed up, the Terminator was screwed.

He hoped Black Mr. Burns would get there quick.

• • •

The Harley's big twin engine roared at the night, the sound bouncing off the buildings on either side to fill the street with an echoing, angry gurgle.

John forced himself to breathe. His neck already hurt from trying to look in all directions at once. So many buildings, so many windows, so many places for someone to hide, to point a gun.

He rolled the throttle back and the Harley picked up speed. He slipped around a truck, then lane-split between a pair of BMWs. Maybe someone was aiming at him right now, tracking him, lining up the shot.

The feeling pressed his chest inward like a tightening vise wrapped all the way around his ribs. His breaths came faster. He was starting to hyperventilate.

He shook his helmeted head. Bryan needed him. So did Pookie.

Just this once. He could push the fear down just this *once,* and for a single night be a man again.

• • •

Gun in hand, Bryan walked up the mansion's wide steps. Traffic rolled along on Franklin Street behind him, but it was a part of some other world, some other dimension.

Bryan stood before the front door. The porch roof blocked the streetlights, bathing him in the night's thick black. He reached out a hand, let his fingertips touch the double doors' ornate wood.

Come on, little one, come and taste the end . . .

"Shut up," Bryan hissed. "Shut up, I'm not hearing this."

You and only you hear it. And they call you the Terminator? You're a joke, and here you are walking to your own death. Come on, little one, don't you want to know what's inside? Neverknow . . . neverknow . . .

"You talk too much," Bryan said, then he raised his left foot and kicked just below the door handle. Wood cracked with a cannon-blast sound. The double doors flew open, the right one tumbling into the hallway beyond to crash hard against the floor. The door had looked a lot more solid than that; must have been some cheap pine and not the old oak Bryan had thought it was at first glance.

Then came the blaring shrill of an alarm.

Bryan walked inside. He didn't notice his surroundings. He was looking for one thing and one thing only.

Somewhere in here was a door to the basement.

•••

The break-in tripped a magnetic sensor, which sent a signal down a thin wire to the small alarm-control box in the basement. That had triggered the Klaxon that screeched through the house, but the system wasn't finished. A telephone wire ran out of the control box into a multi-line office phone, the kind that had once been white but had yellowed with well over two decades of age. The phone had a handset, next to which ran a vertical line of eight buttons, each with a red light. The red light next to LINE ONE lit up. The phone's speaker let out a brief dial tone, then seven rapid digital beeps.

•••

Pookie saw the tall turret of Erickson's mansion up on the left. Cars lined the curb, leaving nowhere to park. He saw the house's driveway — it was wide open. He didn't want to park there and draw attention from anyone who might be in the house, but he was out of time. He pulled in, locking up the breaks to skid agross the gravel. He grabbed his Streamlight Stinger flashlight and was out the door even before the Buick rocked back from the sudden stop. He heard the house's ringing alarm. Pookie ran to the mansion's steps, up to the porch, and saw the smashed-open front doors.

Bryan was already inside. Pookie had to get him out.

In the distance, over the alarm's blare, he heard the oncoming heavy gurgle of a Harley.

Pookie drew his Glock. Gun in one hand, flashlight in the other, he entered the house, stepping past the fallen door that lay flat on the entryway floor. The alarm screeched its constant, metallic tone. Pookie knelt and aimed his flashlight beam at the door's edge — it was solid oak. Almost *two inches* of solid oak, strong as hell. Had Bryan done that? With what? A pair of deadbolts winked in his moving flashlight beam. Then Pookie saw something else — a three-foot-long steel bar, the kind used to secure a door.

The bar was bent at one end.

Bryan had ripped through a superthick door, two big deadbolts, and a fucking *steel bar*.

Pookie remembered seeing Bryan jump up on top of the van. It had been dark . . . he'd been far away . . . his eyes had been playing tricks on him, et cetera, et cetera. He'd told himself those things, deluded himself into thinking that Bryan was just Bryan and not something else.

Images flashed in Pookie's thoughts: a cloaked man jumping across a street, from one building to the next; a body with the arm ripped off at the shoulder; Robin talking about new genes and mutations.

Everything connected.

"Oh, shit," Pookie said.

Bryan was in more trouble than either of them had ever imagined.

Pookie stood, let his flashlight beam play across the house's dark interior as he walked deeper inside.

•••

The sounds of nighttime traffic filtered up from the street four stories below. The evening wind danced by, not quite strong enough to ruffle his green cloak. His ears had long since tuned out the normal sounds of the city. The only things that he really heard, that he really listened for, were gunshots, screams and — sometimes — the roars.

Below him was Rex Deprovdechuk's house. Police tape across the door. Would the kid come back? Unknown, but where else to look? Rex had vanished, as had Alex Panos.

Staking out Alex's apartment had paid off. Alex had come home. The result? Another dead member of Marie's Children. The Issac boy had died up on the roof, but that was how things went.

Everyone dies eventually.

Beneath the heavy cloak, he felt a buzz from his pager. *The house.* He didn't need to look at the pager to know this.

His hands did a fast, automatic pat-down: bow tight on his back; quiver secured, all ten shafts in place; Fabrique Nationale 5.7-millimeter handgun secure in the holster strapped to his left thigh; four loaded, twenty-round magazines at the small of his back; silver-coated Ka-Bar knife snug in the sheath on his right thigh; and minigrenades strapped to the bandolier across his chest — two concussion, two thermite, two shrapnel.

It had been a very long time since he'd had visitors. He had to get home, show them some hospitality.

•••

Bryan stood at the bottom of the basement stairs. He wasn't sure if he could move. Every atom in his body screamed at him to stop. His dreams, where he'd killed people, *eaten* people, those had been bad, perhaps the worst things he'd ever experienced.

But those hadn't been the only dreams.

The dream of being dragged . . . dragged into *this* basement. Hurt, wounded, afraid, bleeding — dragged into this basement by a *monster.*

A monster that could be down here, waiting.

No, the monster was gone; Bryan had watched it leave.

But when would it return?

The house alarm wasn't as loud down here. His flashlight beam bounced through the blackness, illuminating a glossy wooden floor, crown molding, even a fireplace. The long space looked like a small ball-room from days gone by.

At the back of the room, he saw a door. Engraved letters gleamed from a brass plaque. They spelled out: RUMPUS ROOM.

Bryan walked toward the door.

•••

Pookie had to hurry, he knew that, but he couldn't look away — he needed just a few seconds to take it all in. Everything his flashlight lit up seemed to reek of money. Turn-of-the-century money. The place looked like it was taken out of a movie from the days of the lumber barons, the gold barons, the whatever barons. Back then, men had built places like this for their wives and daughters, to impress the city or simply to let everyone know just how rich they were. Pookie was standing in the nineteenth-century equivalent of a red sports car.

A heavy staircase rose up to his right. To his left, something glowed from within a wide, open doorway. Pookie stepped through. Inside of a marble fireplace guarded by two knee-high brass sphinxes, dying coals gave off a faint, flickering light. His flashlight beam played off endless splendor: a sparkling crystal chandelier; polished redwood paneling with hand-carved trim; marble floors with thick grains of granite and thin streaks of gold; gleaming brass fixtures; ornate picture frames showing faces of spooky-looking rich dudes.

Outside, he heard the distinctive roar of an approaching Harley, an oncoming Doppler effect that didn't transition to the fadeaway because the engine idled, then stopped. Pookie pinched his flashlight under his right arm. He pulled out his phone and dialed with his left hand even as he continued to turn, his right hand pointing the Glock before him.

He stopped when his flashlight illuminated an open door.

Through the door were stairs leading down.

The phone rang only twice before Black Mr. Burns answered: "I'm here, man, but I'm flipping out," he said. "Where the hell are you?"

"Inside."

"Want me to come in?"

"Not yet," Pookie said. "Get on the porch and stay there. Don't let anyone in, not even cops. I'll call if I need you."

Pookie hung up. He had to trust that John could manage his fear and control anything that came up. Pookie took a breath, then started down the stairs.

•••

Footsteps. Heavy ones. Bryan shut off his flashlight. He aimed his Sig Sauer back across the ballroom floor toward the base of the stairs. He saw a flashlight beam sliding down the steps, flicking around, followed by legs, then a portly, black-sweater-clad belly that could only belong to one man.

The flashlight beam whipped across the walls, then landed squarely in Bryan's eyes.

Bryan blinked, held up a hand to block the light. "Pooks, do you mind?"

The beam dropped to Bryan's feet.

"Clauser! You are seriously chapping my ass. Come on, man, we have to get out of here, *now.*"

Bryan turned his back to Pookie, played his own beam across the dull-brass plaque. The letters of RUMPUS ROOM gleamed and danced.

"Through here," he said.

"Bryan, *no.* Dude, come on, the game is over and we lost. If we're caught here, we are so screwed."

"I'm not leaving until I figure this out, so you might as well help."

Pookie sighed and walked forward to stand at Bryan's right shoulder.

"Clauser, you are such an A-W-G-M-K."

"That a new one?"

"Yeah, I made it up just now. It means you are an *Asshole Who'll Get Me Killed*." Pookie played his beam across the wooden door's gloss, then let it rest on the intricate brass handle. "Bryan, just tell me one thing. Is this worth going to prison for?"

"It is," Bryan said.

"And you got the memo about what happens to cops in prison?"

Bryan nodded. "It's worth that, too."

"Awesome," Pookie said. "I was afraid you'd say that. I don't suppose this door is open?"

"Nope."

"Double awesome. Well, I guess we can say *aloha* to Honolulu Homicide."

Bryan closed his eyes and shook his head. His career was over, he knew that, but he didn't need to drag Pookie along for the ride. "Pooks, maybe you should just go."

"A little late for that, Bri-Bri. I'm already fired, and you already said this meant enough to you that you'd go to prison for it. I'll finish the job."

Pookie was still all-in. There was no point in arguing, Bryan would have done the same for him.

"I think what we need is on the other side," Bryan said. "Let's figure out how to get this door open."

•••

It wasn't the first time they'd attacked his house. Every ten years or so, one or two of them got stupid enough to forget what happened to the last one or two, and they came for him. They'd always known right where his house was . . . all they had to do was come over and kill him.

They had tried the back door, the windows, even the roof. Over the years he'd sealed all of those things up. As well as he could, anyway — some of them were so strong there was little you could do to keep them out. One industrious little monster had even tunneled in, going right through the basement concrete.

He'd killed them all.

The tunneler was still his favorite. The stupid bastard had dug right up into the rumpus room. Savior hadn't even had to move him — he'd just cut the intruder's spinal cord so he couldn't walk, then went to work.

Oh, how that one had *screamed*.

They screamed, they begged, they threatened. And yet for all their useless words, they never — *ever* — gave up the information Savior most needed to know.

Such was the way of things.

The pager told him the front door had been breached, so he approached from the roof of the building across the street. He looked down at his front porch. Below the peaked roof, he saw a man standing in front of the house's front doors — a black man wearing a purple motorcycle jacket, holding a gun that he kept pointed to the ground.

The man turned. Streetlights played off something hanging around his neck, bouncing off his chest.

A flash of gold.

A badge?

Perhaps the intruders had already left. It wasn't the first time the police had come to his house after a break-in, but he had to be careful. You never knew when the bastards would get clever and try a new tactic.

He pulled off his cloak, wrapping the pistol, the grenade bandolier, the magazines and other gear inside. He stuffed the whole package in a space between an air conditioner and the roof wall, out of sight. Everything except the knife. That he moved to the small of his back, under his shirt — maybe a single knife didn't seem like much against the monsters, but it had never failed him before.

And, sometimes, the knife was just plain more fun.

•••

Bryan watched Pookie slide a thin piece of metal into the lock. "Anything?"

"Yes," Pookie said. "This gives me an idea — in *Blue Balls, all* cops will be able to pick locks. Makes plots so much easier." He stood and put the tools in his pocket. "I give up. Just kick the fucking thing."

The door looked far too heavy for that. Whatever was behind it, the owner didn't want anyone getting in.

"Pooks, look at this thing, it's like a bank vault."

Pookie let out a snort of a laugh. "Bryan, you kicked in the front door of this house, right?"

Bryan nodded.

"By chance, did you look at said door before you treated it to a taste of your Bryan booties?"

Bryan thought of telling Pookie how he'd been distracted because he thought the house was talking to him, but figured that now wasn't the time. "I didn't really look at it. I just, you know . . . I just had to get in."

Pookie pointed his flashlight beam at the door's handle. "Then do me a favor. Realize that you *just have to get in* here."

"But, Pooks, I'm telling you that—"

"Would you just kick the thing? Trust me for once, will you? Kick that motherfucker with everything you got."

This wasn't the time for games, but Pookie would just keep at it until Bryan caved. He stepped back, took a breath, then raised his left foot and pushed-kicked out as hard as he could.

It made a big *bang*, but the door didn't budge.

"See? I told you."

Pookie pointed his flashlight to the door handle. The wood around it had cracked. "Hit it again."

Bryan didn't understand. The door must have looked stronger than it actually was. They'd caught a break. He reared back and kicked again.

The door flew open.

Bryan and Pookie pointed their guns into the darkness beyond. They slowly stepped through.

Something in there. For a second, Bryan couldn't make it out.

Then Pookie's flashlight beam lit it up.

Bryan fired three shots, the gun's roar sharp and deafening in the confined space.

•••

John heard the gunshots. In that same second, he started to shake. He should never have left his apartment. He shouldn't have come here, *shouldn't have come here*! He felt dizzy before he realized he'd stopped breathing. He sucked in a breath so big it wheezed like a marathon runner crossing the finish line.

John stepped into the dark house, feet finding spots around the broken oak door. The alarm blared a constant, undeniable sound.

Pookie and Bryan could be in trouble. John had to go toward the gunshots, he *had* to, but he couldn't—

—his cell phone buzzed, making him twitch with surprise. He pulled the phone out of his pocket and answered.

"Pookie! You okay?"

"We're fine," Pookie said. "Just stay out there."

John returned to the porch. He leaned against the waist-high wooden railing opposite the door. He saw a young couple across the street, huddling with each other against the night's cold; they stared at the mansion.

And farther to the right, a homeless guy, standing there and watching. The lookie-loos had begun to gather.

"Pooks, hurry up," John said. "With this alarm, a black and white will be here any second and the natives are getting restless."

"We're almost done," Pookie said. "Just stay there."

Pookie hung up. John sucked in another ragged breath as he slid the phone into his pocket. He moved closer to the broken door, staying as far back in the porch's shadows as he could.

The Rumpus Room

P ookie's heart seemed to bounce all over his chest, enough to make him wonder if left-arm pain wasn't next, followed by his ticker giving him the bird and just shutting down in protest.

He slid his phone back in his pocket, then tilted his head toward the gunshot victim. "Congratulations, Terminator. You just terminated a stuffed bear."

"Fuck you," Bryan said. "And that's not a bear."

Their flashlight beams played off the target of Bryan's gunfire. It was big, and it was stuffed, as evidenced by the dry strands of dark orange fur floating in their flashlight beams . . . but Bryan was right about one thing — it wasn't a bear.

Bears don't have opposable thumbs.

Bears don't have four eyes.

It had rear legs the size of oil barrels, and long front arms that hung down to the ground. It would have walked half upright, gorilla style. Two bullets had hit the body — one in the shoulder and one in the thigh — ripping off chunks of orange fur and exposing a white, Styrofoam-like material beneath. Bryan's third shot had shattered one of the glass eyes. Two eyes to the right of the squished nose, two to the left — the eyes were so fucked up, so *out there*, that they almost made you miss the mouth full of pointy, inch-long teeth.

Pookie reached out a finger and poked the thing, just to make sure it was, indeed, truly dead. The fur felt dry, stiff and brittle.

"This is messed up," he said. "Erickson makes giant jackalopes?"

Bryan picked up his shell casings and put them in his pocket. "What's a jackalope?" He moved to the wall inside the door, sliding hands searching for a light switch.

"Half jackrabbit, half antelope," Pookie said. "It's fake taxidermy, a rabbit with antelope horns. People with nothing better to do put different animals together to make weird shit. Erickson is doing something like that."

Pookie heard the *click* of a heavy switch. The room filled with light.

The bear-thing wasn't alone.

"Dude," Pookie said, "this is pretty fucked-up right here."

Jebediah Erickson's collection of fake taxidermy lined the room's walls. A dozen creatures, each as monstrous as Ol' Four Eyes. And standing between some of those creatures, five more that didn't look fake, and were even more nightmarish because of their familiarity.

He had stuffed *people*.

Bryan walked up to one. "I don't know much about taxidermy, but this guy looks real."

Pookie walked over to join Bryan. A man, holding a crowbar. A few strands of hair clung to the crowbar's nail-pulling edge. Blue glass eyes stared out from the dead face, each looking in a slightly different direction. He wore tan slacks, brown loafers and a white shirt with a blue Izod sweater vest. His brittle blond hair was feathered in a style straight out of the '80s.

Bryan pointed to a white fleck glued to the edge of the crowbar. "Piece of a tooth?"

Pookie leaned forward to look. "Yeah. A kid's tooth, I think."

If this *was* real, which Pookie doubted, the taxidermist was a long ways from getting his union certification. The man's skin looked taut and leathery. He wore a smile, but Pookie couldn't be sure if that was from the too-tight skin or the "artist's" sense of humor.

Bryan reached out and gently poked the stuffed man's right ear — it was tilted, barely attached. "Can you get DNA info out of something that's been stuffed?"

Pookie shrugged. "No idea. You thinking this is a Zed?"

Bryan nodded. "Too bad we can't test it."

"We can," Pookie said. "Robin has one of those RapScan doohickeys at her apartment. It's worth a shot." Pookie reached into his pants pocket and pulled out a small evidence envelope. He held it up. "You gotta do the honors."

"Pussy," Bryan said as he took the envelope. He gently pulled the ear off the man and slid it inside. The envelope went into his pocket.

He turned, then pointed down and to the right. "I don't like the looks of that."

He was pointing at a little black girl, stiff and rigid, forever frozen in her final pose. She held a knife in her left hand and a fork in her right. Her skin had started to split on the left forearm, pulling away from the white foam material underneath.

Bryan tilted his head back and sniffed at the air. He turned in place and sniffed again, his nose wrinkling.

"Pooks, you smell that?"

Pookie sniffed. The faint odor of ammonia? That, and some other things he couldn't name. "Yeah, I do. You find the source, I'll get some shots of these things."

Pookie pulled out his phone and snapped pictures: the little girl; the crowbar-man; the other stuffed people; a massive, muscular five-hundred-pound thing that looked an awful lot like a predatory human-beetle hybrid; a woman in a summer dress who was normal save for skin covered with inch-long scales that glimmered soft, rainbow reflections of the lights above; a black-furred thing on all fours that was about as big as a German shepherd, but with sharp, foot-long pincers instead of jaws.

"Pooks, come check this out."

Bryan was at the back of the room, staring through an open door. Pookie joined him, looking in at a ten-foot-by-twenty-foot room made of old, ill-fitting bricks. In the middle sat a stainless-steel workbench. Metal workshop shelves full of boxes and pull-out drawers lined the walls. A closed, old-style bank vault door — complete with a spinning wheel-lock — took up the entire far wall.

On the center of the workbench sat a rig holding an unstrung bow. One end of the bench had a polished steel rack holding twenty-four gleaming arrowheads in four neat rows of six. The bench's other end held a custom gun rack loaded with two matched handguns and a blocky, rifle-sized weapon.

"He's got two five-sevens," Bryan said, pointing to the Fabrique Nationale pistols. "Serious shit."

Pookie nodded, memories of the rooftop gun-battle flashing through his mind — those were the same pistols the archer had fired at him. Pookie again realized how lucky he had been; the FNs' powerful 5.7-by-28-millimeter cartridge could punch through typical Kevlar body armor, then tumble through the body behind that armor. The bullet's tumbling action would open up a wound channel far larger than the bullet's diameter.

Bryan reached out and pointed at two empty spots in the handgun rack. "Space for four FNs, only two here. Assume he's got at least one on him."

"Awesome," Pookie said. "Let's hope he doesn't get home anytime soon."

Bryan's gloved hands lifted the larger weapon out of the rack. It sort of looked like an M-16 juiced up on steroids — a thick, composite stock, a flat-black body topped by a rail-handle, a long magazine curved slightly forward, and a midlength barrel.

"USAS-12," Bryan said. "Semiauto shotgun. Ten shots in five seconds. File under *avoid*."

"Consider it filed."

Pookie examined the shelves and drawers. He saw dozens of boxes of ammo for both the five-sevens and for the shotgun — someone was ready to party.

Bryan opened a metal cabinet on the other side of the room. Inside it hung two dark green cloaks. "Maybe Erickson is too old to be the vigilante, but this is definitely the vigilante's home base." He shut the cabinet. "But what's with all the fake creatures?"

Pookie shrugged. "Maybe it's a hobby. A way to kill time when he's not killing people."

Bryan sniffed again. He turned to the old bank-vault door, then walked slowly toward it.

Pookie sniffed as well. "More ammonia?"

Bryan shook his head. "It's not just chemicals. I smell something else."

His gloved hands reached out and started turning the heavy wheel.

Jebediah Erickson

As soon as John saw the old man walking down the sidewalk of Franklin Street, he knew who it had to be.

"Come on, Pooks," John hissed to himself. "Hurry up."

The old man wore black slacks and a dark-brown button-up shirt. Black shoes trod noiselessly on the sidewalk. His hair was so thin it seemed to float above his scalp. He was coming closer, only a few feet from the house.

Just pass on by, just pass on by . . .

The old man reached the bottom steps and started up. He had reached the landing and turned right to climb the rest of the steps when John raised his left hand, palm out.

"SFPD," John said. "Stay right where you are. Please identify yourself."

The old man looked up, stared John in the eyes. "I am Jebediah Erickson. This is my house. What is happening?"

Could this man have a gun? What about those people standing across the street? Were they armed? John's body twitched. He had to control himself. "Uh . . . there's been a break-in. Your alarm. Neighbors called. Please step out to the sidewalk."

"I'm fine right here," the old man said. "Who are you?"

Shit. Should John lie? No, too late for that. "Officer John Smith, San Francisco Police Department."

"Please produce identification."

Shit. Shit-shit-shit. Goddamit, Pookie, get out here.

John lifted the badge hanging around his chest. "You see this, sir? This is a badge."

Erickson held out a hand. "Throw me the badge, Officer. I don't know if you are the police or just acting like the police, so keep your distance."

The old man's house had been broken into and it didn't phase him, not one bit. He radiated confidence. He had every right to ask for ID.

John lifted the badge from around his neck, gently tossed it to Erickson. The old man caught it. He looked at it carefully, then started up the marble stairs.

John raised the Sig Sauer he held in his right hand, just enough to show he was serious. *"Stay where you are!"*

Erickson stopped walking. He looked at the pistol, then back up at John. The old man smiled and tossed the badge back.

John again strung it around his neck. He had to stall, buy time for Pookie and Bryan to finish whatever they were doing. "Now, sir, if I could impose upon you to return the favor? Identification, please."

"I don't have any identification," Erickson said. "Are there more police in my house?"

Shit-shit-shit. "Yes."

"Get them out of there, immediately. The chief of police is a friend of mine and if they don't leave, *right now*, it will go poorly for them."

John nodded, then pulled the phone out of his pocket. It was hard to dial with his left thumb, but no way he was taking the gun out of his right. Something about this old white dude was scary as fuck.

• • •

Bryan turned the wheel until he heard bolts receding into the thick vault door. The wheel stopped. He pulled the heavy door, which slowly swung open on well-oiled hinges.

He and Pookie stepped inside.

The iron-walled vault was all of twelve feet long by eight feet wide. A rack of knives, saws and other disturbing instruments hung on one wall. Shelves containing plastic bottles of chemicals lined the other walls, leaving just enough room to walk around the stainless-steel table in the room's center.

A stainless-steel table with troughs around the edges, just like the ones in Robin's morgue.

On that table, a white sheet covering a body.

Bryan smelled something new, something he couldn't identify. He reached out, grabbed the sheet where it covered the body's toe, then slid it free with a hiss of fabric.

Bryan heard a soft, distant buzz. Pookie's cell phone, he knew, but they were both too stunned to pay attention to it.

The body on the table: naked, lean and muscular. Skin the color of purple grapes. Stomach cut open — a hollow cavity, as all the internal organs had been removed. One leg had been stripped mostly free of muscle, leaving only bones and shreds of meat.

And the body's *head*.

It could not be.

The cell phone kept buzzing.

"Jesus," Pookie said quietly. "Jesus H. Christ on a crutch, Bryan."

The head had a huge, thick bottom jaw as wide as both of Bryan's fists pressed side to side. Inside that open mouth, lining both the top and the bottom, rows of huge, triangular white teeth.

Teeth like a shark's.

Pookie took a step forward. He reached out a shaking hand, pinced one of the teeth between his thumb and forefinger, then gave an experimental wiggle. The tooth didn't move. He did it again, harder, and this time the whole head moved in time.

"That's not fake," he said. "Holy shit, man, there's no way that's fake. Look at it!"

Bryan *was* looking at it — looking at it, and *recognizing* it. He'd seen those teeth and that skin in his dreams.

"This guy is real," Pookie said. "And if he's real, then I'm guessing the ones in the other room are real, too. Bryan, what the fuck is all this?"

They fell silent. The buzzing phone demanded attention. Pookie finally noticed. He pulled it out of his pocket.

"Burns, talk to me."

A pause.

"Fuck," Pookie said. "Bri-Bri, the jig is up. Erickson is here."

...

Pookie climbed the stairs and turned toward the ruined front door. He saw Black Mr. Burns, gun in hand, standing in the doorway, using his body to block entry. Beyond him, Pookie saw an old man standing on the porch.

Gotta be Erickson . . . at least it's just a seventy-year-old man and not the goddamn archer.

"Officer Smith," Pookie said as he approached. "The house appears to be clear."

John stepped to the side, gestured to the old man. "This is Jebediah Erickson. He says this is his house, but he doesn't have any identification."

No matter what happened now, Pookie knew that he, Bryan and even Black Mr. Burns were screwed. Why couldn't Bryan have just backed off? They'd tried, dammit, they'd tried *hard*, and now Pookie's career was probably over for good. His only hope was to try and deal a huge line of bullshit and intimidation to make this go away. Not much of a chance of that working, but he had to give it a shot.

"I'm Inspector Chang," Pookie said. "It's late. Care to explain what you're doing out of your house at this hour with no ID?"

"No, I *don't* care to explain," Erickson said. "I don't need identification to walk outside of my house. Are there any others inside?"

"Sir," Pookie said, gesturing to the porch stairs, "why don't we take a stroll?"

Erickson pointed to the house's open door. "Whoever is in there, get them out here *right now*, or I am calling Amy."

Amy. The guy knew Chief Zou on a first-name basis. Yep, they were all fucked good and proper.

Erickson glared at Pookie. The old man put his hands on his hips. "You've tried my patience enough, Officer. If you don't . . ."

His voice trailed off. He turned to stare into the house. Bryan Clauser stood a foot inside the doorway. Bryan's mouth hung halfway open in surprise, like he saw something he couldn't understand, couldn't quite believe.

Erickson's expression slipped from indignant anger to thin-lipped, focused rage.

A blur of motion — something hit Pookie in the stomach. His back smashed into the porch's thick wooden railing.

Pookie saw John raising his gun, but Erickson was so *fast.* The old man spun, landed his heel on John's temple. John sagged against the house — Erickson reached out and snatched John's gun before John slid down to his ass.

Bryan rushed out of the doorway. Erickson raised the gun and fired, getting off one shot before Bryan buried his shoulder into the old man's stomach. They hit the porch railing and went *through* it in a spinning whirl of bodies and cracked wood. They fell fifteen feet to the sidewalk below, Erickson landed on his back, Bryan on top of him.

Bryan reared back to punch, but Erickson's feet whipped up, black shoes hooking behind Bryan's head, shins scissoring Bryan's neck. Bryan grabbed at Erickson's legs. The old man twisted hard to the left, driving Bryan face-first into the sidewalk.

Pookie tried to draw a breath, but his stomach wouldn't respond. Where was his gun? His hand found it and he tried to stand.

Out on the sidewalk, Erickson snarled as he squeezed his legs tighter on Bryan's neck. Bryan's feet kicked, shoes sliding uselessly against the sidewalk.

Pookie lurched to the broken railing. He still couldn't breathe. He rested his gun hand on the broken rail.

Erickson reached his right hand behind his back — when the hand reappeared, it held a Bowie knife.

Pookie aimed.

Erickson raised the knife.

Pookie fired.

The bullet *whinged* off the concrete just a half-inch from Erickson's hip. The old man flinched, his knife thrust paused. Bryan's left foot kicked forward, the toe driving into Erickson's mouth and snapping the white-haired head backward.

Erickson rolled away. Bryan scrambled to his feet, but the old man was faster, raising the knife and rushing forward to swing it down. Bryan's hands shot up, forearms crossing, catching Erickson's wrist in the V. Bryan turned and twisted, using Erickson's momentum against him even as he wrapped his fingers around the old man's hand.

Erickson flipped, his back hitting the sidewalk for a second time.

Bryan now held the knife.

In that moment, Pookie had a terrifying glimpse of Bryan's face — that wasn't his friend, that wasn't his partner, that was a wide-eyed psychopath. He tried to shout out, to scream *no!*, but he still couldn't draw a breath.

Erickson started to rise. Bryan snap-kicked the old man in the mouth, driving him back down. Bryan closed and knelt, moving *so fast* — streetlight flashed off the Bowie knife's blade as Bryan drove it into Erickson's stomach so deep that Pookie heard the point *chink* into the concrete beneath the old man's back.

Everything stopped. That crazy look vanished from Bryan's face — now he just seemed confused.

Erickson struggled, used his elbows to sit up halfway. He looked at the knife handle sticking out of his belly.

"Well," he said, "I never planned for this." His head lolled. He slumped backward and lay still.

Pookie's diaphragm finally opened up, letting him suck in a deep, halting breath. John stumbled down the steps, then to Erickson's side. He examined the wound even as he pulled out his cell phone and dialed for an ambulance.

Pookie followed, moving down as fast as he could. He saw Bryan stand slowly, saw a patch of wetness soaking the right shoulder of his partner's black sweatshirt.

"Bryan! You're hit!"

Bryan looked at his shoulder. He grabbed his collar, stretched the wet fabric away to see underneath. "Shit. I think I need a doctor." He reached his left hand up and squeezed his right shoulder.

Pookie prayed his hunch was wrong, that Bryan actually *did* need a doctor, but he didn't want to take that chance. If Pookie was right and Bryan went to a hospital . . .

The sound of handcuffs clicking home drew Pookie's attention. Black Mr. Burns had cuffed Erickson's wrists, moved the hands up over the wounded old man's head.

"John," Pookie said, "you got him?"

John looked up. "He's hurt bad and he ain't going nowhere. Ambulance is on the way."

It was bad to leave a scene, double bad as they shouldn't have been here in the first place, and triple bad because Pookie was technically a civilian, but he had to get Bryan out of there.

Pookie put a hand on Bryan's back and started guiding him toward the Buick. "Bri-Bri, come on, we gotta go."

"Go? Dude, I've been *shot*. I need an ambulance."

"I'll take you to the hospital," Pookie said. "Way faster, come on."

Pookie lightly pushed again, and this time Bryan walked toward the car.

••••

Tard saw the brown car pull away from the monster's house.

And down on the ground, with a knife in his tummy . . . *the monster.*

Tard watched all this in utter disbelief. He looked an *awful* lot like the tree in which he hid. He didn't much care for being a tree, because all the bugs crawled into the cracks in his skin. They tickled and sometimes they bit him.

Sirens blared. Tard hated that noise; it hurt his ears. Down the street he saw cop cars, and . . . was that? . . . *yes!* The pretty, white-and-red amberlamps truck!

The monster wasn't moving. A blackish stain slowly spread across his brown shirt. The amberlamps was coming for him, because he was *wounded.*

Sly was going to be *so* excited!

BOOK II

MONSTERS

Sly, Pierre, Sir Voh & Fort

ba-da-bum-bummmm

Rex felt strong arms holding him, cradling him. As he woke, the grogginess faded away — the pain in his belly did not.

Pain wasn't really the word for it. He'd felt *pain* before, courtesy of Roberta, courtesy of Alex Panos and BoyCo, courtesy of Father Maloney. This was something different, something on another level altogether.

Despite that burning agony Rex Deprovdechuk felt warmth exploding in his chest. He took in a slow, deep breath — so powerful, so relaxing. It felt like when he'd met Marco, but more so.

ba-da-bum-bummmm

Rex moved his hand, felt at his belly.

Wet.

Wet with blood.

"You'll be fine," said a voice that sounded like sandpaper on rough wood. "The wound is already closing."

Rex opened his eyes.

First, he saw the night sky, black and starless, the clouds above slightly lit up by the streetlights below. He was on the flat roof of a building. Then, Rex saw *them*.

He should have been afraid. He knew that. He should have been crapping in his pants, screaming, trying to rise and run, but he wasn't afraid. Not in the least.

He recognized them from his dreams and his drawings.

"Hello, Sly," Rex said.

The one with a snake's face smiled wide. A snake-face, but he looked . . . *young*. Smooth features, tiny scales that gleamed with health. A thick body, each motion athletic, confident. He looked like a bodybuilder covered with a rotting gray blanket that hid his bulky form. Only his head was exposed, showing his pointy face with its yellow eyes and angled black irises.

Sly smiled, a mouth full of needle teeth. He looked at the others. "He knows my name."

"It's thim," whispered the second something. "It's thim, I can *thmell* it!"

This one was also covered in a threadbare blanket, and he was bigger than Sly. Well, *taller* anyway, but not as thick. He had a fur-covered face and long jaws, like those of a big dog, but the bottom jaw was a little offset, sticking at a slight angle to the right. His features were also soft, almost like he was in that middle zone between *puppy* and *adult.*

"Hello, Pierre," Rex said.

Pierre's long, pink tongue lolled out the left side of the cockeyed mouth. It dangled, dripping spit down onto the rooftop.

Behind Pierre, a third something stood. Taller than Pierre, wider than Sly. Rex had never seen anything so big.

"My king," it said. The voice was thin and high-pitched. It didn't seem at home in a body of that size. Rex looked closer and understood why — under its blanket, there were actually *two* somethings. One was a massive man, like one of those pro-wrestling guys, with a tiny head the size of a large grapefruit atop a wide neck. The other something rode on his shoulders. The little one had a tiny, shriveled baby's body but a head that would have been normal on an adult. It had spindly legs and arms. It had a tail that wrapped tight around the massive man's big neck.

"I don't know your name," Rex said to the thing riding on top of the big man.

"I am Sir Voh," the big-head said. The end of his tail tapped against the big one's barrel chest. "And this is Fort."

A small moan drew Rex's attention to another figure lying on the roof. Alex Panos.

Blood covered his face, matted down his blond hair. A torn bottom lip showed the cracked teeth behind it. Rex had never seen a nose broken that bad; a bit of white stuck out from between the eyes, and the rest of it angled sharply to the left.

Rex had been face-to-face with Alex many times. Alex had always sneered, smiled, looked angry, looked at Rex like Rex was nothing more than dogshit on the bottom of a shoe. But not now. Alex's eyes pleaded for help from someone, from *anyone.*

The shriveled man — Sir Voh — spoke. "We have been waiting for you all our lives. Now you're here."

The warmth in Rex's chest made him smile. Why should he be afraid of these people just because they looked funny? They were his friends. They were the ones who had made his dreams come true.

"Waiting for me? Why?"

Sly picked Rex up, then set him on his own feet. Rex's legs wobbled a little, but he was able to stand.

"We have been waiting for the king," Sly said. "The king will save us, lead us to a better day."

I dream of a better day. Was that why he'd put that on the drawing?

The pain in his belly remained intense, but it was already fading. "I'm only thirteen," he said. "I don't know much about that kind of thing."

All four of the somethings smiled in unison, even the tiny grapefruit head. The corners of Pierre's long, hairy mouth shrank back like a panting dog.

"You know," Sly said. "You just haven't realized it yet. You've been among the prey for your whole life, because you're a ringer, like Marco was."

"What's a ringer?"

"Someone who looks like *them*," Sly said. "But you are one of *us*. We have come to take you home. We will protect you."

Alex moaned, then reached out with a bloody, twisted hand.

"Rex," he said. "Please . . . *help me*."

Pierre kicked Alex in the ribs. It seemed like just a tap, but Alex's eyes scrunched tight in pain.

"You thut your mouth," Pierre said.

Rex looked down at Alex. How *pathetic*. "What do we do with him?"

Sir Voh crawled out from under the blanket covering him and Fort, then used his spidery arms and legs to descend the mountain of flesh. The big-headed creature reached the roof, then scurried onto Alex's back. He wrapped his tail around the boy's bloody forehead. The tail contracted, pulling Alex's head back until he grunted and made a little whining noise.

"We killed your enemies," Sir Voh said. "The *bullies*, the ones who hurt you. We made examples of them, so everyone would know your greatness. This one" — Sir Voh shook Alex's head — "we saved for Mommy. Unless you want to kill him yourself."

Fort reached inside his blanket, then held out a massive hand as big as a side of spareribs. In his palm sat a long knife.

Alex saw it. He moaned in fear. Sir Voh held him still.

Rex felt his dick stiffen. *Kill Alex kill Alex kill Alex*. The bully now knew what it meant to feel *helpless*.

Rex reached out and took the knife.

Sly's yellow eyes crinkled in delight. Rex wasn't surprised to see a forked tongue sneak out of the face, trace across the left side of the pointy face, flick up over the left eye, then slide back inside.

"Morning is coming," Sly said. "We need to move. Do you want to kill this one, or take him home to Mommy?"

Rex didn't know who *Mommy* was, but the four seemed very excited about the prospect of giving Alex to her.

"Rex, *please*!" Alex managed those two syllables before Sir Voh pulled back so far that Alex started to choke.

So pathetic. So utterly pathetic.

"We'll take him with us," Rex said. "But first, open his mouth."

Pierre knelt and forced Alex's jaws open.

Rex reached out with the knife.

Pookie Gets His Friend to the Hospital

Pookie raced down Potrero Avenue. San Francisco General Hospital loomed large on his left. He saw a parking spot, slammed on the brakes and angled in. The Buick's front-right tire rode up on the sidewalk, but he didn't have time to worry about that.

He jumped out, ran to the rear passenger door and opened it. Inside, a confused-looking Bryan, his hand still pressed to his shoulder with white-knuckle intensity. Bryan looked around. "Uh, Pooks? The hospital is across the street."

"I know," Pookie said. "We're going, I . . . I just want to take a look at your shoulder first."

He heard a siren approaching — probably an ambulance with Black Mr. Burns and Erickson.

"Your wound," Pookie said. "Let me see it."

Bryan seemed to think about it for a second, then let go. He unzipped his bloody sweatshirt and slid it over his right shoulder. Finally, he hooked the fingers of his left hand under his right T-shirt sleeve and pulled it up high, exposing the wound.

The bleeding had stopped. A small red circle of coagulated blood dotted his shoulder, ringed by a thin circle of pink scar tissue. Less than twenty minutes ago, Bryan Clauser had taken a .40-caliber round in the shoulder. The wound looked a week old, at least.

The ambulance scream grew louder.

They both stared at the wound.

"That cut on my head," Bryan said. "From when I fell on the fire escape. How is it?"

Pookie looked at Bryan's forehead. The stitches were still there, but the skin beneath showed nothing but a thin, faded scar. "It's all healed."

Bryan sagged into the backseat, unwelcome realization washing over him. "That door at the mansion . . . could a normal person have kicked that in?"

Pookie shook his head. "No. No way. I should have figured it out when you jumped up on that van with Jay Parlar, but . . . I don't know. Maybe I didn't really *want* to figure it out."

Bryan looked up. His eyes were watering. He looked like a man who had lost all hope.

"I'm one of them," he said. "Those things in the basement . . . I'm one of them."

What the hell was Pookie supposed to say now? *Rub some dirt on it and get back in there?* Hallmark didn't make cards for an occasion like this.

"It's okay," he said. "We'll figure this out."

The siren's scream apexed as the ambulance shot past the Buick, then turned into San Francisco General. Pookie watched as scrub-suited hospital staff rushed out of the emergency room door to meet it. The ambulance's back doors opened. Paramedics wheeled out Erickson, an IV swinging in time to the rolling bed's movement. John Smith hopped out as well and ran alongside Erickson and the others into the hospital. The emergency room door closed. Late-night traffic continued to pass by on Potrero Avenue, but other than that, the night's silence descended.

Pookie again looked at Bryan's shoulder. "Wanna go in anyway? Have them look at it?"

Bryan flexed his arm, rotated it. "No," he said. "Call Robin."

"What for?"

"You know what for. And call John. He's probably got Erickson's blood on him. Tell him to find a blood stain, a smear, whatever, and take it to Robin's right away. Now drive me back to my apartment so I can change. I'll just stay back here for the ride — I need a minute to myself."

Bryan reached out, grabbed the door and slammed it shut, leaving Pookie standing out on the street. Pookie stared at the door for a moment, at Bryan inside, then pulled out his cell phone and got in the driver's seat. Pookie dialed Robin as he pulled out into traffic.

Up on the Roof

Rex flew.

The damp night air whipped by his face and blew his hair back as he sailed over a city street. He was riding on the back of a monster, leaping from one building to the next. Rex kept one hand around Pierre's neck. With the other he held his blanket tight. The end of the blanket trailed behind him, flapping madly as they descended.

This made no sense, no sense at all, and yet it was actually happening. To *him*.

Pierre landed, so light and agile his big feet made barely any noise. Sly landed to their right, Sir Voh and Fort to their left. They moved silently across the flat roof, hopping down to the roof of the next building, then crossed that to the wall lining the building's edge. They knelt, tucking themselves into the deeper shadows.

They waited.

Sly's eyes glowed in the darkness. He leaned in and whispered. "What do you think so far, my king?"

Rex laughed, then clamped his hand over his mouth — that had been too loud. He whispered back: "This is the coolest thing *ever*. Marco had us going through alleys and basements, this is way funner."

Sly nodded. "We take the roofs sometimes, but it is dangerous. Tonight we can — the monster is hurt."

Pierre shook his head. "No, I don't believe it. The monther *can't* be hurt, he'th bulletproof!" Pierre picked up a piece of tar off the roof and started drawing the warding symbol on the brick wall.

Sly sighed and rolled his eyes. "No one is bulletproof, Pierre. Tard called and said they took him away in an ambulance."

Rex looked at the people around him, at Sly and Pierre and Sir Voh and Fort. They didn't look scary anymore, not at all. "If the monster is hurt, why do we move so quietly?"

Sly smiled and winked one yellow eye. "Because if we're mistaken, it's a mistake we only get to make once."

Rex could see inside Sly's blanket. Sly wore normal clothes — jeans, battered leather boots and a ratty sweatshirt with a big hood. Fort also wore normal clothes under his blanket. Pierre was a little more odd — he wore blue Bermuda shorts and no shirt.

It was quiet up here on the roofs. Quiet, and abandoned. Most of San

Francisco's buildings were three or four stories tall. Within a single block, Rex and the others could easily move from roof to roof. To reach the next block, all they had to do was *jump*. Sly led them on a path that avoided known cameras, but he constantly looked for new ones. If he didn't think it was smart to go around a camera, he would come up on it from behind, rip it off and toss it down to the street.

On those streets, there were cars and people and motion. Up here there was stillness — flat, empty roofs in all directions, as far as the eye could see.

Rex heard a soft moan of pain. Alex. He was limp but alive, if just barely. Fort held him under one thick arm.

Sly slowly rose up until he could peek over the wall's edge. He looked around, then lowered himself just as slowly. "A few more minutes," he said.

Each time they leaped over a street and landed on a new building, they stopped and waited. If people were spotted on nearby roofs, Sly had everyone wait until those people went down or he found another way around. When it came time to jump to the next block, Sly would make sure no people were down on the steet below, then time a lull in traffic — no one had seen their crazy leaps.

Rex had never felt so good, so *alive*. He clung tight to Pierre, smelling the delightfully damp richness of his brown fur, the pungent, sour waft of clothes that hadn't been washed in weeks. A feeling of warmth radiated into Rex's chest and arms. Not just the heat from the monster's body, but a deeper warmth, a feeling of love that made Rex want to cry.

They were taking him *home*.

Sly looked over the edge, saw it was clear, then jumped. The journey continued, block to block. Rex recognized Jackson Street when they passed over it, as it wasn't far from his house. Next, they crossed over Pacific and then moved silently from building to building until they stopped and waited at a roof's edge.

Below them was a narrow surface road. Beyond and below that, deep down, four lanes of traffic disappeared into a tunnel that ran beneath a boxy building.

"Pierre, is that the Broadway Tunnel?"

"Yeth, my king."

They waited. Down on the surface street, a man and a woman leaned on a car, making out. They looked old, probably almost thirty.

Rex didn't mind waiting, didn't mind watching. None of them did. That was how things were done. He looked out across the city. He could see the Golden Gate Bridge off to the northwest, the Oakland Bay Bridge to the northeast. Behind him, high above the city, the six blinking red lights of Sutro Tower.

San Francisco. *His* city. He would rule all of it. He would be king.

After a while, the man and the woman walked away from the car and into the building below Rex's feet. Pierre launched himself across the void. Rex sailed through the air, trying not to giggle at the feel of wind tickling his skin.

The group landed atop the boxy building's flat roof. Pierre knelt. Rex slid off and stood still. The sounds of cars echoed up from below.

Sly moved to a hatch in the roof and opened it, exposing a ladder. He smiled his pointy-toothed smile. "Are you ready, my king?"

"Is that the way home?"

Sly shook his head. "You can't go home just yet."

They weren't taking him? But they had *promised*. "Why can't I?"

"Firstborn is dangerous," Sly said. "If we don't bring you home at the right time, my king, he may try to kill you."

Rex hadn't expected that. He looked from Pierre to Sir Voh to even Fort. They all nodded solemnly — Sly spoke the truth.

"So where are you taking me, then?"

"We have *many* places under the city, so many that we can go for months without using the same one twice. Firstborn will not find you, my king." Sly looked to the horizon, stared for a moment, then turned back. "Daybreak is coming soon. If you stay up here, I am afraid the police might find you. You need to trust us and leave all of this behind. Are you ready to start your new life?"

Rex looked at the hatch, then at each of them in turn. He looked around at the glowing windows and twinkling lights of the city, then nodded at Sly.

"I'm ready, brother," Rex said. "Take me down."

Late to the Party

Amy Zou held her Sig Sauer in her left hand, a walkie-talkie in her right. Rich Verde stood next to her. She stared at the eviscerated body on the embalming table.

This was why she did what she did, because monsters were real. The one on the table, the creatures in the room behind her . . . Amy could only imagine those things reaching for one of her twins.

A feeling of hopelessness filled her, dragged down her every thought. She'd spent nearly thirty years with this secret. *Thirty years.* Jesus, how time slipped by. Three decades of her life, and now it might all be over — if it was, many more people were going to die.

Verde clinked the barrel of his gun against the creature's shark teeth, *tink-tink-tink.*

"You are one ugly motherfucker," he said to the corpse. "How many people did you kill with your pearly whites?"

How many indeed. "It's not just the misshapen ones," Amy said. "You see the guy out there with the crowbar?"

Verde looked at her. "Crowbar?" He thought, then nodded as realization kicked in. "Liam McCoy?"

"Yes," Amy said. "Looks like we can take him out of the *whereabouts unknown* column."

Fifteen years ago, McCoy had been a suspect in four child murders. He'd gone missing before Amy could close in on him. He wasn't missing anymore. Justice had been served.

She walked back into the gun room. Verde followed. He holstered his Sig and picked up a five-seven, feeling the weight. No point in worrying about prints; they already knew who owned these weapons.

"What about Clauser?" Verde said. "And that fuck-stick, Chang. Maybe firing them isn't enough."

She watched Rich eject the magazine, which was loaded. He popped the magazine back into the weapon.

"They were just doing their jobs," she said. They had been doing what they were sworn to do, following the letter of the law — just as Amy had done thirty years earlier. "What do you want to do, Rich, shoot them?"

He shrugged. "You're the one who's always talking about the greater good. At least put a BOLO out on their asses, bring them in. Maybe a few days in county will set them straight."

She couldn't do that. Their careers were already over — did she need to publicly humiliate them as well?

Her walkie-talkie squawked: "Chief?" Sean Robertson's voice. He was up on the ground floor, making sure everyone — including cops — stayed out.

She lifted and answered without looking away from the shark-toothed nightmare. "I'm here."

"You sure you two are okay down there?"

"We're fine," she said. "Just secure the grounds and make sure no one enters the house."

"Yes, Chief."

She paused, then thumbed the transmit button again. "Sean?"

"Yes, Chief?"

"Make a department-wide broadcast. Bryan Clauser and Pookie Chang are no longer employed by the SFPD. Make sure everyone knows — they're civilians."

Verde held up his hand to get her attention. He mouthed the words: *And Smith.*

John Smith. The man was afraid of his own shadow. As soon as Pookie and Bryan were out of the way, John would go back to his computer room.

She shook her head and lowered the walkie-talkie.

Verde clearly wanted to argue with her, but he kept his mouth shut.

"I'm going to see Erickson," she said. "Can you and Sean finish up here? Seal the house. *No one* gets in. We'll figure out what to do about all this crap later."

"You got it," Verde said. "You know you can count on me."

"I know I can, Rich. I know."

She walked out of the weapons room. She took one more look at a collection of nightmares that had once hunted the people of San Francisco, then headed upstairs.

Tard's First Time

Out of all Mommy's children, Tard could hide the best. That was why Sly picked him to watch the monster. It wasn't fair that Sly made Tard miss out on all the fun, but now Sly was making it better.

If the amberlamps took the monster, Sly said, then Tard could be free to hunt — just keep it quiet so Firstborn didn't find out. *Hunting!* Tard had never been hunting. Sly was a great friend.

Tard could hide good because he could look like other things. Right now he looked a lot like part of a gnarled tree trunk. Golden Gate Park had lots of gnarled trees on the sides of the dirt walking paths, trees that twisted into corkscrew-trunk patches with little spaces inside. In those spaces, *especially* in the dark, no one could see Tard. There was no light in the park other than a half moon filtering through the tall pines that stretched high above.

Tard looked an *awful lot* like wood, but that didn't stop his heart from beating so hard, making it difficult for him to stay still. So *this* was what it was like to hunt. No wonder Sly always wanted to do it.

Tard moved only his eyes, watching the prey move toward him along the dirt path. A teenage boy, a teenage girl. Holding hands. No one would want to hold Tard's hands, and that wasn't fair. Why should prey get to do that? He had always wanted to punish the people he saw, the people holding hands, the people *kissing*.

The boy looked up, looked right into Tard's little hidey-spot — then looked away. He hadn't seen Tard. That was because Tard wasn't *Tard* anymore, he really was *Chameleon*.

The teenage couple walked closer. Chameleon's heartbeat kicked up another notch. *So exciting!* Would the prey run before they reached his spot? Would they sense him?

He had never killed before. Well, not since he'd been a little boy in the Groom's Walk, but that had been so long ago. Fear of Firstborn and fear of Savior had always kept him in check, but maybe Firstborn wouldn't be in charge that much longer, and the amberlamps had taken Savior away.

This was it. Tard — no, *Chameleon* — was really going to do this.

He held his breath as the couple moved within five steps.

Then four.

Then three.

When they were only a few feet away, Tard reached out cat-quick, one rough gnarled hand wrapping around each mouth.

He pulled them into his dark little fort.

The RapScan Machine

Pookie, wake up."

Robin pushed at Pookie's shoulder. He was on her couch and might as well have been dead for all he moved. She poked him again. "Come on, sleepyhead. Rise and shine."

"Five more minutes, Mom," he said. "I promise all my chores are done."

"You told me to wake you when the tests were almost finished."

That got his attention. Pookie pushed himself to a sitting position. He rubbed his face. "That coffee I smell?"

"Of course," Robin said. "Go to the table, I'll get you a cup."

For the second night — or morning, depending on how you looked at it — her apartment had become their war room. Bryan was already sitting at the dining-room table, his hands around a mug, his eyes staring off into space. John's chair was empty; he was at the hospital.

Robin had turned her dining room into an impromptu sample prep area. The RapScan machine sat in the center of the table, processing the two samples Bryan and Pookie had brought a few hours earlier. She'd loaded the cartridges and set the karyotype test to running. Any moment now, and it would finish.

She walked to the kitchen and came back with the coffee carafe and a mug for Pookie. She filled his mug and refilled Bryan's. Both men looked absolutely exhausted. Pookie had given her the sample materials, then headed straight for her couch. Bryan hadn't said a word since he'd arrived; he just sat in his chair, first drinking a beer, then a scotch, then moving on to caffeine. Robin thought it best just to leave him be, let him work through whatever it was that was on his mind. If he wanted her help, he could ask for it — she was done trying.

"Sounds like you boys had quite the adventure," Robin said. "I'm just glad no one got hurt. Other than Erickson, I mean."

Pookie nodded and took a sip of coffee. "Yes, no one got hurt. Permanently, anyway. How much longer until that test is done?"

She looked at the machine's touch screen. "About five minutes, maybe less. Are you guys going to tell me who the second sample is from?" She knew the first sample was from Erickson, but they had avoided her questions about the second.

"A perp from Erickson's house," Pookie said. "We didn't catch him."

Once again, there was clearly more to the story than Pookie wanted to let on. Not surprising that he did the talking — he was a far better liar than Bryan.

Bryan's head came up. He blinked rapidly, as if he'd been cat-napping and was just becoming aware of his surroundings. "The ear," he said.

"What?"

Pookie nodded. "I forgot about that."

"Me too," Bryan said. He reached into his pocket, pulled out a plastic evidence bag and held it up for Robin to see.

"Bryan," she said, "why do you have a human ear in a baggie?"

"It's from a stuffed person we found in Erickson's basement. Can you run DNA on it?"

She reached out and took the bag, looked at the contents. The skin looked dry and brittle, almost like leather. "When you say *stuffed*, you mean like a big-game animal? Stuffed for display?"

"Yeah. Can you test it for the Zed chromosome?"

"Not here," she said. "The tanning process destroys most of the cellular DNA. I'd need a biology lab, something with the equipment needed to try and extract any remaining DNA and a PCR machine to amplify it. A university lab would work. Maybe SFSU, or I could try the hospitals. But that's going to take a few days, and I wouldn't hold your breath that it'll work."

Bryan just looked at her. His eyes burned with both anger and anguish. He was a cauldron of emotions, so much so that Robin couldn't really remember the old Bryan, the one with the cold, unfeeling stare.

The machine beeped. Robin looked at the little screen.

ERICKSON SAMPLE COMPLETE.

She pressed the icon and read the results.

"Zed-X," she said. "Wow, Erickson is a Zed."

Bryan and Pookie didn't look surprised in the least.

"Related?" Bryan said. "Is Erickson related to the others?"

Robin tapped the touch screen, scrolling through to the familial indicators. There it was — a match.

"Bingo," she said. "Jebediah Erickson, Rex Deprovdechuk, Blackbeard and Oscar Woody's killer all have the same mother."

Bryan seemed to shrink into himself. He leaned back in his chair. His chin dropped to his chest.

Pookie shook his head. "Wait a minute. We think Marie's Children are these Zeds. If so, Erickson isn't just killing his own kind, he's killing his direct family? What is that all about?"

Robin shrugged. "If Erickson is in custody, can't you ask him?"

"Might not be talkative," Pookie said. "You know, considering he's in the ICU after taking a knife to the belly."

Bryan looked up. "He's a Zed. He'll heal fast. We can go to the hospital and question Erickson directly — we just have to get around Zou."

Pookie thought this over, then sipped at his mug. "Robin, you're a doctor — can you find out Erickson's condition without anyone knowing that we're asking?"

She hadn't been part of the hospital system for years, but many of her friends still worked there. "I probably can't get detailed patient info, but I can find someone to tell me if he's out of the ICU."

The RapScan beeped.

SAMPLE TWO COMPLETE.

"Here we go," she said. She clicked the icon and the results flashed up. She saw the marker for an X, then a Zed . . . and also a Y. "This one is trisomal. It's X-Y-Zed, just like Rex. In fact" — she thumbed through the screens, looking for the familial indicator — "yes, once again, the same mother. All these guys are one big, happy family."

Pookie's eyes widened.

Bryan's eyes burned with intensity, maybe even rage. "The same mother? You're absolutely sure?"

Robin nodded.

He stood and held out his right hand to Pookie, palm-up. "Keys," he said.

Pookie looked worried. "Going somewhere, Bri-Bri?"

"Keys."

"Maybe I should drive you," Pookie said. "We could—"

"Give me the fucking keys!"

Pookie leaned away. Robin held her breath. She'd never heard Bryan raise his voice before, not ever, not even during their worst fights.

Pookie dug his hand into his pocket and handed Bryan his car keys. Bryan took them and walked out of the dining room. Emma followed, tail wagging. The apartment door opened and shut. Emma came wandering slowly back into the dining room, looking for someone else to pay attention to her.

Why had Bryan stormed out like that?

"Pookie, what the hell just happened?"

Pookie leaned forward, rested his head in his hands. "I think Bryan needs to go see his dad. Fuck this. I'm going back to sleep."

He stood up and and pulled out his phone. He walked into the living room, his fingers texting out a message as he went. Without breaking stride, he finished the text, put the phone back in his pocket, then collapsed onto the couch, his back facing out into the living room. Emma shot in like a black-and-white streak, jumped up after him and settled into the crook of his legs.

Robin stared at Pookie. He was wiped out. Something big was happening between him and Bryan, and she didn't know what it was.

Why wouldn't they trust her?

She wasn't tired, not at all. She found her phone and started scrolling through her contacts, looking for people that still worked at SFGH.

Aggie Gets a Roommate

Aggie James didn't want to wake up, but a part of his mind pulled at him, tried to drag him out of a dream where a little girl's lips pecked feather-light on his cheek, and her arms wrapped around his neck.

He didn't want to wake, but wake he did.

He sniffed. He rubbed at his face. The real bitch about getting sober? You start to remember things.

Aggie James hadn't always been a strung-out, homeless bum. Once upon a time, in fact, he'd owned a little counterculture Internet café. He'd attracted a certain antiestablishment clientele. All kinds of people wandered in, but after seeing the giant FUCK STARBUCKS mural painted on the wall behind the coffee counter, the visitors either smiled and stayed or frowned and left.

He'd run the place with his wife and his teenage daughter, right up until the robbery.

The robbers shot Aggie first. Shot him *twice*, in fact, once in the leg and once in the chest. He remembered dropping to his ass, back propped up by the counter. His blood ran everywhere. He couldn't move, couldn't lift a finger, but he stayed conscious long enough to see them put a bullet in his wife's head. He stayed conscious long enough to see his daughter run for the door, to see her shot in the back before she could reach it. He stayed conscious long enough to see her crawling across the floor, bloody hands reaching for him, begging for her daddy to help her, to *please help her, please!*

Aggie James even stayed conscious long enough to see the gun pointed at his daughter's face, and just long enough to hear her last scream stop abruptly when the gunman pulled the trigger. Only then had he passed out.

The cops told him the robbers probably thought he was dead, and that passing out had probably saved his life.

His *life.*

What a joke.

Fucking memories. He couldn't shake them, not until he'd done heroin for about a month straight. That made you forget everything. Almost.

He'd lost all that mattered to him. Nothing would fill that inescapable dullness in his heart. Not that he'd tried very hard to fill it, of course. With no reason to go on — and not enough guts to kill himself — he'd chosen a slow route to the grave. A *painful* route. It's what he had coming, after all . . . if a man can't protect his family, does he deserve to live? Aggie had thought not.

That was before the white dungeon.

This horrific place reminded Aggie that life — no matter how crappy it might be — was far better than the alternative. A day and a half ago, as near as he could tell, Hillary had given him hope. If there was even a chance to get out of this, to live, Aggie would do anything she asked.

He finally blinked away the sleep to see that a new man had been chained to the wall on his left, where the Mexican woman had once been. Not a man — a boy, really, but a goddamn *big* boy. The kid's face looked like swollen hamburger: split lip, broken teeth, blood all over his mouth and a seriously fucked-up nose. He was spitting up blood and making low moaning noises, noises that had the cadence of speech but were not words.

The boy opened his mouth to moan louder, and Aggie saw why the sounds had no meaning — someone had cut out his tongue.

To his right, Aggie heard other noises he didn't understand, but that was only because he didn't speak Chinese. The Chinaman was on his knees, tear-streaked eyes shut tight, body rocking back and forth as he prayed to someone or something.

Aggie James couldn't help the Chinaman, and he couldn't help the tongueless boy. He could only help himself, and only if Hillary gave him a chance.

He lay back down and closed his eyes. Maybe he would dream of his daughter again.

Fathers and Sons

ryan pulled up to Mike Clauser's house to find his dad sitting on the front steps, Bud Light in hand. Five more bottles sat in a sixer at his feet. He was shirtless, wearing beat-up jeans and black socks with no shoes.

He was waiting. That meant Pookie had called ahead. Fucking Pookie.

Bryan shut off the Buick's engine. His hands squeezed the steering wheel.

If Erickson was sixty years old or more, and he was Bryan's half-brother, then Bryan's *real* mother would have to be seventy-five or probably even older. Mike Clauser and Starla Hutchon had gone to high school together. Bryan had seen their yearbooks, their class pictures, other pictures of them from their childhoods and their grade-school days. They had been born the same year — Mike had turned fifty-eight a few months back.

Mike, who the genetic test said was *not* Bryan's father.

And Starla, who was younger than Jebediah Erickson — which meant that the woman Bryan had always known as his mother was anything but.

All his life, Bryan had been lied to. He felt that rage swelling up, the same rage he'd felt when Zou had threatened him with jail.

He stepped out of the Buick. Mike stood and reached for the front door, to open it as if to invite Bryan in.

"Don't bother," Bryan said.

His father stopped and turned. "Pookie texted that you had something important to talk about. Come in, we'll talk."

"I don't want to go inside," Bryan said. "What I want is to know who my real parents are."

Mike Clauser stared for a moment. He slowly lowered himself to the front step and sat. He stared at the ground. "You're my son."

"Bullshit."

Mike looked up, his expression caught between the anger that solved most of his problems and a gut-wrenching pain from hurting his boy. "I don't care about biology. I wiped your ass and changed your diapers. I cleaned up your puke. When you got a fever, I felt like someone was chopping up my heart with a goddamn cleaver. You'd just *cough* and the sound scared me worse than any fight I've ever been in."

To think Bryan had loved this man, this *liar.* "Are you finished?"

"I took you to school," Mike said. "I hauled you to soccer practice. I watched every wrestling match you ever had, and when someone put you on your back, I had to grab the damn bleachers because it was all I could do not to come out on the mat and kick the other kid in the head. I'm the one who taught you right from wrong."

Quite a show of concern. But then again, Mike had a lifetime of practice — Bryan's lifetime. "And in all those years, it never crossed your mind to tell me the *god*damn truth?"

"The *truth* is that you are my boy." Mike's lower lip quivered, just for a moment, then he seemed to force his emotions under control. "You will always be *my son*."

Bryan shook his head slowly. "I'm not. I'm just a kid that you lied to."

Mike pulled an unopened bottle out of the Bud Light sixer. He held it between his palms, slowly rolling it back and forth. "I don't know how you found out, but you can forget the guilt trips because I wouldn't change a thing."

What had Bryan been hoping for? Maybe a little remorse? Maybe a *gosh, I'm so sorry*? Mike wasn't apologizing. At least his character was consistent in that regard.

"Who are my parents? You owe me that, so start talking."

Mike set the bottle on the step next to his feet. He looked . . . weak. The expression on his face, the sagging posture, Bryan had seen those things only once before — when his mother had died.

"There was this homeless guy in our neighborhood," Mike said. "Eric. Never knew his last name. He was a combat vet. Marines. The neighborhood kind of watched out for him. We'd give him food, clothes. One day, Eric just wasn't there. When he showed up a week later, he had a baby with him."

Bryan's hands flexed into fists, relaxed, flexed into fists. "Are you telling me that Eric the Homeless Vet is my father?"

Mike shook his head. "He wasn't your father. Your mother didn't think so, anyway."

"That bitch wasn't my mother."

Mike grabbed and threw the beer bottle in one snap-motion, a line drive of tumbling brown glass. Bryan stepped aside. The bottle smashed against Pookie's driver's-side window in an explosion of glass and beer.

Mike Clauser stood up. He didn't look sad anymore. "Boy," he said in a low voice, "you're my son, but she was my *wife*. You blaspheme her name again, and I'm going to string your ass out all over this street."

Bryan felt his father's neck in his hands before he even realized he'd rushed in. Mike's eyes went wide in shock.

Bryan pulled him close and screamed in his face. *"You threaten me again and I'll kill you!"*

He felt Mike's pulse hammering against his fingers. Just a *squeeze* . . .

What the hell was he doing? Bryan released his grip, then took four slow steps back.

Mike rubbed his throat with his free hand. He looked at Bryan more with confusion than fear.

"You've always been so calm," Mike said. "You've never . . . never yelled at me before."

Hadn't yelled, and certainly had never put his hands on his father in anger. This intensity, these highs and lows — all of it was new. He'd had emotions before, of course he had, but nothing this pure, this overwhelming.

What was happening to him?

"Just finish your story, old man."

Mike stopped rubbing his throat. He sat down heavily, opened another bottle and took a long drink. "We didn't know what to do," he said. "I mean, what *could* we do? Eric brought the baby to *us*. He said he had to give the baby to us because he knew we'd make good parents. We watched out for Eric, but he was crazy and homeless. A baby in his hands? That was dangerous. So we took you from him, just to make sure Eric didn't do something bad."

"And you didn't call the cops? You had an infant, probably kidnapped, and you didn't try to find the parents?"

Mike sniffed, slid a hand across his nose. He sniffed again. "We thought we'd try and figure out where you came from, talk to Eric and get some information before we had to call the cops. For God's sake, Bryan, Eric went crazy killing for our country, watching his buddies die all around him. We had to at least try and help him out of a jam."

Bryan breathed slowly. He fought to control the heartbreak and rage swirling inside. This was the man he'd looked up to his entire life? A man who would take another's child?

"I belonged to someone else," Bryan said. "Are you actually going to look me in the eye and say you did it to save some insane homeless guy from a well-deserved felony rap? What, were you hoping he'd bring another so you'd have a matched set?"

"It wasn't like that," Mike said quickly. "Eric was *terrified*, Bryan. I've never seen *anyone* that scared. He said he had to find the baby a safe, loving home, or he'd get into a lot of trouble. He knew your mother couldn't have kids, so he brought you to us."

This just kept getting better. "Eric the Homeless Guy knew you guys couldn't have children?"

"Everyone in the neighborhood knew. That's what God had chosen for us. We didn't broadcast it, but when people asked if we were going to have kids, we told them we couldn't. We'd thought of adopting, sure, but hadn't really focused on it. When Eric brought you to us, we couldn't help but think that maybe . . . maybe it was a miracle."

Bryan's throat pinched. Sadness roared up to swirl side-by-side with the anger. How could they have done this to him?

"A miracle? Are you *shitting* me?"

Mike tilted his head a little, an expression that said *come on, think about it and you'll see.* "Two people are totally in love but can't have kids, then a baby shows up on their doorstep? What more proof of a miracle do you need?"

Bryan's words came out as a cracked yell. "How about making Mom able to have kids in the first place? Isn't that a more logical *miracle* than sending a homeless man with a kidnapped baby?"

"I don't question the Lord's ways."

"That doesn't make you pious, that makes you stupid. What happened then? You just walked out and told everyone you'd suddenly had an immaculate conception and delivery?"

Mike again looked to the ground. "We kept it very quiet. The night Eric dropped you off, I tried to talk to him but he just kept babbling about what they would do to him if he failed."

"And who were *they*?"

"He wouldn't say. The next night, I tracked him down." Mike paused. He took a sip of his beer. "Eric was dead, Bryan. I think he ODed on something. We didn't know what to do about you. Your mother and I read the papers, watched the news, waited for any story about a kidnapped baby. There was nothing."

This was the man who raised him: a liar, a coward who only thought of himself.

"And *still* you didn't go to the cops. The kidnapper was dead, someone had lost their goddamn *child*, and you didn't do anything?"

Mike looked away. "After the second day, your mother and I were already so in love with you we would have risked everything to keep you. If we'd known who the parents were, that would have been different, but there was no news at all. We told everyone we knew that your mother was already four months' pregnant. I sent her away to a cabin in Yosemite — we told everyone she was staying at your grandmother's until the baby came."

Bryan wanted to remind Mike that the women he was talking about were neither his mother nor his grandmother, but he kept quiet.

Mike drained the beer in one long pull, then set it down with a glass-on-brick *clink*. "You mother came home with a baby. Simple as that. The neighbors bought it hook, line and sinker. Everyone commented on how big you were for a newborn. We just laughed and said you were going to play for the 'Niners someday and make us rich."

Mike opened another beer. He tossed the cap away.

Because of this man, Bryan would probably never know who his real parents were. For the first time in his life, Bryan felt tears welling up in his eyes. He blinked rapidly, tried to hold them back.

"What about my birth certificate?"

"Flash enough money around Chinatown, you'll find a doctor who'll play ball. Your birth certificate just says you were born in this house, not a hospital."

"You kept a kidnapped infant and you bribed a doctor. What upstanding citizens. What happened next?"

Mike shrugged again. "That's it. We loved you. You were the center of our lives. God delivered you to us and we spent every day trying to show God that we were worthy."

Bryan couldn't stop the tears anymore. "*Thou shalt not lie.* You ever hear of that one?"

The pain returned to Mike's eyes. His body sagged. He had never looked so old.

"We knew it was wrong," he said. "After a little while, we were able to just block it out. We didn't think about it. You were *our son.*"

Mike Clauser had been a rock: unflappable, reliable, always looking for the positive in all things. Now, he seemed defeated — *deflated*, perhaps, as if someone had stabbed him in the back and let his soul drain away.

Bryan felt torn in two directions; part of him hated this man with every fiber of his being, while the other half saw Mike's pain, remembered all the love given during a wonderful childhood. He wanted to hit him. He also wanted to hug him — but he would never do that, never again.

"You're not my father," Bryan said. "You never were. Don't visit. Don't call. You're dead to me."

Mike's head dropped. His big body shook a little bit as he started to cry.

Bryan wiped his own tears as he turned away. The Buick smelled like beer. He got in and drove away. Fuck Mike Clauser. The man could burn in hell for all Bryan cared. Mike didn't have the answers Bryan needed.

There was one place left that Bryan might be able to get those answers. But not right now. Not today. He'd had enough . . . he'd just had enough.

A Hospital Visit

Chief Amy Zou stared down at Jebediah Erickson. He looked so much older than the last time she'd seen him. Of course, that had been twenty-six years ago, when he'd left the asylum.

The asylum that she'd sent him to.

Amy had once been a snot-nosed rookie who knew better than the older cops. She and Rich had put the pieces together, connecting the symbols to the silver arrowheads, tracking down Alder Jessup, quietly building a case against Jebediah Erickson even as her superiors tried to shut her up, tried to get her to back off. They'd even promoted her to inspector as a form of hush money. She'd taken the promotion, but hadn't stopped — at the time, she thought it poetic justice that she used her new power to further her efforts. She'd found the right judge to hear her case. She'd lined up the right person in the DA's office.

Back then, Erickson hadn't been some old man in a hospital bed, bandaged, loaded with tubes leading into his nose, his arm. Back then he'd been death personified. Just looking into those remorseless eyes had made her cross herself.

Now, he just seemed *old*. Scars covered his arms, his neck, his chest. Nasty scars, too — long, curving things that must have required hundreds of stitches. This man was a warrior. The scars told the story of his battles.

"Goddamit, Bryan," she said. "You don't know what you've done."

She should have fired Bryan and Pookie sooner. Pookie couldn't let something like this go. The Blake Johansson situation had proved that — if Pookie smelled crooked cops, he went after them. Maybe she should have switched him to Internal Affairs years ago.

If she had told Pookie and Bryan the truth about Erickson, about the monsters, would those guys have pursued the case anyway? Based on their track records, she'd assumed they would have done exactly that. And how could she hold it against them? They had done *exactly* the same thing she had done.

When her efforts put Erickson in the loony bin, how many people had died from her stubbornness?

More important, how many people would die now, because of Bryan's?

This wasn't the first time Erickson had been out of commission. He'd been injured twice before that she knew of, but both times he'd left the hospital the very next day. This time, however, he didn't look like he was going anywhere. Was he just old, or was there something else?

Hopefully he would recover soon . . . before Marie's Children realized that they could once again kill at will.

Murder Was the Case

Sleeping until noon had a way of making anything more palatable. So Bryan Clauser was a fleshy-headed mutant. So what? He was still Pookie's best friend. He had saved Pookie's life. Getting all worked up about this wasn't going to fix anything. Pookie would find a way to get his boy through this. Hell, it wasn't like Bryan was a Yankees fan or anything *really* unforgivable.

Emma danced around his feet. Pookie was supposed to just give one treat at a time, but he grabed a big handful and dropped them on the kitchen floor. Life is short; treats are good.

He poured a cup of coffee from Robin's coffeemaker. Nice machine. Everything the girl had was nice. Medical examiners, it seemed, earned a bit more income than homicide inspectors.

He heard footsteps behind him, then a woman's voice. "Did you make coffee?"

He turned with mug in hand. A sleepy-faced, yawning Robin shuffled into the dining room. She wore only a black T-shirt that was too big for her — one of Bryan's, most likely. She sat at the table. Pookie poured a mug for her, then sat as well.

She took a sip. "I made a bunch of calls after you turned in, then I ran out of steam. My friend Dana just called from the hospital, woke me up. Erickson is stabilized."

"He's better?"

"Not even close," she said. "He's still in intensive care. He hasn't woken up yet."

A knife in the belly was worse than a bullet in the shoulder, but Bryan's wound had healed up within hours. "Erickson has the Zed. Why hasn't he healed?"

"Beats me," Robin said. "All I have is a hypothesis. I don't know anything about these people. You heard from Bryan?"

Pookie hadn't. But he had received a voice mail from Bryan's dad. Poor Mike was a mess. Maybe that was the price you paid for lying to your child your whole life, but Pookie wasn't about to judge.

"No word from Bri-Bri yet," Pookie said. "I think he's okay, so don't worry."

She crossed her arms and slowly rubbed her own shoulders. "He's *not* okay. Pookie, *please*, just tell me what's really going on."

She was hurting bad for Bryan. She wanted to share Bryan's pain, help him through anything, but it wasn't Pookie's place to tell her the truth. If Bryan didn't want her to know, that was his choice and Pookie had to back up.

"Bo-Bobbin, you know what? As you've pointed out repeatedly, you're *not* his girlfriend anymore. It's not your business."

She laughed at him. "Right. *Now* you're going to pretend he doesn't belong with me? You've spent six months trying to get us back together."

She leaned forward and put her hand on his wrist. "Pookie, I made a mistake pushing Bryan away. I love him. I also *know* him. Maybe not as well as you do, but I know him, and I think he's real close to doing something bad. If you *don't* let me help and something happens to him, you won't be able to live with yourself."

He didn't have a one-liner this time. She was right, but that didn't change anything — telling Robin, or anyone else, was Bryan's decision alone.

"I can't," Pookie said.

Her eyes narrowed. He had a sudden feeling that she was looking right into his brain with that magic chick-power that women have. She turned and looked at the RapScan machine sitting on the table. Her eyes widened. She covered her mouth. "Oh my God. That second sample, it was from *Bryan*."

What had he said? Was it that obvious, or had he done something to tip her off? He had to cover, and cover fast. "Uh . . . come on now, why would you say that?"

She turned angry eyes on him. "That's why he went to see Mike. The second sample was X-Y-Zed, so Mike can't be his real father."

"Robin, the second sample wasn't Bryan's, it was—"

She slapped the table. "*Stop it!* We both know I'm right, so stop insulting my intelligence." She pointed her finger in his face. "Don't you lie to me one more minute, you understand me?"

Pookie leaned back. He nodded. "Okay. You're right."

Her anger broke. Tears welled up in her eyes.

Oh Jesus, now he had to deal with a crying woman? "Take it easy. We'll figure something out. Bryan is my boy — that's not going to change."

"This isn't about being *boys*," she said. "I can't imagine what he's going through. Oh my God . . . he went to confront Mike and you *let him go by himself*?"

Huh — when she said it like that, it did sound kind of stupid.

She wiped her eyes with the backs of her hands. "I have to find him. He's all alone."

"If he's alone, it's because that's what he wants."

She stood. "This isn't about what he *wants*, it's about what he *needs*. You should have known that."

As soon as she said it, he knew she was right. That Detroit-sized nuke had dropped in Bryan's life, and Pookie had thought the man could handle it solo.

"He's still the Bryan we know," Pookie said. "He won't do anything stupid."

She wiped her eyes again as she let out another derisive laugh. "You mean he won't do anything *stupid* like go into the house of a killer without a warrant or backup?"

Pookie's eyebrows rose. *Touché, Bo-Bobbin, touché.*

His cell chimed the theme from *The Simpsons*.

Robin walked to her bedroom. Emma padded along behind her. Pookie knew she was going to get dressed, then try to find Bryan. There was no point trying to stop her.

So instead, Pookie answered his phone.

"Black Mister Burns. My day is already about as tasty as a St. Bernard turd rolled in rancid salmon poon. Whatever you have to tell me now is going to make my emotional boo-boos all better, right?"

"Only if you like your salmon-poon turd served with a side of tainted clams," John said. "I finished that murder-rate analysis."

Pookie sighed. "Screw it. Go ahead."

"First some perspective. San Francisco's population peaked in the 1950s at 775,000. Right now it's about 767,000. Not much variation in the past fifty years, so the population is a constant against which we can evaluate murders on a basic one-to-one, year-to-year basis."

"Do you always talk like a band nerd that played the French horn?"

"What?"

"For example, when you fuck, do you say shit like *I'm going to insert my penis now, then move it back and forth in a rapid motion until one or both of us achieve an orgasm.*"

"Yes, but only when I'm banging your mom."

For the second time that afternoon, Pookie's eyebrows rose in respect. "Point taken, Mister Burns. Continue."

"The highest murder rate in recent memory was 1993, with 133 murders. Things have been down lately. We haven't had over 100 since 1995. Twenty-seven years ago, however, there were 241 murders. That's the highest the city has ever officially recorded. What that doesn't take into account is the fact that in that same year, from January to June, there were 187 murders for an average of *31 a month.* In July, it dropped to nineteen. After that, the murders dropped off to *7* a month, which is about the normal murder rate. Now, guess when Jebediah Erickson was released from detention in the California Medical Facility?"

The coffee felt funny in Pookie's stomach. He felt like he was going to throw up. "I don't want to guess."

"I'll tell you anyway. He got out that same July. Erickson gets locked in the loony bin, and a few months later the murder rate skyrockets. He gets out, things almost immediately come back down to normal."

Yes, he was definitely going to puke. Vigilantism was one thing, but to have that kind of impact on a murder rate?

"There's more," John said. "The crime spike wasn't just for homicides. Missing persons cases *tripled* in the same time frame. And *serial* killings were up 500 percent. Records indicate the Bay Area may have had *seven* serial killers in action *at the same time.* That shit never got released to the press, because Mayor Moscone sat on it like an ugly fat girl riding a willing drunk."

"See, when you talk like *that,* it makes all this death and despair so much more fun."

"I'm doing my best to make it more palatable."

The jokes were automatic for Pookie, but he felt none of the humor. "You said the murder rate didn't spike when Erickson first went in?"

"It didn't. Things were normal for several months, then slowly ramped up to the levels I told you about."

Pookie thought of a stuffed little girl holding a fork and a knife. Erickson probably hadn't killed her on a whim. Would people like that girl run wild if Erickson was out? More important, were there more creatures out there like the four-eyed bear-thing?

Chief Zou's words rang through his head. She'd asked for his trust. She'd told him there was more going on than he could know. If only she'd just come out and *explain* this. But even then, would Pookie have gone along with it? Zou had known he and Bryan might push too far, possibly get Erickson committed again, leave the city open to mass murder. But they hadn't put him away — instead, they'd put him in the ICU.

"One more thing," John said. "I have a hypothesis about Erickson and why the killings didn't go up right away."

Pookie made a mental note to write that down — two friends using the word *hypothesis* in the same day? Maybe he was moving up in the world. "Hit me, BMB."

"Do you know what a keystone predator is?"

"Is it a Pennsylvania pedophile?"

"No, but that was clever," John said. "It's a predator that keeps a population in check. Like hawks that hunt lemmings, or sea stars that feed on sea urchins that would eat the kelp roots and therefore kill the kelp, throwing the whole ecosystem into crisis and—"

"Get to the point, Bro."

"Sorry," John said. "A keystone predator keeps a prey population in check. Remove that predator, you get a population explosion of the prey species. Let's say Marie's Children were responsible for that murder spike. Maybe Erickson is their keystone predator. Take him out, the killers go crazy. Put him *back* in the ecosystem, he kills them or sends them back into hiding, maybe both. Think about the things you said you saw in Erickson's basement."

The bear-thing, the blue bug, the shark-mouthed man. Had those once been lurking around the city, killing people? "You think that seventy-year-old Jebediah Erickson is the keystone predator of goddamn monsters?"

"Yeah," John said. "We fucked up, Pooks. If Erickson doesn't get out of that hospital, things could get real bad."

Could get bad? Like they weren't bad enough already.

"John, thanks. It's a shitty picture, but now we know."

"Computers are my business and business is good."

"Not just that," Pookie said. "You really stepped up last night. If you hadn't come out, Erickson would have come in after us. It could have been Bryan in the hospital, or in the morgue. I'm proud of you, man."

John was silent for a few minutes. "Thanks," he said finally. "You got no idea what that means to me coming from you."

Pookie heard the apartment's front door open and slam shut. Emma came treading into the kitchen. Ears up, she stared at him with a face that said *it's just you and me, kid.*

"Burns, I gotta go. Do me a favor and call the Terminator. He won't answer, so just data-dump all that goodness in his voice mail. If you reach him, though, you call me."

"Will do."

Pookie hung up. He walked to the kitchen and grabbed the half-empty box of dog treats. He was about to drop another handful, but instead just up-ended the box. Emma started eating them like they might suddenly grow legs and run away.

Pookie headed out of the apartment to find his partner.

The Hidey Hole

Rex paced.

There wasn't much space to do even that; it only took ten steps to cross the room. A damp cold put a moisture sheen on the stone walls, making them reflect the candles that lit the room. The place looked like it had started out as a crack in the rock, then had been chipped away at to make room for a bed, a bookshelf, a table and a chair.

A skull sat on the floor in a corner. A human skull. Maybe someone had put that there to see if it scared him. It didn't. There were gouges in the skull's face bones, like someone had scraped at them with their teeth.

Moldy books sat on the shelves. To pass the time, he'd tried to read one called *On the Road*, but he'd only made it five pages before the spine split and page six crumbled when he tried to turn it.

He didn't want to read, anyway.

There were no clocks, yet somehow he knew the sun had already set. He could *feel* it. His whole life he had felt tired and sluggish during the day, had trouble sleeping at night. He'd always felt exhausted at school, felt *slow*, like the world was slipping by him in a way he couldn't understand.

Well, now he knew why. The day was made for sleeping. Night was the time to *hunt*. There was a word for creatures that lived at night and slept during the day — *nocturnal*.

Rex paced. Sly would be back soon, and he would take Rex home.

The metallic sound rattled through the white room. Aggie and the Chinaman ran to the wall, put their backs to it, pressed their collars to the flanges as the chains started to rattle and draw tight.

The boy with no tongue was lying flat on his back.

"Get up, boy! Get to the wall or that chain's gonna yank you!"

The boy's eyes opened. He looked at Aggie with an empty stare. Aggie had seen that look on the streets many times — the look of someone who's given up.

The chain snapped taut, yanking the boy by his neck. That got his attention. His eyes scrunched tight with pain as hands flew to the collar. He slid along on his back, spitting up fresh blood. The chain pulled the boy up the wall until his collar *clanged* against the flange. He coughed and stared out, wide-eyed and confused.

The white gate opened.

Seven white-robed masked men came in: Wolfman, Darth Vader, Tiger-Face, Frankenstein, Dracula, Jason Voorhees and was that the green Power Ranger? Seven of them — and this time, *two* dragging sticks.

Aggie's breath lodged in his lungs, stayed there like a rock that kept him from inhaling or exhaling.

Who had the masked men come for this time?

Wolfman, Tiger-Face and Frankenstein headed straight for the Chinaman, who screamed in terror. The other four moved to the big boy — he screeched a mewling, sad sound that tried and failed to form words.

Aggie's body sagged in relief. A guilty feeling of knowing joy at someone else's demise once again overwhelmed him, filled him with bottomless self-hate, but there was nothing he could do to help either of them.

The white-robed men closed in on the boy. He kicked out, or tried to, but he slipped and fell, yanking the collar hard against his neck and chin. Before he could get his feet under him, the monster masks were on him, black-gloved hands reaching in, grabbing, hitting, pulling, holding.

The Chinaman tried to fight, but he wasn't like that scrappy Mexican. The masked men easily overpowered him. Frankenstein reached in with his stick and hooked the Chinaman's collar. He screamed and cried as they dragged him out of the cell.

Aggie looked back at the boy. Darth Vader hooked the boy's collar. The robed men wasted no time pulling him toward the door. The boy kicked, he screamed gutteral sounds. Splatters and streams of blood bubbled out with each desperate breath, the red marking his path along the white floor.

They took him out of the white cell.

But this time, the door didn't close.

Aggie stared, waiting, wondering.

Hillary walked through. No cart this time. No sandwiches. She walked right up to Aggie. She leaned in close. He forced himself not to flinch away, not that there was anywhere he could go. She was his only hope.

She sniffed him. She smiled, showing her missing teeth.

"You are better."

Aggie shook his head so violently it rattled the chain in his flange. If he was better, they would take him away like the others.

"I'm still real sick! I need my medicine."

Hillary laughed, a light sound that anywhere else in the world would have sounded delightful. "You understand," she said. "You are smarter than most of those we bring down here."

Aggie kept shaking his head.

She reached out a wrinkled hand and grabbed his jaw, holding him still. He started to talk, but she put a finger on his lips.

"Shhhh," she said. "Now I show you what happens if you don't help me. Now we go and see Mommy."

Loneliness

Robin sat on her couch, Emma's blocky head in her lap, a half-empty glass of wine in her hand. No lights. Sometimes you just have to sit in the dark. Outside her apartment window, the breeze rippled a tree, making shadows of the branches and leaves weave curving patterns against her linen curtains.

A day's worth of searching for Bryan had taught her that she didn't know the first thing about finding someone who didn't want to be found. She'd checked his apartment, the Hall of Justice, the Bigfoot Lodge — no Bryan. She'd even walked around Rex Deprovdechuk's house and visited the spot where Jay Parlar had died. Nothing in those places, either.

She'd left at least ten messages. He hadn't called back, not even when she called to let him know that Erickson had just been downgraded from critical to stable condition.

How much more messed up could things be? Her poor Bryan — what must he be feeling right now? How would *she* feel if she were the one with that mutation? And as if that weren't enough, Bryan knew the family he loved so much wasn't his real family at all.

She took another sip of wine.

The little bit of light filtering through the curtains reflected off Emma's inner eyes, making them flash a luminescent green. When Robin was upset, Emma always knew and tried to get close. The dog let out a little whimper.

"I'm fine, Sweetie," Robin said. "It is what it is."

And what was *it*? *It* was going through the rest of her days without the only man she wanted. All the wine in the world couldn't chase that away. *It* was living half of a life.

A knock on the apartment door made Emma's head snap in that direction. The dog scrambled up, inadvertently digging her claws into Robin's thigh as she pushed off hard and ran for the entryway.

Robin winced, stood up and set the wineglass down on the end table. She followed Emma to the door. The dog had her nose down at the base of the door. Her oversized tail swished so madly her rear end almost toppled her over.

But she only acted like that when . . .

Robin held her breath as she opened the door.

Emma shot into the hall and started circling Bryan's legs, throwing her body against him. He reached down and picked her up in his familiar way. Her rear legs dangled limply, her tail pounded against his leg and her pink tongue flicked madly at his face.

"Easy, Boo," he said. He set Emma down, then turned his green eyes on Robin.

"Hey," he said.

He looked like he hadn't slept in days. He looked . . . hopeless.

"Hey," she said.

He started to talk, then stopped. He looked away. "I didn't know where else to go."

She stood aside and held the door open. Bryan walked in, Emma at his heels. He seemed to be in a daze. He walked into the dark living room and sat on her couch. She sat near him, but not right next to him. Emma wasn't as cautious; the black-and-white dog flopped down on his feet and looked up at him lovingly, her tail thumping a regular pattern on the throw rug.

Robin watched him for a moment, then spoke. "I looked for you today," she said. "I couldn't find you."

"Oh. I was sleeping."

"Where?"

"Pookie's car," he said. "I think. I just kind of . . . wandered."

His beard had grown so frizzy. It reminded her she still had his beard trimmer in the bathroom. She had always meant to get rid of it, but found reasons not to. She wanted to touch that beard, gently stroke it and take his pain away.

"I was having some wine. Would you like a glass?"

He stared out into the room, into nothing. "Got anything stronger?"

"Your scotch supply is still here. Talisker on the rocks?"

He nodded in a way that said he'd have taken anything she had. She made him his drink, flashing back to the time they'd lived together when she had loved making him drinks. They'd been equals in most areas of life, but she couldn't help the fact that she liked to wait on him a little.

Moments later she handed him the glass. Ice cubes rattled as he took it. He liked as much ice as the glass would hold. He drained it in one pull and handed it back to her.

"Want another?"

He nodded.

Emma's tail kept up its steady rhythm.

Robin refilled his glass, then sat down next to him. She picked up his hand, gently, pressed the glass into it.

"Robin, what am I going to do?"

"I don't know," she said. "It's a bit of an unusual situation, to say the least."

He nodded, took a small sip. She picked up her wineglass. They sat in the dark, in silence, together. This time, she waited until he spoke first.

"What am I?"

"You're Bryan Clauser."

"No, I'm not. That part of my life is a lie."

She wasn't going to argue with him about that one. Maybe she could talk to his father later, see if there was anything she could do. But for now, she wasn't about to feed Bryan platitudes.

"You're a cop," she said. "Yes, I know you're fired, but that doesn't change the fact that you're a man who's dedicated his life to serving the greater good."

He took another sip. "I used to think that was why I did it. But now, I'm not so sure."

"What do you mean?"

He finally turned to look at her. The room's shadows hid his face, took the light out of his green eyes.

"I think I drifted into the job because of what I really am. I think I became a cop because I like to hunt."

Robin wondered if she looked afraid, because suddenly she was. Bryan had said *because I like to hunt,* but what he meant was *because I like to hunt* PEOPLE.

He took another sip. "Some cops kill a guy and it messes them up so bad they quit the force. I've killed five men. *Five.* All in the line of duty, all righteous shoots, okay, but still — I don't feel bad about any of them."

He turned away, again looking off into nothingness.

This new Bryan, the one with the emotions turned full on, he was a frightening man. If she didn't already know him and met him in a dark alley, she'd run the other way. But she did know him. There was so much pain in his face. She wanted to take him into her arms, pull his head to her chest and slowly stroke his hair.

"Bryan, there's a difference between being a *murderer* and being a *protector.* Cops carry guns for a reason."

He turned to face her again. "But shouldn't I feel *something*? Some kind of remorse? Or guilt? Or whatever the fuck the psychologists kept asking me after every time I put someone down?"

"What do you want me to say? If you hadn't done what you'd done,

Pookie would be dead, John would be dead, and *you'd* be dead. You saved lives. It's not like you have an urge to go out and eat babies."

He said nothing.

"Because if you want to eat babies, Bryan, I'm going to have to go ahead and ask you to put down the scotch."

He kept staring, then she saw the corners of his mouth turn up just a bit — he was fighting a smile. She waited, knowing him well enough to know exactly what would happen next. His mouth trembled once, twice, then he lost his battle with the laugh.

He shook his head. "You have to be kidding me. Jokes? *Now?*"

She shrugged. "Maybe I've been hanging out with Pookie too much."

Bryan's smile faded. The sadness returned to his eyes, and in that moment her soul felt like it would splinter and blow away on the wind.

She turned her back to him, then slid onto his lap. He started to react, but before he could say anything she reached one hand up to the back of his head and used his rigidity to pull herself in for a kiss. Her lips hit his. She felt his beard on her upper lip, on her chin. She breathed in the scent of him, felt it spread through her chest. He started to pull away, so she held him tighter.

Her wineglass fell away. She put her other hand on the back of his head, pulling him even tighter, feeling the texture of his hair between her fingers. He resisted, but only for a moment more, then she felt his arms around the small of her back, squeezing her tight, lifting her as if she weighed nothing at all. His tongue — cooled by the icy scotch — found hers.

She didn't know how long the moment lasted. It lasted a second. It lasted forever. Finally, his strong hands slid to her shoulders, gripped them and pushed her away so that their faces were only an inch apart.

She felt the heat of his breath, smelled the Talisker that came with it. "I missed you, Bryan. I missed you so much."

Bryan sniffed.

She gently kissed his left eye, let it linger there. "I should have never pushed you away," she said.

He nodded. "I shouldn't have let you."

Her hands slid to his face, felt his beard in her palms, felt the warmth of his skin. "I'm not playing stupid games anymore," she said. "I love you. I think I have loved you from the first moment I saw you. The genetics don't change the fact that you're a good man, Bryan. They don't change the fact that you're *my* man."

He closed his eyes. "Everything feels so much . . . just *more*. Before, all my feelings were kind of, I don't know, kind of *muted*. Now they're on full bore. It's hard to manage."

She kissed his nose. "All I need from you is one emotion. Nothing else matters. Nothing at all. Just look in your heart and tell me — do you love me?"

Her thumbs slowly moved back and forth on his cheekbones. He stared at her, his eyes still full of pain but now also filled with longing.

He started to talk, then stopped. He swallowed. He licked his lips, then spoke.

"I love you," he said. "I always have, but I couldn't say it."

She blinked back tears. "You can say it now. We'll figure this out together. I will never leave you, no matter what happens."

"It's not that easy," he said. "I mean, the Zed chromosome, other people have it and the things that they do . . . I don't know what *I* might do."

She kissed him again, hard. His fingertips pressed into her back.

Robin pulled away from him only enough to speak, her lips still touching his when she did.

"Stay with me," she said. "Stay with me tonight."

He looked at her again, then it was his turn to pull her close.

Hands

Just look at them. Holding hands. *Kissing.* He could see their tongues flicking in and out of each other's mouths. So *unclean.*

The rage built in Tard's chest. So did the excitement. Everything seemed sharper, more intense, from the breeze blowing off the endless ocean to the sand grinding under his belly to the smell of a dead fish that couldn't be far off.

They couldn't see him. People couldn't see at night, not like he could. And these people had a fire, blazing orange and hot, a spot of light surrounded by this long, dark stretch of beach. Their eyes would be adjusted to that light — they wouldn't be able to see anything twenty feet outside of their little bonfire. Tard could cover twenty feet in just a couple of seconds. They wouldn't have time to react. They probably wouldn't even have time to scream.

There was no one to stop him anymore. He'd killed once, and no one had told him to stop.

Off in the distance, a few other bonfires lit up the evening fog of Ocean Beach. Probably bums. No one cared about the bums, but these two — they looked like they would be missed.

No one was supposed to touch a will-be.

Tard thought about slinking away, maybe looking at the other bonfires to see what was there . . . but these two, lying there, holding hands, *kissing.*

The boy crawled on top of the girl and started to move.

It made Tard feel funny to watch, and that funny feeling made him even angrier.

He slowly lifted off his belly and onto his feet, a sand-colored shape that rushed forward, out of the darkness and into the bonfire's light.

Rex let his fingertips trace along rough tunnel walls made of dirt, rocks, mismatched bricks and half-rotted timbers. The timbers formed steep, inverted V-shapes that supported larger boulders above. The whole thing looked horribly fragile and delicate, as if it might collapse at any moment.

"This doesn't look very safe," he said. Sly was ahead of him, Pierre behind him and Sir Voh and Fort in the rear. Rex didn't need to ride Pierre anymore, nor could he — Pierre had to duck to get through the tight space. The big creature looked up frequently, constantly checking his head height. He seemed quite wary of bumping the timbers above them.

"It's safe," Sly said. "Except for this." He stopped, pointed to an overhead boulder that had been spray-painted with an orange arrow pointing back the way they had come. "The tunnels are all set up to collapse if we knock down supporting rocks. We call them *lynchpins*. If you knock this one down, the entire tunnel behind us collapses."

Rex wondered what it would be like to feel all of this weight falling on him, crushing him, suffocating him. "Why are these here?"

"We have lairs all over the city," Sly said. "But only a few tunnels lead home. If the monster discovers any tunnels, we destroy them so he can't trace the tunnels back to where most of us live."

The lynchpin rock looked like it might fall out at any moment. "Do they ever fall down by themselves?"

Sly smiled. "Sometimes. That is our existence, being forced to live underground like animals."

"What happens when there's an earthquake?"

Sly shrugged his big, blanket-covered shoulders. "When there are earthquakes, people die." He turned and continued back down the tunnel. Rex and the others followed.

Rex lost track of how long they walked. The narrow tunnel made for slow going, especially considering the size of Pierre and Fort. Sir Voh seemed to compress on Fort's shoulders, to *flatten* somehow, take up less space. At times Rex had to stoop over and walk in a crouch, which meant Pierre, Fort, even Sly had to crawl through the dirt. It probably explained why their clothes and blankets were so tattered and filthy.

Crawling deep in the dirt, like insects — this was no way for his family to live.

Finally, the narrow tunnel opened up into a big cavern. Rex stood tall and looked around, amazed at what he saw. The cavern was about as big as a city block. The uneven ceiling rose thirty or forty feet above. Dim light filled the space, cast off by assorted light fixtures and naked bulbs attached to any number of things: chunks of dirty concrete, old logs, a rusted-out old streetcar straight from a gangster movie.

And in the middle of the cavern, encrusted with lights of all shapes and sizes, sat a pair of wooden ships. *Big* ships. They looked old, like the *Nina*, the *Pinta* and the *Santa Maria* he'd learned about in school.

Neither ship had masts. The closest one pointed away at an angle, its black hull cracked and broken in a hundred places. The bottom was buried in the ground, as if it were sailing a sea of dirt, frozen in time like a movie on pause. The deck angled a little to the left, matching the ship's slight tilt. On the ship's wide back end, Rex saw chewed-up wooden letters that spelled out the name *Alamandralina*.

To the right of that ship sat the second, this one rolled all the way over on its side so the ruined deck pointed up at a forty-five-degree angle. The hull looked barely intact, as if some giant had picked up the whole ship, lifted it up a hundred feet in the air, then dropped it to crack like a melon hitting pavement. He could only make out a few of the letters on the back of this one: an *R*, then space for two missing letters, then an *AR*, another space, then an *O*.

Rex saw lights coming from inside the ships. Through the cracked hulls, he saw beds, walls and makeshift doors. All these things were level with the ground — people clearly lived in there, even though no one seemed to be home.

Some cars were parked in the space between the ships: a battered school bus with windows blacked out, and two pickup trucks that looked like they belonged in a scrapyard.

All this, under the streets of San Francisco? And this place looked *old*, like it had existed since those ships actually sailed the ocean's waters. A hidden world that had always been here, just waiting for him to find it.

"Sly, this is amazing."

"This is *Home*," Sly said. "Welcome to your kingdom."

Rex tried to take it all in. So stunning, so overwhelming. But if this was his "kingdom," where were his subjects?

"It's empty," he said. "I thought there would be more of us."

Sly laughed, a hissing, scraping thing that a few days ago would have made Rex piss his pants in fear.

"There is," Sly said. "Tons more. They're in the arena. That's where we're going, to announce to the people that you have come to lead us to a better day."

Sly kept saying that phrase. What did it mean? Maybe it was like in the fantasy novels, where a *chosen one* led people to overcome evil. If it was a prophecy, Rex hoped he could fulfill it.

"The arena," Rex said. "How do we get there?"

"More tunnels," Sly said. "It will take us a little while. When we're there, everyone can see you and you can see Mommy. Hillary said it was real important you meet Mommy."

"Who's Hillary?"

Sly grinned his toothy grin. "She's the reason we came to get you, my king. You'll like her. But this won't all be fun — Firstborn will be there. He will not be happy to see you. But don't worry, we will protect you."

Rex looked at Sly, then at Pierre, at Sir Voh and Fort. These men were so big, so strong. How could Firstborn possibly threaten them all?

From the tilted ship, an echoing voice called out. "My king!"

A little man stood on the high rail. As Rex watched, he jumped off and dropped to the ground twenty feet below. The man should have *splatted*, but he landed on his feet and didn't even slow down. He ran forward, covering the distance faster than Rex would have thought possible.

He's really fast. Marco was fast, too. Is everyone like that?

The man stopped a few feet away. Rex felt the *ba-da-bum-bummmm* in his chest. Such a great feeling! This man was family.

He was short, only a few inches taller than Rex. He had a bald head with yellow, mottled skin. His nose was so strange — a hooked, hard thing that curved down and out to end in a sharp point. It started out yellow where it grew out of his face, fading to black at the sharp tip. It was more like a beak than a nose. Rex saw two little holes above the beak, just below and inside the eyes. Ah, those were his nostrils.

The man smiled a wide smile. Behind the wickedly curved beak was a mouth full of tiny, stubby teeth. He wore raggedy clothes, just like the rest, all dirty and smelly and torn up. His right arm was in a white sling. Rex could tell that he was young, like Sly and the others.

"My king! I am Sucka! I have fought and killed for you." He stuck out his left hand, the skin there as yellow as his face. He wanted to shake Rex's hand, like Rex was a grown-up or something.

Rex shook it.

Sly reached out and held Sucka's left shoulder. "Sucka proved himself, my king. He killed Issac and the mother of Alex. Then he fought the monster himself."

Rex drew in a surprised breath. "You fought the *monster*?"

Sucka grinned and nodded. "He shot me with the magic arrow! It was real scary. He would have taken me, but a cop came onto the roof just in time. I jumped away. I haven't healed as quick as normal, but they got the magic arrow out and it's getting better."

Sly's green hand mussed Sucka's nonexistent hair. "Sucka is a brave one. He'll serve you well."

Sucka's face turned a pale orange. He was blushing.

Sly's smile faded. He looked very serious. "My king, are you ready to go to the arena?"

It would be dangerous. Firstborn would be waiting, but Rex's new friends would protect him.

He nodded. "I am. Take me to meet my people."

Mommy

The white dungeon led out into a white hallway. The hallway had the same poorly fitted stones, the same countless slathered-on coats of white enamel paint. Mismatched lights lit the curved roof. A thick, brown electrical cord, painted over in some parts, ran from light to light, hanging down slightly in some places, nailed up to ceiling beams in others.

Where the ceiling was only stone, the stones looked well fitted, like the angled blocks of some medieval craftsman. In more places than not, however, random pieces of rock, tile and chunks of wood patched the ceiling in a white enamel kaleidoscope of shapes.

Aggie saw smears of blood on the white floor — the path of the boy with no tongue. Hillary pushed Aggie on. They walked past a white-robed man wearing a Richard Nixon mask: the long nose, squinty eyes and wide grin. The man stood behind a scratched yellow mop bucket that stank of bleach. He swabbed a wet mop across the trail of blood.

"Wait," Aggie said. "Can I ask a question?"

"Maybe," Hillary said.

Aggie didn't know what that meant, but she hadn't said no. "What's with the masks? You don't wear one."

Hillary let out a huff of disgust. "Because I am *la reine prochaine*. The *ouvriers* wear the masks in tribute to the *guerriers* who risk their lives to bring us food. You understand?"

Aggie didn't. Was she speaking Italian?

His confusion must have shone on his face. Hillary shook her head, then reached out and pulled off the Nixon mask. As it slid free from under the white hood, Aggie held his breath, expecting to see something horrible — but it was just a man. A light-skinned black man. He stood there, mop still in hand, half-lidded eyes staring out. His mouth hung open. The tip of his tongue was touching the inside of his lower lip.

"Hey," Aggie said, "is he retarded?"

"He is an *ouvrier*. He does the work that needs to be done. Now you stop talking and walk, or we will miss it."

Hillary pushed Aggie in front of her. Each shove was just hard enough to keep him going, but he felt strength every time her hands connected with his body. They moved quickly. He got the feeling she didn't want to be seen.

The narrow hall curved and twisted. Soon the white gave way to browns and blacks and grays, the colors of deep earth. Other tunnels branched off. There was no pattern to the branches, no regularity, just a seemingly endless choice of dark options. Stone and brick walkways changed to dirt floors. The hallway widened at one point. When it did, Hillary pushed Aggie into a side tunnel. He walked in, eager to please, but she grabbed him, turned him and held him so close that they were almost kissing.

"What you see now, no one sees," she said. "You be very quiet, go where I tell you. You make one noise, they will tear you to pieces. Understand?"

Aggie nodded.

She pushed him through a hall so cramped he had to turn sideways to fit. Dirt and stone ground up against his face and chest. The walls here looked like an archaeological dig: dirt and stone, sure, but also blackened wooden boards, rotted timbers, worn bits of broken glass bottles, ceramic shards and rusty metal from old tools, gas cans and pipes. This was a tunnel dug by laymen's hands, carved through old landfill. The junk hallway led up at an angle steep enough to make him winded after only twenty steps.

As he climbed, a heavy scent started to fill the air. It wasn't a perfume, it was thicker, more . . . *animal.* He stopped to breathe it deep into his nose. Whatever it was, he couldn't get enough of it.

Hillary pushed him. "Hurry. You must see this."

He kept climbing. Of all things, his dick twitched. He couldn't *possibly* be horny at a time like this, could he?

The floor leveled out. Aggie found himself in a tiny room with a ceiling so low that he had to crawl in on his hands and knees. The floor was a random collection of metal grates and old jail-cell bars set into the ground — he could look through them into the dark void below.

Hillary leaned in close to his ear. "We made it in time."

He whispered back: "Made it for what?"

"To see what will happen to you if you don't do what I say."

A tiny light appeared below — a single candle, carried by a white-robed man. This one wore the mask of a twisted, smiling demon. Aggie saw the floor was perhaps ten feet below the grates. He was close enough that if he reached through the bars and stretched, he might be able to touch the top of the masked man's hood.

Another white-robed masked man entered, also carrying a candle. Then another. And another.

The candles began to chase away the darkness, revealing a rectangular room maybe twenty feet long by fifteen feet across. At one end of the room, the feeble light illuminated a patchwork tarp that covered something big, a mound about the size of an elephant lying on its side.

More candle-carrying, white-robed masked men entered. They walked through a narrow door that was in the middle of one of the long walls. The door appeared to be the only way in or out. Aggie saw that the earlier masked men were leaving, saw that it was a procession — they entered, found a place to set their candles, then quietly shuffled out. The room grew brighter, as did the flickering light playing off the patchwork tarp.

One end of the tarp moved. From that end, Aggie heard the moan of a woman. A masked man ran to the tarp's opposite end. It reached under, picked something up, then stood, holding that something tight to its chest. What was that stain on his white robe? Was it blood? *Fresh* blood? The masked man pushed past his own kind and left the room.

Hillary grabbed his ear, twisted it. "Make no noise. If they see you, you die."

That strange smell intensified. Aggie's face felt hot. His dick started to stiffen.

The stream of incoming masked men set their candles down on shelves, on a table, on the floor, on whatever space was available, then they turned and walked out, sliding past other masked men who were bringing in more candles.

The room grew brighter.

Music started playing, a thin, plinking, metallic melody. Aggie looked to the side of the room opposite the mound. A white-robed man was sitting at a white wooden table. Another masked man walked up to it, this one holding a metal stand with eight candles, all tall and parallel — a candelabra. And wait . . . it wasn't a table, it was a little *piano*, like a smaller version of one of those big grand pianos.

A second candelabra joined the first. Now there was enough light that Aggie could see the piano player wore a Donald Duck mask. The small piano wasn't really white, but more of a pale yellow, the paint chewed up and scarred, chips showing the dark wood beneath.

Aggie's hands locked onto the iron bars holding him aloft. His dick was fully erect now, pushing out his secondhand pajamas. Not just *erect* — it was so hard it *hurt*.

More candles.

The room grew brighter still.

Wait . . . was the entire tarp *moving*?

Hillary's hot breath on his ear. "Now they bring the groom." Her lips were so close. Her breath sent hot tingles up his spine. He wanted her, his throbbing cock calling out to him to *take* her. But how could he want this old crone who kept him prisoner?

The music grew louder. It wasn't a piano — it was harsher, thinner. He knew that sound. He'd heard it in an old TV show . . . *The Addams Family* . . . it was a harpsichord. The white-robed Donald Duck started to rock back and forth as he worked the chipped keys.

More candles, more light.

That tarp *was* moving. Not just the end, oh no oh dear Jesus the *whole thing* was moving what the fuck is underneath that thing it can't be alive it just *can't* because it's so big as big as an elephant. *What is it what is it?*

The squeaking of wheels. A dolly, the kind movers use, rolled in through the narrow door, pushed by a white-robed man. And strapped to that dolly . . .

The boy with no tongue.

The light of at least a hundred candles flickered off the blond-haired boy's blood-covered mouth, his jaw, his neck, his shirt. He cried with big, heaving sobs that shook his thick chest. The boy . . . he had a *boner*? Even from up here, the boy's erection was clearly visible under his pajamas.

The masked men gathered at the tarp, ruffling it, preparing to remove it. The flapping of the giant cloth sent waves of that *smell* shooting up to Aggie's nose. He had to blink away the lust, had to press his face between the cold iron bars beneath him, had to fight the pure *heat* that roiled through his body.

"You do what I say," Hillary whispered in his ear, "or it will be *you* that experiences Mommy's love."

The harpsichord's plinking tones filled the air.

The masked men yanked the tarp away.

Aggie reared back. His stomach churned, tried to push his last meal up into his throat.

Bloated, *huge*, a mass of white flesh like a giant scoop of lard held together with pockmarked skin. Were those *legs?* They were, so fat they looked like giant gray-white sausages with tiny feet, too-small doll parts affixed to the corpulent body that spilled out under them, around them. And above the legs, a bubble of a belly arcing close to the ceiling, a belly that seemed almost translucent, that twitched and wiggled every time the body moved.

If there was a head and arms, they were hidden somewhere behind the fat.

The feet kicked uselessly, like those of a new baby trying out its new muscles.

Aggie had been told not to make any noise. He opened his mouth and clamped his teeth on the iron bar below him. The metal felt cold on his lips. He tasted rust. His jaws squeezed harder and harder, until he heard his right molar *crack*. The pain felt like a burning nail driven into his jaw, but it cleared his mind a little bit — it stopped him from screaming.

White-robed men circled the thing. Aggie realized that it was lying on a thick table . . . no, on a *cart,* with black car tires mounted at the corners. The kicking feet hung suspended over one end. Six masked men moved near those feet, three at each corner. They reached underneath and came out with big T-bars that they slid into rusty fixtures mounted on the cart. The men leaned back hard and started to pull. More white-robed men squeezed in between the wall and the back of the cart. They pushed with all their combined weight.

The cart rolled slowly, the old-wood floor groaning beneath the tires. The masked men slowly turned the cart, moving it away from the wall until the end with the feet faced the strapped-up boy with no tongue.

The harpsichord played louder.

The white-robed men in the room started to sway and moan in unison.

Aggie felt a piece of tooth floating in his mouth. He swallowed it.

He saw the body in profile — a giant slug made of human flesh. Now he saw the arms, at least the right one, endless waves of fat so thick he couldn't make out the forearm from the upper arm.

"Venez à moi, mon amoureux," said a deep, resonant voice that rang with erotic promise.

The voice had come from the body on the cart.

Aggie looked left, beyond the bell curve of the bloated belly and elephantine chest. He saw the head and knew this was the *Mommy* that Hillary had brought him to see.

Aggie James started to whine.

Hillary flicked him on the ear. Hard. The stinging pain again helped him hold on to some semblance of sanity.

Her head. Oh good God, her *head* was inside some kind of box, a metal, leather and wood box affixed to the cart. Bloated shoulder meat swelled up and around the rig. She was so morbidly obese that without it Aggie knew her own fat would engulf her head and suffocate her. A few stringy, brown strands of hair clung to a head wrinkled with deep rolls.

"Venez à moi, mon amoureux," Mommy said.

The light of a hundred candles played off of her white skin. Not *pale,* but actually *white*, like a grub dug up from the dirt, a grub that had never felt the heat of the sun.

There seemed to be a glow from within her swollen stomach. Aggie realized he could see *through* her belly, just a little bit, the translucent skin and tangle of veins pink-backlit by dancing candle flames on the other side.

Inside that belly, he saw something *moving. Several* somethings.

Fetuses.

A dozen? *Two* dozen? Some twitched, some kicked, but most didn't move at all; they were just still, black dots inside that horrific parody of a fleshy water balloon.

A white-robed man walked to the boy's dolly. He tilted it back, then moved the boy toward Mommy's legs.

The boy started to scream.

"Mon chéri," Mommy said.

A baby slid from between her legs in a splash of fluid. It wedged between the wet fat of her thighs. Bile filled Aggie's mouth. He forced himself to swallow it down lest it spray out and land on the white-robed men below. The baby didn't move. Its tan skin contrasted with her gray-white flesh. A masked man rushed in and pulled the still fetus out from between her tree-trunk-sized legs.

The blond boy's screaming changed to rapid-fire syllables — he was begging, but had no tongue to form the words. The masked man behind the dolly reached around and stuffed a rag in the boy's mouth, muffling the sounds.

The masked man then pulled down the boy's pajama pants. He tilted the dolly back again and rolled it between Mommy's legs.

Aggie felt Hillary's hand on the back of his neck. Strong, ready to snap his spine if he got noisy. The message was clear . . . *you ain't seen nothing yet, and when you do, keep your fucking mouth shut.*

"Now," Hillary hissed, "Marie Latreille takes a husband."

The white-robed men moaned louder, the harpsichord played faster.

Mommy's head thrashed inside its metal-and-wood box. "Mon chéri," she said.

Her stubby legs reached out, wrapped around the back of the dolly and pulled the boy into her. Her fat surrounded him — he looked like he was standing in waist-deep curdled milk.

The boy with no tongue lurched against the ropes holding him fast to the dolly. His struggles did no good.

"Mon chéri! *Mon chéri!*"

Hillary's hand tightened on Aggie's neck. She leaned forward, inadvertently pushing his head into the rusty iron bars. He reached back and spasmodically pulled at her dress.

She relaxed the grip, but didn't let go. "Tonight, the king will come to her," she whispered. "We will be saved."

Mommy's legs contracted over and over, pulling the boy into her, making the dolly rattle. Her obscene mass jiggled in time.

The *smell.* That smell that made Aggie so hot, so hard, it cranked up to a new level, filling the room, filling his *head.* Aggie twitched once, then came in his pajamas.

The boy's scream changed, briefly, from one of terror to one of horrified ecstasy.

The harpsichord music stopped.

Aggie blinked. The heat dissipated from his head, his body. He pushed his face away from the iron bars. He couldn't look at the scene anymore, not for another second. He turned and put his lips to Hillary's ear.

"I'll do whatever you say, *anything,* don't let that happen to me, *please!*"

Hillary turned to face him. She smiled, the candlelight from below gleaming off what yellow teeth remained. She held his face, fingertips gently stroking his cheeks. She leaned in. "It is not over for him. You have one more thing to see. Now, Mommy's husband will do the Groom's Walk."

The Groom's Walk

illary told Aggie to get up. He did so, carefully, lest his feet slip through the bars and that *thing* below know he was there. She guided him back out the way they had come. As they exited, Aggie heard the hum of machinery, then a distant, heavy click. One last peek down through the bars showed a strong light coming through the door to Mommy's room. Fully lit, Aggie saw wooden floors and walls that were black with age.

Hillary pushed Aggie through more narrow tunnels until they reached thin well-worn stone steps that led up. After forty or fifty steps, the path leveled out into yet another confined tunnel — but this one led to an open space. In that space, the flicker of torches.

Hillary stopped him just before the opening. She reached into a hole in the dirt wall and pulled out a filthy, gray felt poncho with a hood. She put it on him as if he were a three-year-old. The fabric reeked of mildew and of strange, sour body odors. She reached into the hole again and pulled out a moth-eaten, moldy plaid sleeping bag. She wrapped this around his shoulders, obscuring his shape. Even at his worst moments as a human, sleeping in gutters filled with dirty rainwater, going weeks without bathing, pissing on himself, maybe even shitting himself, he'd never smelled *this* bad.

She led him out on a flat ledge made of rocks, old timbers, what looked like a dented highway sign, and other pieces of societal refuse. Before him sprawled a huge, oblong space maybe three hundred feet long by two hundred feet wide. The ledge ran all the way around, a path four or five feet wide that dropped off into the open space thirty feet below. Seats of all kinds lined the ledge: folding metal chairs, plastic chairs, benches, logs, barrels, buckets — hundreds of them, all near the edge so people could sit and look down to the cavern floor. Behind those seats, running along the back of the ledge, he saw many dark spaces — tunnels that led deeper into whatever hell he found himself in. A curved, uneven ceiling of dirt and rocks arced above.

Hillary led him to the edge and made him sit on the old highway sign. His feet dangled in open air.

Down below and to his left, at one end of the oblong cavern, he saw the wreck of a huge wooden sailing ship, the kind he'd seen in those pirate movies. The ship's bottom sat on a little plateau of sorts that held it aloft from the cavern floor. The long, wooden prow pointed to the other end of the oblong space, while the rear of the ship seemed to be buried in the cavern's wall.

Aggie had never seen anything that seemed so out of place. The ship's deck looked uneven, but was mostly intact. Some of the chewed-up railing still lined the edges. He saw hatches in the deck, hatches that appeared to be well used, as if they still led down to areas below. A mast reached up from the ship's center — a mast made of human skulls. The top of the mast was at Aggie's eye level, thirty feet above the deck, topped by a crossbeam that turned it into a giant *T*. A combination of burning torches and blazing, mismatched electrical lights clustered at each end of the crossbeam, illuminating the deck below.

At the back of the ship, where steps should have led to a higher rear deck, the wreck merged into the cavern wall as if excavators hadn't quite finished the job. A door at the deck's back end looked like it would have led under that hidden, second deck. Through that door, Aggie saw a glimpse of something white and sluglike.

Mommy.

Aggie put it all together. Mommy lived in the captain's cabin of an old wooden sailing ship. Hillary's people had put in jail-cell bars and metal grates in the ceiling of that cabin, so that people could look down at Mommy. But how could a big ship like that get underground? Just where the hell *was* he?

He saw that the cavern floor wasn't solid. The sides of the mound holding the ship aloft sloped down to a series of dirt trenches that wound in every direction, running all the way to the end of the cavern and also stretching from side to side. The trenches twisted and intersected. They looked to be about ten feet deep, varying from maybe five to eight feet wide. From his spot high up on the ledge, Aggie could see into most of the trenches near him. He couldn't see into the ones on the far side unless they pointed right at his position.

He realized what the trenches were: a maze. He shuddered, imagined wandering through those spaces, wondered what might chase him.

A flash of gold caught his eye. On the ledge directly above Mommy's cabin, he saw a golden throne padded with red velvet cushions. Everything in this cavern looked dirty, used, rejected and beat-up, but not the golden throne. It radiated an aura of importance.

"Hillary, what is this place?"

"The arena," she said. "It is very important to us."

She patted him on the back as if they were old buddies, as if they were two kids sitting on a bridge during some idyllic summer afternoon. "Now you will see why you must help me."

Like she needed to show him anything more? "I'll do whatever you say. I swear to God. I just need to get out of here."

Hillary patted him again. "Just watch."

Movement from the captain's cabin door drew his attention. Masked men wheeled out the boy with no tongue, still strapped to his dolly. His pajama bottoms had been pulled back up. The thin fabric clung to him, matted down by Mommy's wetness.

Another masked man walked out of Mommy's cabin. His white, red-eyed mask had exaggerated cheekbones decorated with red spirals. In his hands he held a trumpet.

"Now, the call," Hillary said.

The masked man lifted the trumpet and blew a long, low note. When he stopped, the note echoed briefly, the tone slapping back and forth from cavern walls made of dirt and rock and brick.

In the shadowy tunnels that opened onto the ledge, Aggie saw movement. People filtered out and started sitting in the seats. No, not people . . . *creatures.* Some wore heavy blankets draped over their heads and bodies, but far more wore normal clothes — jeans or shorts or sweatpants, T-shirts, sweat-tops, dresses, tattered suit jackets. The various pieces of clothing covered so many shapes, *horrific* shapes. He saw skin of all colors, the gloss of fur, the gleam of hard shells, the winking of oozing wetness.

"Yes," Hillary said. "*Everyone* comes. Oh, look" — she pointed across the arena to the far side — "I see Sly and Pierre. They are the ones that brought you in. Isn't that nice?"

On the opposite side of the oblong ledge, two hundred feet away, Aggie saw a thick man with a face like a snake. Next to him, a taller man with a dog-face. Behind them, someone so big the size seemed incomprehensible. And between these three, a tiny form hidden inside a blanket.

Aggie felt the presence of people on either side. He slowly turned to his right. Not ten feet away sat a stubby, bleach-white man with snakelike hair that seemed to wave of its own accord. The man turned toward Aggie, but Aggie looked away quick and pulled his blanket up higher to hide his face. He couldn't stop himself from a peek to the left — only five feet away, something that looked like a man-sized cockroach.

Hillary nudged Aggie. "Best if you look straight ahead," she said quietly.

Aggie did just that.

The trumpet player blew a three-note blast, then walked back into the cabin. Everyone on the ledge stood and looked to Aggie's left, to the golden throne.

From the shadows behind that throne, figures emerged. The first wore a brown trench coat. He had a massively oversized head with an even more oversized forehead, the skin there gnarled and wrinkly. He stood on the throne's right side. A woman walked out to stand on the throne's left. She had long, glossy-black hair that spilled over both shoulders. Even from this far away Aggie could see that she was beautiful. She wore knee-high rubber boots, shiny pants and a cut-off Oakland Raiders sweatshirt that revealed a flat stomach. Something dangled from each hip . . . were those coiled chains? A tattered brown blanket hung down her back, secured by a white rope around her neck.

"Bonehead and Sparky," Hillary said. "They are Firstborn's guards." Her tone had changed. She no longer sounded happy — she sounded disgusted, bitter. "And here he comes, our beloved leader."

A tall man walked out of the shadows. He wore a long, black fur cloak clasped at the neck with something that gleamed like silver. Aggie saw blue jeans tucked into black combat boots, a black gun holster strapped to each thigh. The creature wore no shirt — short black fur covered a six-pack and a lean, defined physique. When he moved, his muscles twitched like those of a panther. The face looked vaguely catlike, with long, slanted eyes and green irises, a slightly extended mouth and large ears that angled back against the blocky head. He moved to the front of the throne, every motion smooth and easy.

He sat.

Hillary's lip curled into a sneer. "Firstborn has decided to grace us with his presence. Now we may begin."

Down on the ship, masked men moved the boy with no tongue. They rolled him to the center of the smashed deck and rested his dolly against the mast of skulls. The mast's combination of burning torches and blazing, naked electric lights cast harsh, flickering shadows on his terrified face.

Less than an hour ago, that boy had been in the white dungeon with Aggie.

"Hillary, what happens to him now?"

She smiled. "Now the children come out to play."

Halfway between the mast and the prow, a hatch wiggled. A black-gloved, white-sleeved arm pushed it open.

Two little kids climbed out.

Hillary let out a breathy *awwww*, then slapped Aggie's leg. "They are so *cute!*"

Just kids. A boy and a girl, maybe three or four years old. They wore filthy, secondhand pajamas. The boy was white and blond. He could have been any of the rich little brats from the Marina part of town. His shirt had the faded remains of a San Francisco 49ers pattern. The girl had darker skin and red hair. Her pajamas were blue with a flopping, almost-off iron-on of Barney.

Even from his perch over a hundred feet away, he could see that both of them held something metallic in each tiny, dirty little hand. They moved a few feet from the hatch. As they did, the lights played off the metal enough for Aggie to realize what it was they carried.

Each of them held a fork and a knife.

More kids crawled out, but these weren't even remotely human. One looked like a wrinkled yellow bat. Another had a bumpy shell, with fingers as long as its whole arm and a huge, hard, long thumb that formed something like a crab claw. Still another resembled a little white-furred, red-eyed gorilla. That one wore a Sesame Street T-shirt and red flannel pajama bottoms.

These creatures waited with the blond boy and the red-haired girl. More creatures came out behind them, but Aggie had to look away — he'd seen enough.

Two white-robed masked men walked toward the boy with no tongue. They undid his restraints. He fell forward. A masked man knelt and tapped the boy on the shoulder, then pointed to the right side of the ship, the side facing Aggie. The boy looked that way. Aggie saw the object of attention: a ladder leading down into the trenches.

The masked men hurried their dolly to another hatch halfway between the mast and Mommy's cabin. They lowered the dolly, crawled inside and pulled the hatch shut behind them.

The boy with no tongue stood up. Aggie saw muscles under those pajamas. The teenager looked around, clearly stunned by the cavern's breadth and strangeness — then his eyes fell upon the small monsters.

From inside Mommy's cabin, the hidden trumpeter played a long, single note.

The boy with no tongue ran for the ladder. He grabbed it and scrambled down, athletic and graceful if a bit sluggish. He hit the bottom and sprinted down a maze trench.

The crowd suddenly cheered, a sound just like every sporting event Aggie had ever seen.

Like a pack of tiny wolves, the children rushed to the side of the deck. Tumbling, little-kid running carried them forward, pajama-clad feet zip-zipping across the dirty wood. They didn't bother with the ladder — they just *leaped*, dropping fifteen feet down to the uneven trench floors below. Some landed gracefully. Others hit hard in a clumsy mess of arms and legs. The children screamed and laughed, stepping over each other to chase after the boy with no tongue.

Hillary giggled an old woman's giggle. She clapped her hands. "So *cute*!"

The teenager sprinted through the trenches. He banked left and right, without pattern or thought, sometimes turning a corner so fast his momentum would slam him into a wall. Pieces of rock and dirt fell wherever he hit. A trail of dust followed behind him, almost as if he were smoldering. Sometimes the trench walls obscured any sight of him, and sometimes Aggie could see all of the terrified boy.

The chasing children split up and rushed down different trenches, little feet pounding away in pursuit.

Hillary pointed toward the one with the long fingers and the pointy thumb. "Crabapple Bob is my favorite," she said. "He's a nice boy. I hope he gets the groom." She sounded like any old aunt or grandmother watching kids run and play, like this was nothing more than an Easter egg hunt and she was rooting for her favorite to find a hidden chocolate bunny.

The teenager turned down a trench that led straight toward Aggie's spot. Aggie saw the look of panic on the kid's face, the wide-eyed stare, the open mouth, the blood-streaked chin, the snot hanging from his nose and trailing across his cheek. And from this angle, Aggie saw the little blond boy with the faded 49ers shirt coming down an intersecting trench from the left.

The little boy turned the corner to block the teenager's path, then raised his fork and knife. The crowd cheered in excitement. The teenager didn't slow a bit — he kicked out with all the strength of a muscular, nearly full-grown man. His foot smashed into the little boy's face, throwing his tiny body backward and into a trench wall. Blood instantly poured from the kid's mouth.

The crowd booed.

"Aww, that's too bad," Hillary said. "I like little Amil."

The teenager's running kick had thrown him off balance. He stumbled, then fell to his knees, hands skidding across the rock-strewn path. From behind him came the bat-thing and the nightmarish Crabapple Bob.

Hillary clapped. "Go, Bob!"

The teenager scrambled to his feet. Blood poured from his left knee. He hopped in a mad lurch that threatened to spill him to the ground again.

Kids closed in from trenches on the left and on the right. A mass of shapes and colors, the glint of forks and knives reflecting the flickering torchlight, the happy squeals of children at play. The gorilla boy came from the left, running fast on all fours to pass the others. At an inter-section, he shot out and tackled the hopping teenage boy. Together they tumbled into a trench wall, kicking up a cloud of dust and dirt.

Crabapple Bob and the bat-thing dove on the pile. The teenager punched and kicked. The little monsters stabbed. The rest of the children poured in, burying the teenager beneath a pile of twisted, tiny bodies. Forks and knives rose up and down, up and down, flashing clean at first, then trailing arcs of blood.

Aggie watched. That could have easily been him down there. "Why?" he croaked from a dry throat. "Why would you do this?"

"Well, they have to learn how to hunt, don't they? They have to get the taste."

Aggie saw the little red-haired girl dart out of the swarm. She held a bloody, severed hand. She ran away from the pack, giggling and gnawing on the thumb like a kid working a caramel apple.

"They're *eating* him!" Aggie said, managing to yell without yelling, to pack all his panic and horror into a hissing whisper.

Down in the trenches, body parts came loose. A curl of intestine flipped up, arced wetly, then fell on top of something that looked like a blue-furred wolf boy wearing a Hannah Montana sweatshirt. Blood spread across the trench floor, turning it into red mud. The giggling kids tore at the body, played in the blood-mud like any child in any sandbox anywhere in the world.

Hillary sighed. "They always get so dirty."

A swarm of masked men, *hundreds* of them, ran through the trenches and closed in on the kids, white robes swishing with each step. Some of them carried hacksaws. They rushed to the mass of bloody-muddy chil-dren, pulled them off and held them up while little hands and feet kicked in protest. Aggie had a brief glimpse of the teenager's body — pajamas soaked head to toe in blood, right shoulder ripped open, left foot gone, intestine strings spread about and trampled flat into the dirt.

The masked men went to work with the hacksaws.

Aggie felt eyes upon him. He turned his head to the right, as little as possible, and looked out of the corner of his eye — the man with the snake hair was staring right at him.

A tap on his shoulder, Hillary's mouth near his ear. "Follow me. They have smelled something on you. Keep your eyes toward the ground and make no noise, or *you* will wind up as the next groom."

He felt her hands pulling up his blanket, hiding his head and face. It reminded him of being a small child, when his mother would adjust his jacket for him to make sure he stayed warm.

Aggie stood. He kept his eyes cast down as instructed. He followed Hillary's feet. With each step, he waited for hands to grab him, yank him back, toss him down into the cavern floor where the children would dig into him with forks and knives.

He barely breathed until he again slid into the tunnel from which they'd come, leaving the ledge behind. "Hillary, what happens now?"

"Now they cut up the groom to make the stew. Except for the brains — Crabapple Bob gets to feed those to Mommy. Or maybe they think Vanilla Gorilla got the kill? Either way we will have much stew tonight."

Stew. The Tupperware. Aggie had been eating *people*? The realization should have shocked him, he knew, but he'd seen more than he could handle and he just didn't give a fuck. As long as he got out of here, it didn't matter at all.

"No, Hillary, what I meant was . . . what do I have to do so *I* don't wind up as stew."

They exited the narrow tunnel into the hodge-podge hall that led back to the white room. Hillary gave him a missing-tooth smile, her eyelids and cheeks crinkling so deeply he would have thought her blind.

"Oh, *that*," she said. "All you have to do is deliver something for me, then you are free."

Free. Just the thought of it. He would deliver whatever she wanted, no matter what the risk.

They reached the white room. It shocked Aggie that he was actually relieved to see it, to once again be locked behind those white bars. For the moment, he had the place to himself — but he knew more prisoners would come.

Aggie could only hope that when the masked men brought in the next bum or illegal, he wouldn't be there to see it.

Long Live the King

So many.

All along the ledge, down in the trenches, on the cracked deck of the old shipwreck: *his* people, his *kind*. How had he gone his whole life without knowing this feeling? His heart felt like it might swell up and choke him, push his lungs out of his chest. So much *love*.

"Sly, I don't know what to do."

A big, strong hand on his shoulder. "We've got your back, my king. Everyone is here. This is your time. Are you ready?"

Rex glanced to the right, to the ship cabin and the ledge above it where Firstborn sat in his golden throne. If Rex was going to claim his birth-right, he'd have to face that frightening creature in the fur-lined cape.

Rex took a deep breath, then nodded. "I'm ready. Yes. Let's do this."

"Can you jump?"

Rex looked over the edge — at least a thirty-foot drop to the meandering trenches below. "I can't jump there. That would kill me."

The big hand patted his back lightly. "I'll show you how to do that later. Pierre?"

Strong hands slid around Rex's sides, lifted him, set him behind a big, skewed-jawed head. Then Pierre dipped, and leaped.

The ceiling came so close Rex had to duck tighter into Pierre's fur. They soared under rocks, bricks, broken pieces of wood and jagged bits of rusted metal, then they were dropping down fast.

They landed on the shipwreck, Pierre's big body rattling the dry wood. Sly *thumped* down on their right, Sir Voh and Fort on their left. Rex slid off Pierre's back. They stood in the middle of the deck, near to the big mast. This close, Rex saw that the mast was old wood with human skulls all around it, running from the base right up to the T-bar with all the lights. Sly ran to the ship's cabin and disappeared inside.

Rex looked up and around at all the strange faces peering down at him from the ledge above. Everyone was standing now, looking down — clearly, this was something new to them.

Sly came out of the cabin. He carried a man in a white robe. The man wore a mask from the *Saw* movies and held a trumpet in his hands.

Sly set him down in front of Rex.

"Blow," Sly said.

The man with the *Saw* mask did as he was told, blowing a long, single note.

Sly waved his arms, turning quickly to face one side of the cavern then the next. "Attention! The moment promised to us is here! This" — Sly turned and pointed at Rex — "is our *king*!"

A murmur rippled through the cavern. Rex felt anxious at being put on the spot, excitement at being the center of attention in a *good* way for once, and pride at knowing he was here to help these people, to lead them.

Then, a too-deep voice echoed through the cavern.

"The king? Impossible."

Rex looked up toward the throne. Firstborn stood on the ledge, looking down. The man with a big head stood on his right, the black-haired woman on his left.

Rex noticed Pierre take a step back.

"He cannot be the king," Firstborn said. "Sly, what lies do you speak?"

"No lies," Sly said, more to the audience than to Firstborn. "Everyone, come and smell the truth!"

More murmurs of excitement. People started jumping off the ledge, sailing through the air to land on the deck. Such *strength*, such *agility*. They gathered around Rex. So many shapes. So many sizes. So many colors. They sniffed him. And after sniffing, they all whispered the same thing.

The king.

Some were as scary looking as Pierre and Sly and Sir Voh and Fort, and some were even worse — like the one with the blue scales that looked like a boll weevil. But some looked like regular people, men and women with unwashed hair and multiple layers of ragged, secondhand clothes. They could have been the bums and street ladies Rex saw every day; some of them probably were.

They sniffed, they whispered, they reached, they touched.

Rex's heart filled with love.

"Enough!"

Firstborn's roaring rang off the cavern walls and ceiling. Everyone stopped. Everyone looked.

The black-furred man jumped off the ledge. He sailed through the air, his fur cloak trailing behind. People scrambled out of the way, giving him room to land. He hit the ruined ship's deck with a thud, knees bending to absorb the shock, left hand pressed flat to the ground.

The big-headed man came down to his left, the black-haired woman to his right.

Firstborn slowly stood, rising up to his full height. He was as tall as a basketball player on TV. Six-foot-six? Even taller than that? This close, Rex saw the gray lining Firstborn's mouth, and streaks of that same color running from his temples to above his ears. He looked *old*.

"So, this tiny boy is our *king*?"

"He is," Sly said. The snake-faced man again played to the crowd. "Can't you all feel it? Can't you all *smell* it?"

The crowd murmured with excited agreement — excited, but *cautious*. Rex saw the way they looked at Firstborn. They all feared him.

"Smells can be faked," Firstborn said. "This *boy* is just a human."

Rex saw many people shaking their heads.

Firstborn stamped his big boot, rattling the boards beneath. "He is *human*! You are all being tricked!"

There was anger in Firstborn's voice, but also desperation. He sounded like one of the kids in school who — when caught in a lie by a teacher — just kept repeating the lie louder and with more intensity, hoping to wear the teacher down.

Rex knew he needed to say something, but he couldn't even form a word. Firstborn seemed so powerful, so . . . *cool*.

Now Firstborn played to the crowd, raising his arms, turning and staring at anyone who would meet his gaze. "What all of you smell, it is a ruse. It is impossible!"

Then a new voice, the cutting hiss of an old lady. "And how do *you* know it is impossible?"

The crowd parted for a woman wearing a long gray skirt, a brown sweater and an orange scarf tied over her head and under her chin. She was kind of fat and hunched over a little bit. Everyone fell quiet as she walked across the deck. Firstborn watched her approach, but her eyes were only on Rex.

The woman stopped right in front of Rex. Rex didn't move. She put her hands on his shoulders, leaned in and took a big sniff. Her eyes closed. She leaned back.

"Finally," she said. "We have waited for so long."

Firstborn's gray-speckled lip curled up, showing the sharp teeth behind. "Not you too, Hillary. This can't be the king."

She turned on him, wrinkled eyes narrowing. "And how would you know that? How would you *know* this boy could not be the king?"

Firstborn started to answer, then stopped. All his power seemed to vanish.

She stepped closer to Firstborn, reached up to shake her bony finger in his face. "You say it is impossible because you have killed babies that could be the king!"

The crowd gasped. The mood of the cavern seemed to change instantly. Rex stood very still — it suddenly felt like something bad was about to happen.

Firstborn spoke in a calm voice. "That's ridiculous. The only babies I killed are the ones that came out human. We have enough mouths to feed as it is."

"You *lie!*" Hillary wheeled to face the crowd. "I have *seen* Firstborn kill the babies, the babies that could be kings, the ones" — she pointed at Rex — "that smelled like *him.*"

Firstborn laughed, but the sound was hollow, forced. "And if I killed these babies, Hillary, then how is it that this boy stands here claiming to be king?"

She spoke in a low hiss that was easily audible over the silence. "How do I know? Because for eighty years, I have been taking the ones that could be kings and sneaking them out of Home. This boy, the one who stands here, I made sure he made it to the surface thirteen years ago."

Firstborn stared. He blinked, slowly, almost as if he couldn't understand what Hillary was saying. "You took them out? You know not what you have done."

"But I know what *you* did," she said. "You kill our kings because you want all the power for yourself!"

"Don't be insane," Firstborn said, but the crowd's growing roar drowned out his words. A circle of strange bodies started to close in around him. The big-headed man and the black-haired woman pushed back against the crowd.

Firstborn stood tall. "This isn't about *power.* This is about keeping our kind alive. A king will lead you all to your deaths — I will do what has to be done."

The big, black-furred man's eyes locked on Rex's, and in that moment Rex felt the depths of Firstborn's rage, knew that the creature wouldn't think twice about killing anyone in this cavern to get what he wanted.

Rex saw a brief sneer, then Firstborn rushed in, claw-tipped hands reaching out. The tall creature bellowed a roar that rooted Rex to the spot.

Sly and Pierre shot forward and slammed into the oncoming Firstborn, stopping him short — the points of his black claws swiped just inches from Rex's eye. Firstborn's knee shot up, snapping Pierre's head back. Two black-furred hands lifted Sly as if the snake-man weighed nothing at all, then threw him hard into the crowd.

Rex had never imagined someone could be that fast, that powerful.

As Firstborn turned again to attack, a shadow passed over Rex's head — Fort stepping over him to block the way.

From Fort's back, Sir Voh raised a tiny hand. "Save the king!"

The crowd roared and rushed in. Bonehead swung and hit a white-scaled man, but then went down under a pile of bodies. A normal-looking man reached for the black-haired woman. She reached for the chains on her hips but the man was on her before she could get them. She ducked a punch, then shoved her hands against the man's chest — there was a flash and a loud *crack*. The man twitched violently and fell. The woman turned to do the same to her next attacker, but a blanket-clad person hit her from behind, knocking her to the deck. In seconds, a dozen people covered her, twisted her hands behind her back.

The crowd cautiously closed in on Firstborn.

He let out a primitive growl that made people flinch away, then reached for the guns strapped to his thighs as he once again rushed at Rex.

Fort stepped toward Firstborn and swung his big right fist. Firstborn sprang high — Fort's punch whiffed harmlessly beneath. Still arcing through the air, Firstborn aimed his pistols. Rex moved by instinct, diving between Fort's barrel-like legs, hiding under the bigger man's mass.

Firstborn fired, *bam-bam-bam-bam-bam*, trying to adjust his aim even as he descended, but it was too late for him. When he came down, dozens of hands reached up to grab his feet, his legs, his arms, his chest. The leader of Marie's Children went down under a kicking, punching pile of bodies.

Sly stood. "Kill Firstborn! Kill him for the king!"

Bleeding from bullet holes in his shoulder and the leg, Fort lumbered to the pile of bodies. He tossed people aside until he reached his giant left hand down and pinned Firstborn facedown on the deck. Fort put a knee in Firstborn's back, then grabbed the man's wrists and held them firm.

As strong as Firstborn was, he couldn't move.

Sly walked forward. He picked up one of Firstborn's pistols. His snake mouth smiled and laughed as he pressed the muzzle against Firstborn's gray-streaked temple.

"I've been waiting for this, asshole," Sly said. "Been waiting a long time."

The crowd shouted for blood.

Firstborn looked at Rex. The green eyes looked lost, desperate — the brave knight, brought low.

Rex held out a hand. "Stop! Don't kill him."

The crowd's murmur died away.

Sly didn't move the gun. His smile faded. "But he has to die, my king. He just tried to kill you."

Rex couldn't shake off Firstborn's words. The tall man had said his murderous ways weren't about keeping power. Why would he say that? He could have been lying, but it didn't *seem* like he was.

Sly looked down at Firstborn. "He *must* die," Sly said. "Him and all his rules, and the way he treats us!"

The crowd murmured approval — they wanted Firstborn dead almost as much as Sly did. But they weren't thinking straight, none of them were. Rex knew he had to step up. His destiny began right now.

He walked forward and held out his hand, palm up. "Give me the gun."

Sly stared back for a moment, then once again smiled wide. "Of course. The new king should kill the old ruler." He handed the gun over butt-first.

Rex took it. He'd never held a gun before. It was heavier than he'd thought it would be. It felt good in his hand.

Firstborn was pinned down and overwhelmed by numbers, yet even now he seemed more dangerous than all the rest.

Rex squatted on his heels. "Firstborn, you said I'd lead everyone to their deaths. What did you mean?"

Sly shook his head. "Just *shoot* him already. Don't let him speak his lies."

Rex looked up at him. "Sly, be *quiet*." Rex didn't even recognize his own voice — such command, such confidence. Sly's eyes narrowed in frustration, maybe even in anger.

Rex again looked down at Firstborn. "Tell me. Tell me what you meant."

Head craned to the side, Firstborn stared back. There was no fear in his eyes. "You aren't the first," he said. "The kings bring disaster upon us."

Rex looked at the gun in his hand. He could kill this man and be done with it. He would be king, but he didn't know how to rule. Firstborn had been in charge for how long? Decades? *Centuries?* Firstborn was tough and strong and smart — he wouldn't die in some accident like Rex's dad had.

Firstborn would always be here.

Rex set the gun on the deck's dry, splintered wood. "I am your king, Firstborn. Say it."

Sly grabbed Rex's arm. "No, my king! You *can't* let him live! He will try to kill you!"

Hillary walked up, her hands clasped in front of her as if she were praying. "Sly is right," she said. "Firstborn killed the other kings. I have seen him crush babies in his bare hands when he thought no one was looking."

Firstborn said nothing. He just kept staring.

Rex felt a new strength surging through him. All these people, they were *his* to command. This was his birthright. If he wanted Firstborn to follow, then Firstborn *would* follow.

Rex stared into the slanted green eyes. "You killed babies. I'm not a baby anymore. I am your king."

Firstborn managed to shake his head. "It cannot be."

His nostrils flared, then his eyes widened. Had his pupils dilated? In that instant, Rex knew what to do — he didn't know how, but he *knew*. He held out his right wrist, pushed it close to Firstborn's face. The black-furred man tried to look away, but he was pinned facedown on the deck and there was nowhere to turn.

Rex reached out with his left hand, simultaneously pinning Firstborn's head to the deck and tightly covering the black-furred mouth. He shoved his right wrist closer.

Firstborn held his breath.

"I am your king," Rex said. "Things will be different this time."

Rex waited. Firstborn could avoid it no further; his nostrils flared wide as he drew in a big breath. Rex sensed a calmness spread over the pinned man.

He's yours. Just like all the others.

A desperate, sandpaper voice whispered at his ear. "At least make it so he can't just kill you and take power again. Remove his temptation and he'll follow."

Yes, that was smart. If Rex suddenly died a day from now, a month from now, the people would again fall under Firstborn's rule. Take that away, and Firstborn would truly be his.

Rex stood. He felt like a different person. "I am the king now," he said, turning slowly to look at each and every one of them. "I am king, and you all have to do what I say. My first command is this — if anything happens to me, if I die, then all of you will *kill* Firstborn. Do you understand?"

Many heads nodded, but not *enough* heads. Rex's lip curled into a sneer — who did they think they were dealing with?

"I said, do you understand? *You hear me talking to you?*"

His words echoed off the walls. Was that really his voice? Could it *really* be that loud, that powerful, or was that a trick of the confined space?

Now the heads nodded, nodded and looked away from him as if they were afraid to meet his eyes. Maybe they should be afraid, at least a little.

Rex looked at Fort. "Let him up."

Fort stood. So did Firstborn.

Off to Rex's left, Hillary knelt on one knee. Like living dominoes, the others did the same, everyone dropping until only Rex, Sly and Firstborn stood.

Sly stared at Firstborn, then Rex, then he, too, knelt.

Some of the kneeling people were still taller than Rex, but Firstborn towered over them all.

The big creature moved closer.

Rex stepped forward to meet him. To stare into the man's eyes, Rex had to look almost straight up.

"Kneel," Rex said. "I am your king."

Firstborn snarled. Sly started to rise, as did Pierre, but Rex held up a hand to stop them.

This was real, this was destiny. Rex was the chosen one. He stared up into Firstborn's eyes. Rex feared no one. Everyone would submit to him. *Everyone.*

Firstborn's snarl faded. His grayed muzzle relaxed. He tried to hold eye contact, but he could not — he looked away.

And then, Firstborn knelt.

"My king," he said. "Welcome home."

The cheer of the people rang off the cavern walls.

A New Day

Bryan shut the Buick's door. He looked up at 1969 California Street. The Jessups would have answers, *had* to have answers. If they didn't . . . well, then for their sake he hoped they knew someone who did.

Bryan walked to the rusted gate door. He pressed the buzzer. He looked through the diagonal bars to the house's door atop the stairs. Nothing moved.

The air felt cool on his face. He reached up, felt the short, neat beard on his cheeks and chin. He'd left Robin in bed, asleep, but he had trimmed his ridiculous tangle before coming out here. He'd left her a fresh pot of coffee and a note on the dining room table: I LOVE YOU.

They'd slept through the morning and well into the afternoon. Robin must have needed sleep in a bad way, as she didn't wake up when Bryan slid out of bed. That was good — he had to do this alone. No Robin, no Pookie. Those two might try to temper Bryan's reactions, but he didn't want anyone to temper anything. Playtime was over. Pookie had left a dozen voice mails, each funnier than the last. There was concern within that humor, but Bryan wasn't ready to talk to him yet. John Smith called as well. He'd left a long-ass message that connected a lot of dots about Chief Zou and Erickson.

Bryan pressed the buzzer again. He ran his hands along the stylishly rusted gate's half-inch-thick crisscrossing bars. The thing looked like it could hold back a charging rhino. Yeah, the Jessups knew what kind of dangers ran through this city, and they guarded against them.

Moments later, the interior door opened. Adam Jessup bounced down the stairs. His silver jewelry and black rocker outfit looked identical to the last time except now he wore a BULLET FOR MY VALENTINE concert T-shirt instead of the one that had read KILLSWITCH ENGAGE.

"Not you again," he said with a sneer. "You ain't getting in this time without a warrant, cop. You got a warrant?"

Who did this little *fuck* think he was?

In one whip-snap motion, Bryan reached through the bars, grabbed the back of Adam's neck and yanked him forward, pinning the man's face hard against the rusted iron.

"If *warrant* means will I break your fucking neck if you don't open this door, then yeah, I got a warrant."

Adam clawed at Bryan's hand, so Bryan squeezed harder. Adam winced, tried to say something, but he couldn't get a word out.

"You should open the gate now," Bryan said. "Then the pain might go away."

Adam's hands flailed at the gate's inside handle. Bryan heard a *click* and the door opened. He pushed Adam away — it seemed like a light push, but Adam flew back to crash into the stone steps.

Byran walked inside and closed the gate-door behind him. He saw Adam lying there, moaning, hands rubbing his throat. Bryan's mind seemed to clear. Had he done that to Adam? He had, and for what?

Because he pissed you off.

Bryan stepped forward and reached out a hand to help Adam up when the *whuff* of a silenced gun coincided with a shredded white spot appearing in the floor between his feet.

Bryan froze, moving only enough to look up to the stairs that led into the house. On the top step stood Alder Jessup, who was pointing his cane at Bryan's chest.

"That will be quite enough," Alder said.

A thin curl of smoke wafted out of the cane's hollow bottom.

"A cane-gun?" Bryan said. "Seriously?"

Alder nodded. "Just sit down where you are. I've got four more shots in this weapon. Move and I'll kill you."

Bryan studied the old man. Alder was leaning against the wall — he couldn't even stand without using the cane for help. And yet the man's hands looked rock-steady, as did the barrel of the cane-gun.

Bryan sat.

Alder eased himself down until he sat on the top step. The cane-gun now rested on his right knee, barrel still pointed at Bryan.

"Why are you here?" Alder said. "Why are you assaulting my grandson?"

Adam held his lower back with one hand, his bleeding nose with the other.

Bryan shrugged. "Sorry about that. I, uh, I guess I got a little mad."

Alder nodded. "Then I would hate to see you when you lose your temper. Again, why are you here?"

"I want answers," Bryan said. "I want *all* the answers. I want to know how Jebediah Erickson can do what he does when he's in his seventies. I want to know why he kills Marie's Children. I want to know why he tried to kill *me.*"

Adam stood, wincing from the pain. "Uncle Jeb didn't try to kill you, shit for brains. He wouldn't try to kill a cop."

"Then I guess he just shot me for shits and giggles."

Alder's eyes narrowed. "He shot you? You must have been with someone else. Who was with you at the time?"

"Other cops," Bryan said. "But he didn't try to kill them. He wanted *me*."

Alder and Adam exchanged a nervous glance.

Adam started slowly backing up the stairs. His arrogant attitude had vanished. "I don't believe Uncle Jeb shot you. Show me where."

Bryan reached to unzip his sweatshirt before he remembered — the bullet wound had already healed. Healed because he was a Zed, because he was one of Marie's Children. In his morning optimism, flush with the good feeling of finally opening up to Robin, he'd managed to keep that little fact out of his thoughts. He let his hand drop to his lap.

"Grampa," Adam said, "he's one of the monsters. Kill him now."

Bryan didn't say anything. He stared at the bullet chip in the floor. He *was* a monster. He'd lost it with Adam, and for almost no reason. He could have snapped Adam's neck. A part of him had *wanted* to do just that.

Maybe Alder's bullet was the best thing for everyone.

"Do it, Gramps," Bryan said. "Pull the trigger."

Alder shook his head. "I will not."

Adam walked up the stairs to his grandfather. "Then give me the cane. I'll do it."

"Shut up," Alder said.

"But, Grampa, he—"

"Adam, *shut your mouth*!"

Adam took a step back and fell silent.

Alder lowered the cane. He slowly pushed himself up. He put the end of the cane on the top step and left it there, using it to help him stay standing. "Inspector Clauser, you said Erickson tried to kill you. I've never known him to fail. Why didn't he finish the job?"

Bryan again looked at the chip in the floor. "Because I stabbed him."

"Stabbed him," Alder echoed. "What, exactly, did you stab him with?"

"His own knife," Bryan said. He looked up. "A big silver one."

Alder and Adam exchanged glances again. Their expressions hinted at panic.

"His knife?" Adam said. "Is he *dead*?"

"No. Not yet, anyway. He's in the hospital."

Alder shook his head sadly. "This is my fault. I just assumed Zou would handle it. She always has in the past. How could she let this happen?"

"Don't blame her," Bryan said, surprised to hear those words come out of his mouth. "She tried to stop us. We didn't listen. We couldn't let a vigilante run wild."

Alder's face wrinkled in scorn. "A *vigilante*? I can't believe anyone could be that naive. Do you have *any* idea what we're dealing with?"

Images of stuffed monsters flashed through Bryan's thoughts. He nodded. "I saw Erickson's basement."

"Good," Alder said. "You seem smart enough to believe what your eyes show you."

Even from the first dream, a part of Bryan had known it was all real. The basement only confirmed that. "This wouldn't have happened if Zou and Erickson — and *you*, for that matter — hadn't kept this a secret."

Alder sighed and shook his head. "Clearly, I was wrong about you being smart."

"People need to know," Bryan said. "We're talking about actual fucking *monsters* here."

Adam spit blood onto the stairs. "Uncle Jeb tried telling the truth once, after Zou tracked his ass down back in the day. He told people all about the monsters, and you know where he wound up? The loony bin."

"But there's proof," Bryan said. "All those stuffed creatures in his basement."

Alder walked down the stairs, again using his cane as just that — a cane. "You're missing the obvious, Inspector. You never heard of *monsters* before this, because the monsters can't be found by the police. They are hunters, so skilled that no one knows they exist, even when they murder their victims or take people away to wherever it is they take them. The only one who can find them, who can *stop* them, is Erickson. And, now, maybe you.

"The nightmarish ones Erickson stuffed — maybe the public will believe those are real, maybe they won't, but believe it or not those creatures aren't the biggest problem. You saw that some of Erickson's trophies looked like regular people?"

Bryan thought back to the man with the hatchet. "Yes, there were a few."

Alder reached the bottom step. "Stand up."

Bryan did.

"The problem is the ones that look like *us*," Alder said. "Erickson looks like us. *You* look like us. If you show the world the monsters, and show them that some of the monsters look like regular people, what do you think would happen?"

Bryan thought of Robin, of her little machine that could quickly and easily test for the Zed chromosome. If people knew that some of the monsters looked like regular people, there would be a campaign to test everyone. And if someone other than Robin tested Bryan, found out he was one of them . . .

"Maybe they find a reason to put me away," he said.

Alder nodded. "And if that happens, Inspector Clauser, who will be left to find the monsters that can't be found? Who will stop them from killing at will?"

What if Alder was right? Would anyone trust a man with the Zed chromosome? No, not if they also found out about the creatures. This was all so fucked up. No one would trust his kind, not without a civil rights campaign, education — things that took years if not decades.

Erickson had been locked up once. Because of that, hundreds of people had died. Erickson was still in the hospital — did that mean Bryan was the only one who could find the monsters?

Maybe someday soon Bryan would let the world know. Robin could help. She could get the scientific community behind it, try to use facts to temper the public's probable reaction. Someday, but today was not that day.

"Okay," Bryan said. "You're right. We keep the secret. So what do we do now?"

Alder tapped his cane on the floor twice, *click-click*. "We have to go to the hospital. If Marie's Children find out Savior is hurt, they might come after him. You need to help us protect Erickson until he heals."

Bryan shook his head. "I can't go to the hospital."

"Why?"

"Well, I sort of got fired."

Adam rolled his eyes. "Well, that's just fucking fantastic. Thank *goodness* we have you on our side. Such an asset to the team."

Alder didn't seem phased by the news. He looked Bryan up and down, then turned to his grandson. "Adam. I think the time has come for a new Savior."

Adam stared at his grandfather for a moment, then started laughing. "A *pig*? Grampa, have you been taking too many meds? There's no way we can—"

"Adam! There isn't any other choice! It has to be Bryan."

Has to be Bryan? What were they talking about? Alder didn't mean . . .

"Me? You want *me* to be a Savior?"

Alder nodded. "Except for Jebediah, all the other Saviors are dead. This is your destiny."

"*Destiny?* Give me a break, man. I've got some messed-up genetics and a family that lied to me my whole life. That's *tragedy,* not *destiny.* What's next? You going to tell me *everything happens for a reason?*"

Alder shook his head. "No. I'm going to tell you that if you don't help us, Erickson may die and this city will turn into a hellhole."

Bryan thought of the shark-toothed man on the embalming table. He'd *felt* that man's fear in a nightmare, *felt* the terror at the unforgiving hands of Savior.

"Erickson tried to kill me. If I save him, am I going to wind up stuffed in that basement?"

Alder shook his head. "Jebediah reacted on instinct. For so long, he's been the only one hunting Marie's Children. But if you join us, Bryan, we will have *two* Saviors. You could hunt together."

Hunt together. Erickson was his half-brother. So were all the other obscenities, but Erickson wasn't like them; he was a *protector,* not a *murderer.* A harsh reality hit home — Jebediah Erickson might be the only true family Bryan could ever have.

He shook his head. "I don't know. This all sounds crazy, I'm just trying to figure out what to do next."

Alder nodded. "That's logical. But won't you at least see what we have to offer? I realize the last basement you saw may have been disturbing, but if you're anything like Jebediah, you'll find our basement far more to your liking"

Alder and Adam walked deeper into the house.

Bryan didn't know what else to do, so he followed.

The Kingdom

So many babies.

The nursery was the final stop on Rex's tour of his new realm. Hillary had been so eager to show him everything. Sly and Pierre came with, of course.

Realm. That was a cool word; he'd read about realms in his many fantasy stories, played in them on video games. It was just a cooler word than *kingdom.* And this really wasn't a kingdom, anyway. The tour showed him that.

A *kingdom* was a huge thing, sprawling as far as the eye could see. Home wasn't that big, just a collection of the two large caverns, two smaller caverns, thirteen isolated clusters of caves, and — of course — tunnels, tunnels and more tunnels. He'd seen the library (it had dehumidifiers to keep the books dry), the kitchen (complete with what was left of Alex, who tasted delicious), the theater (they had an old, giant-sized TV and a copy of just about every movie Rex had ever heard of) and the armory that held all the guns. *Lots* of guns. Hillary and Sly told him that there were other tunnel clusters elsewhere in the city, but those would have to wait. He had seen the main areas of Home, then finished up at the nursery.

Dozens of old bassinets, beat-up cribs and even metal tubs with blankets lined the edges of the small room. Babies of different shapes and colors lay in most of these things. Women — both strange-looking and normal — tended to the babies, cuddled them, took care of them when they cried. *So much love.* Secondhand toys littered the floor.

Giggling little kids also scurried through the room. When they saw Rex, they ran to him. He recognized Vanilla Gorilla, Crabapple Bob and the other children who had chased Alex down and torn him to pieces. Hands reached to Rex, tugged at his clothes — these children wanted to be picked up and held. Some were too big for that, and at any rate, that probably wasn't kingly behavior.

"Sly," he said, and that was all he had to say. Sly made fake roaring noises and picked the children up, tossing them lightly away. The children squealed and laughed, but they gave Rex space.

Such a happy place, at least on the surface. The more Rex looked around, the more he noticed the bad things — many of the babies just lay there. Some were coughing lightly, some cried and whimpered. Most of them looked *sick*.

"Hillary, what's wrong with them?"

Hillary reached into a metal tub and gently lifted a yellow-skinned child who had just one big, blue eye in the middle of its face. The eyelid drooped half shut, and the eye seemed to stare out into nothing. She cradled the child in her arms.

"Mommy is old," Hillary said. "Old even for us."

"How old is she?"

Hillary shrugged. "I was born in 1864. Mommy was at least fifty when she had me."

Hillary was a hundred and fifty years old? Holy shit! Would Rex live that long? Maybe even longer than that, because Mommy was already *two hundred* years old.

Hillary lifted the child and kissed its forehead. "Mommy has as many babies as she used to, but the older she gets, the more of them that are born dead. Those who live are often sickly. Most of the children do not make it past their first birthday."

Rex again looked around the room, taking in the numbers. These babies were his brothers and sisters — how many of them would just *die*? It was terrible and heartbreaking; it hurt to even think about it. "What about doctors? Can't we take them to a hospital?"

Hillary shrugged as she gently rocked the one-eyed baby. "Could we take this one to the hospital? I think not. We do all we can, but even if we had medicine, we wouldn't know which kind to give. This is why I worked so hard to bring in a new king, so that the people could spread. If our kind is to survive, we *have* to spread."

Many of these babies would die, and yet Firstborn killed baby kings? Why would anyone kill children? Rex wondered if he had made a mistake by sparing Firstborn's life. Maybe, but there was something about that tall man, something great.

There had to be a *reason* why Firstborn killed babies.

"Sly, where does Firstborn live?"

"In a room on the *Alamandralina*, the ship you saw when you first got here," Sly said. "Firstborn has it good — his room is the nicest place in all of Home."

"Take me there," Rex said. "If he's not there already, you take Pierre and Fort and whoever else you need and *bring* him. He doesn't have a choice."

Gear

The Jessups' basement had a workbench identical to the one at Erickson's house. Bryan looked over the gear — rig for bow maintenance and repair, barrel of arrow shafts, rack of polished arrowheads, a custom gun rack holding four Fabrique Nationale five-sevens and three USAS-12 semiautomatic shotguns. It was clearly a backup base of operations for Erickson, in case anything happened to his house.

The Jessups also had several spotless fabricating machines: drills, presses, grinding wheels and more. One entire wall held a rack of gray plastic pull-out bins, each neatly labeled with names of various parts or components. A place for everything, and everything in its anal-retentive place.

At the back end of the basement sat a fully equipped hospital bed. A wheelchair sat next to it. Like everything else in the basement, both bed and chair gleamed from what had to be a daily cleaning. They also had a heart monitor, an autoclave, a portable x-ray machine, a rack of medical supplies and some other equipment Bryan didn't recognize. He wondered if the stainless-steel fridge next to the bed contained supplies of Erickson's blood.

"You guys into home health care?"

"It's for Jebediah," Alder said. "Occasionally he is injured when fighting Marie's Children."

Had the bear-thing in Erickson's basement drawn blood? Maybe taken a pound of flesh? He wondered what happened if Erickson/Savior was wounded in the field. Who would bail him out?

"You guys ever help Erickson go after Marie's Children?"

Alder shrugged. "Sometimes he asks for our assistance."

Bryan looked at the Jessups for what they were: an old man who could barely walk and a scrawny loudmouth. He made a mental note that if he did become a monster-hunter — as ridiculous as that sounded — he'd find more reliable backup than these two.

Alder seemed to sag a little. He walked to a chair and slowly sat.

Adam ran to him. "Grampa, you okay?"

The old man nodded. "I'm fine. I just need to rest for a second. Adam, give Bryan what he needs."

Adam nodded. His snotty attitude seemed to vanish as he pulled two flat-black five-sevens out of the rack and set them down on the workshop table. Bryan picked one up, feeling the weight. He ejected the twenty-round magazine and saw that the bullets were tipped in black — the rounds were armor-piercing SS190s.

"These are illegal," Bryan said.

"Uh-oh," Adam said. He held out his wrists. "Better slap the cuffs on me. Oh, wait, you sorta got fired."

He walked to a bin and pulled out a rolled-up canvas rig. "Try this on," he said, and tossed it to Bryan.

Bryan unfolded it. The rig held two holsters at the small of the back, three loaded magazines on the left shoulder strap, another three on the right. He unzipped his sweatshirt and set it on the workbench, then slid his arms through the rig's shoulder straps and fastened the belt around his waist. Bryan picked up the five-sevens, reached behind his back and slid them into the holsters. The guns clicked home, the barrels pointing down toward his ass and the handles pointing out to his sides. He imagined they looked like a buck-steel butterfly back there.

He held his hands in front of him, then whipped them to the small of his back, grabbed the handles and drew. The guns came out smooth and clean. He repeated the action three times — so natural, so intuitive.

He holstered them again. "What about a knife? Like Erickson had?"

Adam pulled a box out of a bin and handed it over. Bryan opened it to find a flat-black Ka-Bar knife. The edge gleamed with sharpness, but the flat of the blade also had a strange shimmer. Bryan ran his finger along the flat, wiping off a streak of gel.

"Don't do that," Alder said.

"Why?" Bryan said, but even as he said it he felt his fingertip start to burn.

Alder sighed. "Because it's poisonous to you, that's why."

Adam handed Bryan a rag.

Bryan quickly rubbed off the burning material. "We found paste on Erickson's arrowhead. Is this the same stuff? How does it work?"

Adam nodded. "In case you haven't figured it out yet, Marie's Children heal very quickly. Uncle Jeb says they can heal up from just about anything shy of a disembowelment or decapitation. The silver paste blocks that ability, meaning a wound that would be fatal to a normal man is also fatal to them."

Bryan fastened the knife through his belt to hang on his left hip. "So why the arrows and the knives and shit? Why not just make the bullets out of the material?"

"The specific material won't form a solid," Adam said. "As a paste, it sticks to the damaged tissue. If it's a liquid or even a powder, the monsters' systems just move it along and they heal up. The paste would just burn off of a bullet in flight. Bullets also have a nasty habit of going through a body, not lodging in place. The best way to kill these bastards is to stick them with something that has the paste on it, and make sure that something *stays* stuck. That's why we make the broadheads the way we do."

Bryan drew the knife. "Does this stick?"

"Does if you hold it in," Adam said. "Shove it in and stay there for a while, which isn't as naughty as it sounds."

Bryan put the knife back in the sheath. "So why is Erickson still in the hospital?"

Alder stood, grunting a little as he rose to his feet. "Because he's like me — he's *old*. He's not healing as fast as he used to. You must have hit him in a vital spot. His body is healing, but the paste slows it. Let that be a valuable lesson to you, Inspector — if you want to kill one of them, it's best if you stab them in the heart, not the belly."

"Or the brain," Adam said. "Or cut off their heads, that'll work."

Bryan realized he might have to bury that blade in the chest of a bear-thing, or maybe even a little girl holding a fork and a knife.

"How'd you guys come up with the paste?"

Alder laughed. "Oh, for that part we are merely cooks reading from a recipe. The formula originated in Europe several centuries ago. There was a time when these creatures were more plentiful. Alchemists, and then eventually chemists after them, had many subjects upon which to experiment."

"Experiments?"

Alder nodded. "Monsters were cut up very slowly. Alchemists experimented with different mixtures, slowly testing them on their subjects. Sometimes the creatures stayed alive for months. The researches finally found a compound that worked, and it has been used ever since. But we can talk about that some other time. Adam, show Bryan the greatest prize of them all."

Adam walked to a metal case set against the wall. He set the case on the workbench, opened it and pulled out a beautiful bow made of steel and wood. He offered the bow to Bryan.

Bryan didn't take it. He looked at it, then looked up at Adam. "What am I supposed to do with this?"

"Shoot it, stupid."

"I don't know how to shoot a bow. I've never shot one in my life."

Alder seemed stunned.

Adam started laughing. He set the bow back in the case. "What did you think, Grampa, that he'd just be a natural?"

"I thought . . . well, yes," Alder said. "It never crossed my mind he wouldn't know how to shoot."

Bryan reached out and ran his fingertips along the bow. He had to admit that it was a beautiful, elegant weapon. "Maybe I'll work my way up to that. Got anything else that would give me a little range?"

Adam pointed to a drawer. "Stun grenades?"

"In a hospital?" Bryan said. "I don't think so."

Adam nodded. He walked to another drawer and pulled a contraption of straps, buckles, and a lethal-looking blade packed in on top of a compressed metal coil. "Spring-loaded knife," he said as he handed it over. "Six-inch titanium blade that will arrive at its destination with an agenda and a bad attitude. And before you try to test the edge, genius, the answer is *yeah*, it's poisoned."

Bryan strapped it underneath his left forearm. Adam showed him the mechanism — a rapid wrist-flick up would fire the heavy blade.

Alder tapped his cane twice on the floor. "And now for the *pièce de résistance*." He walked to a cabinet. With great dramatic flair, he opened the cabinet and pulled out a green cloak. He held it forward, a proud smile playing at the corners of his mouth.

"Inspector Bryan Clauser, this cloak is the mark of the Saviors. We are asking you to embrace this role, to become one of us."

Bryan stared at the cloak. "I'm going into a hospital," he said. "I don't think Sherwood Forest is on the way."

Adam started laughing again. He covered his face with his hands, as if to say *oh man, you stepped in it this time.*

Alder's face screwed up into a mask of contempt. "A half hour ago, Inspector, I could have shot you as a monster. Now you are a Savior, and you won't wear the cloak? Just who in the *hell* do you think you are?"

Bryan tried not to laugh, but he made the mistake of looking at Adam who still had his face in his hands and was shaking his head. Despite the mutant chromosome, the killing dreams, a ruined career and a trail of corpses, Bryan couldn't suppress a smirk as the situation's absurdity caught up with him — this old man not only wanted to dress Bryan up like a superhero, but he couldn't fathom that Bryan wasn't oh-so-excited about the idea.

Alder held the cloak up again, as if Bryan hadn't really seen it the first time. "But it's bulletproof."

Bryan tried to squeeze back the laughter, but he couldn't. "Uh, can't I heal real fast?"

"Of course," Alder said. "But healing won't put your liver back in your body if they shoot it out of you."

Bryan stopped laughing. "The monsters use guns?"

"Of *course* they use guns," Alder said. "Guns work. They're monsters, not idiots."

So they could claw him, bite him, *and* they could put a couple of rounds in him as well? As Pookie would say, *awesome.* Still, though, the cloak was too damn conspicuous.

"As far as I know, Chief Zou is going to throw me in jail the second she sees me," Bryan said. "So I'll stick to my usual clothes."

Adam took the cloak from his mystified grandfather and hung it back up in the cabinet. "If you change your mind, cop, I've got some other stuff you could try." He shut the door.

Alder huffed. "Adam, he is not going to wear that ridiculous outfit you came up with. We have *tradition.* The disrespect of today's youth, I swear." He turned back to Bryan. "And don't you worry about Amy Zou. I'll handle her. We'd best get to the hospital."

The old man was right. If Bryan wanted to help Erickson, he couldn't do it from the Jessups' basement. Like it or not, Jebediah Erickson was Bryan's brother. He was *family,* something that Bryan wanted desperately.

"Okay," Bryan said. "Let's do it. Am I driving, or do you guys have a car?"

Adam started laughing again.

Council Meeting

During Rex's tour, he'd seen that the people of Home made do with very little. Some had electricity, but most did not. Dampness hung in the air. Gleaming moisture covered many walls. In some places tiny streams trickled along eroded rivulets in tunnel floors. For most, Home was whatever they carved out of centuries-old landfill.

That made Firstborn's quarters in the *Alamandralina* look like a palace.

Rex knew the room wasn't part of the original ship, because the floor was level. The wood here was beautiful — deep browns sanded smooth, any holes long-since filled in, glossy lacquer reflecting light from both the electric chandelier hanging above and the dancing flames of dozens of candles in each corner. Thick rugs lined the floors. Decorations hung on the walls, mostly designs carved into human bones and skulls. Where there weren't bones, Rex saw maps: tourist maps, Muni maps, hand-drawn sketches, a map of the Golden Gate National Recreation Area, another of Alcatraz Island — and every map showed hand-drawn tunnel systems.

The maps illustrated something Sly had said: there were many places to hide.

Rex sat at the head of a long, black table. Behind him and to the left stood Fort, Sir Voh curled up on his thick neck. Behind and to the right stood Pierre, who held a shotgun with some kind of a drum clip. It was a big gun, but in his hands it looked like a toy.

Sly sat at the right side of the table, Hillary at the left.

Firstborn sat on the other end — no weapons for him. Was he still a threat? Sly thought so. Rex trusted Sly, but he had to figure this out for himself.

The black-furred man was the oldest of them all except for Mommy. It wasn't just his age or the gray muzzle — he had this air about him, a sense of importance. He really was like a knight, plucked right out of a movie and brought into the modern world.

"I have stuff I want to know," Rex said. "First of all, what's happening to me? I'm getting stronger, I can feel it. And I can heal, like, *really* quick. I wasn't like that before. How come I am now?"

Hillary answered. "If you had grown up here, you would have been strong and fast like the other children. It's because of smells. Down here, smells are everywhere. Up there, no smells, so you were like *them*. But I knew where you were, my king. I waited until the right age to send Sly up to put smells by your house."

"Smells," Rex said, the word drawing forth the wispy memory of a strange scent. "Wait a minute. Before I got real sick, I smelled pee around my house. Are you saying I changed because someone *peed* on my house?"

Sly stood and bowed dramatically. "I had the honor, my king. I'm so proud to know my scent brought you to us."

"But that's gross," Rex said. "Totally gross."

Hillary laughed. "Smells are just another way of talking. Soldiers mark their kills, a way of telling everyone *I am the one that did this*."

That made Rex think of Marco peeing on the dead cop. Poor Marco.

Firstborn stared at Sly, slowly shook his head. "I should have known it was you, Sly." He looked at Hillary. "You told Sly to do this?"

She nodded. Hillary glared at Firstborn with defiance and anger, but also a bit of fear.

Firstborn cracked his knuckles. His every motion drew tense looks from Pierre, Sir Voh and Sly.

"You said he wasn't the first, Hillary," Firstborn said. "Have you really been doing this for eighty years?"

Her smile widened. "You think you know everything, but you know *nothing*. Eleven kings I smuggled out, right under your nose. Some I lost track of. Maybe they were taken away by the people who took them in as their own. Some I could not find until it was too late, until they had passed the time that matters for becoming a true king."

Firstborn leaned toward her. Rex heard the shotgun rattle lightly as Pierre adjusted his grip on the weapon.

"But *how*?" Firstborn said. "How could you get them out? How could I have never learned of this?"

"I have secrets," Hillary said. "Secrets I will keep. We can't have new queens without new kings. The people know this, Firstborn, and they hate you for trying to stop it."

His fist banged against the black table. "With your own eyes, you saw the death that a king brings. We don't need new queens. We are fine here."

"Fine?" Hillary scowled. She spread her arms out, the gesture clearly indicating the ship and the caverns beyond. "There is more to life than *this*. Even if we get a new queen, she will never change if she can smell Mommy's scent. If our kind is to spread, we must send kings and queens to new cities. *That* is why I took Rex away. *That* is why I had soldiers watch him grow." She looked at Rex again. Her warm smile returned. "If we had waited too long, you would not have the power to call others to you, to *bind* them to you."

The power to call others — Rex had done that before his fight with Alex Panos. "My dreams. Were my dreams part of calling to others?"

Hillary nodded. "Yes. A king must get the smells while he is young. By fourteen or fifteen years old, if you have not changed, then the ability to call is gone forever."

Fourteen or fifteen was too late. Maybe it had something to do with puberty. Was there science behind it, or was this some kind of magic?

"But *how* does it work?" he said. "What changes me? And how do you know what to do to make someone like me change?"

Hillary clasped her hands in front of her. "It happens because it is God's will. It has always been this way. I know how to make someone change because Mommy told me how when I was little. It was before, when her words still made sense."

God did it? Rex had seen many wonderful things, but he wasn't sure if *God's will* explained all of it. Could it be that his people really didn't know *why* they were so strong, or *how* they changed? He would have to worry about that later — what mattered now was finding out if Firstborn could be trusted.

"Firstborn," Rex said, "what did you mean when you said *the death a king brings*?"

Sly leaned back and crossed his big arms, as if he'd heard this story so many times it bored him. Hillary grew quiet.

Firstborn closed his eyes. "King Geoffrey was born after we arrived in America. San Francisco was much smaller then. It was lawless. Every day, ships brought more people. I was young then — I felt Geoffrey's dreams in my sleep, felt his visions when I was awake."

His shoulders slumped. He looked so sad.

"What about *my* dreams?" Rex said. "Did you get visions from me?"

Firstborn shook his head slowly. "I did not. Perhaps I am too old. Perhaps it is because I did not go up to the surface enough. But I know the power of a king's mind touching mine. I felt it from Geoffrey. We would hunt together. I was by his side, always, but death came when Geoffrey grew so proud he abandoned our rules."

Sir Voh scrambled down Fort's chest and jumped onto the table next to Rex.

"The *rules*," he said. "The rules make us cowards."

Rex looked from the shriveled man with the big head back to First-born. "What are the rules?"

Firstborn opened his eyes. He stared at Rex with a pleading expression that said *listen and truly understand.*

He held up one black-furred finger. "*Never* hunt those who will be missed — take only vagrants, immigrants, people with no home and no one to report them missing." He held up a second finger. "*Never* allow a soldier to be seen. Because of cameras and cell phones, this is a far greater challenge now than when I was young." He held up a third finger. "Finally, *never* let the humans know we exist. We are stronger and faster, we prey on them, but they are so many. Mommy told us stories from the Old Country, handed down for generations, stories of times when the people forgot the rules, and of how the prey would rise up and overwhelm us with numbers. We survive, my king, only because they don't know we exist."

Firstborn looked off to a corner of the room. He stared at a tall candle burning there.

"Geoffrey was arrogant," he said. "He ignored the rules. He let the people hunt openly. Instead of culling the herd for the weak and the un-wanted, we took whoever we liked. Some of us were seen. The *police*" — he spat the word like it was poison — "they found us. Them and the Saviors. They attacked us, *butchered* us. They captured Geoffrey and doz-ens more — soldiers, *ouvriers* . . . even our children. I saw them tied to poles, some with ropes, others with shackles and chains. I saw the towns-folk gathering wood, saw them light the flames. Sometimes when I sleep, I still hear the screams of our people and it makes me want to claw out my own ears."

Rex thought of all the people he'd met down here. He thought of Sly, Pierre and Hillary, the children, the *babies*, all tied to poles and set on fire. Only animals would do such a thing.

That was what humans were . . . *animals.*

"Why didn't you do something?" Rex said. "Why didn't you save them?"

Firstborn hung his head.

Hillary stood. She walked to Firstborn and hugged him. He did not look up.

"He saved Mommy," she said. "And he saved me. I was just a little girl. Firstborn was so *brave*. He killed so many to get us away. He saved the queens so our kind would live on."

Firstborn nodded. A black-furred hand covered his black-furred face.

"Mommy was smaller then, but it was still difficult," he said. "We had to start over." He looked up. Rex saw the pain in his eyes, the fear that all his work would be for nothing and the people would die out.

"The city was changing," Firstborn said. "The ships that brought us and thousands of others, they had been buried in landfill as the city expanded the shoreline. I dug down to one of those ships and made a burrow in the captain's cabin. I brought Mommy down there and sealed her in."

Rex leaned back. "Wait a minute. The ship she's in now, that's the same one?"

Firstborn nodded. "She hasn't moved from that room in a hundred and fifty years. I brought her new grooms. She gave birth to *ouvriers,* to ringers and soldiers. Hillary raised the *ouvriers* until they were old enough to work, while I taught the soldiers how to hunt, taught the ringers how to be our eyes on the surface. We survived. We rebuilt."

Rex looked at his gray-muzzled warrior with a new respect. Everything in these tunnels, every room, every brick, every person — it was all here because of *him.* Firstborn had brought the people back from disaster.

"The rules keep us safe," Firstborn said. "Sometimes the prey has money. The ringers use that money to buy what they can, but most of our food comes the way it always has, from hunting."

Hunting. The word sent a shiver through Rex's spine, made his stomach tingle. He remembered the thrill of stalking Alex all the way to April's house. Rex had *needed* that. The feeling had faded with Alex's death, but the urge was calling once again.

Sly had sat silent during the story. Now he leaned forward and rested his elbows on the black table.

"Our history is important," he said to Firstborn. "But it's just that — *history.* You're forgetting the parts where you ruled like a tyrant, where you didn't just kill babies, you killed people who hunted without your permission."

"We *must not* be discovered," Firstborn said. "That is what drove every decision I made."

Sly rolled his eyes. "Whatever, old man. You're so brave? Then why do you let Savior slaughter our people?" Sly turned to stare at Rex. "Savior is nothing but a *bully,* my king. And Firstborn lets Savior live."

Bullies. Rex thought of Alex, Issac, Jay and Oscar. He thought of Roberta.

Firstborn's eyes narrowed. "You know nothing. My way *works.* You are too young to understand."

Sly stood and snarled. "We *cower*. We are murdered and you ... do ... *nothing*! You forbade us from attacking Savior, from killing the walking nightmare."

Firstborn looked away and waved a hand dismissively. "Everyone knows that Savior kills anyone who tries. To attack him is suicide."

"*Lies!*" Sly pounded a fist against his chest. "If I die trying to kill the killer of my people, that is a life better spent than burrowing in the dirt like a worm." He turned to face Rex. "Savior is hurt, my king. If we could find Savior before he heals, we could end the monster's murdering ways *forever*."

Rex felt Sly's anger, felt it and shared it. Maybe Firstborn didn't know what it was like to be bullied. Firstborn was big and strong. He'd been in charge so long, he couldn't possibly understand what it felt like to live every day in fear.

"Savior is devious," Firstborn said. "He is probably trying to trick us, Sly, tyring to lure us in so he can follow you home and kill Mommy."

Rex looked carefully at Firstborn. The man was lying about something, Rex could tell. What Firstborn said didn't make sense — if they killed Savior, then the people could hunt without fear. Firstborn had secrets. To keep the people safe, he had killed his own kind for over a century. What else had he done? What else had he allowed to happen?

"Sly is right," Rex said. "If you *really* wanted to protect the people, you would kill Savior."

"We have tried," Firstborn said. "Savior kills all who go against him."

Sly crossed his arms and shook his head. He was angry, but also excited — he finally had a chance to say what he wanted to say. "That is not so, my king. Some have gone off on their own and never come back. But others have tried, failed, and come back Home — when they did, *Firstborn* killed them to send a warning to everyone else."

Firstborn stared down at the table. Rex didn't have to ask if the accusation was true — it was clear he had done what Sly said. Rex could *feel* emotions inside of Firstborn: rage, shame, a horrible burden of responsibility ... *loneliness*.

Rex stood and walked to the other end of the table. Hillary stepped aside. Rex put his hand on Firstborn's muscled, furred forearm and gave a little squeeze. "Tell me why. Tell me the truth."

Firstborn looked up, big green eyes hard at first, then softening. There was desparation in those eyes, even *relief* — he had been a villain to his own people, and now he finally had a chance to share the reason.

"We *need* Savior," he said. "Sometimes the urge to hunt becomes too much for some of us. When it does, soldiers hunt beyond the need for food. They hunt just to *kill*, over and over again. They draw attention. If the police find these rogue soldiers, these *insane* soldiers, then the police are that much closer to discovering us again, *slaughtering* us again. By killing the rogue soldiers, Savior unknowingly keeps our secret safe."

Rex let go of Firstborn's arm. *That* was why he let Savior kill? To remove people who disobeyed Firstborn's orders? A true leader — a true *king* — would let no one hurt his people.

He walked back to his seat. "Do the police know about Savior?"

"Of course," Sly said, disgust thick in his words. "The police help him kill our brothers."

The police and Savior, nothing but bullies who wanted to hurt and kill Rex's people. "Sly, how do you know Savior is hurt?"

"I told Tard to watch his house."

Firstborn stood up. "I gave orders that *no one* was to go near the monster's house!"

Rex pointed at him. "*Sit down!* Your orders don't count anymore unless I say so!"

Firstborn's lip curled, showing the edge of a tooth, but he sat.

Rex let out a slow breath. People shouldn't do stuff to make him mad like that. "Do we know where Savior is?"

Sir Voh skittered to the middle of the table. "The police will know," he said. "Tard said cop cars came to his house and followed the ambulance that took him away."

Rex leaned back in his chair. "Do all the police know about us?"

"We think only some," the little creature said. "If all the police knew, the newspeople would probably talk about us but they never do. Fewer people knowing makes it easier to control information."

"So then which ones know?"

Sir Voh shrugged his tiny shoulders, a comical expression considering his much larger head. "We have no way of knowing."

"Sure we do," Sly said. His yellow eyes narrowed in time with his smile. "When you wanted to know the secrets of Marie's Children, you asked Firstborn — you asked our leader. We can do the same with the police."

That made sense. If there was some kind of secret among the police, a pact or whatever, then someone high up would probably know about it. Why not start at the top?

"I won't let the police bully us," Rex said. "We'll get their leader to tell us what she knows. As soon as it's dark, we visit the chief of police."

Hillary stared at Rex like she couldn't believe what she was hearing. "We can't do that. To go after the chief of *police*? It is madness."

Then Firstborn spoke, softly and slowly. "My king, doing that could expose us to discovery."

They wanted to be safe, to play along with the way things had always been? *No.* Firstborn and Hillary had grown too old to do what had to be done. Maybe that was what happened after so long without a king.

Now that a king was here, the way things had always been done wasn't good enough anymore. That night, things would change.

Aggie's Price

Aggie James was alone in the white dungeon. If he'd been a religious man, he would have prayed, but he knew there was no God. God wouldn't have let his wife and daughter be murdered right in front of him. God wouldn't have allowed these monsters to exist. And if God did exist and allowed these things to happen, Aggie sure as fuck wasn't going to worship him.

So while he didn't *pray*, he most certainly *hoped* that he could get out of this horrible place.

The white jail cell door slowly screeched open. Hillary entered, alone, carrying a heavy knit bag and a familiar-looking, familiar-*smelling* blanket. But there was a new scent . . . faint, just a tiny sensation in his nose. It smelled beautiful.

Hillary walked up to him. She held the bag out by its handles, offering it to him. "Are you ready to help me?"

"If you'll let me out of here, hell yes." Aggie took the knit bag and opened it. Inside . . . a baby?

A sleeping baby boy with deep black skin, far blacker than Aggie's, the skin of a child from lower Africa. He was swaddled in a blanket marked with crudely drawn symbols. One symbol looked like a triangle with an eye in the middle, another seemed to be a circle with a jagged lightning bolt through it.

"You take this boy," Hillary said. "I thought the king would make things right, but he is going to do dangerous things. And Firstborn, I think he will try to kill the king. If he succeeds, then he will come for me. I have to act while I still can, get one more baby out."

She stopped talking. She just stared at the child, as if she forgot that Aggie was even there.

"Uh, Hillary?"

Her eyes snapped up. She blinked, seemed to come back to the moment. "I am going to hide you and the baby somewhere."

"Somewhere up on the surface?"

"No," she said. "A special hiding place. You will stay there with the boy until I come to take you above."

Aggie nodded violently even though he didn't really understand. "Yes, I'll do whatever you ask."

She smiled a smile of power. "Of course you will." She unfolded the smelly blanket and draped it around Aggie. "You wear this and be quiet, just like you did yesterday."

He nodded. He really had no idea if he'd last seen her yesterday, the day before or just a few hours ago.

She finished adjusting the blanket, tugging and twisting in her motherly way. "Good," she said. "Now hold him close. *Very* close."

Aggie pulled the baby-filled bag to his chest. Whatever this kid was, it was evil. Aggie would play along, say whatever he had to say, do whatever he had to do until he got out of here. Then he could toss the baby into the bay for all he cared about it.

He smelled that beautiful smell again. It was the baby . . . the smell came from the baby.

"Time to leave," Hillary said. "Follow me."

"Where are we going?"

"You know the place," she said. "We are going back to the arena."

Origin Story

Bryan drove Pookie's Buick, following the Jessups' jet-black, highly modified Dodge Magnum station wagon. Passing streetlights cast sliding reflections off the Magnum's polished body. Bryan had never really thought a station wagon could be sweet. The customized Magnum, however, would make any gangsta wannabe green with envy. It rode on black chrome rims. Tinted windows hid the inside from view. Pull-out drawers packed the cargo area, hidden from view by the rear hatch. Bryan could only imagine what kind of arsenal the grandfather/grandson team had stashed away in the back of that car.

Adam, oddly, drove like an old lady: slow, obeying every traffic light and sign, giving people plenty of room to pass him if need be. Bryan didn't know much about cars, but even following behind he could hear the Magnum's engine gurgling with unused power.

The Magnum turned south on five-lane Potrero Avenue. Two-story houses and small trees passed by on Bryan's right. Just a few blocks now. He had time for one quick call. He dialed. She answered immediately.

"Hello?"

How could just the sound of her voice make him feel better? "Hey."

"Bryan, are you okay?"

"Sure. Didn't you get my note?"

She paused. "I did. Thank you for that. But a nice note and a pot of coffee aren't a replacement for knowing that you're okay."

"I'm okay." He wasn't sure if that was the truth, but it was what she needed to hear. "I just wanted to check in."

She didn't say anything. He waited. Up ahead, he saw SFGH coming up on the left.

"Robin, I gotta go. Erickson might be in trouble tonight."

"Forget him," she said. "Come get me and we'll just *go*."

"What are you talking about?"

"All this death," she said. "You and I could just leave, Bryan. We get in my car, we pick a direction, and we go. Together."

She was afraid for him. Or maybe she was afraid of what he might do. The sentiment broke his heart, but her solution wasn't an option.

"Robin, I can't."

She sighed. "I know. I hope we don't regret it." Her tone of voice changed again, from melancholy to business-like. "Listen, I've been trying to figure out what happened to you. When you were a kid, you had the usual cuts and scrapes, right?"

"Sure," he said.

"And this rapid healing thing, that's new?"

"Yeah. I always seemed to heal a little faster than most people, but nothing like it is now."

"It's because your Zed chromosome was *suppressed*," she said. "That means you had all this genetic information, but it was dormant, your body wasn't doing anything with it. Basically, your Zed information was switched off."

That didn't seem possible. How could you have parts of your body that were shut off? Still, he wasn't about to argue with an expert. "So what switched it on?"

"When you came to see me in the morgue, you were sick, right? *Really* sick, as in body aches, chest pains, all of that?"

How awful he had felt — the fever, the hammering aches, the joint pain. "Yeah, it was bad."

"We need to take x-rays. I bet they'll show the same strange organ we found in Blackbeard. I also bet we find your bones have changed, or at least are starting to change. The sickness was because your body underwent a *massive* physical transformation. The question is, when did you *start* to get sick?"

So much had happened in the past few days. It seemed like an eternity since he *hadn't* been dealing with Erickson, Rex Deprovdechuk, the BoyCo kids, Father Paul . . .

. . . that was it. The roof, where he smelled something that made him dizzy.

"I started getting sick the same day I saw Paul Maloney's body."

"Did Maloney's body smell like urine?"

He nodded. "It did. Urine and something else I couldn't identify. I started feeling crappy soon after that."

"Bryan, I know what happened to you. Well, the general idea, anyway. We're sure Paul Maloney's death was a symbol killing, like Oscar Woody's. We know Woody's killers had the Zed chromosome, so it's logical to assume Maloney's did as well. I'm pretty sure there are hormones in the urine that activated your Zed chromosomes, made them start *expressing*. You had all this dormant code inside you, waiting for a signal. When that signal came, *boom*, your body was off to the races."

That was one for the comic books — he had superhealing and,

apparently, some level of superstrength, and what was his origin story? *I sniffed pee.* Not exactly as cool as being bitten by a radioactive spider.

"But why would my Zed be dormant?"

"I have no idea," Robin said. "Based on everything else we've seen, it's got to be some kind of species protection strategy. If one of your kind is—"

"My *kind*? I'm *not* one of them."

"Scientifically speaking, you are. Don't be a Sensitive Sally. Anyway, maybe tens of thousands of years ago — no, *hundreds* of thousands, but that creates a whole primate family tree issue that—"

"Robin, I'm almost at the hospital." He saw the SFGH complex coming up on the left. "Can you get to the point?"

"Sorry. My guess is that way back when, if one of your kind was isolated and their genes *did* express, maybe normal people killed them. So maybe suppressed genes contribute to survival. Maybe the genes evolved to only express if others of your kind are around — a safety-in-numbers kind of thing. Nature triggers suppressed genes all the time with hormones and other signaling mechanisms. You started out suppressed, *normal*, until your body detected others like you, then your latent genes activated."

He didn't understand a quarter of what she was saying. Not that any of it mattered right now.

"I gotta go," he said.

"Have you called Pookie?"

Shit. He'd forgotten about his partner, and the fact that he'd had Pookie's car for going on twenty-four hours now.

"No, I haven't. Can you call him and tell him he can pick up the Buick at the hospital?"

She paused. "Bryan, he was looking for you all day yesterday. He called me this morning. He's pretty pissed you didn't let him know you were alive."

As well he should be. But Bryan had too much to deal with at the moment — he really couldn't handle Pookie's disappointment on top of everything else.

"Look, Robin, just call him for me, okay?"

"Okay," she said. "I love you, Bryan."

"I love you, too." Those words were surprisingly easier to say the second time around. He hung up.

San Francisco General Hospital had many buildings, but the northernmost one housed the mental health wing — where Erickson was being kept. A head-high brick wall lined the sidewalk, with a ten-foot-high red fence rising from the top of it. Bryan wasn't sure if the fence was to keep people in, or out.

Adam slowed, then did a fast U-turn to slide into an open parallel parking spot just before Twentieth. Bryan struggled to turn the Buick as sharply and realized that not only was the Buick a crappy car, Adam was a far better driver. Bryan parked right behind the Magnum. The Magnum's rear passenger door opened. Alder leaned on his cane as he slowly got out. Bryan got out to meet him.

"Wait here, Inspector," Alder said. "I'll find Chief Zou and straighten this out."

"Are you good friends with her?" Maybe Alder could help patch things up, get Pookie his job back.

"I haven't seen her in twenty-eight years," Alder said. "And we're far from friends. Adam? Let's go."

Alder's cane clicked against the sidewalk as he and Adam walked toward the opening in the wall that led into the hospital complex.

In the Maze

The electric lights were off. Atop the mast of skulls, a few torches burned, casting out a weak light that failed to penetrate the arena's trenches.

There was no noise except for the crunch of dirt under their feet and a faint, regular echoing rumble that came from the shipwreck behind him and to his left. Trench walls rose up on either side. Aggie couldn't see the cavern's ceiling high above, it was too dark for that. He kept moving, tried not to think about the fact that he was walking through the maze — the same place the teenage boy had been killed, then butchered for food.

"This way," Hillary said as she turned right.

Aggie followed. That strange, echoing noise picked up in intensity, and Aggie realized what it was — Mommy was snoring.

Hillary had led him from the white dungeon, taking a different path than she'd used before. This time, instead of coming out on the ledge, he found himself sliding through a narrow, hidden passage and into the arena maze. Aggie hadn't known what to expect. He certainly hadn't expected the place to be empty, nor would he have dreamed that a place of monsters and death and terror could be even more disturbing when it was empty and mostly dark.

A tug on his arm. Hillary gestured all around, showing off like a proud homeowner. "Tonight, everyone will be here to watch the king join with Mommy and give our kind a future. That is when I will take you out. Until then, I have a place for you to wait. Come."

She turned left. Aggie found himself at the cavern's wall — a dead end. Hillary slid past a tall boulder and into a hidden space. She vanished from sight.

Aggie gently adjusted his grip on the knit bag, then followed.

A Blast from Amy's Past

It was like walking into a time warp.

Amy hadn't seen this man in decades. He had the same eyes, the same mouth and the same face, although wrinkles had blurred and softened his features. But all the time in the world couldn't fade the memory of their last meeting.

"Alder Jessup," she said.

He smiled and nodded. "Amy Zou. It's been a long time."

She looked at the man just behind Alder. Again that time-warp sensation. The man looked like the Alder she remembered from so long ago, if that Alder had been a metal-hipster douchebag.

"Hey, cop," the younger man said. "Gestapo stare-downs might work on the trust-fund kiddies, but I'm past that level."

Alder closed his eyes and sighed. "Chief Amy Zou, this is my grandson, Adam. Adam was just going to get himself a cup of coffee."

Adam smiled and nodded. "Nice meeting you, Chief. If I stumble upon a rampaging herd of wild donuts, I'll break out the speargun and bring you breakfast."

The angry young man walked off, his chains and jewelry rattling with each step.

"My apologies," Alder said. "All I can say is that his talent is well worth the trouble."

"Mister Jessup, why are you here?"

"I came to watch over Jebediah. I assume you're here to do the same. If you are, perhaps you should come out to my automobile. Adam has brought several items that could be of use to you should Marie's Children attack."

Those words nearly made Amy flinch. She looked up and down the hall. No one was paying attention.

She leaned in. "Alder, we have this covered. I have people on duty to protect him. I just came from Erickson's room. He's not awake yet, but he's getting better."

Alder sighed in that way old men can sigh and make you feel like a child no matter what age you are. "All this time, my dear, and you still don't truly understand."

She thought back to the nightmares she'd seen in Erickson's basement.

Alder was right — she hadn't truly understood what was out there, how *many* were out there.

He patted her on the shoulder. "I am not just here to protect Jebediah," he said. "I would like to have a word with you about a police officer of yours. I think we need to discuss one Bryan Clauser."

Zou Talks to Bryan

Bryan stood on the sidewalk of Potrero Avenue, watching Pookie stare at the Buick's driver's-side window. Streetlight gleamed against the cracks in the glass, lit up the tentacle-like sprawl of beer tendrils that had dried in place.

"Awesome," Pookie said. "You know, sometimes when people borrow my car, they get it washed and leave me with a full tank of gas. But this? This is so much better."

"I said I was sorry. I'll pay for it."

"With what, food stamps? We're fired, remember?"

Bryan rubbed his eyes and shook his head. "Really, man? I think we've got more important things to worry about than the window of your POS Buick."

Pookie shrugged. "Yeah, we do. Like the two hundred bucks you owe me for my trip to Oakland."

"You thought I was in Oakland?"

"Did I mention, *I looked everywhere?* Why, yes, yes I think I did mention that."

"But two hundred dollars?"

"I took a cab," Pookie said. "You know how I hate public transportation. Kinda the reason I bought a car, know what I'm saying?"

Pookie didn't get pissed that often, but when he did he didn't stop talking about it. He wanted — and deserved — an apology. "Look, I'm sorry I didn't call you, okay?"

Pookie nodded. "Apology accepted, but too bad you're not talking to your dad — I'd have him ground you for trashing my ride."

Pookie Chang, lone resident of *No-Subject-Is-Off-Limits Land.*

"That man is not my father."

"And I'm not chubby," Pookie said. "Amazing how we can just wish things into existence."

"With what I'm going through, are you really going to go there? *Now?*"

Pookie shrugged. "You need to get over it. I think you've filled your quota for feeling sorry for yourself."

"*Feeling sorry for myself?* You jackass, I'm a goddamn mutant or whatever."

Pookie used his jacket sleeve to wipe at the dried-beer tentacles. "So you got an extra chromosome. It's not like you got cancer, Bro. It is what it is, so accept it and let's move on."

Maybe Bryan should have done this solo after all. Only Pookie could reduce being a mutant, finding out your entire childhood had been a lie and tracking down serial killers that were actually your half-brothers to just *get over it*.

Pookie stopped wiping at the cracked window. He turned to stare at Bryan. "You thinking you should ditch me? For my safety, maybe?"

Bryan looked down at the sidewalk. He hated it when his partner did that.

Pookie feathered back his hair. "Forget it, my Young Rebel Detective. No one wants a show about a loner cop. I told you I'm down for the gun-fight. You're stuck with me. Agreed?"

Bryan looked up. Before he could answer, Pookie pointed down the sidewalk.

"Uh-oh," he said. "Here come da judge."

Bryan followed Pookie's gaze and saw Amy Zou walking quickly toward them, dress blues pressed, hat positioned perfectly on her head.

"She doesn't seem happy," Pookie said.

"Does she ever?"

"No," he said. "Should we make a run for it?"

"Too late. And I've got a few things I want to hear from her." Bryan crossed his arms, leaned against the black station wagon and tried to look disrespectful. He wasn't sure how to do that — maybe he'd have to get some lessons from Adam.

She stopped in front of them. "Clauser," she said. "Chang."

"Chief," Bryan said.

"MILFy woman who fired my ass," Pookie said.

Zou ignored the comment. "Clauser, we need to talk. Alone."

Bryan looked at Pookie. Pookie shook his head slightly. Even if Bryan wanted the man gone, he wouldn't go anywhere.

"Pookie stays, Chief," Bryan said. "Anything you want to say to me you can say in front of my partner."

"*Life* partner," Pookie said. "But only for tax purposes. Oh, and the Bed Bath and Beyond registry."

Zou turned her humorless stare on Pookie. She held it until he looked away. She turned back to Bryan. "Alder told me that you're one of them."

She said it with such a matter-of-fact tone. Zou was right, and so was Robin; he *was* one of them.

"I don't understand any of it, Chief. I have no idea what's happening and it's freaking me out."

"But you came to the hospital," she said. "Why?"

Bryan looked at Pookie, who just shrugged.

Bryan nodded to the building beyond the brick wall. "We put Erickson in there. Alder said Marie's Children might come for him, so we're here to protect him if we can."

"I have a full SWAT in and on that building," she said. "They have Erickson's floor on lockdown. Marie's Children are hard to find, sure, but it's a different battle if they have to come to us."

She stared at him. Bryan stared back. She seemed to be sizing him up. He wasn't in the mood for whatever power game she wanted to play.

"Look," he said, "we were just trying to do the right thing."

The hardness around her eyes faded. Now she was the one to turn away. "I know that feeling. This time, maybe we'll fix the damage you caused before the really bad shit starts." She met his eyes again. "At least now you guys understand what has to be done."

"Yes and no," Pookie said. "You can't keep this a secret forever. People need to know what's going on. The victims' families deserve to know what happened to their loved ones."

"Their loved ones *died*," Zou said. "Knowing what killed them won't bring them back. What do you want, Chang? Do you want to tell the world that San Francisco has a killer cult, or that it has real-live monsters?"

"*Both*," Pookie said. "People need to know that there's something out there that can kill them."

"No, they don't need to know. When a killer shows up, Erickson puts it down."

Pookie threw up his hands. "Are you insane? If you don't make this public, more people could die."

"People die every day," Zou said. "That's life in the big city. We're talking two, maybe three murders a year on average."

"On *average*? Those are human beings!"

"In San Francisco proper, eight hundred people a year get hit by cars," she said. "Twenty of those accidents end in death, give or take, and then you have life-changing injuries, but do we take out the roads and make everyone walk because traffic is *dangerous*?"

"That's ridiculous," Pookie said. "You can't compare shit like that."

"Really? Well, can I compare apples to apples? Or should I say, murders to murders? We had fifty murders in San Francisco last year, forty-five the year before that and ninety-four three years ago. Most of those killings were gang related. So we know gangs kill far more people than Marie's Children, yet we don't get rid of the gangs."

Her logic was faulty, fractured. Bryan couldn't understand her reasoning. "Chief, we're talking about serial killers. *Monsters*. We're talking about the public's right to know. The public *knows* about traffic deaths and people stay. Fine. Same for the gang activity. Fine with that, too. They *don't* know about Marie's Children."

She shook her head as if Bryan and Pookie just couldn't understand the obvious. "Sure, we tell the public," she said. "And that makes property values plummet."

Property values? Why would she say that? What did a cop care about property values? What wasn't she telling them?

Bryan heard Chief Zou's cell phone buzz. She pulled it out of her pocket and read.

She looked up at Bryan. "I've got to take care of something. Don't go anywhere. We'll talk about this later."

Pookie raised his hand like a schoolkid in class. "Uh, Chief? Does this mean we have our jobs back? Maybe with a couple of accoutrements known as a *badge* and a *gun*?"

She looked at Pookie, but this time without her trademark cold stare. Then she looked at Bryan. She sighed and shook her head as if she'd already made a decision she knew she'd regret. She looked up at the darkening sky.

"I'll get you back on the rolls tomorrow," she said. "For now, I'll let the watch sergeant know you can enter the hospital. And move your cars into the parking lot; we've got space allotted for police vehicles. You don't have to sit out on the street all night."

She turned and walked away, the phone clutched tightly in her right hand.

Bryan let out a sigh of relief. He had his job back, but more important, so did the friend who seemed willing to stand by his side no matter what.

And Chief Zou . . . that ridiculous logic of hers. Property values? He'd talk to her about that later. For the moment, however, he was a cop again, and his primary duty was to protect Jebediah Erickson from any harm.

Phone Home

Amy Zou walked through the hospital parking lot toward her car. Jack never sent texts like that. Had his father finally passed away? Had something happened to the twins?

She reached her car and got in. She shut the door, took a deep breath, then dialed her husband's cell phone.

It picked up on the second ring, but it wasn't her husband who answered.

"Hello, Missus Zou."

A boy. It sounded like a teenager, or someone just about to enter his teen years.

"Who is this?"

"I want to meet you," the boy said. "I've already met your family."

Amy closed her eyes and took in a deep breath. A knot of fear blossomed in her belly. Amy knew what it was to be afraid for herself — being afraid for her children was infinitely worse. This might be nothing; maybe Jack lost his phone and some kid thought this was funny. She had to stay calm.

"What's your name?"

"Rex."

That feeling in her belly swelled into her chest, her throat. "Rex . . . Deprovdechuk?"

"You already know me," he said. "How nice."

Rex, the boy who had strangled his own mother to death with a belt. The boy who was somehow mixed up with Marie's Children, somehow connected with the deaths of Oscar Woody, Jay Parlar and Bobby Pigeon.

The boy her entire police force hadn't been able to find.

"Rex, listen to me. I don't know what you think you're doing, but you need to turn yourself in."

"I'm at your house," he said. "My family came to visit your family. You have a very nice house, Missus Zou."

He was at her house? Oh, God, what was going on? Amy had to keep control of this, make the boy understand he was in deep shit.

"That's *Chief* Zou," Amy said. "As in *chief of police.*"

"Yes, ma'am. Why else would I want to talk to you?"

"Good," she said. "Then maybe you know how much power I have, and what I'm capable of if you do anything to my family."

Rex laughed. "Come home right now, Missus Zou. Don't call for backup. I have people watching your neighborhood. We see cop cars, even those unmarked ones, and your family is in a lot of trouble."

Amy's eyes squeezed shut. She forced them to open. "Let me talk to my husband."

"Sure," Rex said. "Hold on one sec."

Amy waited, her heart hammering in her chest, every inch of her body crawling and churning. How could this have happened? How?

"Baby," Jack said.

"*Jack!* The girls—"

"We're all okay," he said. "But . . . they'll hurt the twins if you don't do what they say. Oh my God, Amy, these *things . . .* they're not human."

Images of the shark-mouthed man flashed through Amy's thoughts. She felt tears streaming down her face.

The boy spoke again. "Twenty minutes, Missus Zou. Then we start slicing."

"If you hurt—"

A click from the other end cut off her threats.

She set the phone in the passenger seat. She jammed the keys in the ignition, started the car and shot out of her parking spot.

Chillin' Like a Villain

R ex tried to relax in a big La-Z-Boy recliner. Sly said it was the chair most like a throne, so Rex should sit in it. His feet didn't quite reach the extended footrest — his heels dangled in the space between the pad and the seat cushion.

"I like this movie," Sly said, laughing. "I've seen this one fifteen times. No, sixteen."

They were watching *Reservoir Dogs* on Chief Amy Zou's TV. Rex had never seen it. Roberta hadn't liked gangster flicks. Rex was having a hard time concentrating on the movie, but it would pass the time until Chief Zou made it home.

Pierre was upstairs with the father and the girls. Rex had worried that Pierre might kill someone, kill them early, but Sly assured him that Pierre could follow orders.

"I wish she had *Lord of The Rings*," Rex said. "That's my favorite."

On the TV, Mr. Blonde danced a slow shuffle across the screen, straight razor in hand, as the bloody, duct-taped cop breathed heavily through his nose.

"Love this part," Sly said. "Mister Blonde is going to cut off that cop's ear."

"*Hey*, no spoilers."

"Sorry, my king."

"It's okay."

Rex watched. Such a nice house. Way nicer than where he'd lived with Roberta. Way, *way* nicer than Home. Home was really cool, but Rex wondered if the dampness and the dirt had an effect on everyone. There had to be a way to find them a better place to live, yet keep them hidden from all the humans that would burn them, kill them.

Sly pointed at the screen. "See that Mister Orange, my king? Firstborn reminds me of him."

"Which one is Mister Orange?"

Sly walked to the screen and put a finger on the actor lying on a ramp, his white shirt bright red with blood. "This one. You can't trust Mister Orange. He's looking out for himself. He's not looking out for the gang."

Sly wouldn't stop talking about Firstborn. Sly was Rex's best friend, but his hatred of Firstborn was starting to get in the way. Firstborn seemed like a good guy. It was so complicated. Firstborn had saved the people from extinction, saved Rex's *real* mother, but he had also killed babies, killed Rex's grown-up brothers and sisters as well. Sly hadn't killed any babies. Sly had killed Rex's enemies, had given Rex his new life.

And Sly had fought Firstborn when Firstborn wanted to kill Rex.

It was hard to figure all this out.

"Firstborn will be cool," Rex said. "He knelt. He declared me king."

Sly shrugged his big shoulders and returned to the couch. "Sometimes people lie, my king. Don't forget — if something should happen to you, he'd be in charge again."

"But I told the people to kill him if anything happened to me."

Sly shrugged again. "Firstborn has ruled for over a century. His rule is all we've ever known. Unless you name someone to succeed you, then he might kill you and just take his chances, see if he can take over in the confusion."

Rex fell silent. He watched the movie some more, watched Mr. Blonde's white shirt blaze in the afternoon sun as he fetched a gas can out of the back of a white Cadillac.

Maybe Sly was right. Firstborn had led for . . . what . . . like a hundred fifty years? Maybe it was hard to give that up. Rex needed to take that motivation away.

"Sly, what if I actually named a . . . what's that word? The word for who takes over if I'm gone?"

"Successor?"

"That's it," Rex said. "If I named a successor, made it real clear, do you think Firstborn would support me? Do you think that would work?"

Sly's eyes narrowed in thought. "Maybe. You'd have to tell everyone all at once, I think, so there's no misunderstanding about who would take over. If you did that, he'd know he can't win." Sly nodded slowly. "Yeah, then I think he'd follow you for sure."

On the screen, Mr. Blonde doused the duct-taped cop with gasoline.

"You'd need someone you can really trust," Sly said. "Otherwise, that person might try to kill you, too. I don't want to see anything happen to you."

Mr. Blonde flicked his lighter. Just before he could set the cop on fire, gunshots rang out — Mr. Orange shot Mr. Blonde several times. Mr. Blonde fell dead.

Sly said Firstborn was like Mr. Orange.

Rex turned in his chair to look at the snake-faced man. "Can I trust *you*, Sly?"

Sly looked down. Rex didn't know if a man with green, pebbly skin could blush, but Sly seemed overwhelmed with emotion.

"Of course, my king. I'll always do your bidding. If you're going to name someone as successor, you could do it tonight, when everyone is assembled to see you enter Mommy's cabin."

Rex fell silent. Hillary said Rex had to go be with Mommy, start making new queens as soon as possible. "I'm kind of nervous about that. What if I don't want to do it?"

Sly smiled. "Whatever you want to do, I'm there. If you don't want to be with Mommy, well, I won't let anyone mess with you. I'll carry you out of the tunnels myself."

Rex had never had a real friend before. Not one like Sly, anyway. Sly would do anything for him.

They heard the garage door open.

"Tell Pierre to bring them down," Rex said. "Let's get ready to meet Chief Zou."

A New Need

A ggie James stared at the bassinet.

No, he couldn't do it. He couldn't allow himself to succumb.

Just ride it out . . . you'll be free soon.

He looked away, not that there were many places *to* look. The tiny room must have once been part of the sewer system, back in the times when they built things out of rough-hewn rocks. At least it was warm. The room had power — Hillary had turned on a beat-up heater and an old dehumidifier as soon as they'd arrived.

He wore the same clothes he'd had on when Sly and Pierre had taken him to the white dungeon. The clothes had been waiting for him here. Hillary had cleaned the jeans, shirt and jacket. She'd given him a pair of tan work boots that were almost new, if you didn't count the blood stain set into the suede.

For the first time Aggie could remember, he was clean, both inside and out.

Yet now he felt a powerful urge . . . an urge that made him feel *dirty.* How could he want that? How in the *hell* could he want *that*?

Aggie turned. He stared at the baby. So tiny. So helpless. But what would it become? Would it change to look like those things that had chased down the teenage boy?

The baby hadn't hurt anyone. The baby just *was.*

Aggie walked to the bassinet and looked down. The baby slept so peacefully. So quiet, all bundled up in that blanket with the strange symbols. Aggie thought of the day his daughter had been born, thought of her tiny fingers and the way her eyes had closed when she'd slept against his wife's chest. But this boy wasn't like Aggie's lost child. The boy was Hillary's kind, the killing kind.

This was a creature of evil.

So why did Aggie wanted to pick the baby up? Why did he want to hold it? The urge consumed him. It was even more powerful than that inexplicable lust that had overtaken him while watching Mommy in her cabin.

It was more than a *want* . . . it was a *need.*

He *needed* to pick up that baby, *needed* to protect it.

He could fight it no longer. He reached into the bassinet and gently lifted up the tiny, sleeping form. Aggie held the baby to his chest, one hand under the baby's tiny bottom, the other hand on the back of the baby's head.

Aggie started to bounce lightly.

"Don't you worry," he said. "It'll be okay. It'll be fine."

It was just a baby, goddamit. This child was no more responsible for what his kin had done than Aggie was responsible for the actions of his asshole grandfather. The boy didn't have to turn out like Hillary — he didn't have to turn out like those kids in the maze.

The small room's metal door screeched as it opened, the bottom scraping heavily against the cinder-block floor. Aggie instinctively turned the baby away from the door, protecting it with his body. He looked over his shoulder to see who had come.

Hillary.

She entered, and smiled. "How nice. You are holding the baby."

Aggie nodded.

She reached out her wrinkled hand and smoothed the baby's blanket. Aggie fought an instinct to pull the baby away from her. He had to keep his cool.

She again looked at Aggie; her happy eyes returned to their normal hard-ice stare. "Are you ready to learn what you must do?"

Aggie nodded again.

"You are to find this baby a good home," she said. "You take him out of here, find him a good home, a loving home, a *safe* home."

She stared at him, as if waiting for an answer, waiting for confirmation. He had no idea what he should say.

"Repeat it," she said. "A safe, loving home."

"Yes, ma'am. A safe, loving home. But . . . well, how do I do that?"

Hillary pointed a finger at the ceiling. "You live up above. Find someone who wants a baby. Someone who will stay in San Francisco, do you understand? They have to *stay* here. You *must* find someone. Do you know people?"

Aggie had zero idea of who would take in a little black baby, but he nodded. "Sure, of course. I know people just like that."

"Good," she said. "I knew I chose right when I chose you. When you find the people who will take him" — she reached into her sweater pocket and pulled out an overstuffed brown envelope — "you give them this."

Inside the envelope, Aggie saw a thick stack of hundreds.

"You listen to me now," Hillary said. "You listen *carefully*. I have people up there. No matter where you go, we can find you by your *smell*. You do what I say, and you are free. You do not do what I say? Then wherever you go, I will reach out from here and pull you back in, and then *you* will be the groom."

That giant slug of a woman, being tied to the dolly, then the maze, the monster children . . . Aggie nodded madly. If this was the price of freedom, he would fulfill her mission.

"Yes, ma'am, I understand, but . . ." His voice trailed off. He wanted to ask a question, but what if the answer made her change her mind? No, with all the trouble she'd gone through, she wasn't going to suddenly take the baby away. He *had* to ask.

"Why don't you take him?" Aggie said. "I mean, I'll do what you ask and thank you for letting me live, *thank you,* but why wouldn't you just take him up yourself?"

She caressed the sleeping baby's cheek. "I can't go far from Home. When I am away from Mommy for too long, I start to change."

"Change into what?"

She didn't say anything. For a long moment, it was so quiet Aggie could hear her fingertips sliding across the baby's cheek.

Finally, Hillary looked up. "You ask too many questions. Don't you want to help me?"

Oh shit, had he blown it? Aggie nodded, *hard.* "Yes! I want to do this for you. Never mind I asked, just let me take the boy up, *please.*" He would find the boy a home. Forget the questions, that was stupid — all Aggie wanted was to get away from this crazy place and this crazy old woman.

She reached out again, but this time her fingertips caressed Aggie's cheek. It took everything he had not to recoil in disgust.

"Now I let you go," she said. "I give you life. In return, you give this baby a future."

He nodded again, couldn't stop himself from nodding. "Thank you, Hillary," Aggie said, and he meant it. "I'll do it."

"Follow me, and be very silent. I will show you the way out."

None More Black

Bryan Clauser at his side, Pookie Chang stepped out of the elevator onto the third floor of the SFGH mental health wing. Pookie had sweet-talked their way into the building. The staff was on edge, but Bryan's badge helped overcome initial objections.

Pookie couldn't wait to get his own badge back from Zou.

They walked down the hallway of Ward 7A. Pookie took note of the reinforced doors with their electronic locks. SFGH was one of the few places with a "psychiatric emergency room." The hospital took in patients with all manner of psychiatric issues, and at all times of the night. It was to be expected that some of those patients were violent and needed secure holding facilities. That made 7A the most locked-down, defensible spot in the hospital, which was probably why Zou had put Erickson here.

Pookie and Bryan turned down a hall to their left. It wasn't hard to spot which door led to Erickson's room — the two men in full SWAT gear standing outside of it gave things away.

They wore thick black jackets made even bulkier by the body armor that covered them. The men had armored gloves and kneepads, heavy black boots, and black helmets with goggles waiting to be pulled down in front of their eyes. Black AR-15 assault rifles hung from their necks, barrels angled to the floor.

"They look serious," Bryan said.

"You're just jealous because they wear more black than you do," Pookie said. The men did look serious, though, and not at all happy about pulling what appeared to be guard duty. "I know those guys."

"Shocker," Bryan said.

"The one on the left is Jeremy Ellis. The other guy is Matt Hickman. Come on."

Pookie walked toward them. Bryan followed.

Helmeted heads swiveled toward them. Hickman's hands flexed on his AR-15. Ellis held up a black-gloved hand, palm out.

"Hold it, Chang."

Pookie stopped. "Jeremy, my man. How's the softball team? Still doing the department proud with that three-fifteen average?"

Jeremy looked surprised. "Uh, three-seventeen."

"A hitting streak? Awesome."

Jeremy smiled, but only a little before his oh-so-serious cop face returned. "I'm guessing you want in here, but it's not going to happen."

Pookie thought of bringing up the fact that Hickman's son was the starting point guard for Mission High, but it didn't look like small talk was going to get him anywhere.

"Maybe you didn't get the memo," Pookie said. "Chief Zou reinstated us. She told the duty sergeant."

Jeremy shook his head. "News to me. Last word I have is you guys aren't cops. I'm not supposed to allow anyone in this room, *especially* you, Clauser."

Bryan looked at the door. For a moment, Pookie wondered if Bryan might rush it. Hickman must have wondered the same thing, as the barrel of his gun moved up a tiny amount.

Jeremy pointed a black-gloved finger back down the hall. "Guys, do us all a favor and hit the road, okay?"

Bryan shook his head. "We just want to make sure Erickson is safe."

"He is," Jeremy said. "We have three guys on the roof and four more in a ready room they made for us downstairs. No one is getting in here. I'm not going to tell you again — get out of here."

Pookie flashed his best smile. "All right, gents. Keep up the good work. Bryan, let's go."

Pookie started heading back down the hall. Bryan paused; his hands flexed into fists, then he followed. Pookie stayed tense until the elevator doors shut and he knew Bryan wouldn't try to go back.

"Bri-Bri, Zou's got it covered."

Bryan didn't look convinced. "I don't know, man. What if one of those basement creatures attacks?"

"Then those creatures get shredded. Zou mapped it out for us, Bro. This isn't chasing shadows in a darkened alley. The SWAT boys are serious business. They've got this."

Bryan chewed at his lower lip. He nodded. "I guess. I'm still going to hang out on the hospital grounds tonight. You good for that?"

Pookie shrugged. "Sure. I'll hang out here. Got to be some hospital-centric plotlines for *Blue Balls* that I can work on. And it's not like I have to be up early for work tomorrow, as apparently we're still unemployed. I wonder why Chief Zou didn't call the sergeant like she said she would."

When Amy Zou said she would do something, you could bank on it. Whatever the reason for her dragging her feet, it was probably a good one.

Home Sweet Home

Chief Amy Zou pulled into her garage. She came out of the car with her Sig Sauer up and at the ready, sweeping the barrel in a 360-degree arc around the garage.

Nothing.

No one had ever threatened her family before. No angry gangsters trying to get her to back off, no druglord's promise of revenge, not even some thug receiving a sentence of twenty-to-life looking at her and saying *you're gonna pay.* Nothing. Not until today.

She couldn't quite draw in a full breath. Her chest seemed compressed, constricted. Over the course of her career, she'd been shot three times in the line of duty, shot *at* more times than that, and yet she had never felt this terrified.

The garage's interior door led into the kitchen. She heard a movie playing in the living room. She moved as silently as she could, not really knowing why, hoping Rex and his creatures were dumb enough to be overconfident. Maybe she could sneak up on them and end this quick.

She heard something else — her daughter Tabz, crying softly.

If they hurt you, baby, if they laid a hand on you, I'll kill them where they stand.

Amy Zou moved into the kitchen. Finding it empty, she followed the sound of crying into the living room, the barrel of her pistol leading the way.

Her husband was on his knees, a gag tightly wrapped around his head and mouth, his hands tied behind his back. On Jack's left stood a whimpering, gagged Tabz, her face streaked with tears, her arms wrapped in a death clutch around a teddy bear. On his right stood Mur, head tilted down, eyes glaring out from beneath her thick black hair. Mur was also gagged, but she didn't really look scared — her expression reeked of anger and hatred.

Standing behind Amy's family . . . *monsters.*

Two of them. The first had short brown fur and a face like a dog. He was so big his head seemed to reach up to the ceiling. His bottom jaw skewed to the right, and his long pink tongue hung down off the left side. He wore flower-print Bermuda shorts and nothing else, save for a heavy, dirty blanket draped around his shoulders. He held a stockless, drum-fed automatic shotgun — an Armsel Striker — in his left hand. He was so big he made the bulky weapon look like a pistol.

The shotgun was pointed at the back of Tabz's head.

The other monster had a snake face and the girth of a bodybuilder, most of that bulk hidden beneath another ratty blanket. He wore jeans, work boots and a blue San Jose Sharks sweatshirt that strained at the seams. He had a gun, too — a .44 automag, the muzzle hovering less than an inch from Mur's temple.

In between the two hulking nightmares, standing as calmly as you please behind her bound-and-gagged husband, was Rex Deprovdechuk. Amy knew, instantly, that this boy was completely in charge.

She pointed her Sig Sauer directly at his face. "They're going to drop those guns and *get out* of my house. Tell them to do it now, Rex, or you're going to die."

Rex smiled. It was a pleasant smile, tolerant but not quite condescending, the kind a nice kid gives to adults he thinks are okay but still way uncool.

"Then both your daughters will have their brains blown all over your living room carpet," he said. "Put down the gun, Missus Zou."

Amy realized her hand was shaking. With a flick of her wrist and a pull of the trigger, she could kill the brown-furred one, then maybe get a snapshot at the snake-man. But could she do that before either of them fired, murdering her beautiful girls? And would her aim be dead-on if she couldn't even keep her hands still?

In a hostage situation, you were never, *ever* supposed to give up your weapon. If she did that, she had no power.

Rex sighed. He seemed bored. "Missus Zou, just put it down."

The dog-faced man pressed the shotgun barrel to the back of Tabz's head. She cried louder. Her little body shook with sobs.

She's just a baby don't hurt my baby . . .

Amy lowered her weapon.

Rex pointed to a spot in front of Jack. "Right there, please."

Don't do it don't give up your weapon don't do it

Amy tossed the Sig Sauer. It hit the carpet with a light thud. The boy calmly walked around Tabz, picked up the pistol, then walked back behind her family to once again stand between the two monsters.

Amy was naked, helpless. "What do you want?"

Rex grinned and nodded slightly, an expression that said *I really want to help you out.*

"Tell me where Savior is," he said. "Then, I want the names of everyone who knows about Marie's Children. Finally, I want to arrange a meeting with those people."

She couldn't give the boy Savior's location. They'd attack him, kill him. And what would they do to the other people who knew about Marie's Children? Rich Verde, Sean Robertson, Jesse Sharrow, the mayor, Bryan and Pookie, Doctor Metz, Robin Hudson — Amy couldn't put those people in danger.

"No one knows but me," she said. She had to buy time, get word to Bryan, maybe, see if he could move Erickson to another location. "And Savior checked out of the hospital this morning. I don't know where he went after that."

The boy's grin faded. He sighed and shook his head. A put-upon, exasperated teenage killer could decide if her family lived or died.

"Choose," he said.

"Choose what?"

The boy spread his hands, the gesture taking in Amy Zou's daughters and her husband. "Choose which one dies."

Amy's throat tightened. She tried to speak, but nothing came out. Why had she given up her weapon? *Why?*

"Missus Zou, we're wasting time. Choose."

"I . . . no. Please, don't kill anyone."

Rex shook his head. "It's too late for that. You can either choose one, or I can choose two."

Her vision blurred briefly before a hot tear streaked down her cheek, leaving a cool tingling in its wake. She saw no doubt in Rex's eyes.

"No . . . no *please*. Kill me instead. Let them go."

Rex held up a hand, palm toward her, fingers pointed to the ceiling. "I'm going to count down from five," he said.

"San Francisco General." The words rushed out of her mouth. "Savior is there. I know which room."

The boy nodded. "That's great, Missus Zou. But you already made me tell you I was going to kill one. I can't go back on my word. Choose."

"But I told you! I know access codes to the building!"

"Five . . ."

"No! Wait, *wait*, I can get you those names."

He bent his thumb in. "Four . . ."

Monsters with guns counting down her family her daughters the love of her life . . .

He bent his pinkie in, trapped it with his thumb. "Three . . ."

This can't be happening this can't be happening don't kill my babies this can't be happening

"Look," she said, "I *swear* I can give you what you want."

He bent his ring finger in, trapped that with his thumb as well. "Two . . ."

Amy's gaze snapped back and forth across her family, Tabz then Jack then Mur then Jack then Tabz . . .

He bent in his middle finger, leaving only his pointer extended. "One . . ."

Oh Jesus Christ how could this be happening not her daughters *not my daughters*

"Zer —"

"Jack!" Amy screamed.

Jack's eyes went wide with terror. Or was that anger? Betrayal? He started to scream but she couldn't understand him through the gag.

Rex reached up and patted the dog-face's shoulder. "Pierre, do what the chief says. Chief Zou, if you make a move, one of your daughters will join your husband, so you better stand real still."

The snake-face reached down and picked up Mur with one arm, pinning her arms to her sides. She looked like a frail little doll. The monster pressed the .44's barrel under her chin, pushing her head back a bit. Now the girl was scared; her wide eyes betrayed genuine fear.

Pierre's right hand grabbed her husband by the top of his head, big brown fingers wrapping down across her Jack's cheeks. Effortlessly, the monster lifted him right up off the ground. Jack started to kick, but his feet were bound as well as his hands. His body thrashed as he fought to break free. The boy stepped back to avoid Jack's heels.

Pierre never moved the shotgun from the back of Tabz's head. Tabz shook with sobs, but she made no move to run.

Pierre lifted Jack higher. The monster tilted his dog-head to the left, so the skewed jaws opened horizontally rather than vertically. The long white teeth glinted colored plasma reflections from the TV. Pierre slowly bit down on Jack's neck. There was the briefest second as the teeth penetrated the skin, then came the blood. Thin, spraying jets splashed against Pierre's face, splashing on Tabz, falling on the carpet.

Jack's body lurched madly. His knees whipped up then drove down, his bound feet kicked back and forth, his shoulders twisted as arms fought against ropes that would not break.

Amy heard herself screaming, heard words torn by panic and denial and anguish.

Pierre let go of Jack's head, but the man didn't fall — his ravaged neck remained tightly pinched in the skewed jaws. Pierre shook his head like a dog with a chew toy. The gag blocked most of Jack's gurgling screams.

Amy heard a *cracking* sound. Pierre paused and drew in a deep breath through his long nose. As he did, Jack looked at her, eyes pleading for help. Then monster gave one final, hard shake.

Jack's head sailed across the room.

Trailing blood, it bounced once on the La-Z-Boy, then came to rest on its side, eyes facing Amy. The pupils dilated, as if Jack saw her, *recognized* her. His lids closed once, then slowly opened — dead, unmoving eyes stared out.

The girls' screams brought Amy back. She found herself lying on the carpet. She'd passed out. For the briefest of moments, she allowed herself to imagine it had all been a dream. But then she saw Tabz, gagged and screaming, her father's blood matting her hair and dripping down her face. Amy saw the monster holding an automatic shotgun to Tabz's head, a monster soaked with that same blood. Amy saw Mur tucked under the snake-man's huge arm. Mur kicked and fought, but snake-man just ignored it.

And in the middle of it all, Amy saw a smiling, teenage boy.

"There," Rex said. "That's all done. Now I'm going to ask you more questions. Unless you want me to make you choose again, you'll answer them."

Amy nodded, and kept on nodding, over and over and over again.

Handiwork

Rich Verde was just about maxed out. Too many years of this bullshit. Time to start thinking about retirement. Someplace warm. Someplace with rich divorcées and enough booze to drown out any memory of this fucking city. Boca Raton, maybe?

The wind whipped at a blue tarp tied up inside a cluster of Golden Gate Park's gnarled Australian tea trees. The trees were spooky enough all by themselves, even without the corpses that had been found hidden among the twisted, contorted trunks.

Rich and several uniforms stood just outside the tarp. He didn't want to be in there, not with those bodies. He'd had his fill of symbol killings; more than enough for one lifetime. Baldwin Metz was on the way. The Silver Eagle would get this body out of here lickety-split.

That was the process. That was how things were done. Rich just didn't want to be part of that process anymore.

He wondered how he was going to tell Amy. How would she take it? Well, that wasn't his problem. She could go cry on the shoulder of that needle-dick husband of hers. Rich had put in his time. *Thirty years'* worth of time, fuck you very much. He didn't owe Amy a goddamn thing.

This latest killing, though, it was a problem. The media had got to the bodies first. Pictures of two corpses with missing hands would be all over the front page of the *Chronicle*. Hell, it was probably already up on the paper's website.

Whoever this killer was, he had struck twice in as many days. Yesterday morning, the first set of bodies had turned up at Ocean Beach. And now, less than twenty-four hours later, a second set. All four victims showed the same m.o. — broken necks, missing hands and gnawed feet. *Gnawed feet*, for fuck's sake. And, of course, someone had given the bodies a golden shower.

Naw, not Boca Raton. Maybe Tahiti.

The symbol had been found at both sites. He'd been at this game long enough to know it was a new killer, not the same one who had whacked Paul Maloney and those BoyCo kids. He could just tell. The only break was that this time the symbol had been carved into the back of one of the tea trees, and the media had missed it.

All this, and Amy had yet to call him back. So unlike her. Robertson was on the way, though. Sean could run things. Hopefully he'd get here before the rest of the media did.

A uniform walked down the dirt path, then ducked under a line of yellow police tape and approached.

"Inspector Verde, more media is showing up," he said "We've got CBS-4 setting up now, KRON-TV's van just pulled up into the park, and the ABC-7 chopper is closing in."

"Just keep them all back," Rich said. "The last fucking thing we need is for them to start asking questions about a serial killer, you know?"

"Might be too late for that, sir. I think they already have a name for him. They asked me if I knew anything about *the Handyman*."

The Handyman?

Yeah, Tahiti. That would do the trick.

Aggie Gets Out!

Aggie James wasn't sure how long he'd been following Hillary.

She had led him out of the bassinet room and back into the dark arena maze. Many twists and turns later, she'd started up a narrow set of rough steps cut into the wall. Carrying the baby, Aggie had moved so carefully, keeping his left shoulder against the wall as he made sure his right foot didn't slip off the uneven edges.

Those steps rose forty feet to the spectator ledge. She had led him into a narrow tunnel at the back of the ledge, just a few feet away from the last step. Aggie had turned for a last look down below before going in. The ship was off to his right, back end buried in the cavern wall, front end pointing across the oblong cavern. There had been activity on the ship's deck — Hillary's people preparing for some kind of an event, maybe?

They'd been following the tunnel for fifteen minutes, maybe thirty, he wasn't sure. This time, at least, she had a battery-powered Coleman lantern to light the way. She seemed to know the location of every rock, every turn, every jagged outcropping of rusted metal or moldy wood. He knew this because those things caught him, poked him, snagged him while she avoided them all with a subtle turn, a simple twist.

He cradled the knit bag in his right arm. Inside, the baby boy slept. Aggie felt the child's faint warmth through the fabric. The boy weighed almost nothing. Aggie could carry him forever if he had to.

Finally, Hillary stopped and turned.

"Move carefully here," she said. "Step only where I step."

She set the lantern down and stepped aside so Aggie could see a small stone forest; fifteen or so piles of stacked rocks rose from floor to ceiling. No, not piles, *columns*. The columns supported big slabs of concrete, chunks of old brick wall and blackened squares of timber. This strange ceiling ran the final fifteen feet of tunnel, right up to where it dead-ended at a giant, dirty sheet of plywood. It didn't take a genius to see the plan — make any column fall and the whole kit-and-caboodle would collapse, filling the tunnel with tons of dirt and rock.

Hillary gestured to the ceiling. "You understand?"

Aggie nodded.

She slid around the first column. Aggie watched her. She looked like an old lady, but didn't move like one. Her agility and balance complemented the ridiculous strength Aggie already knew she possessed.

With each step, she wiggled her shoe in the dirt, leaving a clear footprint to show the safe path.

She slid around the second column, then waved him on.

Holding the baby-filled bag to his chest, Aggie followed in Hillary's footsteps. He took his time. She didn't seem to mind.

As he passed the third column, he felt something . . . some kind of trembling beneath his feet. An earthquake? The rumbling increased. With it came an echoing, grinding roar. How could there be an earthquake *now*, when he'd almost made it out? Aggie held the baby close, looked up, and waited for death.

The rumbling subsided. The roar faded away.

Hillary was laughing silently, again waving him on.

Two minutes later, they'd passed all the columns save for one. The final column was less than two feet from the piece of plywood. Hillary grabbed the plywood by a pair of metal handles screwed into it, then slowly slid it aside, revealing a hole perhaps three feet wide. The hole led into a deep blackness.

Aggie felt the tender kiss of something he hadn't known for days . . . a *breeze*. Fresh air. Well, not *fresh*, it smelled of metal and grease, but it was far fresher than the still air he'd breathed since he woke up in the white dungeon. He again felt the rumbling — something big, something mechanical, something getting closer.

Hillary held up a hand, palm out. The gesture said *stay there, don't move*. Aggie waited. She turned off the Coleman, leaving a blackness that made the walls close in.

The sound grew louder. The tunnel rumbled. Suddenly there was a flash of light, the roar of metal wheels on metal tracks.

A Muni train.

He was in the San Francisco subway.

Aggie tried to calm his breathing. He couldn't allow himself to believe this was it, that he was really getting out.

The Muni train passed, its roar a fading echo.

Hillary turned the lantern back on. The columns hadn't collapsed. "Now you go," she said. "Do you remember what I told you?"

Aggie nodded. She was giving him life. He would honor his promise to her. No way he was going to wind up as a groom. *No way.*

He turned to hand her the baby so he could duck out of the hole, then paused. A sudden, all-powerful twang of anxiety ripped through him: What if Hillary took the baby and ran?

She waited.

"I'm going to set the baby down," he said. "Can you step back?"

She smiled, nodded, then backed away. Aggie gently rested the bag on the ground, then stepped through the small hole and out of the death-trap tunnel. He stood on a narrow ledge that ran perpendicular to the tracks. He bent, reached back, and was again holding the boy.

Aggie clutched the bag tightly; the anxiety faded away.

Far down the tunnel to his right, he saw the light of a station.

Hillary worked the plywood shut behind him. Aggie's eyes slowly adjusted to the darkness. The hole he had crawled from was gone — all he could see were the hexagonal tiles of the subway's walls. The plywood was a tile-covered plug that perfectly fit the hole, sliding home as sure as a puzzle piece. If he hadn't just come through there, he would have never known it existed.

But that didn't matter anymore.

He had *survived.*

Aggie kept his right hand on the tile wall as he walked. He didn't know which rail was the "third rail," the one that might electrocute him and the boy. It was probably the one in the middle, but he wasn't taking any chances.

He drew closer to the opening into the station. The tracks led out of the tunnel's darkness and alongside the station platform. He saw a few people up on that platform — the trains were still running, so it wasn't early in the morning.

Aggie carefully stepped off the ledge and over the tracks, moving to the platform side of the tunnel. He slid along with his back to the wall. He felt a hint of a rumble — another train was coming. He had to move fast. The people on the platform would see him, but he didn't have a choice.

He was still draped in the stinking blanket. That's how he would get past those people, by just looking, acting and smelling like the homeless bums who wandered down to the Muni stations all the time.

He reached the end of the tunnel. The platform came up to his chest. He lifted the knit purse containing the boy and gently set it on the platform's warning stripe of yellow. Aggie crawled up. People turned to look, saw what he was, then immediately turned away. Aggie picked up the bag. He held the baby with one arm, and with the other pulled the blanket around them both. His heart hammered in his chest.

So close so close . . .

Aggie saw the brown sign in the white ceiling, the white letters that spelled out CIVIC CENTER. He looked at the digital sign that told of the next train and saw that it was 11:15 P.M.

He forced himself to walk — not *run* — toward the escalator that led to the surface. Homeless people didn't run. All he had to do was keep up the illusion and everyone would ignore him. Illusion? How odd to think of it that way. Wasn't he a homeless person after all?

No.

Not anymore.

Aggie had done his time in the gutter. He'd lost *years* mourning, feeling sorry for himself, feeling sorry for his losses. He'd given up and tuned out. That time was over.

He was *alive*. His wife and daughter were gone. Nothing could bring them back. He should have died down in the tunnels, in the white room, but he had a second chance and he wasn't going to screw it up. He had a responsibility now, a responsibility to protect the child he held in his arms. He had sworn to find this child a home.

Why don't I just raise the kid?

He realized that hidden thought had been lurking at the edge of his mind ever since he looked in the bag and saw the tiny baby. *You were a parent once. A good parent. That robbery wasn't your fault, there was nothing you could do.*

A second chance . . . a second chance to get things right.

Aggie felt full of hope, full of a sudden and overpowering love for life. He moved toward the escalator that would lead him to the surface.

And then, the baby cried.

Not a soft cry, not a muffled *I just woke up cry*, but rather a full-blown *I am not at ALL happy cry*. Loud. Piercing. The dozen or so people on the platform who had gone out of their way to *not* look at him now turned to stare.

The baby screamed again.

The kid was probably hungry. This was just a baby being a baby, but Aggie knew what it looked like — a shabby, smelly bum with a screaming child hidden somewhere beneath a filthy blanket.

Aggie saw hands reach into pockets and purses, then come out holding cell phones.

He turned back to the escalator.

A woman stepped toward him. "Stop!"

Aggie took off, his newish boots thumping out a staccato drumbeat on the escalator's metal steps. He heard and felt similar pounding behind him — the heavy steps of men.

The first escalator took him up to the station's main floor. One more escalator and he'd be out on the streets. There were more people up here, heading home from bars or from late nights at work.

"Get out of my way!" Aggie ran, carrying the baby-bag in both arms. His legs felt weak. He was already exhausted.

"Stop him!" the men behind him screamed. Most of the people in front of him quickly got out of the way, but one man, a kid of no more than twenty, stepped in front of him.

Aggie slowed, then tried to cut left.

His foot landed on his blanket — the blanket slid across the polished floor, and his foot flew out from under him. In the split second it took him to reach the ground, his only thought was to protect the baby.

The back of Aggie's head cracked against the marble, and everything went black.

Date Night

The faint but beautiful sounds of a plinky piano echoed from inside of Mommy's cabin. There were no lights in there, just darkness and music. People lined the arena's ledges, holding torches that flickered like big stars against the cavern's blackness.

Alone, Rex stood on the ship's ruined deck. He held a wicker basket with a present for Mommy. Tonight, he would become a man.

Everything was happening so fast. He and Pierre and Sly had brought the chief of police and her daughters back Home. The chief had given up a bunch of names. They'd even printed pictures of those criminals on Chief Zou's computer, so the soldiers would know if they had the right people.

The chief's husband was cooking in the stew. Most of him, anyway. His head was in the basket. Mommy liked brains.

As soon as Rex finished this ceremony with Mommy, he and Sly were going to plan how to use Chief Zou to round up the criminals. Firstborn had allowed the bullies to live, but Rex would not. Once those who knew of Marie's Children were gone, Rex's people would become even more of a secret.

Hillary wanted the people to spread, and so did Rex. She said the only way for that to happen was to make new queens. The only way to make a *new* queen, she said, was for a king to mate with an *old* queen.

Rex was the king, and that was that. If he was the king, though, didn't he need a crown? Maybe someone could make one for him — the people had built all these amazing tunnels, surely they could make a kick-ass crown.

He felt so nervous. He'd never had sex before. Would he get it right?

Two white-robed men walked out of Mommy's cabin. They stood on either side of the door, waiting. The one on the left wore a devil mask. The one on the right wore a mask that looked like Osama bin Laden.

They both waved Rex forward.

Up on the ledge, all the people waited for him to enter. Rex turned slowly, looking up at the ledge, at the torchlight-illuminated faces of his people. *Everyone* was here. Now was the time to make Firstborn understand that all of this belonged to Rex, and Rex alone.

"I have made a decision," he shouted. His voice echoed off the arena's walls. "I am not going to hide in the caverns and let other people go fight. I'll fight with them. I'll lead like a real king. But that means Savior might get me, or the cops might or someone else. I've decided who will rule if anything should happen to me. I name Sly as my successor."

Rex heard applause. Not as much as he would have thought, though. Didn't everyone like Sly?

"Sly is also a fighter," Rex shouted. "If he and I both get killed, then Hillary will be our ruler." He hadn't seen Hillary around, but she was probably somewhere up on that ledge.

Rex knew it was a good decision. Firstborn hated Sly, so maybe he'd try to kill both Sly and Rex. But Firstborn had saved Hillary once — would he kill her as well? Was his need for power that great?

The announcement was done.

That meant no more stalling — Rex had to go into that cabin and be with Mommy.

A smell tickled Rex's nose. He sniffed lightly, then deeper. What *was* that?

He turned toward Mommy's cabin. He sniffed some more. His face suddenly felt hot. Another step, and he stumbled a little on a loose board. He managed to catch his balance before he fell — wouldn't *that* be embarrassing? To fall in front of everyone?

Rex stopped. He looked down. He had the boner of all boners. Wow, did his face feel *hot*.

And then a deep voice came from inside the cabin. Mommy's voice.

"Venez ah mwah mon rwah."

He didn't understand her words. He didn't care *what* she said, didn't care about anything anymore but that smell in his nose and what waited for him there in the darkness.

Rex walked through the cabin door.

Bryan & Pookie Meet Aggie James

They weren't officially back on the force yet, but a lead was a lead. Bryan wasn't going to let a little thing like being fired get in the way of pursuing it.

They'd heard the call come in. A bum had been picked up at Civic Center; a bum carrying a baby. The bum had been injured. Paramedics had brought the bum and baby both to SFGH. When the arresting officer called it in, he described the baby's blanket as being covered with *circles and slashes, occult kind of stuff.*

A bum with a baby. Just like Mike Clauser had described.

Most of the cops at SFGH were preoccupied with Erickson's security. That — combined with the flurry of activity that had blown up surrounding this new Handyman Killer, and with Zou not being around to direct traffic — meant Bryan and Pookie weren't really on anyone's radar at the moment.

They stepped off the elevator onto the second floor of the hospital's main building, far away from the mental health wing. The injured bum was on this floor.

Bryan looked down the hall. It wasn't hard to spot the right room, because a uniformed officer sat on a chair outside of it.

"Shit," Bryan said. "Think you can talk your way past this one, Pooks, or is the Force no longer strong with this one?"

A dismissive huff escaped Pookie's lips. "Nigga, please. Don't you recognize him? It's Stuart Hood."

Bryan did recognize Hood: he was the guy who'd first interviewed Tiffany Hine after Jay Parlar's death.

"Come on," Pookie said. "I'll talk my way in there. Let's see if Daddy really has lost his touch, or if the SWAT boys were just a fluke."

They started walking. Bryan hadn't made it ten steps before he slowed, then stopped — a new smell. A strong yet faint scent, cut with the normal hospital odors of medicine and disinfectant.

He knew that smell . . . it was a lot like the odor from Rex Deprovdechuk's house. Similar, yet subtly unique. The baby or the bum, or both, were Zeds.

"Bryan," Pookie said. "You okay? You're stumbling a little."

Bryan blinked, shook his head. "Yeah, fine." He'd have to learn to control this stuff. What if he ran into one of those basement critters and they had some stink that made him lose focus? Losing focus against something like that bear creature could get him killed.

Pookie put his hand on Bryan's shoulder. "You sure?"

Bryan took a breath, gave his head and shoulders a quick shake. "Yeah, I'm good."

He followed Pookie to the room.

"Stuart Hood!" Pookie said. "Good to see you again."

Hood looked up and gave Pookie a wide smile. "Inspector Chang."

"Hell, call me Pookie. Hey, did you hear that Zou reinstated us?"

Hood looked from Pookie to Bryan, then back again. "No, I hadn't heard that. That's great news, congrats."

"Gracias," Pookie said. "And we're back on a case that's related to what Tiffany Hine saw. You remember her?"

"The werewolf lady?"

Pookie snapped his fingers. "That's the one." He tilted his head toward the door. "We got an ID on the bum who had the baby?"

Hood nodded. "Prints came back already. The guy's name is Aggie James. A few minor drug possession charges but he doesn't have any priors of note. No permanent address. Witnesses said he came out of the subway tunnels. I heard the docs say he has a concussion, but it doesn't sound like anything major."

"What about the baby," Bryan said. "Is it his?"

Hood shrugged. "No idea. No ID on the baby yet. Kid's in the maternity ward."

Pookie pulled out his notepad, sketched out the same triangle-and-circle symbol Bryan had first drawn, then held it up so Hood could see.

"Was this the symbol on the blanket?"

Stuart looked, then nodded. "Yeah. The blanket's in there with him. Ambulance brought him right here, so his personal effects haven't been processed yet. I was told this might be a kidnapping, so someone has to watch him."

"We need in that room," Pookie said. "Just a few minutes. You mind?"

Stuart shook his head, then stood and opened the door to let Bryan and Pookie enter. Inside, a black man lay in a hospital bed. Blankets covered him up to his chest. He had a white bandage wrapped around his head. Handcuffs kept his left hand locked to the bed's frame.

Bryan waited for the fluttery sensation in his chest, but it didn't come. The man in the bed was just that — a man.

There was a cart against the wall. Pookie walked to it and picked up a clear evidence bag holding a blanket. "Symbols all over it," he said. "Take a look at this." He tossed it to Bryan.

Bryan caught it. Even wrapped in the plastic, the smell was nearly overwhelming. The scent seemed to fill up his brain. Just like at Rex's house, the odor made him want to do something — except now that urge was a hundred times more powerful, maybe a thousand times. Bryan handed the blanket back to Pookie.

The smell wasn't just coming from the blanket. Bryan checked out the cart. On it were bags containing the bum's clothes and one holding some kind of knit purse. They all had that powerful odor.

Bryan walked to the hospital bed and leaned in. The bum had the scent on him as well, but not as strong.

The man seemed to sense their presence. His eyelids fluttered open and he slowly turned his head to look at them. "You . . . cops?"

Pookie sighed. "I gotta remember to turn off that neon sign above my head. Hello, Mister James. I'm Inspector Chang. This is Inspector Clauser."

Bryan nodded once. "How you feeling, Mister James?"

The man blinked slowly, as if it hurt to move even his eyelids. "I'm alive," he said. "Where's my baby?"

"Here in the hospital," Pookie said. "He's fine. You claim he's *your* baby?"

Aggie stared first at Pookie, then at Bryan.

"He is," Aggie said. "Bring me my boy or I'll sue your asses."

Pookie shook his head. "Child Protective Services has to verify the child's identity."

Aggie tried to sit up. He seemed surprised to find he could barely move his left hand. He looked at the handcuff holding him in place, then lurched so suddenly the bed rattled. "No! Don't you chain me, *don't you chain me!*"

Chain me. A strange way to describe a handcuff.

Aggie's wide eyes stayed fixed on his restrained wrist. "Lemme go," he said in a thin whisper. "Bring me the boy and lemme go."

"We can't," Bryan said. "Mister James, tell me why you drew those pictures on the blanket."

"I didn't draw them. Lemme go, don't chain me, *please*, lemme go before Hillary finds out I failed."

Bryan looked at Pookie, who shrugged.

"Hillary," Bryan said. "Is Hillary the baby's mother?"

Aggie shook his head violently. His breathing grew more and more rapid. "Mommy is a *monster*."

Bryan felt a cool sensation in his chest and stomach. The baby, the bum, *monsters*, they were all connected, all a part of Bryan's past.

"A monster," Bryan said. "That why you drew those pictures on the blanket? To save the baby from the monster?"

"I said I didn't draw the pictures! Lemme go. Don't let them take me back into the tunnels. *Lemme go goddamit!*"

Pookie leaned in. "Tunnels? Where? Tell us more."

Aggie shook his head. "Don't remember. Don't take me back to the white room. Lemme go. Lemme go."

The room door opened. Stuart Hood leaned in. "Guys, just letting you know I'm out of here. Dispatch said Zou is pulling all security from the hospital. I'm supposed to clear out right away."

"Clear out?" Pookie said. "Who's your relief?"

Hood shrugged. "Someone's coming soon, I guess. I don't know, man, I was told to get out of here pronto. The SWAT team is pulling out as well. Later."

Hood shut the door, leaving Bryan and Pookie alone with Aggie James.

"Pooks, something is wrong."

"Really? Was your first clue Zou wants to leave a child-napper unguarded, or was it that she put a friggin' SWAT team on Erickson and now she thinks he's fine and dandy on his own?"

Pookie's cell phone rang. He looked at it, then held up the phone so Bryan could see the caller ID:

CHIEF AMY ZOU

Bryan nodded.

Pookie answered. "Good evening, Chief. What's up?"

Pookie listened, nodded. "I see." He listened some more. "Sounds nasty. No, actually, I don't know where Bryan is, but I'll find him and bring him. Yes, Chief. Okay."

Pookie put the phone away. "Zou said there's a *third* Handyman killing. Two bodies in the Fort Mason Tunnel."

"I know that place," Bryan said. It was an abandoned train tunnel cut under Fort Mason. It had been closed off and boarded up for years, but people still got in there all the time. No lights, no traffic — the perfect place to drag in a victim and do what you pleased. A new serial killer, a crime-scene location that made sense . . . yet it didn't feel right. "Did she say if we were reinstated to active duty?"

Pookie shook his head. "She didn't mention it."

Two people in the SFGH complex were involved with Marie's Children: Jebediah Erickson and Aggie James. Zou had suddenly ordered that they be left unguarded.

And it was dark outside. Dark, and getting darker.

"Pooks, I think Zou's been compromised. That or she was setting this up all along."

"You think Marie's Children are coming?"

Bryan nodded. "Yeah, and fast. Got a handcuff key? We have to get Aggie out of here."

Pookie nodded, produced a key from his pocket. Bryan unlocked Aggie's handcuff from the bed frame. Aggie's eyes seemed to light up, then fill with betrayal when Bryan clicked the open link on his own wrist.

"Get up, Mister James," Bryan said. "Come with me if you want to live."

Pookie helped the man out of the bed. "Where are you taking him?"

"I'll lock him in Jessup's car for now," Bryan said. "I have to get something out of there. Can you get up to Erickson's room?"

Pookie nodded. "Just hurry the hell back. I just made an executive decision — you can handle all the monster shit."

Bryan put a hand around Aggie's waist and guided the confused, weak man out into the hall.

Calling in the Troops

I t's about time, Chief," Rich Verde said into the phone. "Media is sticking their nose all up in this one. Where have you been?"

"I . . . I don't know."

Her voice sounded strange, maybe a bit hoarse.

"Chief, you okay? What do you mean you don't know?"

"Hold on a second." He heard her sniff, clear her throat. Maybe she had the same bug that had knocked Clauser on his ass a few days ago.

Rich Verde remained just outside of the tarp. The Silver Eagle was in there, doing his thing with the bodies. Rich stared up at the pitch-black night sky. The tall pines surrounding the Handyman crime scene were actually a touch lighter than the dark sky above them, making him feel as if he were deep in the forest. Sometimes it was hard to remember Golden Gate Park was a swath of greenery in the middle of a major city — from here you couldn't see a building, barely any lights, and the sounds of civilization were little more than a dull, distant buzz.

"Sorry," Zou said. "There's another Handyman murder. It's pretty rough."

Amy Zou, the unflappable rock, was shaken up by the third Handyman scene? Rich could only imagine what a Cleveland steamer of gore that had to be. "That bad?"

"Yeah," she said. "Uh . . . is Doctor Metz still there?"

"Yeah. He's finishing up. Robertson hasn't bothered to show up, though."

"I told Sean to come here," she said. "And I need you and Metz here as well. Fort Mason Tunnel. Get here as fast as you can."

Amy cleared her throat again. She sounded like she was on the verge of tears. As far as Rich knew, Amy hadn't cried since they'd found those two half-eaten kids in Golden Gate Park nearly three decades ago. But all this shit . . . it was too much. Rich closed his eyes and saw what he saw every time he did: the mental loop of that hatchet crunching through Bobby Pigeon's shoulder and ribs, the look of fear on his young partner's face.

"Chief, I think I got to take a pass this time. I just can't deal with this anymore."

She said nothing. He felt like a piece of shit. She had always counted on him. He had always delivered. But he was tapped out. He just couldn't look at another butchered body.

"Rich, I need you here."

He looked down, shook his head. She'd have to find someone else. "I can't, Amy. I can't."

She coughed. She *was* crying.

"Just one more, Rich. I promise. Please. Just . . . just do this last thing for me."

Amy Zou gave orders and people followed them. She rarely asked. She had to be as much on the edge as he was.

"Okay," he said. "We're on our way."

He hung up.

Dr. Metz came out of the tent. He nodded at Rich.

"We're all done here," Metz said. "Same as usual. I'll get these two back to the morgue and get to work."

"Change of plans," Rich said. "We're going to the Mason Tunnel."

L emme go," Aggie said.

"For the last time, shut the fuck up." Bryan moved Aggie out of the hospital and toward the parking lot. "I'm trying to keep you alive."

"But I need that baby."

Aggie started to pull away, so Bryan squeezed the man's elbow, just a little.

Aggie's eyes widened. He looked like he'd just realized something about Bryan — something terrifying and abhorrent.

"Don't take me back there," Aggie said. "I swear to God I'll get it done."

Bryan wanted to ask this guy a million questions, but there wasn't time. "Wherever *back* is, I'm not taking you there. But you can bet we'll talk about it later. Now shut up and walk."

Bryan saw the Jessups' black Dodge Magnum at the edge of the parking lot. Adam and Alder were standing outside. They seemed agitated. Adam saw Bryan, waved at him to come quickly.

As Bryan crossed the lot, he pulled out his cell phone and dialed Robin. It was 2:00 A.M. — he expected it to ring a few times, but she answered right away.

"Hey, handsome."

"What are you doing up?"

"Chief Zou called," she said. "She needs me to assist Doctor Metz at a pickup."

Bryan stopped walking. His tight grip on Aggie's elbow made Aggie stop walking as well. "Fort Mason Tunnel?"

"Uh-huh," she said. "I'm just dropping Emma off at Max's, then I'm heading out."

Adam couldn't wait anymore. He ran over.

"Robin, hold on a second," Bryan said. He put the phone to his shoulder and looked at Adam. *"What?"*

"Someone broke into our house," Adam said. He wore a gray jacket against the night's chill. "We have automated alarms that send me pictures." He held up his own phone. The bright screen showed a shadowy image of a massive man with a strangely shaped head. Bryan couldn't make out many details, but he saw enough to know it wasn't a normal person.

Marie's Children had found out about the Jessups, had gone to their house.

Zou had pulled Erickson's security detail.

She wanted Robin at the Mason Tunnel.

Bryan held up a finger, telling Adam to be quiet.

"Robin," Bryan said into the phone, "I need you to listen to me carefully. *Do not* go to the Mason Tunnel. Zou's just as crooked as we thought. Worse. I think she's going to kill everyone who knows about Marie's Children."

"What? Bryan, that's crazy. Why would she—"

"I don't have time for this," he said. "I think shit's about to go down. If you run into trouble, *do not* call 9-1-1 or any other cop. We have no idea who we can trust."

"Okay," she said. There was fear in her voice, but she wasn't about to panic. "Shouldn't I just get out of here?"

Bryan pulled Aggie to the Magnum as he tried to process all the variables. The Jessups' house had already been hit. Would Zou give Robin a certain amount of time to show up at the Mason Tunnel before sending someone after her? Marie's Children could jump across streets. They could scale buildings. They seemed to be at home hiding on building roofs. One might be on top of Robin's building right now, waiting to see if she came out, ready to stalk her just as he'd stalked Jay Parlar in his dream. If she did leave her building, but didn't go right to the Mason Tunnel, would they attack her?

Robin's neighbor Max was a big guy, a bouncer. He knew how to take care of himself. He probably wouldn't stand a chance against one of Marie's Children, but Robin was far safer with him than alone.

"Go to Max's apartment," Bryan said. "Stay there. Keep quiet. Don't call anyone. I'll come for you."

Bryan stopped at the Magnum's rear. Adam opened the hatch and started pulling out equipment drawers.

"Robin, I have to go. I'll call back as soon as I can."

"I love you," she said. "Do what you have to do."

"I love you," he said, then hung up.

She could be in danger, but he didn't know that for sure. Erickson *was* in danger, of that there was no question; Zou had pulled the SWAT detail to clear the way. Bryan wanted to get in the car and go straight to Robin's, but he couldn't just leave Erickson unprotected.

Bryan needed to be in two places at once. The answer was obvious: put those two places together. It would only take a few minutes to pull Erickson out of the hospital, then everyone could head to Robin's.

"Alder!"

The old man slid out of the rear driver's-side seat. "I'm here."

"We have to move Erickson, now. You think he's well enough for that?"

Alder nodded. "I think so. At any rate, it's probably worth the risk if you think they're coming for him."

"I do," Bryan said. He unlocked the handcuff around his wrist. Aggie's face lit up, then faded when Bryan clipped the cuff around Alder's wrist.

"Alder, Aggie, Aggie, Alder," Bryan said. He handed the key to Alder. "I don't care what you do, but make sure Aggie doesn't go anywhere. If you have to convince him this is a wise idea, convince him."

Bryan turned to Aggie. "I'm sorry about this, Mister James, but I need to know what you know. If you run, I'll find you. Oh, and something else you should know. That" — he pointed to Alder's cane — "is a gun that will blow your head clean off. Understand?"

A wide-eyed Aggie stared at the cane, then at Alder, then at Bryan. He nodded.

Bryan clapped Aggie on the shoulder, then turned to the younger Jessup. "Adam, a shit-storm is coming our way fast."

"Then let's gear up." Adam reached into a metal drawer, then handed over a black coat. "Take off your hoodie and put this on before you start babbling questions."

Bryan shrugged out of his sweatshirt and slid into the stiff coat. He gave it a quick look in the Magnum's curved, tinted window. He also saw the reflection of Alder behind his left shoulder, his face deeply wrinkled in an old-man frown.

"That looks ridiculous," Alder said.

The reflection of Adam's face appeared behind Bryan's right shoulder. "Gramps, that shit looks *tight. Real* tight. I been waiting to try this shit out forever."

Bryan stepped back, looked himself up and down.

Long sleeves, black. Two rows of flat-black buttons down the chest. The wide collar lay flat against the coat, but flipped up it would wrap around Bryan's head from temple to temple. The fabric felt heavy. He could see why Adam had chosen this design — navy peacoats *looked* stiff and heavy to start with. Bryan could walk down the busiest street in San Francisco wearing this, and no one would give him a second glance.

Alder used the silver wolf's head of his cane to point at Bryan. "*This* is better than the tradition of the cloak?"

"Hey, cop," Adam said. "How did you know Savior when you saw him?"

"Because people don't wear cloaks," Bryan said. "I mean outside of science fiction conventions or a gay pride parade, that is."

Alder angrily shook the cane at his grandson. "You could have at least given him a trench coat! Like Humphrey Bogart."

Adam rolled his eyes. "Hey, cop, tell my grampa what you pigs do when they see a guy wearing a trench coat."

"We watch him," Bryan said. "A guy in a trench coat could be a perv, a gangster wannabe or a psycho hiding weapons on his person. Usually it's just a businessman, but a trench coat always gets our attention." He smoothed his hands down the rough fabric. "This is supposed to be body armor?"

"The best you can get," Adam said. "You think I fuck around, *ese*?"

Bryan turned on him. "Look, lives are on the line here. I don't have time for your attitude. This is *cloth*, okay? Tell me you have a bulletproof vest in one of those drawers."

Adam's eyes narrowed and his head tilted to the right. "Hey, cop. Remember when you gave me that bloody nose?"

Adam snapped his arm forward. A long-barreled pistol slid into his hand. Before Bryan could even move, three silenced *puffs* coincided with three hard hammer-hits against his chest.

Bryan took a step back, blinking in surprise, then his hands felt up and down his chest, feeling for blood. There was none. There wasn't even a hole in the jacket.

Adam smiled, lifted the gun and blew smoke from the barrel. "Field testing. Good thing that armor worked, huh?"

"Asshole!" Bryan said. "What the fuck, man? What if you hit me in the face?"

"Sorry about that," Adam said. "I, uh, I guess I got a little mad."

The same words Bryan had used after hitting Adam. This guy didn't forget a thing, it seemed. Bryan's hands kept feeling up and down the coat, hands searching for any sign of the bullet impact, but the fabric felt normal. "What the hell is this made out of?"

"The core is a layer of shear-thickening fluid," Adam said. "It's sandwiched on either side by nanocomposite and fronted by spider-silk protein fiber-matrix."

Nanocomposite? *Spider-silk?* "What are you, a mad doctor or something?"

"He's not mad," Alder said. "But he is a doctor. Thrice over. My grandson holds doctorate degrees in physics, metallurgy and medieval history."

Adam pushed his pistol back into its hidden sleeve holster. "That's okay, pig. I'm sure your community college associate's degree stacks up quite well. Don't you worry your pretty little head about the jacket's material, 'cause it gets the job done. There's hidden slits in the lower back so you can get at your guns."

Bryan reached to the small of his back. His hands naturally slid into the slots. He felt the cool handles of the FNs. He pulled the guns out, smooth as silk, then slid them back in — they clicked home into the hidden holster.

Bryan realized he might have to reconsider his opinion of Adam. This stuff was amazing.

"There's more," Adam said. "Check out the similar slit just in front of your elbow."

Bryan slid his hand into the slit and felt a handle. He pulled and found himself holding a knife with a narrow, six-inch blade. "That's amazing. I didn't even know that was there. Other arm too?"

"Of course."

"Remind me not to wear this coat in a metal detector."

"You can," Adam said. "The knives are ceramic. The sheaths are loaded with the silver paste. Every time you put the blade back in, they get a fresh dose."

Bryan slid the knife back into the elbow slot, where it clicked home. "Nice. Any other toys in here?"

Adam pointed to the front pockets. "Hat and gloves of the same material. Check out the hat, it has an extra feature."

Bryan found a black skull cap in the pocket. He put it on.

"Now feel for a snap in the back," Adam said. "Unclip it and pull it forward."

Bryan did. A flap of the thick material came off the top. He pulled it forward. It hung down in front of his face, but he could still see thanks to eye slits. He looked at himself in the Dodge's tinted window. The heavy black fabric reached down below his Adam's apple. Not a single identifying feature showed — he could be anyone.

"Don't get cocky with that," Adam said. "The mask will stop knife cuts, maybe even a small-caliber bullet, but kinetic energy still gets transferred to your head. Someone shoots you point-blank in the head with a Magnum, your brains are going to be bouncing all around the inside of your skull."

"I'll make a note." Bryan pulled the fabric off his face and rolled it back behind his head. It snapped into place. Once again, it looked like he was wearing nothing but a skullcap. "Give me a gun for Pookie."

Adam reached into the back of the Magnum, opened up a case and handed over a five-seven and three magazines. Bryan wondered what other goodies the Jessup boys had in the back of that car, but that was for another time. Bryan put the gun and magazines in his coat pockets.

"You guys be ready to haul ass when I get back," he said. "Make room in that car for Erickson."

Adam reached into another drawer and handed over a small black box with a red button.

"If you get in trouble, hit that," he said. "Gramps and I don't want to go near your mutie littermates, but if you need us, we'll come."

Bryan nodded. Maybe he had underestimated the Jessups. He slid the box into the pocket of his new coat, then turned and jogged toward the hospital. He pulled out his cell phone as he ran.

Bee-boop: "Pookie, you there?"

Bryan waited. Pookie didn't answer.

Bee-boop: "Pookie, you okay?"

Still no answer.

Bryan ran faster.

Into the Breach

The north wall of San Francisco General Hospital's mental health wing faces a small, wooded area. That wooded area slopes down on the east side, leading to the eight lanes of Highway 101. The trees on that slope are surprisingly thick. In those trees, hidden in the blackness of night, stood three still figures draped in dull blankets.

Rex wasn't going to be some pussy king, hiding in the safe tunnels while he sent his brothers and sisters out to fight. Doing things himself was important. He had to be *part* of this; he had to have a hand in bringing Savior to justice.

Sly was on the phone. He talked quietly, nodding at certain points. Rex waited patiently for the update.

Pierre just stared up at the building, his head turning slowly from side to side. Rex had learned two things about Pierre. First, he was head and shoulders above the others when it came to hunting. Pierre knew where to move, how to move, and he saw things that others missed. Second, he wasn't that much fun to talk to. Pierre was a badass, but he was a dumb badass.

Sly slid the phone into a blanket pocket, then stared up at the building just as Pierre did.

"Well?" Rex said.

"Sir Voh and Fort said the Jessups' house was empty," Sly said. "Dragonbreath and Devil Dan got their target, they're on their way back home. Bonehead and Sparky are waiting for the doctor girl to leave. Everyone else said their criminals are heading to the Mason Tunnel."

Rex nodded. "Tell Bonehead and Sparky to wait another thirty minutes. It's best if the criminals come to Chief Zou, but if the doctor-lady doesn't leave, they need to get her. Tell them to bring her in alive if they can. If not, that's the way it goes."

"I'll call them," Sly said. "It was wise of you to leave Firstborn behind to watch the chief, my king."

Firstborn had desperately wanted to come after Savior, but that wasn't smart. Rex wasn't ready to trust Firstborn. Not just yet. Besides — Firstborn had had decades to do the right thing, but he chose instead to stay hidden in the dirt. He didn't *deserve* to be part of this.

A small, blanketed figure appeared on the building's roof. The figure swung over the edge, dropped to a balcony, hopped from the balcony down to a window ledge, then vanished behind the dark trees as it fell to the ground. Moments later, the blanketed man appeared between the trees, walking slowly down the steep slope to join Rex and the others.

"My king," Sucka said. "The roof is clear. I tested the access code and it worked."

Chief Zou had done her job. "Good job, Sucka. Did you see Clauser and Chang?"

Sucka shook his head. "I looked off the roof, but didn't see them. There are too many buildings — they could be in any one of them. Maybe they already left for the Mason Tunnel."

"Maybe," Rex said. "They should have been there by now. Missus Zou said she would take care of them if they didn't show, but they could still be here."

Pierre's long tongue flicked up over his long nose. "Ith okay. If they're here, I'll kill them. Are you ready?"

Pierre knelt down on one knee. Rex needed to learn how to scale the buildings like the others, but that would come later. He crawled up onto Pierre's warm, soft back.

Pierre stood. Suddenly, Rex was eight feet tall.

Rex pulled his blanket tight around his shoulders.

"It's time for the bully to get what's coming to him. Pierre, take me to the roof."

Bryan Fights Sly, Rex, Pierre

Bryan stepped out of the elevator onto the mental health wing's empty third floor. At 2:15 A.M. the hallway was empty.

He pressed the two-way button on his phone.

Bee-boop: "Pooks, you there?"

No answering tone came. What if Marie's Children had come while he was at the car?

Bryan walked quickly down the hall. His hands drifted to the small of his back.

If they hurt Pookie, I swear I'll gut them alive.

Bryan turned the corner and froze. Twenty feet away, in front of Erickson's door, Pookie Chang lay facedown, hands cuffed behind his back. Standing over him with AR-15s in hand were Jeremy Ellis and Matt Hickman in full SWAT gear.

Jeremy raised the barrel of his assault rifle until it pointed halfway between him and Bryan. "Stay right there, Clauser," he said. "Put your hands where I can see them."

Bryan's hands were behind his back, just a quick grab away from his guns. "Pooks, you okay?"

Pookie looked up. "I'm fine. Seems Chief Zou *really* wanted us at that crime scene."

Hickman gave Pookie a light kick in the shoulder. "Shut up, Chang."

Bryan's anger swelled. "You kick him again and I'll rip that foot off your body."

Jeremy took a step to his right, moving to the other side of the hall to create distance between himself and Hickman. "Hands, Clauser." Jeremy raised his barrel farther — now it pointed to Bryan's feet. Could Bryan draw faster than Jeremy could flick the AR-15 up and shoot? No, no way.

Bryan moved his hands out to his sides.

"That's good," Jeremy said. "I hate to do this, but I'm under orders from the chief to arrest you on sight."

What had happened? These guys weren't even supposed to be here. "Arrest me for what?"

"She didn't call me to get my opinion," Jeremy said. "She said if you guys came back, to take you into custody. That's exactly what I'm going to do."

Bryan evaluated his position. Looking down the hall, Jeremy stood on the left side, Hickman on the right. Pookie was on the floor on the right, just in front of the door to Erickson's room. Hickman took two slow steps forward, increasing the space between himself and his partner. Bryan knew the maneuver. That was basic positioning, but it seemed so surreal — *he* did that to other people, people didn't do that to *him*.

"Clauser, come on," Jeremy said, "Make this easy and get on the ground. You know the drill."

Bryan couldn't let this happen. He had to get Pookie off the ground, get Hickman and Jeremy ready to fight whatever was coming. "Jeremy, listen to me. Zou's turned bad. Just give me a chance to explain."

Jeremy raised his weapon the rest of the way; the barrel pointed at Bryan's chest. "Get on the ground, Clauser. *Now!*"

"I can't."

Now Hickman took a half-step forward, weapon also aimed at Bryan's chest. "Put your *hands* behind your *head* and get on your *knees!*"

This was the how the game worked: start out calm, polite, then raise your cop-voice volume until the perp gets the picture.

These fuckers wanted to threaten him? Threaten *Pookie*? Bryan could rush them, draw and *hurt* them, *kill* them, he—

He shook his head. He couldn't lose his temper, not now. "Guys, stop yelling. We—"

That scent, the one he'd smelled on the baby's clothes, but weaker . . . he knew this smell *exactly* — it was the scent from Rex's bedroom.

ba-da-bum-bummmm

Bryan stepped back. That warmth in his chest . . .

Oh shit, not now . . .

Four figures stepped into the hall behind Hickman and Ellis — four figures draped in blankets. In that split second, Bryan saw their faces and knew that his dreams, the monsters in the basement, Rex's drawings, that *all* of it was real.

The snake-man (*Sly*) the dog-face (*Pierre*), a little guy with a giant hooked nose (*the one Pookie saw on the roof*) all striding forward along with the tiny Rex Deprovdechuk.

"Behind you!" Bryan started toward Erickson's door but hadn't made it half a step before two bellowing cop voices roared at him.

"*Get the fuck down!*" Jeremy screamed at exactly the same time Hickman shouted, "*Do not fucking move!*"

Four blankets flared open. Four gun barrels rose.

Bryan reached for his weapons and ran for Erickson's door, knowing full well in that horrid, frozen moment of time that he couldn't do anything to save Ellis and Hickman.

The *crack* of a high-caliber weapon, the *roar* of a shotgun.

Jeremy's head rocked forward. His helmet went flying, chin strap flapping as it spun. Hickman was moving his AR-15 to match Bryan's run when a round caught him in the jaw, shredding flesh, splintering bone and teeth. He fell away to Bryan's right.

Bryan felt the five-seven grips in his hands. He drew and fired without aiming as he lowered his shoulder and launched himself over Pookie. Bryan smashed through the door and landed on his right shoulder, big splinters of wood dropping around him.

ba-da-bum-bummmm

More warmth in his chest, this time from Erickson.

Bryan caught a flash glance of Erickson: an old man in a hospital bed, tubes in his arms and under his nose.

Bryan rolled to his ass. He planted his feet and pushed, sliding on his left shoulder back out the door. Bullets ripped into the door frame above him as he slid between Pookie and the monsters, his fingers flash-flicking the five-seven triggers and sending ten rounds down the hallway.

The monsters ducked and turned. He saw Rex fall backward, spinning to the right, saw Sly stumble backward. Pierre was a blur, scooping Rex up and smashing through another door farther down the hall.

Bryan popped up on his feet and fired twice more. He felt a round hit him in the left shoulder as he put his right foot on Pookie, turned his partner so that his head pointed into Erickson's room, then *shoved;* on his belly with his hands cuffed behind his back, Pookie slid through the door. Bryan dove in behind him as more rounds ripped into the ravaged door frame.

He'd pulled each trigger twelve times, leaving eight rounds in each pistol.

Pookie rolled to his back and sat up. "Bryan, get me out of these!"

They were outnumbered four to one by motherfucking monsters with guns. Bryan wouldn't be able to get Erickson and Pookie out through the hall — he'd have to go out the window. He stood, aimed at the glass and flicked each trigger two times. Four rounds flew out in less than a second. Big spiderweb cracks radiated out from four small holes, but the window didn't break. Security glass. And not just that, there were *bars* on the other side.

He'd forgotten he was in a psych ward.

"Bri-Bri, get me out of these!"

Bryan slid his left-hand five-seven through the slot in his back, clicking it into the holster. He reached for his pocket before he remembered — he'd left his handcuff key with Jessup.

A blur ripped through the door. Bryan raised his right hand to fire, but the thing ducked under the barrel. It hit him hard in the chest, wrapping him up and driving him to his back where they both slid across the floor. Bryan's head smashed into the wall below the window. He felt the attacker slide up to straddle him. Bryan tried to bring his right hand up to shoot, but the attacker grabbed the gun with both hands, ripping it away with shocking strength.

The attacker drove its head forward. Bryan twisted his head to the right. A jagged pain ripped through his left cheek, fire-brand hot as it tore across his lower-left gumline.

The thing pulled back, trailing an arc of blood. Bryan saw the weapon — a sharp, blood-covered, hard needle-beak where a nose should have been. In a hundredth of a second, Bryan recalled Susan Panos's chest, the gaping hole, the lack of blood. This thing was Susie's killer.

The monster reared back to drive forward again, but before it could Pookie slammed into it, knocking it off Bryan. Pookie and the thing crashed into the foot of Erickson's hospital bed.

Bryan lurched up, his right hand sliding into his left sleeve to grip the handle inside.

The beak-nose stood and turned just as Bryan stepped forward. Bryan drove the ceramic knife into the thing's chest with all his newfound strength, punching through the breastbone and into the heart beyond. The eyes above the bloody, curved beak went wide with surprise. Bryan kicked low with his right instep, knocking the monster off his feet while simultaneously pushing down hard on the knife handle, driving the monster to his back.

"Pookie! Hold this in!"

Hands still cuffed behind his back, Bryan's partner threw himself facedown across the stunned monster. Pookie's belly pinned the knife in place.

Bryan grabbed his five-seven off the floor just as Sly's big body came through the doorway. They fired at the same instant, the *cracks* of gunfire filling the small room. Bryan felt a round hammer into his right hipbone, twisting him back and making him miss twice, but he instantly corrected and put two shots center-mass in Sly's chest.

Bryan's five-seven's slide had locked on empty — he was out.

He reached back for his left-hand gun. Before he even gripped the handle, Sly spun away from the door and back into the hall.

Bryan ejected the spent magazine from his right-hand weapon, slid his hand into a chest slot to grab a fresh one and slammed it home.

"Monster!"

Bryan turned. Jebediah Erickson was awake. He looked half drunk and as psycho-angry as an old man could be. Erickson reached to his left with both hands and grabbed a rolling table next to his bed. He hurled it back-handed. Bryan ducked the table, which smashed into the wall.

Now he had to fight Savior as well? "Knock it off, old man!"

"Monster! I'll kill you!"

"Bryan! A little help here?" Hands still cuffed behind him, Pookie was trying to stay on top of the squirming beak-face. The monster fought, but it didn't have much strength left.

Bryan walked over and stepped on its neck, pressing down hard. The creature tried to breathe. Its hands pulled weakly at Pookie's jacket.

The clutching hands slowed, then fell away.

Something big smashed into Bryan's head. He stumbled back. Erickson was throwing anything he could get his hands on.

Bryan's temper *snapped.*

He slid the five-seven into its holster as he stepped to the side of the hospital bed. Erickson groggily reached for Bryan's throat. Bryan hit him in the mouth with a short right. Erickson sagged back.

"Sorry," Bryan said. "I hope you're as tough as they say, old-timer."

Bryan bent at the knees. He reached below the bed, grabbed the heavy machinery underneath, then *lifted.* His arms and legs shook with the weight. He didn't know how strong he really was, but this wasn't the time to doubt it — he took three stumbling, running steps to the window, then *threw.*

The foot of the bed smashed into the bullet-ridden safety glass. The wire-embedded glass folded out like a stiff blanket. The bed, with Erickson still in it, sailed out into the night sky.

Bryan turned to grab Pookie, but before he came all the way around he had a glimpse of a massive, moving pile of brown fur — and then a tank smashed into him.

He flew backward out the window.

Finish Him

Blanket still draped over his shoulders, Rex Deprovdechuk clutched his bleeding arm as he walked to the edge of the broken window. He'd been shot again, but *way* worse this time. He couldn't move his right arm at all, and there was an awful lot of blood.

Down below, Savior's hospital bed was a ghastly gray-white against the nighttime grass. The other man, the one in black who had killed Sucka, was facedown, not moving, still lying where he'd fallen after Pierre had knocked him out of the window.

"I got him," Pierre said. "I kicked his ath."

Rex turned back into the room. Sly was hurt bad, but he had one arm wrapped tight around the neck of a handcuffed man covered in Sucka's blood. The man looked like he might crap himself. Rex couldn't blame him. Rex used his good hand to pull papers out of a blanket pocket. He set them on the ground and unfolded them, his hand smearing the photo printouts with blood. The third sheet matched this man's face.

"Pookie Chang," Rex said. "Sly, that's one of them."

The man struggled, but Sly held him fast.

"I'm a cop, goddamit," the man said. "Let me go!"

Sly squeezed, his bicep pressing into one side of the man's neck, his forearm into the other. Chang's eyes widened, then wrinkled shut. His legs kicked, but he couldn't escape. His kicks slowed, then he went limp.

One-handed, Sly tossed the man over his shoulder.

"My king, we have to go," Sly said. "I have to get you to safety."

Sly had also been shot. His blue San Jose Sharks sweatshirt was soaked at his right shoulder, and also at two spots on his chest. He moved much slower than normal.

Rex pointed back to the window. "Savior is down there. I *want* him."

"Let Pierre take him," Sly said. "Zou said the police with the machine guns would be gone, but they weren't. There could be more of them. I have to get you out of here." Sly looked to his taller brother. "Pierre, can you finish the job?"

Pierre nodded rapidly. "Doth a bear thit in the woodth? I'll kick his ath!"

Sly adjusted his blanket so it covered both him and the policeman on his shoulder. He walked to the room's ravaged door, turned and waited. "My king, we have to go, *now*."

Rex had to trust his best friend. He pulled his own blanket over his head, his arm screaming with protest as he did. He grabbed his wound with his left hand to try and squeeze the pain away.

Pierre leaned out the broken window. "Hey, that guy I clobbered. I think he'th moving. And he'th one of *uth*, I felt it."

Rex looked down again. The man in the black coat was struggling to rise to his knees. Chief Zou had said Bryan Clauser was like Savior, that he was actually one of Marie's Children.

If so, he was a traitor.

"Pierre, make me proud," Rex said. "Get down there and finish him. Then bring Savior back Home."

Pierre smiled his happy-dog smile. His long tongue fell from his mouth and dangled on the right side of his skewed jaw.

"Yeth, my king."

Rex followed Sly out of the room.

•••

Get up, get up, get up.

Bryan pushed himself to his knees. He was on grass. A little clearing in a wooded area. He heard sporadic traffic on the other side of a head-high brick wall not too far away. His left arm wouldn't respond. Every motion he made ripped a stabbing sensation through the top of his chest. Broken collarbone. Had to be.

What had happened? *Pierre* had happened. Bryan ignored the pain as he struggled to his feet. He looked up at the mental health building. He remembered the gunfight, remembered how hard the brown-furred creature had hit him.

Motion from above. From out of the broken third-story window, Pierre sailed into the night air, a long blanket trailing behind him, a stockless shotgun with a drum magazine held in one huge hand.

Bryan looked to where Pierre would fall — fifteen feet away lay the bent and twisted hospital bed, and a few feet from that an unconscious Jebediah Erickson barely covered by a rumpled blue hospital gown.

Pierre landed with far more grace than Bryan had. The dog-faced man stepped toward Savior.

Gunfire opened up on Bryan's left and his right. On his left, the cane-gun, fired by the wobbly old Alder Jessup. On his right, Adam, ripping off short bursts from an Uzi. Pierre covered his face with an arm and turned away. Bullets tore through his blanket, shredding the fabric and spraying blood onto the grass.

"Bryan!" Alder screamed. "Get the creature, we'll rescue Savior. *Go!*"

Bryan quick-glanced for his gun, but the flat-black weapon was nowhere to be seen on the dark grass. He didn't think, he just ran, sprinting straight for the ducking Pierre.

The Uzi fire stopped — Adam's weapon was empty.

Pierre turned and reached for Erickson. Before the big hands could grab the old man, Bryan closed in at full speed — his *new* full speed — and put his right shoulder into Pierre's ribs.

The creature sailed backward and smashed against a tree.

Bryan had hit with his right shoulder, but his left suffered greatly from the impact. Something ground away inside his arm, his chest and his shoulder, liquid fire coursing all up and down his side and neck.

Pierre rolled to his knees. He smiled a dog smile, his pink tongue dangling down off the left side of his skewed lower jaw — he raised his shotgun.

Bryan turned away as the *bah-bah-bah* roar of the automatic weapon tore at the night air. Hammer blasts hit his right shoulder, his back, driving him to the ground.

Then the stuttering crack of the Uzi sounded once again.

Bryan fought through the pain and pushed himself to his knees. When he turned toward the threat, he saw the swirl of a dark blanket, a bit of blue hospital gown, and the pink of an old man's naked ass disappearing over the head-high brick wall that bordered Potrero Avenue — Pierre, with an unconscious Erickson over his shoulder.

Just like that, they were gone from sight.

Bryan heard sirens approaching. How far away was the rest of the SWAT team? Would they have the same orders as Ellis? Would they try to arrest Bryan, or would *shoot to kill* be Zou's new order?

A hand on his good shoulder, grabbing, pulling. "Cop, *get up*," Adam said. "He got Erickson!"

Bryan leaned on Adam as he struggled to his feet. "I gotta go after him."

"No!" Alder's voice. The old man limped over, reloading his cane by taking a bullet from his pocket, putting it into a hidden slot, then twisting the silver wolf's head handle with a click. "Bryan, you have to heal. There could be more of them."

"But they'll kill him!"

Alder shook his head. "He's already dead." His eyes showed he was resigned to an inescapable truth. "Jebediah is gone. The only variable is whether we have one dead Savior, or two."

Bryan started to argue, but the railroad-spike pain driving through his neck and into his lung cut off his words. He couldn't even give chase, let alone fight.

"Okay, *shit*." Bryan let Adam help him toward the wall. "Where's Pookie?"

Adam stopped.

Alder pointed his cane up to the broken third-floor window. "Your partner? Was he with you? Up there?"

Bryan looked up. Some of the safety glass hung loosely like a thick, stiff piece of cracked crystal cloth. "He didn't come down?"

Alder shook his head. "Not yet. Bryan, *move*, we have to get out of here."

Bryan stared, waiting to see Pookie's face pop into view, waiting to hear him shout down some kind of obscenity. Pookie's face didn't show. He had to be in the stairwell, on his way out, or maybe he was already at the car.

"Adam, in my pants pocket, my phone."

For once Adam didn't make a smart-ass answer. He pulled the phone out of Bryan's pocket. Bryan took it. With his right hand, he pressed the two-way button.

Bee-boop: "Pookie! You there?"

There was a pause, then an answer.

Boo-beep: "Hello?"

A boy's voice.

Bryan's body vibrated with instant, overwhelming emotions of *rage* and *fear* and *hate* and *loss* — he had to do something but he knew there was nothing he could do.

"Is this Rex?"

"Uh-huh."

Bryan closed his eyes. He felt like he was there and not there all at the same time. "Is my partner alive?"

"Sure," the boy said. "Don't you also want to know if Savior is alive?"

"I don't give a shit about Savior," Bryan said, not the least bit surprised by his automatic honesty. If it came down to a brother by blood or a brother by actions, there was no question. "Keep Savior. Just let Pookie go."

"No," Rex said. "Mister Chang has to pay for his crimes."

Bryan knew that smell on Rex was supposed to make him want to follow the boy, help the boy. He knew that at a base level, but all the scent in the world couldn't change his urge to find Rex, to wrap his hands around the boy's little neck, to squeeze the life out of him and make him *beg*.

"Let Pookie go," Bryan said. "If you don't, I'm going to find you, Rex. I'm going to kill you. But before you die, I'll make you *hurt*."

"You won't find me," Rex said. "But we'll find you soon enough. You're a murderer, Mister Clauser. You killed Sucka. We'll put you on trial just like the others. Good-bye."

Rex hung up.

Bryan closed his eyes. His best friend was gone.

Pookie had stood by him through everything. Pookie and Robin.

Robin.

His eyes snapped open. "Adam, get me to Shotwell and Twenty-First, right now."

As the three men shuffled toward the Magnum, Bryan texted the one person he hoped he could still trust. He needed backup, and he wasn't about to be picky.

They hobbled to the Jessups' station wagon and climbed in just as the first police cruiser pulled into the hospital parking lot. Bryan and Alder got in the back of the Magnum, Adam hopped into the driver's seat. Bryan saw that Alder had handcuffed Aggie to the inside door handle of the front passenger seat. The bum looked at Bryan, his expression fearful and sullen.

"Jesus, man," Aggie said. "Who fucked up your face?"

Bryan ignored him, waiting to see if he'd have to fight his way out of there.

Adam drove out of the parking lot and onto Potrero just as a second and third cruiser pulled in.

At least Bryan wouldn't have to hurt any cops to go after Robin — and hurt them he would, kill them if he had to, because *nothing* was going to stop him from getting to Robin Hudson.

Bryan reached up and grabbed Aggie's shoulder. Aggie winced; Bryan relaxed his grip — he had to remember his new strength.

"They took my partner," Bryan said. "Do you know where they might take him?"

Aggie nodded. "Probably the same place they took me."

"What will they do with him?"

Aggie shrugged. "Depends on how hungry they are, I guess."

Bryan had to get to Pookie. He had to get to Robin. An impossible decision, but if he could get Robin out of harm's way, then he could focus all of his energy on saving his partner.

"Start talking, Mister James," Bryan said to Aggie. "You've got ten minutes. Tell me what happened to you down there."

Voyeur

Big Max held a glass of wine in his left hand. His right was against his ear, cupped to the wall that separated their apartments.

"Max, quit it," Robin said. "You're making me nervous."

He leaned toward her in that way people do when they whisper. "There could be someone out to get you, but me *listening* to see if anyone is in your apartment is making you nervous?"

"Yes. It's making me think about it and I don't want to think about it. I just want to sit here and have all of us be quiet."

Sitting there, on the couch, was about all Robin could do at the moment — Emma was on one side of her, weighing her down from the left, while Billy's big head and shoulders weighed her down from the right. She couldn't even reach out to the coffee table to set down her wineglass. At some point in the evening, she had become furniture for a combined 155 pounds of cuddly canine.

Max walked away from the wall and waved a hand in casual dismissal. "All right, honey, I'll leave it alone. Not that it matters — I can hear just about everything that goes on over there. I sure did last night."

Robin felt her face flush red. "You heard?"

Max smiled and nodded. "I did. All four times."

Robin covered her face with her free hand. "Oh my God."

"Yeah, I heard that, too," Max said. "I need a boyfriend like Bryan."

"Ho-kay, Max, you've now embarrassed the hell out of me."

He laughed and sat next to her. He scooped Billy up and dragged the limp pit bull onto his lap. Billy's tail gave two thumps, then the dog went back to sleep.

"Well, I'm glad you guys took care of business," Max said. "Was this just ex-sex?"

"What is that?"

Max sighed. "And they call you smart. *Ex-sex* is sex with your ex."

"Oh. Actually, I don't think we're *exes* anymore."

Max held up his wineglass. "Well then, here's to true love."

Robin flushed red all over again. She clinked her glass against his. "And here's to friends — I'd be going crazy if I didn't have a big, strong man to protect me right now."

Max laughed quietly. "Yeah, right. You're the one who's packing heat."

She shrugged. "Still, I'm pretty freaked out. Thank you for letting us stay here."

He flipped his hand dismissively again. "Honey, please, you—"

A metallic *clang* from outside the building cut off his words. Emma and Billy lifted their heads. The arms of both owners slid around their dogs' necks, holding them tight, sending them a clear signal to *be still*, and *be quiet*.

"Max," Robin whispered, "what was that?"

Max nodded toward his curtain-covered window. "Fire escape."

Robin thought of Pookie's claims about people jumping across streets and scrambling up buildings.

Another clang. Then nothing.

"Robin, are you sure we shouldn't call 9-1-1?"

She shook her head. "No. We can't. We don't know if it's safe."

And then Robin Hudson realized just how thin the walls really were, because she heard heavy footsteps coming from inside her apartment.

Pedal to the Metal

A dam wasn't driving like a grandfather anymore.

He didn't seem to give a shit about other cars, the Magnum's finish, traffic lights or even pedestrians. A few days ago, this kind of driving would have made Bryan want to throw Adam's ass in jail. Now he wished Adam could be even more reckless, cut off a few more cars, drive just a little faster.

Aggie was still handcuffed to the front passenger-seat door. The guy spent most of his time staring at the handcuffs.

Adam raced the souped-up Magnum down Twenty-First Street, moving into the left lane to pass whenever the opportunity presented itself. The engine's roar echoed off the buildings on either side, playing off the tinny squawk of a police radio mounted in the dash.

The Magnum hit a pothole; Bryan flinched from a deep sting in his gums.

"Bryan," Alder said, *"sit still!"*

"I'm trying," Bryan said, or at least he *tried* to say it — he wasn't sure what words actually came out of his wide-open mouth. Alder sat next to Bryan in the rear seat. He had to stitch Bryan's torn gums together before he moved on to the ripped cheek. Blood covered the old man's surgical gloves.

There might be more action coming. Alder had wanted to stop so he could fix Bryan's wounds. Bryan told the old man to do the work en route — every bump in the road, every swerve or sudden braking brought more pain from the needle, but Bryan didn't care.

"One more," Alder said. He leaned in, then pulled the needle back. "Done. Now for the cheek, then we have to do the collarbone. It will refuse in the next fifteen minutes or so. If it heals wrong, we'll just have to rebreak it anyway."

Alder opened a kit mounted in the back of the front passenger seat. He pulled out a device Bryan didn't recognize and started prepping it.

"Hey, cop," Adam called from the front seat. "Bad news. Police band just said there's a BOLO out for you. They're saying you killed those two SWAT guys."

That dirty *bitch*. Zou wanted Bryan so bad she'd instantly framed him for the murder of two men. Every cop in the city would be gunning for him. His brief moment of believing Amy Zou was doing the right thing? Bryan had been a fool, and now everyone was paying the price for it.

He closed his eyes, tried to manage the pain radiating through his body. The coat had stopped the shotgun slugs, but like Adam had warned, it didn't stop all of the kinetic energy. Bryan's back throbbed. His right arm hurt almost as bad as his left. He tried to store up the pain, file it away — he'd return it with interest when he got his hands on Rex Deprovdechuk.

Bryan's phone buzzed. A text — the message made his chest lock up.

ROBIN HUDSON: SOMEONE IS IN MY APARTMENT.
CAME IN ON FIRE ESCAPE. PLEASE HURRY!

He started to dial her number, then stopped. She'd texted, not called, which meant she didn't want to make any noise. What if he called and she didn't have her phone on vibrate?

"Adam, how long?"

"Five minutes," the younger Jessup called back.

Bryan texted:

HANG TIGHT, I'M ALMOST THERE.

Alder finished prepping. Now Bryan recognized the device: a power stapler.

Bryan turned his head, offering up his torn cheek, and let Alder get to work.

Dog Fight

Robin hissed through clenched teeth.

"Max, *put it down*."

Big Max held an aluminum baseball bat in his big left hand. In his right hand, he held a thick leash attached to the thick collar surrounding his pit bull's thick neck. Every muscle in Billy's taut body seemed to vibrate — he'd picked up on his master's agitation and was ready to follow Max into any fight.

At least the dogs had kept quiet.

"Robin, come *on*," Max said in a hissing whisper. "You're a cop, you can't let these assholes break into your place."

"I'm just a medical examiner. *Please*, this isn't some meth-head. These people are really dangerous."

Max's muscles twitched just like his dog's. He wanted to mix it up in the worst possible way. He tensed for a second, then sighed. "Fine. You're right. I hope Bryan gets here quick."

Robin nodded. Bryan would be there any second.

She had one arm around Emma, trying to keep her baby on the couch. She felt Emma suddenly stiffen. The dog started to growl. Emma stared at Max's front door, the one that led out into the hallway. A ridge of fur stood up on her back like a furry black fin.

Billy started growling too. He leaned toward the door.

Then Robin smelled it. Coming from the door, from out in the hall, faint but unmistakable . . .

. . . the smell of urine.

Robin reached into her purse and pulled out her gun. She held the subcompact .380 in her right hand, Emma's collar in her left. Someone was out there. One of Marie's Children? The Zed-chromosome people?

Max looped Billy's leash around a heavy wooden chair. Two big steps took Max to the front door.

She tried to say *Max!* but no words would come out.

He held the baseball bat in both hands as he leaned forward to look out the peephole.

The door smashed inward, knocking Max to the floor.

Through the door stepped a man covered in a rancid, blue-and-green-striped blanket. He had a huge head. The forehead alone was two feet wide and misshapen by lumpy, gnarled skin. Beady black eyes beneath that forehead stared right though her.

he's one of them he's got the Zed chromosome he's going to kill me

Dogs barking, the sound of a wooden chair scraping across the floor an inch at a time.

In his right hand, the intruder held a boxy weapon that had a long magazine sticking out of the handle. He glanced down at his left hand — it held a piece of paper. He looked at the paper, then back up at her. He stuffed the paper somewhere inside the blanket, then he smiled.

Shoot him shoot him shoot him echoed in her head, but she couldn't move.

The big-head walked into the apartment, stepping over Max, reaching, grabbing, iron-hard fingers suddenly digging into her shoulders.

A flash of white and black. Emma's teeth locked down on the man's thick thigh. The dog shook her head like a wild thing, putting all of her weight and muscle into it, yanking even as blood sprayed across her snarling muzzle.

The man's beady eyes widened in surprise and pain. He let go of Robin and swung the butt of his weapon hard into Emma's face. She flew across the room, yelping.

Robin raised her pistol and fired three times before she even registered the motion. The big-headed man flinched away, covering his face with his arms.

A flash of metal arcing through the air and a ringing *thonk*. The big-headed man crumpled forward, hands moving from his face to the back of his head. Behind him stood Max, baseball bat in hand.

Billy kept lurching at his leash and barking madly, trying to pull free as the chair holding him back scooted a little closer.

A sound of clinking metal, then a *crack* of electricity. Max contorted so hard his head snapped back. The bat flew out of his hand. He dropped to the ground.

Behind him stood a raven-haired woman — a stunning, strange image. She held a chain in each hand, one set of links on the floor in front of her, another set trailing behind. Robin registered knee-high boots, vinyl pants and a cut-off Raiders sweatshirt that revealed a slim stomach. A brown cape — no, not a *cape*, it was another dirty blanket — hung from her neck. Billy lurched again, dragging the chair closer.

Robin raised her weapon to fire, but the woman flicked a wrist. Robin didn't see the chain move, just felt an electric *zing* in her hand that made her jerk away, throw herself back against the couch. Her hand and arm felt like they were on fire.

The gun was gone.

The black-haired woman smiled and walked forward.

The big-headed man stood up, rubbing the back of his head.

The woman looked at him and laughed. "He did a number on you."

"Shut up," the big-headed man said. "I'll fix him."

He reached down and grabbed Max, who had curled into a fetal position. He flipped Max onto his back, grabbed Max's wrists and held them to the ground. Max opened his eyes and saw what was over him. He struggled, but from the first second it was clear his strength was no match.

Billy roared like a demon. The chair squeaked against the wood floor.

The big man raised his big head, leaning back until his neck muscles popped out like flesh-covered cables. Robin leaned forward to push off the couch and stop the man, but the black-haired woman snap-kicked — the boot smashed into Robin's mouth, driving her back into the couch again.

The world wavered. Robin's body felt numb and unresponsive, but she could still see.

The man slammed his big head forward in a lethal blur. Max's face vanished in a crunching splash of red and gray, like someone had hit a watermelon with a bowling ball.

Robin knew she was screaming, but she wasn't controlling it, it was someone else, someone still there because she wasn't really there, *couldn't* be there, couldn't have just seen Max die like that.

A final screech of wood accompanied the sound of a chair hitting the floor.

Billy the pit bull lunged, locked his massive jaws on the back of big-head's neck. The man let out a scream that sounded like it belonged to a little girl. He fell facedown in the gore of Max's blood and brains, flailing at the back of his head and neck.

•••

John Smith was as afraid as he'd ever been. He thought he might puke at any moment. He had to force himself to watch the road ahead and not look up at the windows of the passing buildings.

There are no snipers up there. There are no snipers.

And even if there were, he had to go anyway. The text message had seen to that.

BRYAN CLAUSER: MARIE'S CHILDREN HAVE POOKS.
GET TO ROBIN'S NOW.

John saw Robin's place coming up on the right. He pulled in the clutch and squeezed the brake as he downshifted. A flare of headlights suddenly blinded him as a car cut over from the left lane, tires screeching. John angled his Harley up onto the sidewalk, barely avoiding the collision. He righted the bike, hopped off and dropped the kickstand in one smooth motion. He ripped off his helmet and drew his Sig Sauer.

The car was a black station wagon. The rear passenger door opened. A man lurched out, clearly hampered by pain.

"Bryan?"

Clauser looked like a completely different person. It wasn't just because of the black peacoat and the skullcap. A makeshift rifle-strap sling held his left arm against his body. A line of metal staples covered a ragged wound from his left upper lip down to the base of his jaw. He held a flat-black sidearm in his right hand. His green eyes burned with a focused rage that promised very bad things to anyone who got in his way.

A high-pitched scream came from Robin's building.

Bryan ran to the apartment building's front door, a classic San Francisco–style door of glass and wood fronted with a black, wrought-iron grate. Without slowing, Bryan kicked out with the flat of his right foot. The iron grate bent, glass shattered, and the whole thing flew inward, hinges tearing free from old wood. The ruined door skidded across the Spanish tile floor, glass pieces skittering in all directions.

Bryan sprinted for the stairs and started taking them three at a time.

John ran after him.

•••

Billy *yanked* and *lurched*, pulling at the man's shredded neck like he was trying to tear the head right off.

"Sparky," the man cried out, "*help me!*"

The woman stepped up and snap-kicked Billy's hips. Billy yelped, his rear legs spinning away, but his teeth stayed clamped on the back of the big man's neck.

The raven-haired woman was laughing.

Robin's eyes shot to a spot on the floor — *her gun.*

She meant to dive for it, but her sluggish legs gave out as she came off the couch. Robin tumbled to the hardwood floor, then urged her unresponsive body forward. She reached for the pistol.

The big-headed man stood, Billy's jaws still locked on his neck. The dog's rear legs flopped limply — he made a sad, hateful sound that combined a deep growl and a long yelp of pain.

Robin reached out. Her hand closed on the gun. As she started to sit up, the man turned sharply, screaming, twisting, trying to aim his semi-automatic behind him — Robin recognized the weapon: a Mac-10.

The black-haired woman raised a hand in an instinctive warning gesture. "Bonehead, don't—"

The Mac-10 stuttered.

Robin felt something sting the left side of her neck and slam against her chest and right shoulder. She fell to her back, stunned.

•••

As he cleared the third-floor landing, Bryan heard the growls of a dog and the screams of a person. He shot down the hall toward Robin's apartment and the sound changed — the growl became a pitiful yelp of dog's shock and pain.

Bryan smelled urine.

Just before he entered the apartment, he felt the *ba-da-bum-bummmm* that marked one of the monsters.

Five-sevens in hand, Bryan turned left into the open apartment door. His eyes caught many things all at once: a man with a big head shooting a Mac-10 madly, trying to hit a pit bull dangling from the back of his neck . . . a big body that could only be Max lying on the floor, his head smashed in like a bloody, broken hardboiled egg . . . a woman with long, thick black hair and a blanket around her shoulders, her hand reaching back . . . and to his right, *Robin.*

Robin, on her back, her chest and shoulder red with blood.

Bryan heard a *crack* and felt a massive shock as something hit his arm. His body lurched away of its own accord. He landed hard on his right hip.

Another Mac-10 stutter, a short yelp, then no more growl.

He saw the black-haired woman move, saw her whipping a chain. The metal rang as it shot forward in a blur toward Bryan's chest. He turned and ducked — the chain hit his face, then a bright flash and a *crack* as numbing pain engulfed his body.

Bryan cried out, tried to roll away, but strong hands grabbed his shoulders and slammed his back into the floor hard enough to crack wood. Stunned, Bryan looked up to see a man with a forehead two feet wide, the gnarled skin smeared with blood, bits of bone and some grayish clumps that were probably Max's brains.

The electric shocks seemed to reverberate through his body — his muscles wouldn't respond fast enough.

The man reared back and lifted his head high. He snarled, he—

Gunshots from Bryan's right, a fast and steady *pop-pop-pop-pop-pop-click* that made the big-headed man twitch, lurch, fall away to the floor on Bryan's left.

Bryan looked to his right: Robin, lying on her left side, right arm extended and gun in hand. She had just saved his life.

The chain flew across the apartment and *cracked* into Robin's hand with a bright spark. Her hand jerked away, sending the gun flying.

"Fuck this," the black-haired woman said. She moved the chains to hold them both in her left hand. Her right hand reached into her blanket and drew a Glock, which she aimed at Robin.

Time moved like it was dragging through hot asphalt. Bryan raised his left hand, felt the rifle-strap sling tearing away, felt his collarbone *snap* again. He was already bending his hand up to shoot the blade mounted along the underside of his forearm, but he wasn't fast enough, he wouldn't be able to—

Gunfire from behind him brough the world crashing back to fast-forward speed. Bryan saw a splash of blood on the black-haired woman's right cheek, another on her right shoulder, then she was turning away, her blanket spinning out behind her, making her seem twice as large. She sprinted to the wall and dove through the window, broken wood and shattering glass following her out into the night beyond.

She was gone.

"Bryan! You okay?"

John Smith, standing in the entryway, dropping an empty magazine from his pistol and loading a fresh one.

Movement on Bryan's left. The big-headed creature, already recovering, standing up, lifting the Mac-10 toward John.

Bryan's extended left hand hung in the air — it was the tiniest thing to point it at the man and flick the hand up.

A metallic *khring* sounded as the blade shot out. Six inches of titanium slid into the man's neck, *chonked* home as barbs dug in, making the blade stick. Eyes wide, the man stumbled to his right, but his foot wouldn't hold his weight. He collapsed like a big bag of bones, blood spraying out of his neck in high, arcing bursts.

John stepped forward and pointed his gun at the man's chest. "*Stay down!* Don't fucking *move!*"

Bryan scrambled to Robin's side. She rolled to her back just as he reached her. He slid his right arm under her neck, lifting her gently. Blood gushed out of the left side of her neck.

He pressed his hand hard against the wound. A growing bloodstain spread across her chest. He slid a hand behind her back and felt wetness. The bullet had gone through her right lung.

"John, call a fucking ambulance!"

The direct pressure to her neck didn't stop the bleeding — the wound continued to pulse blood from under his hand and between his fingers. He'd seen wounds like this before. An ambulance would take ten minutes or more to get here — Robin didn't have ten minutes.

Maybe I'm wrong, please let me be wrong.

"Bryan," she said, her voice quiet and resigned. She knew. They both knew.

"I'm sorry," he said. "I'm so sorry."

She shook her head slowly, once to the left, once to the right.

"Not . . . your fault. Where . . . is my girl?"

"John! Get the dog!"

Bryan stared down at Robin. Why had it taken him so long to realize what she meant to him? "Please don't die."

She coughed. Blood sprayed out of her mouth and onto her chin. Her eyes closed tight as waves of pain ripped through her body, then she opened them. "Bryan, I love you."

"I love you," he said. "I always have. I always will."

Her bloody lips smiled. Somehow, that made it even worse. It opened the floodgates of emotion that had been blocked by the adrenaline. Tears filled his eyes, blurring her a little.

She reached up and wiped them away.

"Tears?" she said. "From you? Nice timing, champ. You got that in just under the wire."

John stood over them, cradling a whimpering Emma. The left side of her face was a sheet of blood.

Only now did Robin looked scared. "Oh God, is she—"

"Cut on her head is all," John said quickly. "She'll be okay." He knelt down and set the wounded dog in Robin's lap.

Now Robin smiled at John. She reached up and touched his cheek, her fingers tracing a line of her own blood on his dark skin. "Looks like you're not afraid to be a cop anymore."

John said nothing. Tears trickled down his face.

Robin turned her attention to Emma. The dog lifted her torn head and licked Robin's face. Emma's blood dripped down to Robin's chest, indiscernible against Robin's own blood.

"It's okay, baby," Robin said. "It's okay."

But it wasn't okay.

Robin looked up at Bryan, Emma's tongue still dancing on her face.

"Bryan, she's all I have. You take her. You love her."

Bryan nodded. He wanted to talk, but he couldn't. His throat locked up tight.

She reached up to him again, her cold fingertips tracing the shape of his eye. "Do you promise?"

Bryan nodded again.

Robin sagged in his arms. Her eyes didn't close, not like in the movies, but he saw the life in them fade, then vanish forever.

She was gone.

All the Teeth

A hand gently pulled at his shoulder.

"Bryan, we have to go."

Bryan ignored John. He cradled Robin closer. He should have never let her out of his sight.

He couldn't handle the whiplash of emotions — fury, blind hatred, a crippling sensation of loss, the desire to punish, to *kill*. She was gone . . . he couldn't move, couldn't do anything other than to gently rock her body.

"Bryan, I'm so sorry, but we *have* to go. You're wanted for murder. Get up!"

Bryan shook his head. "I don't want to go. I want to be with her."

Now a hand on each shoulder, lifting him.

"Bryan, she's gone. Everyone thinks you killed two cops. They're going to shoot as soon as they see you. *Get up!*"

Dead. Robin was *dead*.

He would make them pay for this. Not an eye for an eye, not a tooth for a tooth — *all* the eyes . . . *all* the teeth.

Bryan leaned in and kissed Robin's forehead one last time. His lips stayed there — pulling away was the hardest thing he had ever done.

He gently set her down, then he stood.

He looked across the floor at the three other corpses — Max, who hadn't done anything wrong, the big-headed member of Marie's Children, and Billy, broken and shot as he tried to avenge his master's death.

Blood continued to spread across the hardwood.

"John, get Emma."

"Bryan, we don't have time to—"

"Get the fucking dog!"

John leaned back, a little scared. Bryan didn't give a shit. He wasn't about to ignore Robin's final wish.

John ran to the sink and grabbed a dish towel. He placed it over Emma's torn face and scooped her up. Emma yelped horribly, then tried to get away, tried to lurch toward Robin's body.

"Shhhhh," John said. He squeezed the dog tighter. "Bryan, I'm leaving. Hurry."

John ran out of the apartment.

After all the noise and chaos, now there was only silence.

Bryan took a final look at the love of his life.

"All the eyes," he said. "All the teeth."

He walked out of the apartment.

The Rude Awakening

Pookie's eyes opened slowly to nothing but whiteness.

Don't take me back to the white room . . .

That's what Aggie James had said. Terrified, freaked-out Aggie.

Pookie blinked against the pain in his throat. He reached up to touch his neck — his hands felt metal.

A collar.

MMMMM HE'S AWAKE.

Pookie sat up and looked around. He was in a circular white room. All around him were people with collars, chains leading from the collars through metal flanges in the white walls.

Rich Verde.

Jesse Sharrow.

Sean Robertson.

Mr. Biz-Nass.

Baldwin Metz.

Amy Zou, twin girls with black hair on either side of her, clinging to her.

Pookie stood. He looked from person to person. "What the hell is this?"

Rich tilted his head toward Zou. "Ask her," he said. "She sold us out."

Zou dipped her head, pulled her girls in tighter. She squeezed them. One of the girls was crying hard, her body shaking with tired sobs. The other stared out with murderous eyes through scattered, heavy black hair, as if she was looking for someone to hurt.

Pookie turned back to Rich. Rich had never looked like a pleasant person, but now he stared at Chief Zou like he'd put a fire ax in her head the first chance he got.

"Verde, what do you mean she sold us out?"

Rich spit in her direction. "Lying *whore!*"

"Knock it off," Robertson said. "She had to do it. They killed her husband. They took her daughters. The Mason Tunnel murder was a setup. She called me, Jesse, Rich, Metz, got us all to the tunnel, and then . . . these *things* took us."

Robertson wasn't wearing glasses, not that they would have fit over his horribly swollen right eye. A cut on his head oozed a thin trail of blood.

Someone had worked him over real solid. Pookie wondered what their assailants had looked like. Then he realized he didn't want to know — his own run-in with beak-nose and the human snake was plenty to think about.

Maybe Zou had had a choice, maybe not. All Pookie knew was she had sold him out, sold Bryan out, and if there had actually been a fire ax within reach, Pookie would have sharpened it, polished it, then handed it to Polyester Rich with a dramatic flourish.

Pookie took a better look around the room. A floor of white-painted stones, walls of the same material curving up to form a domed ceiling, and the white bars of a jail door.

"So where the hell are we?"

Robertson shrugged. "We don't know. Underground, we think."

MMMMM MARIE'S CHILDREN HAVE US. WE ARE FUCKED. YOU SHOULD HAVE SEEN THE MONKEY-THING THAT CAME AND TOOK ME. WE ARE SO FUCKED.

At least they'd left Biz his voice box. He had to jam it up under his collar to talk.

Pookie tried the collar again: tight, solid, didn't feel like he'd be able to get it off. Behind the collar, a heavy chain led back into the wall. There was a way out of this, there *had* to be — he *would not* die down here.

Down here . . . with the *cannibals*.

"Chief," he said, "what happens now?" He could judge her later. All that mattered now was getting out of here alive.

She pulled her daughters a little closer, but stayed quiet.

"Answer him," Verde said. He pulled at his collar, as if it was the only thing stopping him from attacking her. "You traitorous cunt, *answer* him."

She looked up. Her *eyes* . . . Pookie wasn't even sure if she knew where she was. Amy Zou had gone bye-bye.

A metallic sound clanged through the walls. Pookie was yanked backward by his collar. He stumbled, tried to stay on his feet — his back hit the wall. The collar clanged into something and the pulling stopped. Pookie tried to pull away, but he couldn't budge.

A squeal of metal drew all eyes to the opening jail door. A fat old lady walked in. She wore a dowdy, knee-length dress, a gray sweater and a babushka — yellow with a pattern of purple plums.

"You are all criminals," she said in a voice as pleasant as you'd expect from a wrinkled gramma. "It is time for your trial."

She stepped back out of the white room.

A swarm of men rushed in, all wearing hooded white robes and rubber masks. They filled the room, groups of them moving to each chained person. As if that wasn't surreal enough, the first one to rush Pookie looked like the Burger King. Pookie threw a straight right jab that knocked the King off his feet, then quickly went down under the weight of the others.

Cloaks and Daggers

John Smith didn't know what to think.

His Harley roared down the street. He followed the black station wagon. For once, he wasn't afraid of some random gunman. He didn't have the bandwidth to fear them, not with trying to process what he'd seen. That woman had delivered electrical shocks with metal whips. Did the whips generate the shocks, or did *she* generate them? Oh, and the small detail that he'd shot her *in the face.* Instead of hitting the deck and joining Club Bodybag, she'd jumped out of a third-story window. She should have been a broken thing on the sidewalk, but when he got down to the street, she was gone.

And it wasn't just the girl with the chains. What was the deal with the gigantic, bony head? Robin had shot that man four or five times at point-blank range, yet the man had *stood up.*

So, yeah, maybe there were worse things to fear than snipers.

Robin, dead. Murdered like a goddamn druglord, gunned down in her own apartment. And her last words to John: *looks like you're not afraid to be a cop anymore.* Well, she was wrong about that. He was still terrified, but Bryan needed help and that was that.

Lives were in danger. Time to step up and do his part.

The Magnum's brake lights flashed. The car pulled into the parking lot of a closed Walgreens. The drugstore itself was on one side of the empty lot. Two-story buildings lined the rear and the other side, creating a walled-in space viewable only from the road. The Magnum drove to the back and parked. John pulled up next to it.

Bryan got out of the station wagon, a flat-black pistol in his right hand. A mask, the same color as his peacoat, hung down over his face. He looked around, then aimed the pistol up at a corner of the parking lot and fired. A camera erupted in a small cloud of sparks. He did it again with a second camera. Another look around to be sure he'd got them all, then he opened the front passenger door, reached in with his left hand and dragged out a black man by his neck. The man had a handcuff locked on his right wrist; the cuff's partner dangled free from the short chain. John didn't recognize the guy.

Bryan pulled the man to the front of the Magnum, then pushed until the man sat on the hood.

"You came out of a Muni tunnel at the Civic Center," Bryan said. "You're going to show us where."

The man shook his head, shook it hard. "No sir, I don't know where I was."

Still holding the man's neck, a masked Bryan leaned in. "Aggie, you're going to show me."

The man — Aggie, apparently — shook his head so hard his lips bounced from side to side. "No way! I'm not going back there!"

Bryan's right hand came up; the barrel of his gun pressed into Aggie's left cheekbone.

John's hand shot inside his motorcycle jacket to the handle of his own weapon. "Bryan, stop it!"

"John," Bryan said without turning around, "you're either with me, or you're an obstacle. Back off."

Bryan was way past the edge. If John moved too fast, if he did anything wrong, that poor guy's brains could splatter all over the car's hood. Bryan had already killed one person that night, and acted like he wouldn't hesitate to kill another.

"Backing off," John said. "Just take it easy."

The Magnum's driver's door opened and a man got out slowly. John didn't recognize the heavily pierced, thirtysomething rocker.

Bryan pushed the gun in a little harder, tilting Aggie's head to the right. Aggie's eyes scrunched up tight.

"I don't know you," Bryan said. "I don't care what happens to you. You're either going to take me into that tunnel and show me where they kept you, or I'm going to pull this trigger."

Aggie's breath came in fast, short bursts. "Tunnel is hidden," he said through clenched teeth. "Don't know where it is, exactly."

Bryan shook his masked head. "Not good enough."

The rocker raised his hands, palms out. "Cop, listen. He can't help us. Erickson has been hunting for their lair for fifty years. He never found it."

"I'm not Erickson," Bryan said.

John thought of going for his gun again, but that would only aggravate Bryan. Any added stress could make him pull that trigger. *Come on, Terminator, snap out of it, he's just a civilian.*

Bryan leaned in until his eyes were only an inch from Aggie's. "You're going to take me down there, Aggie. I know that'll scare you and I don't give a shit. The only way you see the sunrise ever again is if you show me what I want to see."

Aggie opened one eye. He raised his eyebrow in an expression of a man hopeful to make a deal. "The baby?"

Bryan shook his head. "No fucking way."

Aggie opened the other eye. He stared back with fearful defiance. "Then shoot me. I'd rather eat a bullet than go out the way they do it."

Bryan paused. He nodded. "Okay. You take us in there, and I'll see what I can do. But I can't promise anything."

"If you did promise, I'd know you was lying," Aggie said. "Now can you let go of my throat and get that goddamn gun out of my face?"

Bryan leaned back, pulled Aggie to his feet. Bryan's right hand slid behind his back and into a hidden slot in the peacoat. Like a magician's trick, *prest-o change-o*, the pistol vanished.

"One more thing," Aggie said. "I ain't going in without a gun."

Bryan seemed to consider this.

"No way," John said. "Bryan, he's a civilian. Do you even know this guy?"

Bryan turned. Green eyes stared out through mask slits. "He's taking us down. The man wants a gun? The man gets a gun." Bryan turned to the rocker. "Adam, let's see what you've got."

Bryan started walking to the back of the station wagon.

"Hold on," John said. "Bryan, what the hell is going on? Taking us down? Down where? And would you lose that retarded mask?"

Bryan lifted the black fabric and tucked it somewhere in the back of his skullcap. He suddenly seemed like the old stone-faced Bryan, emotionless save for a wide-eyed anger that didn't waver.

"The monsters have Pookie," he said. "Aggie said there's a tunnel complex under the city. If Pookie is alive, that's where Rex took him. I'm going in there to get my partner, and to get some payback for Robin while I'm at it."

Payback for Robin. That was obviously shorthand for *I'm going to kill anything that moves, and I want you to help me with the slaughter.*

"You said *Rex*? You mean Rex Deprovdechuk? That little kid?"

Bryan nodded. "He's the leader of the monsters, Marie's Children, the things with the Zed chromosome that Robin told you about, whatever you want to call them. I don't have time for this, John. I'm going to get Pookie. Those things in Erickson's basement we told you about? Aggie says there are hundreds of them down there. That's where I'm going. You can come with me, or you can leave."

They'd taken Pookie. Robin hadn't done anything to anyone, yet they'd killed her. She wasn't the first person killed by Marie's Children. The cult — or monsters, or whatever the hell they were — had a centuries-long history of murder. On top of those things, the man who had saved John's life was asking for help.

John nodded. "I'm in."

Bryan slapped him on the shoulder. "Good man. Let's get geared up. Adam?"

Bryan walked to the back of the Magnum and everyone else followed. Another man, much older, got out of the back of the car. He walked with a cane. He offered his hand to John.

"Alder Jessup," he said. "The younger fellow there is my grandson, Adam."

John shook the older man's hand, a normal action that seemed somehow bizarre considering the situation. "I'm John Smith."

"*Inspector* John Smith," Bryan said. "John is a cop."

Adam rolled his eyes as he opened the back of the station wagon. "Another cop. If I was any luckier I'd piss rainbows and shit a pot of gold."

The older man sighed. "Please excuse my grandson. He is on less-than-friendly terms with law enforcement."

Metal pull-out drawers packed the Magnum's payload area. Up on top of the drawers, in the narrow space where the driver could see out the rear window, sat Emma. Someone had bandaged the dog's face, wrapping it with gauze and tape that was already stained with her blood.

Adam looked at Bryan. The rocker rubbed his hands together as if he were about to open a stack of presents on Christmas morning. "What do you need, cop?"

"Armor," Bryan said. "Whatever you've got. And firepower."

Adam started sliding out drawers as Emma looked down from her perch.

John looked all around, then back at the cases full of weapons, then at Bryan Clauser. A few hours ago, John had been cowering in his cozy, warm apartment. And now? "Bryan, are we really standing in a Walgreens parking lot passing out guns so we can find an underground complex and shoot monsters?"

Bryan nodded. "That's right."

"Hoo-kay," John said. "Just wanted to clarify."

Adam reached into a drawer and pulled out what looked like an M-16 on steroids.

"Jesus," John said. "Is that an automatic shotgun?"

Bryan jerked his thumb at John. "Give that to him."

Adam handed it to John, then passed over six full magazines. "That's a USAS-Twelve. You know how to use one of those, Piggy Pigerson?"

"I'll figure it out," John said.

"Knives," Bryan said.

Adam opened a smaller drawer to show three sheathed knives. "Only got three, and I get one."

The old man reached out and tapped one with his cane. "I get one as well."

Adam looked up. He didn't look excited anymore. "Grampa, you can't go in."

The old man regally drew himself up to his full height. "I've been a part of this for my entire life. If there's a chance we can find the home of these creatures and wipe them out, I'm going."

"But, Grampa, you—"

Bryan reached in, took a knife and handed it hilt-first to Alder. "He knows the risks. We don't have time for this."

Adam looked angry, but he said nothing. He handed the last knife to John. John pulled the Ka-Bar out of its sheath. The flat-black blade absorbed the dim streetlights. Only the edge gleamed.

"A knife," John said. "They eat bullets like candy, so you want me to *stab* them?"

Bryan nodded. "The knife is poisoned, just like the blade I put in bighead's neck. Stab them in the heart, hold it in till they stop moving."

John hoped he wouldn't get close enough to put the blade to the test. He slid the knife back into its sheath, then attached the sheath to his belt.

Adam pulled out another drawer. Inside were three handguns just like the one Bryan had. Now John recognized them: FN five-sevens.

Bryan grabbed one, then held it in front of Aggie.

"Self-defense only," Bryan said. "You *will* show us where to go, but I don't expect you to fight. And if you point this weapon at me or anyone else here, even by accident, you'll be dead before you have a chance to realize how stupid you are. Understand?"

A wide-eyed Aggie nodded and took the gun.

Bryan handed an FN to Alder, and one to John. Adam passed out magazines. John was running out of room to hold it all, so he made a little pile at his feet.

Adam again rubbed his hands together. "Now the good stuff." He pulled a case out of the back and set it on the pavement in front of him.

He opened it, then turned it toward the others as if it were a display case of fine jewelry.

John looked in the case and wondered if it wasn't too late to get on his Harley and just start driving to anywhere but here.

Aggie leaned in. "Grenades?"

"Yup," Adam said.

"Cool," Aggie said. "Can I have one?"

Bryan shook his head. "Not for you."

Adam pointed to the twelve grenades packed into the black foam in three rows of four. "Four thermite, four shrapnel, four concussion."

Everyone but Aggie took one of each.

John looked down at his pile — USAS-12, FN five-seven, magazines for both, three grenades. "How the hell am I supposed to carry all this?"

Adam smiled. "That's the best part." He pulled out another long drawer, the biggest of them all. He reached in and handed over a bundle of cloth. John held it, let it unfold.

It was a dark green cloak with a hood.

"You've got to be shitting me," he said.

"Put it on," Bryan said. "When this is all done, you're still a cop. You need to hide your face. It's all armored up, might save your life."

Adam handed another cloak to Alder, who rested his cane against the Magnum and started to put it on. Adam pulled one more thing out of the case — a jacket like Bryan's.

"Hey," John said, nodding at the jacket, "can't I have that instead?"

Adam shook his head. "I made it, I get to wear it." He slid it on, then looked at John. "Put on the goddamn cloak already."

John did. He slid into the sleeves The front zipper turned out to be magnetic, a simple strip that sealed tight when he pressed it together. Inside the cloak, he found several deep pockets. He scooped up his toys and put them away.

Bryan took off his hat. He undid the mask and looked at the dangling fabric. "Adam, you got a marker? Something I can use to draw on this?"

Adam looked at him with a *why would you want that* expression, but he didn't say a word. Instead, he reached for another case, opened it, then handed over a white paint pen. "Will that do?"

John watched Bryan take the pen, look at it, and smile. It wasn't a healthy smile.

"Time to go," Bryan said. "John, you're in the car with us."

Bryan opened the back door. "Aggie, in the middle. We need to talk on the way there."

Aggie got in, followed by Bryan. Alder climbed in the other side, leaving John the front passenger seat. John looked at his Harley and wondered again if he should just get on it and get the hell out of here. His apartment was ten minutes away. He'd spent six years afraid of his own shadow, and now Bryan wanted him to go into tunnels and shoot monsters?

John *wanted* to leave, but he couldn't — not if they had Pookie.

He got in the car and shut the door.

Bryan sat in the back, drenched in shadow. He took off his hat, opened the pen, then started to draw something on the mask. "Aggie, while we drive, you tell me everything you can about what happened to you in those tunnels, about everything you saw. Adam, get us to the Civic Center station, fast."

The Magnum's big engine growled as the station wagon rolled out of the Walgreens parking lot.

The Crown

Blindfolded and bound, hanging from a pole like a butchered pig, Pookie bounced in time with the steps of his captors. His wrists and ankles hurt from too-tight ropes, from his own weight pulling against his bones. He lost track of how long they carried him — *fifteen minutes? thirty?* — through tunnels so narrow he felt dirt walls scraping against his left and right sides at the same time. At one point, they had set him down and dragged him through an area so tight Pookie felt the earth pressing into his back and face as well.

Finally, the echoing noise of a crowd and a sensation of openness told him he'd entered a much larger area. Was this where he would die? Would it be quick?

Hands lifted him to a standing position. The knots around his wrists and ankles were cut free, but those same hands — *strong* hands — held him so tight he couldn't even try to escape. New ropes wrapped around his chest, his stomach, his legs. The ropes pulled him tight against a thick pole at his back, but at least he stood on his own feet again.

The blindfold came off. Pookie blinked as his eyes adjusted to the lights. He was in a wide cavern. About thirty feet up, a ledge lined the wall like the deck of a football stadium, a ledge lined with . . .

Mary mother of God . . .

People and *monsters*, hundreds of them, stood up there, looking down at Pookie and the others.

On his left, tied to vertical poles, he saw Rich Verde, Mr. Biz-Nass, Sean Robertson and Baldwin Metz. On his right, Jesse Sharrow, Chief Zou and then her two little girls.

Pookie pulled at his ropes, but his body didn't budge. What was he standing on? Broken wood? He craned his neck, trying to take everything in. It looked like he was on the deck of a shipwreck. He faced the broken prow. If this was an old ship, which was impossible, the pilothouse would be somewhere behind him.

Only fifteen feet away, a mast rose up from the deck — a mast covered with human skulls. Thirty feet up, a wooden pole crossed that mast making a big *T*. And there, still dressed in a hospital gown, hung a crucified Jebediah Erickson. Spikes driven through torn flesh held his bloody hands to the wood, pinned his bloody feet to the mast. The old man was awake — he was obviously in great pain, but he also looked pissed as hell. He tried to shout something, but the gag in his mouth kept him from forming words. On his left and right, lights clustered each end of the *T* — flaming torches as well as the mismatched electric rigs you'd see on a construction site.

The crowd started to cheer. Someone walked past Pookie's left, between him and Rich Verde. It was the boy, Rex Deprovdechuk, dressed in a red velvet cape . . . was he wearing a *crown*? He was, a crown of twisted iron and polished steel.

Jesus, deliver me from this evil.

Rex looked up to the crowd on the ledge. He spread his arms outward like a stage performer, turned left, then right, so they could all see him. The crowd screamed for him — some screams sounded human, some didn't, but they all resonated with righteous rage.

Something sniffed at Pookie's right ear. He tried to flinch away, but he could barely move. He turned . . . he was only inches from the yellow-eyed gaze of the snake-face.

"*Clean,*" the snake said quietly. "We don't get that often, but things are changing."

Out front, Rex raised both hands high, then dropped them. The audience fell silent. When he spoke, his adolescent voice echoed off the cavern's walls and ceiling.

"For centuries they have hunted us," the boy said. "And this one" — he pointed up at Erickson — "has killed more of us than any other. First-born could not deliver him to you, but I have!"

The crowd roared again. Hundreds of monstrous creatures shook their fists. They screamed, some even jumped up and down like a revival meeting.

The boy raised and dropped his hands again, cutting off the cheers, commanding everyone's attention. His diminutive size didn't seem to matter; he had an aura about him, the charisma of a born leader. Pookie couldn't look away.

"Soon we will pass judgment on the monster," Rex said. "But first, we have criminals to put on trial!"

Rex turned to look at Pookie and the others, and for the first time Pookie saw the madness in the boy's eyes — Rex was psychotic, drunk with power, smiling a madman's smile. If there had ever been a normal boy inside Rex Deprovdechuk's body, that boy was gone.

Rex pointed. Pookie shuddered, thought Rex was pointing at *him*, but Rex was pointing to Pookie's right.

At white-haired Jesse Sharrow, his blue uniform streaked with tunnel dirt.

"Bring him forward," Rex said. "Let the trials begin!"

Civic Center

ggie had changed his mind. There *was* a God, and whatever God was, it *hated* Aggie James.

The Magnum pulled into the parking lot of Trinity Place at Market and Eighth. The psycho cop on his left finished his drawing and dropped his pen on the floor. He held up his black mask, examining his handiwork.

Aggie stared at the design. *What did I ever do to deserve this?*

"You ain't much of an artist," Aggie said.

Clauser nodded. "I'm not looking for fans."

The mask had already been disturbing enough. With the paint pen, the crazy cop had added a childish, skull-smile line drawing that glowed an electric white against the flat black fabric.

And this man, this scary-ass Bryan Clauser, was going to force Aggie back into the tunnels.

If going in meant there was a chance Aggie could get his baby back, he had to take it. He had a plan — he just had to wait for the right moment, have a giant set of balls, and hope to *finally* get some luck to fall his way.

The cop set the skullcap-mask in his lap. "Everyone, listen up," he said. "The entrance to the Civic Center station is right behind us, on the sidewalk. At this hour, the station is probably closed so we shouldn't run into anyone. We walk out of the car and head straight down. There's cameras all over and we can't get them all, so ignore them and just descend. If there are any BART cops, I'll handle them. We move fast, we'll be down there in twenty seconds and into the main tunnel before anyone can react. Muni trains have stopped running this late, so Aggie will lead us right off the platform and into the tunnel. Right, Aggie?"

Aggie nodded.

"Good," Clauser said. "Everyone does what I say, when I say it. Hoods up, tuck your weapons in, and let's go."

"Wait," Aggie said. "I need one more thing."

The cop stared at him with those cold eyes. He put the black skullcap on, then lowered the mask. The white skull smile grinned.

"You already asked for *one more thing*, Aggie. What do you want?"

Time for the giant set of balls; it was now or never.

"A badge," Aggie said. "I know we're going to fight monsters and all that, but cops are gonna show up and I already got two strikes. If you all get killed, I need enough bullshit to get away."

The skull-smile shook his head. "No way."

"Then I ain't going." Aggie crossed his arms and gave his best hard stare. He'd never been much of a poker player, but now everything was on the line.

Bryan Clauser stared back. Angry green eyes glared through slits. The skull-smile grinned. "Fuck it," he said. "Not like I'm going to need this thing anymore."

He reached into a pocket and handed over his badge. Aggie took it, amazed that his bluff had worked. Now all he had to do was stay alive just a little bit longer.

"Time to go," Clauser said. "Everyone follow me. If you fall behind, you're on your own. Aggie, you stay with me, and don't try anything."

Doors opened. Out of the black station wagon stepped two men in hooded cloaks, two men in black peacoats and black masks, and a scared-shitless black man with a gun and a badge. They crossed the dark parking lot to the brick sidewalk, then to the U-shaped concrete wall surrounding the escalator down to the subway.

Terror tried to tangle Aggie's feet. He felt like his head might explode, like he might go crazy at any moment.

He was going back down . . . maybe he was already insane.

Aggie kept moving for one thing and one thing only: *for the baby.*

Clauser went down first.

Everyone else followed.

Innocent Until Proven Guilty

The biggest man Pookie had ever seen held Jessie Sharrow tight, only it wasn't a man, it was *two* men, one with a professional wrestler's size and a tiny head, the other with a withered body, a huge head, and a tail wrapped around the bigger one's thick neck.

A bunch of monsters stood on the shipwreck's prow. The snake-face; Tiffany Hines's dog-face, who wore a too-small tuxedo jacket and orange Bermuda shorts; a black-haired girl with a pair of chain whips curled on her hips; a tall, black-furred, cat-faced man wearing jeans and a black-fur cape; the wrinkled old babushka lady; and a little guy with wire-rim glasses and an obscenely distended belly who kept flicking a gold Zippo lighter. These creatures, along with the two-men-in-one, seemed to have some privileged standing with Rex.

Rex stood on the prow's farthest point, arms again raised to address the audience. "You have heard the arguments. Now, we must pass judgment."

There hadn't been any *arguments*, just a long list of accusations against Sharrow — accusations like *aiding and abetting murderers, conspiring to kill people, being a bully,* and *hating on us like a dick.* They were the accusations of an awkward teenage boy who suddenly had all the power in the world.

Rex raised his left fist, his thumb pointed in parallel to the ground.

The crowd roared *guilty! guilty!*

Jesus . . . the kid thought he was a Roman emperor or something, and this was his coliseum. Rex turned slowly, letting everyone see his fist, his thumb. He gazed up at his people, his eyes wide with murder, his upper lip curled and his teeth gleaming in the lights of the ship's skull-encrusted mast.

Guilty! Guilty!

Rex lifted up on his toes, then pointed his thumb down.

"Sir Voh," he said. "Carry out the execution."

Pookie shook his head in denial, pulled at the ropes, wished for a miracle.

The big one lifted Sharrow and set him down on the deck. A sprawling right hand the size of Pookie's chest pressed down on Sharrow's stomach, holding the police captain in place. Sharrow's blue uniform — which had always been so clean and perfectly creased — was covered with dirt from the long haul to the ship.

"Please," Sharrow said. *"Please!"*

The little one crawled higher to perch on the top of the big one's head. Tail still wrapped around the big one's neck, he stood on emaciated, spindly legs. He looked down at Sharrow. "For the king. Fort, finish him."

The big man raised his left hand to the sky and made a fist.

Guilty! Guilty!

"No!" Sharrow grabbed at the hand on his stomach, he punched, he scratched, he even lifted his head to bite but his mouth wouldn't reach.

The fist slammed down onto Sharrow's chest, crushing him like a fluid-filled lightbulb. Blood sprayed out of his mouth, the droplets arcing high into the air to fall on the deck, the dirt, and on Sharrow himself. His legs and arms spasmed briefly, then fell limp.

The monster stood. Sharrow's bloody chest had been smashed flat. He didn't move, didn't twitch — he was just gone.

Rex pointed at the corpse. "Remove the criminal!"

White-robed men scrambled out from somewhere behind Pookie. Four of them lifted the shattered body, which flopped in the middle as if the chest were the broken spine of an old blue book. As the masked men carried the body past Pookie to somewhere behind, Pookie closed his eyes.

Jesus save me from this madness.

"Him!"

Rex's voice again. Pookie couldn't look — was Rex pointing his way? Would he be the next one to face the boy's judgment?

"No, leave me alone!"

The voice of Dr. Metz.

Pookie opened his eyes to see the white-robed men dragging the silver-haired medical examiner up to the prow. Rex was watching, nodding, smiling wide with a closed-jaw grin.

"Bring that bully here," Rex said. "Let the next trial begin!"

Can't You Smell That Smell?

It was four in the morning and the Muni station was empty. The only obstacle had been a pull-down gate, which Bryan had attacked with his gloved hands, bending and twisting and snapping until he and the others could slip through. From there, they'd hopped turnstiles and headed down unmoving escalators. Even Alder made good time, fast-hobbling on his cane.

The Muni platform spread out in front of them, a long, empty, light-colored floor with deep, blackish tracks below on either side, tracks that led into shadowy tunnels. Aggie led them off the platform and onto the tracks. Adam pointed out the third rail, told everyone it had nine hundred volts, four thousand amps, and to steer clear.

Bryan wasn't sure if Aggie would make it. The man was literally shaking. On the drive here, Aggie had told his story of a white dungeon, of masked men, of an old shipwreck buried deep underground and a bloated nightmare known as *Mommy*. With all Bryan had seen and experienced in the last few days, he had no reason to doubt Aggie's story. There was no question that Aggie believed every word of it — you couldn't fake that kind of fear.

This had to work. He had to find these things, find the one with the chain-whips, find Pookie.

They walked through the tunnel, along a narrow ledge that paralleled the rails. Flashlights played off grimy white-tiled walls and cinder-filled tracks. They didn't have long before the station opened again for morning trains. Bryan led, followed by Aggie and the others. John Smith brought up the rear.

Only five minutes into the tunnel, Aggie tapped Bryan on the shoulder. Bryan turned. "Is this it?"

Aggie's hands shook, making his flashlight beam jitter on the white tiles. "I don't know, man. I think I walked about this far. I can't really remember."

"You better," Bryan said, "and fast." Aggie looked up the tunnel, down the tunnel. He looked at the walls, searching for something.

That scent . . .

Had Bryan imagined it? He breathed deep through his nose . . . there it was again, the smell that made him want to do something, made him want to *protect*.

He put a hand on the tile wall, then knelt on one knee. He looked left, sniffed, paused, looked right, sniffed.

Stronger to the right.

He stood and gently pushed Aggie behind him, then walked on. *Yes, stronger.*

Footsteps behind him.

"Yo, pig," Adam said. "What is it?"

Bryan sniffed deep, kept walking. "Aggie brought a baby out of here last night. I think I can smell it."

The odor grew stronger as he walked. This same exact scent had made him dizzy in the hospital. Bryan felt his hunter's excitement building. The smell started to fade, just a little, but he could tell it was *weaker.* He turned and retraced his steps. The scent again grew in intensity — when it was at its peak, he stopped.

He knelt . . . stronger still the lower he got. Bryan dropped to his hand and knees, bent his head and sniffed where the tiled wall met the narrow walkway.

Strongest of all.

He looked up at Aggie. "Is this it?"

"Maybe," Aggie said. "I just don't know."

Bryan stood. He raised a foot.

Aggie grabbed his shoulder. "Wait! There's like pillars and stuff right behind there. It's booby-trapped to collapse. Be careful."

Bryan lowered his foot. He tapped on the tile wall with his knuckles. It sounded hollow. He reached to the right, knocked there to test the sound — solid, like a tile wall should be.

"Give me some light."

Flashlight beams danced, reflecting off the dirty hexagonal tiles. Bryan leaned in. Right there . . . was that a darker line of mortar? He drew his knife and slid the point along the line . . . the blade slipped through. He angled the blade down and pried. A thin, black gap rewarded the effort.

"Shine it in here."

Adam pointed his flashlight into the gap. Bryan saw bits of a tunnel beyond. He slid his fingers into the gap. "Everyone look out," he said, and then he *yanked.* The fake wall split down the middle, shreds of plywood and bits of tile flying onto the tracks.

Four flashlights played into the narrow tunnel. Inside, Bryan saw a line of hodge-podge brick-and-masonry pillars extending off into the distance.

"That's it," Aggie said.

Bryan didn't need the confirmation, because he could *smell* that this was it. He leaned down until his nose touched the ground. *Here.*

Aggie leaned in. "That's where I set him down. Go in and you'll see footsteps in the dirt, follow them real careful."

Bryan stood. He took a flashlight from Adam, then entered the tunnel. He played the beam across the ceiling, the walls, the floor. He saw the footsteps Aggie described.

Aggie grabbed his sleeve. "I did my part, now lemme go. Please don't make me go back in, *please.*"

Bryan felt bad for the man, but not *that* bad. Aggie could be the difference between finding Pookie alive or not finding him at all.

And no matter what, someone had to pay for Robin.

All the eyes . . . all the teeth.

"You're coming with us," Bryan said. He turned and looked at John. "You watch Aggie. If he tries to leave, shoot him in the leg."

John nodded. "Sure thing."

John wasn't going to shoot Aggie. Bryan knew that, but hopefully Aggie didn't.

"Everyone follow me," Bryan said, then carefully put his left foot in the first footprint.

The Eagle

The snake-face man lifted Dr. Metz up high, one hand curving up under the old man's ass, the other cupped around the back of his neck.

Guilty! Guilty!

Pookie couldn't draw a breath. It felt like he wasn't taking in air at all. He closed his eyes again — he couldn't watch this.

Rex's horitzontal thumb lifted, then pointed down. "Sly, execute the sentence!"

Metz screamed, but it was a short scream that ended with a sickening *snap*.

The crowed roared in bloodthirsty approval, a passionate chorus that hurt Pookie's ears and shook his body.

He heard and felt the masked men brushing past him to remove Metz's body, then felt them brush by again as they returned to wherever they had come from.

"Next criminal!" Rex's every word was a hoarse-throated scream, every syllable thick with madness and psychotic lust.

"Him! Bring me that one!"

Open your eyes, open your eyes.

But Pookie could not. He just couldn't.

Hands grabbed at his body. His eyes opened of their own accord as panic gripped him, pulled at his heart and kicked his stomach, and when he looked forward he saw only one thing.

Rex Deprovdechuk, pointing his way.

Bloodhound

Bryan couldn't *see* the smell, but it might as well have been a glowing rope hanging in the still air. There wasn't much circulation down here — what had been barely detectable in the train tunnel now filled his nose and mind. The scent called to him at a base level, made him want to kill anything that might harm the source. It was so powerful; Bryan hoped he didn't find that source somewhere down here — if he did, he didn't know what he might do.

After leaving the booby-trapped pillars behind, they moved faster — as fast as he could through a narrow tunnel made of dirt and broken brick, chipped concrete, bits of rusted metal and charred wood.

Then, noises. Faint, nothing but a whisper at first, a whisper that was lost in the sounds of Bryan's movement. He stopped, made the others stand still. He listened and understood: it was the sound of a crowd, tinny and thin from traveling some length down the tunnel.

Aggie had said this tunnel led to the arena with the shipwreck.

Bryan faced the others.

"We're close," he said. "Turn off the flashlights. Stay close to the person in front of you. Move careful, but move *fast*. And from this moment on, not another word."

He turned off his flashlight and slid it into an inside pocket of his peacoat. One by one, the other flashlights blinked out. Darkness filled the tunnel.

They weren't far away. He was going to get Marie's Children for what they had done to Robin, for what they had done to Pookie.

Monster, human, alien, angel or demon — whatever was down here, Bryan Clauser was going to make it pay.

Arena Rock

Bryan saw light — a distant, narrow arch of illumination just a hundred feet away.

Shapes moving in front of that light.

He kept moving forward, his steps quiet and sure.

The sound of a single person talking from far away, words blurred by echoes and the crowd's murmur, until the crowd roared in unison.

Guilty!

Closer. Fifty feet.

The shapes up ahead took form. Mounds that were people covered with blankets, sliding in front of each other as if craning to see something beyond.

Bryan stopped, turned. Adam was right behind him. Not so brave now. Mouth pursed, Adam was forcing himself to breathe slowly. No, not so brave, but still *here*, ready to fight — was bravery really anything more than that?

Behind Adam, Alder. Not afraid. Maybe he'd had decades to accept his mortality. Everyone dies. You can go out swinging, or you can die shitting yourself in a hospital bed as they feed you through tubes.

And in the back, John Smith. He had to be scared, but he didn't look it. Maybe six years of cowardice had taught him how to hide it. Or maybe John was just ready, because one thing was for certain — no one could call him a coward anymore.

Bryan stepped closer. Twenty-five feet.

ba-da-bum-bummmm

He stopped. He closed his eyes tight, opened them again. The smell of the baby, the *thrumm* of his people buzzing in his chest. Those behind him were *not* his people.

ba-da-bum-bummmm!

Why was he going to kill Marie's Children? Why was he going to kill his brothers, his sisters, his *real* family?

He closed his eyes. He pictured the two people who had stood by him through everything.

ba-da-bum-bummmm!

Why was he going to kill Marie's Children? Because they had taken Pookie. Because they had murdered Robin.

Bryan opened his eyes and again looked down the tunnel. He was only fifteen feet away, close enough to see the feet under one of the blankets. Blue feet. Furry. The feet of a monster.

ba-da-bum-bummmm! ba-da-bum-bummmm!

Wait a minute . . . had he missed Aggie? Bryan looked back and took in the faces: Adam, Alder, John, all ready to fight alongside him.

But no Aggie?

Bryan signaled to John, held up both hands in a questioning gesture. John looked confused, then understood. He quickly looked behind him, saw nothing, then turned and shrugged apologetically. Aggie had slipped away. It didn't matter. The man had done his job. Bryan hoped he made it out alive.

Five feet. So close he could reach out and grab the blue-footed person at the back of the ledge, probably grab it so fast the ones in front wouldn't even know.

That echoing voice again, coming from an unseen spot beyond, close enough now that Bryan could make out the words, close enough now that Bryan recognized the speaker.

Rex.

"And for crimes of hating on the people, how do we find the defendant?" *Guilty!*

A new voice: "Killing me won't change the fact that you're a worthless douchebag, you little shit!"

Bryan stopped. Pookie's voice — *he was still alive.* Bryan drew in a slow breath.

Rex started shouting again, his hoarse words far louder than seemed possible from such a small person. "And for the crimes of making sure we all die, how do—"

"U-G-L-Y," Pookie yelled, his voice echoing just as much as Rex's. "You ain't got no alibi. *You're all fucking ugly!*"

"Stop it!" Rex screamed, so loud Bryan heard the boy's vocal cords starting to fray. "Stop interrupting me, or I'll cut out your tongue!"

Bryan drew his knife.

He stepped forward. His hand reached out, wrapped around a furry mouth and pulled hard. Blue-foot fell back into the tunnel. Bryan had a glimpse of shocked blue eyes, felt a scream try to escape his hand, then he slid the knife under the chin and pushed up at an angle. The creature started to kick. Bryan pushed the knife in deeper and twisted it.

Blue-furred eyelids stared, blinked, stared, then lost focus.

Bryan pulled the knife free and sheathed it. He pulled the smelly blanket from under the corpse, then whipped it around his shoulders.

Out in the cavern: "And for the crimes of, uh, wait a minute . . . oh, right, the crimes of making sure we all die, how do you all find the defendant?"

Bryan waved John and the others forward as the crowd shouted *Guilty!*

Bryan's companions moved in close. They looked at him with shock, with fear — like *he* was a monster, a brutal killer. He was all that and more. He stared back at them: John and Alder, their faces deep inside dark green hoods, and Adam, his black jacket collar flipped up around his neck, his skullcap pulled down to his eyebrows.

"Pookie is down there," Bryan whispered. "I'll find a way to reach him. With this blanket I'll blend in — maybe they won't notice me right away. I'll get as close as I can."

"What then?" Adam said.

Bryan reached into his pocket and pulled out the button-box Adam had given him back in the hospital parking lot. "Will this work down here?"

Adam nodded, pulled out a small device from his own pocket. "Yeah, if that cavern out there is open and you don't go into more tunnels, I'll get the signal right here."

Bryan held up the button-box. "When I press this, you guys start killing. Shoot them in the head and they'll go down. Move onto the ledge and *hold this position.* We don't know any other way out. Cause as much damage as you can, I'll try and use the confusion to rescue Pookie."

He didn't wait for them to answer. He flipped up his peacoat collar, adjusted his mask, then pulled the blanket over his head to hide his face.

All the eyes . . . all the teeth.

Bryan Clauser walked out onto the ledge.

Pookie Chang's Last Moments

"You have heard the arguments," Rex shouted. "Now, we must pass judgment."

Guilty! Guilty!

Pookie had always known that someday he would die. He'd always hoped it would be as an old man in bed with four women, each a quarter of his age. A quadruple Chang Bang with a final orgasm into oblivion. That was how a real pimp checked out.

Not like this.

Rex raised his emperor's fist, thumb pointed in. The psycho kid had done this act twice already — you'd think the crowd would be over it. Hardly. They screamed and roared, waiting for the decision.

•••

A surging sense of *belonging* overwhelmed him.

ba-da-bum-bummmm, ba-da-bum-bummmm, ba-da-bum-bummmm

The ledge was four feet wide, five in some places. Chairs sat near the front edge — lawn chairs, metal chairs, cinder blocks, logs, beat-up pieces of society's discards set up as front-row seats for an execution. In every one of those chairs, standing behind them and between them: Marie's Children.

Bryan moved to his right, along the bumpy, irregular wall. Through the packed bodies, he saw the narrow set of stone steps leading down — just like Aggie had said. No one seemed to be using it. He couldn't take that way down, lest he draw attention to himself.

He kept moving right, sliding along between the wall and the spectators. Most of the monsters/people didn't even bother to turn and look at him. And why would they? Bryan *felt* right, Bryan *smelled* right, because he was *one of them*.

He could see down into the cavern below. Nothing Aggie had said could have prepared Bryan for this. It *was* an arena, an oblong, irregular dome big enough for a hockey rink. The floor, some thirty feet below, was lined with winding, intersecting trenches. At the back of the oblong, to Bryan's right, sat a shattered shipwreck from centuries past.

Down on the blood-spattered prow stood Rex Deprovdechuk, dressed in a red velvet cape and wearing a crown. Monsters surrounded Rex.

Bryan recognized Sly from his nightmares, the dog-face from the fight at the hospital. He knew, instantly, that the tall one with the black fur was Firstborn.

Firstborn held someone in front of him, someone in an ill-fitting sport coat — Pookie Chang, tied at the hands and feet, helpless.

Bryan instantly started forward but stopped himself. He only had one shot at this and couldn't afford to miss anything.

Next to Firstborn stood a nerdy kid with a horribly distended belly flipping a Zippo. Bryan didn't recognize that one. The nerdy kid moved to the side, revealing a raven-haired woman.

Robin's killer.

A white, broken mast rose high from the ship's center. High atop that mast Bryan saw Jebediah Erickson, *crucified*, hands nailed to a wooden pole atop the mast.

Past the mast stood a line of posts jutting up from the deck, each with a person tied tightly to it: Zou, her daughters, Mr. Biz-Nass, Rich Verde, Sean Robertson. Three posts stood empty.

Beyond the posts there was what looked like a squashed captain's cabin. Something moved inside there, but Bryan couldn't make it out. The crowd screamed for Rex's decision. The boy stood tall. He held his fist high, his thumb pointed in, parallel to the deck.

Bryan couldn't wait a moment more. He slid farther down the ledge, pushing past his family members and moving closer to the ship.

He reached into his pocket and pulled out the button-box.

•••

Pookie didn't bother struggling anymore. He'd tried. The devil himself held him in a crushing grip. Seven feet tall, the lean, muscular, black-furred creature wore combat boots and jeans with MK23s in sidearm holsters strapped to each thigh. Gray hairs peppered the black-furred face.

Pookie couldn't move.

A crazy thought — maybe Rex would find him innocent, maybe the thumb would point *up*.

Rex lifted up on his toes. He looked back at Pookie and smiled a madman's smile. Rex pointed the thumb down and threw his fist toward the deck like a singer finishing off a rock crescendo.

"Firstborn," he said. "Carry out the execution."

This time, Pookie would not close his eyes.

Mother Mary, full of grace . . .

A furred hand closed on the back of his neck. Firstborn pulled Pookie close. Slanted green eyes glittered with excitement for the task at hand.

Deliver us from evil as I walk in the shadow of the valley of . . . the death-shadowy valley in . . .

Shit. What a time to forget the Lord's Prayer.

The hand slid to the front of his neck, lifted him, started to squeeze . . .

I don't want to die oh shit oh shit . . .

•••

John Smith's hands flexed on the reassuring bulk of his automatic shot-gun. The cloak surrounded him, hid him, made him feel like a different person. Any moment now, he'd be called upon to step up, step forward and start shooting. Were all these monsters guilty? Would he be firing on individuals who had nothing to do with the crimes committed by others? Would he be killing based on nothing but race?

It was too late to debate morality — Bryan was out there, exposed and alone. Pookie was a captive. If John hesitated, both would surely die.

John heard a barely audible buzz. He turned to look at Adam, who held up the receiver — it blinked red.

Bryan had hit the button.

John leaned in close to Alder and Adam.

"Hit the head if you can, but if you're rushed just shoot center-mass," he said. "Clear the ledge, then start chucking grenades to cause more confusion. We need to make them think there's hundreds of us, so they run instead of attacking. You guys ready?"

Alder and Adam nodded.

John wasn't ready, wasn't even close, but the time had come.

He turned and walked down the tunnel toward the ledge.

•••

Black-furred hands held him aloft as if he weighed nothing more than a child.

He couldn't breathe.

This was the end.

From off to the left, Pookie saw something small flying through the air. Had a spectator thrown a rock? It landed somewhere behind Pookie, clattering against the old wood.

Then he heard a hiss, like a hundred sparklers going up at once. Light flared from behind him, *intense* light, casting his shadow forward onto the prow and the people gathered there.

"Mommy," the creature said, and then Pookie felt his back start to get hot.

The crushing hands let go. Pookie fell to the deck, surprised at the sudden freedom. Firstborn stepped over him and ran toward the back of the boat, as did the snake-face, the dog-face and the girl with the metal whips. Pookie turned to see where they were going, but had to flinch and avert his eyes from the bright light blazing near the ship's cabin. He looked back at Rex, who stood there, blinking, not moving, flickering shadows playing off his face.

Echoing gunfire sounded from up on the ledge to the left of the prow. Pookie looked in that direction. Some kind of commotion up there: muzzle flashes, people scrambling, bodies falling off the edge and plummeting to the floor below.

And then, off to the ship's left, he saw something amazing — a man leaping off the cavern's ledge thirty feet above. He sailed toward the ship, rising up nearly to the ceiling before arcing down, his blanket falling away behind him. Legs bicycle-kicked the air. Arms rowed forward like a long jumper's. He wore a black peacoat.

Bryan?

Pookie locked in on the black mask, on the scrawled white death-grin coming closer, closer.

In midair, Bryan's hands shot behind his back and came out holding pistols.

Pookie had a moment to think *that's pretty fucking impressive, homeslice,* then Bryan started to tilt forward, out of control. Arms flailed and legs kicked awkwardly — Bryan smashed into Rex's back, knocking the boy's body forward and driving him face-first into the deck's broken planks. Bryan and Rex skidded through the wood, spraying up jagged splinters and bits of board, then they fell through the deck and vanished from sight.

Battle Royale

Bryan dropped into darkness, things smacking him in his face, his arms and his hands as he fell. He hit hard on his head and shoulder and came to a stop. *Landing* — something he'd have to work on.

He struggled to stand. He still held a five-seven in his right hand. His left hand was empty. He'd lost that gun and it was easy to see why — his pinkie and ring fingers flopped sickly, both broken at their base knuckle.

Cracked boards surrounded him. Old dust choked the air. He'd smashed through the upper deck and apparently one below that. Fifteen feet above, he saw the jagged hole in the deck and the mast lights rising above it. He had to get up there, had to reach Pookie and the others. Bryan struggled to stand amid the angled pile of wood. He got his footing, then bent and *jumped.* He cleared eight feet and landed on the second deck. Another quick leap took him back to the main deck.

Gunfire and screams echoed through the cavern. At the back end of the ship, the cabin wall and door blazed with crawling flame. Something inside cried out in a deep voice. Monsters beat frantically at the flames, trying to put them out. Bryan saw Pierre and Sly and Firstborn, the whip-woman who had killed Robin, all of them trying to fight the fire, but he couldn't take them on now: he had to get the hostages out first.

He looked toward the poles holding Verde and Chief Zou and the others. Blocking the way stood the nerdy kid with the distended belly. He wore bent horn-rimmed glasses and held a silver Zippo in his right hand.

In a practiced motion that would have made the most hard-core hipster chain-smoker green with envy, the kid brought his left hand up, flipping open the Zippo and lighting it with the same motion.

The kid's cheeks puffed out, like he was about to puke. His stomach made a gurgling noise Bryan heard even over the crackling flames. The kid held up the Zippo and let out a sound that was half-belch, half-roar.

Flames billowed out, a spreading fireball ripping toward Bryan's face.

Bryan stepped back over the hole in the deck and dropped down as the fireball ripped the air above him.

•••

From John's right, an insectile monster scrambled over the dead body of one of its brothers and rushed in. John spun to face it, pulled the shotgun trigger twice — the first blast hit it in the chest, the second in the head. The thing flew back, half of its obscene face ripped away. Something hammered John's left shoulder, driving him against the cavern wall. Clumps of dirt and stone broke off around him — someone was shooting at him.

"Alder! Sniper!"

"I have him," Alder said. Alder knelt, aimed his cane at a blanketed gunman on the cavern's opposite ledge.

Fingers scraped at John's left foot. He looked down — a little redhaired girl, no more than ten, crawling up from under the ledge, her tiny fingers reaching out for his foot. The look in her eyes: *murder, hate, hunger.*

John swung the shotgun muzzle down, held it an inch from her face and pulled the trigger. A cloud of brain and bone, the girl spun away down to the trenches below.

Alder's cane-gun fired; the sniper fire ended.

"Damn, I'm good," the old man said.

More monsters were closing in from the right and also from the left, where Adam fired away with his five-seven.

John reached for his grenades.

•••

Hands and feet tied, Pookie fought to standing position. He had to act. The fat kid — the one who had *breathed fire* at Bryan — was only a few feet away, looking down into the hole in the deck. Pookie pushed off both feet and hopped toward the boy.

Got to keep my balance, I swear I'll hit the treadmill if I get out of this alive . . .

The boy heard Pookie coming; he started to turn but he was too late. Pookie threw himself at the boy's legs. The boy wavered for a moment, arms whirling, then he fell into the hole.

•••

Bryan saw the fire-breathing kid fall through the hole in the deck. The dying words of a burn-covered teenager flashed through his mind: *demon, dragon.*

He aimed his five-seven and fired three times as Jay Parlar's killer crashed down to smash face-first into the broken wood. Bryan jumped high again, this time putting his right foot on the second deck and pushing off that, the one-two leap carrying him up to the main deck — he had scrambled fifteen feet *straight up,* just like that.

Bryan found himself standing over Pookie Chang.

"Untie me for fuck's sake!"

Bryan holstered the five-seven and drew his Ka-Bar knife. He sliced through Pookie's ropes and helped the man to his feet.

A big, resonant voice screamed from inside the burning cabin. "Elle brûle . . . elle brûle!"

Explosions echoed from the ledges, joining the cacophony of gunfire, crackling flames and the echoing screams of fear, pain and anger.

Bryan drew the five-seven, then gave it and the knife to Pookie. "Cut everyone loose!"

Pookie nodded and ran toward Chief Zou.

Bryan's other five-seven had to be around here somewhere, or maybe he'd lost it below, but either way he didn't have time to find it. He looked up at the crucified Erickson thirty feet above — he couldn't leave the man up there. Bryan ran to the mast . . . made of *human skulls*?

All the eyes . . . all the teeth.

Bryan jumped onto the mast, his feet breaking skulls as he climbed. He was so strong now, so agile; he scaled the mast like a chimp shooting up a tree trunk. His ravaged left fingers screamed in white-hot complaint, but there was no other choice.

He found himself face-to-face with the Savior.

ba-da-bum-bummmm

Bryan stared at Jebediah Erickson. Jebediah Erickson stared back.

This was his *brother.*

Bryan hooked his left arm over the crossbeam. With his right hand, he grabbed the spike sticking out of Erickson's right palm.

He met Erickson's eyes again. "You ready?"

Erickson's bloody, split lips smiled. "I'm glad I was wrong about you."

Dangling thirty feet above the deck, Bryan yanked the spike free. Erickson snarled, but he didn't cry out. Blood splattered down on the white skulls and the dry wood below.

Bryan swung behind the mast and moved to the other side. He again hooked his left arm over the crossbar, grabbed the spike pinning Erickson's left hand and ripped it free.

The old man slid his right hand behind the mast, holding himself up as he bent at the knees and reached down with his left to yank at the spike nailed through his feet.

Another explosion, more screams — John and the others were using their thermite grenades, using everything they had. The air started to fill with smoke. Bryan felt the cabin fire's heat even from up here on the mast.

"Bryan!" Pookie's voice from below, followed by gunfire.

Bryan let go and dropped. He bent his legs as he landed, absorbing the impact but still stumbling to the right. Mr. Biz-Nass cowered at the base of the skull-mast. Zou and her daughters ran to him. Robertson had the knife and was cutting away at Verde's ropes. Pookie stood tall, firing away at an advancing wave of white-robed men. The masked men would fall or flinch, but there were too many for him to stop them all.

Spreading flames danced up from the deck's dry wooden planks. Some of the white robes were already burning. Blast-furnace heat billowed away from the ship's cabin — in those flames, shimmering images of man-shaped creatures moving, trying to get inside.

The slide of Pookie's five-seven locked. Empty. Bryan hadn't given him the extra magazines.

Bryan gripped his broken pinkie and ring finger. With a grunt, he snapped them back into place. He slid his right hand into his left-arm sheath and came out with the ceramic knife. He forced himself to do the same with his ruined left hand — each fist held one of the slim killing blades.

Pookie backed up. His foot caught on a broken board and he fell to his ass. The Halloween-masked white-robes reached for him but Bryan rushed forward, cutting and stabbing. *Slice-slash-slice* — bodies fell, red blood painted long, wet splashes on white fabric. He kicked out, the sole of his foot smashing into a chest, sending the man flying back into the flames. In seconds, not a single masked man remained standing.

A flash of heat made Bryan reactively stamp his feet — flames licking the cuffs of his pants. He turned and ran back to the skull-mast. Biz-Nass and Robertson were there, helping Erickson to his feet. Zou held one of her daughters, Verde held the other. The fire's heat seemed to press invisible fists against them all, forcing them to lean away, to shield their faces. They blinked madly, coughed against the thick smoke that filled the cavern like a fog.

He urged them to the tip of the shipwreck. "To the prow, go, *go!*"

"Bryan!"

Pookie was pointing back down the deck.

Fifteen feet away, the nerdy kid crawled out of the hole in the deck. Blood sheeted his face. His glasses were twisted and wobbly on his broken nose. He stood, golden Zippo in hand. Behind him, Pierre rushed out of the flaming cabin, long mouth open in a roaring, skewed-jawed snarl, flames dancing on his back and from his shorts.

Pierre and Bryan locked eyes; the dog-face was coming for him.

Erickson grabbed the knife out of Bryan's left hand. The bleeding, half-naked old man stepped forward and threw it.

The blade whipped through the air and slid into the nerdy boy's distended belly. The boy dipped inward at the waist like he'd been punched, shock and surprise etched behind his bent wire-rims. A stream of thin, white vapor jetted out of the hole in his gut.

A flaming Pierre ran right through that stream.

The flame caught the vapor and shot back into the boy's bloated stomach like a reverse flamethrower. His belly blew open in a fireball that swallowed Pierre and threw the monster forward. Engulfed in flame, he tumbled into the people packed on the prow, knocking Erickson and Biz-Nass hard to the deck before landing heavily on top of Amy Zou, pinning her beneath his burning body.

Bryan dropped his knife and grabbed Pierre's ankles. The flames scorched his hands, but he ignored the pain long enough to yank Pierre off Zou and toss him a few feet back down the deck. The big creature seemed limp, weak. The skin on Bryan's hands sizzled. He started to reach down to beat at Amy Zou's burning clothes, but Sean Robertson and Rich Verde were there, rolling Zou over to smother the flames.

A girl's voice: "You killed my daddy."

Bryan turned toward the voice. Little Mur held the knife he'd dropped. She stood over the smoldering dog-man. Pierre lifted a hand to stop her, but he was too weak and too slow. Before Bryan could reach Mur, she clutched the knife in both hands, point down, and plunged the blade into Pierre's right eye.

Pierre flailed and swung out blindly. Mur fell away. Bryan rushed in and grabbed her, pulling her away. Knife handle still sticking out of his eye, Pierre rolled to his hands and knees. He tried to rise, but his shaking arms wouldn't support him. He slumped to his right side and moved no more.

The flames had engulfed most of the ship, driving everyone to the tip of the prow. Mur held tight in his arms, Bryan became aware of a whistling sound, some kind of low, airy hiss. He looked left, eyes scanning the ledge — there, a man in a dark-green cloak, another in a black peacoat, bodies piled up on the ledge around them.

John and the others had held.

And just to the left of John's position, barely visible through the growing smoke, Bryan saw the thin ribbon of steep steps angling up the wall from the cavern floor to the ledge. He and the others would have to cross the trench maze to reach it. The maze walls rose up to flat islands of dirt, like little mesas that defined and separated the trenches. Bryan could jump from mesa to mesa, but the trenches were too wide for the others to do that and he couldn't carry them all. They'd have to go through the maze while he stayed up on the islands, calling down directions.

He cupped his free hand to his mouth, shouted to be heard over the roaring flames. "Off the ship and into the trenches. Stick together, we have to move fast. Erickson, help me get them down."

Bryan and Erickson each grabbed one person at a time and jumped off the deck to drop to the trench floor twenty feet below. As soon as Bryan hit, he scrambled back up the side of the shipwreck for the next person.

In seconds, everyone was down. A growing wind whipped dirt, dust and smoke through the trenches, feeding oxygen to the hungry flames. The survivors gathered together for their run to freedom. Verde and Biz-Nass were under Zou's arms, helping the badly burned woman walk. Blisters dotted her red face. Most of her hair had melted away. Robertson handed Bryan the Ka-Bar knife, then scooped up Tabz. Erickson lifted Mur.

Bryan slid the knife into his belt-sheath, then vaulted onto a mesa fifteen feet above, putting him at the same level with the dying shipwreck. It blazed like a burning ship at sea. Bryan turned away to scan the trenches, searching for the best way through the maze.

He looked down to the people and pointed. "That way! First right, then first left, move!"

The huddle of people made good time. Bryan jumped across two trenches, moving to a new mesa. So close now, so close.

He looked down to give them the next direction just as a shot rang out — Rich Verde's forehead ripped open in a cloud of red and pink. He and Zou dropped hard. Bryan dove into the trench, using his body to shield the rest.

The gun fired three more times, two rounds hitting him in the back — the bullets dug into his coat like a sledgehammer tipped with a small nail.

Armor-piercing rounds, had to be.

He looked over his left shoulder.

Rex Deprovdechuk stood on the inferno ship's prow. One hand held the broken, smoldering rail, the other held the missing five-seven in a rock-steady grip. The left side of the boy's face dangled in a fleshy flap from his lower lip and chin, exposing the teeth and part of his cheekbone. A bloody, unlidded eye stared out. His jaw hung slack, as if he couldn't close it. Rex seemed to ignore the smoke, the heat, even the flames that were already crawling up his long red robe.

A hand on Bryan's shoulder, a mouth near his ear.

"Get them out of here."

Erickson.

The old man tossed a little girl at Bryan. Bryan reacted automatically, grabbing her, and as he did the old man snatched the Ka-Bar out of its belt-sheath. Erickson rushed back down the trench toward the shipwreck. He ran faster on ruined feet than any normal man could sprint.

Bryan's brother rushed away to fight the enemy. Bryan wanted to go with him, fight by his side, but the little girl in his arms had done nothing wrong, had made no choices that brought her to this horrid place. He looked at the others: Pookie, helping Zou to her feet; Robertson, face bleeding again, holding the other little girl; and Biz-Nass, coughing and cowering, looking left and right for the next threat. They were all crouched low, waving away smoke and waiting for Bryan to lead them out.

Gunfire from the ship. Bryan looked back to see Erickson, arms in front of his face, leaping up to the rail, Rex firing the five-seven as the old man came on.

Good luck, brother.

Bryan turned his back on the ship and ran down the trench.

•••

Rex tried to scream *come on,* but his jaw wouldn't move. The monster landed on the burning deck, knife raised, his old face snarling with evil. Rex pulled the trigger two more times, put two more rounds in the monster's chest, and then the monster rushed in. They tumbled back into the flames.

These demons had invaded his world, his *kingdom.*

Kill them kill them all killthemkillthemkillthem

Rex scrambled to his feet. He tore off the burning cape, tried and failed to find a place without flame. Erickson stood on ruined feet already scorched black. His skin bubbled, his scrap of clothing disintegrated into floating bits. Rex reached down to grab a flaming piece of wood, then stepped deeper into the fire to attack Savior.

Rex would slaughter the monster, then gather his people and start over.

•••

"Go right!"

Bryan held the girl tight as he leaped across the trench to the next mesa. Sweat soaked the shirt under his armored jacket. Below and to his left, the others ran through the trenches as fast as they could. Pookie was in the lead, carrying Zou in his arms. Robertson, Biz-Nass, the girls; all of them were coughing heavily — Bryan didn't have much time before people started collapsing.

They were almost to the cavern's wall. He looked at the trenches, traced the path toward the stairs that would take everyone up to the ledge. *So close!* The smoke burned at his eyes, shoved its way down his throat to scorch his lungs. Wind whipped through the cavern, scattering dust, blowing the smoke around like some vision of hell.

"Take the next right!" he shouted down. Pookie adjusted his grip on Zou, then led them forward. The group exited that trench and stood at the base of the stairs. Bryan jumped down to join them. His feet hit, then his legs gave out and he fell, turning to shield the girl as he did.

A rattling cough shook his chest. Hands pulled him to his feet. He looked at Pookie, saw the man was just about exhausted. Bryan set the girl down, then took Zou out of Pookie's arms. He threw the woman over his shoulder in a fireman's carry.

"We're almost out," he said between coughs. "Just make it up these stairs."

Bryan coughed once more, then started climbing. He kept Zou on his right shoulder so his left hand — with its blistered skin and broken fingers — could feel along the wall. Fifteen feet up, he was high enough to look to his right, out across the maze to the burning ship.

Flames soared so high they kissed the arena roof some fifty feet above. Old pieces of wood all along the ceiling had caught fire — they burned like little flaming suns set into a smoke-filled sky made of dirt, brick and rock. Bits of the roof broke free, plummeting down to smash into the burning ship or pummel maze plateaus and trenches.

Bryan kept climbing.

Three steps from the ledge, a *crack* and a *whuff* drew his attention back to the ship as the captain's cabin sagged, then collapsed in a billowing puff of swirling flame. Bryan saw an impossibility: Firstborn, fully ablaze, straining to pull a flaming cart out of the cabin.

On that cart, even through the shimmering heat, Bryan saw the thing Aggie had described — *Mommy*.

His mother.

Bloated beyond comprehension. Little arms flailing. Little legs kicking. And in that massive, distended belly, Bryan saw things moving, *twitching*, saw bubbles forming and joining and popping.

The fluid in her massive belly was *boiling*, boiling and *swelling*.

Her stomach tore — a thin, high jet of steam shot out, but the belly continued to swell like a filling helium balloon. Another jet of steam appeared, then she *popped*, exploding outward in flame-spinning chunks of sizzling flesh.

Bryan climbed the last three steps toward the ledge, toward John and Adam and Alder.

•••

Rex tumbled off the rail and crashed down hard to a trench floor below. The monster was too strong! Rex looked back up to the prow to see his enemy — the old man stood on the rail, naked and blistered, blood and soot covering his skin. Savior looked more like a monster than ever before.

He had a knife in his hand and madness in his eyes.

The old man gripped the handle in both hands, bent his legs, then lunged out into the air.

Rex reached up in time to catch the monster's wrists. He fell back hard, struggling to keep the knife point from driving into his eye.

•••

Eyes watering, his vision a shimmering blur, Bryan fell to a knee. He couldn't make it. He heard screaming — Adam's voice — shouting over the whipping wind, urging him and the others on, telling them to hurry. He looked up to see John Smith holding the black-haired girl tight, his green hood up around a face that dripped with sweat.

"Get up, Clauser," John said, then carried the girl into the tunnel. The others ran past Bryan, a coughing mass of legs and arms following John in.

How could Amy Zou feel so heavy?

Bryan felt hands on his shoulders, dragging him up by his coat.

"Bri-Bri," Pookie said, then coughed so hard bits of blood flew out of his mouth. "This is *not* nappy-time. *Move*."

Bryan stood, adjusted Zou on his shoulder, then followed Pookie to the tunnel entrance. They stumbled over corpses stretched out all over the ledge — John and the others had been busy. Before he entered the tunnel, Bryan looked back out at the cavern one last time.

The flames were already dying down. The ship glowed like living coal, waves of orange light washing through the sagging vessel. The mast burned like a torch; a steady rain of skulls dropped off to tumble into the embers below. As Bryan watched, the mast tilted, then fell, smashing through the deck in a shower of sparks and spinning cinders.

The arena spectators had fled. The place was empty.

Almost empty — in a trench in front of the ship, Bryan saw Rex on his back, Erickson on top of him trying to drive a knife into the boy's throat. Rex fought, his torn face screwed up into a horrid mask of rage, his shaking hands holding Erickson's wrists. Smoke swirled through the trench around them, reminding Bryan of the thick San Francisco fog that rolled down streets in the late-night hours.

The knife pushed closer.

Then a blur of smoldering black hit Erickson and drove him into a trench wall. The Ka-Bar knife spun and dropped to the ground.

●●●

Rex slowly rolled to his feet. So much pain. His knight had saved him. Firstborn looked horrible — his fur gone, his blistered skin smoking in places, sheened with oozing wetness in others. Burns from head to toe, yet still he fought for his king.

Rex pushed past the pain. He bent and picked up the knife.

●●●

"Bryan, come on!" Pookie's voice. Bryan carried Amy Zou to the tunnel entrance, never taking his eyes off the scene below. Wind shot out of the tunnel, sucked in from beyond to feed the hungry fire. In the center of the cavern, a large chunk of ceiling gave way, dropping down to smash the trenches like an asteroid hitting a planet. The place was collapsing.

●●●

Rex watched.

Rex waited.

The end of one era, the beginning of another.

Firstborn's back muscles flexed and rippled. He had his hands around Erickson's neck. Erickson reached up to claw at Firstborn's face, but the old man was already weakening.

Movement on Rex's right. He turned to look — his heart surged with joy.

"My king," Sly said.

Rex tried to talk, tried to say *you're alive!* but winced at the pain shooting through his mouth.

"Don't speak," Sly said. "I am here." He smiled wide, his needle-toothed grin full of love. He had a few burn marks on his clothes, but looked mostly unharmed.

Sly held his hand out, palm up. "May I kill the monster?"

Rex looked over to Firstborn. The great knight still had his hands locked around the monster's throat. The monster's hands moved weakly — he didn't have long.

Rex nodded, then put the knife handle in his friend's palm.

Sly's green-skinned hand closed around the handle. "Thank you, my king," he said, then thrust the knife deep into Rex's chest.

Rex stared into Sly's smiling face. What was happening? Rex looked down. The knife handle stuck out. He couldn't see any of the blade. It hurt. It burned.

Sly put his arm around Rex and pulled him close. "Thank you for making me your successor," he said quietly. He gripped the knife handle, pulled it out, turned it, then shoved it home again. Rex felt the hilt thump against his sternum, felt the tip poke out of his back.

It *burned*.

Sly had lied. He was just like all the others. Rex's only true friend had hurt him, just like everyone else in his life.

Rex fell to his knees.

Sly knelt with him. "I could never have taken over on my own. Firstborn was too strong. Now, I will tell everyone that *Firstborn* killed you. Good-bye, Rex."

Sly let go. He ran off down a trench, vanishing into the smoke.

Rex closed his eyes and fell to his side.

•••

Bryan saw Firstborn let go of Erickson. The old man didn't move. The smoldering creature turned.

Firstborn stared at the knife sticking out of Rex's chest.

It was over.

Bryan walked into the wind rushing out of the tunnel. Everyone stood there, waiting for him — everyone except Alder Jessup. The old man lay on the ground, unmoving, a neat, black hole in his blood-smeared cheek. Bryan looked up at Adam, had to shout to be heard. "I'm so sorry."

Tears streaked Adam's face. He shook his head. "It's what Gramps wanted. We can't help him. Leave him here."

Bryan started to object, but Adam was right — they couldn't get a dead body through the booby-trapped columns.

He heard another chunk of ceiling give way somewhere behind him. The ground trembled beneath his feet, just a little.

The columns.

"Come on, we have to move!"

He held Chief Zou tight and ran deeper into the tunnel.

• • •

Bryan's flashlight beam danced across a jagged, stacked column. He skidded to a halt before he hit it, sliding feet kicking dirt onto the hodgepodge of masonry. *The people behind him* — he braced his feet just as someone big plowed into his back.

"Everyone, *stop!*"

The sound of panting and coughing filled the air. Almost there . . .

He set Amy Zou down on her feet, gave her a little shake.

"Chief, snap out of it," he said. "You have to walk on your own."

She blinked at him, a glazed look in her eyes. So many blisters, so much scorched flesh; she had been beautiful once, but would never be so again.

"Step where I step, Chief. If you stumble, if you fall, you die and so do your daughters."

That hit home. Zou straightened, seemed to call upon some inner reserve of strength. She nodded.

Bryan looked at the little girls. Now wasn't the time to be nice. "No room for mistakes. Step where the person in front of you steps. You screw it up, you die and kill everyone around you. Got it?"

Their eyes were wide, their little faces streaked with sweat and smoke. They nodded just like their mother.

He looked at the rest: Adam, Robertson, Biz-Nass and Pookie nodded as well. Everyone knew the stakes.

Bryan took a deep breath. The air was clearer here, pouring in from the train tunnel beyond. He eyed the narrow spaces between the columns and the wall.

"Hey, Pooks," he said.

"Yes, my Terminator?"

"You better suck in that gut."

Pookie did, tried to hold it, but he was exhausted and his air let out in a tummy-puffing huff.

"I guess I'll go last," he said.

Bryan nodded, then trained his flashlight beam on the floor and started working his way through.

He made it out, then waited. Zou came next, then Tabz, then Mur, the one who had killed Pierre. Biz-Nass followed, then Adam. As Sean Robertson crawled out of the hole, the ground trembled again.

Bryan leaned in. Pookie was halfway through the columns.

"Pooks, *move*!"

A pebble dropped from the ceiling and hit Bryan in the head. Both men looked up — the ceiling above Bryan was a single, wide piece of chipped concrete.

More pebbles dropped from around its edges, trailing little comet-trails of dust.

Pookie drew in a big breath, then scooted faster.

Two columns to go.

"Pooks, slow down."

"*You* slow down."

Pookie was panicking. He moved too fast. His elbow hit the second to last column.

Bryan stepped through the hole and reached. He grabbed Pookie's arm and yanked him forward. Bryan grabbed his stumbling friend in his arms, then threw himself backward out the hole as the tunnel collapsed. A thick cloud of dirt and dust billowed out around them.

As the dust settled, eight people sat on the train tunnel's narrow walkway, coughing and gasping.

They had made it out alive.

Big Pimpin'

Pookie Chang limped up the steps of 2007 Franklin Street. The porch had been cleaned of debris. Yellow hazard tape was strung between posts, marking the danger of the broken rail that Bryan had driven Erickson through just a few days ago.

Pookie glanced back to his Buick. Night was falling. The streetlights were slowly flickering on. John Smith leaned against the passenger door, sipping on a cup of coffee. He smiled and gave Pookie a thumbs-up.

The more things change, the more they stay the same.

Pookie tucked the manila folder under his arm. Someone had replaced the wooden front door. The new door was tasteful, artistically etched, and solid steel.

Pookie pressed the door buzzer.

He still ached. He was beat to hell. His body would recover, but would his mind? That shit had been too much for anyone to see, let alone a modest, God-fearing boy from Chicago.

The door opened. Bryan Clauser stood inside. He looked fine. Days earlier, he'd had burn blisters, broken fingers and a line of staples up his ravaged cheek. Now the only thing marking that face was a neatly trimmed dark-red beard.

At least his face looked okay. His eyes? They stared out in a way they never had before. Bryan had seen too much, too soon.

"Bri-Bri," Pookie said. "How're they hanging?"

Bryan shook his head. "Sorry, Bro, the name is Jebediah now, although I may just go by *Jeb*."

"That does have more of a *Dukes of Hazzard* feel to it, but I'd rather not see you in short-shorts."

"In that case, just call me *Mister Erickson*."

Pookie laughed. "Yeah, sure, I'll get right on that. You gonna invite me in or what?"

Bryan nodded quickly and stepped aside. Pookie walked in. Like before, the house's old-time finery overwhelmed him. Only now the place didn't belong to some crazy old man . . . it belonged to his crazy best friend.

Pookie followed Bryan into the living room, again taking in the teak, marble, polished brass and fancy-pants picture frames. Emma sat curled up in a beautiful, gold-gilded Victorian-era chair. The dog had a white bandage wrapped around her head. She saw Pookie and started wagging her tail, although she made no effort to get up.

Pookie pointed at Emma. "Bri-Bri, I know you have all the culture of a stale Milwaukee's Best spilled in the bleachers of a tractor pull, but you might want to get the dog off a chair that costs more than my Buick did when it was new."

"Emma can sit wherever she wants," Bryan said quietly. "She lives here."

Pookie heard the tone in Bryan's voice. Emma was the man's last connection to Robin. The dog would have the run of the house, to say the least.

Pookie walked to Emma and carefully twirled her ear. Her eyes narrowed in a quiet doggy smile. He patted her rump, then turned back to Bryan.

"So you own all this now?"

"Sort of."

"What do you mean, *sort of*?"

"Well, Erickson still owns it," Bryan said. "It's just now I'm basically Erickson."

"You're looking pretty fly for a seventy-year-old."

Bryan nodded. "Yeah, well, the mayor is going to take care of that. He knows some people."

"What kind of people?"

"I'm not sure," Bryan said. "Powerful people. All I know is now I'm the Savior. I'm willing to go along with it for now."

"So you're *not* going to make this insanity public? You suddenly buying into Zou's line of BS about property values and how people don't need to know?"

Bryan chewed his lip, then shook his head. "I don't care about that right now. I think Sly got away. So did Firstborn, maybe. There were hundreds of those things, but we didn't see hundreds of bodies. The tunnel we came out of is gone. I need to figure out where the rest of Marie's Children went. And if Robin's killer is out there, I have to find her. Hunting is going to occupy my nights, Pooks. I don't give a shit who foots the bill."

Pookie nodded. His moral imperative to bring a vigilante killer to justice wasn't quite the same when said vigilante had saved his life. Twice. And after the things Pookie had seen, how close he'd come to death . . . maybe this way was better after all.

"Hey, you clean out that wacky basement yet? Could have one hell of a yard sale, I imagine."

Bryan shook his head. "Hell no. A trophy room is for trophies."

A trophy room?

"Uh, Bri-Bri, you're not taking up taxidermy, are you?"

Bryan shrugged, said nothing.

Pookie could only pray that Bryan kept at least a *shred* of his sanity and didn't go down the same path Erickson had.

"I've got some good news," Pookie said. "Word at Eight Fifty is that *Chief* Robertson is clearing you of the murder charges for Jeremy Ellis and Matt Hickman."

Bryan nodded. "The mayor made sure that would happen. Robertson brought him to the hospital yesterday to talk to Amy."

Chief Amy Zou was now just *Amy?*

"Is it true she's staying here?"

"Once she gets out of the burn ward, yeah," Bryan said. "Amy's a wreck, Pooks — physically and mentally. She won't talk at all. She's not all there, man. I don't know if she'll ever recover from what she did. I'm getting her help, the best money can buy. The girls are staying here until she gets out."

Bryan Clauser, former bachelor-cop, now the caretaker of two little girls. "You know anything about raising kids?"

He shook his head. "Nope. Until a couple of days ago, I didn't know anything about killing monsters. You figure out which one is more complicated. What about Aggie James? Anyone pick him up yet?"

"Yeah, that's the not-so-good news, Bri-Bri. It seems there was a lot of confusion at the hospital after the shootout. At about six A.M. that morning, an Officer Johnson walked into the maternity ward."

Bryan shook his head, then laughed admiringly. "No way."

"Way. Funny thing about a badge and a gun is most people don't stop to validate your ID. Once he got in the maternity ward, he just took the baby and ran. We're looking for him, but as of yet he and the baby are nowhere to be seen."

"Jesus," Bryan said. "That baby, he's like Rex. We have to find him."

Pookie nodded, but wondered what Bryan would do if he found the child. Killing a monster was one thing — murdering a baby was quite another indeed.

"So, Bryan, if His Highness the Mayor cleared your name, why don't you go back to being my good buddy Bryan Clauser?"

Bryan paused. He looked at Emma. "Because Bryan Clauser never really existed at all. And after all that went down . . . well, he's just *gone*, Pooks. Leave it be."

Pookie would, but only for now. Chief Zou wasn't the only person wrecked by all of this — so was Mike Clauser. No matter what it took, Pookie would patch things up between the father and son.

Bryan looked down to the folder in Pookie's hands. "That for me?"

Pookie handed it over. "The Handyman struck again last night."

Bryan opened the folder and glanced over the crime-scene photos. "Victims five and six," he said. "And again with cutting off the hands."

"We've got nothing, Bri-Bri. He leaves the symbols, but that's it. You and I both know the police will never find this guy. It's you, or he keeps going."

Bryan nodded. He closed the folder. "That seems to be the way things are. Pooks, it's getting dark. You want to come out hunting with me?"

Pookie had known that question was coming, yet all his well-rehearsed and oh-so-clever answers had vanished. Bryan was made to do this — Pookie Chang was not.

Pookie shook his head as he walked to the front door. "I can't. Me and my new partner have to look into a murder in Japantown."

Bryan seemed confused at first, then he opened the front door and looked out to the street, to Pookie's Buick. John Smith waved.

"Black Mister Burns is your . . . your *partner?*"

"If I'm lyin', I'm dyin'."

Bryan stared, then nodded. "Yeah, that's good. John came through big-time, Pooks. You could do a lot worse."

Pookie wanted to say *I could do a lot better, if only I was man enough to go hunting with you*, but he didn't.

Bryan forced a smile. "If you don't mind, I gotta get ready to go to work."

"Say no more, Brother."

Bryan held out his hand. "Thank you, man."

Pookie shook it. "Thank *me?* You saved my life for the second time."

Bryan looked down. "Yeah, well . . . I don't know what I would have done if you hadn't stood by me. Now that Robin is gone, you . . . well, you're all I've got."

Pookie pulled him in and hugged him. "Gimme some sugar, you big lug. I'm glad you pinched off that emotional nugget before you go back to being all reserved and resigned and whatnot."

Pookie thumped Bryan on the back, then let go. "Good hunting, my friend," he said, then walked away from Bryan's mansion.

Pookie felt like a loser for not backing Bryan's play, but it was just too much. All that death — Robin, Baldwin Metz, Jesse Sharrow, Rich Verde, all killed by something that Pookie still couldn't truly accept as *real*. And what he'd seen in that cavern, how close he'd come to dying himself.

For now, at least, Bryan Clauser was on his own.

Holding Hands

Kissing.

Two girls, kissing, hands rubbing on backs, soft and tender, hidden in the shadows of Lafayette Park, holding hands.

Chameleon felt that cold rage churning inside his chest. Why did *they* get to kiss? Why did *they* get to have each other, when he had nothing?

No one could stop him now. Sly said Savior was dead. The police had staked out Ocean Beach and Golden Gate Park, Chameleon's favorite killing grounds, but the police were just human. One pair of detectives had walked within two feet of his position. They didn't notice Chameleon because Chameleon looked just like the tree behind which he hid. He hadn't killed that night, but the next night he had.

It wasn't hard to wait. He waited like a spider. If you sat still and quiet long enough, eventually a couple would come to you.

Then you just took them.

Chameleon stood at the base of a small tree, his chest and left cheek against the trunk, his arms wrapped around the other side. That was how you hid. You just hugged the tree, then made your skin feel and look like the tree. The shadows took care of the rest.

The girls drew closer. He wouldn't have even known one was a girl from looking at her. She had short hair and wore a boy's shirt and pants. But he knew how women smelled. No matter what she wore, that was a girl.

A girl who would soon be dead.

Chameleon thought it was funny to kill in Lafayette Park, so close to Savior's old house, the house Sly had told him to watch for so long. But Savior was gone. Sly was in charge now, and Sly gave Chameleon respect. If Chameleon wanted to hunt, that was fine with Sly.

Maybe this time, Chameleon would cut off a head and bring it home for New Mommy. She was changing, changing so fast, but she wasn't ready to have babies yet. Maybe the reason Old Mommy could have babies was because she ate brains. Maybe New Mommy needed the same kind of food.

Closer still. Only thirty feet now. Walking, holding hands, smiling, *kissing*. The cold rage blossomed. The lust to kill swirled through his brain.

A noise to his left. He couldn't turn to look, because trees didn't turn to look. Moving might spook the prey.

More noise. The smell of a dog.

Chameleon didn't worry. The dog would pass by like all the others.

He watched the girls. Just another ten seconds or so, and he would grab them, pull them into the deeper shadows beneath the tree. Sly liked boy livers better, but he probably wouldn't mind so much since this was two girls.

The dog smell grew stronger, closer.

A growl — low, deep and aggressive, the kind that would make the hair on the back of your neck stand up if you hadn't made the back of your neck feel just like tree bark. A growl so quiet the girls didn't even hear.

Was the dog growling at *him*?

He had to take a look. Chameleon slowly turned his head, heard his stiff skin crackling like a bending branch.

Just ten feet away, a black-and-white dog with something wrapped around its head stared at him. Its lip curled up, revealing long teeth that glowed softly in the pale moonlight.

Go away, dog, Chameleon thought. *Just go away.*

But the dog did not go away.

For some reason, the dog frightened Chameleon. Dogs weren't that dangerous, but there was something in this one's eyes. Not hunger, but *hate*.

The dog took a step closer. The lip curled higher. A string of drool swung from the dog's lower lip. The jaw opened — the growl sounded gravelly, disturbing.

The girls' footsteps stopped.

Stupid dog.

Chameleon started to slowly push away from the tree. He would have to pounce on that dog and kill it fast, then maybe chase the girls down. Everything was ruined!

A hissing sound.

Something punched him in the back, pushed his chest into the tree. Chameleon started to pull away, but found that he could not — he was stuck.

Then the pain hit.

It *burned*!

He squeezed the tree, as if hugging it might take away his pain.

The girls' footsteps quickened, faded away — they had run.

He opened his eyes to look at the dog again. Now it sat on its haunches. The growling stopped, but its head remained low, its eyes fixed on Chameleon.

More footsteps, heavier footsteps . . .

ba-da-bum-bummmm

Family! He was saved!

"Help me!" Chameleon whispered. He couldn't see who was there. "I . . . I can't move and this dog is bugging me. My chest really hurts. I don't feel so good."

The footsteps came closer, from behind and to the right. Chameleon turned to look — a man in black, his face covered by a fabric mask painted with a white skull-smile. Chameleon saw green eyes through the mask's little eye-slits.

"You've been a busy boy," the man in black said. The skull-smile didn't move when he talked. That looked weird.

Chameleon felt cold. Sleepy.

"Crap," the man said. "Emma, I think I nicked his heart. I really have to work on this bow-and-arrow business."

That was where Chameleon felt the burning, in his chest. "You nicked my heart? I'll heal up, right?"

The skull-smile shook his head. "Not this time. You're gonna die, right here, right now."

"Die? Like . . . like *prey* dies? No, *please*, I don't want to die!"

"*Please?* So polite. Did any of your loving couples beg you to let them live?"

The man took a step closer. Chameleon reached with his right hand, hoping to grab the man's throat, but the man stepped back effortlessly. Moonlight flashed off metal. Chameleon felt something hit his right hand, just past the wrist.

Then he felt a new pain and heard something hit the ground.

Chameleon looked down to see a hand on the grass, a hand with skin that looked an *awful* lot like tree bark. He raised his wrist, now a stump gushing blood. Chameleon stared at the stump, disbelieving — it couldn't be real, couldn't be happening.

The man shook something near Chameleon's face.

It was a string of twelve severed hands, six pairs wired together from Chameleon's victims, all the pairs then wired together in a long chain. The hands at the bottom were blackened, shriveled, crawling with maggots. The ones in the middle were almost as bad. The ones at the top were still fresh — he'd taken those just last night.

"I found your collection," the man in black said. "You killed six people."

"Help me, please! They aren't people, they're prey! You know this, brother!"

The skull-smile man nodded. The metal flashed again. Chameleon felt a burning sting on his left wrist. The man bent to pick something up.

Then, the man in black held up Chameleon's severed hands for Chameleon to see.

Chameleon's *hands.* "Oh, no." His eyes slowly closed. So cold. So sleepy.

Another flash of pain, this time in his right cheek.

"Stay with me," the man said. "You can't check out yet."

This man, he was *family.* Family was everything!

"Who are you? Why won't you save me?"

"Think of me as the nasty uncle you didn't invite to the family Christmas."

Man in black. Chameleon thought back to the night Savior was shot. A man in black had done that. But that man hadn't worn a mask, so it couldn't be the same person.

Something tickled Chameleon's face. He blinked awake — had he gone to sleep? He saw what was tickling his face: the dead, cold fingers of his keepsakes touching his rough skin. It was like the hands of his victims reaching out from hell, grabbing him, pulling him down. Some of the maggots fell free, bounced off Chameleon's face and fell to the ground below.

"I was going to torture you, find another way into your tunnels," the man in black said. "Or maybe you guys have a new home, I don't know. I figure you have about fifteen seconds or so. Any chance you can tell me where Sly lives?"

Chameleon had to focus, but he shook his head. When he did, the dead fingers caressed his cheeks even more. Chameleon thought of Hillary. Beautiful New Mommy Hillary, all safe in her chamber, her body growing bigger every day.

"I won't tell you."

A heavy sigh from behind the mask. "I figured as much. Well, it looks like your time is up. But as you go, know this. I'm going to find your home. I'm going to find your family. I'm going to kill them one by one. All the eyes, all the teeth. But you can keep the hands."

Chameleon felt colder than ever. His eyes closed.

The last thing he felt was the dead fingers of his victims caressing his face.

While I always strive for as much accuracy as possible in these books, I was forced to modify some aspects of the policies and procedures of the San Francisco Police Department and the Medical Examiner's Office in order to create a more streamlined tale. Remember, folks: this is a story about a race of monsters lurking beneath the streets of San Francisco — it's quite possible I made up a detail or two.

The buried ships of San Francisco, however, are real. The discovery of gold in 1848 generated a migration to the Bay Area, resulting in over six hundred ships being abandoned in the bay. As the city expanded, many of those abandoned ships were buried. Special thanks to Ron Fillion for his map of the buried ships and the historical information available at http://www.sfgenealogy.com/sf/history/hgshp1.htm.

> "Certainly, there is not any dust of empire sepulchered below, nor is there anything resembling dust in the ooze beneath those bay-born thoroughfares. But we do know, or every San Franciscan ought to know, that that ooze is the winding sheet of many a gallant craft that once proudly plowed the bounding billows of the open sea, and which formed one of the great fleet of vessels that brought the fortune-hunters to the Golden Gate — that made up the Argonauts' Armada of golden dreams that was soon to be scattered and strewn even as was that maritime pageant once assembled under the management of Philip of Spain."
>
> — WALTER J. THOMPSON, "The Armada of Golden Dreams"

ACKNOWLEDGMENTS

San Francisco Architectural Heritage for their help researching the Haas-Lilienthal House in San Francisco. Yeah, that's where Savior lives, and you can visit it. See www.sfheritage.org.

Richard Vetterli of the San Francisco Medical Examiner's Office for all the fantastic information about how the ME staff deal with the city's dead.

Officer Dwayne Tully for his information on San Francisco Police procedures.

The SFPD Community Relations team for additional research help and fact-checking.

The Scientific Secret Agents: Joseph A. Albietz III, M.D., Jeremy Ellis, Ph.D., and Tom Merritt, Ph.D.

Chris Grall, Master Sergeant, A 3/20 SFG(A), Florida National Guard.

Det. Richard Verde, NYPD (retired).

Dan "ARaiderFan" Garcia for help with Spanish.

Glenn Howell, Deputy Sheriff Retired, Jefferson County SO, Golden, Colorado.

BOOKS THAT INFLUENCED THIS NOVEL

Carroll, Sean B. *Endless Forms Most Beautiful*. Norton, 2005.

Dawkins, Richard. *The Selfish Gene*. Oxford University Press, 1976.

Gould, Stephen Jay. *Ontogeny and Phylogeny*. Belknap/Harvard, 1977.

Hölldobler, Bert, and Wilson, E.O. *The Super Organism*. Norton, 2009.

Oakley, Barbara. *Evil Genes*. Prometheus Books, 2007.

Tinbergen, Niko. *The Study of Instinct*. Clarendon Press, 1951.

Turner, Scott J. *The Tinkerer's Accomplice*. Harvard University Press, 2007.

ALSO BY SCOTT SIGLER

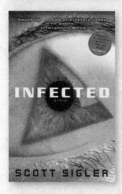

INFECTED

"Riveting...even hardened genre fans will find themselves whimpering at each new revelation."
—*PUBLISHERS WEEKLY*
(starred review)

CONTAGIOUS

"An inventive, amped-up yarn... full of pressure-cooker mind games."
—*ENTERTAINMENT WEEKLY*

ANCESTOR

"Sigler writes as if he is channeling a collaboration between Stephen King and Michael Crichton, as edited by H. G. Wells."
—BOOKREPORTER.COM